The Last Gate

9-8-01

To Kathy
best Wishes
Elizabeth A. Merz

The Last Gate

by

Elizabeth A. Merz

ISBN: 1-58721-908-5

1stBooks - rev. 6/29/00

About The Book

The Last Gate begins a story spanning four generations of Ver dala Ven, a cursed race of magical beings that once flourished among Ordinary Ones as voluntary servants, healers, seers and advisors. Urged by compassion and the singing spirit guide of Ver dala Ven, Betnoni took her own life on the shores of an underdeveloped nation in order to gain enough power to protect millions of innocents from a relentless invader. To punish the Ordinary Ones for their part in compelling Betnoni's actions, Ver dala Ven's spirit guide, called the Masing Star, fell silent and disappeared, and Ver dala Ven began to disappear, as well.

In a prophecy Betnoni left for her son as a legacy, she described events that would lead up to the return of the Masing Star, and the renewal of their kind. She instructed her son to pass the prophecy along to his children, and children's children, while keeping it a secret from all others.

Two thousand years passed, and her Ver dala Ven descendants kept her secret, though over time few believed her words were more than the ravings of a mad woman. Betnoni's name became the favorite curse of aristocrats and modern peoples, and school children were taught that she bore the responsibility of the death of her own lineage, causing the disappearance of an entire race. Ver dala Ven endured only as an oddity in Betnoni's family line, one born per generation with the mark of gold eyes and a magical gift, a trait given from parent to child.

On the eve of Ver dala Ven Voktu's accidental death, he passed the secret to his only gold-eyed son, Cobo, along with a cryptic prophecy of his own. "Betnoni will watch over you and your descendants. You have nothing to fear, and there is no shame."

Cobo didn't give thought to his father's prophecy until the day he chose to leave Ona and Jantideva, to run away from a broken heart. Wrapped in regret and jealousy, he believed his father's words were like curses leveled against him in anger. In his faulty memory, he did not see his father's forgiveness, and he did not recognize the advent of the first sign of Betnoni's secret prophecy.

Prologue-The Death of the Grand Lineage

Shodalum's shore, once rich and green had been transformed to grim and gray, a fortress of stone and filth. Beyond the stone walls lived a simple people, unwillingly industrialized by the Alliance and desperate for justice. Their pleas for mercy went ignored too long, and they took action in the Shodite way. They passively stopped working, and their neglect shut down the Alliance's deadly lume chemical plants. An insignificant and weak seat on the Alliance managed with a single act of defiance to cripple mighty Jantideva.

The passive resistance lasted far longer than Redd's tenuous patience could endure. He refused to listen to their demands, simple and humane demands of autonomy and self-determination. He did not care that their exposure to lume dust killed them at an exponential rate, each day twice more gone than the day before. They hadn't wanted war. They wanted freedom from oppression, a given right being an original member of the World Alliance Council, where all nations were made one, equal and proper. They wanted freedom from Redd's lume death.

Redd wanted the lume they produced. He wanted fuel for his huge flying devices, his windriders. In a society that had not known war in five thousand years, he wanted weapons.

Betnoni stepped onto the ornate open-air deck of Redd's beloved battle cruiser, and breathed deeply the acrid stench of pollution. The smell of lume was not fatal, not at the distance they'd placed themselves, but unpleasant enough to make her wince. She crinkled her pretty nose.

Noticing her, as well as her distaste for the smell that formed a halo over Shodalum, Redd snorted a contemptuous laugh. "And you'd have us relocate the lume plants in Jantideva? The stink would drive all decent Janti from their home."

Her monarch and friend of fifty years looked out on the ugly sight of a dying land, determination in the curl of his lip. Of all his predecessors, this daka's hunger for conquest was sharpest. Born in an era of peace he was out of step with his own time. It wasn't enough for him that the world bent to his opinion on all matters. He yearned for much more. He yearned to win all he already owned. It was the reason, she mused, that he rejected Shodalum's overtures to form a treaty. He secretly hoped it would come to this, wishing to cart out his new devices, his new weapons and prove them in battle. He declared the Shodite's peaceful protest an act of war. The universal truth of the matter didn't touch Redd, for there would be no war in the conventional sense, where a worthy and powerful foe fought with equal prowess. It would be nothing more than a massacre of an underdeveloped people, who's cultural disposition toward peace prevented them from fighting back.

Betnoni moved toward Redd, a gentle reproach that drew a wrathful glare, for he'd already heard her arguments. She ignored his defensive posture, and put forth her hands, together and open, an ancient prayerful pose taught by Thranlam'Sum. She appeared ready to entreat his mercy once again.

"I've seen your future, Redd." She disclosed, her words halting and unsure. She was taught by her mother to be gentle with her gifts, and to refrain from interfering with the natural course in the affairs of the Ordinary Ones. Betnoni was Ver dala Ven, and belonged to the Thranlam'Sum lineage, those who possessed and were possessed by the magical entity known as the Masing Star. They were born into the service of the dakas, to serve as receptive and helpful friends. In the use of their gifts, Ver dala Ven often chose to be healers, teachers or seers, though their gifts far exceeded those simple tasks. Betnoni's finest gift as Ver dala Ven was the sight, to see deeply into the future and past, and understand the consequences of even the simplest of actions, though in keeping with her faith of noninterference, she kept her visions to herself.

She set her faith aside with difficulty. "You will bring upon yourself, your children, and the entire world two terrifying curses if you continue with your campaign."

"Curses." He uttered a laugh, and it sharpened with indifference, cutting cleanly through her reservations.

"Beginning with your family," she stated in a firm, strong voice, "from now until the atrocity against Shodalum is fully recompensed, the dakas will lose one child in each generation." His skepticism caused her to turn pleading. "Redd, my dearest, if you do not turn back from your planned attack, I have foreseen that your son Andelis will be the first to fall to the curse, and he will fall this very day, by my hand."

Redd's defiant features twitched with fury, embedded deeply in primal fear for his child's welfare. Snarling at her, he slapped her hands down. "Do not dare to threaten me!"

She rubbed the sting from her palms. "Redd! I do not understand the prophecy myself! For you know I would never hurt Andelis! I love Andelis as I love my own son! I cannot see how or why he dies, I only know that I will somehow be the cause, and the cause is also the beginning of the curse."

"I do not believe in prophecy," Redd spat, "nor do I believe that Shodalum is worth the life of one daka! If so, the Guardian would have seen fit to make them superior to the Janti."

"I believe it was Lord Crag who once said that very same thing to Mo'ghan the First, but it was in reference to the Janti, and their acute inferiority in comparison to the Rathian Dark Lords!"

"You are arguing with me?" Redd thundered incredulously.

"It is your command of the present that sets in motion your accursed future. You are in command, Redd, you can bring the curse to an end before it plays itself out."

Agitated, he paced away from her, his eyes glaring at the approaching shore. "Go away Betnoni." He ordered, "I no longer wish to be in your presence."

Her voice tenuous, she disobeyed him and continued, despite knowing she would not reach him. "The second curse befalls my kind. Ver dala Ven will die away, until there is but one direct line springing from Thranlam'Sum's lineage, and only one Ver dala Ven child per generation will be born bearing the mark and gifts."

Redd grunted a laugh, turned on her, and with a cruel set to his jaw, he retorted, "You've been cursed already my dear."

Her inability to bear but one child in her lifetime had long haunted her, a secret Redd knew and now used against her. His retort felt like another slap, this time stinging her soul.

Fighting hurt feelings, she continued, "You misunderstand. Ver dala Ven will produce many children, but only one per generation will bear the mark of gold eyes and the gift. Ver dala Ven will beget Ordinary Ones."

Her revelation earned his unreserved attention, and amusement. "There will one day be a blue-eyed Ver dala Ven?"

"No, Redd, no. They will be Ordinary Ones, not Ver dala Ven. They will have no gifts. They will not be willing to serve the dakas, either, contributing to the downfall of Ona and the disbanding of the Alliance."

Dubiously, he countered, "The lineage will not die off. Your relations live far and wide, all throughout the world, millions and millions, upon millions. Thranlam'Sum promised that your kind would be with us always. I think you are trying to trick me, Ver dala Ven. It isn't working, except to thoroughly annoy me."

She felt physical pain for the future of her lineage, and for her part in bringing about the end. She was partner to Redd in the coming disaster, he the father of their descendant's pain, she the mother.

"Please believe me, it is my love for you that moves me so desperately to want to help you escape your fate." she said, "If you do not turn away from Shodalum right now, and take the Shodite's side in peace, Itza's prophecy will come to pass. The Masing Star will leave Ver dala Ven, and the Song it sings to all ears will be silenced. Ver dala Ven will dwindle, and eventually leave the service of the dakas, and the dakas will be driven from Ona, as she has foreseen."

His guffaw was not enough to cover his uneasiness.

"Itza also predicted that there were one day be giants, and all sorts of oddities living among us. Itza was deranged!" he retorted, "Angry that the Star chose to join with Thranlam'Sum and not her, driven mad with her jealousy. You expect me to accept that her jealous ravings are showing themselves to have merit now, after ten thousand years?"

Betnoni withdrew from their argument. She would not win, he would not understand until the darkest hour was upon him. Thoughtfully, she murmured, "History will paint me as a wrathful and selfish murderess." To Redd, she said, "Future generations will see you as the legendary daka who ushered in the Age of Contentment. The fuel you provide the world for their needs will advance Ona, Jantideva, the Alliance, for a time. But someday your crimes will be recognized. Your name will be used to destroy Ona."

"Are you prophesying?" he bit back, and with an air of disdain, he tried to bring her around to good reason once again. "For if so, I wish to have Chancellor Vin to hear your presentation!" Without waiting for her response, he continued evenly, as though he was speaking with an insufferable underling, and not his beloved friend. "Shodalum must be brought to heel. Surely you understand that much? I will not allow the Alliance to see me bend to a tiny nuisance such as their strike."

In response to his unyielding stance, the Masing Star made itself seen. The contented aria sung by the Star while ensconced within Ver dala Ven's body rose to a dramatic crescendo as its essence expanded and came to the surface of Betnoni's flesh. Her skin illuminated gold, as gold as her shining eyes, and radiated intense heat and soft light. Redd stepped back a respectful distance from the Star's radiant heat, away from Betnoni's easy reach. Betnoni was a gateway to the Star's interaction with the world, her body prepared in infancy for possession. No one but a properly prepared Ver dala Ven could make contact with the Star without risking injury.

Betnoni had waited many years for the Star to begin preparing her son, Max, and after Max grew into adulthood and past the best age for preparation, she expected her grandson, Maxim, would be prepared. In the lengthy history of the Star, beginning from the ancient time when the Holy Star descended from the heavens to touch twins Thranlam'Sum and Itza, bestowing on them powerful gifts and the mark of gold eyes, the Masing Star and Ver dala Ven host shared a symbiotic relationship, corporeal being and entity of spirit made one in the flesh. There had never been a break in the cycle.

Betnoni's insights into the catastrophic changes that would befall both the Ordinary Ones and her kind began with Shodalum's defiance. She envisioned a future of silence, a future where Ver dala Ven did not share a body with the Star, a future where Ver dala Ven withered, where their gold eyes faded as rapidly as their desire to serve and protect the Ordinary Ones. In her visions, she felt that the Star always knew this day would come, from the moment it blessed Thranlam'Sum and Itza. But knowing she was part of a greater plan did not erase her sadness, or her longing for an alternative outcome.

Engulfed as she was by the precious spirit of the Star, she saw clearly the suffering Redd would inflict upon hundreds of generations of his kin. She could not change the course of his future, or hers.

With a heavy heart, she said, "Goodbye my dear friend."

Redd, the interior of the Peace Cruiser, faded and for a moment Betnoni was bathed in pure white light. The Song carried her to her destination, which would not appear to her until her slippered feet landed on sandy soil. The Star set her down on the beach of Shodalum's coastal city Nari. The toxic waves of the Gryvly sea lapped over her feet, soaking the hem of her yellow gown. Over her shoulder she could see a waste dump tube. It was dry, unused. The Shodites had shut down this plant first, and held their initial strike here on this beach. In a fit of religious ecstasy, some threw themselves into the sea to honor the Goddess that they believed lived there, and had been instantly killed by the toxic lume present in the water. Bodies bloated and half eaten by sand worms and sea creatures, littered the beach.

She turned her gaze upward toward the approaching vessels in the sky. Redd's giant Peace Cruiser was narrow and long, white and gold, and led an assault force of one hundred smaller ships. The armada was a magnificent sight. Redd's creation aloft and breathing, their blowers roaring, the exhaust that kept them airborne pummeling the water, spawning a choppy sea. "His brilliance is wasted by greed." She said to the Star.

Not that it mattered now.

She raised her arms toward the ships and cradling the Peace Cruiser's image between her hands. "From the Silence, a return to the silence." Betnoni intoned, soft words amplified by the Star's will and heard by every living being on the planet.

"I am ready." She whispered to the Star.

The heat of the Star grew intense, painful. It had not left her since the moment they had been joined, and should not have left her until moments before her natural death. Her flesh was on fire, already melting though the Star had not yet done its worse. Ignoring her agony, she reached out for the beloved entity that tormented her with physical pain, and entreated it to give her a gift. A tiny portion of it appeared between her hands, a pin dot of light, as much the essence of the Masing Star as a droplet of water was to the sea, and seeing that it was hers to possess for all time, an anguished grin spread her mouth wide.

As the Star swept her vulnerable form with its furious and destructive heat, she drew the droplet of the Masing Star to her lips as though to kiss it and quickly wove a final spell, her words spoken soft.

"I am the Goddess of the Gryvly Ocean."

࿐࿐࿐࿐࿐࿐࿐࿐

Every Ordinary One alive had to have heard her piercing scream of agony, for it reached Redd's ears over the distance and the roar of the blowers, and caused him to flinch. On the place Redd had seen her deposited by the Masing Star a pillar of fire rose tall as the smokestacks.

"No," he denied his own eyes, his ears as he heard the pitch of her scream rise and descend, settling into silence. The flames receded, cooling into the recognizable entity, the Masing Star. Taking the shape of a shimmering gold bubble, the Star lifted off the beach and hovered over the sea. It dropped something out of its interior, and Redd felt sickened as he realized it had cast Betnoni's fragile ashes into the waves.

Unable to move, to tear his eyes from the place in the churning water where he'd seen Betnoni's ashes fall, Redd whispered his reply, "It is a trick. She is trying to trick me into turning away from my mission."

The world was too still. He felt alone. He knew she was gone.

xiii

"Daka Redd!" Chancellor Vin burst into the private observation deck without heeding the normal courtesy shown to a daka, followed by a gaggle of priests, their white robes flowing long behind them. Vin's manner was imperative, his tone strident as he blurted, "The Song! We cannot hear the song! Where is Ver dala Ven Betnoni? We must see her immediately."

Redd hadn't noticed the silence, and strained to hear the melody of the Masing Star, which in truth was difficult for him to hear in the first place. He'd long despised his inability to hear the Song, delegated to that group of Ordinary Ones Thranlam'Sum spoke of, those who lack the inner ear to hear the voice of the Guardian Spirit of Creation, lacking even more, that which made an Ordinary One whole and sentient. He'd trained himself to hear it, under the tutelage of Kai'mai masters. But now, in its place, a resounding silence.

"She said it would leave us." Redd said under his breath.

"The song has not ceased since Thranlam'Sum was blessed!" Vin fussed on, neglecting to notice that Redd swooned and gripped the rail tighter. "Where is Ver dala Ven? There must be an explanation, she must have comfort for us!"

"No comfort. Only curses." Redd replied evenly, and harder yet added, "She's dead." He shoved Vin aside, ignoring the Chancellor's astonished response. He stormed off the observation deck, Vin and his priests on his heels, keeping an anxious pace, even going as far as to follow him into the transport tubes connected to the ship's blowers. The diverted exhaust from blowers below was strong enough in the tubes to carry the weight of a man, and at a greater speed than the traditional lift, with a drawback. The air blowing through the tube did not ease its momentum to let a passenger leap from the tube through a portal. Few were adept at using the tubes as of yet, preferring to climb ladders from one deck to another rather than risk broken bones or a cracked head after miscalculating a jump through a tube portal. Redd used the tubes most often, finding the flight exciting and the chancy exit challenging. With ease, he spun at a dizzying speed upward and with perfect calculation grabbed the opening to the battle deck at the right moment, pulling himself through unharmed.

The priest on his heels tried the same artful maneuver, missed, and was heard screaming as he continued to plunge upward to the dead end at the end of the tube.

Redd strode onto the battle deck, aware that all eyes were on him. Slack jawed stares told him enough. They'd either seen Betnoni perish, or they missed the Masing's consoling Song.

"Return to your duties!" His angry shout turned their stares off him, but did not remove the shock from their faces.

He sought out his son. He caught sight of Andelis at the co-commander's post, and unbearable relief washed through him. He'd almost feared he'd find Andelis dead. But he was alive, and well, and watching Redd with a worried look on his face. Like Redd, Andelis had studied in the military consortium and rose to a position of authority in the Pliadors by his own merit. The even-tempered young man wore his uniform with pride, and executed his duties as co-commander of the battle deck with precision and good humor. Redd was proud of his son, his fourth born child. Of his seven children, Andelis was his most beloved.

"The Song," his son faltered, at a loss for words.

"I am aware it is silent. Betnoni has taken her own life, or rather the Star took it from her." Redd replied quickly. He gripped his son's shoulders with both hands and grinned. "She is gone. And so are her empty threats."

Confusion knotted Andelis' brow. "There is no joy in her death."

"No, no joy." Redd relented, and though he felt shameless, he continued to smile at the young man. "Take your post, son. We will strike the coast on schedule."

"As you wish, Father." He bowed his head, ever obedient, though perplexed that his father was not moved by the death of their close family friend, and the oppressive silence that followed.

Turning his attention to Shodalum, Redd spoke to his crew, words that were transmitted to all his ships. "A tragedy has occurred and in its wake we are left in silence. Betnoni is dead, and the Masing Star has left us. We are alone, without the guidance and service of Ver dala Ven." He closed his eyes for a second, grief striking through him, and his anger quickly growing stronger than his grief. "So be it. We will not be diverted from our mission by a tragedy we cannot explain or change."

To his crew, he ordered that the attack begin.

The first wave of assault vessels streamed forward, assuming an attack formation in descent. Redd suffered only a moment of indecision as he watched the ships pull tighter together and moved closer to the place Betnoni died. A moment of mercy crossed him like a warm shallow in a deep cool sea.

And then it was gone.

"I want the villages destroyed. Do not touch Alliance structures."

A waterspout burst from the sea, punctuating his order by spiraling upward and swallowing his ships. Redd watched and listened helplessly as his men cried out in terror, unable to control their ships as they were sucked into a watery vortex.

The waterspout dropped into the sea, and the cries of his people cut off abruptly as if communications were ended from the source.

Preternatural silence loomed large on the battle deck.

"Deploy divers. Search and rescue." Redd ordered, swept at once by emotional fatigue. He placed his hand on a console to keep himself upright. "Drop to attack altitude. Ready crysine cannons."

The waterspout emerged in a new location, this time completely blocking the course of the Peace Cruiser.

"Evasive measures!" Redd shouted, and he stepped forward to watch his ship come about to avoid the hungry mouth of the whirling spout. They didn't have enough room to make the sharp turn, and brushed it, enough to jostle the entire vessel. Redd held on, vowing to stay on his feet and see the crisis through.

As soon as clear sky appeared on their screens, the pillar sank into the sea and reemerged in the path of the Peace Cruiser's new course. But this time, as the water formed, it took on the shape of a woman. Her face bent close to the battle deck, filling the viewing screens. As he recognized her, a chill raced up his back.

"I am the Goddess Gryvly Sea." Betnoni declared, her watery voice booming throughout the ship. "Protector of the Shodites. I will not permit you to harm my children. Behold."

Three arms sprang from each side of her torso, and she swiped at the fleet flanking the Cruiser's right, then its left, sweeping them from the sky and sending them crashing into the sea. The action caused uncontrolled panic to arise among his crew. Well over half left their posts and raced for the lift. Going where? He mused. Escaping a goddess who commanded the sea? Impossible. Stunned, motionless, Redd stared at the watery goddess, at the face he once loved so dearly. The menace present on her features was unlike anything he'd ever seen.

After sending his battle fleet to the sea and swallowing up the lives of thousands, she turned on his war ship. She grabbed hold of the Peace Cruiser in both hands as if it were a toy, opened her mouth wide and shoved the entire thing in. Water was all Redd could see on the viewing screens. The sensation of uncontrolled flight made him sick to his stomach, and Redd braced himself for the moment of death, for a watery grave.

The final impact jarred him off his feet. The scream of metal bending and ripping filled the battle deck. He landed on his back, knocking his breath out of him. Panic set in. There was nothing he feared more than drowning. He screamed his fear, his outrage and unwillingness to die, even as the sounds of ripping metal settled and complete silence followed.

He came to his senses gradually. The sky. He could see the sky on all the monitors, on all the viewing screens, save two. On two that were keeping an eye on the blowers under the main deck, he could see solid ground beneath them. Crushed trees.

"Betnoni?" he said, his voice soft. "What have you done?"

Her voice boomed all around them, causing him to cower like a beaten animal. "Heed my warning, Redd. If you attempt to enter Shodalum, you and your people will die. I will protect Shodalum for all eternity, if I must."

Shakily, he stood and glanced over a blinking map board, one of the only instruments still working. Bay of Peace. She'd transported them across the sea to place them on Jantidevan soil. He was home, his mission thwarted.

"We are alive." Vin said, a shaky laugh punctuating his observance.

A reflexive backward glance at the Chancellor, who was lying under the co-commander station, reminded him instantly of the last person he'd seen standing there.

"Andelis."

He rushed to the post, seeing progressively his son's boots, his legs, his hips, his torso and left arm, and a heavy console that had fallen on top of him where his head and right arm should have been. He knelt next to his son, pressing his hand into Andelis' chest, feeling for life that he knew he would not find. As he pressed his son's chest, he'd moved the body just so, enough to see that his son had been decapitated.

৵৵৵৵৵৵৵৵৵

Betnoni's personal message left to her son, opened and read in secret after the announcement of her death:

My dear Max,

Our cherished Thranlam'Sum once said that our kind is strengthened by our compassion and weakened by the same. With the weakness of our compassion in mind, I implore you, my son, do not reveal my prophecy to anyone, even those of our own lineage. I understand the desire to soothe their grief, but in doing so you endanger yourself and your son. As much as I love Redd, I do not trust the easy cruelty of his selfish nature. I fear he might murder you and

Maxim if he suspects it would circumvent Jantideva's fate.

Watch for the signs, my son. If they do not come soon, pass the prophecy to Maxim, and urge him to pass it to his children in secret, while staying ever watchful for the day of the Rebirth. The Masing Star will sing again. I hope it returns in your lifetime.

*With love,
Mother*

ഝഝഝഝഝഝഝഝ

Two hundred and forty six generations of Ver dala Ven kept her secret, though over time few believed her prophecy any more than they believed the ravings of Itza. Betnoni's name became the favorite curse of aristocrats and modern peoples. Her teachings on peace were removed from the Suma libraries and her statue broken and removed from the Hall of Ver dala Ven. School children were taught that she bore a curse on her own lineage, causing the mark of gold eyes to disappear from Thranlam'Sum's descendants, while in truth the mark disappeared from Itza's lineage, as well. Ver dala Ven endured only as an oddity in Betnoni's family line, one born with the mark and gift per generation, a trait given from parent to child. Legend insisted that the single Ver dala Ven born per generation would have been the Star's Chosen, even if Ver dala Ven had continued to thrive in large communities as they once had, but of course, no one could ever confirm that as a fact. It was one of many pleasant myths that comforted Ordinary Ones, and filled their temples with faithful patrons.

On the eve of Ver dala Ven Voktu's accidental death, he passed the secret to his only gold-eyed son, Cobo, along with a cryptic prophecy of his own. "Betnoni will watch over you and your descendants, Cobo. You have nothing to fear, and there is no shame."

Cobo didn't give thought to his father's prophecy until the day he chose to leave Ona and Jantideva, to run away from a broken heart. Wrapped in regret and jealousy, he believed his father's words were like curses leveled against him in anger. In his faulty memory, he did not see his father's forgiveness, and he did not recognize the advent of the first sign.

The first sign of the Rebirth is awakening. A forgotten north shatters and pours forth horror and guilt. To take the hard path, the Lost must deliver the Untrained into the hands of the enemy

Part One

Chapter 1

The exhibition between Master Lodan Kru Dok and the current kai'gam'Mod, Valerian, was meant to be light entertainment for the daka's guests. Watching the intensity in Valerian's dark face, it was clear there was nothing light about his unwillingness to lose to Master Kru Dok. He was playing a grudge match. Valerian took the honor of kai'gam'Mod after Lodan retired. In short, the title had been passed to the second best, not won. Valerian had defended his claim to the title bequeathed to him for five seasons, but none of the victories were sweet. The advent of his career had been spent in the Master's shadows. In youth, he had soared to second place, a favorite against all contenders, except the Master. He made repeated attempts, and failed to take the championship from Master Lodan in a true match. Valerian's appetite for victory was sharpened by his knowledge that this may be his last opportunity to prove his worth to the gaming world.

Jishni was not one to be swept away by sports, but as the contenders' blades crossed, her heart beat a bit faster. The match was brilliant from the start. The sleek and handsome Master Lodan gracefully defended Valerian's muscle bound attacks. His composed features did not hint at strain of mind, body or soul. Valerian on the other hand, scowled and grunted as he heaved his heavy blade about, and shouted out insults to incite his opponent to anger. Lodan was imperturbable. Jishni did not doubt that Master Lodan would take an easy victory.

The blades reflected the spotlight in intermittent bursts as they crossed, Valerian the aggressor forcing Master Lodan back with cruel ardor. Lodan accepted each blow with a step backward, and at the very moment that it seemed he'd be forced out of bounds he did a smart flip, leaping high though he hadn't seemed to exert much effort, the momentum of his legs carrying him through to a perfect landing on Valerian's unguarded side. The Master's blade circled his upper body, floating around him, arcing over his head and coming down on Valerian's neck for the deathblow. He stopped short of his mark by less than a

3

finger's width and shouted, "Ha!" underscoring the judge's call of one point.

The crowd lifted their voices, a deafening roar filling the outdoor arena, drowning Valerian's disgruntled shout in the din. Jishni clutched at the front of her gown and laughed aloud, pleased for Lodan, for there were some who thought he might have lost his edge after five seasons off the circuit.

Bail leaned near her face to be heard, his smile slightly mocking. "Not excited by the games, eh?"

The blush in her cheeks must have darkened, because he laughed at her, fondly, not with malice. She touched her hot cheeks and marveled at how good she felt.

The two competitors positioned themselves in the center of the arena, and once the signal was given, they continued to spar. This time Lodan took the aggressive stance. Unlike Valerian's lumbering power, Lodan's movements were light and like dance steps, rhythmic and yet unpredictable, and his blade floated around him as if his hand didn't hold it at all, but of its own volition in flight. Jishni held her breath as Lodan grew a grin on his features during his attack, a diabolical grin meant to unsettle his opponent.

"Daka Jishni." Nan said close to her ear.

"No, not now." She moaned, unwilling to take her eyes off the match.

Her assistant bent at the waist to speak lowly to Jishni, her eyes also on the match. "I am very sorry to interrupt, but Director Governor Drindle Mos'm and Commander Moba have arrived to Ona and are requesting an emergency audience. You asked that I tell you of their arrival? Shall I tell them to wait?"

Her moment of peace had been too fleeting. She glanced to Bail, whose expression had turned serious.

"Thank you, Nan. We'll see them now."

Bail stood, offering his arm to Jishni.

The match enthralled, and yet it did not escape notice that the dakas left their private gallery before it ended. Chancellor Yana stood and followed, as did his entourage.

Daka Jishni followed Nan's quick pace from the starlit outdoor arena and through a private corridor leading into the

4

Palace. Their Watchers kept pace with them, silent shadows, splendid looking men and women in purple uniforms, their lives dedicated to protecting the dakas. Yet even so protected, court mindreaders were at their backs as well, ensuring that not even the thought of harm may come to the dakas.

Reaching the round antechamber where the corridor branched off in three directions, Nan ushered them into the lift that would take them into the upper levels of Ona. Music and sounds of merriment reached their ears, floating down the corridor from one of the three ballrooms.

"I certainly hope Taen is enjoying the celebration." Jishni said, a note of regret in her voice. Everything they did to further Taen's destiny was met with his resistance. He'd been sulking about the palace for a full season, and Jishni was at a loss as to how to help him accept his new position.

Bail replied, "His friends are here tonight. No doubt they are reveling in high fashion."

"His friends are, perhaps." She murmured.

Bail stood close to her side in the lift, his hand on the small of her back, a comfort to her these days. For the most part, their marriage had been a cold one, arranged for them in childhood and consummated without the benefit of love. Despite their emotional separation, Bail was a most caring partner during her pregnancies. She knew, in her heart, that this was why she let herself become pregnant again, though their youngest son neared the age of decision, thirteen. Despite her increasing responsibilities with the Alliance, her age and fears of health problems, she wanted to once again feel his hand at the small of her back in that reassuring way. Another few days and the warmth between them would pass away as new life once again entered the palace. Twins this time, but no chance at a daughter. Two more boys were on their way, her physician had warned. She was resigned to living in a household of men, and had already chosen names for their fourth and fifth sons.

She reached for Bail's hand, and held it at her back, afraid. Afraid of the birth. Afraid of the future. Afraid for more reasons than bad news coming from Drindle Mos'm.

5

A lift took them to the Vass Chamber, where more than two men awaited their arrival. Grouped in the center of the chamber were Jishni's political advisors, her trans-cultural liaisons, Ona's historian, and the full host of twenty-eight Alliance ministers. They stood in loose groups, discussing matters among themselves. Their abrupt silence as the dakas entered disturbed Jishni further, more so than their pitying looks. Or did she imagine the pity? She wondered. Hers was not an enviable position.

Commander Moba stood facing the lift, his ever present scowl firmly affixed on his thin features. Moba fell in beside Bail as they all entered the Vass Chamber, causing Bail to slip his hand away from her back, as if touching his wife in the presence of one of his officers were taboo.

Left with a cold chill where his hand once rested, she took her place in the circle of seats, resting her hand on the pale blue ariq stone to her right. The stone gave her palm a ticklish buzz, confirming that the library had recognized her. The meeting would now be recorded for posterity.

She waited for all to be seated, noting with a sigh that Yana and his priests entered the Vass to join them. Yana's political aspirations were once relegated to the happenings in Ona. Since their trouble in the north began, his interest in the matters of state had become intense.

The lights softened, and all present settled in a brief silence.

In as smooth and regal tone as she could muster, Jishni bade Drindle Mos'm to speak. "Your report, Director-Governor."

The Director-Governor of the Northern territories inclined his head slightly. "Daka Jishni, the news from the border is grim."

"I assumed so, considering the manner of my summons."

"The Dilgos have refused to come to the peace table. Instead, they have attacked Montrose."

Jishni sat back into her chair as if shocked, but she wasn't shocked at all. She expected no less from the new adversaries. Their demands were outlandish.

"They are a small force, with antiquated weapons." Moba interjected, as if speaking for Drindle Mos'm, "And yet their forces have turned out to be most formidable, indeed. I am afraid we will need more forces to secure the border."

"We do have an alternative to dealing with them." Chancellor Yana said, deliberately measuring his words. "We could repair the Dome of Silence, just as daka Corrinne prescribed, and close them into their exile once again."

"No." Bail stated unequivocally, though it was not his word that moved the advisors, nor the Alliance.

Jishni heeded his wisdom, and made his word her decision. "I agree." She said, "Enough harm has been done to these people by the hands of our ancestors. There must be another way."

"If I may," Moba stepped into the circle of seats, to the raised podium and the main ariq stone linking them with the library. He placed his hand on the stone, and once he was recognized, he said, "Playback Montrose attack."

Lifelike images of war, and warriors, appeared about the podium, projected through the ariq stone's memory.

The sight of the Dilgo aggressors caused Jishni to gasp aloud. They were giants, standing twice the size of the people under attack.

"These are recordings of Dilgos as they entered Montrose," Moba said coldly, "recorded by a City Watcher. The giants of our legends have come to life. The Dilgo warriors are twice the size, twice the weight, and ten times the strength of our average Pliadors. Look now," he said of the moving image that towered over Jishni and Bail's seats, "and you will see among the giants, there are Dilgos of a smaller stature."

The sight of the smaller Dilgos, darting into the action between scores of giants, drew a prolonged silence from all present. First to appear was a man with four arms, each hand wielding a primitive weapon, hacking through the ranks of Montrose Watchers with murderous glee. Behind him were creatures so bizarre in appearance they did not even resemble men. They moved in packs, galloping along on all fours, the scales on their back glimmering red and green in the morning sun, and they attacked like animals, ripping at their victims with sharp teeth and strong jaws. The sight of one lunging at a screaming toddler and ripping it apart caused Jishni to cringe and avert her eyes. Bail set aside his strict public formality to place a hand on her shoulder, and for the comfort she could have wept her relief.

One of the red beasts stood up on its hind legs, ready to pounce on another victim, and they all saw his face, and his face was that of a man.

"A gruesome display of the unnatural." Drindle stated, eyes away from the moving images.

Moba continued, unmoved, it seemed, by the bloodshed or the strangeness of their enemy. "The giants in the attack force are the legion of Rito-Sant, of whom we are trying to negotiate. The rest are called Ryslack, they are no more than slaves to the giants. Their only weapons are those of great antiquity, and yet they swept through the Montrose Watchers with ease, for it would seem that they are all immune to lume dust, therefore completely unharmed by our weapons."

"How is that possible?" Bail demanded, his tone hushed.

Aton Greely, historian and keeper of the library records, cleared his throat self-consciously before interjecting. "By the nature of the Dome of Silence, daka." He said apologetically, "The lume dust introduced into the high atmosphere of their air wasn't enough to eradicate them, as daka Corrinne first hoped. Instead, they were made into the aberrations you see here, strange in appearance and fully immune to the only weapon we have that may have evened the odds against them."

Jishni viewed the bloodshed with tears in her eyes. Their troops fought a useless ground battle against an enemy armed with antiquated weapons.

"What crime could they have committed to force daka Corrinne to lock them into the Coulcoubanna mountains?"

Chancellor Yana replied, self-importance clear in his tone and carriage. "In her communiqué, left to the Ona Suma for safe keeping, daka Corrinne's instructions only warned that the creatures in the northlands were dangerous enough to warrant permanent eradication. She did not reveal their crime."

"I want to see the actual communiqué."

8

Yana balked. "Daka, it was set for my eyes only, or rather for the eyes of Ona's Chancellor by the chance the Dome should fall."

"Yana, I mean no disrespect, but I do not care about Corrinne's instructions. I demand to see that communiqué immediately."

Yana reddened slightly, and balked only in gesture, expression. "I will have it transferred to the main library, momentarily." He replied hesitantly. He lay his hand on the rounded ariq stone before his seat, and asked aloud to view the Northland Message.

A soft whirring sound preceded the disappearance of the Dilgos and the appearance of daka Corrinne. The image was clear, as if recorded on an ariq stone in the present day. Her flamboyant style of dress dated the piece, a gown so thick with material that she looked heavy set and unable to move. The busy print abounded with shaggy metallic streamers, a messy overindulgent fashion that Ona had not seen in twenty centuries.

Jishni's eyes found the proud features of her direct ancestor, a great-many times over-grandmother. The Janti family features were present, dark and plentiful hair and dark features, and hard black eyes that held no compassion.

Daka Corinne spoke.

"The curse has claimed another child of my house. My daughter Anja lost her only son to a terrible accident. The child reminded me well of Porje, my dear son, dead now thirty seasons." Her eyes fell away, grief obviously still with her, even after thirty seasons.

Jishni's hands drifted to her pregnant belly, to feel the movement of her children. The curse had visited her parents, with the death of her older sister, but had not touched her children as of yet. The fear for her sons was always with her, though far in the back of her mind, an eventuality she chose not to acknowledge until the day came, if it came. She hoped, as her children grew older and no tragedy visited them, that she'd be the one daka who did not lose a child to Betnoni's evil curse.

Corrinne's tone hardened. "Ver dala Ven Locat had reason to mourn Anja's child, too, I am afraid, but that information will

9

not leave the Ona Order. Anja's child will remain illegitimate in the eyes of the Alliance, for better he be known as illegitimate than the product of a forbidden union between a girl and a man older than her grandfather." She winced, clearly incensed by the entire situation. "In his grief, Locat divulged a secret to me that Ver dala Ven has kept from the dakas and from the Suma since Betnoni's death-"

The recording broke, and Corrinne's image was distorted, diagonal lines through her face and torso.

In a blink of an eye the image was restored and the recording resumed. "To protect the future generations of dakas, the Dome of Silence must remain in place, intact. I've placed the problem of maintaining the Dome of Silence upon a sect of Suma who are entirely loyal to my cause. They are the Dagnor Sect, and will heed your wisdom if the time comes. If you are listening to this message, no doubt there is trouble. Please, do what you can to replace the dome as soon as possible. The eradication of the Dilgos is not enough to end the threat to the dakas. We must ensure that no Ver dala Ven of any lineage can cross into the northlands. It is the only way to preserve Ona."

Corrinne disappeared.

"What is missing from her recording?" Jishni demanded.

"I do not know." Yana replied, averting his eyes. "The recording was damaged by the time I viewed it."

"Whatever it was," Drindle commented, "that Locat told daka Corrinne, she found it troubling enough to close off an entire people from the world, to strike their names from our history, to strike their location from our maps."

"It would appear that a terrible injustice has been done to them, for a reason we, or they, may never know."

"Jishni, do not grow soft for their cause." Bail intoned, "Whatever injustice they suffered at the hands of daka Corrinne, they do not deserve our most important treasure."

She glanced at Bail, and felt for him what must have been love, for she'd never felt so grateful to have him at her side.

"We must retaliate." Bail added, speaking now to the entire session, "I will take the Daka Redd out of low dock, and I will put down this force of barbarians."

Approval was voiced by all, except for Jishni.

After the dismissal of the impromptu meeting, Jishni asked Moba and Nan to go ahead, so that she and Bail could have a private moment.

"Must you leave us? Can't you let your Co-command put down the rabble? Taen's elevation is so close, and the babies could be born at any time."

He looked into her eyes, and smiled in a way that melted her heart for him. "I'll be back before both blessed events, I promise."

"I will hold you to that promise."

Indecision, torn between two duties, fettered his brow. "I will tell Taen myself that I must leave."

"He will not be happy."

"Nor am I." He admitted.

He embraced her and she melted into his arms, a simple act done by loving couples daily. For she and Bail, she could count on one hand the warm embraces they shared outside those that preceded the satisfaction of their physical needs. She buried her face in his black uniform, breathing in the woody scent of him, feeling his arms firm around her back, feeling the movement of their twins inside of her, and held on.

"I wish—" but she couldn't say it aloud, for it betrayed something she held too dear, and he didn't prompt her for more, for his mind was on war, and he was already gone before he released her and said his goodbye.

ෙ෬෧෨෧෨෧෨ఄఄ

Historically, the elevation ceremony was held in the grand Orin Hall beneath the towering crystal spire of Leila. On the tenth night of festivities, after numerous balls and plays and competitive matches in the kai'gam arena, the succeeding Ver dala Ven, having been recognized as fully evolved, would prove their worth by rousing the spire in song. In the past, different Ver dala Ven used different methods. The most recent to be elevated, Cobo, then a mere thirteen old boy, simply pointed to the interior of the star, touching it with his will, and, it

11

was said by Crier historians, the spire pierced the guests below with a melody so inspiring that it moved daka Janus to tears.

Taen had no idea how to make the spire sing, and no matter what he did, no matter how hard he willed it so, where he pointed his finger, where he gestured with all his might, the spire remained stubbornly silent.

The kai'gam match continued, drawing all in attendance out of the Orin hall to the arena. Alone, Taen tried again. Gritting his teeth, looking upward into the cone of the spire, he threw his hands up, his full body rigid, his jaw tightened until it hurt, in one last effort to force the spire to produce at least a hint of a hum.

Stupid boy, he could almost hear his teacher berating him, *you cannot force the gift! It obeys a gentle will!*

Nothing gentle about the staff Riar Sed thumped across his back to drive his point home.

The enduring silence caused him to laugh harshly at himself, at his mother, at his teacher, at the Suma, at Ver dala Ven Cobo, at the whole host of Ancients, beginning with Thranlam'Sum. Arising from the his deep core of frustration he growled at the spire, a growl that turned into a mighty bellow and he shook both his fists at it for offending his ego.

The spire echoed his bellow.

Again he laughed. His echo would be the only noise he produced in the spire of Leila, today and all the days to come.

"Riar Sed's tutorial skill was, indeed, lacking."

Taen started guiltily at the sound of his father's voice. He spun on his heel. Bail, a daka by marriage and an Ordinary One born of Ver dala Ven Voktu, stood several paces behind Taen, beneath the spire. He'd walked the full length of the hall, with ample time to witness Taen's private angst.

Chagrinned that he couldn't even sense the approach of an Ordinary One, even with conventional instincts, Taen retorted lightly, "I never asked to be trained."

Impatience leapt into Bail's stance, though he kept his reply moderate and simple. "It is your birthright."

Taen's glittering gold eyes swept the high pitch of the ceiling and the interior of the spire, far above them, and he rolled them, succumbing to easy self-deprecation. "And I will no doubt make a fine Ver dala Ven."

His sarcasm softened Bail. "I am certain you will be worthy of the title, as worthy as your predecessor."

Taen's bitterness twisted his mouth into a pained smile at the thought of his predecessor. Despite the efforts of his parents and the court to keep him from the truth, he knew full well of his questionable beginnings. He held the dubious honor of being born with the potential to become Ver dala Ven, as well as being thought of as Bail's heir apparent, future leader of Jantideva. By law and the dictates of good taste he was not permitted to occupy both seats. He would either be a daka or Ver dala Ven. He had little interest in the latter. Indeed the very thought of being consigned to a life of service after tasting a promise of the highest rank in all the world filled him with cold rage. He'd spent his life proving his worth to his court, the Suma and the Alliance, and now his parents seemed all to willing to pass his claim to his younger brother, Bailin. He hated them both for the full sum of their betrayals, past and present. He wanted nothing better than to be rid of them, for in good riddance came his inheritance, that which not even the Suma could dispute. He had no other recourse, but the one they forced upon him, it was not his doing, but their fault. All their fault.

From the moment he'd been placed under Riar Sed's tutelage Taen had worked diligently to hone his meager and dwindling skills, not to please his court or hasten his rise to Ver dala Ven, but to give him the edge he needed to ensure his liberation. If only he had more time, for it seemed the impact of his abilities were so small to be cumulative, like a slow acting poison. He'd made it habit to inject his poison into the mind of the man who'd pretended to be his father since his birth each time they were together, though perhaps this time his fury and frustration gave the poison a more literal kick.

Bail's face twitched and he shook his head, so slight a movement that if it weren't for Taen's knowledge of what Bail was fighting, no one would have noticed. Bail exuded control and strength, rarely showing his true self to anyone, even his family. A respected commander of the Pliadors, a straight-

13

backed assurance in a crisp black uniform, a handsome and confident leader, he was well loved and trusted by the Alliance for the very traits that made him a stranger among his own family, in his own home. Taen knew him well enough to know that Bail would never share his self-destructive thoughts with another living being. They were weaknesses in action. Bail, above all else, deplored weakness, in himself and others. It was his ultimate weakness, and Taen counted on it to protect him from the court's suspicion.

Maintaining an unperturbed mask, Bail continued in a calm manner. "I've bad news, Taen. I must leave for the north tonight. There is trouble in Montrose. Unfortunately, it is a matter that cannot wait, not even a few days."

"I suppose mother will proclaim me elevated before the Suma?" he countered, amused by the increasing mockery his elevation was becoming.

"I should be back for your elevation ceremony. If not, however, since you must be presented by a descendant of Ver dala Ven, Bailin will do the honor."

Taen averted his eyes, and turned away, certain his hatred for Bail had appeared in his face. "Is this your way of asserting his right to your seat, as well?"

"It will establish certain positions in the minds of the court and the Alliance," Bail admitted, ever pragmatic about such matters, "putting to rest their concerns and shutting the mouth of Crier gossip."

Honesty, at least. Bail had never lied to him, at least not openly. There were those lies of omission to consider, but were they really lies? Taen seethed, resisting the urge to press Bail on the reason for the Crier gossips, cornering him on the facts of his true paternity. It took all his strength to remain sensible in the face of an utter loss. Bail possessed the courage to stand before the Suma and admit the truth, and would if he thought Taen knew the truth. He protected his wife's indiscretion for Taen's sake, and Taen's sake alone. He loved Taen, so much so that there were moments that Taen felt a twinge of guilt for returning Bail's love with gut sickening hatred.

Misunderstanding Taen's pensive silence as self condemnation, Bail added, "Please, always remember that I have faith in you. You will make a fine Ver dala Ven and serve Ona well. I will be proud of you for all your efforts, great or small."

A noisy gang of young men galloped into the Orin Hall, laughing and calling for Taen. Their behavior settled immediately as they noted Taen's company. Each young man, their families well connected to Ona and the finest families in Jantideva, came to attention and bowed to their daka.

Bail spoke briefly to them in a relaxed manner, especially to Evran, who'd just entered into the Military Consortium. Evran wore a uniform much like the daka's, save the appearance of the dowager's fortune of medals on Bail's chest and armband, spoke of his teachers and flight training as if he were pleased to be stuck at the Consortium. Taen knew all too well how Evran hated military training. He'd wanted to spend his life and his inheritance inebriated in Olla houses bedding strange women. His parents, however, preferred he appeal to daka Bail, in order to further their own agenda within the court. In private Taen and his friends laughed at aristocratic games, but in the face of daka Bail, Evran fell into the role his parents expected him to play.

Bail obviously admired Evran, never sensing his insincerity. The whole put on made Taen want to laugh aloud.

Once they were alone, Taen taunted Evran by mocking him, "Oh yes, daka Bail, I am ever so excited to become your lackey. May I lick your boots all the days of my life."

"Oh shut up, you skinny slank." Evran retorted, his good-humor intact. "I should be commended and have your highest respect, for I've just performed a feat of perfected boot licking despite being shamefully drunk. My mother would drop dead if she knew!" And he laughed, that laugh of half desperation, half resignation that came from someone who was not the master of his own fate. Taen knew the laugh, too well.

Forgiving his friends their shortcomings was far easier than forgiving his own. He threw an arm around Evran's shoulders and said, "Let's get out of here. Let's go to an Olla house, and watch half naked girls ply us for pleasure."

Their agreement came in hoots and whistles that made the spire ring.

Traveling to the Center-plex, far from Ona, the celebrations and pressures of his fate, was therapeutic. They sauntered into an upscale Olla house called The Golden Door, each wearing a black mask to avoid the recognition of the other members. Membership was supposed to be a secret, and the owners of Olla houses were unscrupulously dedicated to their members, but to be safe, the masks helped.

Taen and his friends took a private table, sitting on the floor in large pillows, and summoned the dancers. The women assembled quickly. Their dresses were yellow, the loose skirts knotted with bells, the bodice tight and revealing. They danced for the young patrons in fine unison, their skirts flowing provocatively upward. Soon enough the Olla girls would be nude, and in their arms.

Taen's eyes drifted from the face of the girl he'd chosen, to the bells sewn in her skirt, and as he listened to the chiming, all else in the world disappeared. An image of Bail's boot heels clicking across the Orin hall's marble floor overlay the sight and sound of the swirling skirts, and Taen threw his spell at the boot heels, hoping with all his heart for Bail's sudden, horrible demise.

Chapter 2

The vision visited him as he woke. Women with bells knotted in their skirts, their faces veiled, dancing around him in a circle. The dance began with slow sensuality, the women demure in movement, and steadily increased in speed and exaggerated gestures, all the while the clamor of the bells rose, intensified. He was bathed in a hot, anxious sweat by the time he came to his senses.

It had to be a dream, he told himself. He'd been sleeping, and the heat of the day must have inspired him to the hot, erotic dream. He'd not had a vision in years. For that matter, he'd not had a hot erotic dream in years, but no, it was just a dream, a product of his prolonged celibacy.

He wasted no time getting up and folding his mat. He ignored his immediate discomfort, his thirst and hunger, and quickly packed his mat into a large bag, company to their supplies and their harvested yava flowers. Gella had let him sleep too long.

"We should wait," she barked as she descended from a craggy hill. She appeared asexual in her travel clothes, layers of leather strips bunched and wrapped so thick about her that one could not see whether she was a woman or man. A hood formed a second skin over her face and head. Only her green eyes were visible, through slits made in the leather. "until the sun has gone down completely."

"We have a full night before reaching the low plains." Cobo replied easily, firmly. "I want to reach Strum before daybreak."

Her incredulity raised the pitch of her voice. "You cannot keep such a pace!"

"I've not been sick in days!" He retorted, and under his mask, cringed a frown. Too defensive.

Her hands drifted to her hips. He could almost imagine her pretty face twisting in disapproval. "Your weakness is worse in the heat of the day. Cobo, I will not carry a corpse home with me!"

"Dying." And he laughed at the very idea of death.

17

"Is that why you insisted we do our trading early this season?" she asked, her voice swaying to fear. "Will you not tell me if you are so sick you expect to die?"

It was a feeling he couldn't describe, an urge he couldn't possibly begin to explain. His sickness of late was linked to his need to rush their normal trades, but it was not death he expected in Strum. "I am not dying. Not today, in any case." He sensed she didn't believe him, and that there was no way he could convince her otherwise.

"We should get moving. I want to be out of the Black Desert before the sun is set."

She nodded, and in the silent gesture lay a heat of emotions and questions. She picked up her pack, already rolled and tied, and heaved it onto her shoulders. Without another word to him, she resumed their journey. He lagged behind several paces, walking alone in order to hide his fatigue from her. The heat was taxing, more so than he cared to admit. Occasionally she would take a hesitant look over her shoulder to be sure he was still with her, as if she expected to see him lying flat on his face in the sand, rather than keeping up. Thus assured, she went on, and he followed.

At dusk they crossed the last remnants of black sand, finally leaving the outermost boundary of their tribal homeland. Calli covered a vast area in the east, a barren desert fit only to grow the intoxicating yava flowers. The Elders thought Cobo mad to want Calli, set apart from all the rest of Shodite society. He being who he was, they were more than willing to offer him a place of honor in any tribe he wished. In the end, they gave him what he wanted, and dedicated him to Calli.

The desert surrounding Strum was forgiving and cool, and as they walked, they removed their protective clothing in gradations. Here, where the sand was clean and alive with desert brush, there was no fear of blood beetles or contaminants. Cobo pulled off his hood, shook out his scraggly brown hair and took a deep, cleansing breath. He felt baked, feverish, sensations that were swept away by a cool breeze scented with wild grass.

Gella stripped to the waist, and more by the time they approached Strum's city gate, until all that covered her was her waist length reddish hair and the wraps on her feet and lower legs. Nudity was accepted in Shodalum, and most of the natives went about uncovered. Cobo, raised by prudish Janti society, could not bring himself to strip more than his outer layer of wraps.

"Is there a festival, you think?" she asked Cobo, eyeing the throng of travelers approaching Strum from the west.

"Early traders, like us." He suggested.

"Indeed?"

Her sarcasm was not missed. "If there is a festival, do you wish to stay on a few days?"

"Hmmm, if you wish to."

A lopsided grin spread across his features. "My Gella's way of saying yes."

"Perhaps." She replied, and she suppressed a smile.

The city was large, and confusing for a new visitor. Eleven minor tribes had settled Strum, and the eleven now claimed various districts in the city as their own. Often there were feuds in progress between one house and another over boundaries, or less important matters, and it paid to know which tribes held the deepest enmity for one another. But knowing was not enough, one needed to know the city in order to stay safe. The city itself was difficult to know, a labyrinth of unmarked streets with homes that looked similar, and a continuous open market that added color and confusion. If a stranger knew that the er Ilanda tribe wove rugs and cloth, they might presume to know that to follow the streets with rug makers would make a safe and direct path to the city plaza. And as long as they continued on an easterly course, they would be correct. One wrong turn onto a seemingly innocuous alley would abruptly change their location to the er Zarnjim, also rug makers who have been active in a feud with a fraction of their own tribe for several generations. During Cobo's first visit to Strum, many seasons ago, he was caught in a flash riot in the er Zarnjim. A man next to him was killed. He learned quickly which sleepy streets to avoid.

The city's plaza lay off center of the maze, and decent lodging for traders could only be found there.

"We may not be able to find a place to sleep." Cobo commented as they worked their way through the crowd. They held onto each other, certain that if they let loose each other's arms that they'd become hopelessly separated.

"There is Estr er Fantoz." She suggested.

Cobo grimaced at the name. "Out of the question." He retorted. The family once housed Cobo in their bordello, before Calli had been given to him, and it was under Estr er Fantoz's roof that he met Gella. She was a child, serving up her flesh to Estr's guests in exchange for meager daily portions of food and adequate lodging. It was not a life she'd chosen, but rather one thrust upon her after the death of her parents. She was the wealthiest member of her tribe, and her aunts desired her wealth. In order to take her lands they needed to get rid of her. Murder was not acceptable, but selling her into sexual slavery was perfectly legal. She was a maiden too young to wed, old enough to use, and of such beauty she exacted a high price. Cobo felt drawn to her from the moment he laid eyes on her winsome face. She was twelve, hardly a woman and yet so jaded by experience she seemed much older. She was beaten often for her defiant tongue, but not cowed in the least. Cobo was certain that had she stayed in the bordello her owner would have eventually murdered her. It was Cobo's deep compassion for her that moved him to do the unthinkable in the eyes of civilized Shodite society and buy her contract. It was acceptable for a man to frequent the bordellos, to live in the bordellos, but not so for him to own a slave for private use. The subtle social moor evaded Cobo's understanding. He assured the Elders he wanted nothing more from her than to free her from her fate, and to appease them he took her tribal name, legally binding them as brother and sister. They became a tribe of two, the al Perraz. For a long time they lived as family, sharing a home and duties, he as a parent and she, the child.

Their relationship became complicated as she matured. Cobo, weakened by his loneliness and her open willingness, took her as his lover. The beginnings were sublime. They sought each other's pleasure often, and Gella had much to teach him, though she was so much younger. She was open with her affections, and gave him her heart.

It didn't matter how good it felt to be with her, eventually his guilt eroded his pleasure, simply because he had so little to give to her in return.

"I should be as a father to you, or like a brother." Cobo said once during an argument, an argument spurred by her light talk of their future, and children, and generations of kin to come. "Your plans should be made with another man in mind, not with me."

His anger temporarily blinded him to the hurt he had inflicted upon her, but ever since he remembered it vividly and with regret a thousand times over.

"I don't want another man."

"I can't give you what you need." He insisted, "You know my heart belongs to another. Why would you want a tainted love?"

"She isn't here. I am here!"

"She is always here," Cobo admitted, "Between us, always on my mind, a torment I cannot escape, nor one I deserve to escape."

Gella stopped sleeping on his mat with him that night and took up residency in the open loft of their small home. Resentment lurked in the background of their daily lives, sour places they did their best to deny and refused to revisit. Neither would leave the other. Where would they go? They were family, of the same tribe, and in Shodite culture tribal ties ran deeper than either resentment or love. Cobo was aware that Gella often took lovers, usually when they traveled to Strum to trade their goods, and she expected he did, too, though she was far too jealous to ask outright.

Cobo preferred to keep to himself.

They reached the town plaza, and the inn where they usually stayed during the trading season, as giant bonfires were being lit. Women draped with yellow sashes about their shoulders sang a dedication to Betnoni.

"Burnt offerings to the goddess." Gella said, her brows crinkling, "It is too early to celebrate our emancipation."

"Yes." Cobo agreed.

Curious, they drifted into the crowd and watched the offerings burn, and the devoted pray. The women's song was mournful, keening, and tugged at Cobo's heart.

"Ho, venerable one!" A thin man wearing the vestments of an Elder came up beside them and presented a warm gap toothed smile. A cloying sweet scent surrounded him, and even in the faded starlight it was clear he was ill.

"I am Radi of the il Ubay, Tribal Elder of Lot."

"Well met, Radi. I am Gella and this is Cobo. We are al Perraz of Calli."

"Calli? Aha!" He switched sides, placing himself between Gella and Cobo. "I have heard someone lives in Calli." He peered hard at Cobo, trying to see his profile better in the darkness. "An immigrant. I've never met a true immigrant. Is it true you are from Jantideva?"

"True."

Radi chuckled, his head bobbing lightly on a rail thin neck. "There are tales of you far and wide, al Perraz of Calli. You've heard them?"

"If they are scandalous, then they are not tales, but truth." Gella threw the jab over Radi's head for Cobo's benefit.

Radi heard, but paid no attention to her. "The tales I heard were concerning your family line. I heard you are Ver dala Ven."

Cobo tilted his head toward Radi to allow the subtle glow of his gold eyes to be seen in the darkness.

Radi hissed a sigh, and smiled. "And so the tales are true. Is it true, also, that the breed is dead?"

"The *breed*." Cobo replied easily, though contempt raced through him for the manner in which he'd been categorized, apart from all others. "I suppose not, at least not until the day I die."

Radi missed the sarcasm. "Oh yes, but the old tales tell of a kin to Betnoni breaking the cycle of Ver dala Ven, and ending the breed. It is told, and you must know this by heart, for you know all, that you are the last link to a bygone era."

22

"The Masing Star made us," Cobo offered, trying to shake off his sudden irritation with the man. "and it unmade us when it left. The why, or how of it never interested me much. And, just for your information, I've never known all there is to know. I am just like you, Radi, I know nothing more than I can see with my eyes, or hear with my ears."

Radi hummed contemplatively. "You do not know of the miracle, then?"

"Miracle?"

Radi laughed good-naturedly. "Don't tell me you have not heard tales of the miracle in Nari!"

Cobo resisted the urge to sigh. The superstitious Shodites, always watchful for miracles.

"What type of miracle?" Gella prompted, which earned her Cobo's weary glare.

He laughed again, this time in bewilderment of their shared ignorance. "Thib of the ul Olun, the honored Elder of Nari, has seen visions of Betnoni and heard the Worshipped One's messages of hope. I have also heard that the place where Betnoni perished is now enchanted with healing properties. I am leaving Strum tonight to make the long journey to Nari so that I may pay homage to the Worshipped One. Oh yes, yes, as do all the pilgrims here tonight, we have traveled as one tribe. I go, also, to lay prostrate on the sand where her feet touched so that I may turn away my illness."

Radi's vivid hope aroused Cobo's grudging pity, for he knew that no amount of sand could turn away a terminal illness. "I wish you well on your journey." Cobo replied, and perhaps it was pity that caused him to reach for Radi's shoulder, for otherwise his gesture seemed involuntary. Contacting Radi, he felt a warm flow move from him and into the sick man. He had not used his gift or sensed it near for all the years he'd been in Shodalum, and figured he couldn't remember how to arouse it, much less use it, if he tried. But it came back to him in the blink of an eye, easily, compelled by compassion. It was as his father taught him, he was the conductor of the gift, no more.

Radi glowed happily, not knowing what renewed his strength, only having faith in his holy mission. "Thank you for your blessing, Son of Betnoni."

Cobo recoiled, "I wished you well. It was no blessing."

Radi wasn't convinced. "Bless us all, and travel to Nari with us to visit the sacred site. I am certain we will be safer in your care."

"Give my regards to Thib." Cobo replied, a dismissal, and he glanced to the fires and the people praying to a woman, long dead. He knew his lineage all too well, and they were not gods. Thib was by all accounts unimaginably old, and was probably succumbing to a disease of age. It was common for the very old to see visions of Betnoni. Shodites believed that once they died Betnoni carried them into the next life, the utopia she made for them at the bottom of the sea. Cobo knew better. Betnoni was gone, done. If there was an afterlife, she was with the Guardian Spirit of Creation. If not, she was a mere historical footnote.

Cobo turned away from the offerings, from Radi's tenacious company, and took Gella's arm to guide her away from madness and ignorance. She did not fight his guiding hand, though she twisted her head to keep her eyes on the prayer vigil.

They found an inn with a vacancy, a small and clean room with a window facing the plaza. They spread out their mats on the floor and left the shutters open to allow in night air. Neither of them could sleep. The smoke from the fires and noise of chanted prayers kept their eyes open, their bodies restless. Gella finally abandoned her sleep mat and sat in the window to look down upon the scene.

"They are preparing to leave Strum." She said softly.

"Good. I need rest." He murmured in return.

"You do not believe in miracles." She stated.

"Do you?"

She sighed, and was silent so long that he thought she'd fallen asleep in the window. He sat up to make sure she wasn't so tired that she might do something so dangerous, and found her staring down at the dying bonfire. Her features were soft in the reddish glow of the fire, her light hair smoldering, loose and wavy. Her lithe body was entirely nude, in repose, her long legs prettily linked and her hands relaxed on her thighs. Sublime sight, her beauty captured his imagination, moving swiftly from a baser fantasy to a shocking revelation; She would have made a fine wife. If only he'd let her be his mate, they could have had many children and a tribe with a future, instead of the barren, mortal tribe they'd become. He loved her in a fashion, a love so overshadowed by his past that it never grew, thrived, flourished. He so easily healed Radi. Who would heal him?

"Gella, do you believe in miracles?" he reposed, his voice subdued by his own thoughts.

She would not look at him, and yet her relaxed features became pensive. "On the day you arrived to Estr's, I had prayed to Betnoni to be liberated from my fate, through death or through a miracle, I didn't care."

He pushed himself all the way up, sitting cross-legged on his mat. "And I was your miracle?"

"Yes."

"But don't you see, I would have come had you prayed to Betnoni, or not. I had been on the road to Strum for days and days."

"But why Strum? Why didn't you travel to Galoxi or Nari? They are much closer to the border than Strum."

Amused, he replied, "I didn't know any better at the time. I was lost in on the plains forever, it seemed, until I found traces of the old roads. I just so happened to pick the road leading to Strum."

"Betnoni lead you to Strum, and to me."

"It was an accident of fate. Of good, or of ill, sometimes I do not know which. Are you happy with me, Gella?"

She turned her head his way, her face half obscured by the darkness inside their room, and answered his sudden question quickly. "I am very happy with you, Cobo."

"You deserve so much more." He admitted, and a pang groped at his heart. "I've taken your youth from you and in return provided a humble existence. I've needed you much more than you needed me, of that I am certain, and knowing it to be so, I would still fight to keep you in our house. I suppose I am a selfish man."

"All men are." She said, and as she turned away he could see her smile.

Heartened by her stab at humor, he added, "I do love you, Gella."

Her smile vanished. "If so, you will never say so again."

He let his admission drop into the chasm her love for him opened between them, and with difficulty, he changed the subject. "You are bored? Would you like to go downstairs for ale?"

"I want to dedicate our crop to Betnoni."

Taken aback, he balked. "We've less a crop this year than most. I was hoping to be able to take home stock enough for the winter, at least. I tire of eating yava root and slank to survive."

"A handful of flowers, and if it bothers you so, I will eat yava root and you may have my portion of the rest."

"Oh, do not martyr yourself on my behalf, my darling, I won't hear of it." He retorted, and knowing the battle was lost, he stood and began dressing, wrapping himself in the travel clothes he wore into the city.

She did not bother to dress, except to wear her prayer sash about her neck. Yellow cloth woven with a repeating hex design, significant as the color and texture represented Betnoni's gown. She opened one of the leather bags that carried the yava flowers, and carefully took a handful. The flowers were still fresh, in their prime. Dried, they were still valuable, but fresh, soft flowers were at their peak. A grown man could chew on one fresh yava flower and become roaring drunk. Medicinally, it was used for pain.

Cobo held back as Gella made her way to the bonfire. Only a few devoted worshippers remained in the city plaza, solemnly praying to the goddess. Gella joined a circle of women and sprinkled the flowers, a fortune rendered by a tainted desert, into the flames as she chanted a prayer of thanks. The murmuring around Cobo about the prize Gella had released into the fire made him uneasy. He fretted about whom may overhear, whether or not unscrupulous thieves were in the crowd, and he looked over his shoulder, from side to side. A group of old women stood directly behind him, and a small boy leaned

26

against the legs of one, his eyes wide and staring into Cobo's face.

"Betnoni's kin." One of the old women whispered as they saw the mark, his glowing gold eyes, and once they put him together with the young woman who'd made the generous offering they assumed that he'd come to Strum to endorse the miracle.

He swung around, a sharp retort poised on his tongue, that he didn't believe in their goddess of the sea, nor did he believe Betnoni deserved to be heralded as a goddess, for being her kin and of her lineage, he knew far better the mortal imperfection of their kind. But before he could unleash his unmerciful conviction, a vision came upon him, beyond his control or desire, and his surroundings changed. The nighttime scene of Strum's city plaza became a beach in broad daylight. There were ruins above were he stood, worn away stone walls and foundations, very much like those on Calli's waterfront, crumbling relics of Shodalum's short-lived industrial age. But unlike Calli, the sand here was pale, soft. He bunched his toes in the wet sand, and marveled at how real it felt. The sun, the spray of the sea, the smell of clean, open air, assaulted his senses.

A figure stood further down the beach. An old woman, so ancient he scarcely believed she was alive. She beckoned to him to come to her, and over the crashing waves, he heard her tremulous voice clearly.

"A prize awaits you in Nari, far greater than a handful of flowers."

Before he could move to join her, the scene changed to an opulent ballroom. He recognized the interior of Ona's Orin Hall. Well-dressed aristocrats surrounded him, women in their embellished gowns and men in their silken suits. His heart quickened as he thought he caught sight of Jishni in the shifting crowd, but it was the appearance of a young man with gold eyes like his that seized his full attention. The dark skinned young man was dressed well in blazing orange and looking a little bored.

"Taen." Cobo whispered as he recognized the grown version of his estranged son. Last he saw of Taen, the boy was but a babe, fresh from his mother's womb.

Instinct and longing made him reach out for the son he'd abandoned. Taen hid nothing, had never been taught to hide, and his true self lay open to Cobo's slightest contact. His spirit and thoughts were shrouded in darkness. Anger and envy had corrupted him and these virulent twins manifested as beasts and lunged at Cobo, screeching in his ears and clawing at his face and neck. Cobo screamed in horror.

His next sight was that of the old women against the backdrop of the dark city plaza, their eyes wide with shock. The boy with them was crying from fright. Though the beasts dwelling in Taen's heart had horrified him, he saw himself in the mirror of their reactions and broke loose with an uneasy laugh, morbidly amused by their shock. They thought him completely mad, shrieking for no reason, laughing for no reason.

He felt Gella's presence and her hand on his arm, and drew in her concerns for his well being. She intoned, "Come, Cobo. We must rest"

In their room, Gella lay him down on his mat and stretched out beside him, smoothing her hand on his bare chest, murmuring that he would feel better in the morning. He held her close, unashamed of how he needed someone to hold. He couldn't sleep, instead spent the night ruminating on the miracle Radi spoke of, and though he didn't believe in Betnoni, his vision left him with the undeniable urge to make the holy pilgrimage to Nari.

Before first light, he woke Gella, who was curled into his chest, and asked her if she would make the journey with him to Nari. Her grogginess sloughed away quickly.

"You've had a change of heart toward Betnoni?"

"Nothing has changed," he insisted, though he felt the opposite was true, "I am curious, that's all."

Her doubt was written in her frown, but she agreed to go with him, for she was as eager as Radi and the others to see the place where Betnoni supposedly appeared.

By morning of their fourth day of travel they reached the hilly outlands of Nari. Cobo was too tired to push on as he'd planned, so they made camp on a hill overlooking the valley plains and slept to dusk.

Cobo woke before Gella, awakened by the dream. The shrill cadence of bells cut off abruptly as he opened his eyes, but not before he felt another taste of his son's evil soul. Sickness twisted his stomach. He rolled off the mat, trembling and weak, and crawled away from Gella to prevent waking her if he got sick. At the edge of the hill's steep slope, he sat back on his heels and took deep breaths, waiting for the sickness to pass. Instead, his dream continued, drawing him deep into visions of the past. He left his sickness and weakness behind as he relived a thousand memories, most painful and filled with regret. Memories superimposing on the present, a present he did not live. Young faces, overlapping many times, aging before his eyes. Drawing him closer, guiding him home.

Gella found him deep in meditation.

Kneeling by his side, tears in her eyes, she asked him if he was feeling well. "Won't you tell me if you are ill?" she pleaded.

"I'm not ill, not in the way you fear." He assured her. He knew that his illness had to do with Taen. The connection between them that he'd severed so long ago had been restored somehow, and the evil infecting Taen affected Cobo's wellbeing, too, because he'd not known enough to protect himself. With every bit of his strength, he protected himself now. In offering her an easy explanation, he said, "I'm having visions again, and they are draining my strength. It's nothing to be concerned about."

"Visions of the future?"

Her ready acceptance of a gift she'd never seen him use caused him to smile involuntarily. He adored her fearless nature, the easy bend of her logic, her quick intelligence.

"Images of the past and present." He told her, "Images of faraway lands I've not seen in a lifetime, and people I never thought I'd see again."

"Is it Jishni you see?"

Her unexpected jealousy cautioned his tongue. "Taen." He said in half-truth, for Jishni had also been in his visions, tormenting him with images of dear pleasure he'd lost long ago.

"You have to go there, don't you?" she breathed, her voice hardly audible. "To Ona, to be with your son."

She struck to the heart of his visions so cleanly that he had to turn away.

"I always knew you would leave me one day."

"I'm not going to leave you."

"You aren't going home, then?"

He faltered over the truth. "I have to. Something terrible has happened to Taen. He's been polluted. He needs a guiding hand, guidance only I can give."

"And once you have given him the guidance he needs, you will return to Calli." The dubious remark told him that there was no convincing her that he would return.

In truth, he couldn't bear to be parted from her, because he feared as she did, that Ona might capture and keep him prisoner, or worse, he might again become the prisoner of his own heart.

"You come with me, and make sure I return to Calli."

His suggestion drew a laugh. "And become a slave? They still enslave my people in Jantideva, Cobo."

"Not you. You are my Chosen Sister, and in Jantideva that makes you an important person. Besides, we don't have to tell them that you are a Shodite. Your language is similar to Zarian, and you know enough Janti to get by."

"I am afraid of Jantideva. I am afraid of their ways, and their evils, and their sicknesses."

He touched her face. "I will protect you, Gella."

Her pretty sun darkened face settled into a frown and the depths of her green eyes withheld her immediate thoughts from his easy reach. He felt her anxiety, though, a match for his own, rumbling around in his stomach and chest. She didn't say she would go with him. She didn't say she would stay, either. She kept her thoughts to herself, leaving Cobo to agonize over leaving Shodalum without his dearest friend.

By dawn they reached the fringes of a sprawling squatter's camp, and from that point the path to the sea cut through a vast community of worshippers. Each tribe or family group burnt perpetual offerings to Betnoni. Smoke was thick in the air. Cobo could hardly see from one fire, to another, until they reached the shore, where the breeze coming off the choppy sea carried the smoke off their backs.

A familiar voice called to them from the crowd below. It was Radi, overjoyed to see them. With the agility of youth, he loped up the craggy rock face to where they stood. He presented himself, grinning. His color had returned, and he no longer looked frail.

"See?" and he sucked in a deep breath to show off his capacity to breathe, and grinning, he announced, "I've been healed!"

"Yes, Radi, I see you are in good health." Cobo replied, and he grinned with the man, pleased his gift worked so well and so fast.

"Come, make your prayers!"

Cobo glanced at Gella, and seeing her eagerness, he relented. They followed Radi down to the beach, to the water's edge.

"This is where I lay to be healed!" he said of a spot of sand where several people now lay prostrate to the Goddess.

Gella dropped to her hands and knees, and carefully lay on her stomach, stretching her hands above her head, and pressing her forehead into the sand. Her prayers were made silently, unlike the others on the beach who entreated Betnoni with loud wails.

Cobo had no intention of praying to a false goddess. He wished to rest, however, and dropped his pack off his back, with the intention of sitting on it for as long as Gella lay on the ground. As he did, he turned just so, and stopped short as he caught sight of an old woman watching him from across the mass of praying devoted. She held a walking stick and wore a juji, a large scarf that was tied around her waist like a skirt. She was petite and bony, her white hair thin and plaited, her skin

31

dappled by too many years in the sun, her breasts sagging long, her back bowed. She cut a deceptively frail appearance, and yet she exuded quiet strength. Cobo had never seen or met the well-known Elder, Thib ul Olun, but he recognized her instantly from his vision.

He left Gella to her prayers, and stepped over bodies to make his way to the Elder. She waited, her head held high and proud.

"You've come." She said, and she grinned a toothless grin. Her eyes sparkled with youth and vigor, despite her advanced age. "I've been expecting you. What took you so long?" She did not wait for him to reply to her cryptic remark. "Come, walk with me."

They followed a path made by fallen stone and toppled ruins, through a time weathered maze that was once buildings with many rooms, and purposes long dead. Few of Thib's tribe lived this close to the coast where the ruins still stood. As they reached the top of the rise above the beach, Cobo could see Nari, a sprawling community that encircled this forbidding place from a safe distance. Thib's windowless stone and mud hut was the only home this close to the sea.

"I've lived here the fullness of my life." She informed him, and she chuckled at the irony of it. "And alone for eighty years, now. Yesho, my Yesho, he died too young, and I lived too long, long enough to see all our children grow old and die. One hundred and twenty four full rounds of seasons I have seen with these eyes. But for all that living, I have never seen you!" And she chuckled at her own joke.

She led him up a gradual incline, one that ended at her doorway, and invited him in with a gesture.

"Sit." She ordered once they were in the darkness of her home, and he did so on a firm rug that bore her family name woven into the boxy design. She lit two lamps, one on either side of the hearth, throwing light on a stark room that that held few possessions. She offered him tea made from special grasses she grew, served in plain ceramic bowls and fed him fresh bread. Though Cobo desperately wished to ask her questions that he felt were more important than the blend of her grass tea, he held his tongue and impatience while she divulged her recipe. "Mollen and diadreinom, good for the constitution and very good for the memory."

He sipped the tea, and though it was bitter and not to his liking, he praised the taste. His praise made her cackle with delight, and she refilled his mug to the very rim.

Sitting with him and sipping her own mug of tea, she began by saying, "I am the caretaker of the Goddess's place of death. I have left offerings to her, morning and night, for as long as I can remember. My mother was also dedicated to Betnoni, as was my grandmother, on and on, back for as long as my tribe has been dedicated to Nari. We've all prayed the prayer of Resurrection, hoping the Worshipped One would return to us. I believe my tribe's steadfast faith is why she came to me to deliver her message of hope."

Thib leaned forward, her active eyes sparkling with enthusiasm. "After you rest in Nari, you have plans to return to your homeland."

"How did you-"

"Do you know why you are returning?"

"An obligation." It was all he would divulge to the old woman.

She sipped her tea, and cackled low. "Betnoni told me everything about you. How you came to Shodalum to escape shame. A son you gave away, and a lover who still owns you, as though you were born her slave."

He drew back, a slight movement that belied his distress at having been emotionally ambushed, darted clear through the heart. He'd not told anyone but Gella his secret shame. "You have the sight, Thib?" he countered, angry that she used it to invade his privacy and pick at his open wounds.

She grunted at his assumption. "You are Ver dala Ven. Do I have the sight?"

He reached out to touch the wiry hair on her head. Her spirit was strong, vibrant, sharp, but he felt no sight in Thib, no extra senses of the unknowable whatsoever. He withdrew his hand, still angry, but no longer angry with Thib.

"Put your doubts to rest, Ver dala Ven." Thib said, "Betnoni is alive, in the sea. She rose from the waves, made of water and

33

not flesh and bone, and she told me that you were coming, and why. The Lost One, she called you, and so right, you are very lost, my dear boy. And of your son, she calls him the Untrained, though she may as well have called him Evil Incarnate, it would have had a truer ring."

Her casual reference to keywords of a prophecy taught to him in secrecy caused the color to drain from his face. His father went to a great deal of trouble to ensure Cobo remembered the prophecy of Betnoni. Ver dala Ven Voktu treated the ancient prophecy as if it were great wisdom that would carry Cobo through hard times, even though the prophet had been disavowed in the Suma, her writings stricken from scripture. She'd been posthumously tried and convicted for the high crime of destroying the Masing Star, and crippling her lineage. Her name was sullied in Ona, her statue removed from the Hall of Ver dala Ven. In truth Cobo hadn't given the prophecy a moment of thought since his father had died.

Thib smiled at his distress, looking a bit relieved. "By the sun in the sky, you do understand, just as she promised you would."

She lifted her hands, the palms facing inward, and between her palms appeared a tiny light, so small Cobo felt he could have been imagining it.

"Hold out your hands, as I hold mine."

He did as she instructed. The tiny dot of light migrated from between her hands, to a point between his. At once his hands and arms tingled, a pleasant sensation.

"This is a gift from Betnoni to you. It is the Spirit of the Masing Star, to guide and protect you." She placed her hands over his and closed his palms on the point of light.

The tingling immediately swept his entire body, and he shivered from the pleasure of it touching every nerve. He saw a light behind his eyes, and in his palm, and felt it in his heart and his loins. He moaned softly, for it was more pleasure than he'd felt in a very long time.

"How is it possible?" He murmured, sensing a new life moving in his flesh, taking up residency. "The Masing Star possesses me?"

"No, not the Star. Its spirit, or perhaps even less. A mere cell of its spirit. It will not sing for you. It will not obey you, for you are not the Chosen. The Spirit of the Star is here to help you find your way. You have work to do, Ver dala Ven. Betnoni's work."

His inner attention focused on the small sun swaying gently inside his chest. The past came alive for him, the events of his life becoming linear in his memory, and at once he saw how his every step, decision, and act seeded his true destiny.

"I am the instrument of Betnoni's prophecy."

He closed his eyes as he experienced once again the dream that had been plaguing him. Women in dresses, bells ringing, swirling, dancing. Warships, headed north.

"Dilgopoche." He whispered, and unimaginable events became a part of his memories. A tender female voice spoke low in his ear, whisking him far from the reality of Thib's home, placing him on the front lines of a war waged in another land. His eyes opened wide as monstrous beings emerged from a cloud of dust, galloping toward and past him, on to their enemy. He glanced upward, and in the sky saw daka Redd's famous war machine. Past and present linked together, inextricably drawn. "The first sign." He whispered, and he shuddered as he remembered the full prophecy, and the awesome tasks that lay before him. "Impossible."

Thib touched his cheek, bringing him back to the present, to Nari and her small hovel. Affection for him shone in her eyes. "I just gave you the Spirit of the Masing Star. A few moments ago, you would have said it was impossible for a simple Ordinary One like myself to even hold your gift, but I did, and I passed it on, and you feel it in you, don't you? Betnoni is inside the Spirit, and she will speak to you as she spoke to me. I have my mission, as you have yours."

"My mission." He murmured, and he mindlessly drank the bitter tea as a timeless voice spoke to his heart of healing his kind. Visions blurred his sight of Thib and her home, not of the past, but misty visions of a possible future. Ver dala Ven, again in great numbers. Cobo had felt very alone for all his life, the last of his *breed*, as Radi so aptly observed. Worshipped by some, revered by others, looked upon as an object, a servant, Ver dala Ven, a thing unlike the Ordinary Ones. He was drawn to Jishni, because she saw him as a man, and then to Gella, because the color of his eyes and stories of his ancestors didn't awe her outright. They were rare, as rare as Cobo.

To be ordinary among his own kind was a fantasy, a wishful one that he'd entertained as a child. To have friends, contemporaries, for his brother to have gold eyes. His childish fantasies were playing out in his futuristic vision, overwhelming him with hope.

Leaving the warmth of Thib's home, he sought out Gella, and found her sitting on the spot where she'd been praying, looking out at the sea. He sat next to her, and took in the vast horizon. The Star, or as Thib referred to it, a single cell of the Spirit of the Star continued to move his inner vision. She and he, and the worshippers shared their space with the ancient dead and Betnoni, who gave herself in sacrifice. Two realities coexisted, their present and Shodalum's past.

"It is very beautiful here." Gella said after a lengthy silence.

"Jantideva is beautiful, too."

"Vast and filled with depraved sluggards."

"Indeed." He affirmed.

"If I go with you, by Shodite law I will lose my right to Calli."

The laws against Shodites leaving Shodalum are strictly enforced. In the eyes of the Elders, Gella would no longer be considered a Shodite. The law was in place to protect their young innocents, lead by curiosity, from wandering across the border and into the bondage of slavery. It, however, did not extend to Cobo, as he was not a Shodite by birth, an unfortunate irony.

"Stay, Gella." He relented, "I am selfish to want you to give up your home to go with me."

She folded her legs and hugged them, and lay her head on her knees, turning to the side to look upward to see his face. "My home is not Calli."

He gently moved a lock of Gella's hair out of her eyes. He stroked her cheek, her hair, his movements leaving trails, as if he'd had several yava flowers and was happily inebriated. The trails encircled her, tracing her outline until it separated from her and became another person. A man. Cobo closed his eyes, and a clear image of the man came to mind. Not a Shodite, or a Janti, but a warrior who would one day embrace Gella and never let her go. He tried to see himself in Gella's future with this man, and could not.

Tears in his eyes, he withdrew his hand.

She embraced him quickly. "I will miss Calli, too."

∾∾∾∾∾∾∾∾

The desolate border was guarded by a broken fence, and the awesome legend of Betnoni's might. They walked across without molestation by Janti forces, which still patrol the borders and pick up stray Shodites.

"Old Peril City is on this side of the big river, over that crest. It is one of the last Rathian cities in a lawless land. Janti would like to believe Old Rathia is theirs, but the Rathians have made it very hard for the Janti to settle here. We will be safe there for the time being. I've heard they protect Shodites."

Their journey took them into the hills of Peril, on steep and narrow trails. Long before they reached the city itself, they could see it glimmering in the distance. A modest city in comparison to most Janti cities, Old Peril sprawled twice the size of Strum. Gella was in awe, not only of its size, but also of the strange glass buildings, and the windriders buzzing around each other in the sky.

Watching the underbelly of a compact windrider fly overhead, she asked, "Will we fly to Ona?"

"Oh yes." And he grinned at her. "If we walked, it would take ten seasons to get to Ona!"

"I am young and have plenty time." She countered, a small smile on her lips.

Several windriders swooped down and attached to a public transport rail that towed them into the city. Cobo explained to Gella that the rail was a safety measure most cities devised to cut down on airborne crashes in metropolitan areas.

The walkways in the city pleased Gella more than imagining two or three, or more, windriders colliding in midair. They reminded her of the walkways in Strum. Narrow, cobbled and full of vendors.

Cobo found the right vendor, and did the talking. He acquired clothing and travel accoutrements, as well as transportation across the Peril River, using their yava flowers in the trade. The vendor treated him like any other customer, for he didn't see him as a being with gold eyes. Cobo had been taught not to muddle the mind of the Ordinary Ones, that it was as immoral as any vice. Having the vendor see him with brown eyes instead of gold was only bending the rule, he decided, and he did his best not to feel guilty.

In a small room of the vendor's home, they prepared.

"This garment is too much." Gella said, pulling at the flowing gown he'd chosen for her. Simple, made with simple material and of a simple design, and it covered her fully, from neck to toes. "How am I expected to move in this?"

"You can't go about naked, Gella, you could be put to death for indecent exposure."

"And they believe we are barbarians."

"It is a discomfort you will have to live with. We must have the appearance of having just arrived from a legitimate Alliance nation."

"Shodalum being illegitimate."

"Don't be surly, and put it on."

Gella refused to leave her wraps and leather travel clothes behind. She tucked them neatly beneath her Janti clothing. "For our return trip." She insisted.

He let her have her belongings, and left his own behind.

Chapter 3

Ona's Suma temple was filled to maximum capacity with an eager audience of citizens and journalists, all present for the historic elevation. A musical introduction was underway. The Janti National Pride orchestra played several numbers in honor of past Ver dala Ven, including the melodic hymn Cobo had chosen for his elevation. Jishni closed her eyes as it began, and with accompaniment she replayed that day in her mind. She was fifteen, he thirteen. Already they were close friends. He was her best friend, she mused, until they became lovers, and as lovers they became like one person in heart and mind. At his elevation, though, they were still innocents, still friends. She was proud of him as he took his oath, and her anticipation for the future knotted in her chest and tingled in her stomach. She had such visions of their being the pair who could change the world and right the wrongs set by the past. Daka and Ver dala Ven, acting in harmony for the good of all people.

The song ended, and she opened her eyes to the sight of Taen on the center stage wearing black Suma robes with a gold sash on his shoulder. Her heart sunk. They had such high ideals. Where were those ideals, today? She was party to a lie. The Suma wished the Alliance, and her people, to believe Taen was ready for elevation, to allay their fears of the future, their restless desire for change. Since Ver dala Ven had fled Ona, there were insurrections and civil wars in nations that once knew peace. The Alliance lacked the cohesion of the past, because the Ministers and their represented peoples no longer respected or trusted the dakas as they once did. Ver dala Ven's presence had kept them together.

Jishni was aware that they were offering hope that was nonexistent. Taen was not ready for elevation. He would only serve as a figurehead. From now on, the children of Ver dala Ven would be mere reminders of a rarified era.

If I died at this moment, Taen's fate would change. He would become daka, and usher in a new age.

She forcefully rejected an urge to climb Aurora's spire and throw herself from the overlook. If she did, she'd be following the suicidal footsteps of daka Corrinne. No one understood the madness that drove her, and apologists tried to pass it off as a tragedy. Jishni thought she understood Corrinne's madness. Her guilt must have been awesome after locking Dilgopoche away. She was not a soulless a monster, after all. Jishni could not imagine bearing the responsibility for the eradication of an entire people.

This is different, she told herself firmly. I've no reason to want to die! It is the pregnancy, it has made me weak. Thoughts of ending her own life had crossed her mind on the odd occasion since the pregnancy began, and for no good reason. The desire to do harm to her self had become stronger in the last few days, and since viewing Corrinne's posthumous message to the Suma, throwing herself from the spire preyed upon her thoughts night and day. Her torment was only alleviated during the careful planning of the celebrations leading to this day. Genuine fear struck through her as she witnessed the end of the elevation, for she did not know what she would do with her time to keep her mind occupied, away from her despair.

The elevation ceremony was less elaborate than in the past, and Taen did not perform the feats usually performed. Cobo had levitated, brought sunshine into Orin hall as if it were midday and not evening, and had made the spire of Leila sing. Jishni's father, a usually harsh man, softened as he heard the song, his face contorting with ecstasy. Daka Janus had proclaimed that Cobo touched the Masing Star, itself, in order to produce so beautiful a refrain.

In the silence of the Ona Temple, Chancellor Yana asked that Taen be presented for elevation, and Bailin stood on cue. "I, a son of Thranlam'Sum, present Taen as Ver dala Ven."

And thus he was elevated. Applause, music resuming, Taen walked off the stage and the ceremony was over, a grave anti-climax that would no doubt be discussed on the Crier, and among the population, for years to come. No one was fooled, Jishni noted pensively. They all knew it was a ruse.

And for their failed attempt to stabilize the Alliance, Taen lost his place in Ona. Bailin sat down quickly, his head low. He was none too happy with the turn of events. He bluntly informed Jishni and Bail that he didn't want to become heir apparent, and was furious for being made to present Taen. And so two of her sons were unhappy, all for the sake of good politics.

She returned to the palace alone. Bailin wanted nothing to do with her, leaving the Temple with friends. Taen had new duties to begin tonight. And then there was Voktu, her thirteen-year-old son, who had returned to the final ball of the elevation. She thought of him fondly. He was very much like Bail in disposition, but it was his friendship with Rabielle that caused her to compare herself to him. Rabielle was the sixth daughter of Jishni's private secretary, Nan, and had been Voktu's best friend since they were toddlers. Rabielle had grown into a beautiful young lady. Voktu now followed her around like a faithful pet. Seeing the two of them together brought back memories of her and Cobo, when they were still young and innocent. She hoped for a better outcome to Voktu's adventure in love.

Ironic that she was ruminating on her love affair with Cobo as she entered her private living quarters. Immediately she saw a man's figure on the terrace. From the back he could have been Bail, wide shoulders and tawny hair, but the hair was wrong and the clothing wrong, and the slimness of his hips wrong. Haggins, her houseman, hovered near the lift doors, and formally announced her guest.

"You are in the company of Ver dala Ven Cobo." He said, and he bowed, after taking note of her stunned expression.

"When did he arrive to Ona?"

"A few moments ago."

Entranced, she started toward the terrace. She paused by the open arch leading outside. Cobo leaned against the railing, facing the Tronos sea, his back to her. In the clothing he wore, he appeared thin. His curly hair was long, plaited down his back like a savage. She wondered where he'd been, and if she had the strength to greet him, face to face. Her hands and knees trembled, and uneasiness descended upon her. She considered turning away, racing upstairs to her private quarters, awaiting Bail's return before confronting this stranger.

Cobo sensed her presence. His head went down, and he turned slightly to look over his shoulder. Seeing her, he turned his full body, resting his hip on the railing. He took in her full form, his hungry eyes finally resting on her face. "You haven't changed." he said. His gaze, his voice, they were like silk against her naked body. His very presence seemed to touch her, and her skin came alive under his steady gaze. The length and breadth of her anger against him for leaving was forgotten as she longed for his hands to caress her, for his arms to embrace her forever.

She was prone to tears these days, but this time her tears had roots deep in her heart.

"It's been a long time." he acknowledged, his gaze steady and self assured.

Cautiously, she stepped into the night air and approached him. She was reminded in an instant of his profound magnetism. Without thinking, she abandoned her bitter grudge against him and invited him with all her heart to touch her.

He did. As soon as they were within reach of each other, he placed his hand on her pregnant belly.

"Two lives." he said thoughtfully, seemingly unaware of how his touch and closeness sent thrills through her. "Identical, and yet their destinies seem to part at a very early age. They will become two very different men. Both vibrant with your life force." A bitter smile touched his lips. "And Bail's."

He dropped his hand from her and moved away, facing the open expanse beneath the terrace and placing his profile to her. The separation between them, of space and time and, now, the emotional separation, caused Jishni to physically ache.

"Where is Taen?" he asked, his tone low.

"He doesn't know you are his father."

"He does." Cobo replied, turning to face her. "Make no mistake, he has been listening to your thoughts since he was five or six. He knows everything."

She suspected as much, but it was surreal, and oddly devastating, to have her worst fears confirmed by Cobo. She faltered, and Cobo caught her by the arm and lead her to a bench.

"Do you need a nurse?"

"I'm fine."

"Are you sure?"

"I'm fine." She repeated, though she was unable to catch her breath. He knelt before her, his face upturned, his expression worried, his hands on her arms. His hands, once soft like an aristocrat's, were now callused and strong. His face, once young, was lined by the sun and darkened. For the years and obvious wear, he was still the most handsome man she'd ever laid eyes on. His touch was an excruciating pleasure.

The children moved within her, as if reacting to her desire. Reminded of Bail's kindness to her over the years inspired her guilt, she pulled her arms away. "Please don't touch me." She breathed unevenly.

He drew back, hardness setting in around his eyes, and he stood, returning to the railing. His back now to the sea, a seemingly safe distance between them, she could still feel the roughness of his hands on her arms.

"Where have you been all these years?"

"Zaria."

"We've had mercenaries in search of you since you left." She countered, "They searched Zaria, and there was no trace of you to be found."

"Where is he, Jishni? I want to meet him."

"Bail searched for you for many years. Did you know? You broke his heart when you left us."

"I did Bail a service by leaving." Cobo replied, his tone sharper. "You can't tell me that he wasn't relieved."

"Taen needed you. We eventually had no choice but to find him a teacher to take your place."

"A teacher."

"When Bail couldn't locate you, he tried to obtain for Taen a suitable teacher, a distant cousin named Riar Sed, but the man complained endlessly about Taen. In the end, he said that Taen too incorrigible to train. Of course, Bail made sure Taen's

43

failure never reached the court. He always had high hopes for Taen."

An odd, unreadable expression appeared on his face. "Riar Sed. I remember stories of a relation named Riar Sed. A healer's son."

"He is from Kanak, and his mother was a healer, yes. He, however, was nothing more than a petty sorcerer. Not an effective teacher. We've elevated Taen, in any case." She blurted, "Tonight. He is performing his duty to the Den as we speak. So that is where he is, Cobo. He is in the Den of the Suma."

Incredulous, he countered, "Did he demonstrate that he was ready for elevation?"

"He couldn't."

"Of course not!" Cobo retorted, "He is untrained."

"Please, don't raise your voice, the servants may hear."

"Why elevate him? What prompted you to do so without my consent?"

"I am his mother, I didn't need your consent!"

"I am Ver dala Ven." he thundered, "I am the only one who can elevate Taen! Who did it? Bail? Did Bail elevate my son before the Suma?"

"No, Bailin gave him away."

"And who is Bailin?" he demanded, then froze as he realized the namesake.

"It was time." She pleaded, wanting now his forgiveness more than anything, "He is almost nineteen. No Ver dala Ven has ever been elevated after the age of eighteen."

"You had no right to elevate him at any age."

"And you released your right to elevate him as Ver dala Ven in my court when you abandoned him at birth."

Hurt erupted in his face, and she immediately hated herself for lashing out at him. Her emotions were a tangle of angers. Old, faded anger at him for leaving her eighteen years ago, and a fresh, electric anger for the way his presence rekindled her intolerable passion for him.

Subdued, he replied, "Jishni, I didn't come to argue with you, or settle our past with insults. I came home to take Taen away. To Dilgopoche."

Her shocked silence caused him to sigh, and a conflict of emotions twisted his features. "I know of Dilgopoche's demands. They want Taen to join their monarchy as a good faith gesture that Jantideva will never repair the Dome of Silence."

She shook her head, knowing full well that there were no secrets she could keep from Cobo, state or otherwise.

"You don't understand the situation, Cobo. Their people...their people are horrifying. They want us to give them Taen, and I won't do that to my son. You shouldn't want that for Taen, either, if you have any feeling for him at all."

Cobo swept toward her, once again on his knee and looking upward into her face, urgency in his manner. "As abhorrent as it seems, this is Taen's destiny. We have no choice."

"There is always a choice."

"Evident by the way you ran away with me when you discovered you were pregnant?" he posed pointedly. There was a trace of bitterness in his voice as he added, "Instead you did as your court expected and gave them a military leader to rule by your side, and my child was given to Bail. I was left with nothing. You said then you had no choice."

"And so this is revenge? You'd consign your son to a terrible fate in order to hurt me?"

"No! I am trying to reach you, to show you that sometimes there are no choices. You were right to take Bail and refuse me. I was wrong for you, our affair was sacrilege, and even I knew it at the time, and yet I couldn't help myself, I was so obsessed with you."

"Don't make what we had seem ugly." She retorted, "I loved you then with all my heart, I love you now, I will love you for all time, until I die. It wasn't wrong, Cobo, how can love be wrong?"

He reeled back on his feet, and with agitated gestures, he was up and paced around behind her. She knew she'd said too much, too quickly, exposing her truth vividly in the heat of the moment.

To her back, Cobo said, "I am here to exert my right as Ver dala Ven and take custody of Taen. I will stand before the Suma, the Alliance, all of Jantideva and expose them to the truth, if I must. I will have my way."

"Cobo!" she cried out, desperate and angry, and she struggled to rise. He was leaving, his stride uncompromising. "Cobo!" and she damned herself for being unwieldy. She wouldn't catch up to him, he wouldn't let her. She reached the lift as it descended.

Nan stood in the corridor by the lift, her mouth open in surprise.

"Was that—"

"Yes."

"By the Guardian's eye, he is incredible. When he looked at me, I felt….." and she was at a loss for words.

"That, my dear Nan, is the magical presence of a true Ver dala Ven." She admitted, and her mouth crooked in a frown. Fighting tears, she said, "Send out word to the entire court and all Alliance Ministers that tomorrow morning they are expected to attend a reception to welcome Cobo home. Arrange for the reception to be held in the Masing Chamber."

"Right away, daka. Shall I send word to daka Bail, as well?"

"I will take care of that message." She replied, sober. "If I can find the words."

ॐॐॐॐॐॐॐॐ

Armored low gliders soared above the battle, dropping crysine pellets. As the crysine hit the air, it began degenerating immediately, turning into a gas that would cause severe breathing difficulties in the Dilgos, as well as the civilians and Alliance soldiers who were unfortunately not prepared with protective masks. From his command center in the battleship christened Daka Redd, Bail watched the pink gas coil downward into the fighting. He did not want to inflict this discomfort on his own people, but he had no choice. If he was going to end the bloodshed, he needed the Dilgos immobilized.

Peace. Rito-Sant spoke of peace, while warning that the bloodshed would not end until his demands were satisfied. He held Jantideva ransom for an impossible price. Taen. Rito-Sant had arrived boldly to the Daka Redd in the company of a Huntress guard, made his demands in person, and left as abruptly as he'd arrived. Bail remembered the meeting, remembered the urge to capture the enemy while at the same time feeling utterly helpless, unable to move, think, unable to function. Unable to react as his instincts dictated.

After the talks, the Dilgos intensified their attacks. The Janti retreated, running south to Talda, despite the Dilgo's antiquated methods of warfare. The Dilgos fought armed Pliadors with spears, swords, moro tubes and spiked moro chains; weapons outdated by ten thousand years of progress. The Dilgos had gone back in time and fought like primitives against trained and armed Alliance soldiers, taking one victory after another.

What choice did they have? What choice?

The sky beneath them was pink with crysine, and surrounding them were black mountains of smoke billowing from fires. In odd synchronicity, the blue and green streams of Janti lume detonators would streak the pink and black skies, creating the effect of dusk in the Southlands of Zaria. It was beautiful, and loathsome.

Bail watched in silence, waiting for the crysine to take affect, and for the Dilgos to fall back. His inspiration came too late. Montrose had been destroyed. But, perhaps he could save Talda. Perhaps he could end the assault on this battlefield.

Minutes passed. His fear mounted that the Dilgos were so hardy an animal that they were immune to crysine, just as they were immune to lume dust.

His lieutenant, Ponch Lelant laughed his relief. He announced, "Dilgos are falling. The crysine has worked!"

Cheers erupted on the battle deck. Bail was not relieved, however. Thousands had lost their lives in this battle. It was not settled.

"Deploy the first wave." Bail ordered. Troops he'd equipped with the same antiquated weapons of war the Dilgos had used against them, as well as breathing masks and armor that would protect them from the crysine, were to take Montrose away from the giants. While the Dilgos were down, he intended to trample them under his boot.

"First wave is on the move." Lelant replied.

"Good," Bail said, though he felt nothing he'd accomplished today was good. They'd suffered a staggering defeat. Bail was not accustomed to defeat, not on the battlefield. As a young man, before he was a daka, he'd fought in the Zarian revolutions and come home a hero. No more than four years ago, he had been the victorious Supreme Commander during the Borysenka range wars. They were wars fought with technological equals, where the odds were even. Defeat at the hands of Dilgos, regardless of their size, carrying weapons made out of stones and steel was an absurdity.

Jishni's father once praised Bail for being a brilliant military strategist, and Bail once allowed himself the luxury of pride.

Now he was an incompetent who couldn't see a way out of the deplorable Montrose situation, except by the sacrifice of one of his sons. Through the first few days of war, his mind drew a complete blank on alternative methods of handling the Dilgos, and his military advisors were no help. In his war room, as his generals began concentrating on strategy, the agitation among them built into a frenzy until the inevitable physical fight commenced. Never had there been such turmoil among the Janti military elite. And never had there been such an ineffective leader as Bail.

And then, this morning, the fog lifted. Bail woke with an idea, so simple that he was amazed it had evaded him for so long. During the planning stages, he received the message from Jishni that Cobo had returned. It nettled him, but he refused to leave before he saw his plan through to the end.

There were those who believed Ver dala Ven had returned to aid in their battle with the Dilgos. Even now, as the battle turned in their favor, Bail heard his own men praising the life of Ver dala Ven. He remained silent. He was unsettled by his brother's timing, and by the news that Cobo intended to deliver Taen into the hands of the Dilgos. The latter information was not passed on to the troops. Bail had no intention of ransoming his eldest son to the enemy.

He was reluctant to leave his soldiers on the front to return home, but not because of the battle in progress. Ponch could handle taking charge of the battle. Bail didn't want to return to the Palace and face his brother and his wife, together again.

Better I die than see them enamoured—

The thought frightened him, because it almost felt as if it didn't belong in his mind. Transient thoughts of self-destruction came to him often during the past year, surprising him each time for he was not depressed, or unhappy. In the beginning he was able to dismiss the awful thoughts soundly, deflating their power by willing them gone, but since the crisis in Montrose had begun, they plagued him constantly and were harder to squash.

If I die before Taen could be given to Dilgopoche, Taen would ascend to the throne. He'd be unavailable for an arranged marriage. Yes, my death would solve a great many problems.

Bail shot to his feet and, agitated, strolled to the viewing screen. Ponch's head jerked up in response, and he watched Bail curiously, his eyes flicking to the reflexive movements of Bail's hands. He frowned, and turned his eyes back to the battle screen.

If I leave now, I could be home in a few hours. Tonight, I could lay next to Jishni in our bed, feeling our children kick my back from inside her belly. Tomorrow, I could wake and see my brother's face with my own eyes. Selfish heart that I have, I must see Cobo before I die.

He closed his eyes, but the thought could not be exorcised from his mind.

"Ponch," he said to his second, "inform General Sot that I am returning to Ona. If he wishes to speak to me, I'll be in my quarters for the next hour."

"Yes daka."

Bail strode confidently off the battle deck and into the lift. He caught the glances of a few of his men, recognizing in their eyes the old admiration he'd grown accustomed to seeing in the past, that admiration which seemed to depart during the fall of Montrose. As if all had returned to normal, but he knew better. Nothing was normal.

Bail rode the lift down to the officers' deck of the Daka Redd. It was the only fully operational Peace Cruiser to survive the days of its namesake's legend. The Daka Redd was the last of its kind ever built, a remnant of Jantideva's once shining military machine.

Though by design it was similar to other warships, it was the first to be defined as a windrider class vessel, equipped with the ability to hover in the sky as a ship would float in the sea. Powered by lume dust and carefully maintained, it had protected Alliance airspace for two thousand years until the vessel was retired after the last of the land skirmishes in Borysenka. At that time, the Alliance council reinterpreted the statutes regarding warfare and decided that it was an unfair distribution of power for the Janti to keep their battle class windrider, while the rest of the Alliance provinces did without. The Daka Redd was decommissioned, and turned into a museum to past wars, past victories.

With the Daka Redd, Bail had expected to crush the Dilgos in a day. The council readily gave their permission, and the ship was undocked for his use. Bail was their daka Warrior, unable to make a faulty decision.

Bail was certain they did not hold him in that high esteem any longer.

He passed through a group of weary pilots on their way to the lift, acknowledging their bows with a curt nod. His quarters were on the same deck as the officers, no better or larger than the quarters of his men, the same quarters he had occupied before he'd been made daka. He refused additional security measures to protect his safety, the traditional security officers and mindreaders to dog his every step, or the better than the standard locking mechanisms for his door, and he absolutely refused to inhabit the royal apartments on the forward deck. He instead converted the sprawling quarters into an all inclusive recreation center for his soldiers. He believed that if he lived and worked among his people, he'd foster their respect, as well as continually remind himself that he was a daka by marriage, only. He was first, and foremost, a soldier. He was happiest living the life of a soldier.

His quarters were stark. A bunk, a desk, gray walls, gray floors. The only color to disarm the eye were the images of his children cavorting across his desk. It was the same scene, looped continuously, a day a few years ago when Bail had the time to spend with his sons. The three of them wrestled with lighthearted glee, while Bail looked on and roared with laughter. Taen, Bailin and Voktu, young men he was proud to love. Taen, as always, got the better of both his brothers. His grin as he pinned Bailin was triumphant, and his eyes gleamed with boyish charm as he looked straight at his father, straight into the eye of a camera, and said, "Got him!"

That boyish gleam left his eyes after Riar Sed arrived to Ona. But Bail tried not to think about that failure. He'd always known that Riar Sed was the wrong man to train Taen. Perhaps it was best Cobo had arrived to take control.

If I were to die, Taen's failure in training would be irrelevant.

The thought hit him hard on the inside of the head, and the pain he felt caused him to cringe, and curse. He waved off the thought as he would an evil spirit, using a hand motion he'd seen his father use long ago, a superstitious signal but one that seemed to work for him in this instance. The headache receded immediately.

He breathed a sigh of relief, and sat heavily on his bunk. He found himself musing as he did in times of trouble about the life he would have preferred to live had he not been forced to become a daka. In his youth, he dreamed of travel and discovery. He'd wanted to conquer the world, to climb the highest mountain and explore untamed jungles, while sampling a world of women. He'd romanticized and coveted the lifestyle of the Rysenk mercenaries. To become a smuggler, a soldier of fortune, a rogue; the prospect excited his young spirit. But Bail's father had loftier ambitions for his eldest son. The highest seat in court.

Bail never felt comfortable as daka. In truth, he had once hoped Jishni would not go through with the wedding. He expected, hoped, that Cobo would take her, trade places with Bail and take on the obligations of daka. Instead, the arranged wedding happened as it was planned. He lost his freedom, and then lost his brother.

In retrospect, he'd long decided that being a daka had not been all bad. He became commander of the Janti army, a post he enjoyed. He'd grown to love Jishni, in a way he'd never expected. She gave her body to him to bear him children, and he respected her for her great suffering on his behalf. Each first moment he held a son's squiggling countenance, fresh from their mother's womb, he had known he'd been given a gift.   He loved his sons beyond all reason. He loved Taen beyond all reason.

What better gift could he give to Taen in return, but his place in court?

A clap outside his open door lifted him out of his miserable ruminations.   General Sot leaned through the opening, his face creased with tired worry.   Kril Sot was twenty years older than Bail, and before Bail married a daka Sot was his commanding officer. Bail often looked to Sot for guidance in many matters.

"We've taken prisoners, and they are being off loaded at this time." Sot raised a brow significantly, "One of them claims to be Rito-Sant's sister."

Bail's depression fell away immediately.

"Take me to her."

He followed Sot's quick pace to the lift.

The cargo hold on the main deck had been converted into a temporary prison bay in order to accommodate the oversized female Dilgo prisoners of war. The warped and distorted male Dilgos they'd captured were housed in the brig, one deck above, as their size was similar to an average Janti.

Few of Bail's men wished to oversee either group of prisoners. The Dilgo men were surreal versions of themselves, frightening in their familiar yet nightmarish appearance. With the women, it was not so much their size, but their smell that put off the Janti soldiers.

Stepping onto the landing of the cargo hold, the stench of the Dilgo females struck Bail and sickened his stomach. The smell was like rotting meat, mixed with dung and musk. He instinctively covered his mouth and nose with his hand.

The female warriors called themselves Huntresses.   The Huntresses were shackled together and lined against a wall, many still suffering from respiratory distress. Bail thought he'd grown accustomed to their unusual appearance, size, but even now he couldn't help but stare. They towered over his biggest men. Their bodies were inconceivably long, heavily muscled and shadowed with fine, dark hair. Most of the women wore a loincloth made with leather, hanging loosely from their hips. A few of the younger women were nude, seemingly a custom of the Dilgos. Those who were of lowest rank among the Huntresses were expected to enter

52

battle completely vulnerable in order to prove their courage. The nude Huntresses were obviously female, yet there was nothing about them except their V shaped pubis to differentiate them from a man. Their actions, strength, mannerisms were male. Bail found their appearance as revolting as their smell.

Sot led him away from the main body of captives.

"She was a fighter," Sot commented, "it took twelve men to bring her down, and another eight to hold her down long enough to get her into irons."

The Huntress Sot spoke of was separated from her compatriots, sitting on the floor in full body restraints and surrounded by wary guards. Bail noted she was dressed in black armor, made with the precious metal, jetsilver, indicating she was a high ranking officer, and she wore a black band around her head similar to the black band Bail had seen on Rito-Sant during their only face to face meeting. He recognized her from Rito-Sant's Huntress guard, and noted that she closely resembled Rito-Sant. Flaxen hair, freckled face, and hard blue eyes. She was pretty, less male in appearance than the other women, Bail decided wryly. Her face had a soft shape, her eyes were large, her mouth pouting.

"Hail, daka Bail of Jantideva." she said huskily as Bail stood before her. Her strange accent contorted his name, as did the sneer on her lips.

Seated, her face was slightly above his height. Despite needing to tilt his head slightly upward to meet her gaze, his response was a stern demand. "Identify yourself."

"Baru-Oclassi, Maiden Huntress, second daughter of Mirpur-Sant." she replied stiffly, and issued her own demand in return. "When may I expect this itching to stop?"

He noted the white blotches of a crysine rash on her face. "Eight days at the most."

"Intolerable," she retorted, "I want it stopped now!"

Bail crossed his arms in front of his chest, and with a sardonic smile that belied his fury at the woman, he replied, "Do your kind know how a peace agreement is supposed to work, Baru-Oclassi? The side that offers peace stops killing long enough to show that they are sincere."

She cocked her head to the side as if she didn't understand him, but replied by saying, "You will call me Baru. No one but Rito-Sant is permitted to call me Oclassi to my face."

"We have not been given time to consider Rito-Sant's demands," Bail fumed, "We cannot make a decision like this while we are still at war!"

"The bloodshed of evil Janti murderers will continue," she replied evenly, "until Taen of Jantideva resides in our court!"

"The fighting will stop, or we will not consider your demands at all!"

"You expect us to trust you to be fair to us?" she countered incredulously, and she punctuated her question with a harsh laugh. Her eyes stony and her mouth stiffened by a cruel smile, she said, "Are you more trustworthy than the dakas before you who imprisoned us? You locked us away and forgot about us, but we didn't forget about you. We remember you, daka Bail of Jantideva. You are the living incarnation of all the dakas who lived before you, those who spit on us and left us to die. We hungered, we suffered, we needed the Alliance to help us, and you ignored our cries. You silenced our cries."

Bail eyed her coldly. He wouldn't be drawn into a political debate with this woman over issues predating his existing by thousands of years. "I will continue to drop crysine on your Huntresses," he warned, "if you do not put an end to your attack."

"Do your worse," she invited, "we will not end our march until Rito-Sant is satisfied that Taen is ours. And we are numerous, daka Bail, as numerous as grains of sand in the Coulcoubanna." She abruptly growled and rubbed the armor against her legs. In a demanding tone, she said, "There must be a way to ease the itching now!"

Bail glanced to Lorma, the Daka Redd's head physician. She was preparing to inject Baru-Oclassi with the antidote to crysine, as she had many of the other sufferers. Bail shook his head, no. He did not want this woman to feel relief. Lorma nodded that she understood, and left them to attend to the rest of the prisoners.

"General Sot," Bail said, spearing a glare at Baru-Oclassi, "are our communication systems with the Dilgos still in operation?"

"They've been off line all day,"

Bail nodded his understanding, frowning. Nothing in the Daka Redd seemed to want to work correctly. "Send a messenger to Rito-Sant. Tell him we have his sister. If he does not end hostilities, she will be executed. We will wait his reply."

Her eyes flashed with fury, but beneath the fury was palpable fear. Bail felt satisfaction to see the latter from the insolent woman.

"Rito-Sant cannot be coerced." she asserted with false bravado.

"If not, there will be one less useless Dilgo thing cluttering our world." Bail countered, and his lips upturned in an unfriendly smile. "Enjoy the crysine, Baru-Oclassi."

He turned on his heel and strode away.

To Sot, who was a step behind him, he said, "Give Rito-Sant one hour to respond. If his push does not end, I want crysine dropped on the Dilgos every hour, on the hour. If the crysine ceases to be affective, use a melathor bomb--"

"Guardian protect us!" Sot hissed at the prospect of using the deadly chemical on their enemy.

Bail knew he committed a moral crime by even suggesting the use of melathor. The chemical was generally used in mining, an acid bomb that cleared heavy deposits of stone from lume deposits. It was capable of dissolving the soft tissue off a living being on contact.

"You just make sure you don't drop it on our own." Bail told him firmly, "If the Dilgos choose to continue their attack, we will be unmerciful. I will not allow them to reach Talda."

"Yes daka."

"And make sure Rito-Sant's sister is uncomfortable." Bail said, feeling a twist of sick pleasure at the prospect of hurting a Dilgo monarch, "Whatever she wants, give her the opposite."

"With pleasure." Sot replied.

Bail returned to his quarters to pack, and wait for Rito-Sant's reply.

The reply came. The enemy would hold their ground, but end their aggressive push into Jantideva. Finally, Bail had won a battle against the Dilgos.

*

Brooding, Bail entered his personal transport, Ona Wizard, and dropped his satchel on a passenger seat in the rear.

He took the co-pilot's seat. Trev, his life long friend, had been his pilot since he'd taken the title of daka. The moment he sat down, Trev ignited the blowers, and the Wizard took a breath.

"Jishni pop you a couple more, Bail?" Trev grinned at his daka with characteristic irreverence for Bail's royal title. Trev was a rather ill kept bachelor, with a sparse beard on his face and equally sparse hair on his middle aged head. His flight suit looked as if he'd slept in it, and he smelled of spice brandy. Nothing new for Trev.

"No," Bail replied unsmiling. "Ver dala Ven has returned."

Trev's jaw dropped. "Cobo has come home? Why?"

"To accompany Taen to Dilgopoche." he said, and suddenly he felt weary of the world. He eyed the console, wishing he could fly as far away from the palace, and his responsibilities, as this small windrider would take him.

Trev heated the main engines without taking his eyes off Bail. "How did he know about what the Dilgos wanted?"

"He is Ver dala Ven." Bail shrugged. It was the best explanation he had for Cobo's strange return.

"The omnipotent, omnipresent, all powerful Ver dala Ven." Trev said sardonically, and he chuckled. "Remember when Cobo was nothing but a mewling, whining brat that ran to your mother if we so much as crossed our eyes at him?"

"That boy is dead and gone."

Bail's low mood had a sobering affect on Trev's humor.

As the flight deck mechanically moved the Wizard onto the launch pad, Trev reached under his seat for his stashed bottle of brandy. He thumped it into Bail's chest.

"You look like you can use it."

Bail accepted the brandy gratefully, and drank from the bottle as if he were still a lowly man, a normal man, sitting beside a friend on a public transport, on his way home from a laborer's job. Bail monopolized the bottle as Trev communicated with the control officer and made his take off, falling in a line with Bail's military escort.

The brandy had melted Bail's tensions, and he slumped in his seat in a manner most unbecoming a daka. He threw his head back and eyed his friend. "What if we were to take off, right now, change our course for the Kanak highlands, and never return?"

Trev chuckled lightly. "Take ourselves a half dozen wives and learn to weave?"

"Drink all night, and sleep all day." Bail replied without humor.

"You drink all night," Trev said with a loud guffaw, "With a harem of wives, I'll be too busy to drink all night!"

Bail snorted a halfhearted laugh at the comment. He drank again from the bottle, and stared vacantly at the oncoming skies.

After a long silence, Bail said, "Montrose is gone. Burned to the ground. Last rough estimate of casualties were around the hundred thousand mark." His voice dropped in pitch, and he said, "They anticipated my every move. If I didn't know better, I'd think they had Ver dala Ven on their side."

"Maybe they do." Trev said offhandedly. "Maybe Cobo somehow got past the lume dome and has been hiding in Dilgopoche. How else could he have known about—"

Bail's anger at the suggestion that Cobo could be behind their devastating defeat blinded him and he lashed out at Trev with his fist. He caught Trev on the side of the jaw with a blow, knocking Trev to the side, Trev released the controls and the Wizard veered off course.

Trev reacted by grappling for the controls. Once the windrider was righted, he rubbed the side of his face and stared at Bail warily. "You son of a dirty slank."

"Don't you ever suggest that Cobo could turn on me." Bail commanded angrily.

The comm link came alive with the anxious voice of the pilot in the escort to their rear. Trev turned their com on, and said, "No malfunction, just air turbulence. Steady, on course." He shut the comm off, and he licked a droplet of blood off his lip.

"Pardon my logic, great daka Bail of Jantideva." Trev replied with contempt, "In the future, I will keep it to myself."

"Logic," Bail muttered. "The easy logic of a simple mind, if you ask me."

"I am a simple man, daka." Trev stated. He touched his jaw gingerly, and moved it to test it for soreness. "With no creative instinct to speak of, only logic at my disposal."

"Cobo would never inflict pain on his own people." Bail insisted irritably, "He would never willingly do harm to his own family!"

"Indeed, why would he want to?" Trev countered dryly, "What did he lose here? A woman? A son? Pah! What would a family be to the omnipotent Ver dala Ven Cobo? I was an idiot to even suggest that he might hold some grudge against you for raising his flesh, and fleshing his woman."

Bail's anger with Trev simmered, and for the first time in eighteen years he regretted confiding in his friend about the situation between he, Jishni and Cobo.

But despite his anger with Trev, he felt the birth of niggling doubts about Cobo's trustworthiness. He struggled with the notion that Trev was right, giving birth to jealousy as he imagined Cobo claiming Taen as his own, and possibly laying claim to Jishni, as well.

"He's taking his rightful place with Taen, who will be Ver dala Ven," Bail stated aloud, defending his brother against his own dark apprehensions, "he's been welcome to do so all along. He is not taking anything away from me!"

Trev glanced cannily at Bail. "Are you so sure? If he's taking Taen to Dilgopoche, he is indeed taking something from you, he is taking your Chosen Son away."

Bail fell into a pensive silence, and drew brandy from the bottle, oblivious of his own actions. Cobo, siding with the enemy. Not possible, but if it were so, Bail faced an insurmountable obstacle within himself, because he wouldn't make war with his brother. Long ago he'd made a vow to his father that his loyalty to Cobo would remain absolute. Despite the unfortunate events leading to Cobo's self-imposed exile, Bail honored that promise. He kept Cobo close, as close as he could under the circumstances, by loving the son he'd made and left behind.

Unendurable situation, supporting Cobo's claim to Taen. "How can I?" he whispered to himself, earning a slight glance from Trev. "How can I?"

Chapter 4

The primary home of the dakas, the palace called Ona, lay in the Sahla hills half embraced by distant mountains and facing the Tronos Sea. The original structure, a Rathian castle that had been partially destroyed in the Necroli War, had been repaired and served now as Ona's main ballroom. Empty and clean today, the ballroom had served the guests celebrating Taen's elevation.

"These five statues," Cobo said of the carved columns before them, his voice echoing in the enormous space, "each represent one of the five moral precepts of the Rathian Knights, a creed that ultimately became the hope of Jantideva during the Rathian occupation. In this hall, the Knights defended the Janti against Lord Crag, a despotic ruler bent on the genocide of our people, and drove him and his supporters from the palace and the Sahla hills. Crag called upon Ver dala Ven Mo'ghan to aid him, but Mo'ghan would not come. His creed as Ver dala Ven prevented him from harming the one he'd served, Crag, and his creed as a Rathian Knight prevented him from confronting his comrades for an unjust cause. So he left Ona to Crag, and Crag to the Knights. Crag's army of conquerors was no match for the Rathian Knights, and Crag was driven from Ona. He withdrew to his castle to the south. Mo'ghan awaited him there, and submitted himself to execution for his part in the Janti conquest."

Gella let her hand slide over the dark blue marble pillar, as her eyes traveled the expansive dome above them. "It is said that the Rathians originated from Shodalum. Is it true?"

Cobo's mouth twitched in a slight smile. "True. In antiquity, they were tribal warlords. Their history breaks from yours, however, with their first conquest, the taking of the territory we now call Old Rathia. The true Elders of the Shodites were peace loving, as those who now sit in council to the tribes."

"War is a pursuit of small men." She said, repeating the Shodite proverb, and she grinned at the image of the knight. She relished the thought of being connected, even in a small way, to so fierce a race. She should have been embarrassed by her avid interest. Most Shodites wouldn't speak of Rathians, for the

Shodite creed was one of peace and simplicity, not conquest. Gella, however, imagined the final stand between the noble Knights and Lord Crag's men, their ancient weapons in hand, fearless and determined. She imagined the sounds of battle echoing under the five domes of the knighthood, where their convictions were tested and made true, and let her imaginings thrill her.

"Why does Janti history still revile Mo'ghan?"

"For his part in placing Crag in power."

"But he saw his mistake."

"And instead of serving the daka of Jantideva, he chose to submit himself to Crag's vengeance. He was the first and only Ver dala Ven ever to be put to death, hence the moniker, Mo'ghan the First."

"Don't you see the nobility in his act? He honored the Knighthood by remaining true to his friend to the end, and yet did not allow his friend to oppress a vulnerable people. He was a hero."

Cobo nodded, seeming to consider her point of view. "Most Janti wouldn't be able to see him as a hero. He, and the twelve Ver dala Ven who had preceded him in the service of the Rathians, are not well respected, nor were their journals or histories recorded and studied in the same manner as those who served the Janti."

Gella expressed her disapproval of Janti bias with grunt.

Cobo eased her in the direction of the grand entrance of the Janti portion of the palace. The dark Rathian influence ended abruptly as they went through the first of four arches. Blood red tile and blue marble pillars became white stone. Opulence was evident throughout the palace, but in the portion built by the Janti the opulence was demure. Lightly gilded designs above the arches formed delicate circular patterns, and the pastel murals on the rounded ceilings between arches depicted peaceful scenes, rather than warriors or battle.

Gella paused to look at a life-size portrait of Thranlam'Sum. "He is dressed like a Shodite Elder." She said of the draped, blue garment.

"I wouldn't repeat that observation to anyone else in the palace." Cobo warned.

In her native tongue, she commented that she found the Janti to have difficulty with the truth.

"In Janti, Gella." He admonished.

She shrugged, "If I must." There was a rebellious air in her reply that set Cobo ill at ease.

Haggins approached from the length of the hall. Before reaching them, he intoned, "Ver dala Ven? The dakas are waiting."

The reminder of their ultimate destination caused Gella to cringe. They had made their way to the reception hall at a leisurely pace, Cobo making a valiant attempt to calm Gella's nerves by giving her an impromptu tour of the palace. She begged Cobo to allow her to stay in his rooms during the reception, but he insisted she attend. He was to meet his son for the first time, and he wanted Gella by his side. But she was not accustomed to so quick a pace. There were no rest periods in Janti culture or politics, very much unlike the deliberate and thorough Shodite way of life. Being hurried along rattled Gella.

Cobo had become a Shodite in the pace he kept, and felt as hurried as Gella. He'd not been given the luxury of meeting with his son or family in private, only served with a summons for a reception that included hundreds. He would have preferred to ease into a relationship with Taen, to prepare his son for what was to come, but Jishni and the court of Jantideva would not afford him the chance.

"Thank you, Haggins, you may tell the dakas that we are on our way."

Haggins bowed, turned on his heel and hurried off to deliver the message.

Cobo steered Gella onward, continuing to take a leisurely pace despite being prompted to hurry. They passed through the final arch and into a wide ballroom. Gella's breath was taken away by dappled refracted light drawn in by the spire of Ver dala Ven Leila.

"Where does the light come from?" Gella asked, her voice hushed in awe.

"The spires draw in warmth and light from any source, including the stars in the heavens."

Gella held out her hands and marveled at the tiny pin dots of color that appeared on her skin. "I feel…"

"Yes?" Cobo prompted.

"At peace." She breathed, and she wandered further into the hall to stand beneath the spire. Blissful, she gazed upward. "I can see stars, though it is still day!"

"They are magnified by the crystal."

"Why do I feel as though I am in a warm bath?"

"It is the effect of the spire." He said, and he followed her gaze upward. "It is said that the Masing Star guided my ancestors in their construction of the seven spires. Beginning with Ver dala Ven Dex and ending with Aurora, seven consecutive generations of Ver dala Ven made it their life's work to crown Ona with the largest gems ever known in history. But you see it and feel it, don't you Gella? That the spires are not an architectural embellishment, but a tool. They calm one's nerves, bringing peace to one's constitution. It is believed that they are here to help the dakas guide the united world in peace by calming their minds and increasing their wisdom." Cobo shrugged lightly, "In truth, we aren't certain of the spires' real purpose."

Gella closed her eyes and held out her arms. "I could live beneath this spire."

Inspired by his love for her, he reached upward into the spire with his will, and palpated the stone. The spire vibrated, coming alive with bursts of multicolored light. Orin Hall thrilled, growing brighter. The vibration in the stone slowly worked its way downward, humming melodiously, softly at first, and growing thunderous as the crystal began to fully resonate to the sound.

Feeling in control of the crystal, Cobo made it sing a mournful prayer he remembered from his childhood. The melody broke into a three-part harmony, the voices lilting sopranos. Building, he added tenors, bass, the voices rising in a tumultuous song. Beneath the voices, pushing them higher, an orchestra of ancient instruments joined in, and in glorious crescendo rose, rose, undulating in waves that shook the floor beneath their feet.

The symphony became a visual feast. The sparkling light transformed into radiant beings, and danced in time to the languid song. They spun in lazy circles, reaching out and touching Gella's face with loving gestures, much to her awe and pleasure. Giggling, she joined in their movements, dancing with them, swirling, her many layered skirts flowing out from her legs.

Approaching footsteps, a stampede of footsteps, caused Gella to stop dancing, and take cover behind Cobo.

Cobo, while holding onto his control of the spire, glanced to the side to see a battalion of haughtily dressed aristocrats disgorging from the Masing Hall and rushing across the ballroom floor.

Jishni and Taen were among the first to reach the underside of the spire. For Taen's benefit, Cobo raised the level of the song, until the pitch shook the rafters and the portraits on the walls. The spell of Leila's spire was known to heal terminal illnesses and to turn the hearts of heartless men. Cobo's hope that Leila could reach Taen through the spire, turn his stone heart to living flesh again, became a part of the prayer.

The song caused Taen to falter and swoon, but he fought the bliss associated with the spire. He stared upwards at the magnified stars, anger causing him to tremble. The sprites danced their way to him, abruptly becoming comely women in gauzy dresses, their skirts adorned with bells, and they danced around him in a seductive manner. Cobo hadn't changed them, they had changed in accord with Taen's alignment to evil.

Olla girls, and as Taen recognized them, Cobo understood the spell his son had been trying to weave in Jishni's and Bail's minds. Murder, cloaked by the appearance of suicide, was the darkest mark in Taen's heart.

Cobo ended the prayer abruptly on a shrill note, the last voice ringing in the spire as silence descended in Orin Hall.

Taen glared at Cobo, all the shades of resentment imaginable present in his expression. Pure dark hatred glowered from the depth of his soul.

Numbers of people gathered around them. Sighs and laughter, applause and joyful shouts of approbation followed the sudden silence.

Jishni smiled beatifically. Her manner regal, relaxed, she walked to Cobo, hands outstretched to take his. Her hands were warm, and welcome within his, and under the calming, clearing influence of Leila's spire, he felt as if he belonged to her again.

"My dearest Cobo, I have not heard so beautiful a prayer since your elevation."

"Nor have I."

His brother's voice did much to break the spell of the moment. Cobo and Jishni released each other's hands, and guilt jumped into her face. She turned away as her husband came up behind her.

The daka of Jantideva stood proudly next to his wife, looking like the dark Knights of legend, dressed in his black uniform and covered with Alliance commendations. He'd aged gracefully, and though he was the elder brother, he was so fit that Cobo was sure that Bail looked the younger. His demeanor was composed as he glanced from his wife to his brother, though Cobo could see clear through him, as always. Bail's emotions were a bedlam of conflict. Old heartache caused by Cobo running away mixed with good memories, as well as new distrust. Cobo's eyes widened as he heard the thoughts his brother volunteered. Distrust lingered in each darkened corner, in each thought.

"You've come home."

"For a short time."

"Yes, I have heard of your plans." Bail replied, his expression carefully controlled, as were his words. All eyes were on them, all ears alert, wishing to hear their first exchange. The court, still an appendage of the dakas, visibly leaned in closer.

Bail sidestepped all the subjects he wished to speak with Cobo on, instead diverting his, and the court's, attention to Gella. His lips tried to smile for her, but he simply could not make the expression come to life.

"So you've brought a wife home?" he asked, his question marred by the jagged edge of emotion.

"A Chosen Sister." Cobo replied, and he averted his eyes as if his brother could read the truth in them, that Gella should have been more, but would never be. "Gella al Perraz, this is my brother, daka Bail."

Bail's brows twitched, his only outward show of the disappointment that Cobo was not attached.

"Sister." Bail said, and he strolled forward, his manner regal and confident. "And where is the rest of your family, Cobo? Surely, you have a family?"

Cobo let Bail's jealousy and lack of trust hurt his feelings. Softly, he said, "I do. I have a Chosen Sister. I have a brother, and a brother's wife, and a brother's sons. You are my family."

Bail paused and stared at Cobo's face, measuring him the way he'd measure an opponent.

"We have much to discuss." he said finally, "But after," and he nodded toward the huge double door entrance leading into the reception hall. "you are presented to the Alliance. As much as the Alliance," and his glare flashed Yana's way, "and the Suma hate to give us privacy, it will be so before the end of this day that I will spend a private moment in your company."

"Yes." Cobo agreed earnestly.

Bail offered his arm to Gella in gallant style. "If you are Cobo's Chosen Sister, you are also mine. It will be my pleasure to get to know you, Gella."

Gella shyly took the arm of daka Bail, throwing a worried glance at Cobo. He nodded, urging her on. The crowd parted and Bail's subjects bowed slightly as he passed with his new sister in tow.

Taen did a smart pivot and stalked from the underside of the spire, ignoring the eye contact Cobo tried to make with him.

"He will not greet me." Cobo relented.

"Give him time, he will come around." Jishni said as she took his arm.

Cobo doubted very much that he'd ever win Taen's affections. It shouldn't have been important to him, whether or not Taen loved him as a father. He'd given that right away, years ago, but he found he wanted Taen's love, nonetheless. It was never to be. Disheartened by the truth, he concentrated on remaining true to his destiny. He would give his presentation to the Alliance, make his demands, destroy his son's dreams, destroy the hopes of the Janti people, and do so in as few words as possible. He would not win supporters tonight, indeed he intended to make as many enemies as possible. He caressed Jishni's hand, while knowing that she may become his enemy as well.

Low, his eyes greeting onlookers they passed on the way into the Masing Chamber, he said to Jishni, "I want you to trust me. No matter what I say to the Alliance. Will you?"

They were one in heart, even after all the years that had passed. She understood that nothing good would come of his reception, and glanced worriedly toward his profile, and on to their destination. Her lips twitching with suppressed emotion, she replied, "I vow to trust you."

*

Lines of ushers dressed in red velvet uniforms flanked the dakas on both sides as they descended a curved staircase that lead into a vast auditorium. The cadence of their step leant formality to the daka's entrance, a garnish in the majestic style of Ona. Everything Gella saw in Ona seemed grand, to the extreme. In Shodalum, a good place to sit was on a soft mat on the ground. In Ona, the auditorium was furnished with ornamental seating, chairs and settees that did not look comfortable in the least, but looked rich. There were four generations of seating surrounding an expansive ballroom, and hundreds of guests, who were pouring into the auditorium from less obvious entrances above theirs. A small stage in a gallery above the entrance held an orchestra that had only just resumed playing after Cobo's interruption, producing music of a kind she'd never heard before filled the vast auditorium. The beauty of it drew her full attention and she twisted around to see the source of the music. Forgetting her feet, she caught the toe of her slipper in the hem of her gown. She stumbled on the last step, and Bail caught her in his arms.

"Are you all right, Chosen Sister?"

Flustered, she righted herself and replied, "These feet of mine, a double assed slank has more grace."

Her use of a profanity caused his mouth to slip open. Her heart sunk, and she faltered over an apology as ungainly as her misstep.

Bail responded by laughing out loud. Amusement twinkled in his eyes, and lightened the sobriety in his features. "I've not heard frank talk from a woman in all my life. Refreshing!"

She giggled nervously, and again took his arm, while inside damning herself for her loose tongue. She did her best to keep her attention on the cumbersome dress and where she put her feet, difficult for all the distractions offered.

The Janti aristocrats and Alliance Ministers, and their hosts of guests and assistants filled the seating area to capacity. There was an air of expectation all around them, of hope, hope that was directed at Cobo.

Bail navigated her toward a stage in the center of the ballroom, going around a statue standing guard nearby. The stone statue was covered with chips of blue and yellow tiles, creating at a distance the effect of a green form. The statue was of a man, his dress simple, his hands held out in offering. Bail paused with her, and together they looked upward at the serene face.

"I was told you are Zarian?"

The question shook her, but she did not show it as she answered. "Yes."

"Where in Zaria do you call home?"

She lied as Cobo had instructed. "The Outlands."

"Ah." Smiling, he said something to her in an exotic sounding foreign language.

Prepared for the eventuality that someone might try to speak with her in her "native" tongue, she replied, "If you please, daka Bail, I prefer to speak Janti. I am new to the language, and I am trying to become fluent."

He smiled wryly, shrugged. "My Zarian isn't the best, I am afraid." Gesturing to the statue, he asked, "What do you think of our rendering of Thranlam'Sum?"

"Very pretty." She said, meaning it, for the tiles were tiny and put together well, and the blend of color pleased her eyes.

He raised his brow, "You are not offended?"

She shook her head, not understanding his meaning. She turned slightly, hoping to catch Cobo's eye.

"No?" Bail prompted, "Most Zarians find it discomforting because Ver dala Ven is depicted here dispensing blessings as a man, with his hands. The Zarian Suma have petitioned the dakas for well on four thousand years to have this particular statue changed. And it does not offend you?"

She was aware that he was baiting her, testing her. Cobo warned her that there would be questions about their whereabouts, and doubts. Fresh out of readily rehearsed lies to deliver, she reverted to her usual plainspoken style. "Daka Bail, I have lived with Cobo for nearly all my life. I'm not impressed by Ver dala Ven, even the ancient ones." and she averted her eyes, hoping the depth of her panic did not show through her calm.

He grinned at her reply. "I am your brother. Call me Bail."

This time she saw affection in his eyes for her, which was far more disturbing for Gella than anything that had happened since they'd left Shodalum.

He guided her to the stage where the dakas would be seated, in the center of the auditorium and on display.

"And here we part company, my dear." He said as they reached the long steps of the stage, and he let her arm go, turned and waited for his wife. Once he took Jishni's arm, the two dakas went up the steps without her.

"Cobo?"

But he went off in another direction, toward a raised platform between the rendering of Thranlam'Sum and another Ver dala Ven, a woman that she didn't recognize, placing himself above the height of the statues. He told her earlier that he was the main attraction, and had an obligation to stand before this court and answer questions until the alliance exhausted themselves, or him.

Alone, Gella was uncertain what to do. She lingered at the bottom step, lost, her eyes darting about the faces of strangers. Already exceedingly nervous, she recoiled in shock as an usher took Bail's place at her side and touched her elbow in order to guide her to her seat.

The usher, a Shodite slave she realized, bowed submissively, and waited for her readiness to be escorted to her seat. Waited, as if she were some high strung daka repulsed by his touch.

Mortified by the thought of injuring his feelings and by what he must have thought of her, in carefully enunciated Janti she said, "I am terribly sorry for my bad manners. Please forgive me."

His eyes shot to hers, shock flickering through his temperate expression. He was young, handsome, very well built and tall, with full lips, pale gray eyes and dark hair. Red looked splendid against his rugged brown skin and the cut of the uniform perfectly accentuated his slender youth. If they had met in Shodalum she would have at least tried to seduce him, if only to run his fingers through his hair or feel his slender hips between her legs. At the very least she would have brought him home with her in her fantasies, for he was beautiful. Perhaps they could have fallen in love, and filled Calli with new life, new hope.

In Jantideva he was a slave who was forbidden to speak to his betters, and unused to being shown simple courtesy.

Tenderness for him, for his situation, his oppression, filled her heart, and wet her eyes with tears. At once she felt ashamed of needing his help. "Will you," she asked low, "please show me where I belong?"

Her prompting, however gentle and kind it had been made, caused him such distress that he quickly dropped his eyes, and obediently took her elbow. To her surprise, he guided her up the steps and to the empty seat next to Jishni. She thanked him in brief. His mouth set in a grim frown, and he snapped a bow and joined a row of ushers against the wall. It was clear that she'd unnerved him, and that he did not trust her courtesy or her motives, because she was a Janti.

Her hands slid from the curved arms of the chair she was in to her silken dress, and she felt ashamed to be sitting next to the daka.

In orderly silence, the gathering took their seats. Cobo's hands were linked behind his back, and he was at ease though he was on display. If he was nervous, it didn't show.

Once all in attendance were in their seats, an elderly man with thick hair of silver and dressed in a glittering black and gold robe swept toward Cobo. He smiled, his mouth a perfect shape, his teeth glowing white. His arm went up to present Cobo, his hand held out, and he lowered it slowly as he said, "Ten thousand years ago, here, where this palace stands, the Masing Star gave birth to Ver dala Ven. In those beginning times, the Masing blessed us with peace, plenty, and happiness. The Guardian Spirit of Creation gave us a great gift, and He returns to give us yet another! We've all prayed for this day, my friends, and it has arrived. It is my great pleasure to welcome home Ver dala Ven Cobo."

The audience shouted their welcome, and fell into reciting a prayer that reminded Gella of a Betnoni Return Prayer.

*

Once the prayer had ended, and relative silence came over the crowd, Cobo said, "I am honored by your interest in my return."

A tall woman from a middle row stood and introduced herself to Cobo as Mother Rea, Minister of Garma. Her dark face gentle, her wide mouth moving in a slow smile, she said, "We are all interested in hearing your story, and knowing more about the timing of your return. Why have you chosen this time to return, and what will your mission be now that you are here?"

"My mission in Jantideva is to offer the Alliance an opportunity to right the wrongs of the past, and avert certain destruction."

The Garman, as did many in the reception, believed he'd affirmed his obligation as Ver dala Ven to the dakas. None of them understood, but he intended to make himself understood.

"I am not here to ease your minds." He added sharply to the entire assembly. "I am not here to renew my position among the dakas. As Itza prophesied, Ver dala Ven has abandoned Ona, never to return. I am here to claim Taen, to take him north, to offer him as recompense for the suffering of Dilgopoche."

72

Cobo could hear his own heartbeat in the silence that followed. Behind him, Bail and Jishni were rigid in their seats, their faces impassive. Taen had gone from sullen boredom to edge-of-his-seat horrified interest.

Disapproval burst from the audience in angry shouts and desperate pleas for mercy. The Alliance ministers wishing to speak stood, some shouting through the din of other voices. Their impatience spurred his.

Cobo continued with a fury that belied his calm entrance into the reception. "The Alliance of Corrinne's age wiped their feet on the Dilgos, then congratulated themselves for their cunning abuse of a vulnerable people! Like it or not, you are the heirs to that abuse, the responsible heirs who must pay the price! The Dilgos want to reunify, and by the spirit and law of the Alliance, you have an obligation to see their desire made real!"

A string of incredulous retorts came clear over the din.

"You cannot be serious!"

"You are here on behalf of the Dilgos?"

"What is your dealing with the Dilgos!"

"The Dilgos aren't like us!"

"They are abominations!"

Cobo's voice rose majestically, "The Dilgos are not my Chosen People, they are not my Chosen Cause! The Dilgos are Taen's cause. They are Taen's destiny!"

"Taen's cause is Ona! By law, he belongs to the dakas!"

The surly retort came from the front row, from a pompous looking man Cobo recognized though he'd aged much and grown fatter. Grav Tulkue, the Minister of Janti affairs, a lifetime appointment given to him by daka Janus, was an important man in Jishni's court, and intended to be heard.

"Taen is elevated to Ver dala Ven before the Suma. You cannot remove him or lay claim upon him!"

To Grav Tulkue, Cobo declared in a full voice, "I dispute Taen's elevation in the house of Ona. I say he is untrained and unfit for duty, and since my word is law in regard to Ver dala Ven, Taen is therefore still my property and mine to do with as I wish. As Ver dala Ven I have ultimate authority over his future! Not one

73

among you, not the dakas, nor the Suma, can dispute my claim on daka Taen."

"No, it isn't true." Taen mewled, and he looked to his father and mother. "He can't take me away against my will, can he?"

Jishni and Bail offered no comfort in the helpless and worried way they glanced at each other.

"Mother, tell me that *Ver dala Ven* doesn't own my destiny!"

"By law," Bail replied, reluctant, tired, trying to soften the blow, "it is true, but the spirit of the law was meant to protect Ver dala Ven-"

Taen did not need to hear more. Rejecting Cobo's claim in gesture, Taen burst out of his seat and fled the reception hall. He made no effort to be discreet, charging gracelessly by Cobo with less than a glance, furiously stomping his feet like a child half his age. His behavior stunned the court to silence, and not a word was spoken until he'd burst out of the auditorium.

Bail nodded toward the purple robed Watchers, and on his unspoken command, four followed the young daka.

The first to break the silence was the elderly Kanacki minister, Virella. The sleek woman stood, her ankle length white hair flowing around her shoulder, and though her voice was soft, it carried easily to all ears. "Venerable Ver dala Ven, if as you say, the Dilgos are Taen's mission, what is yours? Is yours to train Taen to be Ver dala Ven, and if so, who will he serve? The Dilgos?"

Cobo replied in the same soft tone that Virella had posed her question. "Taen is too old to be trained." And he ignored sighs and gasps of disbelief, "His time is past. He will not now, nor ever, act as Ver dala Ven, for the Dilgos or Jantideva."

Chancellor Yana cringed in his seat, and covered his mouth with his hand. He shook, his head at Cobo, as if to beg him to say it wasn't so.

"My mission is two fold." Cobo went on, "I've returned to Ona to ensure that Jantideva pays for the crimes against Dilgopoche, and to do so, Taen must be made heir to the Dilgo throne. I've also returned to ensure that the moral laws set down by the Elders of the Grand Lineage of Thranlam'Sum are reasserted. By the laws of Thranlam'Sum, we are all commanded to refrain from profiting on the suffering of other beings. I am here, today, to urge the dakas to free the Janti-born Shodites from their bondage of slavery."

*

Jishni's hands came together, a casual movement, though Gella could see that Jishni was biting into her own flesh with her nails.

His firm entreaty renewed the babble of too many voices assaulting him with questions. It was the contentious man in front who was the loudest, and who Cobo had placed his attentions.

"You are a fine one to remind us of Thranlam'Sum's laws, Ver dala Ven! You are nothing more than runaway who cannot admit his guilt, or his true responsibilities before the court!"

Bail shot to his feet, causing Gella to jump right out of her skin.

"Grav Tulkue!" he bellowed, "You will show Ver dala Ven respect in my court! Tame your tongue!"

Grav Tulkue's begrudging show of respect came in the form of a muttered apology, and on its heels was another attack, this time against the Shodites. "Your demand is impossible, Ver dala Ven Cobo! If we freed the Shodites, what type of citizens could they possibly make in Jantideva? The Shodites need us to harbor and feed them, to give them direction, for if we did not they would be lost! They are technologically illiterate, and quite often functionally illiterate, as well. We do our best for them, give them work and homes and a place in our society. We should be commended for being their benefactors, for we have already accepted into our society a people which are born stupid as stones."

Gella's courage and fury ignited, and, unmindful of the opinion of the court or the dakas, unmindful of her own well being, she shot to her feet and retorted, "You are ignorant and unfair!"

Jishni's hand shot up, prompting her to sit.

Cobo ignored Jishni's gesture, and recognized her to the guests. "My Chosen Sister, Gella al Perraz, will speak."

Jishni's hand sunk into her lap. Gella was certain the daka wasn't pleased, but she could not restrain herself. She brushed off a cloak of quick regret, and threw her head high, glaring down at the bigoted minister. "Shodites are an extremely intelligent and proud people."

Grav Tulkue guffawed. "You obviously have not met the wide eyed simpletons that stumble into our hands, fresh from Shodalum!" He glanced around him, a gesture that encouraged others to laugh with him at the expense of the Shodites.

Her cheeks burned. "You, sir, obviously confuse intelligence with a knowledge of Janti culture, a glaring example of your own ignorance." she retorted scornfully. He huffed his displeasure at her comment, but before he could rebut, she quickly went on, speaking with passion, "Despite your beliefs, Jantideva is not the hub of the universe! Perhaps Shodites are not taught the Janti language, nor do Shodite schools teach skills to use Janti technology. And why should they? Shodalum has its own language, its own history, and more importantly, its own traditions. Shodites are taught how to survive off the land; how to raise crops in a desert made by Jantideva's greed for technology, where the seasons are fickle and the water tainted, and the land only able to grow yava and spice grass. Shodites survive by their wits, by their intelligence and common sense!"

With an even, and patronizing, tone, Grav replied, "Chosen Sister al Perraz, I agree that the Shodites are resourceful people, and they live hard lives in Shodalum, by the tyranny of their own techno-phobic government. That is why in our society we welcome the Shodites who escape the penal colony their government has become, and freely care for their needs."

"The Shodites you keep as slaves labor so that you Janti may live your lives with lazy ease, and in return, they are stripped of their freedom! They do not have the freedom to live as they wish, or where they wish to live, to perform the jobs they wish to perform. They do not have the freedom to be artists, or farmers, or businessmen!"

"They have more here than they could ever want in Shodalum." Grav countered angrily, "Do you not understand? We are taking care of them!"

"And the price of your patriarchy are their spirits!"

"What would you have us do?" he exploded impatiently. "If we released them from their posts, right here and right now, what would these people do? Live on the streets and beg for food, that is what they would do, because they are not qualified to do anything more."

"What of the services they provide to you now?" she countered indignantly, "Pay them for the jobs they perform, and they will not be beggars, but members of your society!"

"Can you imagine the cost to pay Shodites to work? More money than they are worth!"

Nervous laughter erupted around the councilman. Gella's fury deepened. She wished to lash out at the man physically, and hurt him, a wish that fisted her hands.

Jishni beckoned to Gella's usher, and the beautiful man hurried to Gella's side to place light hold on her arm, as if to prevent her from rushing into the crowd to go after Grav Tulkue. The presence at her side of the man she'd insulted and unnerved with her kindness only incited her anger further. She wanted to grab Tulkue by his wobbly skinned throat and squeeze until his stupidity surrendered.

"Certainly, I cannot expect insight for a most just cause from a pampered fat man with Shodite servants to attend to his every need, including holding your little consha while you relieve yourself."

A slight gasp hushed the auditorium, and her off color insult momentarily dumbfounded the Minister. From her right she heard Bail let out a rueful sigh. His refreshing Chosen Sister no doubt shamed him. For his sake, not her own, Gella curbed the string of insults ready on her tongue.

Furious, yet controlled, she added, "You'd show yourself as an ignorant fool in Shodalum, sir, for you wouldn't last a day in the deserts Jantideva and the Alliance made with their greed and selfishness."

Grav recovered his composure. Calculative, he said, "You speak for the Shodites with uncanny understanding. Where exactly is your homeland, Chosen Sister?" And he glanced to the side, a purposeful look toward the statue of Thranlam'Sum.

Curious, Gella followed his gaze, and seeing the court mind readers keenly watching over the gathering, her heart thumped hard in her chest. Three men, dressed in dramatic black, stood guard over the minds of those at the reception. They seemed to be of the same family, as they had similar features; beaky noses, small eyes, gaunt faces and spindly bodies. The oldest man had to be near eighty. He clung to a blue staff with both hands, and wore a form fitting cap that covered his ears and wrapped around his neck, exposing only his face, giving his face the look of a grinning skull. His appearance, with the staff and head covering, was the personification of evil Janti mind readers in many Shodite moral plays. Gella had thought the costume was for affect, to frighten the audiences. Instead, the costume was as authentic as Gella's fear of the man.

Standing next to the old man could have been his fifty-year-old son, with graying dark hair and reddish cheeks. The third mind reader was a man near Cobo's age. This was the man Grav Tulkue now stared at, as macabre amusement struggled in his features.

The youngest mind reader glanced from Gella, indecision sweeping his features. Finally, he shook his head, a solemn refusal.

She shuddered as she realized Grav Tulkue suspected her ancestry, but for whatever reason, perhaps because Cobo stood so near, the mindreader would not venture into her thoughts in order to confirm his suspicions.

In the background of her fears, she heard Jishni speaking to her, repeating her name. Finally, Jishni's sharper tone tore Gella's attention away from the mind reader.

"Gella, you've said enough."

She expected Jishni's disapproval, as if she were a child expecting the wrath of a parent. Instead, in Jishni's face she saw compassion.

Low, Jishni said to her, "You've accomplished what you needed to accomplish. You have been heard. You have reached me."

Gella was frozen in place, unable to take her eyes off Jishni. In that moment, she felt as if the daka had always understood her somehow, yet they'd never met. They shared a love for Cobo, which should have made them rivals, but did not. The daka enslaved the Shodite people, which should have caused them to hate each other, but did not. As she stared into Jishni's compassionate eyes, she realized that the daka didn't believe in the slavery of the Shodites.

Jishni gestured for her to sit. Carefully, and still shaking with anger, Gella took her seat at the daka's command.

Her usher was dismissed, and was expected to return to his post. Instead, he hesitated, then fell to one knee before Gella. He grabbed her hand and pressed the back of her fingers to his forehead. The gesture of respect was a Shodite custom. She felt honored, and tenderly touched his head, feeling the wiriness of his dark hair under her fingertips.

"No, not for me." She admonished gently.

"For no other." He gushed, and he pressed his lips against the back of her hand.

"Blasphemy!" The elder mind reader shouted, and he cracked the floor with the bottom of his staff.

In less time than it took to comprehend what was happening, two Watchers plunged from behind the daka's seat and wrenched the young Shodite to his feet. His face was alive with pride and fear, and tremendous respect for Gella. His cheeks were wet with tears.

"Bless me in death, Sister of Betnoni," he cried out as they hauled him away from the daka's seats.

Her arms were held out toward him as she rose, trembling now with horror and not anger. She spun around to Jishni, "Please, what are they going to do to him?"

Jishni's mouth was agape, and she shrugged as if she were helpless in the matter. "For treason, he will be put to death."

"No!"

"He pledged himself to you," Grav Tulkue proclaimed, laughing with sickening glee, "and by law he is not permitted to do so, unless you are his benefactor."

Gella threw herself on the ground before Jishni. "I beg you for his life! He was moved by my words, just as you were. Please, do not have him put to death for being moved by the thought of his own freedom! He is like us, with dreams, daka!"

"It is law, Gella." Jishni replied, her tone hushed.

"No, you are the law! Please, oh please!" Gella dissolved into tears, and she crawled closer to press her cheek on Jishni's slipper. "I beg you, daka. I beg you. Forgive him, he did not mean to offend you!"

Jishni's composure faded. Her voice shaking, she commanded that the sentries halt. They roughly turned the prisoner around, and as they did, a look of utter disbelief came over his features as he saw a well-dressed Janti woman groveling before the daka on his behalf.

Grav watched the scene with sordid amusement. "Would Chosen Sister al Perraz give her own life in exchange for this young wretch?"

Cobo, who'd been silent throughout, said quickly, "Gella is a daka in the court of Ona. Take care how you offend her, and me."

This was news to Gella. She bolted upright, her reddened eyes now wide with shock. "A daka?"

"You didn't know." Jishni said softly, and she glanced to Cobo, suspicions twisting in her features. "You are Chosen Sister to the dakas." She said softly, looking again at Gella, "You are daka Gella of Jantideva. Your importance exceeds all in this court, and all in the Alliance, save Bail, my children, Cobo and myself. Didn't Cobo tell you?"

"No," and it was more a denial than a response.

"As a daka you are afforded certain privileges. For instance, there is no need to kiss my feet in order to have your opinions heard."

"I can't be a daka."

"Why?" Jishni prompted, her voice very low so that only Bail could hear, "There could only be one reason you could not be a daka, as explained in the Masing Law of Separation. Why can't you be a daka?"

She fought a resurgence of tears, her earlier courage drained by emotion. She refused to answer Jishni's pointed question.

"What will you do to him?" Gella asked of the slave.

Her eyes clearing, as if enlightened by Gella's evasive response, Jishni looked toward Cobo. "What is your judgement on the matter of the young upstart, Ver dala Ven?"

Gella lifted herself off the floor and she wiped her tears away as she looked hopefully at Cobo. He looked at her with longing and contrition mixed.

"I believe," he began slowly, his eyes creeping back to the assembly, "you should spare this Shodite, and appoint him the living guardian of Chosen Sister al Perraz."

The pampered fat man guffawed. "Splendid suggestion!"

"I disagree," the elderly mind reader interjected, and he started toward Cobo, leaning lightly on the staff. He had everyone's attention, though no one would look directly in his eyes. Undoubtedly, all those present, Janti and Shodite alike, were wary of him, and what he might hear in their random or purposeful thoughts.

"I wish to hear you, Tidio." Jishni obliged. Gella detected a note of fatigue in Jishni's tone.

Tidio spoke slowly, his voice raspy and unkind. "The Janti born's thoughts were most rebellious. As he pledged himself to Chosen Sister al Perraz, he hoped for the death of the daka."

"I didn't!" the usher shouted, struggling against restraint.

Bail barked, "You will keep still and quiet!"

A second mind reader, the middle aged man, said, "He does think of himself as a Janti, daka Jishni. His family has kept count of the generations born in Jantideva—Two hundred and two."

Gella threw her gaze toward the usher. As usual she spoke before thinking, and blurted, "You are more Janti than Shodite."

Tidio's ears were sharper than Gella would have liked. "He is nothing of Jantideva!" he snapped, "He is Shodite! And the Shodite must obey our laws, or die!"

Jishni relaxed into the back of her seat and thought a moment. She sighed, heralding a resolution.

"Bring him to me."

The Watchers led the man toward the daka's place. He was proud now, his head high and his eyes piercing into the daka's, unafraid of his captors now that he'd been damned. "You are Korba, son of Yu-Jakyi." the daka said casually.

"I am." he replied, his voice clear and sure.

The daka nodded. "I knew your mother. She was a fine woman and a wonderful cook."

"Yes, daka." He agreed wholeheartedly.

Jishni again thought a moment, her eyes finding Cobo's. The two stared at one another a long moment.

Addressing the assembly, she said, "I heed the wisdom of Ver dala Ven. From this day, forward, Korba, son of Yu-Jakyi, will be the living guardian of Chosen Sister al Perraz."

Gella wept in relief that his life was spared. Her relief was so profound that she failed to question what really had transpired.

The assembly was in an uproar. A variety of questions about the significance of the daka's leniency were lobbed at Cobo, who seemed not to hear. He gazed at Gella, sadness turning his frown deep. As she found his eyes, a hardness formed in her stomach, a hardness of fear and anticipation.

అలఅలఅలఅలఅలఅలఅలఅల

Cobo escorted Gella to the apartment he once shared with his brother when he was growing up in Ona. Korba was three paces behind them. Gella held her temper the full length of the palace, trying mightily to maintain Janti decorum. As they entered the apartment, she slapped a hand on Korba's chest and pressed him out of the threshold. She closed the door firmly on his face

She lunged at Cobo, coming short of smacking him in the face with both fists. "You made him my slave for life?"

"We'll have to talk about this later, Gella. I have to find my brother, to meet in private with him. I will endure your tongue lashing later, if you are still inclined to abuse me."

"You find amusement in my humiliation?"

"We saved his life, Gella. You'd rather he be dead so that you wouldn't have to feel humiliation?"

"I hate Jantideva!" she spat. "Disgusting, barbaric people who stink of unnatural smells, and these clothes, they have a life of their own, by the Goddess they are driving me to distraction!"

Cobo pursed his lips and opened the door for Korba. "Come in. Don't be afraid, she isn't as ferocious as she sounds, at least," and he glanced backward at her, "she won't be with you."

"Cobo!"

"Stay put. I'll be back soon. If there is anything you need, Korba will be happy to provide it for you." To Korba he said, "Make sure daka Gella is comfortable."

Korba nodded his head in assent.

"Aha, and there is another matter I wish to twist your arm for, what is this? Daka Gella! Pah!" In Shodite, she rapidly spun out a stream of colorful profanities, calling Cobo every vile thing she could think of.

"Ah," Cobo pressed a finger to his mouth, signifying he wanted her to hold her tongue. "Later."

He was out the door before she was finished, so she continued, shouting to the top of her lungs. He was racing to join his son, or his brother, or his pretty little Jishni, despite her emotional devastation.

Furious with him, Gella stomped through the sitting room and let herself into her bedroom. Korba followed, like a well-heeled pet. She took great satisfaction in slamming another door soundly on Korba's handsome, bemused face.

A clap outside her door caused her to turn and grimace.

"Go home!" she told him sharply through the door.

"I've no where to go." he replied earnestly.

She huffed her disbelief and flung the door open to face him. "Surely you must have a home?" she demanded, "Where did you lay your head last night? The ground outside the palace?"

"Of course I have a home, but I don't belong there now. I belong with you." he said earnestly, "I belong to you."

"You don't belong to me," she retorted, feeling shame color her face. "I don't want a slave, nor have I need for one."

"I am not your slave," he corrected, "I am your living guardian. It is my pleasure to spend my life protecting and serving you. Please, don't turn me away."

She liked that his gaze was direct with her, unlike the way he and his fellow Shodites averted his eyes around the other Janti. But the way he held her in awe was disconcerting.

Mindful of the "eyes" Cobo warned her of in the palace, security measures that may or may not be present in the outer rooms of Cobo's apartment, she took hold of Korba's arm and dragged him into her room. Closing the door behind him, she said, "I am not a Janti, nor a Zarian. You do not have to serve me or protect me. I am a Shodite, Korba, from Shodalum."

"A true Shodite?"

To quell his doubt, she held out her hands.

"Feel them." she invited.

His brows hooked together, and he did as he was told. Feeling the rough texture of her hands, his eyes widened with his astonishment.

"You've labored."

"I am consecrated to Calli, matriarch of my tribe." She said ruefully. Matriarch to a tribe of two, but what did it matter now? Calli was gone, Shodalum, gone, and all that was left to her was Ona, Cobo, and this slave before her, holding her hands.

"We are equals, Korba." She added, "I could very well be in your position tomorrow, were my secret be discovered. Do you understand now why I cannot have a servant?"

"The daka allowed you to speak before the council."

"The daka didn't have much choice." Gella replied, and she pulled her hands from Korba's and walked away from him. "She does not know of my origins, and besides, I have a tendency to speak my mind. It's a character flaw, but one I could live with in Shodalum. Not here, however. I have to hide who I am, here." She turned and looked at him, expecting he would no longer view her in the same light. Instead, in his face she saw the same disconcerting awe.

"By Betnoni's holy ass, do you not understand?" she demanded. "I am a Shodite! We are equals! I cannot be your master, no more than I can be a daka in the court of Jantideva!"

He stepped toward her and sunk to one knee. "I have been blessed more than I ever could have imagined. I thought I was being placed into the service of a liberal Janti woman, on the order of the great Solien, but instead I am with a Shodite goddess."

"Goddess? Have you taken leave of your senses, man? Stand up!" she ordered.

He obeyed her. His features bore the light and happy expression of a child being given a great gift.

"I do not deserve your adulation, Korba. I am nothing." she spat brusquely, "Before Cobo rescued me, I was a whore, trading my body to men and women for food. Now, how do I look to you?" she asked sarcastically, "Like a goddess?"

He was looking at her differently. His awe was subdued with compassion. "Is it as hard to live in Shodalum as we have been taught?"

"How hard is hard?" she wanted to know. "A landless woman who only owns her body sells her body. Those with land work the land. I've done both. It didn't seem so hard a life, as living as a slave must be for you."

"But weren't you a slave?" he wanted to know, "If you have no choices, you are enslaved by the law, or fate."

She sighed, and smiled tiredly at him. "So you are a philosopher."

"An optimist," he replied, "I believe in a better future for the Alliance. Are you loyal to the daka, and the authority class?"

"I have no loyalties to the Janti, except for the loyalty I feel for my brother. And he may have been born in this palace, but he is no Janti."

His manner grew urgent. "Will you come with me into the city? I have someone you must meet."

She refused his surprising request with a wide gesture of her hands. "Cobo told me to stay here!"

"If you are worried about the dangers of the city, you'd be with me, I promise, I would never let anything happen to you. Please, come with me. Let me show you how we Janti-born Shodites live, give you a chance to decide which life is easier." His smile told her the latter statement was made in jest, but he was absolutely earnest about taking her into the city.

It was spite, not common sense that prompted her to accept Korba's invitation. She was asserting her freedom to do as she pleased. She did not need Cobo's permission to undertake an adventure!

"Alright. I'll go."

Korba was absolutely delighted.

Chapter 5

Janti born Shodites are given two names at birth. Their legal name was their service name, a traditional Janti name that purposefully distanced the Shodites from their heritage and was used by their benefactors.

In their own homes, among their families, they called each other by the names given to them by their parents, Shodite names handed down through numerous generations.

His legal name was Fisk, a name given to him by his family's benefactor. An insult, as Fisk was a common name Janti socialites gave their pets. His benefactor taunted him with that name, Fisk, calling him *here Fisk, good boy Fisk, do come Fisk*, always certain to give him a pat on the head as if he were an obedient animal. He came, did as he was bid to do, allowed the condescending pats on the head for the sake of his mother, who wept bitterly each time he was beaten for insubordination; all the while growing in resentment as gradually as he grew into manhood.

And as he grew into manhood, he developed the same long body of his benefactor, the same tawny hair and the same pale blue eyes. His face was a replica of the man he hated with all his might. He did not need his mother's deathbed confession to know that his biological father was not her state-approved husband, a man traded from the family before he was born, but their family's slaver.

He was eighteen when he petitioned the Janti Council of Shodite Affairs to allow him to change households. His benefactor did not block the move to keep his only son close to him, but rather behaved as if he'd been relieved of a great burden.

He was transferred to the household of Bret and Solien di Haveran. They were an older couple with four adolescent daughters, and were loosely connected to the royal family. They were aristocrats, and political radicals. They believed in and campaigned for the liberation of the Janti-born Shodites, and though they were benefactors they treated their own servants with respect. He found himself in a house where he was permitted to come and go as he pleased, as long as he also met his daily responsibilities. They did not openly treat him as chattel, even paying him a modest wage for his efforts. They didn't like his legally given name, so they started calling him by his Shodite name, Tryn, which in Shodite meant fine son of the great man.

He understood they were trying to honor him by recognizing his Shodite heritage, so he did not labor to explain to them why Tryn was also an offensive name. He asked them, instead, to change his name entirely, commemorating his entry into a new family. He wanted to be called Shelon, which was his maternal grandfather's name. The di Haverans was agreeable, though amused, too. Shelon was an uncommon given name. It meant Fighting Devil.

In the thirty-two years he lived in their household he served the di Haverans at many state functions. The Janti often spoke freely in the presence of the Shodites; they rarely considered Shodites intelligent enough to understand matters of state. So, while Shelon served drinks or stood by as an attendant to the di Haverans, he learned much about politics and the people running their government. He'd been in the company of Kanaki presidents, and Zarian monarchs, and Rysenk mystics. He'd met, face to face, the dakas. His sworn enemies, and they called him Shelon. He relished the irony. He retained all he learned of the Janti court while working in the di Haveran household, never once realizing the future importance of his knowledge.

Bret di Haveran died the same year that daka Jishni took over her father's seat in the Chamber of Ministers. Solien's heartbreak was assuaged by her cause, her passion for the Shodites. Though Solien was approaching eighty, and not in the best of health, she became more aggressive and open in her crusade to free Janti-born Shodites. She spoke often on the subject before the Alliance Ministers, and campaigned for the Shodites during formal state functions. Many were talking behind her back, saying that she was addled, losing her mind.

Shelon was present, a nonentity in the room serving tea on the day that daka Jishni paid an urgent visit to Solien. He fought to keep control of his reactions as the daka and Solien discussed a myriad of death threats made against the di Haveran family. Jishni begged Solien to publicly drop the Shodite issue. Shelon swelled with pride for his mistress as she refused to give up her cause.

Unable to change Solien's mind, the daka compelled her to accept a unit of Watchers into her home.

"To be honest," Solien said to Shelon after the daka left, "those strutting militarios will not put me at ease. Many in the military do not appreciate my politics."

"I'd be honored to protect you, even to die for you."

Solien smiled upward at Shelon, a sad and tired smile of an old woman. "Thank you, dear one, but no. I certainly do not want you to die for me. If you are to die, be it for a cause greater than my well being. Be it for the children you will someday have, if you decide one day to allow our evil empire to choose a genetically fit mate for you." The bitterness in her tone was clear and she, hearing it in her own voice, waved it away tiredly.

She went on, her voice tremulous with age, but forceful and firm. "And when you do have children, teach them the truth. They are not aliens in this society, but are born to Jantideva, just as the daka was born to Jantideva. They have the right to be treated as Janti."

Shelon was shaken by her strong words, knowing that these must have been the words she used at social functions, words spoken before Alliance Ministers and Suma priests, the words that compelled her enemies to make death threats.

"I've been beating down the Council's door with diplomacy for forty five years." She continued softly, her pale blue eyes falling contemplatively to the floor. "It seems that using diplomacy has failed."

She tilted her head to the side, and met his eyes again, a purposeful glint in their faded depths that made his heart pound frantically.

"If one were to research infamous conflicts throughout history," she said ambiguously, "one would discover that once diplomacy was exhausted, more violent measures of persuasion commenced. Our most significant social changes were preceded by bloodshed. I find violence, in itself, unacceptable. But when one is dealing with intractable people who lack vision, one is often left with no other choice. One must make oneself clear."

She threw her head high, and her lips pressed together in a grim frown. "In every cause, there is a leader. A man of intelligence and integrity who has suffered at the hand of oppression. A Fighting Devil of a man. Do you understand, Shelon?"

He understood, and was speechless that she could suggest he lead a violent uprising against the Janti. He was, after all, just a houseman. A fifty year old houseman. Not a soldier, not a leader. Those positions were left to strong young men who could still dream.

They did not speak together with as much candor again. The Watchers arrived that afternoon, strutting into the di Haveran household, taking over and occupying each entryway, nearly each room of the house. Solien should have been safe, surrounded by so many protectors. Sometime during that first night an assassin entered Solien's bedchambers and smothered her with one of her own pillows. The captain of the Watchers quickly found a ready suspect, a Janti-born in Solien's employ that had been found with an item of her clothing on his person. They called it a crime of sickness, of hatred, a rape gone awry, and having nothing to do with her political agenda. Indeed, the government used the crime to dissuade other liberal aristocrats from trusting their servants, and soon afterward the short-lived era of liberalism concerning the Shodites was at an abrupt end.

Shelon knew that the man they accused of the crime, and summarily put to death, was innocent. Being the head of the household servants, he knew very well where his people were when Solien was murdered. They were all in their sleeping chambers, in the boarding quarters that were apart from the household. Two Watchers were posted outside the only door to the servant quarters, and were still posted there in the morning when the servants arose to begin their usual duties. Shelon believed that Solien was assassinated by one of the Watchers, a man or woman in the service of her enemies, in order to blame a Shodite for the crime. Solien would have made a fine martyr had a Janti assassinated her for speaking out on behalf of the Shodites. Murdered randomly by a sick Shodite, she was mourned, made an example of, and forgotten.

Shelon was heartbroken, and filled with an impotent rage that knew no expression. To speak out would have brought reprisals onto him, and he wasn't ready to die for any cause, not even that of Solien's murder. No one would have believed him, in any case. He was but a Shodite slave.

In her will, Solien granted Shelon a choice. She granted him permission, if he chose, to petition the government for another home, where he would essentially lose all the freedoms given to him by the di Haveran family, or he could accept a position in the home of one of her daughters, and retain his freedoms. Monca was first in line offering him a place. Before Monca married and moved away, it was the sweetest pain to live with her in the same house. He loved her madly, ardently. She never suspected his feelings, or at least she did not let on that she suspected. To him, she displayed only indulgent fondness. She'd never even asked for a night of pleasure from him, though in his youth her older sisters had summoned him to their bedrooms with frequency. Even in the liberal di Haveran household, using a Shodite for sexual pleasure was still practiced. Shelon never complained for being used. Solien's daughters were pretty and kind, a lovely pleasure to be with on a lonely night. He only wished Monca had wanted him, at least once.

He chose to live with Monca, expecting to live the same sweet misery of his youth.

Once he became a servant in her home, however, she made clear what she wanted from him. She was married to an inattentive and cold man. She was lonely, and Shelon had always been a good friend. She trusted him. Becoming Monca's lover seemed to complete his life, and for a year he was happy. He'd forgotten the conversation he'd had with Solien on the day before her death. He'd forgotten, briefly, that he was a Shodite. While he was with Monca, he was a man. A free man.

It turned out that Monca's husband was not as dispassionate, or oblivious, as she had assumed. He discovered his wife's indiscretions, and used the law to deal with Shelon. Since it was his ancestral home that housed Shelon, by law Shelon belonged to the master of the house, and not Monca. He petitioned for Shelon's expulsion from their household, on charges that he had illegally molested Monca. One word from Monca on his behalf would have put the charges to rest, but she would not speak for Shelon. She told him simply that she had no choice but to heed her husband's will. "It was good while it lasted," she told him fondly, and she caressed his face, "but now it is over. I hope you are placed in a good home."

He recognized the way she looked at him, and the quality of her voice, her touch. All the time they were together, he thought she looked at him with love. It was not love. It was the affection reserved for a pet. She looked at him the way his half sisters once looked at him in his biological father's household, as if speaking to an animal with no sense, or intelligence, or self direction. He stood before the Janti Council of Shodite Affairs and was found guilty of a sex crime he did not commit. Because he was considered a felon and impossible to place, he was consigned to a Raal work prison for the rest of his life.

The ultimate loss of his freedom, prison, inspired in him a fire for true freedom, real freedom. He preached vehemently and often to clandestine gatherings of murderers, rapists, robbers and runaways of the rights of Janti-born Shodites to be free and self determined. He excited them with his ideas, with his hopes and his fury. In prison he learned he was a leader, and he attracted a sizable cult of followers.

He did not live in Raal for long. He and several hundred followers escaped from prison during a carefully planned uprising. They made their way back to the Center-plex, and hid in Shod City, the infested slum where five million of their people were forced to live in cramped squalor, those who were laborers and factory workers, owned by large businesses or industry. They were rarely fed well, and many died very young from the wasting disease. From the discontent brewing among the strong, they built their revolution. With his army, he robbed and destroyed Janti holdings, stealing weapons and supplies, and often pillaging Alliance storehouses in order to distribute food to the hungry. In a very short time he became a hero to the Janti-born Shodites.

The Alliance had little information on him, though after two years of enduring his terror, they did manage to get a poorly snapped photo of him from a hidden camera in a military warehouse. They broadcast his picture daily on the Alliance Crier. Because they did not know him by name, and because he sported a beard, they called him Cleses, after a bearded Rathian demon of Suma legend. Shelon rather enjoyed being compared to a Rathian demon, but did not enjoy the need to hide his face from the public. He was no longer as free to roam about, to do as he pleased. Often, he was forced to stay in his room for days on end. While in hiding he recorded a lengthy manifesto, scratched on the walls of his flat, which was destined to become a holy document for the cause. Friends of the movement memorized his manifesto and spread it by word of mouth. Dressmakers stitched his verses on the inside of work clothes, keeping Shelon close to them all the time to give them hope. The practice caught on like a fad, and soon many Shodites wore some form of clothing that bore a verse by Shelon discreetly stitched into the lining.

It was the sash of Ulon Miit that finally brought Shelon out of hiding.

Ulon Miit made the mistake of wearing his sash with the verse showing. It said: *A Shodite born on Janti soil is as much a Janti as a child born to our so-called benefactors.* Ulon Mitt's owner, an austere Janti judge, found the verse and had his servant beaten to death as punishment. The news of his unjust beating and death spread quickly among the Shodites, and reached Shelon on the eve of the very next day.

His followers wanted to retaliate by killing the judge. Shelon's primal reaction was the same, a desire for vengeance to protect the innocent. He knew, however, the price they'd pay for murdering an important Janti. Their cause would lose the meager Janti following it boasted, as well as bring about added hardship for their own kind, who would suffer the fear and wrath of their owners. He chose, instead, to take a stand without taking lives. Using animal blood, he and two of his followers painted

Ulon's name on the great entrance of the Chamber of Ministers building. They did it during the busiest part of the day to ensure it was seen by important members of the Alliance Council before it was cleaned off, and they were forced to run for their lives afterwards.

The daka's reply to their non-violent civil disobedience was to send the Pliadors into Shod city, where they brutally and randomly swept whole neighborhoods in search of Shelon or information on his whereabouts. They invaded Shodite homes and took anyone they thought looked suspicious into custody. In Tract Twelve, a particularly brutal officer questioned suspects on the roof of building seven, and if they did not supply the expected information, they were flung from the roof to their deaths.

Stepping over the remains of an old woman and mangled men, left in the street to rot, his objective shifted.

"Their message was for you." A merchant told Shelon, his words shaky, his hands moving nervously from his hips, to his face, to his hair. "Turn yourself in, or more will die."

Softly, hardly aware that his followers stood at his back listening carefully to his every utterance, he said of a young man spattered on the street, "Better to die here, than live a lifetime cleaning the dirt off the daka's feet." He closed his eyes to his inconsolable pain for the suffering of his people. Under his breath, he said to the ghost who'd inspired him, "Solien, my darling Solien, you were right. You were so right. There is only one way to deal with intractable people."

*

The sunset cooled the skies and darkened the alley. Track Four was like the rest of Shod City. The area was densely populated, the walkways like a maze. Those who did not live here often lost their way their first time through, and to their detriment. Robbers stood on every corner, waiting for the unwary to stumble into their lair.

Today, the robbers were revolutionaries.

94

It was too easy. The Pliadors strolled boldly into a dead end alley. They weren't afraid. A child had tipped them to Shelon's location, and they were tracking stupid, mindless Shodites, after all. Shodites, who couldn't so much as use a simple ariq stone. What threat were they?

They were very surprised to find themselves trapped in a box like canyon of brick walls by shaggy Shodites brandishing lume hand weapons at their backs.

Iada took point, stepping in front of her five comrades and sharply ordered the Janti to surrender their weapons, or die.

They indecisively glanced around to each other, looking for a response in the man next to them.

Iada lifted her lume hand weapon and aimed at the head of the Captain. "You think I don't know how to use this," she purred, "which one of you would like to see a demonstration of my skill?"

The Captain tossed his weapon to the ground. His subordinates followed suit.

Iada smiled. She glanced upward.

"Good work, my brothers and sister." Shelon praised. He stood on a laundry platform, a mere ten feet above their heads, his hands on his hips.

"Cleses." The Captain hissed.

Shelon grinned widely at the Janti, who cringed at the sight of their demon's menacing presence above them.

"Moxom," Shelon barked.

Moxom, and his brothers Vold and Vere, responded to Shelon's prompt, moving out of the shadows behind the Janti. The three brothers were robust, physically large as a result of spending fifteen years working in a Raal mine. They were convicted of a murder they maintained they never committed. Shelon did not doubt them, despite their violent natures. Shelon did not doubt that all his followers were imprisoned falsely.

Acting according to plan, the brothers stripped everything off their ten prisoners except their clothing and dropped what they took into a large black bag. They used the Watcher's own bindings to secure the arms of their prisoners behind their backs.

Shelon grabbed hold of a laundry rope, and stepped off the platform to slide easily down to the ground, landing near Iada. Still wearing his triumphant grin, he tossed an arm around Iada's shoulders.

He leaned close to her ear, "And you thought our trap wouldn't work."

"I said, 'Only a madman could make it work.' I should have remembered that I was talking about you." She smirked.

"Ah, you should have more faith in me."

"I'll never doubt you again."

He chuckled at her wry reply, and planted a affectionate kiss on her lips.

The Captain of the guard grimaced his displeasure as Vere tied his wrists together. "You will be put to death for this outrage!"

Shelon laughed in earnest. "We could each be put to death for glancing at a socialite the wrong way, or offending our benefactors. Personally, if I am to be put to death, I'd prefer it be for a good reason."

The Captain's eyes widened, and hushed, he said, "I remember you. You belonged to the di Haveran household. It makes perfect sense, now, why you called your group Solien's Soldiers. We all figured Cleses was born of her house. All her servants ran away from their new posts after her death. A few went to prison. Like you, I believe. Oh yes, I do know who you are. I have an excellent memory, better than yours, it would seem."

Shelon hid his surprise well, for he felt he was not a memorable sort. He had faded into the background with the di Haveran's other servants, a piece of forgettable furniture.

Memory served, and he was struck by blinding rage. He let the emotion carry him toward the Captain, and with the full force of his strength, he slammed his foot into Edise's crotch. The man whooshed out a breath, crumpled forward and fell to his knees.

Captain Edise's men lurched forward, despite the weapons trained on them and the binders on their wrists. In a fury, Shelon lunged at them, forcefully shoving one back, then another, then another, bellowing vehemently, "You want to aid your Captain? You want to aid him? You want to die? You want to die?"

His insane ranting eased the Janti backwards, and stunned his own people. Shelon didn't indulge in wild displays of fury, or displays of violence. Yet he returned to the Captain and beat him further to the ground, until Iada grabbed hold of his arm and begged him to stop.

Voice trembling, he explained himself to Iada, and the others. "This man was the Overseer of Watchers who was placed in Solien's home to protect her on the night she was murdered. He put one of our own to death for the crime and ignored facts that might have lead him to accuse one of his own men, instead."

Iada released his arm, staring anew at the Captain on the ground. "What will you do to him?"

Still simmering with fury, Shelon gestured to a portion of the Captain's men. "These three." And he gestured at Liv And Dmit. The rough looking revolutionaries came out from behind Iada and gathered the three Janti that Shelon had indicated and led them away.

"Vold, Vere." He said, and he pointed out three more of the Janti. The brothers took their three prisoners, and, leaving the alley, they turned in the opposite direction Liv and Dmit had taken the first three prisoners.

"Khoeg, Ladius, them." He said, indicating the last three. "Moxom gather the weapons."

Shelon turned an icy stare on the Captain. He couldn't predict what he might do to their prisoner, not yet. It already took every ounce of his self-control to keep him from beating the man to death.

He nodded at Syan, and the rough looking revolutionary forced the Captain to his feet.

The crowded trading center in track four hushed as Shelon passed through with his prisoner. A man reached out to touch Shelon's hand, whispering his name worshipfully. Several more hands erupted from the crowds, Shodites who wanted to touch their hero. Shelon had learned how to live with their worship, without needing to acknowledge them, or rebuff them. He knew he was not their object of worship. They all worshipped the same thing he worshipped, freedom. He forged through without glancing to the left or right, making his way to the building he and Iada had called home for the past few months.

His flat was in the dank sub-basement, a room no bigger than the cell he occupied in Raal. It had bare floors, brown walls, no

97

electricity, no running water. It was a copy of the fifteen like it in the sub-basement, and the sixteen on the floor above, and so on, up eight floors. Shelon shared the borrowed flat with friends to the cause, but often had the place to himself. He was lucky. Usually whole families, burgeoning with steps of generations, jammed into one flat. Doors were always left open for air. Privacy was nonexistent.

Children were playing from flat to flat, screaming or crying or laughing. An old man leaned in a doorjamb and smoked a rolled manau leaf. In one flat they passed a couple was making love with abandon as their toddler played nearby. In nearly every room there was at least one person who was sick with the wasting disease. The smell of it clung to the air, a sickly sweet odor the residents had learned to ignore.

Shelon was the only tenant that locked his door, and the only tenant that never left it wide-open, even for air. He stored his weapons here, and Janti money. And now, he would store a prisoner of war here.

He unlocked the door, and let Iada, Syan, then Moxom with the Captain, through. He met the eyes of the old man down the hall. The old man gave him a casual nod, acceptance, a continued vow of silence in the gesture. He returned the nod, and entered the flat, locking the door behind him.

Iada lit an oil lamp that hung from the ceiling, filling the room with wavering light, and the smell of burning oil. The room was furnished with a bench and a rolled mat that was Shelon's bed. In the far corner, they had stockpiled water, and some food. Near the door was the toilet chest.

Syan kicked the hinged top up, sat down and relieved himself as soon as they entered the room.

"Empty it yourself, this time." Iada chided, wagging a finger at Syan. He grunted something that sounded like an affirmative. Emptying the removable box inside the toilet chest was a chore. One had to walk it upstairs, out the building, and around back to the alley.

Edise's disgust pinched his face. "Animals."

A rumble of incredulous laughter erupted from Shelon's chest, and he roughly shoved the Captain into the corner closest to the toilet chest.

"We live as you force us to live." Shelon retorted, and he gestured for the Captain to sit on the ground.

The Captain had sense enough to keep his mouth shut and obey Shelon, but still wore the same pinched expression on his face and turned toward the wall to escape them all.

Shelon emptied the black bag onto the floor, and he sat next to Iada as he went through the personal belongings of their prisoners. Pictures, wallets, identifications. All of which would be very useful.

Shelon picked up the hand held base communicator that had been taken off the Captain. He looked the device over. This one served many purposes. It was a communications link to the Captain's headquarters, as well as a link to the military's database for criminals. Attached to the back was a camera tube, and on the front a screen.

He leaned to the side and reached into the box holding his tool kit. Finding a flat blade, he pried the screen off the base, cracking the cover. He turned the device over. A silver hoop was clamped to the underside. A homing device, activated in case it was stolen or the user accessed forbidden files. He dropped the hoop into his palm, and handed it to Iada, who put it in her mouth and chewed it in half. She spit it out in her hand, and showed it to Shelon.

He placed the screen onto the broken base, and switched it on. It crackled to life, and the mini-screen turned pale yellow, and though there was a thin line across the top caused by damage Shelon had done, it appeared to be in working order.

He used a code Solien had taught him on the sly, many years ago, and was delighted to be welcomed into the government data banks. As the names of the council members slowly scrolled the screen, he ran his finger across the screen to choose those he wanted to contact. It seemed like he had to wait forever for daka Jishni's name to appear on the list.

He pressed the code to record a message, and unhooked the camera from the back of the base and aimed it at the Captain.

Moxom, Syan and Iada were expectantly silent.

99

In an insolently informal tone, Shelon spoke.

"Hello Janti authority class. This is Cleses, of Solien's Soldiers. As you can see, we have abducted Captain Edise and his men. They are now political prisoners for the Shodite cause."

The Captain stared at the camera, squirming slightly for being caught by the Shodites.

Shelon's voice hardened, "Jishni, daka of Jantideva, did you think you could bully us? Did you think we would stop making demands because you are indifferent to Shodite lives? No. We are tired of being Jantideva's great burden. Release us from our contracts with our benefactors, those who enslave us and beat us to death for having an idea that is not like their own, and let us prove to you our worth!" Almost as an afterthought, he added, "Fair warning, if you attempt to send another unit of Watchers or Pliadors into Shod City, we will kill our prisoners, starting with Edise."

"I doubt if they'll care much about me or my squad." Captain Edise said lowly. "The daka has much too much on her mind to concern herself with petty Shodite matters."

Moxom reached over and backhanded the Captain in the mouth, snapping the Captain's head toward the wall. Blood bloomed over his bottom lip.

"Speak when you are spoken to." Moxom growled.

Shelon smiled slightly at the impromptu violence.

He said, "Don't doubt our sincerity, daka."

He shut off the camera. Message sent, mission accomplished.

Chapter 6

Ona's kai'gam arena, was unchanged. The spectator seats rose high above the center arena. A circle of green stone highlighted the gray clay court.

Cobo was in an upper row watching his nephews toy with kai'gams at the instruction of Lodan Kru Dok. Lodan was in full control of the situation, yet Cobo reflected on the last kai'gam lesson he watched. He remembered it as if it were yesterday, and not twenty five years ago. His father, sweating and laughing, capering about like a master. Stumbling, so unlike a Ver dala Ven. Dropping the kai'gam, the grip hitting the clay floor, the blade turned up at the precise angle needed to impale him at the neck as he fell. Cobo remembered every detail. How his father had looked at him, reached for him with is last ounce of strength.

Bail sat down next to him, his eyes also on the kai'gam arena. "They do well." A casual comment, as if they were daily companions.

"I'm surprised you let your sons play the game." Cobo countered. Finally in the presence of his brother, the man he most loved and envied, he felt at a loss to say more of what was in his heart.

"I don't, usually. Lodan offered his service to tutor my sons, and I was hard put to turn down a master in the art.

Besides, my sons are nearly grown. How long can I protect them from my fears?"

"The daka's curse."

"I must let them," Bail faltered, "live their lives as they wish."

"May the curse be lifted in this generation." Cobo said, repeating a blessing said to many dakas, before and after tragedy.

Bail shifted in his seat, now looking at Cobo's face.

"Where have you been, Cobo?"

"Does it matter?"

"I know you haven't been to Zaria. I made a lecherous advance on Gella in Zarian, and she did not respond. She isn't Zarian, is she?"

Wryly, Cobo countered, "Were you testing Gella, or are you interested in seducing our beautiful sister?"

"Don't mock me, and don't presume to see vice where there is none." Bail reproached. "I want to know where you have been."

"I'll tell you where I have not been. I have not been in Dilgopoche."

Bail recoiled at the claim, and returned his gaze to the arena. "I'd forgotten how irritating it was to have my mind picked."

"I needn't pick your mind. You are all too obvious. I've been demonized in your court for leaving Ona, it was easy to jump to the conclusion that I've turned traitor."

"I assure you, it was not easy to jump to that conclusion."

"I have not sided with your enemy, your distrust is ridiculous."

"Yet you would deliver my son to them, without allowing us to negotiate?"

Cobo glanced at him, and away, to Bailin, capering around the arena. "Your heir apparent takes after you, Bail. He also has your fire."

"More than you know." He conceded, "You've made yourself his hero, Cobo, for he, too, is an advocate for Shodite freedom. Jishni's court does not trust him, nor do they want him to reach a seat of power. They love Taen. I'm afraid that Bailin might be assassinated if he takes my seat."

"Oh, indeed, he is in mortal danger. Taen will kill him if you don't let me take him away from Ona, just as he will kill you and Jishni." Cobo continued, begging with a raised hand for Bail's indulgence, "Riar Sed lied to you. Taen has abilities he is hiding from the court, and from you. He has learned how to seed thoughts into a victim, a fairly easy task for any Ver dala Ven, however reprehensible. He has been seeding you with thoughts of self-destruction. Such as throwing yourself off the landing dock of the daka Redd."

Denial was on the tip of his tongue, but what came out was a demand. "Why would he do such a thing?"

"To become the next daka of Jantideva."

"I don't believe you."

"I doesn't matter what you believe. If you allow Taen to stay in Ona, you will all be dead, because his powers of persuasion are

102

growing, as is his desire to secure for himself an undenied position in Ona. He will kill you all to remain a daka, and to remain in Ona."

Pensive, Bail admitted, "In Montrose, I felt as though I was under a spell. I was confused, my thinking backwards. I could do nothing right. Right before I heard you'd come home, my muddled thinking lifted."

"Taen isn't strong enough to effect your thinking so profoundly. Someone else confused you during the battle in Montrose, and once that person found out I'd come home, withdrew his efforts. Riar Sed." Explaining, Cobo said, "There are lingering impressions from his stay here, strong in certain areas of Ona. The fountain garden, for one. The Rathian Hall, another."

"They were the places he took Taen for training."

"In the impressions, I feel bits of his plan, and see his allies. He is allied with the Dilgos. He came here to ensure Taen's delivery into their hands. He'd no idea you'd elevate Taen without his consent, thereby making it illegal to send him away. He was here to defeat Taen, to keep him from being elevated until the sixth cycle after his eighteenth birthday. As you well know, it is the old deadline for elevating Ver dala Ven, and he didn't think the Suma would bother with Taen after he'd become so old. The Dilgos are innocents. They want a Janti heir apparent to join with their monarchy as a status symbol, instant recognition with the Alliance. Riar Sed on the other hand, he wants something more specific from Taen. I've yet to discover what that might be."

"Taen learned something from him."

"He has powers," Cobo confirmed, "but without a gentle nature in acceptance of a position of service he cannot be Ver dala Ven. He is a spoiled, angry boy, Bail. Ruined, by circumstances beyond his control."

"I wish you had stayed for him."

"No you don't." Cobo replied gently, a smile alighting his lips. "None of us could have abided that situation."

Bail agreed with a silent nod, returning his attention to his sons. "I wish father was here. I could use his advice."

"Do you remember what father requested of you last?"

Amusement lifted sorrow from his brow. "What a grand jester he was!"

"Exactly now, word for word."

"Repeat it for you?"

"Yes, please."

"He said," and Bail imitated their father's austere tone to perfection, "'*Bail, after I die you had best keep my statue tidy, for if one speck of dust lands on me, I will haunt you for the rest of your life!*' End quote!" and he laughed.

"I think he knew."

Bail's amusement fled quickly, the somber cast to his eyes returning. "Knew he was to die?"

"Why else would he hurry my elevation?"

"Father was a court Ver dala Ven, wishing the status of having one son the youngest elevated Ver dala Ven in history, and the other a Janti daka."

"Your bitterness would wound him."

"I've kept his statue clean. It was all he asked of me."

"No, he entrusted with you much more, and you never knew it." Cobo pointed at Bail's face, "Tend to his statue today, and you will learn a secret that father told me, many years ago."

Cobo felt Taen's presence somewhere in the arena.

Below, Voktu swung the kai'gam around and slipped. As he fell onto his back, he lost control of the weapon. Cobo saw the outcome before Voktu was on the ground. The weapon turned a neat half-circle in the air, and was heading down, blade first, threatening to impale the boy's neck if its descent was not impeded.

Lodan reacted swiftly. He left his game with Bailin and swung around to attack the liberated kai'gam as if an opponent wielded it. His blade made contact with Voktu's, and he knocked the weapon away. Disaster was averted. The blade landed haplessly on the clay court, far from Voktu's head.

Bail gasped and sprang to his feet.

Lodan scolded Voktu in a loud voice, "A kai'gam is not a toy! I instructed you to keep still until it was your turn! For your disobedience, you must leave the arena!"

Voktu was downfallen. Master Lodan had kicked him out of the game. What a humiliating blow!

Bail loped down to the ring, heading toward his banished son. Voktu looked up and scowled. His humiliation was complete. Not only had he'd been thrown out of the game by Master Lodan, he'd been thrown out of the game in front of his father. What next? Are the Crier's monitors on? *Did all of Jantideva see me fall on my ass?*

Cobo chuckled at the darkly self-deprecating thoughts racing through Voktu's mind. Voktu was something of a comedian. Everything was a joke. Even his defeats.

"And you'd kill a wit like Voktu." he said lowly, directing his words to Taen's ears.

Taen, from his unseen place, replied to Cobo's ears, "His wit is not so amusing when you have to live with it."

He'd felt Taen's hand in the accident. Taen had made his brother trip, precisely where the elder Voktu had died, and guided the kai'gam home.

He said into Cobo's ears, "Did you kill your father like that? Was it so easy?"

Cobo shut out Taen's mind. Taen had read his guilt, but not the fullness of his memories. Cobo had watched his father's accident, without having the power to prevent it. It all happened too fast. Though his adult reasoning had long ago exonerated him of the crime, he'd always feel partially responsible for his father's death.

"Father, Voktu slipped, not I!" Bailin cried out petulantly.

Below, Bail protectively gathered his boys and ordered them to their rooms. Bailin was worst afflicted, for being the responsible Kai'gam student.

Taen's voice rang in the Arena, his tone mocking. "Don't argue with father, he knows best."

Bail looked up to the shadows under the daka's balcony seats. Taen stood there, watching them. He waved at Bail. Bail hesitated, glancing at Cobo, then beckoned Taen into the arena.

Taen's swagger was self-important, cock sure, arrogant. He tossed a malicious smirk toward Cobo as he passed in front of him.

He cannot be saved, Cobo thought bleakly. He is lost.

The kai'gam master prepared to retire from his lessons, in agreement with the daka that they could practice on another day. He gathered his belongings, his eye on Bail and the three young dakas, listening to Bailin's pleas for mercy. As Taen moved closer to Master Lodan in order to look at his carefully etched blade, Cobo sensed another presence among them, one ghostly in nature.

"Father." He whispered, and he felt the machinations of his father's spirit weaving Lodan into Taen's life, with a purpose that was unclear. Lodan's essence radiated intense purity and Taen's sulked in the darkness of evil. It was possible that his father was seeking out an influence that might heal Taen of his darkness.

Or a pure hearted sacrifice that would ensure Taen's slide into oblivion. The latter thought cause Cobo to stand, and reach out to the kai'gam master's mind. *Lodan, can you hear my voice?*

The Kai'gam master looked up to Cobo. Almost imperceptibly, he bent his head, indicating that he could hear Cobo's projected thoughts.

Beware of Taen.

Lodan again bent his head. He understood.

ৡৢৡৢৡৢৡৢৡৣৡৣৡৣৡৣ

"Come along." Trev beckoned. "We didn't come to the Center-plex for this, did we? With Plaetesus just a wing away?"

"I never said a word about going to Plaetesus."

"I assumed." He retorted. "Alright, then, I will leave without you."

"Go on, you whoring sot." Bail retorted. He polished the head of his father's likeness with irritable strokes. "I have better things to do than follow you to an Olla House."

"Oh yes, spending a perfectly fine afternoon in a Suma Temple is a perfectly fine way to spend the afternoon."

"Cobo sent me off on this heinous mission, for what, I do not know."

"I can't stand this place." Trev said, his eyes fixed to the statue next to him, that of Ver dala Ven Amur. "See the eyes? They follow your movements. Like they are still alive. Bail, I am beginning to see their eyes move, and they are all looking at me."

"Keep your drunken ramblings to yourself." Bail snapped, his strokes becoming harsher, seemingly to clean the grottiness from between the pearly tiles that made his father's robe. His father's likeness, however, wasn't that dirty. "My father left nothing to me," he grumbled, "but the legacy of his agreement with Janus, predetermining my future before I was out of my mother's womb. It was a joke to him that I wanted to be a soldier, a damned funny joke, so funny that he made me the keeper of his likeness, as if I was a slave! I've kept his statue well tended, and for what? To have my brother put me in my place?" He finished with a particularly harsh stroke with the oiled rag, right across his father's shoulder. A tile came off the collar of the statue, and he called out, "Trev!"

Though Trev was already so drunk that he swayed, he reached out his hand and easily caught the tile. Seeing what he'd done, he chuckled to himself, pleased by his good fortune.

Bail reversed the controls on the low glider, a single blower vessel once used as personal transportation in the city, and long since banned for the number of fatal accidents the unmanageable vessel had caused. They were now used as recreation vehicles, or to perform specific tasks, such as raising Bail so that he could reach his father's head and shoulders for a routine cleaning.

He descended, and the low glider wheezed a dying breath as it set him down. He stepped down from the disc base, and his self-recriminations rejoined his anger toward Cobo.

"I've broken my father." He lamented.

"Um, no." Trev said, blinking several times as he stared at the stone chip in his hand. "It isn't a tile, Bail. It is an ariq stone."

"Give it to me."

He didn't believe Trev until he held the stone in his hand. It was a slightly different color of pearl than the tiles used for his father's robe. He held it up to the light and sure enough, light shone through.

"There is an inscription. The symbol for Ver dala Ven." He said, and he palmed the stone and stared at it.

"Well? Let's snag ourselves a theater and take a look."

"Not here." He said, glancing down the hall. Not in the Suma Temple. Not in the presence of Yana's priests. His father hadn't trusted Yana. Bail didn't, either.

"Thank the Guardian Spirit for something." Trev exclaimed, "Delivery from this spooky sanctum of statues ready to come to life." Then brighter, Trev asked, "Shall I pilot, or would you rather?"

To that, Bail let out a wry laugh.

In Bail's transport, Trev nodded off in the co-pilot seat nearly as soon as he dropped into it. Bail took them upward, above the glittering Ona Temple, and instead of setting a course to cross the Tronos Sea and return to Ona, he went deeper into the Center-plex, to the Alliance Congress.

လလလလလလလလ

Gella did not like windriders. Among the crowd in the public windrider, she was the only person gripping her companion with nothing short of hysteria.

Korba gladly enveloped her into his arms, taking in her reactions with a mix of interest and amusement. He asked her questions like, "How did you get around in Shodalum?"

"With my feet on the ground!" she replied shrilly, and buried her face into his chest as the pilot released the tram lock and soared.

Returning to another inner city tram, where the windrider locked onto an elevated rail and was pulled along with many others, did nothing to ease her tension. Korba explained how the tram made travel in the city safer, but it did not comfort Gella in the least. They were still high off the ground, traveling at a dizzying speed.

She was so grateful to get off the windrider that she didn't hear Korba say something about needing to make another connection.

"No, no--" she shouted the words as he compelled her toward the transport that would take them into Shod City. "I'd rather walk!"

"You are attracting the attention of city Watchers." he said lowly, and he glanced down the landing platform to a couple of uniformed officers starting their way. "I'm about to be arrested for accosting a Janti woman. Do you know how long I'll be in prison?"

She stopped struggling as she noticed the two in white uniforms approaching them. She smiled in their direction. "All's well!" she said loudly, then lowly, holding her grin, she said, "If you try to take me aboard that contraption I will scream."

"It's another twenty two spans to Shod City." he explained impatiently. "If we ride, we'll be there soon. If we walk, we'll be there sometime tomorrow night."

"Perhaps by morning." She judged, still smiling at the Watchers.

"We'll never make it, we'll be robbed and murdered first." He replied, and he too had grown a supplicant smile on his face.

The City Watchers were upon them. The male of the pair was sleek, and dark, and handsome. He glared at Korba. "Is this Shod bothering you, Mistress?"

The slur against Korba galvanized her fear. The man had judged them on their dress, alone. Korba was in his dress reds from the palace, she in her fine gown. Irate with the unfairness of his bias, she straightened, and eyed the man stonily. "Of course not. We were just making our connection."

"Surely you aren't going into Shod City," As the female Watcher posed her question, she crossed a compact black tube in front of their faces. The motion didn't seem at all threatening, yet Korba's hand tightened around her arm, and at once she felt his anxiousness.

She kept her voice steady as she asked, "And why not?"

"Mistress," the male officer said, "there has been recent violence in Shod City. It isn't safe for Janti at the moment. We strongly advise you to turn back and go home."

She glanced at the hefty, windy, noisy machine that strained against the tram attachments beneath it as it hovered, waiting. She felt she had no choice. She could either stay here on this landing platform and argue with Janti Watchers, or enter the windrider with the surge of Shodites now boarding.

"I will take my chances." She said, and she pressed Korba to lead the way into the crush.

Being on the inside of another metal death trap caused her to tremble from head to toe. There were too many people in the windrider, forcing them to stand. She reached for Korba's hand for comfort, and realized he, too, was trembling.

"You were afraid of them?"

"They are a cruel lot. We do our best to avoid them at all costs. I can only hope they don't send someone after us when they realize who you are."

She looked back at the officers. The windrider's doors were shutting. She caught a glimpse of the man staring hard at a hand held device.

"That thing he has, it can identify us?"

"Of course. They scanned our likeness, and in moments will know exactly who we are. I am surprised they didn't make us wait for the information to return."

"Scanned us?" she questioned.

He faltered, realizing she understood nothing.

"Never mind." she said, dismissing the subject, annoyed with her own ignorance. "What's our next stop?"

"Nari station." and he leaned close to her ear, his breath moving her hair, and said, "Being scanned is like having pictures made of you. Only done instantly, and with more information. A scan can reveal what we are carrying, or if one of us has an infectious disease. For those of us who have been through processing as children, it can even read our genetic signature, identifying our family and our present benefactors."

"How?"

"That," he shrugged, "I don't know."

The coupling hooks on the rail released the windrider, and they ascended abruptly. This time she forced herself to watch out the window, in order to see the magnificent view. The city below glittered in the sunshine like the starriest night she'd ever seen. Korba had told her that the city was not just one, but many cities, each representing an Alliance nation. They were built around the capital, the Center-plex, the largest and most diverse city in the world.

"There we are. The Janti call it Shod City. We call it the Underworld. The city was built for the laborers. I lived here with my mother until she was lucky enough to land a house post in Ona. She didn't live long enough to enjoy it, however."

Korba's Underworld did not glitter like the rest of the Janti Center-plex. It was ugly gray and forbidding.

Korba held her hand as he led her off the landing bay and down a long ramp into a stifling city. Narrow walkways were glutted with people, both busy and at rest. The smell was horrible, open sewers and dirty bodies, and the dirty smell of the lume driven public transport, gagging her and she was forced to cover nose and mouth with her hand. She stared upwards at the dizzying heights of the buildings, built so close they seemed to hug each other, seeing only slivers of sky.

The trading center looked like the trading center in Strum, only the goods were different. There was a wide variety of foods, clothing, gadgets that were against the law to own in Shodalum. The people were haggling over the goods, speaking a bastardized language that resembled Shodite. She hardly understood them.

She saw the usual sights of a city, though much magnified. The children, slipping through the crowds, playing their games. Cliques of prostitutes hanging around the busiest stands dressed in brightly colored Janti gowns, one side of their full length skirts hitched to their waist to show off legs and more.

Not seen in Shodite streets were old and infirm begging for food, and yet here in Korba's Underworld they were vast in number. There were sick drunkards lying face down in the street, or perhaps they were dead. No one bothered with them. No one tried saving them, or preached Betnoni's way of clean living to them, indeed, there were no Betnoni worshippers in sight. No signs of Betnoni on the buildings for luck, no carvings of Betnoni in the stands. Gella was never religious, but without Betnoni's presence, Shod city seemed spiritually dead.

The deeper they went into the trading center, the more she gathered attention. The Shodites of the Underworld sneered openly at her, and jeers were made to her back.

"Ignore them, they don't understand." Korba assured her. "Next time we'll know to dress you appropriately."

"Next time?" she questioned dubiously. If she got out alive, she had no intentions of returning.

111

Korba led her to a nondescript building, numbered 4-5-48. Korba explained: Track four, district five, building forty-eight. "There are fifty resident buildings in a Track; ten per district; and there are five hundred Tracks in Shod city identical to this one. We are in a good district, here, five districts from the Pril, a fair distance from the water….and who would want to be close to that water?" he asked with a grin that she didn't understand.

The interior of the building was very much like the streets outside. Narrow halls filled with people, and a door every ten paces. Candles and oil lanterns dimly lit their way to the back of the building, and down an endless staircase.

"How can you people live without space?" she asked him after pressing through yet another throng of loitering men.

"Ask the Janti," Korba said dryly, "They seem to think these are tolerable living conditions. You've seen how the dakas live. Which would you prefer?"

"Shodalum." she said without reserve.

He tossed look over his shoulder that was filled with respect.

"Here we are." he said, and he clapped before the only closed door in the long hall.

"Yes?" a woman's voice replied sharply.

"Korba." he replied to her.

Gella heard latches moving. The door opened, and Korba took her by the arm and ushered her inside.

Five people were in the cramped room. The woman who'd let them in and four men who had been sleeping. Taking up space in each corner were an odd assortment of gadgets Gella didn't recognize.

The woman greeted Korba with a smile, a smile that disappeared the moment she saw Gella.

"Have you lost your mind, bringing a Janti witch here?" she demanded, and she slammed the door behind them, latching all the locks.

The man who'd been lying on the mat on the floor woke, and rose, and stared, bleary with sleep, at Gella. He was not handsome, his face craggy and his brow heavy, his sterling hair disheveled. It was his eyes, though, that caught her attention. His sharp, blue

112

eyes captured hers, and she felt unable to look away from the depths of him.

"No, Iada, you don't understand,"

"What is there to understand, you buffoon!"

"She is a Shodite, from Shodalum!" he proclaimed with a triumphant grin. "Gella al Perraz. She spoke on our behalf before the daka!"

"Gella al Perraz, a Shodite from Shodalum." The man on the mat rose to a sitting position, crossing his legs in front of him. He smiled, a smooth, dangerous expression. He held her captive in his gaze, and in a mocking way, he said, "You were permitted to speak before the daka on our behalf?"

"It was nothing personal, I assure you." Gella replied stoically. "I was defending my people."

He cocked a dubious brow as his eyes traveled her form, seeming to take too long in certain places. His eyes again reaching her face, he chuckled low with his doubt. In the undulating light of the oil lamp he seemed at once malevolent, as dangerous as a hungry predator. She decided she was afraid of this man, and her fear was the reason her heart raced.

Korba was made nervous by the man's doubt. With a tremor in his voice, he said of the woman standing next to him, "Gella, my sister Iada," and gesturing to the man she couldn't take her eyes off of, he said, "And this is Shelon. He is the hope for Shodites. Our leader."

"And Korba is a loose lipped slank." Iada snapped, and she slapped her brother on the back of the head.

Korba ducked away from Iada, and drew Gella toward the mat on the floor. "Let him touch your hands." Korba insisted. "Tell him what you told me of Shodalum."

Korba eased her forward, and she knelt on the mat. Sitting this close to him made her heart pound in her throat. She held out her hands. He touched them with his own callused fingers.

"Too rough to be a Janti witch." he commented softly. He looked into her face, at the lines, at the tiny scar on her cheek made by a ring on a hand that had struck her after she'd provided sexual services. He touched her face, then her hair. "Course, never been treated. You've never been to a Janti spa."

113

Tired of feeling like an imbecile, she didn't bother to ask him to explain spa. She replied simply. "Never."

Without releasing her hands, he said, "My ancestors are from Zorna. I may still have family there. Are you familiar with the tribal name of Zorna?"

"Zorna," and she thought a moment. "I have an uncle who became consecrated to Zorna. His mate's family name was al Entlay. Yes, I believe that is correct, my uncle took the name of a woman named Rin al Entlay, from Zorna."

He stared into her eyes for a long time. His intensity made her decidedly uncomfortable.

His manner subdued, and he was no longer mocking. "Tell me of Rin al Entlay."

She pulled her hands out of his. "I am sorry, but I can't tell you very much, except that she was a respected matriarch in Zorna. Is she your kin?"

"I know nothing of my kin there, if even we could be called kin. Only the stories my mother told me, stories passed along too many generations to count. I had thought they were myth, until now. It is enough," he said, "to know my tribe really exists. Gella," he said, her name sounding exquisite coming from him, "how do you find yourself here, in Jantideva, living as an aristocrat and not as a slave?"

"My Chosen Brother brought me."

Korba chimed in, "Her Chosen Brother is Ver dala Ven Cobo! He has returned! And at his formal reception, he advocated, no…he outright ordered the daka to free us!"

"What's this?"

"Yes! Of course there was more dissension in the court than agreement." Korba added. "Grav Tulkue was most outspoken against Ver dala Ven Cobo."

"The Janti Minister, who is the daka's voice." Cynically, he shook his head. "They will not listen to Ver dala Ven. He no longer has power in Ona. They will not listen to reason. The Janti are not compassionate by nature. They know only force, and the results of force."

The men who had been sleeping on the floor at the end of the mat woke, and rose. She noticed them out of the corner of her

114

eyes, and looking, she saw that the third man on the floor was tied and gagged. His face was covered with bruises. He stared at her, a pleading note in his expression.

She twisted around to Korba. "Why have you brought me here?"

Shelon threw a glare up at Korba. "Yes, Korba, do explain why she is here."

"For the cause." he said ardently. "Don't you see?" Korba knelt by her side, "She can be our voice in Ona! I can pass along your messages to her, and she can pass them to the daka! You will have a direct communication, short of living in Ona, yourself."

"And how would I get my messages to you, Korba?"

"I would come for them, of course!"

"By who's leave?" Hardness crossed his intense eyes, and he leveled his stare at Gella. "In fact, how is it that you managed to bring Korba to me?"

"I-"

"Korba," he snapped, cutting off her reply, "did you gain permission from the daka to leave Ona?"

"Not exactly. I was in danger of being put to death by the daka, for the least of crimes. Gella saved me."

Understanding made Shelon grin, an ugly and unpleasant expression. "So, Chosen Sister Gella, or should I call you daka? You are now the proud owner of a slave named Korba."

The truth stung her, and worse, he glared at her in the way the Shodites had as she entered their city in her finery. Nothing could have cut her so deep as his open disgust.

"You do not understand."

"Enlighten me." He offered sardonically.

"It was my brother's will that Korba become my living guardian to spare his life for showing respect to me! I'd no idea what it meant until after the deed was done."

"Mercy from a Janti, as always, is perverted. Spare him his life by giving him a living death. Do you think you have done Korba a favor by becoming his Janti benefactor?"

"I am not a Janti!"

"You are a daka!" he retorted, "You are no better than any Janti I've ever had the displeasure of meeting."

Bristling at his stubborn refusal to see reason, she snapped, "Likewise."

"I am Gella's living guardian, but that is not important." Korba insisted. Wary of the live wire of animosity crackling between Gella and Shelon, he withdrew, glancing at them in turn. "Gella you can serve the cause. You can speak for us to the daka. Shelon, she can speak for you. She can help lead our revolution to victory."

Shelon's stare was wrenched away from Gella, and he now stared hard at Korba. "How can she speak for me? What is it she can say of my experience as a slave? Eh, Korba?"

"She has the daka's ear." Iada said from above.

"No, not you too."

"If she is willing, she is the perfect candidate."

"She falls well short of perfection, as she is a slave holder!"

"She is a Shodite!" Korba repeated, as if that were to make a world of difference.

"Therefore she earns our unquestionable trust? I don't trust half my own kind, should I trust this one without question?"

The three of them arguing over her made her head spin. She felt locked in, closed up, suffocating. Korba, her slave. She, a revolutionary? And this man, Shelon, a stranger whose presence awakened her and whose condemnation pained her, muddled her reasoning. She had to get away, to pull herself together. "I need air," she said flatly. She pushed off the floor and went to the door, and struggled with the foreign latches.

Shelon signaled to one of the men sitting nearby. He rose, a giant walking wall of a man, and went to the door. Gella thought he was going to open it for her, and she backed away to let him by.

He stood before the door, his massive forearms crossed before his chest. He glared down at her, daring to her object.

"What is this?" she demanded incredulously, "I'm not permitted to step outside?"

"I can't let you leave, Gella." Shelon said.

"What?" Korba sputtered.

"She's seen our guest," Shelon explained, "We can't let her return to the palace. Besides, Chosen Sister Gella has more value as a hostage."

116

"Shelon, the very idea is reprehensible." Korba objected, "I am her living guardian....I can't let you kidnap her-"

On the word kidnap, Gella turned on the giant man before her, gave him an insincere smile and threw her knee square into his crotch. Because he was big, she felt compelled to continue kneeing him until he crumpled. Instinctively calling upon the survival skills she'd learned on the streets of Strum, she grabbed the closest object she could get her hands on and used it as a club. In this case it was a cold, metal thing, with a handle on one end. As she grabbed it, Shelon, Iada, and the second man shot to their feet with a shout. She ignored them, and cracked it over the head of the man she'd abused, then swung around to hit the second man with it, though he dodged her swing, watching her weapon of choice with a worried look on his face.

Shelon lunged at her. She swung at him, and he caught her arms. He wrestled the thing free from her hands, and handed it off to Iada, who took it gingerly.

Gella's panic heightened once her weapon was taken from her, and she flailed her fists at Shelon's face and kicked at his legs without controlling her assault. Shelon grabbed one of her arms. Grabbed the other. Crossed them, and managed to exact a painful grip on her wrists with one of his large hands. He banded an arm around her body, holding her in a restricting embrace that she fought. It was no use. He was too strong.

In her ear, he whispered with husky anger, "You could have killed us all." In a patronizing tone, he added, "It is a lume bomb, a touchy piece of equipment, easily set off by a good jostling, or in this case, a swing or two around the room."

She froze. Horrors from childhood stories often spoke of bombs. Lume bombs that were once made in Calli, that could kill thousands in a second. Her eyes flew to the object she'd used as a club.

Iada had set it on top of a trunk. "It's unharmed." she announced. "No leaks."

"No thanks to our native daughter."

Shelon released her arms and turned her roughly to face him, holding her upper arms in the same grip he used on her wrists. She feared his wrath, but she would not let him see her fear. "Take your hands off me." She demanded.

"You're a fighter." He commented, and he glanced at the man she'd abused, still not able to straighten. "Isn't she, Moxom?"

"I'd like to put my hands around her neck." Moxom grunted venomously.

Korba hovered nearby, his expression a mix of fury and helplessness. At Moxom's threat, he shouted, "You'd have to kill me, first!"

Moxom heaved a laugh. "Gladly."

"Let me go!" she demanded, and she brutally stomped on Shelon's bare foot with her heeled shoe. He shouted pain, and his grip on her weakened, allowing her to twist out of his grasp. She backed into Korba, who threw a protective embrace across her chest and drew her away from Shelon.

Shelon leaned against the wall and rubbed his foot. An amused glint sparkled behind the sober fury in his eyes.

"I like women who fight back." he breathed, his teeth clenched together as he set his smarting foot on the floor. He took a limping step toward her. His voice low, he said, "Tell me you are more than the pretty words you speak to dakas, Gella al Perraz. What would you sacrifice to gain freedom for the Shodites? Freedom for your slave, Korba?" He paused, his amusement fleeing. "Would you give your life?"

She was trembling again. She felt as if she were on a windrider again, being taken on a terrifying journey. The truth shot out of her mouth. "I would die for the Shodites, but not for you, Shelon of Janti. You are no more a Shodite than the daka, herself!"

Fury clouded Shelon's features. His tone was controlled as he cracked a joke, to which no one dared laugh at. "Imagine! My life as a slave has been a terrible mistake, for I am Shelon of Janti! Yes, I can walk through the affluent Center-plex with my head held high, can't I? I can live like a daka, and bed Janti women, and throw money away in gambling establishments and Olla Houses, and never again concern myself with the miserable, hungry shod, living in their filthy hovels!"

She'd unnerved him. His vulnerability was as plain to her as his fury. Using her advantage, she stepped out of Korba's protective arm, and faced Shelon as an equal.

"Janti take what they want, when they want it, just like you, Shelon. You see me as an asset, and you do not ask me to help, you tell me I am yours to use as you see fit. You treat me the way a Janti treats a Shodite! I am nothing but a shod to you, Shelon of Janti!"

He grabbed the sleeve of her gown. "Look who is accusing me of being Janti."

She looked at his hand, then with sardonic expectation, into his eyes. "Now that I am your possession, Shelon of Janti, will you demand my comfort? Or will you just take it, as you've taken my freedom?"

He jerked his hand away. "This is revolution! You are a prisoner of war!"

"You can't hear your own voice, can you? Tell me, do you know where the Janti in you ends, and the Shodite begins?"

Fuming, he stepped forward, thrusting his face into hers. "The Janti in me ends when I leave this room, and the Shodite begins the moment I take a breath of air outside this miserable slum."

Her jaw set. "Then do not act like a daka. Do not tell me what I will do for you. I am Shodite. I deserve more from you than to become your slave. Ask me to help you, and ask nicely."

"Ask?" he exclaimed indignantly, "Shelon does not ask!"

Gella's eyes glimmered with fury. "Shelon is great, he does not have to ask! These blind fools follow you without question, don't they? Well, I don't follow you, Shelon of Janti! I obey no man!"

He growled, "You have no choice, native daughter. You are my prisoner. Get comfortable. You're going to be here awhile."

Korba stepped forward, "Shelon, please,"

"Enough!" Shelon shouted at Korba, a shout that caused Korba to cringe. "She will be an asset! I intend to use her!"

Piqued by his ready claim of her, Gella speared him with a icy glare. "So be it. Keep me as your prisoner. Do as you wish to me. After all, I am nothing but a lowly Shod, without a right to make my own choices. I submit myself to you, *daka Shelon*. I am your obedient slave."

"Ah, by the Rathian Gods, gag her!"

"No!" Korba objected.

"Leave me to him," she ordered, "I am his now. I came into this land a free woman, and I will live here as a slave to a heartless Janti." To Shelon's back, she said, "In Shodalum, we have a saying that fits the likes of you." She repeated the saying in quick Shodite. His head turned slightly, bending his ear her way, and he looked as though he might have understood her, but she erred on the side of caution and assumed he did not understand her language. She repeated the saying in Janti. "It is a fool who feeds his children to the cattle, to fatten his cattle for his children."

Iada snapped a length of cloth around Gella and tied it over her mouth. Gella accepted the gag, while continuing to glare coldly at Shelon's back.

Korba was made livid by her treatment. "She is right, you are heartless, all of you! I bring you a flower, and you trod upon her with both feet!"

"You are enamoured of your slaver, Korba?" Shelon questioned, "Will her beauty make you turn away from the cause? From you own people?"

"Your ego has blinded you, you forget your own roots!"

"She," he pointed at her, but did not look, "speaks to me thus, but you will not! Now sit still, and shut up, or I will have you gagged, as well! Children and cattle, my consha!"

He pivoted and in two long steps, rushed her, placed his hands heavy on her shoulders and pushed her back. She wondered if she might not succumb to the fate that she'd invited with her angry words, the fate of his proving his mastery over her in rape. Korba wouldn't allow it, and she looked to him for help, but Korba stood aside, powerless against the will of Shelon.

Shelon forced her to sit on a bench near the other prisoner. Backing away from her, he challanged her defiant glare with matching ferocity, though as his eyes crossed over the gag covering her mouth, his conviction faltered, his eyes dropped away.

"Watch her. I'm going for a walk."

120

He pulled his boots on and left them, slamming the door hard behind him. Iada followed him to the door, and locked him out with slow, deliberate movements.

"Korba, you've made a mess." She told her brother.

"It was not my intention."

"I know," Iada said, forgiving him with her soft reply.

"You should have heard her speak for us." Korba's eyes filled with tears as he looked at Gella. "She was poetic and fantastic. The passion moved me to tears as she spoke of our ability to be self-determined." He sunk to her side, looking into her face, "Gella, I am so sorry."

Annoyed with the entire situation, Gella sighed and rolled her eyes to the ceiling.

"Don't weep, boy." Moxom ordered, but he was clearly moved by Korba's show of emotion. He walked, with difficulty, to a chest and drew out a rag. He threw it at Korba, and Korba wiped the tears from his cheeks.

"You should have consulted with Shelon before bringing her here."

Korba nodded at his sister's comment.

The Janti-born passed their time tinkering with the gadgets stored in the one corner, chatting about nothing in particular, gossip or news. Gella was uncomfortable, but would not show her discomfort to them. Her arms crossed defiantly, she bided the time wishing she'd not been so eager to show Cobo that he could not order her about.

It seemed a very long time before there was a clap at the door. Shelon announced himself, and Iada let him inside.

He paused, looking at his prisoner. "She is still gagged?"

"It was your wish."

Gella irritably cocked a brow at his surprise, and began tapping her fingers impatiently against her arm.

"I'm surprised she didn't take the gag off herself." And to her, he said, "Your hands aren't tied, native daughter, or hadn't you noticed?"

She glanced away, her annoyance turning her cheeks hot.

"She is your prisoner." Korba stated, "She is obeying your will."

"And here I thought she obeyed the will of no man."

Her breath caught in her throat as he sunk to one knee before her, head down, his hands on her arms. Looking deeply into her eyes, he unfolded her arms and took her hands in his, caressing their roughness again with his long fingers, his grip gentler. His calm gentleness eased her irritation. Something about him, or in him, warmed her chest, her entire body, and though she did not know what to expect from him, she was no longer afraid. She allowed his touch, knowing as if by instinct he needed the assurance of her rough hands.

He searched her face as if trying to understand her. His magnetism pulled her into his gaze, and she couldn't look away from the desperation in his features; the suffering that made the lines on his face, the everlasting disappointment in the crook of his mouth, and the tiny spark of fury in his eyes. There was hope in his features, too, and she suspected that his hope was what kept him alive.

He sighed, and touched her chin, her cheek, a touch she savored despite her situation. There was an undeniable allure surrounding him, a romantic danger that made his harsh features attractive.

"What am I going to do with you?" he asked rhetorically, a question posed to the fates involved in depositing her in his tenement flat, rather than one directed at her. He shook his head in dismay, reached around and untied the gag, removed it, tossing it aside.

Her mouth was dry, her voice pitched just above a whisper and heavy with condemnation. "Praise yourself, Shelon, you have terrorized me. What more will you do to me now that I am yours?"

"You are afraid of me." he said, as if it hadn't occurred to him that she might be afraid. The tips of his fingers tickled her neck. His touch caused her to shiver, and he took it mean revulsion.

He withdrew his hands, and rocked back on to his heel. Amusement crept into his eyes. "And if I ask nicely, how will you serve me, Gella al Perraz?"

"It depends," she replied, "on what you want from me."

He hummed what sounded like an affirmative response, but grew contemplative. "I want you to go back to your Janti brother."

Her heart hammered with relief against her ribs. "That is it?"

"Not entirely." He stood, going to Iada, again placing his back to Gella.

Released from his intense eye contact, she felt the tension drain from her body. Her skin still tingled from his touch.

Korba gave her a hand and helped her to her feet. She nearly waved off his support, until she felt the weakness in her knees. She clung to his arm.

"Thank you," she whispered to him as he allowed her to lean on him, "for turning my life upside down."

Korba suppressed a smile at her dry remark. "You're welcome."

Shelon spoke lowly to Iada, and she nodded, her eyes wide.

"I will help you, Shelon." Gella told him, a decision she quickly, and for Korba, she told herself. To exact his freedom, but a part of her knew that she wanted to help their cause for Shelon. He was interesting, and even now as he looked at her over his shoulder, his brows raised expectently, she felt his dangerous allure. "I believe in your cause. I will do what I can. But, for now, I'd like to return to Ona. My brother will miss me if I am gone much longer."

Shelon pivoted, and viewed her speculatively.

"Yes, we will return to Ona immediately."

Her brows shot up. "We?"

"You. Korba." Shelon gestured to both of them in turn, and his mouth grew a smile, and he placed his palm on his chest "And me." To Iada, he said, "The uniform."

Iada removed a silken black uniform from the cabinet, of the type Gella had seen on daka Bail's Pliadors, and on the hostage huddled in the corner of the room.

"What are you going to do in the palace?" she asked incredulously, "Take the dakas hostage?"

"Perhaps." he replied evasively, "Perhaps I merely want to keep a close eye on my native daughter."

"You do not trust me." she stated, her tone hard.

Serious, he moved toward her. "Not fully, not yet, but that is not why I am going with you. I am asking for your service, Gella. For the cause. Smuggle me into the palace."

A chill raced into her stomach. "I can't let you hurt anyone." She replied, shivering again for what she imagined he intended. Holding herself with arms crossed over her chest, she said in a tight voice, "Violence is not the Shodite way. I will not be a party to violence. You can keep me until the end of time, make me your hostage if you will, or kill me this very moment. If it is violence you intend, I will not help you. Ever."

She thought she saw respect cross his features, or annoyance, it was difficult to discern for he turned his gaze away too quickly for her to read his reaction.

"I vow, no violence in Ona against the Janti. On my life." He again seized captive her gaze. "On my honor."

She found herself wanting to trust his vow. Softly, she told him, "Even if you did plan to violate Ona, my brother will stop you. He is Ver dala Ven. He will not allow you to harm the dakas."

He eased away, a smirk growing in the corners of his mouth. "And so now it is you that does not trust me."

"Will you tell me what you intend to do?"

"I believe....no. No, I will not." He replied, nonchalant.

He grinned roguishly at her, and yanked his tunic shirt over his head, revealing chest and arms muscled by work, and scarred by abuse. Next, he stripped his pants off without reserve. Beneath he wore more clothing, just as the Janti women wore clothing under their gowns. Layers and layers of clothing. Gella didn't understand the Janti affection for clothing.

Iada threw the black uniform at him, and he dressed, his amused eyes steadied on Gella, watching her watch him.

124

Chapter 7

Aton Greely, the archive librarian for the Alliance Congress, spent his entire life absorbed in his work, the study of Alliance history and law. He could be found any time, day or night, in the library, taking copious notes if he happened to be researching a political or legal subject for the daka, or one of the ministers. He never went out, married, nor had children.

Bail quickly descended the curved steps leading into the library's theater.

A circular screen and stage encompassed a cylindrical ariq stone, the latter which held thousands of years of history, art, scientific discovers, and recordings. Around the ariq stone were seats and benches, arranged to suit whoever had been there last. As always, Aton was in the seat directly in front of the stone pillar.

A voice that did not sound like Aton spoke on the legal history of Dachan bathhouses.

Bail quietly entered the theater. On the screen was the interior of Toboli's bathhouse, in New Dacha. The deep green tiling cast a faint glow over the old man seated in the center of the screen. Projected above a holographic imager was a young historian, who was speaking on the legalities of opening new bathhouses in Dacha. The man, young here, would grow to be an elderly librarian for the Congress one day. Aton was listening to his own report, on laws passed early in his lifetime.

Bail announced himself by saying, "I'm not intruding, am I?"

Aton glanced up, his slack, relaxed features wakening with surprise. "Oh my, Daka Bail!" Bail's appearance had so flustered Aton, that as he stood, he knocked his chair over. Aton quickly bowed, glancing at his chair, and saying, "Oh my...my!"

"Please, at ease, Aton." Bail said, and he righted Aton's chair for him.

"But, this is such an honor,"

He appreciated respect from his subjects, but Aton's shaky veneration made him uncomfortable.

Bail gestured to empty benches set to the side of the screen. "Where are the Suma scholars?"

Aton's mouth fell into a disapproving line. "They will be back tomorrow morning if you wish to consult them. Their prayers come before higher learning, I am afraid."

"Ah-good. I need to view the contents of an ariq stone I found and I'd prefer not to share with the Suma just yet."

Aton's face lit up. "Oh, yes, yes, a finding. A new finding?"

"New to me."

He handed the small ariq stone to Aton.

"Hmmm. The material is fourth dynasty, when ariq stones were still being mined from the Rysenk territories, and the insignia is," his eyes popped open wide, "Ver dala Ven Betnoni!"

"I recognized the insignia." Bail admitted.

Aton sat, then half stood. "Would the daka prefer to sit?" He said, offering his own chair to Bail, though there were chairs everywhere in the theater.

Bail smiled at the elderly man. "No, Aton, I am fine."

Aton replaced his bottom in the seat. He reached to the side and slid the ariq stone into a slim slot in the front of the pillar. The youthful scholar reciting the history of Dacha bathhouses flickered, and disappeared.

"Daka Bail, the library will not recognize your stone."

Bail shook his head. "It has to." And he leaned forward to place his hand on the main ariq stone. The stone turned pale yellow, and the screen around them came alive.

"Ah, it didn't recognize me, that is why it wouldn't play."

"But why would it recognize me?" Bail wondered.

A background of a private room in Ona appeared around them, though the décor was old world. The ornamental furnishings were overdone to the extreme, gilded and bejeweled, to a point past beauty, edging closer to ugliness.

The subject of the recording appeared a half -second after the background, taking the place of the dacha scholar on the silver disc set in the floor before Aton's seat.

Betnoni looked just as Bail remembered from his history lessons as a youth. A normal, luxuriously dressed Ver dala Ven with long dark hair, dark skin, and gold eyes. Her hair was tucked behind ears that stuck out slightly, and her tiny frame had a boyish appearance. Bail had been taught to abhor the sight of her, for she had tainted his line. If she'd not killed herself, he would have been born with gold eyes. It was a lost privilege he often ruminated over in his youth.

Her voice was soft, and she put her hands out as if offering them something. She said:

"From the silence, return to the silence, from the complicated, a return to simplicity."

In her pause, Aton muttered, "Notice, but we cannot hear the song? I find it fascinating that the song spoken of in legend had never been recorded. Was it real? Imagined? Or simple myth?"

"My dearest children, listen carefully." Betnoni admonished, *"The time of purity is done, the Alliance is tainted by disunity. Ignorance will grow in all quarters, and you will see borders where there were once none. No one will show alarm as the world breaks into pieces. The appearance of unity will delude, as the foundations of the Alliance disintegrate. In the final days of the Alliance, seven signs will appear. It is of utmost importance that you watch for the signs, for once the prophecy begins to move you will have but four opportunities to take the hard path and end the curse upon Ona before the return of the Masing Star."*

Aton breathed, "A lost prophecy of Betnoni. Daka, you have brought me a priceless gem from antiquity. The shortsighted dakas of her time destroyed her prophecy, and so much of her writings! I am beside myself with joy!"

Betnoni spoke, a calm rejoinder to Aton's excitement: *"The first sign of the Rebirth is awakening. A forgotten north shatters and pours forth horror and guilt. To take the hard path, the Lost must deliver the Untrained into the hands of the enemy."*

Bail wasn't interested in the rarity of a Betnoni Prophecy having survived to the present day. "The lost," he whispered, and he knew it was Cobo, and the Untrained, "Taen."

In a hushed tone, Aton replied, "Yes, it would almost seem that the first sign has come."

She knew nothing of their awe. She continued, still in offering.

"The second sign of the Rebirth is regret. The Invisible roars in the Vass Chamber and causes much discord. To take the hard

path, the Daka must show mercy to the maligned and downtrodden."

Aton interjected, "Invisible, yes, here she speaks of the Shodites, at least in her day, those who opposed the industrialization of Shodalum referred to the Shodites as the Invisible, for the aristocracy seemed to refuse to see their plight. I am assuming much, I suppose."

Bail hushed him, then asked him to begin her message again, at the end of the second sign. Apologetically, Aton quickly reversed the message.

"-show mercy to the maligned and downtrodden."

She took a breath, and continued; *"The third sign of the Rebirth is mourning. One to the Guardian, One to the invisible; Though the purpose is clear. To take the hard path the daka must free those Redd set into bondage."*

Aton made a funny whistling noise, but kept his mouth shut to avoid interrupting the message again. He recognized the third sign for what it was, as did Bail. Betnoni was echoing Cobo on the release of the Shodites, or was it the other way around?

A pause, and; *"The fourth sign of the Rebirth is Sacrifice. The Masing Star emerges from its isolated tomb, and the last gate is opened. To take the hard path, the daka must have faith in Ver dala Ven."*

She folded her hands in front of her.

"Once the fifth sign makes itself clear, the hard path is no more." She warned, *"Destiny is set, for good or ill, and you only need sit back and watch the movement of the universe, and to wait."*

After a brief pause, she went on, *"The fifth sign of the Rebirth is a miracle. He sees his face in the invisible, and what was lost is returned. Thranlam'Sum will bless the true faith, and destroy the false."*

"The sixth sign of the Rebirth is fear. Mo'ghan Awakens! The Rathians Rise with him, and revitalize their mission in secret and dark places-"

"Mo'ghan? As in Mo'ghan the first?" Aton cried out in delighted shock, and he grinned, enjoying his adventure with Betnoni.

128

Bail hushed him, and Betnoni continued, unaware of the interruption, *"-to destroy Ona and control Ver dala Ven."*

"The seventh sign of the Rebirth is destruction. One become two, and two become one. In trine, the Chosen must correct an injustice to inspire the song to sing."

Betnoni frowned, lowering her hands. *"My friends, if you believe that fate is law set in changeless stone, take the easy path and let the signs come to pass without notice. Endure the consequences. Jantideva will fall, the Alliance will die in the heat of one thousand wars, and Ver dala Ven will pass out of this world for all time.*

"If you are self-determined, seek the hard path early, and do not relent to cowardice or a calloused heart."

Betnoni fell silent and the ariq stone popped from its place in the screen. She, and her surroundings, disappeared.

"Daka," Aton gushed, "Thank you so much for sharing this priceless gem with me!"

Bail was not so thankful for having uncovered the prophecy. "What does it mean?"

"Which part?" Aton countered, "The entire piece is replete with ancient images, echoes of older prophecy, and hidden meanings. The epilogue marks this as a classic form of soothsaying. Predicting doom is a habit of Ver dala Ven of old, in order to jar their dakas into heeding their wisdom."

"A sort of threat?"

"In a manner of speaking, yes. They were taught by Thranlam'Sum not to interfere with our free well or self determination, so instead of telling us outright which path to take, they laced prophecy with frightening images to avert us off the wrong path."

"Then the outcome of the future days may not be all that horrible? One thousand wars—"

"Reference to Thranlam'Sum's era, where before the Masing Star descended from the heavens the world had been embroiled in one thousand wars. In ancient times, the Janti feared the return of those horrific times, which they believed were revisited during the thirteen generations of Rathian rule during the dark ages. Though in all fairness, the Rathians did build the foundation on which the present day Alliance now stands, their unification of the world was done by force, not peace. Citing the specter of Rathianism and the end of the Alliance are well known tactics to persuade dakas and Suma of the severity of a prophecy. I'd say there is little chance of the worse coming to pass."

"Except the Rebirth of the Masing Star?"

Aton became apologetic. "I am ill equipped to offer much insight on the direction of prophecy, daka. Historical lore, oh, yes, I can indeed aid you with a wealth of historical lore, but interpreting prophecy is best left to Ver dala Ven. Have you discussed this with Ver dala Ven Cobo?"

"Not yet." He said, and he took the ariq stone from the screen. "But I intend to."

"Uhh, just out of scholarly curiosity, where did you find this recording?"

"It was in my father's possession."

From the landing bay on the roof of the Alliance Congress, Bail could see the entirety of the Center-plex. They were far above even the flight path of private windriders, higher than any building for spans around. Bail wandered to the edge of the rooftop, and placed both hands on the glass enclosure. He could see Shod City, from this distance looking clean and beautiful. He closed his eyes as he remembered standing in this very place with is father when he was a boy. He, looking up at his father, and his father looking out toward lake Pril and Shod City.

"Suffering, suffering." Ver dala Ven Voktu had muttered, "Beyond endurance. Beyond compassion, compassion is empty in the face of their suffering." And his father turned away, as though he could no longer stand to look upon their suffering. He knelt to look Bail in the face. "You will honor yourself if you at least treat the Shodites with respect. You will honor me if you treat them as you treat a Janti."

He remembered that day. He was present in the Rotunda as a guest of the Alliance Congress to watch his father do nothing more than stand behind an aristocratic couple as they spoke to the body of ministers. At the time, his five-year-old mind didn't grasp the significance of their speech, or his father's support. He didn't understand that his father, along with Solien and Bret di Haveran,

130

had committed a crime by speaking out on behalf of the Shodite cause. It was only later, many years later, that he understood the courage his father had shown by doing what he thought was right, versus what was expected of him by daka Janus.

Again he opened his eyes, and though he tried, he couldn't see how it was possible to free all those millions of angry men and women. Already, their uprisings were causing fright in all corners of the Center-plex. There was talk of moving their colony to the opposite shore of the Pril, where the land was still tainted by old lume mines. There was talk of imprisoning them all in a penal colony, releasing them under guard. Now that another commando of Pliadors had been lost to Cleses, a respected Captain of Bail's own legion among them, the Alliance would be hard put to make concessions to the Shod.

"Suffering, beyond compassion."

He backed from the glass, taking one last long look at the looming menace in the distance, and set out to find Trev. He needed distraction. A bottle of brandy would ease his conscious, his concerns. At least for the moment.

෬෬෬෬ඛඛඛඛ

Cobo preferred the outdoors to being locked down in the palace. Too many years in the desert, he mused. He strolled leisurely in the fountain garden, enjoying the sounds of rippling water and the comfort of nostalgia. If circumstances were better, he'd enjoy his homecoming. There were happy memories for him here, of his parents and his brother, of Jishni. The garden was as he remembered, though he knew nothing of it was the same. The water was not the same water he played in, the plants were new or grown or had died and been replaced with a plant of the same type. Everything changes, and yet nothing changes. The koan described his life.

Winding garden paths connected twenty-eight fountains. Each fountain represented an Alliance culture, with Jantideva as the central point to the maze.

There were two clearings without fountains, the old wells supporting fountains long covered with stones or filled in with dirt.

After an early supper taken alone in his room, he took his walk through the garden, purposefully making his way to one such clearing where sat on a bench to think. He heard the footsteps following him long before he sat down, and knew they were not here to enjoy the sea air or the sight of the fountains. They were trying to find him, to speak with him.

"Interesting that you'd take your respite on the very spot the fountain of Shodalum once poured forth."

"Good evening, Yana." Cobo replied. "Durym." He said to acknowledge the young priest with Yana, and to the Suma Mistress, he said, "Good Sister."

She cracked a smile, which beneath her hideous exterior made her seem familiar to him. She, like all the women entering into the Suma enclave, was hairless, neutralized, and her skin horribly scarred by graining. Neutralization was a surgical procedure to remove all forms and matter of femininity from a candidate's body, done by doctors. The process of graining, however, was the domain of the priests, and took several seasons to complete. The painful process of rubbing a solid, sandy acid on the entire body of a woman, killed hair follicles and left raised and reddened pocks on the skin. The purpose of the treatment was to make the woman less inviting to the touch, therefore less a distraction for the priests.

In ancient times, Suma Mistresses were not subjected to torture. They were the helpmates and concubines of the priests, who were the keepers of Ver dala Ven's teachings, rather than being teachers, themselves. But since the Silence began, both the roles of the priest and the Mistress had changed. The entire Suma priesthood changed. It became a religion of celibacy and self-denial, as the priests watched and waited for the Star to return. Their sacred prayers became invocations to the Masing Star, and because the Star had, in legend, caused the possessor to feel ecstasy, the priests of antiquity decided that the one true act of ecstasy should be used as a dedication to the Masing Star. The Mistresses who were concubines became objects to facilitate prayer, prayers made by the priests during the act of love and especially during the moment of ecstasy. In order to ensure that the relations between the priests and the Mistresses were clean and fully dedicated to prayer, the tradition of disfiguring their female counterparts was born.

She said, "Good brother, don't you remember my name?"

He recognized her voice, paled and stood. "Surna."

"Good to see you again, Ver dala Ven."

Surna was not pretty in her youth. She had thin lips and a crooked smile, large jutting teeth, a hooked nose, and a form like a boy's. Surna once had dreams, though, of becoming a wife and a mother, of being cherished by a family. Cobo knew her dreams well, had learned of them during their courtship. She had been Cobo's promised, the one his mother wanted him to wed. But Cobo loved another, and Surna had no interest in him as a husband, she had her heart tied to a young Pliador under Bail's command, so they were poorly matched, indeed. They carried on a courtship for the benefit of their parents, each becoming the other's confidant, and alibi so that they could meet their lovers on the sly.

Her lover was killed in an accident shortly before Cobo left Ona.

She sent him a thought, an image made to words, just as he'd taught her to when they were friends. *Being wed, you and I, might have been a better life than the fates we were dealt, my love.*

The story of Surna's fate tripped quickly through his mind, and left him with a pang of regret. After he ran away from Ona, the responsibility of her future fell to her brother, Dai, one of Ona's court mind readers. Dai didn't want the yoke of her living in his home, and convinced she was too ugly to attract a husband, he placed her into the Mistresshood.

"I wish I knew." He said to her, for he would have prevented it from happening. He would have taken her with him to Shodalum. Unable to bear how his bright, gregarious woman friend had been abused, he bestowed a high honor on her and sunk to one knee. "I am very happy to see you again, Surna."

Yana viewed the gesture with disdain, unable to understand why Ver dala Ven would choose to honor Surna, who did not deserve such an honor.

Tears glittered in her eyes. "I've missed our chats in the garden."

He rose, and with fondness, he replied, "So have I."

"Indeed," Yana interjected a bit too loudly. "We've all missed Ver dala Ven dearly. It is a great pleasure to welcome you home." He was calling attention to himself, to the fact that Ver dala Ven had not bestowed such an honor on him, the only one present who really deserved to be honored. "I've looked high and low for you, Ver dala Ven. It was only by chance I spied you slipping into the garden on my way to the High Room. Where have you been hiding yourself?"

The warmth he felt for Surna turned cold for Yana's insinuating tone. "I've not been hiding from you, Yana. I've been in my apartment for the better part of the day, in meditation."

Clearly chagrinned that he'd not thought to check Cobo's apartment, he retorted, "I've sought you out to discuss your future in Ona."

"I have no future in Ona. There is nothing to discuss."

"Oh, you are quite wrong. You see, I know where you have been all these years, Ver dala Ven. No need asking how I know, I have my sources. I know you have been in Shodalum, and that woman you've made a daka is a full-blooded Shodite. I can't imagine how the entirety of the Alliance doesn't already know, she has the look of one. Very exotic animal, I must say. Lovely bone structure, and in optimum health for breeding. She'd exact a high price on the market, don't you think?"

The Spirit of the Masing Star crackled through him, reacting to his protective anger. "Careful, Yana," he warned, feeling the power of his *breed* course through his veins, ready for his use, "do not displease me."

"What can you possibly do to me Ver dala Ven?" he laughed, "I will have upheld the highest law. The very worse you can do to avert her slavery is to petition the Janti court for ownership."

"And if I agree to stay in Ona, you will keep your silence about what you think you know about my Chosen Sister?"

Yana's greedy mouth smiled big. "Exactly."

"And if I go to the daka with your threat?"

"Your sister still becomes a slave."

"And if I tell the daka that you altered daka Corrinne's message so that she would not discover Betnoni's final prophecy and how you knew that Taen figured heavily in the first sign, then what will you do?"

Yana's smile dropped away. "She would think you a liar."

"I don't think so." Cobo retorted, "As we speak, the original recording of Betnoni's final prophecy is in the hands of the dakas. They know what you know, Yana."

"What have you done?" Yana breathed.

Durym glanced quizzically at Yana. "What prophecy?"

Cobo leaned forward slightly, "They do not have to know how you hid the truth from them. Lying to the daka, it is the ultimate sin for a Suma, is it not?"

"You will destroy the Ona Order of the Suma for your own selfish ends? Hardly surprising, you were always a selfish and shortsighted boy. Ona will not survive the coming holocaust!"

"'Bear not the worries of the future.'"

"Do not quote Thranlam'Sum at me! I am the foremost authority on the teachings of Thranlam'Sum!"

"Yes, you are." Cobo allowed, and he settled back into a comfortable position, turning his eyes to the cloud dappled sky. The sun would go down soon on his first full day home. "Beware my threat, Yana. I am not afraid to destroy you, nor will it vex my conscience much."

"I will oppose your departure to Dilgopoche with all my might!" Yana promised, and with that he spun on his heel, his cape flowing out, and stalked off into the darkness. Durym quickly followed, but Surna hesitated a moment.

"Come with me Surna, my friend." Cobo offered, an offer made from the heart, "Dilgopoche could mean your freedom."

"Surna!" Yana barked.

With quick steps, she raced to catch up to her master.

Cobo pensively considered the silence. He'd been home one day, and already he'd torn the house of Ona asunder.

Gather strength

Gather strength

He breathed in and dismissed his worries. He breathed out, and felt his strength. In and out, he knew peace. In and out, and he rose from the bench, levitating above the bench, rising.

135

In and out, the Spirit of the Masing Star gently burst from his outer skin, and he gasped at the sheer pleasure of the release. His peace deepened. *Worry not for the future.*

His breath eased in, then out, and he disappeared.

His consciousness awakened, and he knew at once that he'd become the seven spires of Ona. Not possessing them, nor lingering within their crystal centers, but living as them at once, they his body, he their mind.

How am I doing this?

He was not enlightened, only hushed, and told to stay still.

ଏଏଏଏଏ∾∾∾∾∾

Taen rolled off her when he was done and dismissed her curtly. Her name was Jem Jin, but he persisted in calling her "girl" to remind her that she was nothing in his eyes. She was fifteen, on the heavy side with a large bosom, her golden tresses like a flowing river, her eyes as blue as the sky. She always cried when he was done. He hated that part. Usually, after she dressed and just as she was ready to leave his room, he made her forget so her tears wouldn't alert his family and the staff. Bail didn't approve of using the shod women for an easy release. He'd heard Bail warn uncle Kinn that he'd ban the young girls from the palace indefinitely if they were used. Of course, that didn't stop the use. Even Bailin had a little thing that found her way into his bed on too many nights to count. Taen could hear them through the wall even now, giggling and moving around in the next room.

The only saving grace of being forced to make Jem Jin forget was that it made each encounter fresh and new. Each time she was a virgin, timid and afraid, each time she came to his room unaware of what he wanted, each time she resisted enough to incite his lust.

She was still crying as she dressed, pitiful tears that dropped off her fat cheeks and onto the floor.

He decided as he watched her from the bed that he wouldn't make her forget this time. He didn't care if his parents found about her. He wanted her to remember. Tomorrow night Jem Jin would come to him remembering.

Once he was alone, he lay very still and stared at the ceiling. He wouldn't sleep well with Cobo under the same roof. He could feel Cobo's stifling presence. The powerful Ver dala Ven. The man who left him, the man who'd made him a bastard had come home to strip him of his life.

Riar Sed once promised he would be a daka, greater than Bail, greater than any daka that ever lived, because he was Ver dala Ven. Riar Sed made many promises.

He never mentioned the possibility of being exiled to Dilgopoche.

Giving up on sleep, Taen rose from bed to practice the meditation Riar Sed taught him. He could almost hear the old man's barked orders. Erect back! Breathe in the triad! Nose, chest, groin....yes, stupid boy, imagine you are breathing through your chest and groin, imagine you have a blow hole right between your nibs, and imagine the air is sucked in through your infinitesimal consha!

Free my thoughts, Taen thought, then grimaced. Riar Sed would have slapped him on the back of the head for thinking the words. Empty mind, foolish boy!

He had hated Riar Sed.

Empty mind. I'm cold, I'm uncomfortable, what is this, did Jem Jin leave this?

thinking again

Taen sighed and opened his eyes.

He wondered how Cobo maintained mental silence.

His thought was answered. "Self control and mental purity."

Taen flinched, realizing Cobo had been listening in on his efforts. He stood and whirled around, looking for Cobo in his room.

yes, find me

A challenge. Taen smiled confidently. He reached out, touching the minds of everyone in his home. His mother, who was moving about restlessly in her chambers. His brothers, one sleeping peacefully, the other enjoying his concubine. Jem Jin, entering the lift leading to the servant quarters in the basement, her mind a mess of anguish.

Below the daka's quarters he felt the minds of various residents. Uncle Kinn, putting it to a girl who was not auntie Sual. Auntie Sual, in another room, putting it to a man who was not Uncle Kinn, while imagining the man was Lodan Kru Dok. Servants, finishing their routines, relaxed now that the dakas were retired.

He touched Cobo's room, and felt no presence. He moved on down through the entire palace.

Nothing.

"Look harder."

Cobo's voice behind him caused him to whirl around. Cobo stood before him, and Taen blinked.

Cobo vanished.

"Where are you?" Taen demanded, and he looked around the bed, under it, in the closet.

"Taen? Where am I?"

He stopped, and closed his eyes, searching for Cobo again with his senses. This time, as he passed through Cobo's quarters, he felt a presence there.

No, the presence faded. Gone.

"Stop playing with me." Taen demanded.

"This is not a game." Cobo said, his voice clear and again behind him.

Taen glanced over his shoulder. Cobo leaned casually against the wall, a contemptuous grin on his leathered features.

"Teach me how you do that." Taen commanded. "It is my right to learn!"

"You've no rights, but those I afford to you."

The retort stung, but he'd long ago learned how to get his way in his mother's court. Doing his best to affect a pleasant and sincere demeanor, Taen changed his tone of voice and approached Ver dala Ven with both hands outstretched to touch him. "Teach my spirit how to walk, father." His hands went through Cobo's body, and he lurched back in surprise.

"You aren't here?"

"I am here, I am everywhere."

"Teach me," Taen begged, "how to spirit walk!"

"Can you learn?"

"Yes!"

"It is easy." Cobo told him, "My father taught me to spirit walk before I took my first physical step."

"Teach me,"

A hundred thoughts ran through Taen's mind. Thoughts of the excitement of being able to ghost around the house, and spy on his family. Dozens of greedy notions of being able to enter the bodies of others, and guide their actions with the force of his will.

"To spirit walk, you need only to have a pure mind."

Taen's brow crinkled quizzically. "I don't understand."

Cobo's grin faltered, and his features saddened. "I know."

His image faded.

Taen bolted to his feet and ran through the space where Cobo once stood, as if to hold him in his room.

"Cobo! Teach me how to have a pure mind!"

"You can learn that from Jem Jin."

Taen laughed out loud at the audacious comment. Jem Jin was a meaningless Shodite slave. What did she know?

He reached out with his mind, looking for Cobo's presence. Again, he felt nothing in the palace, even in Cobo's room. Wait, no, there it was, above and around him, all around.

"You are blocking me from finding you?" he growled, "Is that it?"

No response.

"You have an obligation to teach me!" he shouted.

This time his response came through the wall between his and Bailin's bedroom. "Do shut up and go to sleep!" his brother hollered irritably.

Taen, in his fury, threw his fist against the wall. "You shut up, beast boy, or I will tell father about your whore!" He threw his fist against the wall several more times for good measure.

The house intercom went off. He glanced at the screen next to his door. A red light was blinking. It was his mother.

"Ha, ha!" Bailin hacked out his forced laugh, expecting Taen would be in trouble for waking their mother.

Taen answered his mother's call curtly.

"Taen? I'm afraid I am in labor." Her breathless voice was laced with pain.

139

He'd seen her give birth to Bail's children before. He wasn't interested in these two.

She said, "I've already called for Nan, but I can't seem to reach your father. He was at the Suma Hall of Ver dala Ven, last I knew. Would you please go and find him for me?"

She wanted him to run to the Center-plex for her at this ungodly hour? He had the urge to tell her that he'd be happy to run and get his father, then return with Cobo, see what the fat rew had to say about that!

He decided that was exactly what he would do.

Smiling malevolently, he said, "Right away, mother."

As he dressed, he considered the possibility he may not be able to find Cobo. And what if he did? How would he explain himself to Bail once Jishni told him about his prank? Bail would admit his paternity, and all hope of being a daka was lost.

It would be easier if his mother died in childbirth.

A glint of spiteful determination sparkled in his eyes as he reached out for his mother's body. As he touched her, he realized she was very close to delivering the babies. No one was with her yet to help her if something terrible happened.

No, Taen, please, came her plea. His mother had sensed him and his intent. How that was possible he hadn't a clue, but now he had to work fast before someone found her. He searched her for weaknesses. Could he stop her heart? Burst a vein in her head? Wrap the umbilical cords around the twins' necks for good measure? He heard echoes of panic in her mind. She began pleading with him for mercy, and pleading with the guardian for help, weeping, screaming out for help. A servant heard her, but she didn't know that yet. Her fear rose. Delicious fear, he drank her fear and reached for a vulnerable artery in her head—

Suddenly, he felt his own heart set loose, beating as if he were running hard. Pain exploded in the center of his chest, causing him to lose hold on his mother. He crumpled to the floor, clutching at his heart.

"Can I stop your heart?"

Cobo's voice rang in his ears. He couldn't respond, because he couldn't breathe. His heart thumped in a wild rhythm, struggling to live.

"Can I burst a vein in your head?"

His vision faltered. His right side slackened, paralyzed.

"Can I, Taen?"

He could see Cobo's boots, his tunic brushing the floor.

"Yes," he hissed, "yes."

Ver dala Ven disappeared, and as he did he released his hold on Taen. The pain in his head and chest vanished, and his sight returned. He moved his right hand, his right leg. Rubbed his chest. His heart had returned to a normal rhythm.

He lay on the floor cursing Cobo with all his might.

Quiet mind, he thought hotly, knowing he had no power while his thoughts were in furious disarray. There had to be a path around Cobo's influence. He had to control his mind to find that path.

He lay for hours on the floor, desperately practicing the techniques for mind control taught to him by Riar Sed.

Not enough, not soon enough, not easy enough. Cobo seemed alive in the walls, protecting Jishni from harm.

"I will not go to Dilgopoche!" he screamed at Cobo.

"You will."

෴෴෴෴෴

The windrider let down in Ona's public landing dock without a bump. Gella had her eyes tightly closed. She didn't realize they'd landed until Korba took her by the arm.

The few people who rode the windrider this far had been picked up in Dralon, the provincial town where Ona's servants lived. The sight of a Janti woman was unusual at this hour, but no one looked too long at her. Their fear for the uniform Shelon wore was clear, and made them blind to how the legs of the pants were a bit too short on him, and the tunic top a bit too tight.

They disembarked, and passed through an unmanned check station. An invisible barrier protected each entry into the palace, and encompassed the common leading from the public landing bay to the palace's main hall. Gella stepped through the barrier, looking into the air as if to see it recognize her on contact. Cobo had tried to explain the security device, but all she really

141

understood was that the Watchers knew instantly who entered and left the palace, and if someone who'd not been programmed into the system tried to enter or leave, an alarm sounded.

She glanced backward at Shelon, who'd dropped back to fiddle with something on his collar. "Korba," she breathed, worried at once that they'd be caught, worried about Shelon's fate, and Korba's, and her own.

And as she glanced back at Shelon, she saw the passengers of a sleek, silver windrider disembark. She went rigid as she saw daka Bail and his pilot start toward the check station. Bail stopped and stared at the stars a moment. He seemed a bit off balance. His pilot came up beside him, and gave him a shove that seemed highly disrespectful, but one Bail took in stride and with a grunted laugh.

As he saw Gella, his wayward course had a destination. He strolled purposefully toward her.

"Gella, what are you doing out this late?"

"Bail," she said uncertainly, and she glanced quickly at Korba. "I suppose it would be poor manners to ask the same of you?"

He chuckled in a relaxed way. "Depends on my mood, and the fairness of the lady asking."

She smelled spice, and realized the daka had been drinking. His smile, his manner, was loose and carefree.

His rumpled pilot bid the daka a good night with a slap on his back.

"See you in the morning, Trev." he replied.

"Not too early!" Trev called back over his shoulder.

Bail laughed.

While the daka was speaking to his pilot, Shelon passed the checkpoint, still fingering the device on his collar. In the transport bearing them to Ona, he had described the item as a highly illegal device that could get him executed on the spot if it were found. The device and how it worked to fool the barrier was not explained to her, he only assured her that it would ease his entry into the palace.

He was admitted onto the grounds without note.

Brazenly, and still fingering the device on his collar, Shelon addressed the daka as he passed through the three of them. "Good evening, daka."

"Good evening, Captain." Bail replied, after a quick glance to the rank on Shelon's opposite collar. "Here on business or pleasure?"

"Business, of course. Routine test of ground security."

"Ah. Carry on." Bail invited, and he gestured at Shelon to go about his business.

Shelon affected a brief bow, and strolled away as if he belonged.

Gella didn't realize she'd been holding her breath, until the discomfort in her chest preceded weak knees. She reached for Korba.

Bail put his hands on his hips and returned his attention to Gella. "Have you been sight seeing? I would have expected Cobo to go with you. Did he? Or did he stay behind and leave you to your own ends?"

The question seemed loaded with significance.

"I thought I'd have Korba show me the sights." she replied, trying to seem normal, though lying always took the normalcy out of her tone.

"I hope you took her to the Congress?" he said to Korba, "The lights in the Congress rotunda are spectacular at this hour."

"Daka!"

They all turned at once to see a Watcher sprinting across the bay to Bail.

"Daka!" she called again breathlessly.

Bail's loose drunk sobered immediately.

"What is it?"

"It's daka Jishni, it's time."

"Time," he said, bewilderment crossing his features. Realization opened his eyes. "Oh, it's time."

The Watcher took his arm and raced him away. The daka didn't so much as turn to say goodbye.

Gella waited until she was sure the daka was gone from sight, then spun around to look for Shelon.

He waited casually by a statue, his foot up on the pedestal, smoking a rolled manau leaf. He nodded to a security officer who was passing by, acknowledging the man. The officer returned the nod, and walked on.

"Is he an idiot?" she asked Korba irritably as they began walking toward him.

"He is a hero." he said, his awe obvious. "I've never known anyone as brave as Shelon."

"Bravery without common sense is called stupidity."

Korba laughed. "You know, I think you and Shelon are a lot alike."

"Don't even say so in jest."

Shelon noticed them, and dropped the burning leaf on the ground and stomped on it with the Janti Captain's boot.

"Are we ready?" he said.

He fell into step with Gella, leaving Korba to his place, several steps behind them. He took Gella's arm as if they were good friends, and wrapped his hand around hers.

"Do you think you could possibly be more blatant?" she asked him lowly. "You want to get caught, don't you?"

"Here's a tip for you. If you behave normally, you are not as noticeable. Skulking around tends to attract attention. Now smile for the Watchers."

Gella faltered a smile as they went through the palace's many open arches. A Watcher looked at Gella, but not to her eyes. His gaze lingered on the roundness of her bosom beneath the layered gown she wore, obviously yearning to see what lay beneath the layers. She mused on the prudishness of the Janti, and how it did not seem to quell their lusts in the least.

They entered the palace, unquestioned.

"See? Easy." Shelon said under his breath, with a maddening smile on his face.

His polished control dropped away as he got his first look at the grandeur that lay beyond the palace doors. He stopped in the center of the main hall, and looked up at Ver dala Ven Dex's spire above their heads, then down to the intricate stone work left by the Rathians.

"Beautiful," he whispered.

Gella smirked. "You behave as if you've never seen the inside of the palace, Captain."

He smiled at her dig, and nodded that she was right.

"Help me keep my jaw off the floor, will you?"

"I'd be happy to knock it back into place for you."

"I bet you would."

Their pace was casual, and he stopped too often for her comfort, to admire a piece of artwork, or gaudy jeweled filigree in the molding above a door. Envy and rage steadily tainted his admiration. Disregarding whose ears might be listening, he made frequent comparisons to his "palace" and that of the dakas. "Look here, what is this? A sitting room? This room is as big as the subbasement of my building."

"Feel this….feel the breeze? They must have air converters. My flat has an air converter….I open my door and a collection of new stale air flows through."

"You are staying here? Look at the size of your quarters, and...bed chamber...and your bed! My, my, I think I might miss my roll mat tonight!"

Korba took his place outside the door of Cobo's apartment.

"It's better this way," he said to her objections, "The household will expect me to be here in the morning, guarding your room."

"You can stay inside, sleep on the lounge."

"No, my people would think I stayed for your pleasure, and I don't want that reputation among my own." he replied, and with a boyish smile on his face, he quickly added, "Not that I mind the idea of being with you, but I care what my fellows in the palace think of me, and if I were to let them believe that of me, I'd lose their respect."

She sighed, and released the light hold she had on his arm. "I think I understand."

He let himself outside the door. Soon he'd be sitting on the floor, blocking the door, sleeping with his forehead on his knees, like many young men they passed in the hall tonight. Special, unpaid security guards, to keep the Janti feeling safe.

"I don't like leaving him outside." she said to Shelon as she followed him into the bedroom.

Shelon was testing the bed for firmness. He hopped in, landing on his back with his feet crossed, and his hands behind his neck. A supreme smile of satisfaction crossed his lips.

"It's been years since I slept in a real bed. You mind?"

"Take it, it is yours."

"You're welcome to join me." Grinning at her, he caressed the coverlet beside him, an invitation.

"Wish all you like, and sleep by yourself." She kicked off the uncomfortable Janti shoes and wiggled her toes with a sigh.

"You'll not share a bed with me? I won't bother you. You sleep on your side of the bed, and I, mine."

"I prefer the floor."

"You don't trust me."

"Should I?"

He shrugged, "At your own risk, I suppose. But if I am the type of man that would force myself on you, sleeping on the floor wouldn't be a deterrent."

"You won't force yourself on me."

"How can you be so sure?" he persisted, and he was growing amused with the subject. "I may be planning to take you right this moment. What would you do? Scream? No, you wouldn't scream, because you'd worry about who'd come, and the questions they'd ask. Who would come to your rescue, my pretty Gella?"

"I would." Cobo replied from the doorway. His undetected presence unnerved Shelon, and he leapt up from the bed.

Gella turned on Cobo, unaffected by his silent arrival. "You and I need to have a talk."

"Gella, what is done is done. We don't need to talk about it." He sank from the door, and entered the sitting room, drifting toward the expansive windows facing the night.

Infuriated, Gella stomped after him. "Oh yes we do need to talk about it, you slank slug!"

Tiredly, he turned on Gella and said, "It wasn't my will to make Korba your living guardian."

"You suggested it to the daka!"

"It was the only way to both save Korba, and put you on your proper path. I was doing what was best for both of you."

"Put me on the proper path? By making me a slaveholder? Well, this is what I think of your good intentions!" She slugged him in the arm.

He jumped back, and threw a hand over the assaulted body part. "Gella, that hurt!"

146

"She kicks and uses her nails, too, so watch yourself." Shelon said sardonically. He now stood in the doorway where Cobo once stood, leaning on the doorjamb, his arms crossed casually in front of his broad chest.

Cobo twisted around and stared at Shelon now, surprise on his features, as if he recognized the Janti-born Gella had brought to their rooms.

Gella didn't note the recognition in Cobo's face. She was far too upset over Korba. "What must I do to free him from my service?"

"Let him be put to death." Shelon interjected, "It would be a far better fate than having him traded off to another house."

She threw her furious glare at Shelon.

"There is no way to free him," Shelon informed her, "not even if that is what you want for him. He is born into slavery, he will die a slave."

"It cannot be."

"It is so." Cobo replied, finally dragging his eyes away from the man blocking Gella's bedroom door. "He lives and dies as a slave. There is no freedom for the Janti-born."

She turned away, a chill racing through her as the shackles of Korba's slavery cinched around her neck. "How can I live like this? I may as well die, too."

Cobo sidestepped her furious confusion to address Shelon. "Your plan to speak before the daka is ill timed. She will be indisposed to company tomorrow, especially your company. But, I can arrange for the opportunity for you to speak before the council, if you will be patient and trust me."

Shelon's arms tightened across his chest. He clearly did not like having his plans known by a stranger.

"In the meantime, you must stay in this apartment. You must not step out, not even for a respite of fresh air."

Shelon glanced around, "As prisons go, it is a vast improvement to Raal."

"Cobo, I cannot be Korba's slaver, I cannot." She entreated, begging him with her eyes to make it go away.

Clearly tormented by her predicament, he shook his head. "I knew in Nari," he faltered, grimaced, thumped his chest in agony,

147

"that we might be separated someday by circumstances beyond our control."

"I promised never to leave you." She retorted thickly.

"I will understand if you change your mind."

He'd made her afraid for her future, their future, too afraid to press him on details, on truth, on his visions or premonitions, because she preferred to remain ignorant.

She stalked into her room, brushing Shelon out of her way as she passed through the doorway. "Shut the door." She ordered over her shoulder.

He edged into the room, and shut the door.

"No, you, out!"

"I can't sleep out there. I might be discovered by a maid."

His sober reply irritated her far more than his usual sarcasm, for she knew he spoke the truth. Like it or not, she was stuck in his company.

She went to the bed and leaned heavily on a bedpost. She felt crushed. She was certain she couldn't survive without Cobo. But she wouldn't weep. No one had the power to make her weep. Though her eyes were hotter than the sun baked sand in Calli, she wouldn't shed a tear.

"I cannot rest until Korba is free."

"You are an honorable woman."

"I don't care about honor! Or you, or the Janti-born." She spat, "I hate this palace, and my brother, all of Jantideva, and everything I have seen and heard since arriving here, I hate windriders, and I hate you! I wish I had stayed home!"

Unmindful of Shelon she undressed, throwing aside her gown and the useless undergarments she'd been given to wear as if they were rubbish, and, fully nude, she untied her sleeping mat and snapped it open and let it fall to the floor next to the windows.

Kneeling down to fix the edges of her mat, she noticed Shelon standing with his face to the wall, and was reminded of the lascivious stare of the Watcher. To the Janti, the unclothed body was forbidden, therefore, erotic.

"Shelon," she chided impatiently, "please don't try to tell me you are modest, not after you stripped before me in Shod City."

He turned slightly, his gaze averted to the floor. "I was never fully unclothed. Call me what you will, but I am not a deviant. I am a gentleman." He glanced at her again, and his expression turned grim. "By the eyes of Thranlam'Sum, please put something on!"

"Nudity is the Shodite way. You Janti, you are enthralled by nudity because you keep covered. You are an unenlightened society."

"Please, you must have a dressing gown?"

"No, I do not." she said, and she lay on the mat without covering. "Leave if you do not like how I sleep."

"You know I cannot!"

"You can go home."

"No, I cannot!" he snapped. And he hazarded another glance over his shoulder, and quickly turned away. "At least a blanket!"

She snorted contemptuously. "A moment ago, you were threatening to take me against my will. Now you are a Janti gentleman that cannot stand the sight of a woman's body? Nudity is natural, but not in Janti! Oh ho! The gowns the women have to wear here, covering arms, legs, neck, bosom, they are a horror! I will wear them in the day, but you ask too much of me to wear them as I sleep."

Shelon dropped his head on the door, and now he glanced toward the bed. "Fine, so be it. Lights off!"

They were plunged in darkness, save the moonlight that painted Gella's body and mat blue. She could not see the bed, but heard him climb onto it and get comfortable.

After a short time, Shelon said, "Gella?"

Sullenly, she replied, "What?"

"Will you tell me about Shodalum?"

Finally it was homesickness that caused a sliver of tears to wet her eyes. Her voice husky, she said, "Shodalum is still and silent. There are no machines to break the silence, none to litter the sky. We have cities, similar to your city,"

"Shod city?"

"With market places and homes and many people, but they are clean, and there are many shrines to the goddess."

"Which goddess?"

"Betnoni, your patron and mine. The patron goddess of the sea, protector of Shodalum."

"Your protector. Not mine." He replied softly.

"Who are your gods?"

"I know no god."

"Hnn."

"Are you a Betnoni worshipper, Gella?"

"She has intervened on my behalf in the past."

"And will she now?"

"I hope so."

"So do I."

His soft, heartfelt words made her tears fall and more appear. She wiped tears from her cheeks, and rolled onto her side.

His silky voice spanned the darkness once again. "What does your home look like?"

"My home." And she cleared sadness from her throat to go on. "It is in Calli, built in the shadows of ruins left by Janti invaders, and near the sea. It is a desert, with subtle beauty many do not see. The land is perfectly flat, and the sky wide open and clear, except during the rainy season. When it rains the sand has a pleasant smell. In the spring, our yava ripens and you can see the orange and purple flowers from a span away. And the sea, when it is calm, is easy to fish."

She heard him sigh, followed by a long silence.

"Shelon?" she whispered.

"Yes?"

"I was in Zorna once, as a girl, before my parents died." She said, "Would you like to hear my memories of that time?"

"Yes." He replied quickly, sounding more awake.

She curled in a ball and embraced her good memories as though they might save her from a horrible fate. "Your tribal land lies between Sidera and the sea, a vast valley thick with trees. Your people live mainly along the shore, as Cobo and I in Calli, and they are fishermen and boat makers. In the mornings, before the sun rises, the men and women put out in their boats, singing all the way to invite Betnoni's grace." She tried to remember the song, singing it in part and in her own tongue, for some of it was far too hard to translate into Janti. Giving up, she smiled at herself. "When there is a large harvest, they have a festival, and at that time they consecrate new members to their tribe. I believe that is why my parents and I went to Zorna, to see our relation consecrated to Rin al Entlay. For the celebration, fires were built along the beach, and through the night we roasted and ate fish, danced and sang with abandon. I fell asleep by a fire at my mother's knee, and woke as the sun rose over the water, pale orange sky, and in the far distance, I could see the outline of boats."

The comfortable warmth of the room and her own happy recollections of youth and of her mother lured her deeper and deeper into a contented sleep.

"Please, go on." Shelon said after a lengthening silence.

"Gella?" He glanced to see her laying very still, on her side and curled in a pretty ball, her wavy hair fanned from her back. Wiry thin, long legs and arms, a wide and sensuous mouth, scars on her here and there. He'd seen enough abuse in his life to know the scars of beatings. Cobo? He wouldn't have been surprised. Ver dala Ven was a Janti. He'd learned of the heartlessness of Janti first hand. She'd not receive a beating again, not as long as Shelon had say in the matter.

Cloaked in the images of Zorna, and Gella dancing around a fire, naked and laughing and singing Shodite songs, he drifted off to better dreams, and sounder sleep.

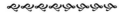

The second sign of the Rebirth is regret. The Invisible roars in the Vass Chamber and causes much discord. To take the hard path, the Daka must show mercy to the maligned and downtrodden

Chapter 8

Lodan Kru Dok was famous, considered a pop culture hero, the greatest kai'gam-Mod in all the Alliance, perhaps the greatest kai'gam-Mod of all time. In matches, Lodan was billed as the reawakening of an ancient Kai'mai master, Ver dala Ven Pletoro, reborn into this life with the ancient knowledge of kai'gam. The claim came close to heresy but was forgiven because many thought it was true. Like Pletoro, Lodan's strength was nearly ethereal, and his hair was so light that when the sunlight hit his head a halo appeared. His weapon was hand crafted, his blade hand sketched with ancient symbols said to be on Pletoro's blade, ancient renderings of the Suma language studied only by Suma priests and Ver dala Ven.

Apart from his uncanny resemblance to the ancient master, his proficiency alone in the art, emerging at the tender age of nine, was proof enough to sway even the most cynical disbeliever.

Privately, Lodan scoffed at the concocted stories about his so-called spiritual pedigree. He was proficient in the art of kai'gam, just as some people were proficient in math, or science, or music, or politics; or in public relations, where a mere man could be made into a god overnight with the right kind of publicity. He didn't play for the sport or the wealth or title. He played the game to strengthen his mental and physical skills in the philosophical art of Kai'mai.

He was called Master, and disliked the rank. In the beginning, he tried to explain to his throbbing followers that he was nothing more than a student of the game, not worthy to teach. Their persistence wore him down, and he agreed to guide them in the way of Kai'mai, teaching them what he knew of the practice they'd viewed as a spectator sport. This was how he began his school. A few of his more centered pupils became independent adherents of Kai'mai thought. The majority either used their lessons as a diversion from a dull life, or as a way to get close to the great man, as if learning kai'gam from him would open them to a new world. In the end, those who were not fascinated with Kai'mai eventually moved on to more interesting philosophies. Lodan bid the transient seekers farewell without regret.

Overall, Lodan had been content during his retirement. When he wasn't teaching, he spent his time practicing, in deep meditation, or forging kai'gams as gifts to his favorite students. The pale imitations of the true kai'gam, blank blades stamped out by robot driven factories in the Kanaki industrial quarter lacked the grace, perfect balance and artistry of the hand forged weapon of the Old Wars. The stories handed down by Suma teachers of the magical kai'gam, part of children's fables, came to life as awestruck spectators watched Lodan meet challenger after challenger in the open kai'gam sporting arena with a weapon that seemed to come alive in his hands. The glittering, shimmering stars that only Lodan could make appear as he used his weapon was hypnotic, drawing the adversary's eye, immobilizing him, opening an opportunity to strike the mock death blow, and win the match.

Under the hot sun of mid-day, the finely etched pictographs on the metal blade shimmered in a race to the tip and back to the hilt as Lodan rotated the blade above his head in a broad circle. The motion and the play of light mesmerized his student, Durym, robbing his attention from the face of his opponent and focusing his attention intensely on the rapturous beauty of the blade. Lodan brought the blade down on his student, at the last moment noticing his student was no longer defending himself.

"Durym!" he barked, and slid his slippered feet aside in the sand in time to narrowly miss taking off his pupil's head. The tip of the kai'gam nicked Durym's ear, and the wake of the heavy weapon violently tossed his upper body aside.

Durym woke from his dull hypnotic state with a shouted obscenity his priesthood normally prohibited him from uttering. He inadvertently stabbed his kai'gam into the ground and stumbled before finding his balance. His hand flew to his ear, and withdrew to find blood on his fingers. Durym's dark eyes pierced Lodan's with a mixture of resentment and grudging respect.

Lodan retreated, his kai'gam lowered in rest. His heart beat furiously as he recovered from the horror of hurting Durym. In the years he taught the art, he'd not hurt a pupil until today, indeed, he'd never drawn blood with his blade in his life.

Durym wiped the blood from between his fingers onto his blue activity smock. Though the kai'gam that Lodan held was not reflecting light while in the resting angle, Durym was careful not to look at the weapon, not even at the harmless black handle loosely wrapped in Lodan's hands.

"I realize I am as uncoordinated as a Rysenk," he said, his tone low with condemnation, "but do refrain from ending my meager life for the crime, Master Kru Dok."

Lodan's reply was made in a carefully modulated tone. "I beg your forgiveness, Durym, for my faulty teaching methods." He took a barest breath and continued, "For, I should have taught you never to look away from my eyes. I should have trained you to use your peripheral vision to judge the movements of my arms, therefore judging the movements of the kai'gam."

The diplomatic reminder neutralized Durym's anger. Lodan repetitively taught his pupils to keep their eyes on their opponent's while sparring. Durym's shoulders slipped down and he frowned at the kai'gam sticking out of the ground before him, one made by Lodan and supposedly imbued with the same hypnotic powers of Lodan's personal weapon.

"Ah," Durym sighed impatiently, "This is impossible. I will never learn."

He allowed himself to show a friendly smile at Durym. "Don't give up so easily. You were doing well. Your movements were becoming less choppy. Much cleaner."

Durym arched a brow and snorted his utter disbelief at Lodan's compliment.

In response, Lodan again grew serious and lifted his kai'gam across his body, a defensive posture, waiting for Durym to make the advance.

Durym glanced sullenly at him, then lifted his own weapon. He braced his feet shoulder width apart, proved his knees loose by bobbing lightly, and fixed his eyes on Lodan's. He waited.

Lodan opened their match by swinging his kai'gam in a wide circle above his head. The sliced air screamed in soprano, and he skipped toward Durym. He resolved to soften his approach, and sure enough, as he executed a sluggish travel right- travel left move, Durym defended himself with ease, and their blades clashed. Lodan saw the blaze of lightning fly off the metal as they connected, and felt the snap of electricity bite his neck and shoulders. A thrill traveled through his body. Until he began making weapons for his students, he'd never experienced the explosive excitement of dueling with an opponent who used a properly made kai'gam. During his years as kai'gam-Mod, in the many tournaments he'd played against opponents who'd had their weapons factory made, when their blades clashed nothing happened beyond the force of their collective strength.

Durym yelped as a mild zap of electrical currant poured into the grip of his kai'gam. To remove himself from the offensive, he popped backwards as lithely as a gymnast, and warily faced Lodan from a useless distance.

Lodan continued to advance, swinging his blade with precise cadence, taking the upper hand. Durym retreated, step by step, blow by blow. Lodan's gaze never left the younger man's dark eyes. He watched Durym, sensing his thoughts as a hot, fluid stream. Lodan's ability to read thoughts did not leave the sparring arena. He'd attributed his ability to his dedication to Kai'mai practice, and continued to expect that, someday, one of his students would begin to exhibit this gift.

Durym was thinking angrily that he wished to throw this match, if only to end the lesson. He was tired, and his ear ached. He felt wetness on his neck and suspected he was still bleeding. And besides, *I'll never learn this.*

Hearing the latter as clearly as if Durym had spoken the words, Lodan brought his assault to an abrupt end. He pointed his kai'gam to the ground.

"That will be all for today, Durym." he said while slightly bowing his head toward the bemused priest.

"We're done?"

"Did you wish to double your lesson for today?"

156

"No, no, not at all. Thank you, Master Kru Dok." Durym said, his relief causing a smile to open his mouth.

Lodan found his tunic on the ground where he'd haphazardly dropped it and draped it carelessly over his bare shoulders without shaking out the sand. Durym fell in step with him as he walked toward the entrance of his modest exercise studio. The day was mild, warm and humid. Durym commented on the unbearable oppressiveness of the air, to which Lodan muttered a polite agreement. The weather conditions never affected Lodan. He had learned to shut physical discomfort out of his mind.

His circular studio had plain white walls and unpainted wooden floors, and high ceilings made with large sections of glass to allow in the maximum amount of light. The few furnishings he owned were old and unfinished. His quarters, which were attached to the studio, were dressed in the same sparse style. Lodan endeavored to ignore societal fads in decor and personal adornment. He wore simple clothing, ate simple foods, and had kept a simple lifestyle since he'd moved away from the city to escape the teeming masses of his fans. He chose to live in Dralon, much to the chagrin of his status conscious family. Lodan's mother had fainted the day he told his parents he would be living among the Shodites.

Durym placed his kai'gam into the serviceable weapons cabinet, being sure to hang it beside Lodan's, and as he cleaned his wound with a damp cloth retrieved by Lodan, a small nick as it turned out, Durym felt it was the perfect time to engage in idle chitchat.

"Did you hear that daka Taen will be turned over to the Dilgos? Daka Jishni made the announcement to the Suma yesterday and will no doubt make a formal announcement to the Alliance council today. Daka Bail did not attend the announcement to the Suma, but Ver dala Ven was at her side. Between you and me, I think Ver dala Ven Cobo has more sway with her than he should, being he is not her husband."

Lodan wondered tiredly why the priests loved to gossip, with tales of sorrow and intrigue ready on their tongues. He'd long ago concluded that, with their limited duties as religious leaders

157

that priests didn't have enough to do with their time except collect tales of woe.

As the priest asked him what he thought of the possibility of an arrangement between daka Taen and a daughter of the Dilgo leader, Lodan diplomatically diverted the subject to the time of their next lesson.

And as the priest began to casually pass on the heartbreak of daka Jishni, Lodan suddenly remembered he had some important matter to attend to immediately, and saw Durym to the door. He bid Durym farewell, and watched from the open door as the priest boarded the small windrider on loan from his temple, and fired the blowers. Four strong breaths of the propelling engine, and Durym was gone, high above Lodan's home.

Alone, Lodan returned to a state of ease.

He picked up his kai'gam and went through several exercises. His studio was small, limiting his movements somewhat, but he adapted to his surroundings. He'd made it a habit to be adaptive. In adaptiveness and simplicity, he'd found peace.

He submerged deep into himself as he swung the blade, dancing in time to an unseen force around him, growing quieter in mind and spirit. This was the true magic of Kai'mai. It was not excitement, or winning contests. It was emptiness of wanting, and peace.

In his peaceful state of mind, he was receptive to the unseen. He kept his visions and encounters with the ancients secret, knowing that if the public discovered he was now as receptive as court psychics, the hero worship that had afflicted him during his championship career would certainly redouble.

As always, his visions began as gentle touch to his full body. A spirit, passing through him, introducing itself as they were one. This spirit had a name Lodan recognized. Voktu.

His motions slowed as the spirit of the late Ver dala Ven Voktu appeared as a light in the center of the room. Lodan never knew the Ver dala Ven, he'd died when Lodan was young, but he knew of him. He'd studied the genealogy of the Ver dala Ven, as had all children under Suma instruction.

Lodan bowed to the appearance of the great man, and waited in silent expectation for Ver dala Ven to teach him as other masters had in the past, giving to him important esoteric knowledge of Kai'mai.

A lesson is not what he received.

Voktu said from the bright light: "You will leave your home and join daka Taen on his journey. Protect him, and guide him."

The light of Ver dala Ven Voktu faded into the wall, and was gone.

Journey? What was it Durym prattled on about? Taen being ushered off to Dilgopoche?

"I am to go to Dilgopoche?" he asked the wall incredulously, expecting a reply.

None was forthcoming.

With his kai'gam, he slashed through the air where the vision had hovered, as if to finish his exercise.

Stepping back, he searched for a meaning of the vision, other than the literal meaning that he'd understood. To join with the daka. To become the daka's protector. Nothing figurative came to mind.

A call at his door brought him around. He glanced out a window, and saw a windrider resting in the middle of his courtyard. He hadn't heard it approach, and wondered if Durym had forgotten something.

He slid open the door to his studio, and instead of Durym, a boy stood at his threshold. He was no older than ten and his face was bright with hero worship. He was dressed in the fine material of a member of the court, in glossy red and gold robes. Behind him, near the windrider, stood two palace sentinels, dressed completely in white.

"I am Jed." the boy said quickly, and he handed Lodan an ornate plaque with golden edging. On the blue screen was the emblem of the dakas, the Masing Star.

"What's this?"

"Please view it, Master Kru Dok. I've been instructed to wait for your reply."

"Is it so important that it needed a personal messenger?"

159

The boy was suddenly chagrinned. He moved uncomfortably from one foot to the other. "I have no information, except that I am to wait for your reply."

Lodan pressed the repeat message bar at the base of the plaque. His pale brows knotted above his eyes as daka Jishni appeared on the screen, looking smooth and a bit tired.

"Master Kru Dok, If it pleases you, I request the honor of an audience with you this day. I have a matter of great importance to discuss with you, and it cannot wait."

He shook his head at the plaque's screen as it returned to blue with the emblem of Ona in the center. "Today?"

"If you choose." Jed said.

He glanced to the place where Ver dala Ven Voktu had appeared to him, and reflected on the duty charged to him, to protect daka Taen.

"One minute." he said to the boy.

He went to the weapons cabinet and found his scabbard. It was made of plain hardened leather, and had a soft brushed strap that fit across his shoulders. His kai'gam was a weapon of sport, long replaced in battle by the lume. But if he was to protect the daka, he would do so in his own way. He slid his kai'gam into the scabbard, and pulled the strap over his head to rest on his left shoulder. Pulling the buckle on the strap tighter so that the weapon fit neatly against his back, he noted the awe in the boy's face.

He smiled at the boy. "You will learn one day?"

"Only if you teach me." the boy blustered.

"You don't need me. You can teach yourself," Lodan replied, "You only need to quiet your thoughts, and the information you are seeking will flow into your mind, like a river flows into a sea."

The boy didn't seem to understand. No matter. Once he secured his kai'gam to his back, he was ready to leave his studio, without a glance backwards. If he never returned, he would not miss this place. He felt no attachments to the material world, something his materialistic parents never understood.

The trip to the palace was short, and quickened by Jed's many questions. Lodan enjoyed the company of children, perhaps more than the company of adults. Children were genuinely honest in their motivations. Deception was an adult art. Jed's interest in kai'gam was hero worship, like most of the adults seeking Lodan for lessons in the game, though unlike Lodan's adult pupils, Jed did not conceal his hero worship with false interest in Kai'mai thought and practices of peace. Jed was interested in the thrill of besting an opponent in the arena. Lodan gave him what he wanted, tales of how he'd beaten the best kai'gam players in the provinces.

They set down in the daka's private landing bay. There, a houseman named Haggins greeted Lodan. He was ushered through a gallery overlooking the Rathian Hall, down a flight of steps, and into the main entry hall of the palace.

Almost immediately, he encountered Ver dala Ven Cobo. Ver dala Ven stood in the entry hall, as if waiting for Lodan's arrival. He watched Lodan walk by, his expression sober. Without knowing why, Lodan distinctly felt Ver dala Ven's approval.

He was ushered into a guest suite, and told to wait for the daka.

&c&c&c&c&c&c&c&c&c&c

Her hard labor seemed to come on quickly, though in retrospect she wondered if she hadn't been in labor the full day before the birth. Her discomfort had been vexing, and cyclical, but not painful enough to drag her away from the problems of state, of her household. She'd felt utterly foolish, calling Nan in the middle of the night as if this pregnancy was her first.

Janus and Archer lay curled together in the baby bed, sleeping peacefully. They cried when they were separated. The baby's physician warned Jishni to not allow them to sleep together, fearing they may form a debilitating attachment to each other. "They may not learn how to assimilate with other children their age if they depend upon each other for comfort."

Jishni threw the man out of her nursery and ordered her nurses to keep the children together. They'd just been wrenched from a safe place and thrust into a cruel world. She would not deny her sons the comfort of their twin.

Bail leaned over her back, and touched Janus's hand.

"If you wake him, you feed him,"

Bail smirked. "Afraid I don't have the equipment for that task." His finger went down the length of Archer's leg. Bail's finger was about the size of Archer's leg. He grimaced, "Still too small."

"The doctor said they are healthy."

"Then why are they still in warming beds?"

Jishni gave his arm a comforting rub, "They have your blood, Bail. Don't worry about their viability. They will grow into huge, brawny boys before you can get used to the idea of having two more children in the house."

He smiled at her. "Thank you, Jishni, for my sons."

He looked at his new sons, wonder taking over his expression. She smiled, content to watch his face as he watched over the babies. Five children and still he treated their appearance as a miracle.

The palace intercom chimed twice.

She stepped away from the warming bed, to the interior of the room, and with a soft voice, she replied, "Yes, Nan?"

"The Alliance ministers have arrived to Ona to meet with you, and I am very pleased to say that Lodan Kru Dok has also arrived. Both parties await you."

"Thank you, Nan."

She paused before turning, very slowly, to Bail.

"You've hardly recovered from the birth."

"I need to formalize the treaty agreement. Taen will be betrothed to a girl named Danati-Zuna. I want to see her likeness before I give my son away."

Crestfallen, he replied, "I see."

"Please don't feel I am being disloyal to you," she said, "but I must heed Cobo's wishes regarding Taen. I will send him away, and your seat as daka will go to your eldest son."

Bail nodded thoughtfully.

Feeling guilt creep up her back for the high handed manner she'd stripped Bail of his rights as a father to Taen, she justified herself. "I don't trust Taen anymore." she said harshly, and the truth hurt her whole being. "Not after he tried to do harm to me and the babies. He needs help. He needs Cobo." she breathed, a lump coming to her throat. She could still feel Taen's cold, murderous touch, curling around her heart, her head, her babies. "And it isn't just my fear of him, it is my fear for our sons. If he's willing to try and kill us to be seated as daka, imagine what he might try to do to his brothers. If he sees them as a threat, then he might…" she couldn't say the words, they were too despicable.

"I agree with your decision, Jishni."

"Do you?" she said hopefully.

"I stand with you." he said, and he smiled sadly.

"I wish," she whispered, "that made me feel better about my decision. I'm giving away my son because I fear him, yet it is I who must bear the responsibility for his evils."

"Don't say that." Bail begged, "You were a good mother."

"You are kind to say so, but I don't believe it." Impassioned, she said, "The Guardian Spirit of Creation is punishing me for disobeying my father and forgetting my betrothal promise to you. I made a Ver dala Ven who was never trained. For my crime, he became a monster, as ugly as the monsters of Dilgopoche. If it is his destiny to be with them, so be it, but I bear the blame. A grave injustice has been done to all that follow. Ver dala Ven is dead in Jantideva."

Bail's features became pensive. "Jishni, there is a matter I have been meaning to discuss with you. It concerns Taen and his destiny."

They were interrupted as the Janti nurse named Bea and a Shodite nanny entered the nursery. The nurse smiled sunnily at her dakas. "How are you feeling, daka Jishni?"

"Like I just climbed Mount Shazzar." Jishni quipped.

"And rolled down the other side, from the looks of it."

Jishni smiled at the irreverent comment, and threw a curious look at the nanny. She was a young woman, chubby, her face pale, her eyes red rimmed. Jishni leaned toward Bea. "Is she experienced with children? She seems awfully young."

"Jem Jin?" and she smiled easily, "She is new to the profession, with experience limited to taking care of her siblings.

163

But according to her genetic profile, she should be a natural care giver."

"But you will be with the children, too?"

"Every moment." Bea assured.

"I shouldn't be gone all day."

"Rest easy, daka. Rest easy."

Bail followed her out. "Jishni, before you go, we must speak. In privacy."

She couldn't bear to discuss her failure with Taen, or her own moral failure, further. "I have much to do this afternoon, and I wish to return to the babies as soon as possible. Please, Bail, another time."

৵৵৵৵৵৽৽৽৽৽

The physical closeness was done. No hand at her back as they walked to the lift, no embrace as they parted, he to his duties, she to her meetings. Four days after the birth, and their marriage had returned to normal, friendly yet distant.

She met Nan in the corridor leading to the guest suites. "You still wish to meet Master Lodan?"

A hungry look appeared on Nan's expression. "Absolutely."

Jishni chuckled. "Nan, you are incorrigible."

"I am a normal woman who recognizes greatness when I see it."

"I hear he is celibate as a practice."

"Not in my dreams, he's not."

Jishni couldn't help smile at the comment, though she reproached Nan with a playful thump on the arm.

Haggins stood outside the closed doors of the guest suite. He bowed to Jishni as she approached, then opened the doors for her. Jed went into the room ahead of her, to announce her arrival.

Lodan Kru Dok stood in the center of the room, his back pulled straight and his eyes closed, as if in repose, and his hands crossed over his chest. His presence in the room resonated peace, and Jishni immediately felt a startling sense of calm. She had heard stories of the amazing influence of Kru Dok's presence, that it was similar to Ver dala Ven, but had dismissed the rumors as the hysterical ranting of fanatics who followed Kru Dok's every breath.

Nan's audible gasp told her that she, too, had sensed the same emanating force surrounding Lodan. They were both compelled to pause at the threshold, their astonishment preventing them from disturbing the Master's deep meditations.

Jed was also in awe by Kru Dok, but with a childish excitement that gave him courage. He strolled right to the Master and tugged at his blue contest tunic to get his attention.

Lodan took a deep breath, as if coming alive for the first time, and he smiled a relaxed smile before opening his eyes to Jed.

"What is the time, Jed?" he asked, his voice smooth and serene.

"Time to meet with the daka." Jed said, and he flourished a hand toward Jishni, standing still as a stone in the threshold of the doorway.

She was struck by Lodan's relaxed manner as he bowed formally in her direction. "I am honored by your summons, daka."

In order to respond to him, Jishni was forced to quickly find her wits. She faltered, but made her feet move. She glided into the room to greet him, performing as regally as she could muster in order to prevent behaving in a gloriously undignified manner, like one of those mindless fanatics who routinely gave their pledge to Kru Dok. If she faltered, even one word, Nan would never let her forget her fumble.

"I am honored you chose to come to me on such short notice." she said smoothly, happy to hear her own voice sound regal and possessed.

"Congratulations on the birth of your sons."

She thanked him, and motioned that they should sit, and as was custom, Kru Dok waited until she was comfortable before taking his seat.

Jed stood near, clearly pleased he was in Kru Dok's company. Jishni would have gladly allowed him to stay in the company of his hero, had the nature of their discussion been benign. She nodded at him, signifying he was to leave, and the excitement fell off his face. She wished she could, as a daka, apologize to him, but royal propriety prevented her from humbling herself to a servant.

Haggins closed the double doors to the guest chamber after Jed stepped out, and they were left to their privacy.

Kru Dok grew serious and stared directly into Jishni's eyes, waiting for her to begin.

"I trust I may confide in you, Master Kru Dok?"

"Yes, daka," he said with such assurance that she didn't need a court mind reader to tell her he was being truthful. The truth was in the profound depth of his eyes, and in the unwavering tone of his voice.

She, at once, felt she'd been delivered. She was unable to keep the tears out of her eyes. "You must have heard by now that my son is to be betrothed to the daughter of the Dilgo sovereign." and she went on without waiting for confirmation. "When he is delivered to the Dilgo camp on the border, he will not go alone, of course. He will have Ver dala Ven. He will take his court, a Watcher escort for protection. But, to be perfectly honest, I have no confidence in the Watchers to keep him safe. Often they have their own political agenda. As for Ver dala Ven, his motives serve a higher cause, and that may or may not include the safety of my son. I would prefer to send with Taen a single protector, someone who will keep him safe from treachery. I fear-" and the catch in her voice betrayed her before she could voice her most terrible fears. Kru Dok was silent as he waited for her to compose herself, his face softening with compassion.

Nan's firm touch on her shoulder was a comfort, and she crossed her arm in front of her swollen breasts to thankfully grip the older woman's hand.

"I fear Rito-Sant does not want Taen bound to his family, as he claims. I fear he will hurt Taen to hurt me. Master Kru Dok, I am asking you, if I must sent my son away, will you accompany him to Dilgopoche and protect him from possible treachery?"

Without hesitation, Kru Dok said, "I am honored you have entrusted your son's life to me. Yes, I will be his protector. I will treat him as my Chosen Brother."

She breathed a sigh of shocked relief. She hadn't expected Master Kru Dok to be so easily accommodating. "Thank you," she whispered. Her voice still low, she said, "It will happen quickly, within a few days. Will you have time to prepare?"

"I've come prepared, daka," he said, his head lowering, "I am at your service."

Her brows hitched together. "I was speaking of your need to close your school, inform your students, pack your belongings."

"I have all I need on my person," Lodan said politely, and he gestured to a nearby table, to his kai'gam. "As for my students, they will be informed of my departure through the Crier. If the news does not reach all my students through the Crier surely they will hear through the rumors spread by well meaning Suma priests."

Jishni did not miss the irony in his tone, though he maintained an even, peaceful demeanor. She smiled slightly, knowing too well of the Suma Priest's penchant for gossip.

"In that case, I invite you to enjoy my hospitality. I will have Jed show you to the guest rooms," she said, and feeling a need to make amends with Jed, she said, "and I will appoint Jed to your services until you are to leave."

He smiled at her as if he discerned the altruistic motives of her gesture.

She gripped Nan's hand as she made an attempt to rise from her seat, rose too quickly and swooned. She faltered, and was about to fall back into the chair when Lodan, breaking with traditional etiquette, shot to his feet and took her by her arm to help her regain her balance. She steadied on her feet, holding onto Nan and Lodan for dear life.

Lodan held tight to her arm for a moment longer than necessary, and stared enigmatically into her eyes. He seemed to delve into her soul, into her thoughts.

Disturbed, Jishni said, "I am quite all right now." She gently pulled her arm free.

He seemed genuinely abashed. "Pardon my hands." he said, dropping them away from her forearm. "I didn't mean to offend. I was caught for a moment in the stress bedraggling you. It is like...." He grew oddly introspective. "An evil spirit."

During her pregnancy it had felt like an evil spirit, the affliction of weak impulses encouraging her toward self-destruction. She would have preferred an evil spirit were haunting her, rather than discovering it was Taen trying to destroy her and his brothers.

Lodan's ease in uncovering a secret she intended to keep to her grave was unnerving.

Nan replied to Lodan with a muttered quip. "It's the spirit of daka Corrinne, throwing a temper tantrum on the borders of Montrose."

Nan's humor broke the taut spell Lodan's observation had cast. Jishni drew herself up, and diplomatically excused herself from Lodan's presence.

Once she'd given her instructions to Jed and Haggins, she strode regally to the lift that would take them to the Vass Chamber.

ৡৡৡৡৡৡৡৡৡ

Cobo had their morning and mid-day meals delivered to his apartment. He, Gella and Shelon sat around the same table to eat. Shelon mocked ease, though his stomach was tied into knots for what the day was certainly to bring. He tried not to think about standing before the council, and the repercussions he expected. Instead, he tried to engage in light conversation with Gella, while watching her watch Cobo, the latter who rarely took his eyes off his plate. The tension between them was palpable. It reminded Shelon of the undercurrent of tension between he and Monca if her husband was present. And Gella claimed Cobo was her brother. Shelon was positive she felt more for Cobo than brotherly love.

The dynamic tension between the two made Shelon exceedingly uncomfortable.

"The juice is divine," Shelon said mockingly after an excruciatingly long silence between the siblings, "and the sweet cakes are the lightest I've ever tasted. Don't you think, Gella?"

"They are too sweet, they stick in the back of my throat." she complained and she tossed her utensil on the plate. "I can't eat this

168

food. What do they think we are, children? Only a child could endure a steady diet of candied this, and candied that."

Cobo agreed with a slow nod, slowly chewing, his eyes drifting to Gella's profile and lingering overlong. The longing that appeared in Ver dala Ven's features made Shelon angry.

"I agree." Shelon said vehemently, "It's no wonder the Janti have rotting teeth. Of course, they can pay to have their teeth replaced, can't they? We Shodites must take good care of our teeth, or end up gumming our dinners."

"Must you constantly proselytize?" Gella snapped, "We aren't your ardent followers, there is no need to keep us in your thrall."

"Pardon me, daka Gella, for forgetting myself in your exalted company." he retorted, his anger flushing cold through his body. This woman irritated him like no other, with her disrespect and her aggravating logic, but worse than enduring her opinions was his own traitorous male function that tortured him with a craving for her that he'd prefer to ignore. Four days and nights locked in her room, enduring more than any man should, he was ready to submit himself to the Watcher guard.

Her eyelids dropped with pique. Her lips parted, ready to issue a retort.

Cobo spoke in Gella's stead, making an announcement to Shelon. "They are almost finished discussing the treaty." he said, "If you still want to go through with it, now is the time."

Shelon's anger drained away immediately. He threw a wary glance at Cobo, for speaking of the meeting in progress, far elsewhere in the palace, as if he had his ear to the Council Chamber door. For centuries, the dakas had been filling Shodite heads with stories of Ver dala Ven omnipotence in an attempt to strike fear into the hearts of their slaves. For centuries the stories worked because Ver dala Ven was a constant fixture in Janti society. Shelon had heard stories of Ver dala Ven Voktu's frequent trips into Shod City to heal the sick. Shodites respected and feared Ver dala Ven, and the daka used the sharp double edge of their veneration by insinuating that not only could Ver dala Ven remove afflictions, but cause afflictions. Indeed, among the very superstitious, Ver dala Ven became the root of all illnesses and bad luck.

Ver dala Ven Cobo's disappearance from Janti society cooled the superstitions of Shodites. Many, like Shelon, thought Ver dala Ven was dead, and the line of omnipotent beings ended. The worship of Ver dala Ven ceased, and contemporary beliefs became god. The belief in freedom, a better life, an end of Shodite poverty, and the death of the Janti authority class.

The slender man who was Ver dala Ven didn't seem like a god, yet Shelon felt as if he were in the presence of a god. Cobo made the back of his neck tingle.

His reply was simple. "I am ready."

☙ ☙ ☙ ☙ ❧ ❧ ❧ ❧

The last motion had been accepted and carried, and the last article of the treaty had been deemed acceptable to all parties, as Cobo entered the chamber.

Heads turned, and silence fell over the Council.

Cobo's shoes made no sound on the polished floor, but the tromping footfall of the unkempt security officer who was with him echoed around the chamber.

The ministers welcomed Ver dala Ven by standing. Jishni did not. Her eyes were trained on the security officer. She recognized him.

Razim Kal Kalar did also, shouting, "Cleses!"

Shouts and a panicked shriek followed. Cobo held up his hand to encourage their calm. "This citizen wishes to be heard by the council."

"We do not listen to terrorists." Grav Tulkue retorted.

"An indisputable fact," Cleses replied smoothly, and with mocking humor, "the Alliance Council doesn't often listen to itself think, much less speak."

"Send for the guard!" Jishni ordered.

Haggins bowed and rushed out of the chamber.

Cobo did not countermand her orders. He obviously expected and accepted Cleses' arrest, as did Cleses, because the fugitive remained calm, composed.

Cobo stepped to the side, and presented Cleses to the council, saying, "I recognize Shelon al Entlay to the Alliance Council."

170

Having effectively entered the fugitive into the council session the members were now compelled to sit and listen to the Shodite terrorist.

Shelon did not stand on ceremony. His tone belligerent, he said, "You call me a terrorist, yet it is you who uses terror daily to keep the Shodites obedient to your will. I know of crimes each and every one of you have committed against the Shodites. None are perhaps as aggressive as the crimes the daka commits," and he gestured to Jishni in a most indecorous fashion, "but she has the Pliadors to back her pernicious will. The rest of you are passive-aggressors. You own slaves. You use them in your factories, your businesses, to clean your homes, warm your beds. To repay their service, you house them in quarters only a step up from Shod City's tenements, clothe them and feed them with your discards, and congratulate yourselves for your grand act of charity."

He held his hands out wide. "Wake up!" he shouted, "Your slaves do not see you as benefactors. To Janti-born Shodites, you are our oppressors. We endure your treatment, afraid of what may happen to us if we defy you. Ulon Miit discovered the cost of defiance in Jantideva. It cost him his life. And for those of you who have already forgotten his name, his high crime was in holding an opinion that differed from his slaver's. For this, he was put to death."

Grav Tulkue sneered. "As I recall, he wore a statement written in his clothing so profoundly disturbing that it moved his benefactor to an act of passion."

Cleses pierced Grave with his irate glare. "He died for an opinion that did not keep him from his work, did not harm another living being. He died for the pleasure of his slaver, at the hands of a man who is supposed to be fair and just, a judge of the Janti courts."

To the rest of the ministers, he continued, "Millions of Shodites live in the rodent infested slums that you own, where there is no heat, no air. Raw sewage runs freely in the alleys between your buildings, and into the Pril, into our only drinking water. You think Shodites smell bad? Perhaps you should bathe in the Pril as we do. You believe we have poor constitutions, therefore we are your inferiors? You live in filth, hungry and cold, your constitutions would fair no better than ours!"

The Watchers rushed in, accompanied by Bail. A collective sigh of relief chased through the council.

Shelon acknowledged them with a slight turn of his head, but their arrival did not silence him. Instead he threw his hand into the air and rose his voice majestically.

"By the laws of your dakas, set down after the Rathian conquest, you vowed to support and comfort oppressed peoples. I am here today to declare the Janti-born an oppressed people in need of your comfort and support! I am here today to request your succor! I am here today, to ask for political asylum and protection from our oppressors!"

The guards surrounded him, and grabbing his arms, they roughly shoved him to the ground, silencing him momentarily. The commander put his knee into Shelon's back and cuffed him on each ear, though it was obvious their prisoner wasn't going to fight.

Horrified by the wanton violence, Jishni stood and shouted, "You will not lay your hand on that man again." And as soon as she reached her feet, the blood rushed out of her head. Her sight dimmed and her knees buckled. She fell limply back into her chair.

Bail called out her name. Her sight resolved quickly, and his concerned face was the first she saw.

In the background Shelon wrestled the guard in order to prolong his time before the council. He shouted, "It will be easy or hard, you make the choice! You make the choice! Shodites will crush Jantideva! Shodites will crush Jantideva!" The guard lifted him by his arms and feet, and carried him out.

Bail caressed Jishni's cheek.

"She's fine." Cobo said, "She rose too quickly."

"How dare you bring that terrorist into our home!" Bail retorted, "You do not have the right to put my family in danger!"

Stoic, Cobo conceded to Bail's fury and left them. Whatever it was he'd come to accomplish, it was done.

The council was now considering the proper punishment for Cleses. Around the table, with anger in their voices, they condemned him to death.

It all happened too quickly, and Jishni lacked strength to fight their will. She grabbed Bail's hand to get his attention. The fury on his face, which matched the fury of the council members, melted into concern.

"Remember Ulon Miit," she whispered tiredly. "Cleses made a martyr out of him. If we kill Cleses, what will he become to the Shodites?"

Bail's eyes widened, and realization blossomed on his features. "Cleses. He is invisible. The invisible. And he roared in the Vass Chamber."

"What?"

"I should have told you. I should have made you listen." Without explaining himself, Bail stood and shouted for their attention, "Good Council!" His eyes were alight with something akin to horror. "We must not kill Cleses!"

Grav Tulkue stood, his face red with fury. "My nephew, Ito Iusco, under the command of Captain Eln Edise, was kidnapped and murdered by Cleses in Shod City! His body was found in the Pril just last night." With emotion, he said, "He'd been skinned alive and his feet and hands burned away!"

"Three of Cleses' hostages were murdered in that fashion!" Della Ston interjected in accord. "Can we afford to allow that bloodthirsty madman to live?"

"I want to see him impaled!"

The council member's voices rose in accord.

"What will it gain us if we kill him?" Bail shouted, "A moment of satisfaction, and then what? Does it bring back the men he murdered? No! That man has a larger following than we have men in the Janti army!"

"They are Shod!" Grav retorted. "Are we to be afraid of the Shod?"

The Zarian Minister stood and became the only voice to agree with Bail. "Cleses is leading an army against oppression! The Pliadors were murdering innocents, the Shodites reacted as you or I would if our families were threatened!"

"The Pliadors used just force." Grav countered, "We all know the Shod are natural born criminals! The Pliadors must be permitted to protect themselves at all costs!"

"I heard reports that there were children murdered."

"A child is as dangerous as an adult in some cases!"

"But you yourself said that we had no concern of the Shod!"

"Don't twist my meaning!"

"You contradict yourself!"

"Without him, the Shodites will lose their heart for freedom." Della Ston interjected, "They will settle into meek acceptance once again, and we will have peace with the Shod."

Razim Kal Kalar stood. "I cast my vote to have Cleses declared a dangerous citizen, and as such to suffer the strictest penalty, death."

Rancor seemed to be catching, like a virus. One after another, the council members sternly pronounced their decision to have Cleses put to death. Plat L'Otu was the only dissenting voice. The Zarians were evangelical in their belief that the Shodites deserved better treatment, and generally Plat irritated Jishni to no end with his constant petitions on behalf of the Shod. But for how beaten Bail looked in the face of so great an opposition, she was grateful that at least one of them took his side.

Once the vote was done, the decision made, Bail's rebuttal was tired and soft.

"We must show mercy."

"It is too late for mercy." Grav retorted.

Bail sat down next to Jishni, and looking deep into her eyes, he said, "We must talk in private. Now."

ͽͽͽͽͽͽͽͽͽ

In one of the High Room's theaters, they viewed Betnoni's final prophecy together. She remained silent as she listened to the historical document, recited by a figure dead over two and one half centuries. She knew it was her son described in the first verse, and went cold as Betnoni recited the second verse. Jishni was certain that the time Betnoni spoke of was the present time.

Once the recording was done, she asked, "Have you shown this to Yana?"

"I don't trust him."

"He is our confessor." She reminded tersely.

174

"I confess little to him, Jishni." Bail countered, "My father once told me that the Suma has not been worthy of trust since the Silence began, because they lost their way and became religious fanatics. Yana would have destroyed this message, because it came from Betnoni. It would have been lost to us."

"What is Cobo's advise concerning the prophecy?"

"To heed Betnoni. That was his only advice. He is no longer Ona's Ver dala Ven. He made that perfectly clear. He has his own destiny, and it is to take Taen to Dilgopoche."

Jishni was disappointed in Cobo for his lack of support, and her husband for his secrecy. "Why wait until now to show it to me?"

"I first viewed the message on the day you gave birth to the boys. And you were already doing as the prophecy said you should, letting Taen go. I thought it could wait. Maybe I really didn't think it was true. I can't imagine any force powerful enough to destroy the Alliance or Jantideva. We've been united ten thousand years."

"No, we haven't." she replied, "Shodalum and Dilgopoche once held seats on the council, now they do not. They are independent nations. As for our united Alliance, we routinely send the Pliadors into the wilder lands to put down rebellions. I can think of seven Alliance seats that would withdraw and become independent if we gave them that option. The foundation of our unity is an illusion, just as Betnoni predicted."

"If we heed Betnoni, we must release the Shodites from their bondage. Jishni, how can we accomplish it? It is impossible!"

"I know."

"Doing so would destroy our credibility before the Alliance and our own people."

"I know."

"We cannot free the Shodites."

"I know."

Bail paced the circle inside the theater screen. "But perhaps we can show mercy to Cleses."

"How? The Alliance has already pronounced his death warrant and the Crier will have it published by tonight!"

"I've an idea. A way to circumvent the will of the Alliance."

175

Concerned he was planning something illegal, she blurted, "Oh, please don't tell me, I mustn't know."

"No, don't worry. Don't think of it again. I will take care of everything."

లిలిలిలిలిలిలిలి

Taen leaned his back to the theater wall, and listened to the prophecy and his parent's conversation afterward. The timing of his entry into the High Room was a fortunate accident. He had wanted to view the recording made by Jishni's peace envoy of his future bride once more. She was a comely woman named Danati-Zuna, a daughter of the Dilgo Monarch, Rito-Sant. Her normal size and appearance relieved Taen of the fear he'd be wedded to a beast. He continued to grapple with living among her giant and disfigured kin, but at least the woman in his bed would be beautiful.

After his mother coldly informed him that his future would be traded away for peace with the Dilgos, he had thought about running away. His mother no longer loved him, that much he was certain, for she knew, all too well, how he'd tried to murder her and her unborn spawn. His life as a daka was done. He packed his belongings, and decided he'd run away to a paradise, maybe Cearse. But as he tried to leave the palace, the almighty Ver dala Ven blocked his passage to freedom. It was clear that he would heed his mother's will, whether he liked it or not.

He wished he knew how Cobo could move from room to room in the blink of an eye, sometimes seeming to be in two or more places at once. There were times he thought he felt Cobo's presence in the spires, and went from one to the next in search of him. Once the trail turned cold, he'd give up, give in, and turn his rage on Jem Jin.

Leaning on the wall, listening to his future mapped out by an ancestor he'd hardly studied, he closed his eyes and imagined finding the Masing Star. He decided that he had to be the one, the Chosen that would be possessed by the Star, and that their trip into Dilgopoche was to retrieve the Star. For the first time since Cobo's arrival, he felt kinship with Ver dala Ven.

"Is it true?" he whispered, knowing Cobo lurked nearby, guarding his every move, his every thought.

"You will live to see the Masing Star."

Taen grinned and closed his eyes. He was happy for the first time in too long. The Masing Star, the heart of infinite power, would make him better than a daka. He could reunify the Alliance under his fist. The Alliance would not die, but prosper.

His pleasant musings were interrupted by the sound of his parents leaving the theater. Bail's determined step, and Jishni's quiet footfall, diminished as they walked through the High Room. He hated them. Whether they were bending to the will of his destiny or not, they were garbage in his eyes for selling him into the wedded slavery of the Dilgos to save their own necks.

"Once I am the possessor of the Masing Star, they will be the first to die by my hand."

Cobo listened, watched from his hidden place. Taen could feel Cobo's eyes on him. There was no response to his threat.

"Are you still jealous? Do you want them dead, too? If we are to be allies, let us begin now, Father. Admit your hatred, your jealousy. You hate them, don't you?"

The presence abruptly disappeared.

Taen grinned. "Oh yes, I think you do."

Taen shoved off the wall, dropped the ariq chip containing Danati-Zuna's likeness on the floor and crushed it under his boot heel. He no longer had to be convinced. He would go to Dilgopoche of his own free will.

Finally, being Ver dala Ven had meaning.

Chapter 9

Gella lifted her skirts and climbed the steps to the Keep. The windowless fortress, built centuries ago to hold political prisoners, capped a steep wooded hill overlooking Tronos lake. Korba had filled her head with stories of torture and mistreatment of prisoners. She expected to see horrors. Dark, dank cells containing wretchedly treated human beings, trapped there at the daka's will.

The anteroom was brightly lit, the walls and floors white and clean. Beyond the front desk was a wide corridor.

A guard sat at his station, idly listening to clamoring music that seemed to come at them in all directions. He was youthful, and brawny, like Moxom.

Seeing Gella with her servant behind her, he quickly turned the music off and stood.

"Daka Gella, how my I serve you?"

"I must speak with Shelon."

The guard's brows hooked together. "Shelon? I don't remember processing a Shelon-"

"Cleses," she interjected, "may be the name he is using."

The guard shot her with a wary look. "Are you sure you want to see Cleses, Mistress? He is..." and he faltered.

Her heart started to pound. Cobo had warned her that Shelon would die if he remained in custody for long. She feared a fanatical Janti had already done the deed.

"By the sun and the sea, he had better not be dead." she fumed, her voice tight.

"No!" he replied quickly, "He is alive and well. Such is the pity. He is a course shod. I've never heard such a foul mouth on any man, not even the Tronos fishermen."

She fought the urge to fling a few oaths at the young man, simply for the shock value. "If he is alive, I want to see him."

"Daka Bail left strict instructions. No one is to see Cleses."

She glanced uncertainly at Korba. His head was down, but he was prepared. A lume hand weapon was beneath his tunic.

The guard also wore weapon on the sash of his uniform.

179

Trembling inside, she threw the man a suggestive look. "Perhaps we could work out a trade?" She stepped forward, placing a light hand on his chest. "Just between you and I, daka Bail need not be involved."

He flicked a glance down at her hand. As his gaze returned to her face, it was evident she'd titillated him with her touch, and her suggestion.

"A personal trade. Is that what you mean?"

She moved her hand over his wide chest in a light circle. "I see Cleses in person, and you can take me in any way you choose."

He smiled so that his teeth showed. They were uneven and dark yellow. "I've no authority to turn down the will of a daka." His hands went to her waist, and he moved forward, as if he intended to have her right there at the desk, in front of Korba.

She took a step back, and wagged a playful finger at him. "Cleses first."

He huffed a laugh. "As you wish, daka."

He held his arm out to escort her through the wide corridor. Noting that Korba intended to follow, he barked, "You, stay here."

Korba threw an anxious look at Gella, but did as he was told. She tried not to show her own anxiety as they left her protector behind.

"This way." the guard said.

Empty cells lined either side of a long corridor. They were sterile rooms the size of Shelon's flat in Shod City, and boasted amenities the flat did not have, a toilet, windows and circulated air.

"Janti felons live better than Shodites." Gella commented.

The guard laughed, as if she'd made a great joke.

"I'm sure Cleses is glad to be here!" he rejoined, still laughing.

The cells were left open, yet the prisoners were held inside by the danger of lume poisoning. Small holes in the floor at the threshold of each cell held a triggering device that once set off filled the cell with lume chemical. If a prisoner tried escaping, or crossing the threshold, he'd die instantly. Korba told her this in fear that Shelon might try to use the device to commit suicide.

The dakas must have worried about that, too. The guard released her arm and gestured into a cell. Shelon way lying on the floor, on his back. He was in body chains, shackled from head to toe, the chains attached to the wall.

"Can I go inside?"

Hearing her voice, Shelon stirred.

The guard put his hand on her back, and ran it from her shoulders to her waist. She held her ground, refusing herself the luxury of bolting away from his loathsome touch.

He hummed his satisfaction with her shape. "Yes, I think you can."

Shelon rolled over onto his side, his chains clanking.

He'd been beaten. His face was covered with purple lumps, his lips were split and bleeding, and his gray prison tunic was stained with blood.

Seeing her, he struggled to sit upright.

The guard looked upward, and said, "Open cell."

A high pitched tone announced that the cell door was deactivated. The guard ushered her inside with a flourish. She tentatively crossed the deadly barrier, and once across rushed to Shelon.

The one eye that wasn't swollen shut watched her face as she sunk to her knees before him. "Come to say goodbye to the damned?" he asked, his tone ever mocking.

"Shelon," she whispered, and tears sprang into her eyes. "What have they done?"

Shelon glanced toward the guard. "What they do best." he said, for the guard's benefit.

"I wish I'd come earlier." She said angrily.

"To prevent my beating?" He breathed a rueful sigh. "They beat me in the palace, and in the windrider, and again, here, in my cell. There was nothing you could do."

She forgot herself, and tenderly touched his discolored cheek. He winced, but did not pull away from her touch.

"You could have prevented all of this by staying in Shod City and allowing me to speak before the council for you as Korba suggested."

"You still can, Gella." he said passionately, "You, and the many leaders in the Shodite community, can speak for me, and you can use my life and death to move our people to action."

181

Disbelief raced through her. "You mean to die."

He didn't reply, but the answer was in his sober expression.

Anger set her jaw. "You want to die?"

"No one wants to die. But it is the only way I can best help my people."

"You are wrong." She tried to convey meaning in her gaze. "Your people need you alive. And I intend to give them what they need."

"What are you planning?" he whispered imperatively.

She hushed him, and backed away, unable to take her eyes off the hope, and naked fear, she saw in his face.

She turned, and found the guard directly behind her blocking her way out of the cell. He was grinning at her knowingly, and there was a cruel glint in his eyes.

"I hadn't realized," he said lowly, "that you and Cleses were friends. But I should have known. I heard on the Crier that you are a Shod sympathizer. Does this dirty Shod excite you, daka?"

She hadn't expected to encounter disrespect. "Please move out of my way." she asked, her voice shaking and betraying her sudden unease.

"We made a bargain." Lightly, he ran his hand from her collarbone to her breast.

At once, she felt cornered. This was not their plan. Korba was at the desk, waiting for them to return, his weapon ready. They were going to surprise the guard, take his weapon, knock him unconscious, and escape with Shelon. They had but a few minutes before the active patrol returned. A few minutes where there was but one guard to contend with if they moved swiftly and silently.

Korba wouldn't enter the corridor unless she screamed. If she screamed, the guards on the roof would come running.

She smiled uncertainly at him. "Couldn't we find some place private? There was an office near your post-"

"It's private here." he said, his tone low with purpose.

She glanced at Shelon. He was rigid, his bruised and swollen mouth pressed into a frown.

The guard's eyes were roaming her body. He laughed at her worried glance at Shelon. "Your friend Cleses won't bother us."

182

and he threw a hateful glare at Shelon. "Hmmm Cleses? You'd like a show, wouldn't you?"

He made his move, clumsily grabbing for her. She darted away, putting her back to a wall. She laughed anxiously, and said, "Please, there must be a better place."

"There is no better place, than here and now."

He lunged at her, roughly pinning her to the wall with his body. She struggled to push him away, ineffectually pleading with him to stop, but he was an immovable object with an unswerving purpose. His hands worked fast, yanking her many layers of gown to her hips, ripping at her underclothes. She lunged at him and bit him on the neck. His mouth cranked open, a silent scream. He was as aware as she of the guards up top, and of their limited time of privacy. He shoved her off him, and backhanded her to the floor. Stunned by the blow, she lay on her back, unable to move, or think. She heard Shelon's shouts echoing painfully in her head. Her eyes began to focus as the guard unbuttoned his uniform and released his aroused manhood, throwing back his sash, and his weapon, as he dropped his trousers.

He swooped onto her, and she was flooded with painful memories of past rapists. Trading her body to survive had been a prolonged rape, healed in part by Cobo's love and the years distancing her from her experiences, or so she thought. She instantly revisited her nightmarish existence, as his hands bit into her thighs to force her legs apart. She keened, tears wetting the sides of her face, but she did not fight him. She traded her body too easily to see Shelon. She'd not changed, not at all.

She covered her face with both arms so that she wouldn't have to look at her tormentor, though she couldn't block out the self-castigating thoughts afflicting her. The guard had entered her with one painful, dry thrust, his body heavy and cruel.

Shelon shouted one last time, a phrase in Janti she didn't understand. The guard leaped off her, his single entry being his only taste of her, and he growled, a noise that could have come from an animal. He staggered toward Shelon, his erection leading the way. She looked through her arms. Shelon had the sash, and the weapon in his hands. He fired. A blaze of blue light flew from the lume to the guard's chest. The sound that came after was louder than Gella expected. It boomed like thunder, and shook the floor.

The guard trembled, and a groan ripped from the back of his throat. He went down on his knees, then his stomach, his body racked with convulsions. His groan turned into a high pitched keen, and Gella realized he was screaming in utter agony.

"Get the keys." Shelon told Gella urgently.

His demand startled her, and made her move. She scrambled to her knees and crawled to the guard.

"His pocket," Shelon prodded her, "roll him over and get into his pocket."

She did as she was told. Hands shaking, she fished in the pocket of his trousers, trying not to glance toward the man's face a second time. There was no wound, no mark on his clothing, though his mouth was wide open in agony, his eyes white, and pink foam drained from his nose and ears.

"I found them." she said, her voice cracking. It mortified to weep openly. She chided herself for not being stronger, and tried to stem her tears. She survived worse in Strum, but that was a long time ago. She'd never humiliated herself in front of a man like Shelon.

"Come to me, Gella." he beckoned to her, his voice subdued.

She obeyed him, crawling to him, weeping all the way, and with shaking hands she undid the shackles on his wrists. His arms free, he took the keys away from her, his steady hands working twice as fast to unlock the rest of the irons on his body.

Once released from the shackles, he stood and helped her to her feet. Her legs and hips hurt, and she felt blood trickling freely down the inside of her legs, but when he asked her if she could walk, she said yes without thinking.

They left the cell running.

Korba rushed to them as they appeared in the corridor. Seeing Gella, tears staining her face and her dress torn, his eyes flashed with anger and he brandished the lume weapon he'd carefully hidden.

"Where is he?" Korba demanded.

"I already took care of him for you." Shelon stated flatly, "Now, where do we go from here?"

"We have a boat waiting."

"Security?"

"There is one more man on duty, and he is in the tower. He won't see us."

"Good,"

"As long as we take the cliff side to the water."

Shelon stared at Korba as if he were insane.

"It is the only way."

Shelon bowed and gestured to the door. "Do lead the way, Korba. I'd like to see how you intend to get us to the cliff side without our dying or being caught."

Outside, there were two ways off the platform leading out of the Keep. Down the steps, or down an incline that was too steep to walk. Korba said, "I've done this before, it's difficult, but not impossible."

Korba tucked the lume under his tunic, and jumped off the platform. He landed into the arms of a tree. Holding onto the trunk with one arm, he reached out for the limb of the neighboring tree. Switching from one tree to the other, he let his legs dangle over the steep drop and, hand over hand, he made his way to the next limb.

"Would you like me to go next, or do you want to follow that crazy young man?" Shelon asked, his irritation for Korba clear.

Gella watched Korba with a grimace on her face. She was strong enough to follow, but wouldn't be able to manage in the Janti gown she was wearing. She stripped the tattered gown off, and threw it on the platform.

In her torn undergarments, she felt safer to perform acrobatics. She took the leap, and landed in the armpit of the tree Korba first jumped into. Her bare foot found a sharp piece of bark, and she was forced to stifle a cry.

She followed Korba's course through the tree limbs, trying not to look down at the drop below. She concentrated on placing her hands exactly where he'd had his, not thinking about how some of the limbs bowed under her weight.

Shelon dropped into the first tree as soon as she'd moved on, and followed her with quick agility. He was easily thirty years older than Korba, yet he moved like he was Korba's contemporary.

185

As they entered the trees under the guard tower, Korba began to descend. Gella tried to follow. Above her, she heard voices. The guard speaking aloud to someone. The answering person's voice was muted, but also audible. The man in the tower had heard the commotion inside the Keep and summoned the patrol.

They were under a cover of wide, fan shaped leaves, and even if the guard took a notion to look over the railing, he wouldn't be able to see them. All he'd see was movement in the trees, and assume it was caused by an animal, or the wind.

Despite the rational voice urging her to go on, the sound of the guard's voice caused her to freeze.

Shelon paused behind her. "Gella," he whispered, "Are you in trouble?"

She lay her head back through her arms and looked at Shelon, and felt her will to live ebb. Shodalum and Calli were too distant. She'd never see Cobo again. Ona would not welcome her back, not after viewing the confession Korba helped her to record. She'd told them the truth, that she was a Shodite, no more and no less. Korba begged her not to make the confession, but she felt it was the only way to ensure that she did not leave Ona as a slaveholder.

She was her own worse enemy. She wouldn't survive in the strange new world unless she fell back on her only talent. Evident in how soon she felt the need to use it after leaving Ona, and Cobo. She imagined a future as a whore, alone for the rest of her life, and began to cry. She closed her eyes and steeled herself to release the limb, to end her suffering before it began.

"No, don't."

Shelon moved quickly. He grabbed the limb she was on with one hand, and took hold of her waist with his free arm as she loosened her grip. The limb bowed under their combined weight, threatening to drop them both.

"Don't let go." He ordered.

"Go on." She replied tremulously, "Hurry, before the limb breaks."

"You turn around and put your arms around me, or we will hang here until the limb cracks in half."

"Leave me!" she sobbed.

"I will die with you, if that is what you want."

186

A dozen retorts were on her tongue, but all she could say was, "I'm afraid."

"I won't leave you." He said, misunderstanding the source of her fear. "Turn around, and put your arms around my neck. I can hold you. Trust me."

Her urge to die was supplanted by a fear that he would die with her. It took all her strength, but she did as he instructed, she turned in his half embrace.

"Put your hands around me, Gella."

Above them, an alarm sounded. Their escape had been discovered.

"Right now."

She nodded stiffly. She released her right hand from the tree, and as she twined it around his back, clinging to his shoulder, her left hand lost its hold. She snatched at Shelon, embracing his full body, arms around his torso and legs around his legs. They swayed uncontrollably. She was sure they'd fall the moment she had burdened him, and she closed her eyes and waited for the end.

To her utter surprise, they started moving. Shelon picked through the intertwined limbs for the thickest, and he descended, following Korba, who was far ahead of them now. He grunted with each movement, a fact she didn't notice until he'd placed some distance between them and the guard tower.

"Shelon, you'd move easier without me."

"Almost there." he grunted.

She turned her head to see if what he was saying was true.

Korba waited for them on a ledge made from the dirt clotted over a twisted knot of tree roots, about twenty feet below. Beyond, and below where he stood, Gella saw water.

Shelon's descent was slow, but constant. As they neared the ledge, Korba held onto a root and reached out to pull them in.

Shelon released Gella as they found solid ground. As he did, she looked up. She could no longer see the Keep through the trees, but it was up there. Shelon had carried her much farther than she'd imagined, nearly the full distance down the side of the slope.

Darkly, she turned on Shelon, "You should have left me. We could have fallen, we could have both been killed."

Shelon's brows pricked up in astonishment at being attacked. "I didn't ask to be rescued. I was happy being a martyr, but you couldn't leave well enough alone."

"Does your life mean so little to you?"

"Does yours? What were you planning on doing up there, Gella? Erasing him from your mind forever?"

She shuddered, and hated him for seeing too cleanly through her motives.

"It was nothing!" she retorted, her voice too shrill, too revealing.

"Don't be so quick to leave us. You are stronger than that, and we both know it." His directness and meaningful gaze alight with fury and affection caused her to shiver once again, and she wrapped her arms protectively around her waist. Shelon, his closeness, and the way he looked at her, the way he knew what was in her mind, made her feel exposed, and less alone, all at once. He seemed to understand her, to care about her, and though she wanted him to care about her, she dismissed her hope as soon as she felt it, because her hopes were always futile.

"Please," Korba said intensely, "They are waiting, but they won't wait long."

Gella and Shelon looked downwards at the fishing boat below, and as one, they looked at the steep, dirt slope leading to the water.

"We'll slide part way. Just watch." Korba told them. He sat down on the edge of the roots, placed his feet in front of him, and pushed off with his arms. He plummeted downward at an incredible speed. Like a child, he threw his arms above his head and shouted a whoop.

Somewhere near the middle of the slope he became airborne. A moment later he plunged into the water. Next, they saw him rise to the surface. One of the fishermen tossed him part of a net, and once Korba grabbed hold, the boat hands hauled him aboard.

Shelon and Gella glanced at each other.

"Together?" he said, and he held out a hand to her.

She took his hand, and they did as Korba had, sitting on the edge of the roots, placing their feet before them, and as one they pushed themselves off and into the dirt. The slide that Korba had made look effortless was not easy, nor was it painless. Sticking out of the dirt were stray fingers of roots and rocks, ripping into Gella's skin as she flew over them. She resisted the urge to claw at the dirt as she felt herself leave the earth and become airborne. The drop into empty space made her stomach lurch into her chest.

She hit the water feet first. The water was freezing, and dashed the sensed out of her.

The next thing she knew, she and Shelon were clinging to a net and being pulled out of the water together. His arm was around her body.

Two sets of hands pulled her out of Shelon's arms and into the boat. First, she saw Korba, then Iada.

Korba swept her off her feet, and carried her below deck.

He took her into a narrow cabin, and lay her on a bunk that was built into the wall. As he covered her with blankets, she noticed that he'd begun to weep.

"I shouldn't have let you go in alone." he lamented, "I should have been there to protect you. I can never forgive myself for what happened to you."

She sat up, and found it was hard to sit after her rocky slide into the water. "Nothing happened to me that I can't handle." She winced, knowing that part of the pain had nothing to do with the slide. Disgusted with herself, she said, "Remember what I was before I came here. I'm not a delicate Janti doll. I'm a whore." The words were meant to soothe Korba, but they came out too hard.

He rejected her bitter assessment of herself. "You are my hero. Don't say otherwise."

"Oh Korba, I'm nothing." Suddenly she was very tired. She and Korba were nearly the same age, but at the moment she felt much older.

A call for Korba from topside brought his head up. "I should see what he wants." Looking down on Gella, his fondness mixed with uncertainty. "Unless you want me to stay?"

"Go, I'm fine." She lied.

He was reluctant to leave her, but a second, angrier shout from above moved his feet. He took the steps upward by twos in quick succession.

She pushed herself off the bunk, and stood with difficulty. Her foot throbbed where she had speared it on the tree. In fact, her whole body throbbed. She stripped off her muddy chemise, and tossed it aside, stretching her back.

A hand touched her, over her shoulder blades. A tactile memory of the guard stroking her back overwhelmed her senses. She bolted blindly from the touch, screaming, throwing herself across the room, knocking over a shelf of supplies, sending them crashing to the floor. She huddled in a corner, her eyes wide with fright.

Shelon stood in the doorway, wearing a shocked expression on his bruised face.

"You had seaweed on your back." He held up a thick cord of green, living material.

She could have wept, but instead laughed harshly at herself. She felt like an idiot, and she finally felt the injury to her pride, as if it bled like the gash on her foot.

Shelon came closer, but did not touch her. "Will you allow me to help you up?" he asked gently.

She consented, saying, "I'm not afraid of you."

"Good, good." He intoned, and he gave her a hand off the floor. Instead of lifting her, he put an arm around her waist and helped her hop to the bunk. In an offhanded way, he asked, "Those scars on your back-"

"What of them?" she retorted defensively.

"Was it Cobo who beat you?"

There was a trace of anger in his question. "No," she replied, wondering why he might be angry over scars so old.

Iada appeared at the door, drawing away Shelon's attention. Gella curled into a ball and watched the two.

Shelon said to Iada, "Tell me that your husband knows the danger he has placed himself in by aiding and abetting my escape."

"He does what I tell him to do." Iada answered flatly.

"I cannot say the same for you, Iada." he replied, "I told you to let me go."

"To die at the hands of the Janti?" Iada sneered, "I'd prefer to kill you myself."

Shelon laughed out loud, a laugh that was stifled by a grunt. He placed a hand over his nose and sucked in a sharp breath.

"I'll take care of that, right now." and Iada ordered, "Sit."

"Take care of Gella first." And to Gella, he said of his friend, "Iada is a wonderful doctor. I'd trust no one else with my body."

"Oh, get out of here," she said, waving off his purposefully lewd comment with a pleased smile.

Gella looked away from the two, unable to witness their happy banter without feeling very alone.

"Well, come on, let's see what's wrong with you."

Shelon was gone, and Iada stood by the bunk in his stead.

"I'm fine, I don't need to be nursed."

Iada looked at her dubiously. "Let me be the judge."

She let Iada look at her foot. "Nasty gash," she commented, "It will need a soak, and maybe a closure."

She got into a cupboard and pulled out a satchel, and from the satchel she took out a bottle of blue liquid.

As she placed Gella's foot in a pan of the cool, stinging liquid, the boat's engines revved to life, and the boat began to move.

Iada said, "Ul Zub must be done fishing this cove. Wouldn't matter if he'd kidnapped the daka, herself, he wouldn't move the boat until he caught fish."

"Ul Zub is your mate?"

"Mate? No. Legal husband, yes," she replied casually, "He is the one I was genetically matched with twenty years ago."

"Genetically?"

"Genes....they are the hereditary traits parents pass along to their child."

"I know what genes are," Gella retorted, "I may be a naive Shodite, but I am not ignorant of scientific facts."

"Ah, I didn't mean to insult your intelligence. Korba said that you know very little about Jantideva's toys." and she shrugged, disavowing Korba's assessment of Gella.

"In the tribe I came from, our Elders taught the sciences and history. Knowledge about technology was not against the law, in fact, knowledge was encouraged."

Iada hummed a response, and dabbed at her foot.

191

Curious about Iada's relationship with Ul Zub, she asked, "How do the Janti genetically match you to a mate?"

"The Testing Centers." she said with contempt. "After a Shodite child is born, they are tested and their genetic information is place in a library. Our strengths and weaknesses are assessed, and we are placed into an occupation based on the assessment. In adulthood, our test results are used as a breeding tool. Prospective mates are matched in order to produce the type of laborers the Janti think they may need in the future."

Gella's mouth fell open. "They breed you?"

"They try," Iada said, amusement twinkling in her eyes. "I didn't know Ul Zub before we were married. My benefactor had me matched when I was thirteen. I was working in a factory, and I was very good at what I did. One day, he comes to me and tells me I am married to a man who is also intelligent and has strong hands, good manual dexterity. He takes me to the docks in Bilk and introduces me to a fisherman. I hate fish. I hate boats. And I hated Ul Zub on sight. Luckily, he hated me too. He had a woman he loved, he didn't want anything to do with me."

She lifted Gella's foot out of the liquid and gently scrubbed the cut. Gella fought the urge to cringe. The stinging of Iada's insistent washing brought a prick of tears to her eyes.

Iada was saying, "The Janti geneticists gave us permission to have four children, which is unusual. Usually, a couple is only permitted two. One child to replace each parent, so our population is somewhat controlled. Ul Zub and I apparently had wonderful genes, to be permitted to have four." She grinned up at Gella. "Too bad we never had a child together. I lay with many other men, and I had four children in four years. I'm not even really sure who their fathers were, there were so many men. The Janti were pleased I was prolific, and after I'd had my allotment of children they had me sterilized. As my children grew, to the amazement of my benefactor, none of them showed skills in factory labor or for fishing."

Gella couldn't help but laugh at Iada's way of circumventing Janti control of her reproduction.

"Ul Zub didn't mind?"

Iada shrugged, "He had his children with other women. My four children made our benefactor happy, so Ul Zub was happy to claim them. We fulfilled our marital duties, as far as he is concerned."

Gella's amusement faded as quickly as it had burst out of her.

"There is no love in Jantideva for a Shodite?"

"Love," Iada huffed cynically. "The Janti, they fall in love and bind themselves in marriage in huge ceremonies in front of their families, and move into big houses, and have as many children as they want. But the freedom is wasted on them. They choose their mates, then they do what Shodites do. They have sex with strangers."

Gella watched Iada dry her foot, her mind on Shelon and the relationship he and Iada shared. She wondered if it was love, but couldn't bring herself to ask, for fear of sounding speculative, and offending Iada. She liked the tough, yet kind, woman. She didn't want to hurt her in any way.

"No, it isn't bleeding. A bandage may be enough, if you stay off your foot a few hours."

"I don't think I could get up if I wanted to. I feel like I was beaten with a stick." she commented, "Korba's escape plan seemed easier when he explained it to me at the palace, as my behind sat in a cushioned chair."

Iada harrumphed a laugh. She wrapped Gella's foot, her eyes on what she was doing, saying, "I'm grateful to you for going through with it. For rescuing Shelon. If it weren't for you, our cause would have lost an important leader."

Gella stared at the bunk above her as she affirmed, again, that the cause for Shodite freedom was the only reason she'd agreed to attempt Korba's foolhardy plan.

Once Iada was done with her foot, she said, "I put your satchel in the cub," and she patted the cupboard over Gella's head. "you should dress. Ul Zub and those two panting hounds he calls a crew will be through from time to time. No sense in inviting trouble. Eh?"

Iada left her alone.

She sat up with care, and reached into the cupboard for her things. She'd packed only what she'd brought from Shodalum, and had given it to Korba to pass on to Iada. In her satchel made from the velvet skins of a slank, she had desert wraps, a hooded robe, a set of work clothes, and her mother's red juji.

She chose the desert wraps. She'd almost lost them at the palace. The Shodite who'd gathered her belongings had assumed they were rags, until Gella set her straight.

The wraps were softer than they'd been in Shodalum. They were cleaned in the palace, and returned to her in a neat folded pile. They smelled floral, a scent that to a Janti's nostrils was pleasant.

She missed the arid scent of dust on the cloth. She wrapped herself in the leather, covering most of her body to the eyes of the Janti-born, as Iada had suggested, leaving only one arm and shoulder exposed. In the palace, Cobo told her that even the skin hugging wraps were unsightly to Janti eyes. If that were so among the Janti-born as well, the entire populace of Jantideva could hang themselves. She wouldn't don another gown for as long as she lived.

Once she was done dressing, she was sufficiently fatigued to lay down and stay down. She stared at the bunk above her as she waited for sleep, her mind resting on Cobo. Not so long ago she was laying next to him in Nari on a bed of soft soil. If she'd known then that they were destined to part, she would have never left Shodalum.

Or perhaps she would have. Shelon was a compelling enough reason to have come to Jantideva. Even on the run. Even without Cobo or a homeland.

With Shelon's face in her mind, she drifted off to sleep.

❧❧❧❧❧❧❧❧❧

The fishing boat headed away from the sunset, and the palace. There were other boats in the waters, some close. Ul Zub shouted a friendly hello to a passing fisherman.

A dozen military windriders flew overhead, their destination, the Keep. Troops sent in to help with the fugitive search. Shelon watched them, his good eye shaded with his hand. He imagined the surprise of the Janti. They obviously didn't expect a rescue

194

attempt, not on palace grounds. That was the only reason Shelon could think of for their light security.

That, and the Janti didn't believe that the Shodites were so bold.

They didn't reckon on Gella.

Shelon didn't reckon on Gella, either.

If it had been anyone but Gella, he would have refused to leave his cell. His suffering was nothing. He knew what would happen if he'd died at the hands of the Janti. Chaos. And from chaos, leaders would have sprung. Leaders like Yegi Hahn and Praj Xsang.

But then Gella showed up in his cell saying things about the Shodites needing him, and he weakened.

A pleasant breeze lifted off the waters and struck him in the face. He lifted his lips into a painful smile. He could be a martyr on another day.

Iada came up the cabin steps into the sunshine. She carried her medical bag. Iada was a medic in Shod City, and would have made a fine doctor with real training. Her mind was quick, and she had an uncanny understanding of the human body. But Shodites weren't born to be doctors.

"How is she?" Shelon asked.

"Better than you look," Iada quipped, "Now, if I may attend to you?" she pointed at Shelon, and gestured for him to sit on a crate by the hold.

"If you must." he replied, and he sat. His good eye was on Ul Zub's crew, and Korba, who had a congenial relationship with his brother-in-law. They were tossing barbs at each other, and Korba made Ul Zub laugh. Iada's husband was a good sort. A very obedient Shodite, but Shelon tried not to hold that against the man. He had the life he wanted, fishing on the Tronos. Why would he not be an obedient Shodite?

"You trust Ul Zub not to turn us in?" he asked lowly.

"He knows I would implicate him, and he'd find himself in an iron works, or worse."

Her assurance drove Shelon's concern away.

She dabbed at a cut on his head, and he tried not to flinch as it stung him, deeper and deeper.

"Did they do this to you before or after they had you in chains?"

"Some before, and more after."

"Of course. You couldn't fight back."

"I expected to be questioned," Shelon said sardonically, "I guess they weren't interested in finding our friend Edise. You've moved Edise, haven't you?"

"Oh yes."

He grunted his approbation.

She looked at Shelon's nose, and touched it.

He couldn't suppress a cry of pain.

"It isn't broken." she announced flatly, "It does look nasty."

"The Janti changed my looks for me, without surgery." he quipped.

She took a roll of bandage tape and gauze from her bag. Without missing a beat, and as if they were on the same subject, she said to Shelon, "Our people are rioting. They started in Bryn, lead by Praj and his militants."

Shelon whistled through his teeth his dismay. The Janti social elite lived in Bryn.

"They heard about your arrest, and assumed you'd be executed. Praj was heartbroken....no, more like incensed beyond reason." she explained, "Many of our people have died, but many Janti have died, too, including three of our prisoners."

"What?" he snapped, and he pushed her hands away from his nose to look at her.

"Vold and Vere swore they were overcome by a mob." she said, "Their three charges were hung by their ankles in the market place of track forty-seven and skinned alive. The bodies were left to rot in the sun for a day, and then thrown into the Pril. They were found by a Dachan ferry."

Shelon was filled with disgust, and anger. "I knew I shouldn't have trusted Vold and Vere on their own."

"Yes, I think they did do it, but I also think that no one minded seeing the Janti brutes hanging like meat in the trading center."

"I've no doubt that is true." he said evenly, "But it wasn't the plan. They are no good to us dead."

Iada pursed her lips. "Neither are you."

Hearing Iada echo Gella's words made Shelon shake his head. "How did I surround myself with sentimental revolutionaries?"

Iada suppressed a smile, and finished taping his nose.

"Are we putting in at Bilk?"

"In a hurry to return to a Janti jail cell?" she asked sarcastically, and she straightened and barked at Korba to bring her some ice.

"Then where are we going?"

"As far as Ul Zub is concerned we are laying low in Padra." she replied easily, "But, clever girl that I am, I've arranged for you to go to Moom from there."

He tried to laugh, but it hurt his nose too much. "Am I being exiled?"

"Gella's brother warned us to keep you out of Shod City for a few weeks." she replied, trying to keep her tone neutral. She appeared to be as uncomfortable with subject of Ver dala Ven as Shelon. "He said you'd do more good separating yourself from the violence taking place right now."

"And you took his word?" Shelon said irritably, "He is Janti! Think, Iada, of all the reasons he might have to keep me away from the action!"

"Shelon, the Shodites do not need you in order to kill Janti, they can do it on their own." Iada replied sharply. "They need you to help them see your vision of living as equals among the Janti. You cannot do that if you are dead on a Bryn street. Can You?"

"I'm not the leader to bring them peace," he retorted, "I am the destroyer. I leave peace and government to the man behind me."

"And who will rule in a community where bitterness is easy and anger, cheap? No, they need a strong leader they can respect and love, someone to show them the way to peace. That leader is you."

Shelon shook his head dubiously. "You over estimate me, Iada. But you're not the first." he said, thinking of Solien.

Korba brought the ice Iada wanted, wrapped in a cloth. Iada took it from her brother, and gently placed it on Shelon's head. "Hold this here, and don't move unless I say you can move."

Shelon obeyed her will, and sat still as she inspected his swollen eye. She gently forced the folds of flesh open, and he

197

could see her peering at him. His eye was undamaged. She washed it, daubed it with ointment, and put a patch over it.

At her direction, he took off his tattered shirt. Ul Zub and one of his men, Les, drifted toward them, watching Iada wash and dress the strap marks on his back. They'd each felt the strap at one time or another, and they commiserated with Shelon in silence.

"No broken ribs, a mild concussion, a few cuts and bruises." she reported matter-factly once she was done with him. "I've seen worse."

"Don't forget my crunched consha." he informed her blandly.

"You rest." she informed him, "And keep the ice on your head. It'll shrink the swelling." and her lips curled in a wry smile, "And if your consha really hurts, you can put the ice on that, too."

Left alone, he watched the sunset from where he sat, holding ice to his aching head. His thoughts rested on his friends and fellow Shodites who were pillaging the Center-plex. He would have loved to be a part of the melee, and to have personally set fire to the house of Tuv Grethian.

Perhaps he'd get a chance, soon.

Cheered by the thought, he decided he was happy to be alive.

Chapter 10

In a sunny cove of Ona's fountain garden, Lodan did his morning exercise. He chose a series of eight defensive poses, and alternately moved through them quickly, then very slowly. His concentration was in perfecting the transition between poses. The fluidity of his movements became a fluidity of mind, and soon he was aware of everything around him. The shifting breeze. The boredom of the Watchers on the daka's gallery above. Animals and bugs in the garden; and Taen, approaching from behind.

Heeding Ver dala Ven's warning, and his own instinctive internal alarms, he gracefully moved so that he was facing the young daka's approach.

"Good day, Master Kru Dok."

"Fine day, daka Taen," he replied, his fluid movements unceasing.

"May I watch?"

"If you participate." Lodan replied, "Move with me. Movement is the masterpiece of the universe."

"Pletoro." Taen said, showing he'd recognized the quote. He stood before Lodan, and attempted the graceful arm movements. His movements were like a beginner's, angular, choppy.

"You want something from me?" Lodan asked directly.

"As a matter of fact, yes," he said, his eyes on the movement of Lodan's feet now. "I need you to teach me how to purify my mind."

Lodan's movements did not falter, though he was taken aback by the request. His students rarely went past wanting to learn kai'gam. Taen's interest in Kai'mai thought was refreshing.

"To purify the mind," Lodan obliged, "one must first define, and understand, the concepts of purity, and that of the mind. Define purity, Taen."

"To be devoid of weakness, imparities, and pollutants." Taen replied readily. "Purity is something that is clean, like good water."

Lodan crossed his hands over his chest, once with the kai'gam in his left hand, then with a seamless movement he switched the hilt to his other hand and again crossed his chest, this time with the kai'gam held in his right hand. "Would you say that the water that runs through the fountains in the garden is pure?"

"I wouldn't drink it." Taen said with humor.

"And why?"

"It runs through algae coated pipes, fish live in it," and he grimaced, "No telling what kind of parasites thrive in that water."

"And that makes the water impure?"

"Absolutely undrinkable."

"But is it impure?"

Taen's movements stopped. "I don't understand."

Lodan prompted him to keep moving, "Arms up, like this, knees slightly bent." and once Taen started to move again, he replied to Taen's question. "You say the water is impure because you wouldn't want to drink it. But is it impure? Algae, and the plants fed by the fountains, fish and the birds and insects, even the microorganisms you'd prefer not to ingest, they thrive because of this water. To them, it is drinkable. It is pure."

"But they are just plants and animals."

"They are no more, and no less, than you."

Taen laughed sharply. "Are you saying that a bird is equal to a daka?"

"I knew an amusing priest once," Lodan replied easily, "who said that until mankind evolves beyond the daily need to defecate, he may not deem himself more important than the animals who crawl on the ground."

"An outrageous idea." Taen retorted, "The animals don't think, or feel, or believe in the Guardian Spirit of Creation. And I really don't understand what this has to do with purity of mind."

Lodan finished the last movements of his morning exercise, and stopped, took a deep breath, and gave thanks for another day, holding his blade with both hands to the sky, to the sun.

Returning his blade to its scabbard, he turned strolled across the grass toward the nearest fountain, expecting Taen to follow. A vast and ornately carved bird stood on a pillar, spitting water straight up in the air out of his long beak.

As Taen came up alongside him, Lodan gestured to the water below the bird, gurgling and moving in a thin layer over the rocky bed of the fountain. In the undulating mirror made by the water, he spoke to Taen's reflection.

"The water serves its purpose without thinking about purity. It provides a home for fish, and microorganisms and algae, feeds the plants and hydrates the animals, without questioning mind. It moves, or stands still, but it does not worry about moving or standing still. It exists, alone, but it is never truly alone."

Taen huffed a laugh. "Is this a riddle?"

Laboring to find patience for the boy, Lodan said, "Taen, a pure mind is like the water. It serves its purpose without question. It feeds others without asking for food. It moves when it must, and stands still when it must, and does not worry about where it will go next. It exists, alone, but not alone. Do you understand?"

He was shaking his head, frustration written deeply in his face.

"To have a pure mind, one must act without artifice, accept what is given and take only what one needs, to go where one is needed, or stand still if the time says to do so, to exist alone, but not alone."

"I understand existing alone." Taen said, his unusual eyes on the water. "I've always been alone."

Lodan nodded that he understood. In the days he'd spent as a guest of the daka, he'd learned much about Taen. Taen did not maintain deep, abiding relationships with anyone, not even family members. Outwardly, he wore a personality that was fabricated, and it was that very fabrication that cut him off from all others. Even as he had moved with Lodan in exercise in order to form some sort of connection, Lodan saw clearly the impenetrable walls surrounding Taen. He was utterly alone in a fortress of his own making. A man this alone did not empathize, or sympathize with his fellow man, because for him, there is no one but Taen.

"There is a difference between feeling alone," Lodan said, "and being alone. Being able to exist alone means being able to live in your body, your mind, without craving constant company, or entertainment, without seeking out food or sex or the clock or a hero to tell you how to feel, how to be or what you are."

Taen's false mask slipped, and as he looked into Lodan's eyes, his misery was plain on his face.

"How do you do that?" he whispered.

Lodan thought for a minute, then smiled wanly. "It is the easiest, and the hardest, state of consciousness to accomplish. The first step is to give up controlling your life."

"Give up?"

"Yes. Accept all that life has to give you, and enjoy each moment as you are in it. The second step is to never think about the future. The future is a lie."

"How do you mean?"

"What are your plans for this afternoon?"

Taen faltered reflectively, as if he were searching for an answer to a math or geography question.

"I'm going riding." he offered finally.

Lodan nodded. "And what if, after breakfast, you trip and fall down the steps and break your neck and die? What will you be doing this afternoon?"

Taen's brows shot up.

"Ah," Lodan said, expressing Taen's realization for him, "So your plans for your future was a lie, yes?"

"But only if I die."

"What if you find you have a more pressing matter to attend?" Lodan offered, "Or you simply change your mind. All the thinking, and planning that went into your future was wasted."

"Then I must never think about the future?" he asked incredulously.

"Does the water? As it flows, does it think 'Oh, look, there is a rock ahead, I need to prepare to flow over top of it.' No, when the time comes it merely exerts the proper amount of effort to get itself over the rock."

"I don't understand how I could live like that."

Lodan placed his hands on Taen's shoulders. "If you'd like to try, there is a meditation I can suggest. Sit here, by the water and watch it flow. Imagine you are the water. Become like the water."

"For how long?"

"That can only be answered by you."

He left Taen sitting by the fountain, staring at the water. Hours later, as he was on his way out for a walk, Taen still sat by the fountain, waiting for enlightenment.

Purity of mind is like water.

Taen spent the entire day watching the water. Contemplating how it streamed from the bird beak and flowed over craggy rock. The water was relentless. Encountering a nook in the rock it gathered its strength to plunge over the blockage. Encountering a barrier, a large rock that stuck out further than the rest, it made a path around, cutting the earth deep with its ceaseless movement.

That evening, his mind was still moving with the flowing waters as he sat with his parents in the sitting room. His father offered him brandy. His father had never offered him brandy before. Bail had never treated him as a man before, but here, and now, he was being treated as a man. Water flowing rapidly through a frightening gorge. They broke the news to him cautiously, though he already knew he'd been given away to the Dilgos. His mother watched him, her expression well guarded, but distrust in her thoughts. There was talk of the journey they would take in the morning, of his impending marriage, of his need to sit with Aton and be briefed on what they knew of Dilgo customs.

Odd, he did not become enraged. He saw his family as if they were, a dam of rocks, and he was the water accumulating strength. Eventually he would cut a path through them, or drown them, and continue onward to his destiny.

Jem Jin arrived to his room that night at the normal time, to turn down his bed. She came, her head down, frightened as a mouse.

Taen was fully dressed tonight. He had no interest sexual pleasures as he beckoned her and made her stand before him. With a gentle hand, he touched her flowing hair. Flowing, like a river.

The power of the river surrounded them. They were no longer in his bedroom, but in a desert sliced by Taen's river. Jem Jin gasped as she felt the water flowing over the rock they were standing on, ice cold water flowing over her bare feet, and saw the unending wasteland around them. Stunned, her mouth slightly parted in awe, she found Taen's eyes.

With the crashing water all around them, Taen felt impervious to Ver dala Ven. He did not understand why, he only knew that

Ver dala Ven would not be able to listen in on him as long as he stood in the river.

"What is purity of mind?"

She trembled harder. She did not have the courage to answer.

"It is a mind that is ceaseless, unbound to thought." he told her. "Why do you have a pure mind, Jem Jin? Is it because all you think about is little girl things? Or do you think about womanly things, now that I've made you a woman?"

Still, no answer. Just the wide-eyed look of a dumb animal, frozen in the face of danger.

"No," he said, seeing into her mind as clearly as looking though pure water. "You think about babies. Dolls, but living dolls. You love my little brothers, Jem Jin? You love babies, but you also resent my little brothers. I feel it in your gut. You love to hold them, but wish in your gut they weren't dakas." He stroked her hair again, cocking his head in a paternal way, looking at her lovingly, because he did love his little pet, his little thing, Jem Jin. "You worry they will grow up and be like me. And they may."

She shook her head, fearful to speak, but fearful, too, to stay silent as he made his accusations.

"Don't lie," he whispered, "because I can see the truth. I am the water, Jem Jin. I am the river that flows through your mind. My river flows ceaselessly, and cuts its own path."

She cringed, and grabbed hold of her head. The pain was cutting her, deeper. Cutting a path for his river.

"What is it, Jem Jin?" he asked innocently.

She whimpered.

"You hate the new dakas, don't you Jem Jin?"

"No," she denied.

He poured more of his river into her mind, flooding her, and she cried out and fell on her knees before him.

He touched the top of her head. "I can make the pain go away, Jem Jin. Do you want the pain to go away?"

She nodded fervently, sobbing, pressing her hands hard to the sides of her head.

He knelt down beside her, and put his cheek close to hers. She smelled sweet, of flower petals she'd rubbed on her neck. "I will release you from the pain if you admit how you feel about the new dakas. Admit it aloud, Jem Jin."

She groaned her agony, and tried to hold back the words, but couldn't. "Hate them,"

"You hate the babies?"

Her sobs became keening.

"How can you hate babies, Jem Jin?"

She could no longer take the pain. She crumpled into a ball, and began twitching uncontrollably.

He brushed the hair away from her face, exposing an ear. "Listen to me, Jem Jin. Can you hear me?"

She was unresponsive, and her eyes were closed to slits. She was listening, however, and understood him.

He said, "I want you to do something for me. I want you to kill Archer and Janus."

She began to convulse. Despite her pain, she was fighting the proposal.

"You hate them." he replied, made incredulous by her resistance.

He saw her conscience as if it were an entity outside her, moralizing cretin that it was, making her despise the thought of murder.

"Would you prefer to die?"

Her convulsions stilled as she considered her own mortality. She struggled between her fear of dying, and her fear of committing a horrible act in the sight of the Guardian.

"Ah, Jem Jin. Do you really believe the Suma priests?" he asked dubiously, "They are liars, all of them. They know there is no guardian. They preach about a Guardian that watches over us, rewarding the good and punishing the evil, to keep you shod from misbehaving. In truth there is nothing for you Shod, no gods and no hope. We dakas took it all away."

Her morals were too deeply entrenched to be uprooted by ridicule. She wouldn't do this on her own will.

"Yes, I see Jem Jin. You are pure. Like the river. But I am stronger. You can't fight me, nor can you defy me. I am Ver dala Ven. Delicious, isn't it? Riar Sed laid the foundation, and Lodan filled it in, doing the job my coward of a father was meant to do. I am Ver dala Ven. Feel me in your mind. Know that if you defy my will, you will feel excruciating pain. Worse pain than you are feeling now. Do you believe that is possible?"

She keened a response. She was pleading. Pleading with him, with her eyes and her throaty noises, and her mind, begging him to release her.

"My mother intends to force me to marry." he said with slow deliberation, "I want her to suffer as I will. On the day of my wedding, the moment I take my bride, you will enter into the nursery, and you will smother Janus and Archer."

"No," she shouted miserably, and she wept.

"Oh, yes, you will." he said, sure of himself. He saw her fear of the pain. The terrible pain. She wished he'd taken her again rather than give her this terrible pain.

"No, my love," he said softly, and with a sardonic smirk on his face, "I am betrothed. I must be true to my bride. But, I am flattered by your desire."

He reached into her mind, and found a place she didn't often go. "You'll forget we ever spoke, until the day I take my bride. When you hear the news, you will smother Archer and Janus. If you do not do my will, you will be in constant pain for as long as you live. You understand?"

"I understand." she whispered.

"And because I am feeling benevolent, I want you to forget last night. You are a virgin again, Jem Jin."

He removed the pain. It flowed out of her, like a river, releasing her. The river, the desert, faded to the walls of Ona. She lay limp on his bedroom floor, gasping, exhausted in the aftermath of agony.

Her eyelashes fluttered, as the memory of the abuse she suffered was chased away by his will. Melancholy lines that had appeared on her face since the night before disappeared.

She looked up at Taen, then noticed herself, laying supine on the floor with a start.

"You went to turn down my bed, and fainted." he explained.

"Oh," she huffed, and twisted around to push herself up on her knees.

Taen offered a gentlemanly arm. "Would you like me to call for a physician?"

"No...." she hurried to his bed and turned it down.

"Are you certain?" he insisted.

"Yes, daka Taen." she said obediently. She stood by his bed, her head down, waiting to be dismissed.

This was where they usually began their evening.

He dismissed her, saying to her, "I hope you are feeling better."

Her departure was his river, cutting a path through Ona.

જ્હ-જ્હ-જ્હ-જ્હ-જ્હ

Trev sauntered into the office of the Keep, sat down before the commander's desk and propped his feet up. Bail glanced across the desk at Trev, then returned to the viewing screen to watch yet another security disc depicting Cleses's escape.

This particular disc was taken from the camera in Cleses's cell. It showed the officer clearly dying at the hands of Cleses, but only after he'd assaulted Gella.

Bail was racked with anger and guilt. He'd let the escape happen, and now Edan's wife and children were without him. If Edan Julestria hadn't been such a fool to rape Gella in front of Cleses, perhaps Cleses would have shown mercy.

A fat lot of good it did to set him free. Edan was dead, his wife a widow, Cleses at large, and still the Shodites were tearing apart the Center-plex. Houses, businesses, government offices were set on fire. The building that housed the Janti Council of Shodite Affairs had been burned to the ground. The Pliadors had been dispatched to put an end to the insurrection, at any cost. Many Shodites were being killed, and yet the riot raged on. The Shodites had tasted blood and they wanted more.

Trev's eyes were on the screen, watching the rape with detached interest. "So Edan is dead. At least he died happy."

Bail lifted his head. "She is Cobo's Chosen Sister, a daka of Jantideva." he chastened, "If that were Jishni, I would have killed him myself."

207

Trev rolled his eyes as if it didn't make a difference to him who she was, because she wasn't really a Janti, but a Shodite and a traitor. She deserved to get stuck.

Many would feel as Trev felt when they discovered her native land was Shodalum. Even Bail fought those feelings, though he'd admired Gella and had wanted Cleses to escape.

He'd tried to heed Betnoni's warning, and show mercy. Instead of easing her dire predictions, the Guardian slapped Jantideva in the face by giving the Shodites unbounded courage to tear their benefactor's homes apart. Worse yet was Gella's confession that she was a Shodite, after having been declared a daka. Absolute heresy.

Bail lifted the disc from the viewing screen.

"I should have released Cleses in front of Crier cameras, in a huge ceremony in his honor." Bail said sardonically, "Given him a medal of valor and kissed his bare ass for having the audacity to enter my home to spout his political garbage."

Trev chuckled.

He placed the discs with the stack he intended to take. No one would see Edan compromise his post for the promise of sex. No one would see his attempted rape. No one would see Cleses kill him.

It was an accident. Edan Julestria's weapon had discharged accidentally. It happened sometimes.

Bail set his head into his hand and rubbed his forehead.

"I have some ale packed in the cargo hold." Trev said, and grinned, "It's good for what 'ales' you."

"Keep it for yourself." Bail told him curtly, and he stood. "I'm not in the mood to get drunk."

Trev followed him out of the office, muttering something about always being in the mood for a good drunk.

ৡৡৡৡৡৡৡৡৡ

Cobo looked Janus over, a wistful expression settling on his face.

"You are thinking about Taen, aren't you?" Jishni asked softly, to avoid disturbing her suckling child.

208

Cobo nodded mutely. He'd been reluctant to see the new dakas, and now she understood why. He pined for his son, what he remembered of his son, the tiny infant he'd left behind.

Tears again. She tried mightily to control herself, tired of feeling emotional tears flow down her cheeks. Damn hormones. Carefully modulating her tone, she said, "They look the way Taen looked when he was born. Black hair, and fat cheeks, and skinny little legs and arms."

"Yes." he whispered.

"Taen was quiet." she remembered, "He was a good baby. Full of smiles, never a tantrum."

"I wish I'd known him before-" and he faltered. He didn't have to finish his thought. He was wishing he'd known Taen as an unsullied being, a sweet child.

"I do too." she replied earnestly.

He straightened and gazed at her. Here, alone with her, in this setting filled with bittersweet memories, he did not hide himself from her. His love was plain on his face, in the depth of his gold eyes, and she felt it touch her, envelope her.

Archer disengaged from her breast with a loud smack, and she was compelled to look away from the love of her life, to her new child. Archer slept, his tiny face serene. She smiled, feeling happiness overwhelm her. Hormones again, she tried to tell herself, but she knew it was the combination of holding her infant, and having Cobo near. She wished this moment could last forever.

Cobo knelt on one knee by her chair, and placed his hand on Archer's small head. The warmth of his fingers radiating to her bosom made her heart race.

He answered her unspoken desire, and moved his hand to caress her breast. Her skin came alive.

"Cobo," she whispered breathlessly, "I'm hardly up to a seduction."

He moved to pull his hand away, and she quickly covered his hand with hers to hold him. She stared earnestly into his face. "Not yet."

His ache for her plain in his voice, he whispered. "I'll always be yours."

Janus made a noise from the warming bed. Soon he'd be crying for his dinner, and her precious moment with Cobo would be over. Holding his hand to her breast, she wondered what might have happened between them had he returned home a year earlier. Before her pregnancy, she'd pined for him so deeply that she felt she might have died of a broken heart if she'd not become pregnant.

He clearly struggled with his desires. He stood, turning the hand he had on her breast into her hand, and he held it tightly as he leaned forward to kiss her on the forehead. As his lips touched her face, she felt him change his mind. His lips drifted to her mouth.

She greedily accepted his kiss, reaching for him, clinging awkwardly to him with her free hand while still mindful that she held Archer.

He ended it too soon, pulling away from her eager lips, and away from her grasping hand.

"Bail has returned from the Keep." he said lowly. He stepped away from her, returning to the warming bed. "He's on his way to see you, he'll be here any minute."

She withdrew her arm, and looked down at her baby.

"The guilt will never change, will it?" Cobo observed bitterly.

"It's difficult to set aside my guilt, I desire you as I hold Bail's son."

Cobo quickly turned away.

Bail entered the nursery cautiously, quietly, to prevent waking the babies, or Jishni if she happened to be sleeping.

Seeing Cobo standing over the warming bed, he lost all pretense of caution.

"What are you doing here this late?" he asked of Cobo.

"I invited Cobo to meet his nephews." Jishni replied, covering her breast. She felt a flush of shame warm her cheeks. She gazed down at Archer, afraid her face revealed adulterous deception.

"Just as well that you're here." Bail said to Cobo, "Gella did just what you said she would. She helped Cleses escape, but at the expense of one of my officers."

"What did the man do to Gella?" Cobo asked, but his tone insinuated that he knew.

Jishni glanced at Bail. "What happened to Gella?"

210

Bail ignored her. To Cobo, he demanded, "Can't you soothe the savage Shodites? End their uprising and stop the killing!"

"No, I can't."

"And why not?" Bail demanded hotly. "Imagine the lives you'd save! The property, and the goods-"

Janus reacted to his father's raised voice with a cry.

Jishni frowned at her husband, and stood to place Archer in the warming bed and pick up Janus.

"Can you guarantee," Cobo interjected, "that not one Janti will have his Shodite slave put to death for their part in the riots?"

"Is it better that the Janti army must kill every Shodite on the street in order to protect the public?"

"If you decree that no benefactor is free to murder a Shodite, I will end the riots."

Bail's voice shot up with his fury, "I am not in the mood to bargain with you, Cobo!"

Both babies began to cry.

"I am not bargaining with you." Cobo replied tersely, "I am exerting my prerogative as Ver dala Ven. Decree that no benefactor is free to murder a Shodite, or let the Center-plex be torn asunder. It is your choice."

Jishni hushed her sons, and she warily glanced from brother to brother. Their eyes were locked, each staring furiously at the other.

"You want me," Bail fumed, "to tell my people that I believe a Shodite's life is of equal value to a Janti life?"

Cobo didn't reply, or avert his stony stare.

Bail said, "It will never be accepted. Even if I passed such a law, no Janti lawman would enforce it! It would be words, useless words!"

"It is a start." Cobo replied, and he brushed by Bail to get to the door.

Bail stopped him, planting his hands on Cobo's shoulders. "You are Ver dala Ven, you are to serve the dakas."

Cobo stared coldly into Bail's eyes. "Ver dala Ven is no longer yours to command, daka Bail of Jantideva. You've lost the Guardian's gift as a punishment for irreconcilable sins against people entrusted in your care. I've helped you because you are my

211

brother, but I will not turn my back on Betnoni's chosen people, not even for you."

Bail pushed him away.

Jishni's heart lurched. Bail's fury fisted his hands, and she thought he'd succumb to an urge to strike Cobo.

"Not in the nursery!" she shouted. Little Janus flinched in her arms, and wailed pitifully.

Bail stiffened at Jishni's cry.

Tautly, he said, "I will not protect the Shodites from Janti reprisals. They do not deserve protection after what they have done to us."

"It is the easy path, Bail."

"Don't use that tone with me, little brother. You won't help us, but you will judge us as if you are still Ver dala Ven! Go into Bryn and use that tone to a family who lost their ancestral home to the riots!" To Jishni, he said, "We showed our mercy and Betnoni is punishing us still."

He stalked to the screen on the wall, slapped his hand on its face and said, "Daka Bail, Crier, current events, Bryn."

The Crier came on, and a soft-spoken man described a scene playing out on the screen, of protesters lighting the rails of public transports on fire.

Jishni sat back down and watched the mayhem unfold.

"This is happening because Cleses escaped! The Shod are throwing a victory party, and we are the main entrée!"

Without word, Cobo left the room. Bail pivoted in time to see the door shut. With purpose and fury, he went after his brother.

Jishni shook all over. The anger reverberated off the walls and saturated her mood. Her sons cried with impassioned pleas for comfort, and she gently bounced Janus in her arms as she watched the Crier report on the devastation in Bryn.

ৡৡৡৡৡৡৡৡৡ

In the temple, Surna's place for the morning prayers was at the altar of the private prayer chamber, in an enclosure that bore the shape of the Masing Star. It was made from a pliable, form fitting material that clung to her body. Her legs fit into two of the Star's

212

ten beams, her body in the center, and her arms in two beams extending from her side. The porous material used to make the star allowed her to breathe, but not to see more than moving shapes and light. At the seat of the star, covering her most private place, was the portal. As a priest came in to make his morning devotions, if he felt seized by the spirit to make a passionate plea for the Star's return, he'd open the portal to give him access to the Guardian's welcoming delights. In this way, neither he, nor the Suma mistress, could see one another.

When he was done, he'd close the portal, and leave Surna waiting for the next priest.

There were rules in this practice, and Surna had to learn all of them. While in the temple, during the morning devotions, the priests were not permitted to touch her flesh with anything but their manhood. To do so implied that the priest was more interested in having a woman than prayer. They were not permitted to speak to her, nor was she permitted to speak to the priests. If any of the priests forgot themselves, she was instructed to immediately inform the Chancellor.

She believed that most of the priests approached her with devotion to the Guardian in their hearts. Their prayers were passionate as they copulated, and she was a forgotten part of an altar.

There were a few however who used their time with her as an outlet for pleasure. She could tell the difference between a devout priest and a priest who used her as his sexual toilet. It was subtle, in the way they hurried their prayers, or said none at all, feigning silent prayers, or how they pressed hard against the star to feel the form of another being under the protective cover. She disliked serving those unchaste priests, but since they did not speak to her or act in a shocking way, she could do little but endure their daily visitations.

In the fifteen years she was a Suma Mistress, only two priests had actually spoken to her, calling her by name, and asking that she remove the star. Both times she did as they asked, pressing the control with the back of her head to release her from the star, just to see what they might do. She believed they might turn away from her ugliness, but no. Her ugliness did not matter. One wanted her to climb back into the star, face first, and present her fanny to him for his use. The other desired her hairless body and her flat chest, and he wanted her to call him daddy like a little girl.

In both instances, she refused them and went straight to the Chancellor. Both priests were expelled from their vocation.

It had been several years since her last encounter with a priest who treated her like a woman, however objectified she was in the star. She'd grown accustomed to being the Guardian's surrogate, her resentment mellowing with age. And then one morning, about a year ago, she met the sniffer.

The first time it happened, he shocked her so that she'd lost count of the priests she had serviced, and couldn't tell for certain which one it had been in order to go to the Chancellor and report him. The priest made his devotions, and opened the portal, and then put his face right into her private place! He smelled her, and smelled her, and smelled her, and after he'd had enough of her scent, he climbed onto the Star and did his duty.

Several days went by and it didn't happen again, though the incident made Surna look at the priests with more care than usual. Was that old one the sniffer? That young one? That handsome one? That ugly one? The question beleaguered her mind.

The second time it happened, she was no less shocked, for this time the sniffer didn't just sniff. He had to taste, and he did so with the relish of one licking honey off a plate. She had again forgotten how many priests she'd serviced that morning, because never in her life had she experienced such primal pleasure. Once the priest heard her moaning with delight, he climbed on the star to finish his devotions, but there was nothing mundane about the feeling of him inside her on this morning. Prepared by him, the devotion became enthralling for her, and she moved with him, sighing and moaning.

The third time, the fourth time....she started forgetting the order of her priests on purpose. She decided that her sniffer had a different kind of devotional style, and she didn't mind his style, not in the least.

One morning, while in the throes of passion with her sniffer, she had a vision. She saw the ocean, and heard a voice tell her that Ver dala Ven was returning. *"When he calls you, go to him. Do not look back, and do not be afraid."*

She heard through Durym later that very day that Ver dala Ven had indeed returned.

This morning, before she climbed into the star, the Chancellor came to her, and told her that Ver dala Ven had requested her to be his attendant in Dilgopoche.

"I give you the choice, Surna." the Chancellor had said, though he knew she wasn't really happy in the temple. Her choice was easy.

She waited for her sniffer. He would be the only one she missed in this miserable temple. He came to her, and as usual he pleasured her before his prayers were made. He took her to the edge of ecstasy, pulling back at the critical moment, and he always seemed to know when that moment had come, and began his devotional as she squirmed, wanting him. Sliding his ready hardness inside her prepared place, his form, a shadow bearing down on her, lay on top of the star. His face lay near hers, and she imagined he could feel her panting breath through the star's material. They moved together, he grunting and sighing, she sighing and crying out and resisting the star's constraint to be closer to him, feel him deeper inside her. They found their climax together, and he moved his face as if he wanted to kiss her, but finding the star between him, he groaned. Groaned, and she groaned, wishing she could see him, touch his face, feel his lips on hers, taste his mouth like a lover.

He lay on her for a long time, their bodies still one, resting inside her, recovering from passion. Her heart was still pounding. Moved by her pleasure, and more, she broke the rule of silence.

She said, "I am leaving the temple today." She got his attention, and heard his breath draw in sharply. He listened. Silent.

"I will never return." she said softly, "But I wanted to tell you that....I love you."

He laid with her for a long time, his hands caressing the outline of her face under the Star's form. She felt tears come to her own eyes, but they wouldn't shed. She wanted to know who he was, but knew by his silence that he preferred not to reveal himself to her. He was a Suma priest, and she his mistress. They could have nothing more together.

The whole body of priests seem to come to her that morning. The Chancellor obviously spread the word that Surna would no longer be with them, and they felt it was their duty to use her, at least one more time. She endured them, her mind reaching for that moment when she'd be free.

As she left the star, she felt giddy. She had yearned for escape so long that even the idea of living in Dilgopoche sounded wonderful.

഍ഌ഍ഌ഍ഌ഍ഌ഍

Daka Jishni spoke sweetly to Janus, and wept, telling him she'd be home soon. Surrounded by nurses and nannies, and still she worried about his well being. She promised him that she didn't want to part from him this soon after he'd come into the world.

Jem Jin stood by her, silently scoffing the daka's sentiment. Shodite mothers had their babies taken from them a day after giving birth, so they could be sent to testing centers. If the child returned from the testing centers, it was given to their benefactor, and often raised by someone other than the woman who'd given birth.

Jem Jin raised her younger brother so their benefactor could have free access to their mother. She was his concubine, and though she lived a more lavish lifestyle than the average Shodite, everything of value to her was taken from her. Her children, for instance. Jem Jin was thirteen when her benefactor traded her for three grown, and comely, women. He gained three more concubines, and his favorite concubine lost her eldest daughter.

The state permitted Jem Jin to see her mother once a year. The contact was hardly enough mothering for any child.

But she wasn't a child anymore. She didn't feel like a child anymore. She felt old, and broken, and weary.

The daka handed the baby to her, and another nanny came forward, bearing Archer. Jem Jin walked Janus to his warming bed. Before putting him down, she gazed into his face. The sight of him caused her terrible anxiety.

She took extra care in laying the tiny baby down, and she was reminded of his vulnerability. His scrawny neck could break like a stick. With a sharp pinch to his throat.....

Jem Jin moved away from the baby bed. She trembled, but no one noticed. They all watched Jishni weep over Archer, their faces filled with compassion.

୶୶୶୶ଡ଼ଡ଼ଡ଼ଡ଼ଡ଼

"What will we find in Dilgopoche?" Surna asked once they were on their way.

Voktu piped in, a sneering smile on his face. "Freaks."

"A wasteland." Taen added, and a strange calm smile bent his lips.

To Surna, Cobo said, "You'll find a new life there."

She smiled at the prospect.

"But what kind of life?" Durym muttered to his window.

Surna shifted in her seat to put her back to Durym, brushing off irritation. He'd come along to preside over the uniting of daka Taen and Danati-Zuna, a great honor that no ambitious young priest would turn down, regardless of the circumstances. He wasn't staying, however, and she was no longer a Mistress he could boss around. She no longer had to put up with his childish petulance or his annoying anecdotes. She no longer had to suffer his presence at all, and she made that very clear by the way she put her back to him.

"I am so excited." She confided in Cobo.

"You were always adventurous." He replied fondly.

"Thank you." She whispered, and she grinned. Her eyes twinkled, and he could almost see her as she was in youth. The Suma devastated her appearance, but hadn't managed to devastate her spirit. She reminded him potently of another strong woman he loved dearly.

His eyes went to the windows across the aisle, and scanned Tronos as they crossed over. At once, he felt her, though he could not see the boat with his physical eyes. She was well. In good company.

He would miss her.

217

Chapter 11

The chilly morning breeze forced Gella to wear two layers of wraps, along with Janti work trousers and tunic to keep warm, but the sight of sunrise on the sea was worth the cold. Gella marveled at the endless expanse of blue-green water, for as far as her eyes could see, and the blue sky that touched the horizon, like a huge upturned bowl. In Calli, as she fished or swam in the Gryvly, she often wondered what it might be like to be in the middle of the water. The Tronos wasn't as large as the Gryvly, but it was big enough for her imagination.

Ul Zub and his crew were casting their fishing nets as she came up on deck. Without prompting, she fell into helping them as they brought the nets in. Her foot was sore, and her back and arms still ached from their escape, but activity felt better than idleness. Ul Zub rewarded her hard work with an assortment of off color jokes that she found splendidly funny. He seemed to know a thousand jokes, and he seemed to like to make her laugh.

Korba emerged from the crew cabin as they were casting the nets into the water for a second run. He joined in to work beside Gella, and Ul Zub's jokes became vulgar banter between the two men. On Ul Zub's boat, Korba was a much different man than the usher she'd met in Jishni's court. He was relaxed, and carefree. She found he had a penchant for teasing that bordered on the sadistic, and he teased her about everything from her skills as a fisherman to the cloth she'd used to tie up her hair. It took her several hours to realize his unmerciful torture was flirtatious. He'd smile at her a certain way, or keep his eyes on her too long, as if trying to make her understand his bold behavior. He was handsome and brown, his grins infectious. To clear away her doldrums she flirted back, which made him even bolder.

Later in the morning, while Gella was picking fish out of a net, Shelon and Iada appeared in the doorway of the crew cabin. They were arm in arm, and seemed content, as if they'd just made love. Gella found she didn't like being confronted with the confirmation of Shelon and Iada's relationship. She returned to the work, glad she had something to keep her hands busy, and glad for the diversion of Korba's company to keep her mind untroubled.

Iada, like Korba, went right to work.

Shelon didn't do much at all. He climbed the ladder to the deck above the crew quarters, and reclined. Occasionally, Gella would glance his way, and each time she did, she found his one good eye was trained on her. He'd smile, or nod, and look away, as if his stare was purely accidental.

His casual attention did more to incite Gella's interest than Korba's tireless pursuit.

When the sun was high Ul Zub was ready to move on to their next destination. He gave Gella a cloth bag of dried and salted fish as payment for her work, and took her company away.

"Engine is faulty," Korba apologized with a shrug, "It needs to be kicked while Ul Zub turns it over, otherwise it won't start."

Ul Zub scowled at Korba's fresh sarcasm. "Hey! You turn one valve and it starts right up!" he said defensively.

Korba chuckled at his brother-in-law, and followed him into the engine room.

Iada strolled past Gella, saying in her ear, "It needs to be kicked." and she winked as if they shared a great secret, though Gella didn't understand the significance of the joke.

From inside the pilothouse, Ul Zub shouted down at Korba to turn the valve in question. The engine turned over, and came to life.

Gella leaned against the railing surrounding the hold, bracing herself as the boat began to move, and opened her bag to eat. She found a small piece a fish to test. Tasting it, she savored it on her tongue. The fish in Calli didn't taste this good. It was velvety and light. Finding another small piece, she placed it in her mouth and closed her eyes at the exquisite taste. She relaxed fully.

The boat crossed through the wake of a larger ship, and suddenly lurched to the side. Gella's eyes flew open in time to watch her feet leave the deck. She sprawled on her back with a gruff exhalation of air.

Shelon cracked a loud laugh at her expense.

Indignant, she pulled herself up and gripped the railing with both hands. In retaliation, she yelled upwards, "Do you know what we do with lazy slanks like you in Shodalum?"

He pursed his lips into a smile. "I don't really want to know, but I'm sure you'll tell me."

"We take them far into the desert, and leave them without food and water. By the time they've made their way back home, if they do make it home, they are sufficiently inspired to work harder than anyone they know."

He gestured to the sea. "I don't see a desert around anywhere."

"I'd kick you out of the boat and circle, see how long you can tread water."

He laughed heartily. With an imperious gesture, he beckoned her to join him.

Her smoldering stare refused him. Her ego, as well as her backside, still smarted.

"Oh come on, I won't bite." he assured her, and prompted her with another imperious gesture.

He was infuriating, but too compelling to resist. She made a show of being reluctant, even as anticipation twisted her middle. She wanted, very much, to sit with him.

With care, she picked up her bag of fish and tottered across the deck to the ladder.

As she reached the top, Shelon was there to give her an arm up. He stood with ease on the rocking surface, his feet firmly placed. She stood next to him for one heartbeat, and immediately dropped down to her backside to prevent from pitching over the railing and to the deck below.

Shelon sat next to her, his legs folded comfortably.

"May I?" he asked of her fish.

"Is that what you wanted from me, my food?" she asked scornfully.

"If I'd only wanted fish, I could have had Ul Zub bring me some." he replied, and he gestured to the bag.

She took another long and well-salted piece for herself, and handed the bag over. He folded down the sides and set it before him and chose a piece at random.

"Are you going to Moom with us?" He asked casually as he ate.

"I have no where to go, but where you go."

"You have left your brother?"

"He has left me." she replied flatly, and she glanced at Shelon. "I'll probably never see him again." The words put a hard lump in her throat. Avoiding his gaze, she let her eyes be drawn by the endless waters.

"You react as if he were a lover, and not a brother."

She shot a wary glare his way.

"It's just an observation." he said, and he tossed a segment of fish in his mouth. "How long were you and Cobo together?"

"We've been a tribe for eighteen years."

"Hm. You were......ten or eleven when he took you in?"

"Twelve."

"Hmp." The second grunt held more significance. "Was he a father to you, a brother? Or more?"

"What does it matter what Cobo is to me?" she retorted defensively.

"I'm curious." he said in an offhanded way, and changing the direction of his questions, he asked, "How does a young Shodite girl become entangled with Ver dala Ven?"

She looked away again, but this time, instead of seeing a beautiful sea, she gazed into the past.

"He saved me," she offered, "I was abandoned after my parents died. I spent a year," and she faltered, finding she wasn't able to tell Shelon about her past as a prostitute. She demurred, saying, "Surviving. Cobo found me, and took care of me. He took me home, gave me food and a place to live. I fell in love with him for his kindness. I stayed in love with him because....he is Cobo. He is my brother, though for a very short while he was more. He is my first love, and the only family I have."

He made no comment. Shelon's features were sober as he finished his fish. He slapped the salt off his hands.

His silence made her uneasy with self-doubt. She pulled her knees to her chest and hugged them protectively, and watched Shelon's profile. Under the bandages, bumps and bruises, he had rugged features she found utterly appealing. A weathered and imperfect face that was as interesting as the man, and a hardened and imperfect body which housed a mighty spirit.

He brought her out of her reverie by asking, "Why did you throw away so much? You had everything. A Janti life, a Janti brother, and now you have nothing."

She considered telling him that she'd left Cobo because she couldn't bear to see him killed, but there was more to that truth than she cared to admit, so she held her tongue. Instead, she mocked wrath and grabbed the bag of fish away from him in time to prevent him from taking another piece. "I'm not left with nothing. I have my fish!"

Her stab at levity caused him to look at her as if he couldn't fathom her. "You are a funny one. Laughing like a fool at Ul Zub's old jokes and eating this awful fish as if it were fine Janti cuisine. If the planet spun out of its orbit and crashed into the sun, would you find humor in that catastrophe, too?"

"Life is hardship," she replied matter-factly, quoting a Shodite aphorism she'd heard her grandfather say often, "so I laugh when I can. There's no mystery to it. And this fish is wonderful. You are just spoiled."

He guffawed. "I've never been accused of being spoiled."

"It's my pleasure to be the first to point out your dreadful flaw."

An amused smile turned up the undamaged corner of his mouth. "You see my flaws too clearly, I think. And voice them too readily."

"I'm not intimidated by your magnificence like the cattle that follow you, daka Shelon." she said, and she grinned, challenging him to defend himself.

He grunted a laugh. "Your lack of courtesy is perhaps your best quality. That, and your temper."

"Oh, no, no, no, you are wrong." she assured him, her tone colored with the playful innuendo she'd been honing all morning on Korba. "You have not seen my best qualities, Shelon."

"I will," he replied with brash aplomb, "before long."

His steady, assured gaze left his intentions in the light, and inspired a thrill to race through her body.

Before she could respond, Korba bounded out of the engine room and started up the ladder. Gella felt a pang of annoyance for his interruption, yet managed to muster a smile for him as he stepped onto their deck.

He sat next to Gella, and said to Shelon, "Ul Zub is going in to Padra."

Shelon grunted a laugh. "I'm surprised he's not keeping us out for another day, with you two providing free labor. His benefactor will be overjoyed with the amount of fish he brought in on this trip."

"His benefactor is why we are going in." Korba said, "He has called in Ul Zub. The weather is predicting a storm for tonight. He wants his boat docked."

"Thank the Guardian for foul weather."

Korba leaned back on his arms. One arm was a bit close to Gella's back, a presumptuous intimacy that Gella didn't really mind. "Ul Zub is putting us off on a raft before we get to Padra. He's worried that his benefactor will have the boat searched once we dock."

Shelon seemed irritated by the news, though his irritation began the moment Korba sat too close to Gella. "He'd put us off in a storm?"

"He will. He plans to."

Shelon shifted abruptly, and stood. "We'll see about that." He plunged down the ladder, wearing a scowl on his face.

Gella was instantly concerned by Shelon's concern, and moved to follow him down the ladder.

Korba placed a gentle, restraining hand on her arm. "Wait one moment. We need to talk." He wore a boyish smile, and was apparently unconcerned about Ul Zub and the raft and the storm.

She looked from his face to the hand on her arm, and slowly returned to his side, at once uncomfortable.

"What is it that you want from me, Korba?" she asked, suspecting she knew the answer, that he, like all men, wanted only one thing from her. He managed, however, to shock her. "I wanted to tell you," and his color deepened, "I don't want my freedom from you. I accept you as my benefactor for all time."

224

Anger creased her features, and she twisted her arm from his grip and thumped him on the chest with the back of her hand. "Are you out of your mind?"

"I am in love," he breathed passionately, "with the most beautiful woman I've ever known. How could I want my freedom, when it could mean I'd be separated from you?"

"In love?"

"I understand if you don't feel the same," he said hurriedly, "I accept that it may take time."

"Korba, you shouldn't sell your freedom for love." she berated him, "Nothing is worth being in servitude to another. And love......love is fickle. It doesn't last. You say you love me now, but you may not love me next week, or month, or year. And then where will you be? You will be a servant to a woman you detest. Is that what you want?"

"I want you." he said softly, and he touched her face, his fingertips lingering on her cheek.

"Oh, Korba," she breathed, and she returned his touch, framing his face with her hands. His face, so dark and perfect, his beauty would have, at one time, been enough to draw her into his bed. "We can never be more than friends."

Her rejection hurt him, and pain glittered in his eyes. She felt compassion for him. She knew what it was like to love someone and be rejected. Cobo had rejected her love every day for ten years.

She smoothed his cheek, and to ease his pain, she gently kissed his lips.

"Korba!" Shelon shouted sharply from below.

They bolted apart, and Korba twisted to see Shelon staring malevolently up at him.

"Help me with the raft!" Shelon demanded.

Korba didn't hesitate to obey Shelon, and scrambled down the ladder.

Shelon's gaze switched from Korba, to Gella. He was furious. It was Ul Zub, and the prospect of being abandoned in the Tronos on a raft that had sparked his fury, but she indulged herself and imagined it might be more, that Shelon didn't like seeing her lips on Korba's.

But no, she saw his disgust, his judgement. She'd seen it on the faces of her own people so often that it wasn't hard to recognize. She'd last seen it on Thib's wrinkled old face. Once a whore, always a whore. He'd never think more of her than she could think of herself.

Her tormented thoughts stirred resentment for Shelon, and any person who'd judge her. She glared defiantly at him, refusing to look away.

Disappointment crossed his features, and he turned his back on her. She turned cold.

She told herself she didn't care. She didn't need his approval to breathe Janti air.

She descended the ladder and joined them. Despite her proud bearing, as she stood near Shelon on the deck, inside she felt small and frightened. She wished heartily that she'd gone to Dilgopoche with Cobo. At least with him, she knew herself.

ન્ન્ન્ન્ન્ગ્ગ્ગ્ગ

The storm moved quicker than expected, and was upon them before dusk. Despite the risk of being seen, Ul Zub shut down the engine, and let his boat drift.

Shelon and Korba lifted the tethered raft over the boat railing and tossed it into the choppy water. The raft was not what had Gella expected. In Shodalum, a few foolish and daring people had fished the Gryvly on woven mats of sticks, and they called that a raft. Ul Zub's raft was spongy, and was shaped like the cupped palm of the goddess. Bobbing in the water, it looked much smaller than it had on the deck.

The wind picked up the moment the raft hit the water. A free edge of the raft's folded and tied canopy flapped wildly.

Korba stood beside Gella, and said, "There, you can see the coast." He patted her back, as if all would be well.

Gella could see the coast. It was a sliver of dark green in the distance.

"It will take all night to row to shore, fighting the currants the whole way." Shelon told her, still fuming at Ul Zub. "Are you prepared to laugh at the hardship, native daughter?"

She was nervous. She glanced at the raft being pushed about by the agitated waters.

"You swim well?" Shelon prodded.

"I can swim." she said, still staring at the bouncing raft.

He took her face in his hand and turned her head so that she'd meet his serious expression. "Do you swim well?"

She shook her head lightly. "I was born inland, and lived in a desert."

Worry creased his features.

"Get us an extra rope!" Shelon barked at Korba.

Despite Ul Zub's objections, Korba brought Shelon a berthing rope. Shelon looped it around Gella's waist.

As he tied it, he said, "The three of us will be connected by this rope. That way, if one of us falls off the raft, we can pull the idiot out of the water before he, or *she*, drowns."

He measured the rest of the rope, using the length of his arm. Finding the center, he tossed it at Korba, and helped the younger man negotiate the length of the rope in order to tie himself to Gella.

Shelon tied himself on the opposite end, and grimly watched the sky.

Gella felt a raindrop kiss her cheek.

"I must go now!" Ul Zub shouted at Shelon. Squinting his eyes against the fine, misty rain beginning to fall, he went to Gella. He said to her, "A pretty woman with a foul mouth is a rare find! You can stay, work on my boat if you like. I can hide you in Padra."

"If I make it to shore alive, I'll be sure to give your offer consideration!"

Shelon frowned grimly to the comment. To Ul Zub, he pleaded again, "Take us closer!"

"We'll be seen from the docks, I won't take that chance!"

"They can see us here!"

"I'm already taking a chance by letting you have the raft! Do you know what my benefactor paid for that raft?"

"I couldn't care less!"

Ul Zub scowled at him irritably. "Maybe I should let you swim through the Harda."

Iada put herself between the two men. "Stop it! Ul Zub, he gets the raft!" and to Shelon, she said, "Ul Zub is certain to be beaten for losing an expensive piece of equipment."

Her tone told Shelon he needed to show some gratitude. Shelon pursed his lips, and pulled his eyes away from Iada's. To Ul Zub, he said, "It's too cold to swim."

Ul Zub took his comment with a curt nod.

"I'll see you soon." Shelon said to Iada, though his pensive scowl revealed his own doubts.

Iada nodded, looking no less apprehensive.

Shelon gestured to Korba that he was ready, and he climbed over the railing to the knotted rope that Ul Zub used as a ladder for the raft. He went hand over hand down, and Korba followed. Shelon released the rope half way and dropped into the raft on his back.

Iada gave Gella a half embrace, her arm around Gella's shoulders. "Take care of them!"

Gella nodded, shivering and frightened. She stepped over the railing just as the rope between she and Korba grew taut.

As she went down the knotted rope, she saw Korba land onto the raft on his back, just as Shelon had done. She nodded to herself, assuring herself that it was easy, Korba and Shelon had made it look easy. Once Korba rolled out of her way, she released the rope.

She fell, and landed in the raft on her back. The spongy raft that seemed to welcome Korba and Shelon felt like a rock face to Gella. The fall knocked the wind out of her, and she lay on her back, immobilized by the shock.

Shelon untied the rope holding the raft to the fishing boat, and tossed his end up to Ul Zub. The currant quickly carried the raft away.

"May the Guardian protect you!" Ul Zub shouted, and he waved.

Gella struggled to sit. The raft seemed to want to engulf her hands and knees as she moved around. Shelon was already at the front, using the oar to prevent the currant from taking them too far off their course.

Korba grabbed her by the waist and pulled her to the side of the raft. He held her back close to him, and placed her hands on an oar. Speaking into her ear, he gave her a crash coarse in rowing while showing her how it was done. He placed his hands over hers, and helped her put the oar through the water for a few strokes.

Shelon looked over his shoulder and scowled. "You think you can wait until we get to shore to make love to her, Korba? We are being swept away!"

Gella glared at Shelon. To Korba, she said, "I'm fine, go on, before daka Shelon breaks a blood vessel."

Shelon sullenly turned away, and resumed his struggle with the active water.

Korba grabbed an oar, and threw his body to the other side of the raft. Working together, they managed to stay in the same place for what seemed like forever.

In the meantime, the fishing boat disappeared into the horizon.

As the sun set, the storm began in earnest, and rain slashed their faces. Darkness continued to descend on them, until they were engulfed and could see nothing except their destination, which was no more than a dotted line of faraway lights. No matter how hard they rowed, they didn't seem to get any closer to the shore. They actually seemed to be drifting farther away.

The cold was unbearable. Gella's hands became numb, and her arms and legs cramped. Her movements became as choppy as the water as her muscles began to surrender to the cold. Her fingers finally lost all strength, and she fumbled with the oar. It splashed into the water.

"Clumsy slank sucker," she berated herself, and she held onto the side of the raft and reached into the water toward the place she'd heard the oar enter the water.

Deciding it couldn't have gone too far, she shouted, "Shelon, I've dropped my oar, I'm going after it!"

"No!"

Before Shelon could stop her, she rolled over the side of the raft and plunged into the icy water. She expected to sink under for a second, then float to the surface, swim, and reach the oar with no problem.

She sunk, and a powerful undertow embraced her, and pulled her deeper into the liquid blackness. She didn't panic, at first. She made swimming movements, expecting to be able to pull herself to the surface, which she thought was right within her reach.

Panic set in as she realized she was swimming as hard as she could and continuing to swiftly sink. The desire to breathe overwhelmed her, and she stopped swimming in order to cover her mouth and nose with her hands to keep herself from trying to take a breath.

A tug at her waist reminded her that she was attached to Shelon and Korba. Abruptly, she stopped sinking. Her waist rose above her head. She was moving through the rushing waters, but now she was going upwards.

Not fast enough. Her body became light, and her thoughts slipped away from panic. The inky blackness of the water brightened, and Shelon's face resolved clearly before her sights. His eyes twinkling, amused. She wanted him, but not for simple pleasure. She wanted him because she sensed he was the one who completed her.

His voice was clear. *"We'll never know for sure if I am for you, and you for me, because, Gella, you are about to die."*

The rushing black waters squelched her day dream, and world began to spin. She felt strength rush from her arms, and her hands floated aimlessly away from her face. Surrendering, she took an involuntary breath of salty water-

-and cold air.

She coughed, her body convulsing violently in order to push the water out of her lungs and through her nose and mouth. Two sets of hands pulled her out of the water and into the raft. She flopped onto her side and struggled to breathe.

"Is she all right?" She heard Korba from somewhere in the darkness above her.

She felt arms around her, gentle but strong. She was pulled into an upright position. A hand rubbed her back as she sputtered and coughed up more salty water.

"Talk to me, native daughter." Shelon said, his voice close to her ear.

"I lost my oar," she croaked, which prompted another round of violent coughing.

"She'll be all right." Shelon told Korba. And close to her ear, he said, "Should I have warned you about the Harda surge? It is forbidden to swim in the Padra bay because the Harda surge will carry an unwary swimmer straight to the bottom, and hold her there forever."

She continued to cough, unable to reply.

She felt him move away. His voice was near, and he spoke to Korba. "See that?" he said, "We're heading straight into the Eller peninsula. If we stop fighting the damn currant and let it work for us, we'll wash onto the shore there."

"But....Eller?" Korba breathed.

"It'll be the middle of the night by the time we land. No one will see us."

"We'll be seventy....eighty spans from Padra!" he objected.

"One problem at a time, Korba." Shelon replied sardonically.

Gella took a deep breath, which was exhaled with a dozen sputtering coughs. Her chest ached.

She heard Shelon say, "The Shelter."

She felt their movement around her, and heard snaps come undone from her right. The canopy. Shelon murmured instructions to Korba on how to raise the canopy, and as abruptly as they had released it from its binding, it rose above their heads. The sheets of rain that sliced at their skin became the patter of rain on the canopy.

"That's it." Shelon said. "Lace the flap, but leave a window so we can watch the shore."

Next to her head, the provision box unlatched.

Shelon muttered, "In the past few days I've aged twenty years. Another day with you, and I'll be volunteering for my own grave just so I can rest my nerves!"

Piqued by his irritation, she retorted in a hoarse voice, "If you need help getting there, let me know, I'd be glad to kick you in the hole myself."

"By the gods, you are most definitely alive."

She felt him move toward her, the surface of the raft sinking beside her as he came closer. Unsure what to expect from him, she cringed.

A blanket fell on her full body. She felt his hands on her as he blindly tried to get her tucked into a cocoon of warmth. His hands on her legs, her arms, shoulders--Nothing was more welcome to Gella than Shelon's touch.

"That should help get you warm." Shelon said to her, patting her legs. He sounded subdued, weary.

Sensing he was moving away from her, she reached out and grabbed his wet shirt in two handfuls, holding him in place. "Shelon," she whispered.

He hesitated, and did not pull away. "Yes?"

Tears sprang into her eyes. She wanted to thank him for having the foresight to tie the rope to her, and for his part in fishing her out of the deep waters, but the sentiment was lost in a tangle of emotions she couldn't articulate.

Her silence spoke to him. His voice softening, he said, "You are a nuisance, Gella al Perraz, and I must be a glutton for punishment, because I'm not ready to let you go."

The tenderness in his voice, and the way he seemed to know her heart, touched her. Following the impulses of her desire, she whispered his name and pulled him closer. Heart aching, female aching, she slipped her arms around his back and prompted him closer. He answered her embrace, lying down next to the full length of her and draping an arm over her. The indentation he made in the raft drew them in a natural embrace, turning them toward each other, nestling them in a cozy groove. His face was close to hers and slightly above, she heard his rapid breathing, felt it moving her hair.

"It is colder than the daka's heart out there." Korba said, teeth clattering, "The lacing is too short, Shelon. The flaps wouldn't close all the way, if we wanted them to."

Shelon sighed. "It'll serve us." His embrace tightened, a prelude to his release. He whispered to Gella, "You are safe now."

Realizing he had misunderstood the meaning of her embrace, she objected by digging her fingers into his back and refusing to release him. She found his skin with her lips, wanting his mouth

232

but finding his chin. She kissed his face until she found what she was looking for in the darkness, his mouth.

He hesitated in returning her kiss, groping for understanding. She thought he might pull away, rebuff her advance, and leave her in an agony of humiliation, cloaked mercifully by the darkness.

His breathing deepened, and his mouth moved over hers to make the kiss his. His lips were still swollen and misshapen, limiting their kiss to a gentle moment of holding their mouths together.

Behind them, Korba rifled through the provisions. "I know that Iada packed blankets in here. Shelon, have you already taken them out?"

Shelon lifted his face from Gella's. His breathing was irregular, alerting Gella to his quickening arousal.

Gruffly, he said over his shoulder to Korba, "They are on your right."

As Korba fumbled in the blind darkness, Shelon rolled on top of her and his mouth again found hers. Ignoring his own discomfort, he insisted on deepening their kiss, and as he did, he rocked his hips into hers, introducing her to his smooth, hard heat. His swift intensity chased her mind away, and she reacted to him with abandon. She kicked away the blanket and opened her legs to him, wrapping them around his hips, ready for him to make love to her.

He lifted his face away, brushed his lips on her cheek, found her ear, and bit her earlobe lightly. His voice tremulous with desire, he whispered low in her ear, "What about Korba?"

Thinking he was referring to the innocent kiss he'd seen her give Korba on the boat, she sighed, "I want you, Shelon, only you."

Above them, Korba said, "What are you two whispering about?" He was crawling toward them, trying to find the warmth of another body in the cold.

Shelon abruptly rolled off her, leaving her to squirm with frustration and chagrin. The heady ache Shelon caused between her legs made her oblivious of Korba's presence in the raft.

"Trying to choose who will stay awake for the first watch." Shelon answered readily, though he sounded as chagrinned and frustrated as Gella. "I say it will be me."

233

Korba lay beside her. "Good. I feel like I could sleep a hundred years."

She turned to face Shelon as Korba spooned his body into her back and got comfortable. By chance she found Shelon's leg, and after finding his leg, she purposefully found his aroused male and gripped it possessively.

Shelon's tone was sardonic as he answered Korba's comment, "I don't think I could sleep if I wanted to."

Gella said, "If I must suffer, you must suffer."

"Hm?" Korba questioned tiredly, obviously not following the intricacies of their conversation, and not concerned by their exchange.

Shelon placed his hand over hers, and gripped her hand as tightly as she had hold of him. "I must sit by the opening, to watch the shore."

Understanding, she reluctantly released him. He lifted her hand to his face and kissed her palm. Touching his face, a disturbing realization overwhelmed her. In too short a time, Shelon already owned her heart. Her passion for him was potent and undeniable. She was giddy with happiness, because she was in love.

He moved away, leaving her side cold. He opened the window Korba left in the flap, and a cacophony of rain ushered a chilled breeze underneath the canopy. She could see Shelon as a faint outline against the lighter darkness of night, and yearned for him.

Korba huddled closer to her.

"Don't become attached to him." Korba whispered.

She turned her head slightly, realizing that Korba must have intuited more of what was happening in the darkness than she or Shelon suspected.

Korba spoke, so low she was certain Shelon couldn't hear. "He loves no one but the cause. Besides, Iada will be reunited with him in Moom. He and Iada have been lovers for many years. He barely knows you. What would he want you for, except to keep him satisfied while he is parted from Iada?"

Though she could hear the jealous note in Korba's voice and understood why he might want to stand between her and Shelon, her happiness sunk like a stone into the abyss of her entrenched cynicism. In the darkness, where she couldn't see Shelon's face or motives, she'd released herself to a romantic fantasy in a moment of weakness, without considering the reality of their situation. Shelon was a man living a reckless life, and she was a young and easy harlot.

As if he felt the jolt of pain that coursed her system for a rejection she hadn't even experienced yet, Korba's arm slipped around her waist and he held her tighter.

"I'll never leave you." he whispered.

Cobo had said something to that effect to her once cr twice. Hearing those words from Korba turned her lips up in an ugly, and jaded, smile.

࿇࿇࿇࿇࿇࿇

Shelon's shout woke Gella from a dream. Hazy images of dipping her hands into the black soil in Calli to harvest impossibly huge yava roots disappeared and the interior of the raft appeared. She could see.

"Is it day?"

A wave surged under the raft and she was tossed against the canopy. She heard the canopy rip, and as she flopped back into raft's belly, water splashed around her.

Korba was on his knees and fighting the shimmering raft to get to Shelon.

To where Shelon should have been.

Shelon wasn't in the raft.

Horror seeped into Gella's bones. He'd fallen into the water. She imagined him fighting the Harda surge, drowning. She scrambled to Korba, to the opening, to the rope around Korba's waist. Pulled it, hand over hand. It was slack, and the end that had been tied around Shelon was coiled next to the opening. She hung her body over the side of the raft with Korba, immediately soaked by rain. Day hadn't broken, the sky was still black, but they were in a halo of undulating orange light.

"A beacon!" Korba shouted.

She could see the shore through the storm. They were close enough that she saw the metal erector set tower that was built on a rocky out cropping.

She was uninterested in the shore. "Shelon!" she screamed.

"Here!" he shouted back. He was in the water, hanging from a grip on the side of the raft, struggling against the waves "Korba, drop the shelter, and row!"

Korba, seemingly forgetting that Shelon was in the water and untethered, hurried toward the ties that held the shelter on the raft.

Gella reached for Shelon, and shouted, "I'll help you!"

"Row!" he shouted at her, refusing her help. His free arm splashed wildly in the water to keep his head above the surface.

"Korba, help me get Shelon into the raft!" she screamed hysterically.

Korba released the shelter and it took off like a windrider, flying up to be carried off by the winds into the heavens.

He grabbed an oar, and handed it to her.

"Help me with Shelon!"

"He doesn't need our help!" he shouted back, and he dropped the oar before her, grabbed the second and went to the side to row.

Misunderstanding his motives, believing Korba's jealousy would lead him to let Shelon drown, she grabbed him by the arm and pulled him away from the side with all her might.

"Gella!" he shouted, "we must row to get to the shore, or we will hit the rocks!"

Shelon, angry and soaked, pulled himself easily over the side of the raft. Glaring at them both, he shouted, "Must I do all the work?"

Shaken both by her fear for Shelon's safety and her distrust of Korba, Gella flinched at the sound of his voice. As she released Korba's arm, he quickly returned to the side of the raft, and pushed the oar through the water.

Shelon said to Gella, "Row hard, away from the beacon spit!" and dropped back into the water.

Gella looked again at the outcropping where the beacon stood. She could now see the sharp rocks, eager to shred their raft, and them. She struggled to get to the opposite side of the raft. From where she rowed, she could see Shelon trying to maintain a foot hold on a silty beach, his arm wrapped in the grip and yanking, as if he were trying to single-handedly pull them to shore. Each wave that kicked them in the air tossed Shelon about like a doll, then sucked him deep under the water. Each time she lost sight of him, she held her breath until he bobbed to the surface, and resumed tugging.

Prompted by Shelon's shout, Korba grabbed hold of a strap on the other side of the raft and plunged into the water to help Shelon drag the raft out of the water. The waves pushed, while Korba and Shelon pulled.

The raft beached itself, and Shelon stumbled tiredly into the sand on his knees, coughing wildly. Gella jumped out of the raft into the moving waves, and ran, splashing, to Shelon's side. She dropped down next to him, and put a gentle hand on his back, waiting for him to be able to take a full, deep breath, without his lungs rejecting water.

She felt a tug at her waist. Glancing back, she saw Korba rolling the rope over his arm, walking toward her. Her hands went to the knot to her waist, and she struggled to untie herself from the tether.

Shelon sat back on his heels, and seeing her difficulty in releasing his knot, he moved her hands out of the way and took over. Though he trembled from over exertion, and huffed water out of his lungs every other breath, his fingers were strong and deft. The knot obeyed his will.

He threw the rope away and met her eyes, and he gazed at her the way she thought he might have been gazing at her in the darkness of the raft. A gaze filled with longing, and a secret feeling they hadn't yet had time to explore.

Her heart thrilled painfully. If he were using her, as Korba suggested, she'd allow him to possess her for as long as he wanted, just to see him look at her like this.

Shelon wordlessly stood, pulling her to her feet. "The Eller patrol are ever present near the beacons. We need to move, now."

Korba tossed the rope into the raft, and shoved it back into the waves. It drifted toward the rocks surrounding the beacon.

He trotted to them, saying, "Which way do we run, Shelon? The Janti are all around us!"

Shelon didn't reply. He took Gella's hand and started them up the beach.

As they found darkness and cover in the thick grove of trees that fringed the beach, Shelon made them pause, and crouch. Gella could hear music, somber music accented by a clear toned soprano. She peered around Shelon, and saw lights twinkling through the trees.

"A party," Korba whispered. "Eller is a vacation spot for rich Janti, and it is famous for its raucous parties. Iada's benefactor once owned a house here."

Shelon hushed him irritably.

Gella and Korba heard at that moment what Shelon had heard. Voices, approaching. A woman's tinkling laugh. A man's lower, suggestive tone.

They receded into the under brush and lay on the ground.

Sandal clad feet came into view. The couple was faltering their way to the beach. He was saying, "-the storm is an aphrodisiac, the electricity in the air-"

"-being hit by lightening enhances love making, is that it?"

"Oh, yes,"

She laughed heartily.

Lecherously, he breathed, "I'm going to lash you to the beacon and-"

"If we get caught, we'll be the talk of-"

"-strip you," he breathed.

"-my father-" she said pointedly.

"-let him watch, he might learn something useful-" he suggested lasciviously, which inspired the woman into another fit of tittering laughter.

And on they went, making their way drunkenly to the beach.

Shelon gave her arm a tug, and he quietly slid out from under the bush. She followed, and she threw a quick look down the trail. She could see the outline of the departing couple against the orange glow of the beacon.

In the cushion of trees and gardens lay the Eller vacation home. It was designed to look something like Ona, though by many measures smaller. Seven glass spires crowned the house, an excessive architectural doo-dad that did not match the beauty of the originals.

The music came from a courtyard near the garden. The dome covering the courtyard blazed with twinkling colored light, but for the trees surrounding the courtyard, Gella could not see the guests. There were many voices, and they sounded close.

Shelon took her hand, drawing her gaze from the sound of the Janti revelers. He gave her an assuring nod and drew her away from the courtyard and the noise.

Out of sight of the main house, far from the party, was a long and narrow windowless building. Staying in the shadows they made their way around the building to a door. After taking a quick look around, Shelon rapped loudly on the door, using a purposeful rhythm. A short rap, three long, another short, and two long.

An elderly man dressed in service white threw the door aside. He carrying a long stick and brandished at the three strangers in the darkness.

"Go away, we aren't one with you here."

"I am Shelon." Shelon said soberly. There was no narcissism in his tone, no vanity whatsoever, though revealing himself to the elderly Shodite had an incredible affect. The Shodite plucked an oil lamp from a hook on the wall and rushed outside to take a closer look.

"It is you. We'd heard you'd been killed by the dakas."

"We need your help."

The man backed away from Shelon, reluctance in his features. Gella expected he'd slam the door in their faces once he crossed the threshold, but he replaced the lantern and soberly rejoined them, closing the door to the night.

"You have allies, but not in this house. Follow me."

He led them through the darkened and narrow pathway that wound its way around the house. At the end of the path was a metal gate. The old man pushed it open, and hurried his pace. They emerged into a well-lit common in the middle of a neighborhood resplendent with Janti homes. Afar, across the common, the Janti leisurely made their way to and from the party. Gella hesitated crossing into the light. Korba came up behind her and put a supportive arm around her in order to compel her forward. With his quick step guiding her, they caught up with Shelon.

They crossed a brick walkway, went around a private windrider that was berthed near the neighborhood's landing site, and crossed through another gate.

In the back there was another plain building, servant quarters Gella realized, narrow and windowless. The old man rapped on the door, his eyes twitching from right to left.

"You've put us all in danger, Shelon."

Shelon acknowledged the truth with a nod.

A young woman answered. "Lagos," she said, seeing him, and her eyes went to them with wary curiosity. "Are we needed for service?"

Lagos quickly ushered them inside, closing the door after throwing another wary glance behind them. "Juana, tell your mother I've brought Shelon to her home."

Juana gasped at the name, and recognizing Shelon, she gasped again. She went running for her mother.

The interior reminded Gella of the buildings in Shod City, though it was better kept. The entry opened into a hall that ran the length of the building. There were doors on either side of the hall, one at the end, all closed. Oil lamps hung outside each door, only a few were lit.

From a door toward the middle of the hall a woman not much older than Juana burst through and came running, her long straight brown hair flying straight off her back.

She rushed Shelon, hesitated only long enough to see it was really he, and fell to her knees laughing and crying.

"I've never felt such joy!" she gushed, and she kissed his hands. "I wish my husband was here! He would be more honored than I!"

"Benin's husband died in a Raal work camp for your cause, Shelon." Lagos informed him curtly.

Shelon gripped her hands and brought her to her feet. "I am sorry to hear of your loss. Many good men died for the cause."

"A cause for fools and dreamers." Lagos spat, and he left them, slamming the door behind him, causing the lamp next to Gella's head to sway.

"Lagos lost his son in the riots, only yesterday."

Shelon dropped his eyes, and nodded. "Tragic that our freedom comes at so high a price."

"Yes." Benin whispered, her eyes shining with hero worship. The tragedy seemed lost on her while in Shelon's presence.

"Good lady," Shelon intoned, "we are in need of rest, warm clothing, and food. We don't want to cause you trouble, and will leave as soon as we have gathered our strength."

"You are welcome to stay as long as you like. In the name of my husband, Ranjee, I will treat you as my family."

Benin took Shelon by the arm and led them down the long hall to the door on the opposite end. To her daughter, she said, "Warm a room for Shelon." To Shelon, she said, "I will fetch you fine clothing, and the finest food available from my benefactor's larder."

"Do not cause yourself harm, we wish the very least, that which the Janti will not miss."

"They won't miss a thing." She scoffed, "They stay drunk night and day. Worthless scum."

Benin released his arm and threw open the door at the end of the hall.

The sultry heat of the bathhouse soaked into Gella's skin, and she sighed. Unlike the simple exterior of the building, the bathhouse was elaborate, rivaling the bathhouse in Cobo's apartment. Light green tile covered the floor and walls, and there were two deep bathing pools recessed in the floor, both full of water. A row of indoor toilets lined the back wall, one of the few luxuries Gella encountered in Ona that she understood. A wash basin and drying rack for clothing was near the toilets.

Near the latter, two naked toddlers played in soapy water, splashing about. Juana plucked them up in spite of their objections, and whisked them out of the bathhouse.

Benin said, "Strip off those wet clothes. Bathe if you like. The water is fresh, filled only this afternoon and used once, I bet it is still warm. In the meantime, I'll find you something dry and warm to wear."

Gella put her foot in the bath water to test its temperature. Warmth embraced her toes. Without hesitation, she stripped, dropping her clothing and wraps in a wet heap on the floor, and quickly descended into the water. Dropping to her knees, the water was to her chin. She threw her legs forward and let herself sink, submerging, and she rested a moment, allowing the warmth to thaw her to the bone.

Rising for air, her first site was Shelon and Korba, looking as though they were deep in conversation, though seeing her rise silenced them. The tension between the two men was obvious.

She sidled closer to the edge, wondering what they had been talking about.

"We'll leave Gella to her privacy." Shelon said, not to her but to Korba, and in a way that told Korba he had no choice but to leave. "Understand?"

"Perfectly." Korba replied, seething.

Shelon nodded, and threw a hungry look Gella's way before following Korba out. Anticipation finished warming her, and she pushed off from the side of the bath to sink once again into the water, a happy smile on her face.

Benin brought her a robe to wear, and tried as the servants in Ona had to throw away her leather wraps. She set Benin straight, and took time to hang them to dry on an empty rack next to the wash basin.

Benin's lips pursed with dislike, disapproval, she showed Gella the room she'd prepared. It was a simple abode, sparse, much to Gella's liking. A fire was in the hearth at the back of the room, warming the space nicely. Mats were rolled out on the floor.

"Where are Shelon and Korba?"

"You won't be alone for long." Benin spat coldly.

Gella did not understand Benin's sudden coolness toward her, until Korba found her. He was in a robe much like hers, and wearing an urgent expression.

"This is Shelon's room, Gella. He instructed Benin to bring you here, and put me in a different room so that you and he might have privacy. If his intentions are unwelcome, you can sleep in my room."

Her body prickled with interest as she discovered what had caused tension between Shelon and Korba.

Without second thought, she said, "I want to stay."

Korba lowered his head, and he scowled. "He is-" and he fell silent as he heard footsteps pass by the door, waiting for Shelon to interrupt.

The footsteps continued on, and Korba did as well. "He is using you!"

She nodded, as if she understood the minds of men and their motivations, even though her middle twisted at the thought of Shelon using her like the men who'd used her in Strum.

Becoming quite angry with her complacency, Korba took her by the arms and scowled into her face. "Are you so taken by him that you could let him use you? Or do you think you need to lay with him because he is the great Shelon? He is not a god, he is a man, an old man! He has done nothing for you that requires you to give him your body!"

Gella's jaw set. "I have not sold myself since I was twelve, and I am not selling myself now. I want him, Korba. If it is only a brief affair, I accept it. I see my interest in him hurts you, but I made no promises to you. You have no reason or right to be hurt!"

His voice loud, and furious, Korba said, "I am your living guardian, it is my job to protect your life and your virtue!"

Her reply was stiff and caustic. "Perhaps you should be more concerned about Shelon's virtue, considering my immoral past."

Shelon's disembodied laughter reached them through the closed door. He was right outside, he'd eavesdropped and now he was coming in, and yet Korba reacted just the same. Turning dark crimson with fury, his jaw tight, he retorted, "You are callous as well as immoral."

The door flew wide and Shelon entered, draped in a robe, his long sterling hair still dripping.

"Enough, Korba."

Gella was stung, but she maintained a cool exterior. "I will not be needing protection tonight, Korba."

Korba's lids dropped with his pique. "Very well. Your will is my will, benefactor."

"Don't call me that!" she demanded hotly.

243

"Would it be better if I called you whore?" he retorted venomously.

Gella's mouth dropped open, silenced by an insult she felt was truth.

"Korba!" Shelon barked in her defense, "You will correct yourself!"

Korba woke from his fury, and genuine contrition bent his head. "Gella-of course I didn't mean to insult you-"

Shelon threw a hostile fist in the air, gesturing toward the door. "Leave us."

Korba blinked, and threw a wary eye at Shelon. Obediently, he shrank from them, leaving the room they would share.

Subdued, Gella said in Korba's defense, "He was upset."

"Oh yes, I know why he is upset," Shelon replied ruefully, "but a pining heart is no reason to forget himself and call you foul names."

He closed the door, and turned to face her. In the muted lighting of a small lamp, his expression seemed fierce.

Her heart fluttered, and she turned away in order to keep her composure. His presence was palpable, and she could feel his eyes on her. She yearned for his touch.

"Are you cold still?" he asked softly.

"No."

"Then why are you shivering?"

She threw her head back and met his steady gaze. "Because I am finally alone with you."

He crossed the room to her and touched her, her neck and face. His hands were hot against her cool skin, and she invited him to explore her body by throwing off her robe.

He looked at her, hunger entering his expression. His hands drifted to her shoulders and down her arms as he drank in her body with his eyes.

She was made breathless by the way he looked at her, and, in paradox, she was suddenly self conscious about the muscles that could be seen in her arms, her legs, her midriff. Unevenly, she said, "I'm not soft, round or delicate."

He stepped closer, and touched her upturned breasts. She closed her eyes as he kneaded her breasts. One of his hands dropped down to follow the contour of her waist.

"You are perfect, a precious beauty." he murmured.

He kissed her lips, a soft touch that closed her eyes.

"Tonight we rest." He told her, "As willing as my desire may be, I've been beaten half to death by the Harda Surge."

She was disappointed. Her fatigue had left her as soon as she discovered she'd be lying in his arms. She couldn't let him go to sleep right away, fatigue or not.

She made him take his robe off, and he let her look him over. Approving of what she saw, she took him by the hand and they lay together on the mat. In embrace, she hooked her leg over his hip to inspire his tired male to action, and kissed his neck and chest. Enveloped in a warm haze, the smell of the fire and of him, the comfort of being in his arms, fatigue claimed her in spite of her lust.

She woke, she did not know how much later. There was activity in the servant quarters, and she felt as though it might be morning. Still in Shelon's arms, she moved to see his face, to find he'd been watching her sleep.

He kissed her, and her heart thrilled, because she knew it was time.

He was gentle in how he touched her and kissed her, and he took his time, seeming to watch her reactions. Between kisses, tender nips with is teeth, he spoke sweet things to her that she'd never heard spoken for her, things that made her sigh and moan and giggle. He stroked her slowly, finding her private hair and tickling her sweetly, touching and kissing her whole body, livening her senses, and filling her with heady anticipation. He enticed her with his sweet play to surrender herself entirely to him, and as she did, Shelon's play turned to passion, and he pulled her atop him as they became one. He rocked her slowly, fluidly, his hands on her hips, his thumbs pressed into her wiry female hair, his eyes staring into her face.

Afterwards, they lay tangled in each other's arms, too numb and tired for renewed passion. His voice velvet, Shelon said beautiful things to her, things that she wanted to believe. He told her he'd recognized her, from the moment they met, from his sweetest dreams. He told her that she was the most beautiful woman he'd ever been with, and the most exciting, and that he'd sorely anticipated the moment they could be one, and that she had exceeded his expectations.

Silence passed long between them, and his breathing became even and deep. Gella tried to go back to sleep, too, but couldn't. She watched the play of dying embers in the hearth, her head on his chest, toying with the masculine hair beneath his belly, and ruminating on the future.

Chapter 12

Hundreds of tents had been erected on the outskirts of Montrose, on land blackened by the Dome of Silence. From the Daka Redd, it had looked like a huge carnival or traveling stage show.

Once arriving, they'd spent the afternoon being briefed on the Dilgo's customs by Baru, the sister of Rito-Sant. Aton had briefed them before leaving the palace, still yet Jishni believed her council members needed to be familiar with the actual size and appearance of the Dilgos before entering into peace talks. Sitting in a room with the giantess, enduring her strangely sulfuric smell and her horrid manners, did nothing to engender acceptance in the envoy for the Dilgos.

Early the next morning, just hours before their peace talks were to begin, Jishni toured the prison quarters, as was the custom when a daka boarded a ship of war. Bail had no intentions of making their tour a lengthy affair. He quickly guided her through the cargo hold where they kept the women, and as quickly took her through the brig where they kept the men.

Seeing the men for the first time, she was shocked by the level of the physical deformities, shock that inspired the deepest guilt she'd ever felt. As she saw a man with four legs, or one with skin as scaly as a slank's, or another with a jutting jaw and fangs and fur and a caper that made him look like a beast, Jishni was reminded that it was her ancestor that caused their suffering.

To Bail, she murmured, "I haven't seen a man yet who couldn't benefit from surgery. You can't tell me that the Dilgos don't have physicians who couldn't help these poor unfortunates."

"They wouldn't if they could." Bail said lowly, "Baru calls them animals."

"Baru is a barbarian." she replied vehemently, "If she is the best of the Dilgos, Taen will be miserable in their company."

"He seems all too happy to join them."

"Strange, isn't it?" she said of her son's sudden change of heart. "I wonder if Cobo spoke with him?"

"If so, what could he have promised to change Taen's outlook so dramatically?"

Jishni held her reply, pausing at one cell where a sullen young man crouched in a darkened corner. His body seemed naturally proportioned, and the profile he showed Jishni was strikingly handsome, his hair shiny black and the eye she could see brilliant blue. She was intrigued to find a normal man among the Dilgos.

"What is your name?" she asked of him.

He turned his full head, and as he did Jishni saw that his skull was malformed, lumpy and bulging on the sides and cleaved in the center. He tilted his head to the side, revealing two faces to Jishni. The eyes of the profile face were blind and the mouth closed and useless. On the other side were functional features, identical to the handsome defunct twin. It was a surreal distortion, his head looking like a cell that had tried to divide, but didn't quite finish the act.

Jishni lost her composure, and gasped.

His functional mouth sneered, causing the defunct mouth to open slightly and form an o. "Buhj." he replied.

She struggled to behave naturally with him. "Buhj is your name?"

"Are ya deaf?" he asked.

Grappling for something to say that might hide her horror, she countered with a stilted question. "Are you being treated well?"

He stared at her sullenly. "No understand Janti," and he turned his perfect profile to her, dismissing her.

Irked by his obvious lie, she demanded, "You understand me, don't you?"

He didn't react, his profile remained still.

She feared her own morbid interest in the deformed men, and for that reason hadn't looked too long at anyone of them. But this one intrigued her. Perhaps it was his dismissing silence, or his utter sadness, she wasn't sure. She stepped closer to the bars, despite hearing Bail's impatient sigh. Intent on drawing the young man out of his corner, she asked, "Can you tell me anything useful about Dilgopoche? What is your view of your country?"

Her question brought his functional face up. He looked at her quizzically. "In comparison to Jantideva?"

She suppressed a smile, and said, "Your Janti is getting better, I see."

He shrugged away his chagrin for having let her lead him into revealing that he knew her tongue.

He said, "I can't compare Dilgopoche with Jantideva. I've never been to Jantideva, except here, in Montrose. The fires make it too hot here. The food is horrible. But it is interesting to see your type after hearing about you in old stories. Though I don't see how the storytellers could have called you beautiful. You are like the Men and Women-you all look alike to we Ryslacs."

"But....I'm confused, Buhj. Ryslacs?"

"We are the race apart from the Men and Women."

"The Men and Women. You mean the giants."

"I am Ryslac. A different race."

"So, you and all these men are Ryslac?"

"Most of them. Some of them are Inferes."

"And the difference is?" she prompted.

"The Inferes are sexless, the end of their lines. Inferes, it is Dilgo for the end."

"Why would you see us as like Rito-Sant? He is different from us, don't you think?"

Buhj stood and stepped closer to the bars to look at Jishni. He was taller than Bail by a few inches, and slender, with arms longer she'd expected. His neck was broad to support his larger head, and split like his face to accommodate what appeared to be two throats, two spines, and yet only one nodule bobbed in his throat as he spoke. His hands were splayed, fringed with digits. He put his hands on the bars, and she counted seven fingers and two thumbs on each hand.

He turned his face so that his seeing eyes looked through the bars. Jishni could see now that he was very young, perhaps Taen's age.

"You're tiny." he conceded. "All you Janti are tiny little Men and Women. Especially you. Never seen a Woman so small."

"I'm average for a Janti female." she informed him easily.

"Hmmm....then maybe you are different. A different race?"

She shook her head, "No, Buhj, we are the same race. We are human. You and I."

His functional face brightened with amusement. "The same race? You are deaf, blind and dumb!"

"Buhj, your deformities do not take away your humanity."

"Deformities!" he retorted, "What deformities? I am Ryslac-Toscocti."

"I didn't mean to offend you Buhj. I was only trying to make you understand that there isn't that much that makes you and I different."

He viewed her, and in a mocking tone, "Hmm, oh yes, I see now how similar we are." And his functional eyes rolled his disgust, much the way Bailin had taken to doing if he thought Jishni was behaving like a stupid mother.

"You have two faces." she offered, "And I don't."

"Aha!' Buhj cried out with discovery, "She can see! I am amazed."

"But can't you see how we are the same?"

He looked at her as if she were insane. "I am Ryslac-Toscocti. How are we similar?"

"How are we different?"

"I am Ryslac-Toscocti." he repeated with emphasis, as if it was obvious and she was obtuse.

"Tell me what that means, because I don't understand."

He frowned. He called out, across the walk way to the corresponding cell on the other side, saying, "Uylle, wake up! Uylle! Wake up!" and he snapped his many fingers impatiently. A man lifted off a cot, and looked at them. He had the same deformity as Buhj, the oddity of a head nearly split in two, with two faces, and a broader neck that supported his larger head, and a splayed hand with many digits.

Buhj said, "He is Ryslac-Toscocti."

Bail's brows hooked together. "You are similar."

"We are the same. We are from the same clan. Toscocti. Eh?" he threw his wide hand in the air, expecting them to understand whether they liked it or not.

"You are from a clan? The Toscocti's, they all share the same defor-" she bit back the word, and continued, "the same appearance."

250

"Oh, I've heard the Men and Women say that of us, that we are deformed. They especially say so when our kind are born of them. It happens. We don't know why. But for as far back as we can remember, the Toscoctis have been made this way. You understand? We are not deformed. We are as we are because we are Toscocti."

"And what of him?" Bail asked of the cellmate of the Toscocti Uylle. The man paced along the back wall, wringing his hands, all four of them. He had short legs and a long body with two sets of shoulders and four well proportioned arms.

"Ryslac-Vubushi." Buhj replied.

"And his kind...they are all like him?"

"Oh yes," he said readily, "Vubushi are known for their kindness, and their intelligence. They are intelligent, Man would say too intelligent, but Man wouldn't deny himself the useful Vubushi inventions."

"How many subgroups of Ryslac are there?"

"Seven clans." Buhj said. "Four mountain clans, three clans of the plain. Vubushi, Fjurd, Yesvectu, and the Denmen are the mountain clans. Bladz, Middrilrich, and my people are clans of the plain."

"Seven," Jishni mused. To Bail, she said, "The way Benu spoke of the untouchables, it sounded as though they were a varied group."

She felt a brush across her arm, and realizing Buhj had reached out to touch her with his many fingers, she bolted away from the bars. Bail reacted by slamming his fist on the bars and demanding that Buhj step back.

Buhj backed away, a look of sardonic amusement on his face. "I touched you. Have you become Ryslac-Toscocti?"

Jishni touched her arm, realizing that she'd offended Buhj with her thoughtless comment about the untouchables.

"I am sorry, Buhj. My only contact with Dilgos thus far has been with Baru-Oclassi. She'd misled us about the Ryslacs. She lead us to believe that you were....essentially ignorant beasts of burden."

Buhj tilted his head to the side and looked at her with a bitter smile. "Yes, they believe they are superior. Perhaps they are.

251

They united the Ryslac Clans, and compelled us to wage war for them. They and their sorcerer."

Angrily, Bail said, "Riar Sed?"

Buhj sneered at the name. "That's the one."

"Is he with Rito-Sant?"

"I'm not a slave of the Men. I don't know what happens in Rito-Sant's tent, or who is there. You are questioning the wrong Ryslac."

"Then why did you cross the mark of the barrier to fight for Rito-Sant?" Jishni countered, "Was it your will to kill Jantis?"

He grew pensive.

"We of the Toscocti clan," he began, "were taught that the land beyond the mark of Eral-Cra was the edge of the afterlife. If one were to walk across, one would meet god. I had long prayed that after I died, I would walk across the mark of Eral-Cra and live in place of beauty and peace with god."

All four of Buhj's eyes grew wet with tears as he mourned the loss of his god, his beliefs, his heaven.

"Are you saying you did not want to attack Jantideva?" she asked significantly.

"The Toscocti are not like Men and Women." he said lowly, "We do not yearn to possess what is not ours. We are a clan of the plain. Nothing more."

"Do all the Ryslacs feel as you do?"

"Not all. The clans of the plain are peaceful. There are other clans, though, that feud among themselves. The Yesvectu and the Fjurd; they are always feuding and warring. And Men and Women feud with all Ryslacs. And now, Men and Women feud with......Janti." he said, deciding that the Janti were a different race despite Jishni's assertion otherwise.

Jishni nodded thoughtfully, worrying that Baru had misled them about more than the Ryslacs. She didn't trust Baru, or Rito-Sant.

"Buhj, how did you learn our language?" she questioned.

He laughed. "How did you learn mine? This is the language of the Clans of the Plains."

"Interesting.....then do you know the language the Dilgos speak?"

He said something rapid in the harsh, guttural language of the Dilgos, and smiled. "Fluently." he bragged.

Jishni looked over her shoulder to her husband. "Bail, I need to speak with Cobo, right away."

She wordlessly canceled the rest of their tour and quickly made her way back to the lift.

Behind her, she heard Buhj shout, "And a nice day to you too, Janti!"

⚜⚜⚜⚜⚜⚜⚜⚜

Taen stalked through the corridor, his senses alert. He held the kai'gam light in his hands, the blade crossed over his body. The blade was an extension of his body. An extension of his arm. A living extension of his spirit.

He detected breathing. Heart beating rapidly. But the heart was too big to be Lodan's, too out of shape. He sensed the size by the way it pumped, sensed the subtle differences in heart rate and flow of blood.

An officer was in the conveyance tube, climbing the ladder from a lower floor, and seeing Taen with kai'gam in hand, he stopped, and watched, an interested gleam appearing in his eyes. Taen pressed his finger to his lips, asking for the officer's silence.

Taen heard movement ahead, and he jerked toward the sound. He moved forward rapidly, his feet making no sound on the open grate that made the floor of the corridor. Approaching an intersection, he slowed. Listened. Hearing nothing, no breathing, no heart beating, no thoughts emanating from a mind. There was a ringing in his ears that he did not notice. He took a step forward, bringing him into the intersection.

He circled cautiously. He saw nothing. He looked down both corridors, and could have sworn they were empty.

After making nearly a full circle, he heard Lodan cry out from behind him in a loud voice, "Aiy Heeeeee!"

The warning spun him on his heels and he lifted the kai'gam in time to deflect Lodan's blade. Taen's heart raced as Lodan attacked, his kai'gam singing. He realized, too late, that the ringing in his ears had been Lodan mesmerizing him with the blade of his

253

kai'gam. Lodan had probably been standing, right there, in the open, in plain sight. Taen's thoughts boiled with defeat. He tried imagining the rushing water, to reach a pure mental state where he was in control of himself and the elements, but since arriving to Montrose his mind was a stagnant and poisoned pool. He feared meeting with the Dilgos. He feared accepting his fate. His fear sidetracked the brief progress he'd made with Lodan.

Lodan chased him down the corridor, he swinging his blade easily in the cramped space, and Taen defending himself clumsily, cracking his blade against the walls and ceiling, slicing and denting the metal. The piercing, and melodic song of Lodan's kai'gam wrenched officers and enlisted men alike away from their stations. A crowd gathered in the corridor behind them. Taen sensed their presence, retreating as Lodan pushed him back. They thrilled to see Lodan in action. He moved with the grace and strength of an eel cat. Taen, on the other hand-

Sweat made his hands slick, and as he reached back, preparing to throw his weapon forward to cross Lodan's, the kai'gam slipped out of his grip. It went sailing behind him, and there were cries of consternation as the onlookers dodged the flying weapon.

The kai'gam lodged in a wall at the bend of the corridor. A man who'd narrowly missed being impaled stared at the jutting weapon, his features white.

Lodan lowered his weapon. "Where is your concentration, Taen? I sense your thoughts are bedlam."

Taen grimaced. "They are bedlam." he said without reserve. He found he could easily talk to Lodan, and confide in him, and take criticism from his hero without falling into a waste of anger.

Feeling beaten, he walked to the kai'gam, grabbed the handle, stuck a foot on the wall beside the embedded blade, and pulled it out, the metal wall screeching its protest.

Taen ignored the onlookers, the Lodan fans, and said to his teacher, "I heard you in the corridor back there, as a ringing in my ears, but it didn't register until after you appeared to me."

Lodan made a thoughtful noise in the back of his throat.

"I listened for your heartbeat as you suggested, but I couldn't hear it." Taen went on, "I heard the heart of a man who surprised me in the corridor, but not yours."

"Ahh, there is a simple explanation." Lodan offered, and he allowed himself a rare smile, "My heart was not beating."

Taen threw a skeptical glare his way. "And how is that possible?"

"Through a Kai'mai relaxation technique called The Rock. I can still my heart, and my lungs, all my internal organs if necessary."

"How can you do that? You'd be dead!"

"No. Death is final. I do not die, obviously, because I am still alive. I simply have taught my body how to subsist without air or blood flow." Lodan said matter-factly, "In a resting state, I can still my heart indefinitely, and maintain a life force. In the active phase, I can still my heart for up to an hour."

Taen laughed. "You tricked me. You told me to listen for your heart beat, then stopped your heart!"

Lodan turned serious. "I taught you the value of using your own judgement. You rely too heavily on the teacher, and you lose sight of the potential that is yours."

"Yes," Taen agreed, "I see my mistake clearly."

"Then today's lesson was a success."

They walked down the corridor they had just been jousting through, to the lift.

In the privacy of the lift, Lodan said, "Tell me what makes your mind a bedlam where nothing flows in or out, only agitates."

"Danati-Zuna." Taen said readily, "In a few hours I will finally meet her and I am nervous. I want to go home, and forget about the Dilgos, and my so-called destiny. Betnoni's prophecies be damned. Her prophecies could be interpreted in a thousand different ways, but because it is easier for mother and Bail to send me away, they choose to believe Ver dala Ven."

"Ver dala Ven was sent to us to serve us in times of need," Lodan reproached, "their wisdom is only turned away by the ignorant and the selfish."

"And I am both." Taen stated with blunt sarcasm.

"It is understandable that you are nervous." Lodan replied, "You will be meeting your bride for the first time. That is enough to make any man nervous."

255

"What if I hate her?" Taen mewled, "What do I do then? Take concubines? But what will I have to choose from? Deformed women, or those stinky Huntresses?"

"Have you married her already?" Lodan asked, his tone vaguely sarcastic, "Did I miss the signing of the treaty agreement, and the joining ceremony? Oh..no..wait, you haven't actually met her yet."

Taen cracked a smile at Lodan's stab at humor. "I get the point. I'm agitating on an event that hasn't even happened yet."

"Correct."

They stepped off the lift together and strolled to the guest quarters. A high pitched note filled the air as they passed the parted door of Bailin's room. He was listening to the latest musical sensation, Gilibea, a singer known for his unnaturally high pitched voice and his mournful songs of lost love. Taen frowned at his sentimental brother. What kind of leader would he make for Janti? Janti needed strength. Janti needed more than Bailin had to offer.

Passing Cobo's quarters, he heard his mother's voice, murmuring low. Feeling a jolt of hopeful spite, he paused outside to eavesdrop.

Hearing Bail's voice join the conversation, he frowned. No illicit interlude between his mother and Cobo would include Bail.

Immediately bored with the three who so recklessly took charge of directing his life, he trotted to catch Lodan, who'd continued on as if Taen had not stopped.

Over his shoulder, and without looking to see that Taen was, indeed, behind him, Lodan asked, "Do you wish to prepare for today with meditation, or do you wish to give your agitated thoughts control over your mood and intellect?"

The question was rhetorical.

Taen replied anyway. "Meditation is preferable over agitation."

"I will guide you." he stated, and he paused at the threshold of Taen's quarters, gesturing for Taen to enter. Lodan had Taen sit on the floor. He began his guided meditation by taking Taen back to the fountains. His smooth voice, like the kai'gam, was hypnotic, and Taen immediately found himself sitting on a bench beside trickling waters. Lodan sat in front of him, speaking to him, the sun shining through his light hair.

Taen's point of reference changed, from sitting by the water, to becoming the water. He was the water, rushing through the creek, molding himself to the contours of the soil and rocks, ever moving to reach his goal.

this kai'gam athlete is dangerous

The voice shook Taen, yanking him abruptly from his peace. He found he was no longer the water, no longer a part of the water. He was in the fountain garden, alone.

"Lodan?"

Silence. Lodan's voice, his form, was gone.

He backed up, looking around, and turning slightly he saw Riar Sed. His old teacher was dressed in faded blue robes, and standing on the other side of the fountain. His image sparkled. His narrow, wrinkled face scowled a smile at Taen.

"The stupid boy has learned to spirit walk." he said, "And taught by an ignorant blade banger, no less. Amazing. I suppose I should congratulate you."

Taen looked at his own sparkling body, his hands, and realized it was true. He was spirit walking! But, how?

"Aha, you don't actually know how you've done it, do you Taen?" he said with nasty glee curling his lips.

"I am the water." Taen replied, feeling it was his connection to the water that had brought him to leave his body and return to his home, Ona.

"But are you the sky?" Riar Sed asked, and he laughed at Taen's expense.

Taen felt potent. He reached out his hand and a droplet of water appeared, hanging suspended above his palm. His eyes on Riar Sed, he projected the water with all his hatred, and from the droplet poured a raging river. The waters splashed down into the fountain, and gushed out the other side, rumbling toward Riar Sed. The force of his river took Riar Sed off his feet, and washed the sight of him away, but did not wash away his voice.

"You fight me," Riar Sed said, "without considering what I offer you. I can help you find the Masing Star."

257

He was blinded by his surroundings, except the sight of a luminous gold orb hovering before him.

Taen came out of his meditation with a gasp.

ઌ⁊ઌ⁊ઌ⁊ઌ⁊ও⁊ও⁊ও⁊ও⁊

Cobo followed Bail and Jishni's rapid pace through the brig. Among the Ryslacs he sensed a mild curiosity at the sight of the Janti, but no hatred, no fear, none of the emotions which he'd felt from the Huntresses. The Ryslacs weren't especially interested in the political motivations of Rito-Sant's war. Besides, they'd been taught by experience that the Janti were weak, stupid, easily conquered, and ridiculously merciful in victory.

Jishni and Bail halted abruptly before a cell, and faced the prisoner. "Buhj." Jishni said, "I have someone I want you to meet."

"And she returns." the Ryslac replied, "But does she greet me? No, she is not at all polite. Are all Janti so impolite, or only this little woman?"

The Ryslac glanced casually at Cobo, expecting Cobo to gasp in shock, as Jishni had when she'd first seen him. Cobo was not shocked, or interested, or diverted by Buhj's appearance. He stared at Buhj, touching his mind….minds….two minds in one body. Two beings in one body.

"Toscocti are united." Cobo said lowly, "You call yourself Buhj, but your silent brother calls himself Drell."

Shock widened Buhj's eyes.

"They are two people in one body." he said to Jishni, "Buhj speaks for them both, but he doesn't always have control of the body."

Jishni's mouth went slack with wonder.

"Two? How is that possible?"

"The Toscocti are a race of twins who are not physically separated. The spirits seem to prefer the togetherness. Drell enjoys the quiet of his own mind, and Buhj enjoys the company of his brother."

"Do you feel Buhj is trustworthy?" she asked.

258

"Drell and Buhj are both very trustworthy men. You must not ignore Drell as you are dealing with Buhj. Drell is the thinker of the two, because he has so much time to himself, behind blind eyes and a mute tongue."

"How do you know of my brother?" Buhj demanded.

Cobo frowned. "You have no need to hide Drell. He will not be extracted from you."

Jishni noted the look of alarm on Buhj's functional face. "Extracted?" she prompted of Cobo.

"You wondered why the Dilgos didn't help their people with surgery. Well, unfortunately, they have. In the beginning, when surgical medicine was still practiced, physicians believed they were removing a dead part of the Toscocti by surgically separating the brains, and spinal chord. Usually, the operation left the Toscocti dead, or worse, a vegetable.

"In time, the Men and Women ritually separated the twins, mistakenly believing that they were liberating a tormented spirit by finishing the process of dividing the two, leaving the twin who had contact with the outside world alive and murdering the twin who was hidden in the dark."

A tiny, guttural cry ripped from Buhj's throat, and he sank into the deepest recesses of his cell.

Cobo said, "His mind, and Drell's, are now filling with nightmarish images of religious rituals and medical experimentation once performed regularly on the Toscocti. In order to avoid being caught in the Men's religious crusade against them, the Toscocti had long ago stopped speaking aloud to, and speaking of, their twins. The Men believed they ended the Toscocti's possession of tormented spirits hundreds of generations ago."

Two hundred ten generations, Drell informed him staunchly.

Cobo smiled briefly at the interjected remark. "Two hundred ten, to be exact."

"How alone the Toscocti must have felt after their sibling was killed." Jishni murmured, appalled, "It must have been better to die."

Seeing her compassion for Buhj and his kind, Cobo could no longer hold in place the aloof mask he'd used to hide the warmth he felt for her, even in Bail's presence. He moved closer to her, and said, "They now fear we might try to do that to them. Maybe you should tell them what you really want from them."

Jishni glanced to Bail. "Let me in to speak with him."

Bail was hesitant.

Cobo said, "They will not hurt her. Jishni is safe."

Bail frowned. He glanced upward at the control panel above his head. He pressed his code into the panel, and said, "Access cell three, six, three." The monitor recognized Bail's voice, and opened the cell door by his command.

Jishni entered, her step light and cautious.

"Buhj," she said, "I want you and Drell to consider a proposition."

Buhj was leaning in the corner, looking at her with tears in his eyes. "What kind of proposition?" he asked thickly.

"I need an interpreter, and an expert on Dilgo society whom I can trust. I was going to use Baru, but I do not trust her, nor do I like her." she said flatly. "I like you....and Ver dala Ven tells me I can trust you, both of you," she amended.

Buhj looked to Cobo, a kind of awe coming over his functional face. "You are Ver dala Ven?"

Cobo heard Drell speaking to Buhj, telling him in quick bursts of images of the many stories about Ver dala Ven he remembered. From the legend of the Masing Star to Betnoni's sacrifice in the Gryvly.

"We are less notable now, since Betnoni left us." Cobo admitted to Drell, "But I am Ver dala Ven."

Drell was impressed.

"Buhj, will you be my interpreter at the peace table?"

Buhj said, "Drell is the linguist."

And Buhj is the playboy.

Cobo chuckled at Drell's droll brotherly jab.

Glancing away from Jishni, Buhj smiled at Cobo. "You can hear Drell?"

"Clearly." he replied.

Drell's mind flooded with questions.

"My brother would very much like to speak with you sometime."

"We will have plenty of opportunities." Cobo assured them both.

Buhj looked at Jishni, and smiled. "Drell and I would like to help you." Cobo heard Drell voice his concerns, which caused Buhj's smile to fade. "As long as you do not openly address Drell in front of the Men. They do not understand Ryslac-Toscocti."

Jishni moved closer to Buhj, and reached out to take his wide hand. Peering earnestly into his eyes, she said, "While you are by my side you are Buhj. And the Men will have no say in your fate."

His smile slowly returned.

৵৵৵৵৵৶৶৶৶

Every time she turned around, there was Durym. He spent his day and part of his night dogging her steps, speaking to her of the joys she was leaving behind at the temple, and she spent her time doing her utmost to avoid him. She'd finally thought she'd been relieved of his presence once the dakas called him away to advise them on some matter of importance, and reveled in the peace of being alone.

He was not gone long enough for Surna.

Durym appeared at the open door of Cobo's quarters. He noted with a hitched brow that she was gathering Ver dala Ven's clothing for the wash, tidying the small room.

"And this is better than spending your mornings in devotions?"

The sound of his voice grated against her nerves. He was tall, fairly attractive, a virile twenty year old boy with thick lashes around his eyes and the soft hands of a priest. A boy, a silly boy. Twenty years younger than her, and pretentious, acting as if he were as aged as Chancellor Yana and twice as wise. He liked to tell tales on the other priests, especially if it enhanced his position in the temple. He also enjoyed the rush of dropping names, bragging that he knew this famous person or had met that political figure, all the while a flush came to his cheeks, the flush of power and influence. The boy wanted to be powerful, influential, and in the spotlight. She imagined he'd volunteered for Taen's wedding, then used his father's influence over Yana to be assigned to the

261

task, simply to be able to say he resided over daka Taen's historic wedding. See how important I am!

Surna did not conceal her contempt for Durym's presence. "Why do you ask, dear priest? Are you feeling the need for the Guardian's carnal satisfactions this morning? You know, I hear that some of the priests know how to satisfy themselves without the holy altar, perhaps you should give it a try."

Durym turned crimson, and pursed his lips. "How could you speak of the beautiful act of devotions with careless heed?"

"Oh Durym," she sighed, "I hope your inexperience is the cause for your lack of sensitivity. Because if it is a character flaw, you'd do well to find an occupation more suited to your talents. Perhaps as a gossip columnist for the Crier."

"I lack nothing," he said, becoming defensive, and blind because of his defensiveness. Fuming, he went on the attack. "Obviously you lack, Surna, for not being able to stick with the discipline. Oh, yes, it is easy being the mistress of one man. Cleaning his room, running his errands, pleasing his body. Does he whisper prayers in the high moments, or do you?"

His unholy outrage, as well as his erroneous assumptions about her relationship with Cobo, scorched her. "You let your imagination go where it is not welcome, Durym!"

"Where is your shame, Surna?" he said, pleading with her now, "You were blessed, a surrogate for the guardian!"

She frowned dangerously, feeling at once like an old mother ready to beat her unruly son. "Perhaps you should lock yourself in the star for a day and see how you like it."

He gaped at her, horrified she could blaspheme.

"And you put up with the degradation of being used for fifteen years," she went on, "and the female infections that come with having sex with twenty men a day, and the knowledge that your youth, and your dreams, have died with your womanhood. You experience all I have experienced, and then come chastise me for not being able to stick with the discipline. Until then, get away from me, Durym. I didn't like you in the temple, I don't like you now, and I'd prefer not to hear your voice or see your face ever again."

His vanity was utterly hurt. His lower lip quivered, like a little boy who'd been smacked in the face. Wordlessly, he fled Cobo's quarters.

Surna breathed a sigh of relief. Finally, some peace. She went through Cobo's simple clothing.

"Surna,"

Durym's return caused her back to bunch with tension. Tiredly, she turned toward him.

His deep-set brown eyes were filled with misery. "I wanted to let you know that I-" He faltered, his words seemingly stuck in his throat. He looked away.

She crossed her arms and waited, nearly expecting some sort of harsh rebuke for how she'd spoken to a Suma priest, all the while preparing a retort sure to skewer his ego to the bone.

With difficulty, he said, "I wanted to let you know that I wish you a happy life."

Her brows shot up. Almost an apology. Perhaps there was hope for Durym, yet.

"Thank you, Durym. Happy life to you too."

A strained smile curled his lips. "Thank you." he said softly, and he left her.

Odd boy. No doubt he'd be a Chancellor before long. His connections, and his drive to become an important member of the Janti court, assured him success.

To bad he'd make a terrible Chancellor.

❧❧❧❧❧❧❧❧❧

Trev circled the Dilgo encampment twice before descending toward the landing sight. Jishni held Buhj's hand as they landed. His many fingers felt strange to her, but his hand was pleasantly warm and dry. She was trying to put him at ease, assure him of her acceptance, and of his safety with the Janti as they entered the peace talks.

He leaned close to her, and said, "Your hand is cold and clammy. Is that normal for your species?"

Jishni suppressed a smile. "It is when we are nervous."

"Oh, you are nervous?"

"Frightfully."

"You don't look nervous."

"Good."

Nan was on her other side, stealing glances at Buhj. His appearance had a subduing affect on everyone in the treaty envoy. She hadn't heard a word spoken among them, but could feel their stares on the Ryslac-Toscocti at her side.

Buhj seemed utterly oblivious to their stares. He watched the ground approach with amazement.

"Wonderful sensation of lightness." he said, and he touched his midriff. "Will we be riding in the windrider again?"

"Yes, in a few hours." she replied to him, and now her stomach felt light, but not from Trev's flawless landing. According to Rito-Sant's demands, they were expected to turn Taen over without a fight, or a treaty. They hadn't brought Taen with him for this meeting. Only their own demands, and resistance. They had no way of knowing how Rito-Sant would respond. Suddenly, she felt vulnerable, though they'd brought an armed military escort.

As expected, a Huntress guard of eight waited for them at the landing sight. They carried crudely made kai'gams, and stood in a line, like soldiers.

Jishni gripped Buhj's hand reflexively.

Buhj leaned over and whispered, "Don't fear them, they are clumsy and stupid as stones. You ask them where their feet are, they show you their tongues."

She suppressed a nervous laugh.

They disembarked as Aton instructed. The four male Pliadors on their windrider stepped out first, followed by Bail and Cobo, Plat and Aradon. The men of all human breeds were considered of higher rank than women, and therefore more deserving of a place of honor. Jishni allowed Buhj to lead her down the ramp. Behind her were Nan, Della, Feblen, Virella, and the two female Pliadors they'd brought with them.

As she and Buhj stepped off the ramp and onto the ground, a Huntress casually blocked Buhj's path. She said something menacing in Dilgo.

Buhj translated. "She has informed me that I am not welcome."

264

Curtly, Jishni said, "Inform her that you are a part of the envoy, as my personal translator."

Buhj replied calmly. The Huntress became enraged, and roughly shoved Buhj back. He faltered a few steps before regaining his balance.

Buhj said unnecessarily, "She is unhappy with the arrangement."

The Huntress sneered at Jishni, and spat what sounded like a curse.

Buhj translated. "Word for word, she said, 'I will not be addressed by a breeder and a Ryslac.' Jishni, we have offended her."

Jishni had encountered a similar attitude of hauteur with Baru. From what she understood, there were three sexes among the Men and Women, the male giants, the masculine female giants, and fertile females of a much smaller size than their counterparts. The latter were called Breeders, and they were the only females of the giant's culture who could reproduce, although how reproduction was possible between the giant men and tiny women escaped Jishni. The Breeders were also considered of low rank, only slightly above the untouchables. Through Baru, they discovered that pretty Danati-Zuna was a Breeder, and had been given some sort of increased rank in order to be made Taen's mate.

Baru, and this Huntress, unquestionably viewed Jishni as a Breeder because of her size. In both instances, she chose to take the reference as an insult.

Irritably she threw her head back to look up into the face of the Huntress. Without wavering, she issued a command. "Bail, we will return to the daka Redd."

To the Huntress, she said, "Tell Rito-Sant that your bad manners sent away the daka of Jantideva, and ruined his chances to marry his daughter off to my son."

Buhj translated quickly. Before he was finished, the Huntress belted out an angry yelp and stalked away, the guard marching closely behind.

Bail's mouth crooked in a smile as Jishni regally strode up the ramp.

Once inside the windrider, Jishni said to Buhj, "She didn't hurt you, did she?"

Buhj assured her she was fine. His seeing eyes were on the departing Huntress guard.

With the envoy in the windrider, and Trev at the helm powering the engines, it certainly appeared they were ready to leave.

Bail said to Cobo, "How long do we wait before we actually leave?"

Cobo's eyes were closed. He was eavesdropping in his own way on Rito-Sant. He shook his head, and said, "Something is happening."

The Huntress guard returned quickly, minus one of its members. Bail set down the ramp, and gestured to Buhj to follow him out.

They all watched as Bail held a heated discussion with a Huntress, aided by Buhj's translation.

Something was decided. Bail and Buhj returned inside.

He looked into Jishni's eyes, and scowled. "Rito-Sant wants you to know he will put the woman that insulted you to death if that is what we want."

"No!" Jishni said sharply.

"Yes." Cobo replied, and he looked at Jishni urgently, "He is testing us. If we appear weak, he will not take us seriously. Mercy is weakness in his mind. He will measure Taen's strength by our actions. We don't want him to find Taen lacking."

"Cobo," she whispered, and she reached for his hands, "Please tell me there is another way to deal with Taen. That he can be rehabilitated. I can forgive him, perhaps even trust him again, I know I can! I can't do this to my son. These people," and she used the word loosely, "aren't fit to live among."

Despite the presence of Bail, and the treaty envoy, Cobo stepped closer to her, bending his face low so they were only inches from each other. Lowly, he said, "You must be strong for Taen. We want Rito-Sant to respect our kind. He is unsure of us, because we are led by a breeder, and he certainly does not like your bringing a Ryslac into the talks. But he is desperate for Taen. I feel he will agree to anything you demand. And there is a reason for that-" Cobo closed his eyes and his voice dropped lower, "-his daughter has fire, Jishni. She is willful, as much a prisoner of her father as his Ryslac slaves."

Jishni closed her eyes, and imagined the beautiful Danati-Zuna as a willful woman. The images came clearer in her mind. Danati-Zuna was an impetuous and thrill-seeking teen, running her father ragged with her outrageous behavior. She had threatened to run away if he tried to force her to mate with a Janti, especially one small and weak. Somewhere close Danati-Zuna also waited for their reply on the Huntress's fate.

Jishni opened her eyes sleepily to peer into Cobo's. "You gave me a vision, didn't you?" she whispered.

Cobo didn't reply to her question. "You will step out and give the order to have her put to death. Her name is Vero, use her name, speak it loud, with malice and anger."

He released her hands and stepped away from her, opening the path to the windrider ramp. She found Bail's eyes. He was clearly troubled by the order she was about to issue.

"Come Buhj." she said.

At the top of the ramp of the windrider, where she nearly stood the height of the Huntresses surrounding them, she issued a sharp and angry demand for Vero's death. Buhj translated.

The Huntresses marched away to relay her demand.

"Guardian forgive me." Jishni whispered.

They waited. Jishni nervously paced the aisle of the windrider seats, avoiding eye contact with her treaty envoy. More and more she questioned her actions, her fears, and the prophecies; indeed, she questioned her own perceptions. Had she truly felt Taen's malevolent touch on her heart, her babies, on that fateful night she gave birth? It seemed like years had passed since that night, and in those years Taen had changed, became a quiet, peaceful boy again. With each glance at the primitive Dilgo encampment, her uncertainty grew. The daka Redd could easily destroy the Dilgos. They could return to Jantideva as victors, and replace Taen in his home, Ona.

The Huntress guard emerged from the tent. The leader carried a tall staff with something affixed to the top. Jishni gasped. Vero's head was impaled on the end of the staff.

Jishni sunk into a seat, terrorized by Rito-Sant's gesture.

Bail said to Cobo, "Is this a good sign?"

Cobo replied soberly, "He sacrificed a valuable soldier for Jishni. It is a very good sign."

The Huntress stuck the staff into the soil near the end of the ramp, so that Vero's slack features stared into the windrider.

Cobo went to Jishni's side, and helped her to her feet. She was reluctant to continue on, to meet the man who'd so callously murdered one of his own for a simple transgression.

"You must look at Vero, and be angry. Do not let them think you are sickened by her death. The same goes for everyone. We must all look at Vero, and show no sign of weakness."

They again exited the windrider, the male Pliadors, Bail and Cobo, Aradon and Plat, followed by Buhj, and the women, Jishni, Nan, Della, Feblen, Virella, and the female Pliadors. Bail and Cobo each paused at the end of the ramp, and glared at Vero's head. Jishni mustered the courage to do the same.

This time, the Huntresses did not address Buhj, nor was he prohibited from entering the camp. The Huntresses avoided his eyes, and the eyes of Jishni, out of respect. Jishni imagined the idea of displaying respect to a Ryslac and a breeder revolted the Huntresses, but they did not reveal their revulsion openly.

The Huntresses marched them into the encampment, where there were more Huntresses milling about. The watched the Janti curiously, staring at Buhj, but no one uttered an objection. No one dared.

Rito-Sant's tent was the largest in the encampment, and was made of shiny silks, in many boldly colored stripes that flowed from the peak of the tent to the black dirt.

Jishni's eyes grew large as she entered. Her gaze flew to the peaked roof of the tent, to the flimsy looking bands that held it aloft, then to the interior. It did not seem as large as she first assumed, then quickly realized the tent was sectioned off with flowing pieces of material. The main section was larger than the Suma Auditorium, and filled with Dilgos, hundreds upon hundreds of Men. A few Huntresses stood guard on the periphery, but the main body of Dilgos were males. They were seated on the ground, reclining on pillows.

Rito-Sant waited, his back erect and his features grim. He looked the part of a barbarian monarch, with long golden hair in a thick braid that snaked over his shoulder to lay across on his bare chest. He wore a black band across his forehead, signifying his rank, and a brief loincloth fringed with beadwork. Jishni noticed immediately, and to her chagrin, that the cloth he wore was not enough to fully cover his slumbering manhood. Its head jutted from beneath strings of beads, its one eye seeming to watch her as she entered the hall.

Disconcerted by his exposure, she did her utmost to keep her eyes upward and on his face. Equally disconcerting, however, were his hard blue eyes. Rito-Sant was an imposing figure.

Jishni fought the urge to reach for Nan and Buhj for support, or worse, to flee the sight of a giant. She held her head high, and followed the procession of Huntresses until they stood before the Dilgo monarch. Here, Bail and Cobo dropped back behind Jishni in obvious submission to her authority.

A hushed silence persisted, where all that could be heard was the laborious breathing of the Dilgos. Jishni waited for Rito-Sant to welcome her.

Finally, he sighed, and it struck Jishni that he seemed as reluctant to be a part of these talks as she.

Rito-Sant began to talk, his grave voice booming, filling the tent.

Buhj translated Rito-Sant, word for word. "'I wish to welcome my honored guests. We have waited an eternity to be in the company of our Janti brothers.'"

Jishni nodded, and replied, "I only wish our meeting could have been on friendlier terms, and not held in the rubble of one of my cities."

Rito-Sant frowned deeply as Buhj translated.

He replied, his tone spiteful.

Buhj's tone held the same spite, as if to portray Rito-Sant's retort correctly. "'Jantideva owed us a blood sacrifice for the suffering we have endured.'"

Anger took hold of Jishni, and she forgot her fears. She took a step forward and replied loudly, so that her wrath was

269

unmistakable to his ears. "The people of Montrose did you no harm!"

"'Their guilt is written in the history of their race. There are no innocents in Jantideva.'"

"You could have come to us in peace, and we would have somehow made reparations for all that you have lost."

Rito-Sant laughed harshly.

Jishni added vehemently, "Instead you have alienated the Alliance! You may have won my cooperation, but the world is against you. Do you think you can trade for goods in a world that distrusts you? Do you believe you will be welcomed with open arms into the Alliance after what you have done?"

"'We are not interested in the Alliance.'"

Jishni's brows shot up at Buhj's translation, and she retorted, "Your attack on Montrose implies interest."

"'You spoke of reparations,'" Rito-Sant said, pausing as Buhj shadowed his words, "'Reparations are inconceivable. The damage is done, and irreversible. Jantideva cannot pay us enough for the wrong committed against our people. We are now, and forever will be, your responsibility. By joining our houses, we become kinsmen. I expect Jantideva to behave as an elder brother, providing sponsorship and succor to our ailing nation.'"

Cobo had moved, coming up behind her. Lowly, he said, "He is sincere. He wants Taen in his court to compel Jantideva to take care of Dilgopoche. Ultimately he wants Dilgopoche to become a part of the Janti nation."

Buhj turned, and translated what was meant to be a private comment. Jishni barked his name, but not before the damage was done.

Rito-Sant stared hard at Cobo. He addressed Cobo, his tone flat.

Buhj translated, though it was hardly necessary for Cobo, who could read Rito-Sant's thoughts.

"'Present yourself.'"

Cobo's voice was clear and sure, and his reply needed no translation. "Ver dala Ven."

Rito-Sant's hands flexed, the only sign of his shock. His eyes steadied on Cobo.

"'I was told you were dead.'"

"Your source was mistaken," Cobo replied, "I suspect he has made many mistakes. One comes to mind, as he attempted to manipulate the Janti into a laughable defeat. But he failed, didn't he? The Janti were victorious."

Rito-Sant eyed Cobo, considering what he'd said. To Jishni, Cobo murmured, "He is dubious of my claim."

"One only need look at you and know the truth."

"My appearance does not seem out of the ordinary to him."

"Why?"

Cobo shook his head as he stared at Rito-Sant, and perplexed, he said, "I can't see why, just that I seem….ordinary to him for some reason."

Rito-Sant issued an impatient sounding epithet.

Buhj said, "He wants you to prove that you are Ver dala Ven."

"Very well."

Cobo stepped forward, holding out his hand, and something happened that Jishni had never seen him do. As he reached out his hand, in his palm he'd conjured a small point of light. The point grew in size, reaching out and encompassing the entire assembly. A gasp riffled among the Dilgos as they were touched, and some of the men on the floor inched away from the glow. Jishni held a similar reaction in check, until the golden glow enveloped her. Calm took hold and released the stress she held in her shoulders. A new certainty that what she was doing for Taen was right and timely came over her in waves of warmth.

A look of amazement grew on Rito-Sant's face.

The golden light expanded toward and gently enveloped Rito-Sant. He braced himself, as if he expected an attack.

A huge smile grew on his face, and in seconds he sighed content.

Cobo held a restraining hand toward Buhj, demanding his silence, and he spoke to Jishni. "Because of their size and rapid rate of growth in infancy, the Men and Women suffer from debilitating bone diseases. Rito-Sant is elderly for his kind, though he is only thirty-nine. He hasn't been able to walk for many years, due to a failure in his knees and hips."

271

The glow faded, sinking into Rito-Sant's legs. He relaxed fully. Staring at his legs, he tried moving his right. He laughed heartily as his foot rose off the podium. He moved the left, and again he laughed his joy.

He stood, and the entire congregation stood with him, gaping in wonder at their restored leader. Grinning, he strutted around the peace envoy, brandishing his arms outward, presenting himself to his subjects. A roar of approbation went up, whistles and the thumping of their feet caused the ground to shudder.

As he completed his circuit, he returned to the chair, this time jauntily standing aside it, his hands planted on his hips. The cheers among the Dilgos seemed never ending, yet when Rito-Sant spoke, silence fell all around them.

Buhj translated, "'Welcome to Dilgopoche, Ver dala Ven. I am especially honored by your presence.'"

"I have come as a member of daka Taen's court," Cobo informed him, "another measure of recompense from Jantideva to Dilgopoche."

Rito-Sant faltered, his face brightening with elation at the unexpected good news.

Jishni's pain in her heart for losing Taen doubled. Her voice hard, she said, "But before we turn over our precious heir and Ver dala Ven, we have demands that must be met."

Rito-Sant listened to Buhj with more patience, and readily agreed to hear their demands.

As was previously planned, Aradon took the floor. He stood proudly in the shiny green costume of his native land, Dacha. He listed, slowly for Buhj's benefit in translation, the demands of the Janti court. None were rejected, even the amendments concerning the limits placed Dilgos entering into Jantideva. The Janti wanted them to stay within their own boundaries. Jishni expected Rito-Sant to be offended by that particular point, but he seemed more than willing to let it be law.

The treaty agreed upon, Jishni, her heart breaking, agreed to release her son to Rito-Sant in betrothal to Danati-Zuna.

Rito-Sant crossed his arms and peered thoughtfully at Jishni. His low voice rumbling, he spoke his language slowly while Buhj interpreted.

"'Of all my children, Danati-Zuna is the only breeder I have produced. She is precious. She will carry my blood, and give birth to my descendants. I give her to your son, in trust and hope for the future of Dilgopoche.'" he said it with difficulty, as if the thought of turning her over to Taen sickened him

Their size and cultural differences disappeared as Jishni saw him as a parent, as conflicted as she about giving his child away to a loveless union with a stranger. In spite of her anger toward the Dilgos, her fear of them and revulsion, she found common ground with Rito-Sant that would forever soften her heart toward him.

Rito-Sant moved on to the subject of Janti's prisoners of war. He requested they be released.

Buhj added to his translation, "Jishni, give him the huntresses, and refuse him the Ryslacs. They will only kill us, or enslave us. If we are freed separately from the Huntresses we can go home, instead of being taken to the city of the Men and Women."

"Very well, you tell him what you want, and make them my words. You know your people's plight better than I."

Rito-Sant agreed to the return of the Huntresses without the Ryslacs. His sole concern was with the welfare of one Huntress, his sister. By his manner, Jishni gathered that even the rest of the Huntresses were expendable.

"'It is done.'"

The simple statement inspired the giants to stomp their feet and chant what sounded like a fighting song. Rito-Sant's sober mood lightened, and he joined them, gaily stomping his feet and shouting at the top of his lungs.

The rumbling beneath Jishni's feet felt like an earthquake.

Buhj shouted to explain, "The treaty has been accepted and passed by the majority. I see two men who do not agree."

She looked in the direction Buhj gazed. Two men, both fair and youthful, though perhaps not at all youthful, considering how young the Dilgos die a natural death. They glowered at Rito-Sant, their hands stuck defiantly under their arms, their feet planted solidly on the ground.

Jishni moved to Cobo. "What of them?"

"Taen's competition," he said matter-factly. "Rito-Sant has no sons, only brothers. If it weren't for Rito-Sant's desire to unite

Dilgopoche with Jantideva, one of them would be the next Dilgo with Sant after his name. They have every intention of killing Taen as soon as the opportunity arises."

A chill raced through Jishni.

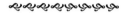

The third sign of the Rebirth is mourning. One to the Guardian, One to the invisible; The purpose is clear. To take the hard path the daka must free those Redd set into bondage

Chapter 13

Jishni would have preferred a lengthy betrothal between their children, for by Janti standards, Taen was far too young to take a wife, and she wished him to have a traditional wedding ceremony, held in the exalted Ona Temple. As expected, however, Rito-Sant would not delay the claiming of his prize. He gave them but four days to make preparations and gather the important members of the court and the Alliance for the event.

During the late evening of the fourth day, Taen was brought to Rito-Sant's tent for the first time. He wore a black Suma wedding robe, the very robe Bail had used to wed Jishni, his face covered with a cowl. Lodan Kru Dok attended him, by his request, as well as his brother Bailin, by his mother's decree.

They entered into a joyous celebration, a somber troop of small people. Giants danced and sang around Rito-Sant's throne, stomping in time to lilting, rhythmic music played by an ensemble of Ryslacs. Others lounged on pillows on the periphery of the main floor, eating, drinking, and to the shock of the Janti, publicly copulating. Nearest the tent opening, Trev sat among a group of Dilgo men, dwarfed by them yet treating them like old drinking buddies, telling tales of his adventures with daka Bail in broken Dilgo and hand gestures. Whether or not they understood him, Trev amused them, evident in their full laughter.

A section of the tent had been cleared for the Janti and Alliance guests. Tables and chairs and customary accoutrements had been prepared for the daka's comfort. Jishni employed Janti servants to wait on them for this occasion, wanting nothing to go awry, though noting as they entered into Rito-Sant's den of iniquity that there was no way to prevent the event from being a complete disaster.

Baru-Oclassi proudly stood by her brother's empty seat, while her brother danced a jig with a fresh, young Huntress. He laughed, and sang, and behaved like a boy half his age. Rito-Sant's happiness for feeling young again was in his great smile. He spun in a circle, and caught sight of the Janti as they entered the tent, and specifically caught sight of Cobo, and he let out a joyous whoop.

He clapped his hands, and the music ended abruptly. With a broad smile on his face, Rito-Sant welcomed his guests.

With ceremony befitting a daka, Jishni and Bail led the procession of the Janti court through the Dilgo tent. Behind them were their sons and Cobo, Lodan, and in succession, the full membership of the Alliance, the latter taking their places in the seats provided. Finally, bringing up the rear, Durym and Surna.

Rito-Sant watched them, his eyes finding Taen. Melancholy touched his features, though he struggled to keep his smile alive. Taen halted in the middle of the great space, and once silence and calm had descended upon the giants, Durym began the ceremony. He placed his hands on Taen's shoulders, and said a prayer for the couple, for health, wealth and happiness. Rito-Sant took his seat and looked down at Taen, watching the Janti custom impassively. Ceremony meant nothing to him, nor was he interested in the strange custom of tying two hearts together for life, except for how uniting Taen to his family could serve him and his people. The Dilgos did not use ceremony to unite. The Men and Women shared each other equally, openly. The Breeders remained pure, or if they didn't, they were put to death. It was their law, and their custom, and as easily as Rito-Sant looked upon the open orgy in his tent among the Men and Women present, he equally abhorred bending the law for this little Janti, especially with his daughter. But Rito-Sant tried keeping his eyes on his people's future, and this little Janti's happiness meant much to that future.

Once Durym was finished, Baru-Oclassi came forward give to Taen a gift from Rito-Sant. It was a gold pendant, and he was told it was a symbol of the Men and Women, and his entry into Rito-Sant's family. The shape was unmistakably the symbol of the Masing Star, a ten-pointed star. She placed it around his neck.

Taen glanced at the pendant speculatively. Cobo sensed from his son an interest in the Masing, with an undercurrent of avarice. Taen's thoughts behind the emotions, however, remained elusive. Cobo noted that Taen's new sense of peace, taught to him by Lodan, had created a private space around him in which he could not penetrate, unless it was done vigorously and violently. Cobo thought better of invading Taen's mind. For the time being it was useful to him that Taen thought he was impervious to Ver dala Ven's perceptions.

Far behind the throne, from a private area inside the tent made with silken material, Danati-Zuna appeared. Following her were two fair, blond Breeders, sisters to Rito-Sant, and her chaperones. Danati was covered with a flowing, loose fitting gown, one of the many in the trousseau Jishni had given to her, and she wore it proudly. It was a resplendent red hue, and moved gracefully with each step she took. Her head was veiled with a sheer cloth that was secured by a black rope around her neck, as the custom dictates. Her attendants escorted her to Baru-Oclassi, and Baru-Oclassi escorted her to her place, where she was instructed to kneel before Taen. In keeping with the Janti marriage ceremony, Surna draped a black cloak over the bride. She stood back, next to Baru-Oclassi, as Durym had Danati-Zuna repeat a prayer to the Guardian, where she promised to love and be faithful to Taen for the rest of her life.

Danati-Zuna's Janti was flawless, and her voice resoundingly strong, though she was apprehensive. Cobo sensed in her a knowledge of men, not Janti men or Men, but of Ryslacs. She was not as pure as her father thought her to be, and though she was attracted to Taen, she worried that he might not satisfy as well as her court slaves.

Taen had similar worries, and a similar distaste for being attached to one woman for the rest of his life, even one as fine as Danati.

Cobo felt sorrow, for he sensed the dark future of their union.

Taen said his vows to Danati. Afterwards, Durym said a few trite words about the joys of love, keeping his portion of the ceremony short as Jishni had instructed, and said his final blessings. He removed Taen's cowl and Danati's veil, careful not to remove the rope around her neck, to allow the couple to look upon each other's faces. Danati then removed the length of the rope from her neck and handed it to Taen, a very old Janti tradition symbolizing a woman's surrender of her freedom, and her acceptance of the man she'd been joined with.

Durym declared them married according to Janti law.

Taen held fast the rope, and smiled happily, relieved that the first half of their stressful ordeal was over. The entire congregation of Janti relaxed, their sober expressions turning to smiles with Taen's smile, for finally one Janti among them smiled. None thought it was possible to find a moment of respite among the stink and immorality of the Dilgos. Even now, on pillows and in plain view of all present, a Man climbed upon the back of a Huntress and went at her, they both grunting like animals as they fed their passions, despite the ceremony and the host of witnesses present. The Dilgos seemed not to notice the couple's poor timing, oblivious that their actions were barbaric and just plain wrong, a fact that further outraged and scandalized the prim and proper Janti.

Jishni could not reach Bailin, but Voktu was right next to her, and she made her thirteen-year old son cast his eyes to the floor, much to his chagrin.

Getting on with it, Surna removed the black cloak from Danati-Zuna's back.

Jishni squirmed in her seat. It was time for Danati to perform. The Dilgos had no ritual for marriage, but the breeders often danced for the court in a ritual that was a part of their breeding practices. Buhj had explained the custom. The dance was supposed to excite the Men's seed out of them, for later implantation into the breeders. When Jishni wondered how a Breeder as small as Danati could carry the child of a giant, he explained that the giants were born small, beginning their great growth during the time they changed from children, to adults. The Breeders stayed small, the Men and Women grew large. And what of the small men, she wondered. Weren't there small men, counterparts to the breeders? Buhj reported that, yes, there were small men, and once puberty was upon them and their growth did not begin, they were executed.

Rito-Sant had assured her that all Taen's children with Danati would be protected, even if they were small men. His assurance did little to assuage her fears, and Jishni knew that her worries for Taen, and whatever grandchildren came from Taen, would never end.

A Dilgo boy raced onto the dance floor holding a cylindrical tube made of what appeared to be clay. He sat beside Taen, and placed the tube between his feet.

278

Danati stood, and stepped off the pillows and onto the dance floor. She rolled her head, her shoulders, preparing. Facing Taen, she struck a pose, once hand pointing gracefully upwards, the other lifting the gown to display a sinewy calf, bare feet and ankles adorned with many gold bands.

The boy began to play, tapping his fingers along the length of the tube, creating a hollow, tinkling song, gentle and light. She started to dance, her movements slow and seductive. Her hands found her waist, holding down her shapeless gown to accentuate her form, and her torso undulated beneath the filmy material. She danced in a circle around Taen, with each step rocking her hips. As she went behind him, she teased his cheek with the end of her silken gown. His head went back and he watched her progress as she made her way to her original place.

Before him once again, her hands moved to her hips and bunched her gown to raise it to her knees. She performed a few steps of a Dilgo folk dance Cobo had seen the Huntresses doing during the celebration. Danati's version was lighter, and quicker. She performed the complicated moves with ease.

Dropping her gown, she twirled, the gown teasing her legs, and she lunged forward to land on her hands and knees. She crawled toward Taen, acting like an animal on the prowl. Climbing onto the pillows, she lay on her back with her legs parted in the air and her gown falling aside to reveal her female to him. She simulated the act of coupling for Taen's benefit, caressing herself and issuing guttural cries that were supposed to be passion, all the while the music grew faster, building to a climax.

Jishni, as well as many of the members of the Alliance present, found this portion of the dance offensive, and averted her eyes from the display.

Taen was transfixed by Danati-Zuna's open sensuality. His mouth was agape as he watched her writhe on the pillow before him, making a promise to her husband of the delights he could expect all his life.

The boy's playing stopped, and Danati-Zuna rolled up into a sitting position. Her eyes blazed with desire and her bosom rose and fell with a quickened breath. She yearned to try this small man, and reached out for Taen intending to seduce him right there and then, grabbing at his clothing with greedy hands. As she untied his belt, Taen realized that she wanted to copulate as the rest of her people did, with abandon and in front of everyone, and his own Janti prudery caused him to push her away, to withdraw. His actions brought Rito-Sant to the edge of his seat, and Baru-Oclassi from her place by her brother.

Danati's aunt yanked her roughly off the pillow and to her feet, and speaking her strangely accented Janti, she demanded. "Do you find this one lacking?"

Taen nearly choked on his reply. "No, no, absolutely, no, she's beautiful!"

"Take her then." Baru-Oclassi shouted, repeating the shout in Dilgo, which encouraged the Dilgos at the celebration to begin chanting, urging Taen on.

Taen glanced around, anxious lines appearing around his mouth for what the Dilgo's expected of him. It was clear that he didn't know what to do.

"Cobo, please, make this stop." Jishni entreated.

Cobo nodded, and stood, an action that earned Rito-Sant's immediate attention. The crowd silenced as Cobo spoke, and Baru translated. He explained that the Janti were uncomfortable with open copulation, and wished that the couple be allowed privacy.

Murmurs raced through the giants, and Baru retorted to Cobo that the Janti were barbaric creatures, and that Rito-Sant would have none of their barbaric ways.

Rito-Sant, however, was agreeable enough to giving his daughter and her lover privacy. He had dreaded witnessing the small man defile his daughter. He preferred to hold Danati in his mind as a Breeder, pure and untouched, even if it were no longer true after this night.

Danati and Taen were instructed to leave the staging area and retire to Danati's private space in her father's tent. Taen stood, and took his wedding cloak off and placed it on Danati's shoulders, covering her. Looking eager, he embraced her, and as one they followed Baru-Oclassi to the farthest reaches of the tent.

Lodan Kru Dok rose, and followed, to stand guard near the screen and protect Taen from his enemies. A gathering of youthful

Dilgos also crept near the screen, and listened. Whatever they heard caused uproarious lewd laughter and shouts.

"In Ona we could have made his wedding a beautiful affair." Jishni said downheartedly.

A corrupt grin opened Bail's mouth, "I don't think Taen minded how his wedding turned out. He looked pretty cheerful."

Jishni shot him with a hot glare. "There is nothing holy about craven deviants eavesdropping on their first innocent tryst."

Bail threw his hands up in surrender to avoid an argument. "I stand corrected, yes, we could have made it beautiful for them in Jantideva."

Trev joined them, sitting between Bail and Cobo. He winked at Bail. Lowly, so that Jishni could not hear, he said, "Danati-Zuna's dance will live in my fondest fantasies for as long as I shall live."

Bail couldn't help but laugh at his friend's lecherous comment.

The Dilgos began a celebration that involved full abandonment and succor of all the senses. Eating, drinking wine, clamoring tribal drums, dancing, and public copulation involving two or many more Dilgos; the Dilgo brand of merriment held no bounds of good taste or restraint. The Janti were expected to participate. The majority begged fatigue after a short time, Jishni included.

"I need air." she said flatly. She stood, ordered her sons up and out of their seats, and with them in tow, she strode purposefully out of the tent.

Durym agreed, "They are savages." and followed his daka.

Surna, who had taken her place beside Cobo after the ceremony, scoffed at Durym, saying to Cobo, "Is it more savage to be joyful for a couple to love each other, than for a body of priests to have sexual relations with one woman at dawn each morning?"

Cobo smiled at her sarcastic comment. "You don't find the Dilgos the least bit revolting, do you?"

Surna's brown eyes glanced around the room of giants. "Do you think I am odd?" she asked, as a way to evasively answer him that no, she did not find them revolting.

"I think you are accepting, and embrace all that the Guardian Spirit of Creation offers us." Cobo replied, his eyes twinkling at her.

"I feel comfortable among them." she said, encouraged by his acceptance, "I know intellectually that I am not like them, but in a way I am. I have been altered by the Janti to suit the purpose of the Janti. Just as they had been altered."

"Betnoni must have known you'd be happy in Dilgopoche." Cobo said casually.

A look of content came over Surna's face.

ఇఇఇఇఇఙఙఙఙఙ

The announcement of Taen's wedding was made over the Crier the following morning. Jantideva mourned the loss of their heir, but heaved a sigh of relief that the conflict with Dilgopoche had been resolved.

Jem Jin heard the announcement as she was eating breakfast. She had just put a sweet cake in her mouth. She froze, and her jaw locked. She couldn't swallow, couldn't spit the sweet cake out.

"Jem Jin?" Ovu said gently, "Are you all right?"

Nodding, she stood and left the kitchen table, her breakfast unfinished. Once she was out of earshot, her peers around the table clucked and shook their heads. For well over a year they'd seen her entering and leaving Taen's room, calculating the length of time she spent with him each night, knowing full well that something was going on between the daka and the Shodite girl. They felt sorry for Jem Jin, assuming she'd been in love with Taen and was now heart broken.

Jem Jin rode the lift to the nursery, cloaked as if in a dream. Her movements were sluggish. She didn't have full control over her body. Her vision was hazy, bordering on blindness, where only the tiniest pin dot of sight was available to her.

She stepped off the lift, and saw a nurse. A woman she liked, very much. A Janti that treated her with respect. She was named Leila, after the great Ver dala Ven.

Leila smiled, "Jem Jin, you're early, love! You oughtn't work too hard-"

Jem Jin's hand reached out for an item off a nearby table, and she silenced Leila's greeting by clubbing the nurse on the head with it.

She looked at her hand, and saw that she held a spiraling luck stone, a gift to the babies from the Minister of Dacha. Looked down. Leila was sprawled on the ground, unconscious, blood trickling from her ear.

Jem Jin's dream became a nightmare. She tried to scream, but as her mouth cranked open, no noise came forth. The sweet cake that was lodged between her teeth fell on the floor.

Pain poured into her, a scalding, stinging sensation. The harder she tried to push the scream out of her body, to cry for help, the more intense the pain became.

A voice in her head urged her to do something hideous and promised dire consequences if she did not follow through. Sucking in a shuddery breath, she gave up on screaming for help. The pain was immediately swept away.

She heard one of the babies crying. Janus. She recognized his cry. His was usually more insistent than Archer, more demanding. Just like a daka. Insistent, demanding, just like Taen. She went into the nursery and stared down at the tiny infants in the warming bed. Janus cried, kicking his feet and legs robustly. They were early births the doctor said, but they were thriving as if they were full term babies. Janus was the strong one.

Archer, the weaker. The sweeter. He lay curled next to his squalling brother, his eyes open slightly to the bedlam. He seemed to see Jem Jin, and he seemed to smile, though babies this young didn't smile, she told herself.

She gently touched Archer and spoke his name, and he reacted to her, recognized her, as if she were his mother.

Involuntarily, as with what she'd done to Leila, Jem Jin took hold of a pillow off Jishni's bed, and pressed it on Janus's full body. Silence filled the nursery.

Janus struggled mightily beneath the pillow as his air ran out. He grew still.

Archer began to cry.

She woke to her own actions as she heard Archer's thin cry, and gasped, throwing the pillow aside. As soon as she tossed away her weapon, the pain returned. But this time, in spite the pain, she focused her thoughts, her fears, her guilt, her compassion, on Archer, and how he cried for his older brother. She knew she could not kill Archer. The pain flowed through her, ripping her in two, and yet she could not bring herself to reach for the pillow again.

She lifted Archer out of the baby bed, doing her best not to look at his still twin, and lay him on a blanket and wrapped him so that he looked like a bundle of clothing.

As she cradled him, he quieted.

She left the palace carrying her bundle. She had informed Ovu she had vomited and needed to go home, in Dralon, to change. His eyes filled with pity for her, and he let her go.

On the windrider destined for Dralon, her head cleared and the pain ebbed to a dull ache in her heart. She remembered all she had done, and remembered, too, why she killed Janus, why she had kidnapped Archer. Daka Taen had enchanted her. She remembered it all, every night of rape, every day of blissful unawareness.

In Dralon, she took a windrider into the city. She had a cousin who was a laborer, and lived in Shod City. She would seek his help. She couldn't go back, not after killing a daka.

Seated on the windrider, she unwrapped the baby and peered lovingly into Archer's little face. He was a sweet baby. With a proper upbringing, he wouldn't turn out like the other dakas. He'd be a good man.

A Shodite woman near her cooed her delight at the sight of the child. "Is it yours?" she asked.

"Yes, my son." Jem Jin lied, perhaps too readily.

"And what is his name?"

Without hesitation, Jem Jin christened Archer, "Gidnea," after a fellow she once thought she loved.

"Gidnea," the woman said with approval, "A good Shodite name."

"Yes, it is." she said, and she smiled at her adopted son.

৵৵৵৵৵৵৵৵৵

Jishni managed the efforts to divide the Ryslacs into their respective groups in order to transport them to their homes. It was busywork to keep her mind off the Dilgos and their preparations to leave for their home city, Zadoq. Taen seemed only too willing to leave with his new family. He was blissfully bewitched by his bride's charms. Trev had imprudently passed on information that Taen and Danati-Zuna had hardly left their bed since their wedding.

"Last time I saw him, he was wearing a stupid grin and a woman's robe." Trev told Bail. "He raced out from their cove to grab a plate of fruit and a bag of wine, Danati crying out his name from their bed the whole time, and raced back as if he had a fire on his backside. He probably couldn't decide which hunger to feed first."

Bail had the audacity to laugh.

Jishni preferred Buhj's company to Bail's this morning, and the business of being a daka to being the bridegroom's mother.

Buhj helped to separate the respective clans of Ryslac, speaking to each in their own unique dialect of Janti. She was impressed by how well he went from one of his kind to another, addressing them as friends and gaining their confidence. Like a diplomat, she decided.

As they were on their way to the docking bay to add another destination to their flight list, Jishni complimented him on his organizational skills.

Buhj took the compliment with a diffident smile.

"Buhj," she said, "would you and Drell ever consider leaving Dilgopoche?"

Buhj halted abruptly. "To go where?"

Candidly, she said, "Here is what I am thinking. If we are to incorporate Dilgopoche into Jantideva, we need to understand your country and your people. We need to know your history, and your geography, and the names of your clans, and your languages. What I'd like for you to consider is a position in the Janti Library, aiding in our research of your people."

"Me?" he said, "Us?"

"You'd be faced with many challenges." she admitted, "The most important is educating us about your many cultures, your history, your collective suffering. Least important, but perhaps most uncomfortable, will be in facing the reaction of the Janti people during your visits to the Center-plex. In all fairness to you, I must truthfully say you will encounter fear and distrust, and perhaps revulsion from many Janti. But not from me. You will be a guest in my house when you visit on business."

"Drell says yes, but I am undecided." he said, and he shifted uncomfortably. "I already see the looks we get from the Janti, how they stare and turn away if I catch them. They are afraid to say hello, for fear I might reply. You see, in truth I am very vain." He joked, and shrugged, and nodded, a way to show the joke was at least partially true. "Among the Toscocti, I am considered handsome. I have many girlfriends. Here, among you, I am ugly. In Jantideva, I'd have no one."

"Yes, that is true." she replied, "If you decide you cannot work among us, I understand. I will be disappointed, but I will understand."

"Yes, yes, I will tell her." Buhj said, patting his brother's cheek. "Drell wants me to tell you that if he didn't have a scoundrel lady's man for a brother, he'd gladly go to Jantideva with you. Personally, I think Drell has a crush on you, Jishni." and he grinned, "If you were Toscocti, I might too."

"If I were Toscocti," she replied playfully, "we wouldn't be having this conversation. I'd take one look at your young faces, and send you home to your mother."

"Oh, that hurt." Buhj replied in jest, grabbing for his broken heart.

They'd resumed walking as a call came through for Jishni. She paused and ordered the ship's communications to connect her. Doctor Poulin's face appeared, hovering in midair before her and Buhj. His features were grim.

"Doctor? Are the babies well?"

"Jishni, I have some bad news. Perhaps you should find Bail, and we can discuss this together."

"You will tell me now. What is wrong?"

"Are you alone?"

Jishni glanced at Buhj, who was watching her with genuine concern. She'd told him about her new babies, and shown him a likeness of twins who were born in separate bodies. He'd been fascinated by the concept, and bit repulsed, too, that two beings so alike could be separated by flesh.

"Speak freely." She insisted.

"This morning," the doctor began, "one of your Shodite nannies attacked Leila Gaulden, and attempted to murder Janus."

A breath was pushed from her body. "How is he?"

"He is in critical condition. We have him in a respirator at the moment. Daka, you must return to the palace. Janus may not survive." he said sympathetically.

Her feet prickled cold, and her head grew light.

"Archer?"

His lips compressed into a thin line. "Daka, I am so sorry to have to inform you that he has been kidnapped."

"Kidnapped?" she said incredulously, "Who? Who took my baby!"

"A young woman named Jem Jin. The Pliadors are presently searching Dralon, but as of yet she has not been found."

Jishni rushed to Bail, oblivious of Buhj racing along behind her through the corridors of the Daka Redd. She found Bail drinking with Trev in his quarters on the officer's deck. Breathless, hysterical, weeping, she poured out the news. Bail came to his feet and tried to comfort her, though his features twisted with the same gamut of emotions she felt, from helplessness to hysteria.

She would not be comforted. She pushed his hands away and uttered, "I must find Cobo."

Bail flew into an uncharacteristic rage. He swept the bottles and glasses off the table, causing Trev to duck away from flying, smashing glass, and in doing so landing on his backside on the floor. Lunging at her, his finger shaking in her face, Bail shouted, "He is not the father of Archer and Janus! You have no business going to him!"

She backed away, frightened of Bail for the first time in her life. "He is Ver dala Ven! He can help find Archer!"

He reeled, obviously drunk. Weeping, he said, "I couldn't save Taen, but I will save my own son!"

"You'd put your pride ahead of Archer's welfare?" she asked him incredulously, "If Taen had been your son, it would be you asking Ver dala Ven to help us find Archer!"

A bitter smile twisted his lips. "But Taen isn't my son, is he?" He turned to Trev, who was bemused, sitting on the floor in the center of a pool of brandy. "Get my transport ready. We are returning to Ona." He barked an order at the impersonal ship communications system to connect him to Ona's Captain of Watchers, Varian. In moments Varian's likeness was projected into the room with them.

Jishni quietly slipped out of Bail's quarters with Buhj. "I've got to get to Cobo." she said urgently.

"Is there anything I can do?"

"Attend to your people."

She rushed off, leaving Buhj staring anxiously at her back.

๛๛๛๛๑๑๑๑๑

The tents came down, and were loaded into primitive carts. The Dilgos once had windriders a long time ago, but they had run out of fuel quickly after the Dome of Silence was erected. Like Shodalum, they returned to their aboriginal state once technology died. They used carts for their supplies, and carriages for their important people, pulled by beasts of burden or hundreds of slaves.

Rito-Sant's carriage was once an ancient seafaring ship, stripped and modified to suit Dilgo comfort. The ship's curved bottom fit in a specially formed block to hold it upright. The block was surrounded by hundreds of metal wheels forged by blacksmiths. For his carriage, Rito-Sant did not use animals, but his Ryslac slaves. Hundreds, naked, tied to ropes and driven by Rito-Sant's huntress guard.

Taen, now a part of the family, was ushered inside Rito-Sant's land ship, along with his bride and his protector, Lodan. Cobo was invited to join them, but declined. He still felt like a Shodite. He loved his feet, and disliked very much the idea of benefiting from the sweat of slaves.

He and Surna loaded their belongings into a cart pulled by one beast. Their conversation was pleasant, as they compared their observations of the Dilgos. Cobo decided that Betnoni wasn't just looking out for Surna by sending her on this journey, but for him, too. He wouldn't be lonely as long as he was with her.

As the caravan to Zadoq began its journey, led by Rito-Sant's carriage, activity exploded from the daka Redd. A series of windriders screamed through the sky, going at their top speed, heading south. Cobo recognized Bail's private transport in the lead.

Jishni and Bail had already said their good-byes to Taen, but they hadn't planned on leaving the daka Redd for another day, in order to release the Ryslacs in their custody.

Bail was going home. Cobo touched Bail's mind, and brought back the thoughts troubling his brother. Something unspeakable had happened to his sons.

After the string of windriders disappeared in the sky, a smaller transport left the docking bay of the daka Redd, and made a slow, easy descent toward the now empty encampment.

"Who is it?" Surna asked, shading her eyes from the sun.

"Jishni." he replied, and he started walking toward the place he expected the windrider to land. "Surna, tell the lead Huntress we will be delayed."

Surna nodded and ran toward the front of the caravan.

Jishni emerged from her transport and flew into Cobo's arms, and as she tried to verbalize her tragedy, he held her tightly, willing into her strength to face her worst fears.

"The curse." She wept, "The curse had finally claimed my family. Please, Cobo, don't let this happen to me. I will do anything Betnoni wants of me, if only you will save my sons!"

Looking deeply into her desperate eyes, he said, "I'll try."

He embraced her firmly and closed his eyes, soaking in her pain, her hope. Locked in her embrace, his body firm around hers, his spirit went walking. He first projected himself into the palace, into the medical wing. He found Janus in an observation room. The little daka was pale and struggling to breathe. Without intervention, the boy would die. For his love of Jishni, Cobo touched the baby and restored his health. Janus took a huge breath, and burst into loud, healthy wails.

And now for the missing child.

"Archer." He said aloud, calling to the spirit of the second child. Cobo drifted away from Janus, pulled toward Archer. He was shown the recent past, the moment Jem Jin assaulted Janus, and fled with Archer. He followed her trail, to Dralon, and there her imprint was supplanted by the present terror riffling through the Shodites. It was all linked to Archer, but separate, as well. He followed the scent of terror to a Pliadors security station. A group of officers were brutally questioning a Shodite who was on the premises at the time of the kidnapping. Cobo sensed that none of these Shodites knew where the little daka had been taken, and he sensed the officers believed the same, but that wouldn't stop the interrogations and beatings. These Janti men were angry with the Shodites for more than daka Archer. Their grudge lay in the burning of Loxyn and Bryn.

He listened for the mind of Jem Jin. He felt her aching guilt, and her succor. She had a new son. There were no thoughts about Archer. Only her son. Her son.

He let her delusional mind reel him in, and he found himself in Shod City, standing in a small airless room.

The baby in Jem Jin's care looked like the twin he'd just healed, but it was difficult to identify him otherwise. The mind of an infant is active, and communicated in images and emotions. The baby was attached to Jem Jin, and had bonded with her the way a child would with a mother.

In Jem Jin, he felt the mark of Taen in her mind. Taen had driven her to a sort of obsessive insanity from which she would never recover. In her mind, this baby was hers. She had even conjured memories of giving birth to him, of pulling him out of her body, though Cobo could see clearly by her aura that she had never been pregnant.

The mark of Taen directed his spirit back to Montrose, and placed him at the side of his son. In the back of the lumbering ship-carriage, behind a sheer screen in the hold, Taen and Danati were involved in a passionate embrace, tearing at one another's clothing, craving release. Their passion was mutual.

That hadn't been so for Taen and Jem Jin.

Cobo probed Taen's mind. At first, all he saw was a rushing river, flowing out of Taen. He stepped into the river. It was icy, shallow, and unsubstantial. Cobo plunged his hand into the waters, straight through to the bottom. He worked his hand into the silty sand.

Taen felt it as a sharp pain in his head, and he grunted and cried out. Mistaking his cry of pain for passion, Danati's own passions ignited and she worked harder to free herself from her gown. Taen, in the meantime, looked over his shoulder and saw his father standing in the river, boring into his mind with insistent fingers.

"Get out." he hissed, and Danati hesitated, looking at him uncertainly.

"What did Jem Jin do for you?"

"Jem Jin?"

"Who is Jem Jin?" Danati demanded, her passions turning to jealous fury.

"Nothing," he replied to Cobo.

"If she is nothing, why say her name?" Danati replied petulantly.

Cobo's hand finally reached the truth. It was a feverish and undulating thing, alive in his hand, trying to slither away. He grabbed it firmly, and violently yanked it from Taen's mind, as if he were extracting a particularly tough yava root from the soil. Taen cried out again, clenching his hands to his head.

Danati shrank from him, and Lodan entered the space to see what was wrong with his young charge.

Danati demanded of Lodan, "Who is Jem Jin and why does he wail for her?"

Lodan said, "There is no Jem Jin that I know."

In his hands, Cobo held a writhing, slimy mass of lies and hatred. He saw the spell Taen afflicted on Jem Jin.

"So. You've progressed."

Angry, he threw the glob of ugliness back into the waters, where it was sucked down into Taen once again. *"She didn't do it."* he told Taen sharply, *"You are too weak to impose your will on a strong woman like Jem Jin. You are too weak to be Ver dala Ven."*

Taen shouted his outrage, and began screaming at the wall, "I have only just begun! I will gain strength, and I will destroy you! I will destroy you, and Jantideva, and the dakas!"

Taen was unable to maintain his stream of consciousness during his quivering emotional outburst. The waters ran dry, and Cobo now stood in a desert, dryer and more brutal than the deserts in Shodalum. Taen was entirely open to him.

Cobo saw, and felt, Taen's craving for the Masing Star. Taen expected to find it in Dilgopoche, and use it to his own ends. In the desert, Cobo saw an old man approaching. It was Riar Sed.

Welcome to Dilgopoche, Ver dala Ven

Made uneasy by Riar Sed's habitation in Taen's consciousness, Cobo left Taen, who was only now realizing he'd have to explain his irrational behavior to Danati, Lodan, and Rito-Sant, who had thrust his huge face through the screen and glared at his new son-in-law.

Cobo returned to his physical self. His embrace firmed on Jishni.

"What did you see?" she asked breathlessly, sensing his return.

"Janus will recover nicely," he said, and he released her to again look into her eyes, "and Archer....is well, if the baby I saw is Archer. Jem Jin has a baby with her, a boy, who looks like you and Bail, but the baby is attached to her. If only I saw your face in his mind, I could be sure it was Archer."

"Jem Jin is too young to have a baby, of course it is my baby, I want him back!"

"I will tell you where to find him, but take care with Jem Jin. She wasn't responsible for what she did. Taen placed a spell on her, compelling her to kill Archer and Janus. He's driven her mad, but she will not hurt the baby."

"Ugh," and Jishni grabbed her stomach with one hand and her mouth with the other, and all the color drained from her face. Cobo was sure she would throw up, but instead, her eyes rolled back into her head and she fainted.

He caught her, and lifted her off her feet. As he returned her to the windrider, Nan and Jishni's Watchers rushed out to meet him half way. Inside, he lay her down and allowed Nan to tend to her as he contacted Bail. He passed along the location of Jem Jin, and his warning that he should treat the woman with mercy. Bail took the information with a curt word, "Understood," and ended their communication. It was clear that Bail was angry at Cobo and Jishni, and for more than their immediate collaboration.

Jishni came around as he returned to her side. Cobo gently caressed her face.

"Bail will find Archer." he whispered to her, "Don't worry."

"Come home with me." She whispered back, her eyes filling with tears. "I need you, Cobo, can't you see? Don't leave me again."

He caressed her face, ruminating on his weakness for her. Finally, as a reply, and a farewell, he leaned forward to kiss her lips. The eyes that watched them were forgotten, and she returned his kiss, her lips soft and wet with tears. She held onto his face, tight at first as though she intended never to release him, gradually loosening her grip as she felt his resistance.

"If you ever need me," he said to her, his lips still close to hers, "call upon me."

"I need you." She replied quickly.

"Jishni," he reproached with a half smile.

"It's true."

He touched her face. "Hurry home to Janus. With any luck his brother will be waiting there for you, too."

She relented with a jerky nod.

He left her, and met Surna by their cart.

"Is all well?" she asked.

He looked up at the blue sky, and the mountains in the distance they would traverse in order to reach Zadoq. His thoughts were heavy with what he'd seen in Taen's mind, and with his own renewed loss. He didn't turn to look back as the windrider carrying Jishni away lifted off the ground.

"For us," he said finally, "yes." and through his grief, he smiled at her.

Relieved, Surna waved at the Huntress, eager to get on with their adventure. Their caravan moved.

Chapter 14

They were trapped for several days in the living quarters of the Shodite slaves waiting for an opportunity to escape Eller. Gella would have gone mad if it weren't for Shelon's company, and the duties she took upon herself to perform during her imprisonment. She had a routine. She cleaned out hearths, then scrubbed floors, washed laundry in a wash tub, and filled the oil lamps. After her chores were done, she tackled odd jobs, such as chipping away a thousand years of mineral deposits off the bathhouse walls. The Shodites were amazed at her industry and her energy, more so once they discovered she was not a slave but a true native of Shodalum.

"Do you work this hard in Shodalum?" Juana asked her one day as she was cleaning out Benin's hearth.

"Always. If you do not work hard in Shodalum, you die."

Juana grimaced. "It sounds horrible."

Pursing her lips together, Gella retorted, "Better to labor in freedom, than lounge in slavery."

Juana repeated Gella's retort as if it were a mantra, as if she were putting it to memory. The next day Gella overheard Juana repeating it to a group of her friends.

After that, Gella often had teenagers following her about as she did her chores, asking her questions about Shodalum, but rarely offering a hand to do the chores. Irked, she finally handed one young man a broom and said, "If you want to know what Shodalum is like, sweep the floor."

Shelon spent his days speaking to gatherings of Shodites. Groups of ten or twelve at a time would arrive early in the morning, as the Janti were finally getting to sleep after yet another night of debauchery. Gella sat in on a few of his talks, listening to him fire the hearts of the Shodites. Reluctantly, she admitted, but only to herself, that had she been a slave she would have chosen to follow Shelon.

Not that she was a convert, or anything.

In the evenings, as Eller came alive with parties and the servant quarters emptied, Shelon and Gella retired to their room and made love, or talked about their lives, or did both. Shelon's sad life inspired Gella to reveal to him what had happened to her as a child. He wasn't shocked, or revolted. He accepted her. They were like kindred spirits, both wounded in the same way.

On the morning of their fifth day of confinement, Gella woke to the familiar sound of trampling feet outside the door. Another group had come to hear Shelon speak.

"What if we were to want to make love in the morning?" she asked Shelon as he rolled off the mat, standing, reaching for his trousers. "What would they do? Sit outside the door and wait for us to be done? Or come in and observe the sexual technique of the great Shelon?"

"Hmmm, you're in a mood this morning, my pretty precious one." he smiled at her over his shoulder, "I thought I tamed that mood out of you last night."

"I'm tired of this place." she grumbled, and she got up and dressed with fast, jerky, irritated movements. "If I don't have fresh air soon, I will die."

"Soon, Gella," he promised.

"Soon," she retorted, "I think Benin is lying to us about the security patrols to keep you here. I think she looks at you too hard, with too much lust in her heart. I think that if she looks in the direction of your consha again, I will slap her."

Shelon grinned at her jealousy. Goading her, he said, "I don't mind the way Benin looks at me, or my consha."

Indignant, her jaw went rigid. "Oh, you man, you wouldn't. Why not just take her into your bed, Shelon? I can sleep with Korba tonight!"

Her tone, and the subject of her threat, edged him away from amusement, and toward vexation. Sarcastically, he replied, "By all means, if you need the satisfaction of a young buck like Korba, I wouldn't dream of standing in your way. I'm sure Korba would be ecstatic! And if I get lonely while you are gone, I'll go jump Benin, and maybe her sister, too!"

Fuming with hurt feelings, she said, "Do what you want, Shelon. I don't own your body, and you don't own mine!" She grabbed her tunic and pulled it over her head.

He sighed remorsefully. "Gella," he called out to her, but she wasn't in the mood to make amends. She opened their door and came face to face with Lagos, who'd listened to Shelon's speeches every day in an effort to come to understand why his son had given his life for the cause. In the beginning he was rather contentious with Shelon, a resident heckler, but in a short time his anger at Shelon was redirected at the people who actually killed his son, the Janti. His change of heart pleased Shelon.

Behind Lagos was a throng of eager devotees.

"Did you have a good listen?" she demanded of them, and she fought her way through the crowd and headed toward the bathhouse.

After scrubbing the floor she was calmed enough to realize that their argument had been stupid and pointless. Yet, there was some truth to it. She didn't own Shelon. Nothing prevented him from taking Benin, who so obviously desired him, or from taking Iada back when they finally did get to Moom. She tried not to think about Moom.

She continued her chores, allowing them to carry her through another day.

As she came to the open door of their room, she paused and looked in on Shelon. He had nine men crowding around him on the mat, talking in low tones. Shelon's features were serious, and instead of giving a speech, today he listened, and nodded, and listened. He happened to glance at Gella. The alarm in his eyes, his features, and the fury there, too, told her that something terrible had happened. Something that would no doubt touch them.

She faded away from the doorway, and let herself into Korba's room unannounced. Korba lay spooned with Juana on a mat, both of them nude and sleeping. He had no trouble moving on after being so deeply in love. He'd seduced Juana the first night.

She made a point of making a racket as she cleaned. Juana woke, and seeing her hunched over the hearth, she gasped, and scrambled to cover her nudity.

Korba stared at Gella blearily. "Aren't you early?"

Irritably, she snapped, "I don't know, Korba, I haven't seen the sun in so long I can't tell night from day!"

Juana sighed, "It's early. We haven't been sleeping that long."

"Who could with all the noise coming from the room across the hall?" Korba asked sullenly.

Gella's movements slowed at the thought that she and Shelon had been too loud. Each day, as the soreness from the beating he'd received at the Keep healed more, Shelon grew more passionate, forceful, and far more possessive as he made love to her. He instinctively knew how to take her, how to touch her sensitive places, how to appeal to her heart with his pretty whispered words, and when pretty words were not enough. The way he looked at her with his fierce lust, and the way he stroked her back, and the way he filled her, satisfied her desires, and in tandem, incited her desires. A mere brush of his hand against hers could awaken her female, a throbbing, pulsing entity that rarely slept in Shelon's company.

Last night, their seduction began with play, laughter and chasing each other around the room, grabbing at each other, she teasing him, refusing to let him have her, telling him he would have to take her, rip her clothes away and force her if he wanted release, laughing as she said these things, aroused by the gleam of challenge in his eyes. His hunger for her became stronger than his reasoning mind, and he captured her, wrestled her to the mat, held her arms above her head and controlled her, possessing her, thrusting into her with a violence that was hot and delicious, consuming her until she forgot her own name. Gella was uninhibited, noisy if pleasured by a skillful man. Last night, Shelon had pleasured her very skillfully.

Dismissing a light stab of mortification that she'd disturbed Korba with her cries of delight, she finished cleaning the ashes from the hearth, and poured them in the can Benin had given her for the job.

As she stood, she saw that the men who'd come to see Shelon were now filing out of their room. Shelon was last, and he paused outside Korba's doorway. "Get dressed, Korba." He looked at Gella, frowning deeply, "We're leaving here."

"But what of the patrols?" Juana cried. She wasn't ready to lose Korba's company.

"They've been called to duty in Shod City. One of the daka's children was kidnapped, and they suspect a Shodite of the crime." his voice thickened as he said, "They've massacred hundreds of Shodites."

Korba sat up quickly. "Praj and Iada-"

"There's no news about our friends." Shelon said, "But now is our time to leave, and before we leave, we will have our revenge."

He stormed away, and Gella stared at the empty doorway, numb and afraid of what this day was to bring.

Her son developed a cough.

She kept him warm and well fed, still, in his first hours of life he did not seem well. He was not moving about much and he cried pitifully when she left him in the makeshift warming bed. She worried for his health, that he might end up like his poor dead brother, who came out of her womb quiet, blue, still and lifeless.

Before first light she left for track four. Her cousin had told her that she could find a healer there who was discreet. He'd been helpful, but not as pleased to care for her and her infant as she had hoped. He wouldn't accompany her on the long walk, nearly the full length of the Pril along the boardwalk, leaving her to go alone and in the dark, to fend for herself and risk being accosted. She was afraid, but her fear for her infant compelled her onward, and she walked quickly and as quietly as she could on the dangerous boardwalk.

The building's number was 4-5-48. She went in and to the subbasement, and to a closed door. She couldn't clap, so she called out. "In need of assistance!"

From the other side, she heard, "What type?"

"My baby has a cough!"

She heard an array of locks unlatching, and the door opened. A woman her mother's age, but not as pretty or plump, greeted her with speculative caution.

"Who are you seeking?"

"Iada, the healer."

The woman nodded, and gestured for her to enter. There were men in the room with her, she counted six. They were packing objects into bags.

The baby squealed and she looked down into his face.

"I am Iada. Let me see the child."

She released him into the woman's arms.

"He is light. How old is he?"

"A day." She said, and her mind raced with soft and glowing memories of giving birth the night before. He'd been her son for a day.

"Was he premature?"

"I-don't really know." She faltered.

"Are you feeding from the breast?"

"I can't. I've dried up."

"In a day?"

"My mother was the same way."

Iada grunted a response and nodded. She sat on the bench and uncovered the boy.

"Moxom, bring me my bag."

A big man lumbered to a corner to retrieve a black bag. On the floor where the bag had been sitting there was what looked like dried blood.

Iada listened to his heart and listened to his cough, and said, "Are you keeping him in a warming bed?"

"Yes."

"Then his cough may be due to an irritant in the environment. Where do you live?"

"Track 310."

"Near the Pril."

"Yes."

Iada seemed concerned. "I know of a woman in track twelve who takes care of newborns, a nurse. Could you stay with her a few days so he can be observed?"

"Is it that serious?"

"He sounds good, but with infants this small, it is best to err on the side of caution."

"I suppose, yes." She replied. She really didn't have anywhere else to go, and she sensed her cousin would turn her out if she returned to his flat.

"I will take you there myself." Iada offered.

"Oh, if you could, I would be grateful."

"Save your gratitude," Iada said and she smiled at the baby. "It's been too long since I've held a little one."

Iada led her out of the building and through the alleys to the boardwalk. As the stench of the Pril hit their noses, Iada said, "You walked all this way? Only a day after giving birth?"

"I can't use the public transports."

Iada considered the many reasons why a Shodite was forced to walk along a boardwalk where few Janti Watchers would deign to walk.

"You shouldn't exert yourself so soon after. You should have sent the baby's father to fetch me. I would have come."

"He…..he is a Janti." She replied, frowning at her memory of Taen's rapes, which she assumed caused her pregnancy, for she could not remember lying with another man.

Pity crossed Iada's features. "I understand."

As they walked, Iada prompted, "You didn't tell me his name."

"Gidnea."

"Ah, a fine name. And yours?"

Jem Jin hesitated. "Wedri," she said, using her mother's given name. She was afraid. Afraid of being found by Taen. She remembered little about their last encounter, except that he wanted Gidnea dead. That was stamped firmly in her mind.

They started along the boardwalk as the action in track four began. Narrow Wizard class windriders swooped in between the buildings, their blowers causing the canyon of the city to vibrate. People flooded from the main streets to the boardwalk, terrified.

"Black boots, black boots!" one man shouted at the women.

"Pliadors." Iada muttered under her breath.

Jem Jin prickled cold.

"Hold your child, and stay here, the Pliadors won't venture this close to the Pril, even for the worst of criminals."

Iada left Jem Jin on the boardwalk, racing back through the alley to investigate the action. Jem Jin glanced around at the panicked people crowding the rickety boardwalk, hearing the infected water splashing lazily on the beach far beneath them, and felt fear that the boardwalk wouldn't hold. In her mind, she escaped one peril to flirt with yet another. She followed Iada. As she reached the crowd in the street, a larger military transport passed above them.

Iada noticed her, and grimaced. "They are searching my building. Come, if we go back to the boardwalk, we'll be safe until they are through."

The crowd was in motion, parting and converging, parting and converging. She saw Pliadors entering the building, guarding their transports with weapons brandished at the unarmed Shodites, and she saw a Shodite among them. Her cousin, on his knees, his face beaten, his features impassive as the officer above him shouted curses at his bowed head.

"No," she objected, and without thinking she shouted his name, "Swasdi!"

The officer turned sharply on his heel. His demonic black eyes stared at her, then the baby in her arms. He pointed and barked an order she heard. "That one! Arrest her!"

Shock jolted her from her delusion. She glanced at the daka she held, and grimaced in fear. Keening, she bolted toward the boardwalk, Iada on her heels. She ran as fast as she could, turning two corners, but still feeling heat on her heel, hearing the rapid footfall of another right on her back, she panicked. The boardwalk, and certain freedom in sight, she threw down the bundle she carried and continued to run in order to save herself.

Iada scooped the child off the ground, and ducked behind a sanitation bin a heartbeat before the first of a succession of pursuing black boots turned the corner. From her hiding place, she watched Wedri's mad dash. The black boots passed by the sanitation bin and didn't give a glance back to the woman huddled against the wall with a silent bundle. He undid his lume from his sash, and shot into the crowd on the boardwalk. The Shodites screamed and cried out in horror, and tried to run away, even jumping into the Pril to escape the wholesale murder.

With the black boots beyond her, and a clear route of escape open to her, Iada mustered the courage to step out from the behind the sanitation bin and walk quickly away. Turning a corner, she entered a thick crowd of Shodites at the edge of the building and feeling more at ease, peered over her shoulder at the scene unfolding behind her. What she saw made her stop cold. Wedri lay on the concrete, convulsing as lume poisoning slowly cooked her from the inside, out. The guards stood over her body, kicking her to get her attention. One knelt by her head and asked her a question that Iada couldn't hear clearly.

Iada sank back, her eyes darting through the crowd. Slow and easy, maintain calm, behave normally. Shelon's method for invisible entry and escapes. She tried walking normally, but couldn't help picking up the pace as she found a clear alley to the boardwalk. She paused only long enough to look at the child she carried, because she felt it move, and seeing it was alive, awake, and staring silently at her, a large smile broke into her frightened expression. She'd thought she was carrying a corpse.

Lume thunder rumbled and echoed in the city once again. She looked ahead, uncertain where she would go next.

Escape. It was all she had to do. She started walking away from the sound of lume thunder.

৽৽৽৽৽৽৽৽৽

Bail's knuckles were sore and bloody. In a rage, he'd beaten the officer who'd killed Jem Jin. He'd ordered them not to hurt her, yet they did not listen, and they killed the only person who knew where to find Archer.

They searched every building, threatened every Shodite in the track with death and destruction, yet they found no sign of Archer.

After a thorough interrogation, Jem Jin's cousin admitted that he knew the name of the doctor he'd sent Jem Jin to see, though he claimed before that he only knew of her location.

"Why did you lie about knowing her identity?" Bail demanded.

"She is one with Solien Soldiers, a lieutenant of Shelon." He admitted breathlessly, "I feared the wrath of my people if I turned her in."

And yet after Jem Jin was so heartlessly murdered, even though a child had been in her arms, he chose to reveal all to the black boots.

The child was not found, nor could they find Iada, the healing woman who followed Shelon.

He went to Jishni late that night, knowing she had already heard the news. She was with Janus, rocking him in the dark of the nursery. She fed him from a bottle, because her breasts had dried of milk during their time in Montrose. Janus ate heartily, making loud sucking noises. Doctor Poulin had happily reported that Janus made a complete and surprising recovery after being so gravely ill. To Bail Janus seemed better than fine. His legs were thicker, and he was more active, wiggling, kicking, boxing. He seemed robust.

Jishni was not doing well, however. Poulin had her on medication to keep her calm. She hadn't changed or combed her hair since their journey home. She looked insanely unkempt.

She didn't look up from the baby as he entered the nursery.

"Jishni, my darling." he said, announcing himself.

Carefully enunciating her words, she said, "Cobo told you to handle her with care." Her voice was low and malevolent, and he felt her blame.

"The man who killed her will be punished." Bail promised.

"As will I, for as long as I miss my son." she whispered.

Silence hung heavily in the room, broken only by Janus's loud sucking noises and the creak of the rocking chair.

Bail was heartbroken. He missed Archer, too, and he missed his wife. She had pulled away from him since their blow up on the daka Redd, physically and emotionally. He tried to apologize, to tell her that he was drunk and possessed by grief, but she rebuffed him with silence and open animosity.

"I'll find him," Bail vowed, "Trev and I are leaving tonight. We're going to employ some friends of Trev's. The same men who found Riar Sed. We'll find Archer."

"Riar Sed started this," she said softly. "He taught Taen more than he needed to know, and Taen turned on us. If it weren't for your finding Riar Sed, we would have all our sons under this roof tonight."

"Then I am to blame for Archer's kidnapping?"

She looked at him. Her voice thickened by the medication, and by her sorrow, she said, "No. I am to blame. I took Cobo's son away from him. I destroyed Ver dala Ven. I made a faulty choice nineteen years ago, and I married the wrong man. I should never have married you, Bail. I didn't love you, I loved Cobo, and I am cursed, because I still love Cobo."

Bail reached for the wall for support. "Don't talk like that Jishni," he pleaded huskily. Never had words hurt him so much.

"The Guardian has taken Archer away from us, to punish us." A sob caught in her throat, and she rocked a bit faster. Miserably, she said, "I want Cobo here. I could bear the pain if he were here."

Feeling useless and discarded, Bail left the nursery.

He joined Trev in the High room. Trev was watching a live broadcast of a dramatic play about a woman who betrays her husband with his brother. The play featured several famous actors, and a twist of an ending. On a gold disc in the middle of the room, a skinny man was replicated in full form as he recited his lines vehemently, speaking to the Guardian. "....it can't be my fault! I did not betray her, she betrayed me-"

He sat with Trev, and shut off the recording.

The actor disappeared, his last word ringing in the chamber, mocking Bail.

"He was just getting to the good part." Trev complained.

"He kills his brother, and his wife kills him. The end." Bail said flatly, having once seen and enjoyed the play, but now repulsed by the subject matter.

Trev winced. "Did you have to ruin the ending?"

"Jishni will not forgive me," Bail said tiredly, "until I bring our son home."

Trev nodded his understanding. "We'll find him. The two of us could accomplish a great deal without the Pliadors holding us back. Head thumpers.....they don't have one brain among them. If they'd dress as a Shodite when they entered Shod City, the Shodites wouldn't hide, or become defensive....they wouldn't even blink."

"I showed horrible judgment sending Captain Varian after Jem Jin. I will never stop regretting my own stupidity."

"You showed better judgement putting him in the infirmary," Trev laughed.

"He's going to spend the rest of his life in a Raal work camp with the shod for murder." Bail said flatly, "He may as well get used to being beaten."

Trev threw his head back to peer at Bail under lowered lids. "My contact informed me that a raft was found hung up on a spit off Eller. The raft was traced back to Yuini Vol, who bought it for one of his fishing boats. The master of Yuini Vol's boat is named Ul Zub, and he has a wife named Iada, a healer that sees patients in track four."

Bail leveled an intense eye on his friend. "Where does Yuini Vol dock his boats?"

"Padra."

"Then we'll leave for Padra immediately."

"There is more, Bail." Trev hedged, "Ul Zub's boat was the boat that helped Shelon escape."

Bail ruminated on the coincidence, worried that a terrorist he'd only just let escape might have his hands on his son.

"I want Ul Zub's boat searched, and I want him questioned. If the healer is not there, we will try Eller." Reluctantly, he said, "If we fail to find Archer, we'll go to Dilgopoche, and seek out Cobo. Petition him to come home.....to comfort Jishni."

Trev chuckled mirthlessly.

"Don't say it." Bail ordered, his pain creasing his face. He could almost hear the randy comment that was on the tip of Trev's tongue, concerning the type of comfort Cobo would provide. Bail didn't have the strength for jealousy. He was hurting too hard with loss, and reeling from her rejection, and the knowledge that he was her mistake, a mistake she'd prefer to cast aside.

Trev kept the comment to himself, though the thought left an unrepentant smirk on his face.

చించించించింగింగింగింగింగి

Gella abandoned her chores and readied herself to leave at a moment's notice. Korba and Shelon prepared to wreak havoc on Eller.

From the houses of the Janti, the Shodites gathered a variety of appliances. Bedwarmers, clocks, goblets, a table, and a thing that Shelon described as a hearth that didn't need wood or dung to cook and cooked meals five times faster. He called it a rad steamer.

He didn't explain to Gella what he had planned for the items, other than to explain to her what a rad steamer was, but it was obvious that whatever he had planned, it was dangerous. He urged Lagos to organize an area wide evacuation of the Shodites.

Gella stayed behind, unknown to Shelon, and watched him as he worked. He set everything on the table, and took the outer casing off the rad steamer, exposing a mess of wires and silver plates. He carefully removed the plates. He removed the coils from the bedwarmers, and tacked them to the ceiling in four corners. He smashed the stems off the goblets and gently packed the bottoms of the hanging coils in the glass and turned them upside down on the plates. Using the wires from the rad steamer, he reattached the plates. Last, he took the back off the clock, and wired it to his gizmo. His hands were steady, his body taut, his expression grim. He was quick. He had done this before.

Once he was done, and had stepped away from his creation, Gella drifted into the open doorway.

"What is it?"

His head flew around. Seeing her, he said urgently, "You shouldn't be here, Gella."

"What will it do?" she insisted.

His eyes crinkled with a frown. He looked at it. "It's a lume bomb."

"Lume......like the weapon that killed the guard at the Keep."

"It is the same technology." he admitted, "Applied in a slightly different way. Instead of a quick cooked supper, we're going to quick cook some Janti."

"You're going to kill Benin's benefactors?"

"Yes....all the Janti in this district, as soon as we evacuate the Shodites."

"Shelon," she breathed, "what about the children?"

"Don't worry. Those who don't have families in Shod City will go to Moom with us. The children will be taken care of by our own."

"Not the Shodite children. The Janti children. Will you kill them too?"

He cocked a brow. "A lume bomb doesn't discriminate according to age."

307

She stared at the death machine, disbelief on her face. "You would kill children for revenge?"

"They kill our children." he retorted, "They kill indiscriminately, and they do not pay for their crimes."

"Is this what you are?" she demanded, "A cruel monster who could kill children?"

He was taken aback that she sided against him, and angrily he defended himself. "They are Janti!"

"They are children!" she shouted, "Just last evening I heard them playing a game right outside that wall, and their laughter was no different than the laughter of Benin's grand-daughters. Even you smiled as you heard them. I saw you smile!"

"Ah, yes, they do have more to laugh about than Benin and her kin, don't they?" he countered hotly, "While they play games, Benin's daughters and grand-children clean their kitchens, mend their clothing, and keep their bastard of a father sexually contented!"

"They are innocents!"

"No Janti that uses a slave is innocent. I don't care how fresh their face is to the world." he replied bitterly. "On the inside, they are rotten."

She drew a shuddering breath, unable to see her Shelon behind the bitter, hardened man who stood before her. "In Shodalum," she said lowly, "there is a saying; The hostile man chases his shadow, the meek man is fortunate."

He sighed in exasperation. "Your wisdom from the homeland is getting to be a bore."

Her eyes flashed with anger. "Oh yes I forgot, you aren't a Shodite in your heart.....you are a Janti, daka Shelon! You behave like a Janti, you speak and hate like a Janti, you will kill children, and walk away feeling justified in your vengeance, just like a Janti!"

"They are my enemy!" he thundered, "This is war! I am fighting a war! Do not condemn what you do not understand!"

"You are the son of Tuv Grethian!" she retorted sharply, "The Janti are your brothers! Would you kill your brothers?"

He stepped back, a look of fury overtaking his features.

Her own breath caught in her throat for her vile remark. She quickly said, "I am sorry for invoking that name in your presence."

"Gella, I can no longer speak to you. You must leave, now."

The controlled fury in his tone warned her not to go further, but her principles pushed her into the room.

"By killing Janti children, Shelon, you are asking the Janti to kill more of our kind. And they kill us, and you kill them, where does it end?"

"Gella," he breathed as a warning, and he turned away from her, seeming to fight for control. A tick worked madly in his cheek.

"There are ways to make an impact on the Janti, without taking lives." she said. "Think about your Shodite heritage, where you came from and why your branch of al Entlay were enslaved to Jantideva. The Shodites did not want their land and their people poisoned by the Janti, but they were fervently peaceful, so they fought their enemy without bloodshed. They sat down. They stopped working. The Janti beat them, but they wouldn't move. We Shodites incited the horrible daka Redd to attack our land by acting in peace, and with peace, we earned our liberation through the protection of our patron Goddess, Betnoni."

In a dangerous and mocking tone, he retorted, "Are you suggesting we sit down and start praying to Betnoni?"

"I am suggesting that you fight like real Shodite. Don't succumb to evil, Shelon. I've seen the Shodite within you, in your wisdom and gentle nature. And now I see the actions of a Janti who kills children to make his point. Shelon," she pleaded, "I refuse to believe that a brutal Janti is your true heart."

Tension crackled in the air between them. His arms were rigid, his face a mask of grim control. The last time she'd angered a man to this point, it was in Strum, and he struck her and threw her against a wall, dislocating her shoulder, breaking her ankle, and cracking her head. She trembled in fear at the prospect that Shelon might be inclined to hurt her if provoked.

She decided it was time to leave. She inched away from him. He moved toward her, so fast that she cried out and cringed, preparing for the blows to come.

309

He threw his arms around her in embrace, and she realized then that he hadn't moved to hit her, but to seek comfort from her. He held her in a desperate grip, buried his face in her hair. "Tuv Grethian made me a Janti." he said gruffly, his embrace tightening, his fingers biting into her waist. "I yearn to live as a Shodite. Gella, my precious Gella," he wailed miserably, "how can I soothe this ache in me?" His voice broke with sobs, and he wept.

She threw her arms around his neck and held onto fistfuls of his shirt, shaking in the aftermath of fright, and from the intensity of his embrace. She held him, praying to Betnoni for the first time since she was a girl, asking that Betnoni imbue Shelon with the spirit of Shodalum.

Once his body stopped shuddering, and his misery was spent, he lifted his face and let her wipe the tears from his rugged cheeks. He watched her lovingly. Gradually, she saw her Shelon return to her.

"If you were leading us," he said lowly, his voice gruff from weeping, "what would we do today to protest the deaths of innocent Shodites?"

"I'm not a leader," she replied, and she smiled at him, "I follow Shelon."

He glanced at the bomb. Chagrinned, he said, "You follow a fool." He thought a moment. "We've been very destructive, yet we haven't seen much progress. There have been many Shodite uprisings through history. None have had the impact of Shodalum's initial uprising against the Janti."

"And none were staged like the first uprising." she assumed.

He looked at her, as if seeing her for the first time. "Yes. We behaved.....like the Janti. In a way they understood. Maybe it is time we learned a new way. But first," he looked back at the lume bomb, and said, "I have to dismantle this. I want you to leave, in case I make a mistake."

A stab of dread for Shelon went through her now that she knew what he was doing was dangerous.

"If you make a mistake, we will die together." she replied, and she crossed her arms to prove herself an immovable object.

"You'll make me nervous, standing over me, and I will make a mistake," he retorted, "Now get out!"

310

He stared her down. He was serious and he wasn't going to take no for an answer.

She stepped closer to him, and looked up into his eyes. "Alright. I'll go. But not before I tell you that I've changed my mind. I don't want you finding comfort with Benin. And I have no need to find comfort with Korba."

Her oddly timed statement amused him. He bent and lightly kissed her lips.

"Benin is hardly my type. And Korba..." he shrugged, "I almost think he is too young for you." And he smirked at his own remark.

Gella nodded seriously, and threw a wary glance at the bomb Shelon had made before leaving him to his work.

෧෧෧෧෨෨෨෨

Bail arrived to the seventh neighborhood of Eller with a light guard. They found here what they had found in the last six neighborhoods. Masses of Shodites, sitting peacefully in the plazas of their benefactor's homes, refusing to work. They held signs written on tablecloths that said things like, "Shame belongs to Jantideva," and, "We are united." Most disturbing were signs shouting, "We are brothers to Janti."

The Janti benefactors could do nothing to move their servants. Bail saw one irate middle aged woman beating her old houseman with a broom. He lay on the ground, his hand clutching a sign that read, "The Janti are murdering slavers." He was laughing between blows as if it tickled.

Bail gathered the Janti as he had in the last neighborhoods and questioned them about Cleses. No one had seen anything unusual, until their servants refused to do their work.

"Do you think this is the work of Cleses?" one man demanded.

"I wouldn't rule it out." Bail replied.

He questioned the Shodites. The old man who was being beaten on their arrival, Lagos, sniggered when he was asked about Shelon.

"You've seen him?" Bail prompted.

311

"No, not at all."

"Then why are you amused, old man?" he demanded.

"My great-great grandmother served her body for Ver dala Ven Edum's pleasure. You and I could very well be cousins." and he grinned impudently.

His benefactor swatted him on the back of the head with the broom, sprawling him on the ground. He rolled onto his side and laughed uproariously, holding his stomach.

"By the guardian." Trev said, "I believe he has been hitting the brandy."

"I will have him put to death, immediately." the Janti benefactor promised.

Bail flashed on Vero, the Huntress who made the fatal mistake of insulting Rito-Sant's guests.

"No," Bail replied quickly, "Don't......I don't want you to kill him for an insult. But do keep your eyes open for any signs of Cleses."

"We will, but, daka Bail, what do we do about them?" she said, gesturing widely at her sitting servants.

Bail shrugged helplessly. "Reason with them." he replied, and he strode away.

They landed in the eighth neighborhood and again searched for Shelon. Like the previous neighborhoods, they found Shodites engaged in a peaceful sit down.

"Who would have known they'd finally turn their rage into peace?" One of the residents commented with admiration. A liberal, Bail could see. The man was smiling his approbation at his own servants' defiance.

Bail was tempted to have him arrested, on principle.

312

Chapter 15

Dressed as a Janti couple with a Shodite slave, and bearing a credit slip that Benin had stolen from her benefactor, Shelon, Gella and Korba boarded a public Transport in Eller Central West and rode over the Tronos to Padra.

From Padra, they took a long-range transport to a village named Horp Row, in the deep south green jungles of Jantideva. For half a day, Gella and Shelon sat in comfortable seats, being served drinks and food, while Korba lay cold in the cargo hold below. Gella did not worry about him aloud, for fear one of the Janti might look askance at them and suspect them of being what they were not. Shelon was careful to warn her on how to behave. They only needed to reach Horp Row, and from there, they would be safe.

It was early evening when they reached their destination. They left the transport, claimed their slave, and casually left the travel station.

Shelon took them walking through Horp Row common as if they belonged to the community, smiling and wishing a good evening to the Janti who crossed their paths.

As the sun set deeper into the sky, they took a detour, and went through a neighborhood of small homes, where the Janti were too poor to be benefactors, "but wealthy enough to live better than Shodites." Shelon commented lightly. Their homes were built in the lush, wild foothills of a medium size range of mountains.

Shelon pointed to the highest mountain peak, and said, "Moom is up there."

"We're to climb a mountain?" she said incredulously.

"Yes, we are." he conceded.

"It's not so hard a climb." Korba interjected, "It takes a day, from morning to nightfall."

"What is Moom? A town in the clouds?"

"It is a castle, built by the Rathians," he shrugged, "during the time before the dakas came into power. It was built on Moom so that the Rathian Knights could see the land, and the Sochen Sea, for spans, and detect invaders. But it has long been abandoned."

With a playful smile, Korba said, "The Janti won't go near it. It is said that Ver dala Ven Mo'ghan died there, and that his spirit still haunts the castle, ready for revenge."

"Mo'ghan." She breathed, recollecting the story Cobo had told her of the unfairly maligned Ver dala Ven Knight, and she smiled.

"See, Korba? Our native daughter isn't afraid of ghost stories." Shelon said with a smirk.

The road they were on ended, and turned into a field. Shelon seemed not to notice they were trampling tall grasses, walking with the same casual ease he'd used in the common of Horp Row. He led them to the edge of the forest, through the moonlit darkness of the trees. The ground began a gentle incline. Once far from civilization, and cloaked by brush and trees, they paused to remove the finery Benin had stolen from her benefactor for them. Shelon had worn his Shodite street clothes under a full-length tunic, and had tied his boots to his waist. The latter he untied, and pulled onto his feet.

As Gella wrapped her feet with strips of slank leather, she glanced dubiously at the hard-soled work boots worn by Korba and Shelon. They didn't look comfortable for climbing, much less walking.

They hiked at a brisk pace until the trail of pale moons lowered toward the mountains. On the edge of total darkness, he found a small clearing surrounded by giant trees.

"We'll camp here until morning."

Shelon built a fire to stave off the cold, and sitting by it he drew Gella between his legs and held her, and they watched the flames. Korba sat across from them, eating his portion of the snack Juana had packed for them. The forest was quiet, and a frosty breeze rustled through the trees.

Contented by the crisp smell of the night, Gella said, "If I returned to Shodalum, I would miss the rain....and the green."

Korba glanced at her. "Will you return?"

Shelon tightened his hold on her, as if to silently deny her the right to leave.

"I am dead in the eyes of my people." she said, "Once I crossed the border, I crossed into exile. The law says I cannot return."

Korba sneered, "That sounds like a stupid law."

"It is an old law," she conceded, "Put into effect to punish the traitors and their families that left with the factories once Shodalum became an independent nation. It serves no purpose now, except to exile those who are curious about what lay beyond our borders."

"Laws are made to be changed." Shelon said lowly in her ear.

"You would have me go home?" she asked playfully.

"Only if I go with you." he murmured.

She melted into his chest and sighed happily.

They slept in shifts that night, one staying awake to keep watch while two rested. While Gella slept, she dreamt about the Castle of Moom. In her dream, it looked very much like Ona, except there were spirits haunting the halls. She saw the spirits of her parents, and as she called their names they faded into a brocade tapestry depicting a sparse Shodalum landscape. Cobo walked through her dream, speaking gibberish she didn't understand. She followed him, trying to hear everything he said.

Waking from her dream, she felt the familiar ache for Cobo, and turned to find Shelon's arms, but he wasn't beside her.

She rose. The fire was dying. Across from her, Korba slept peacefully.

"Gella," Shelon whispered.

She found him with her eyes. Dawn was near, and he was purple hued in the subdued beginning of day. He leaned against a tree, a few feet from her. He gestured his head, beckoning her to come to him. She rose easily to her feet, shaking the dirt from her shapeless gray tunic. As she stood by his side, he put an arm around her waist and pulled her close to his side.

"Look out there," he whispered.

The pale dawn had illuminated a pasture below them to softest, palest green. In the pasture, a group of animals grazed on the grass, the white spots on their backs glowing against their darker pelt.

"Are they dangerous?" she whispered.

Hearing Gella's voice, their heads shot up as one and they looked in her direction, their ears pointed forward. Some still had grass hanging out of their mouths. The sight made Gella smile.

"Harmless." he whispered back, "Plus, they are tasty."

"No, you don't kill a thing of beauty," she objected quietly, "Kill the ugly animals for meat....like a slank, or a briarbeast."

Shelon chuckled and embraced her with both arms. "You are an astonishing woman. One minute, a fighter beating a man like Moxom into the ground, and the next an advocate for the beasts. An advocate for peace." he added. He paused and they watched the animals relax and return to their breakfast.

"I've been thinking," he said finally, "about the direction we should take our revolution. I've built quite of following on the idea of purging the Janti from their homes, and their government, and taking over, or, a less drastic measure, taking part in their government as their equals. But, the more I think about Shodalum, I begin to think that the Shodites need a homeland to hold onto, to give them strength as they fight for equality among their slavers."

She looked up into his face expectantly.

"I'd like to go there, and meet my relatives." he said, "I'd like to know what it is to be Shodite. I'd like to take that knowledge, and give it to my people, so they know it too. I'd like.....to call it my homeland. I want a homeland. Right now, we have nothing. We do not remember what it is to be Shodite, and we are not good enough for the Janti to be called Janti. We're in limbo. That is why the uprisings of the past never worked. We never had a firm foundation on which to plant our feet. We never had a home to return to, even in our heads."

"You would immigrate?"

His brows shot up at the prospect. "I don't know. I never thought about it. I don't know if I am ready to face a world without high technology." he said, smiling briefly thought.

"This world moves much faster than Shodalum." she agreed.

He embraced her full body again, and his thoughts turned from contemplative to romantic. "See that sunrise? That sunrise was made for us, Gella. For you and me."

Her eyes ran across the trees in the distance, their wide leaves reflecting a hundred shades of silver and green in the newborn sunlight, and to the beasts, moving along the meadow, and she pressed the sight on her memory. Shelon may return to Iada, but she would always own this dawn.

Once the sun warmed the sky, Shelon woke Korba, and they continued their hike through the hills. They eventually came across a shallow creek, and followed it until they reached a series of stones that looked like steps going up the mountain. In some places, the steps seemed purposely carved. As she noticed the amazing oddity of nature, Shelon informed her that it wasn't amazing, nor was it an oddity.

"There was once a perfect set of steps leading up to the castle. Before the days of windriders, the Rathian knights had to climb their way to the top. The path has worn away some, but not too bad that we cannot use it."

They climbed at an even pace, with Shelon leading the way and Korba a few steps behind Gella. The men seemed accustomed to the strenuous activity. Gella was having trouble breathing, and keeping up. She'd heard about mountains, especially the Sidera mountains in Shodalum, learning about them while in school in Nmar, but had never seen one until traveling to Jantideva, and had never climbed one until today. As a girl, she imagined they were like huge dunes, but found she was wrong. And, she imagined they were easy to climb, especially for one as hardy as herself.

"I must stop." she begged, finally succumbing to the humiliation of fatigue. She leaned against the mossy rock face, struggling for air.

Shelon paused, throwing an impatient look back at her. "We need to push on, Gella. We can reach the summit before sunset, as long as we keep moving. If we don't reach the summit, we'll be climbing in the dark, because there is no place for us to camp. And if we climb in the dark, we run the risk of putting our feet in the wrong place and slipping and falling."

She nodded that she understood, but her rubbery legs and aching chest debated with her. She looked down. The ascent was less gradual than it appeared from their campsite. The drop off here was steep.

"We're not even half way." she complained.

"Come on, Gella," Korba prodded from behind, "You can do it."

"I am suffocating."

317

Shelon stepped toward her, concern in his craggy features. "It's the thinner air. You'll get used to it. In the meantime, I'll set a slower pace. Will that help?"

She had no choice but to agree to move on, whether or not a slower pace would help.

They climbed further, and passed a set of stones embedded in the ground, placed in a circle. Shelon touched it with his foot, and said, "Half way."

Afterwards, the mountain sloped gracefully away from their sides, rolling upwards to the summit, where it abruptly squared, and jutted straight up into the sky. Shelon told her that the Castle Moom was once a gray stone cap set on an emerald green mountain peak. Over the years nature claimed it as its own dominion, and covered it with moss and ivy vines, hiding it from the eyes of the Janti.

"As the story goes," he said over his shoulder to Gella, "Ver dala Ven wanted the Janti to forget this place existed. So they did....in a manner. They remember it, and see it when they look at the odd shape of Moom's peak, but they choose not to know it is here, to keep the spirits happy. Still yet, occasionally, we have visitors. Usually small groups of young men, set on proving themselves courageous. But we spirits of Moom manage to frighten the bravery out of them."

Korba laughed heartily at the prospect of scaring the Janti witless.

The sun had dipped low in the sky by the time they reached the last, and most arduous, leg of the climb. The narrow steps went up a sheer cliff face. Gella did like Shelon, climbing the steps like a ladder, bending down slightly to touch the steps in front of her with her hands for increased balance. She tried not a fear the drop below her, or the fact that the stone had been worn down in places and left little more than token toe holds and hand grips, or that moss and the moist cold air made the stone slippery.

As they reached the top, they entered the jagged mouth of a cave. The interior was dank, dark, and smelled of animal feces.

She didn't care about the darkness, or the smell. She was elated to crawl onto firm soil and sit on her bottom to rest.

318

Shelon crouched behind her, and gently pulled her to her feet. "We've still a ways to go, Gella."

"How far?"

"Not far. Moom is above us."

She clung to him, relieved that their ordeal was nearly over.

Only a few steps into the darkness, Shelon halted. Hushed her question, and listened hard. "We'll have company soon." He murmured.

She heard what he listened for, a scraping noise ahead in the dark and a low groan.

"Is that you, Mo'ghan?" Shelon called out, jeered, "Sounds as though you've a nasty stomach ache."

The groan faded.

"Stones in the Raal river." He stated the code words loudly, and he laughed, adding, "Poor imitation of a great ghost, fellows. I take it you've not had practice in awhile."

Imitation light flooded the depth of the cave, and appearing in the light was a motley group of men. The leader among them was Gella's age. His blond hair hung unevenly over his shoulders, and his face was covered with a wiry beard. Seeing Shelon, amusement lit his features.

"Spoken like a true ghost."

"I'm more alive than dead, but that could change if I don't get a good rest tonight."

Shelon countered, "Be so kind, little man, and move aside and let me into Moom."

"Take a dive, or taste my wrath, shod," he said with mock ferocity, "For you are not getting past me until you take back your foul insult!"

"There's no challenge in suicide....or fighting you." Shelon replied dryly, eliciting a rumble of laughter from the men, "Is there a third choice?"

The man's gaze dropped from Shelon's face to Gella, and his eyes greedily roamed Gella's body. "I'll let you by if you sell me your woman."

"How many nights?"

Indignant, Gella said, "She's not for sale."

He grimaced. "She talks back. Deal's off."

Shelon breathed a laugh. "Praj, you don't know what you are missing."

"She must be good if she brought you back to life."

Praj laughed, and embraced Shelon, breaking him from Gella. He slapped Shelon on the back, kissed his cheeks, his mouth, and welcomed back to the land of the living.

"Iada tells me you've been busy." Shelon said sardonically.

Praj released him, and grinned. "After I heard you were dead, I went insane. I caused a little trouble."

"Little? You burned down Bryn!"

"A trifle," he shrugged, "but I had to leave home for a vacation. Or die. Some choice. Yegi was caught and killed on the spot. Not even a trial before the Council for Shodite Affairs."

Shelon sneered at the news. "The Pliadors think they are above the law."

Praj nodded, and he glanced at Korba. "Where's your sister?"

"She'll be here any time." Korba replied, "She wanted to stay behind and tend to the wounded in Shod city."

Praj nodded, his disappointment evident. "I wish I was among the wounded, then." He glanced at Gella, and smiled lasciviously. "And who is this, Shelon?"

Shelon pulled Gella to him, and said, "Praj Sang, I want you to meet Gella al Perraz. She is a native of Shodalum."

"A native. Where did you find her?"

"It's a long story, one I'll tell after we've had some wine."

Praj grinned, "Much wine." he said, and he turned and led them through the crowd of men.

Gella noticed that many of the men eyed her with earnest interest. "Please tell me I am not the only woman in the castle."

"Relax. They are cut throats, robbers and molesters, but the are my people! We can trust them. Besides," he leaned close to her ear and said, "they have more to fear from you, my pretty warrior, than you have to fear from them."

She smirked at his amusing taunt, and at the way he turned and growled, in jest, at the men who still stared at her. His instant happiness in being with his fellows chased away her uneasiness, and her fatigue kept her from finding insult in the bantering way Shelon had offered to the unkempt man named Praj.

The tunnel came to an end at a set of stone steps that were turned dark gray with dampness. They went up in a circle.

Leaving the dankness of the cave, they entered into an open common and fresh night air. A vine-covered fortress protected a quiet, peaceful village. Tiny thatched roof houses scattered the grounds, protected by the fortress. Small children chased about in the grass. Women stood around a brewing pot over an open fire, talking, laughing. A man was splitting logs, and piling them next to a kiln he was firing. He noticed Shelon, and grinned.

"Hail, Shelon!" he shouted, waving.

Shelon waved back. People who treated his appearance as a delightful occurrence greeted him a dozen more times as they walked through the village.

"Who are all these people?"

"The ghosts of Moom." he replied, a comment that inspired hearty laughter from the men following him.

The castle residence was built to face the east. A huge octahedral dome crowned a plain cut facade. The dome was newer than the older stone walls of the castle, and in many places it was obvious that newly cut stone replaced old. At the top of the dome was the watchtower. The man standing watch whistled and waved. Shelon waved back.

The entrance of the castle residence resembled the palace in structure. A series of lancet archways lead them to a set of double doors, which were indecorously propped open with stones. The interior, however, was a stark contrast to Ona's smooth elegance. The ceilings were lower, and the hall was long and unbroken. In the center of the hall, there was a fire pit, and above, yawning from the low ceiling, was a wide mouthed flue. Around the fire pit, there were fourteen armless stone seats with curved backs, planted in the floor.

A fire roared in the pit, warming the entire hall.

Oil lamps, hanging from the ceilings and lit, exposed the imperfections of the bare stone floor, and the damage, decay and repair of the gray walls.

"The castle was restored by our people, a very long time ago, and though we try to keep the walls standing, it has become a death trap in some areas. Never wander about by yourself. I wouldn't want you to be crushed under a wall or fallen ceiling."

She nodded, her eyes traveling along the script written on the walls. She asked Shelon what it all meant.

"This is the war room," Shelon told Gella, his tone subdued. He waved a hand at the long wall, filled with writing, "There are my plans to destroy the dakas, and the Jantidevan government." He stared at the wall, shaking his head in wonder. "Who was the man who wrote this?"

"What does it say?" Gella prompted.

Shelon smiled self-consciously. "I'll leave it to your imagination."

Praj said, "Korba can show your lady to your room, eh?" and he nodded his head with significance, "You have guests to greet."

"Ahhh," Shelon said knowingly. To Gella, he said, "You go lay down, rest. I'll be up in a few hours."

Shelon followed Praj through the hall, and out the archway at the far end. The rest of the men followed, leaving Korba and Gella behind.

Korba stepped to a wall that was once covered in decorative tile, but now empty except for the outline of a its former design. He pressed his hand into an indentation and pushed. The wall recessed backward, and gave him enough of a handhold to allow him to push his fingers through and slide the wall aside, revealing a spiraling staircase.

"The Rathians hid everything, even the access to their sleeping quarters, in case they were attacked." Korba explained. He gestured for her to precede him, and once they were in the staircase, he slid the door back, pushing it forward until it thumped into place.

The castle had three levels of sleeping quarters. In each level there was a large community sitting room, furnished rustically with handmade chairs and tables and benches. The common area linked many private rooms. Gella found, as they passed through levels one and two, that the castle was far from empty. In each common there were women and children enjoying a quiet evening of conversation and play, communing like a large, extended family.

As they passed through, hails were called out to Korba, and he was made to pause to introduce himself and Gella, and to answer questions about Shelon and Iada. Gella was met with open interest once Korba told them she was from Shodalum, and curious scrutiny once he admitted to one woman's question that she'd be staying in Shelon's room.

On their way up to the third level, Korba said bluntly, "They are whispering behind our backs right now about your youth. Though they love Shelon, they find your age difference unsuitable."

"I don't care what they think." Gella retorted, "I've been spurned for less."

They were silent as they reached the third level. Like the grand hall below, there was a fire pit in the center of the room, with a yawning flue above, and fourteen stone seats surrounding it. And, like the sitting rooms in the lower two levels, there was also an assortment of odd furnishings, rugs, adornments, the personalized touches of the residents of Moom.

"The well room is in this closet," Korba said, "we have no bathhouse, except those that are outside. If you are cold, I can make a fire-"

"Which room is Shelon's?" she asked coolly.

He pointed to the only door that was closed. On the door, there was a symbol etched neatly in the wood that she did not understand, a long vertical line with three short horizontal lines crossing it. She made a mental note to ask Shelon what it meant, and let herself inside his room.

It was a modest sized room, with a Janti-like bed that stood off the floor, and a hand crafted wardrobe almost like the one she had in Shodalum. The window was a narrow crack in the wall that she could fit her hand through and no more, but enough of an opening to let in the cool, night air. She stood at it to look down at the village below, noting instead how the wall flaked away as she placed her palm on it, making Shelon's warnings about the safety of the castle seem all the more real and deadly.

"Where will you go once Iada is here?" Korba asked from behind her. He leaned in the doorway, his arms crossed before his chest.

323

She refused to allow him to see that he'd hurt her so easily with a few words. "I'll go where Shelon sends me."

"And if he leaves you here? What will you do?"

Her lower lip trembled, and she retorted angrily, "I won't be rushing to your arms, that is what I won't do, Korba."

"I wouldn't take you if you did." He countered, and he stalked off. A door slammed shut elsewhere on their level, echoing in the silence.

Gella shut the door of Shelon's room, and went about preparing for his return.

๙๛๙๛๙๛๙๛๙๛

Shelon matched Praj's quick descent into the Rathian torture chamber. The chamber was hollowed out of the mountain, deep beneath the castle. It had been out of use since the Rathians fled Moom, and had been flooded numerously from rushing waters during heavy rains. There was nothing left in the earthen cavern that resembled the devices of torture the Rathians once used, it was empty but for a stone alter deeply embedded in the dark red soil. Suma priests taught that the Rathians worshiped many gods, and according to the Suma teachings, they often sacrificed animals and Janti babies to their gods. Believing the Suma unequivocally, the Shodites that first found themselves in Moom removed the altar from the castle's temple, and banished it into the torture chamber. Unfortunate, because the altar was a thing of beauty.

The seven men chained to each other in the belly of the Rathian torture chamber probably wouldn't agree. They lay on the cold ground, too listless to pick up their heads. They were tired and hungry and mistreated. One was clothed in Shodite coveralls.

Edise was the only one to sit and face the enemy. Seeing Shelon, he grimaced.

"So you aren't dead."

"Maybe I am," Shelon offered, "And we're suffering together in the afterlife."

Edise spat. "I'll be with the Guardian Spirit of Creation in the afterlife. You'll be in the pit of torment with the Rathians."

Shelon chuckled. "Then I'd be with preferred company."

324

"Devil." he muttered.

Shelon ambled around Edise, viewing him speculatively.

"The dakas have yet to demand your return, Edise." he said casually. "In fact, they didn't ask about you at all while I was in custody. An oversight, you think?"

Edise's mouth turned down and he glowered at Shelon.

"The daka feels no loyalty toward you. How does that make you feel?" Shelon prodded.

"What do you want from me?" Edise growled, "You want me to beg for my life? Beg for my men? Side with you?"

Shelon laughed mirthlessly at the latter. "Oh no, I do not want to call you ally. But I do want you to see what kind of scum you follow. As far as the dakas are concerned, you are expendable, like a Shodite. You'll die here, and the daka will hardly give you a thought. She is far too consumed with her own worries to care about your fate."

"You won't shake my loyalty to the daka with lies." Edise blustered. His sallow face turned red.

"You think I am wrong?" Shelon asked, "You are a part of the authority class, not the wealthy class. Don't you feel how they look down at you, Edise? You live in a modest home with your wife and many children, and can only afford two or three Shodites. Doesn't it burn your pride that you manage the wealthy class's Shodites single handedly without recognition? *No,* you say, you are recognized for your hard labor. Your thanks will come in the meager retirement the government will pay you. And when you retire, you'll likely have to give up one or two of your Shodites, probably the one you keep company with when your wife goes to see her mother in the country." Shelon paused meaningfully.

"You are filth." Edise retorted hotly, "I understand why you are unafraid of Moom. You are a Rathian. Only the Rathians could act with utter impunity against the Janti! Be gone evil spirit! Die, die, and forget this place!"

Shelon smiled, bemused by the ridiculous hex. He glanced at Praj, and the men standing around Praj, to utter a witticism. As he laid eyes on them, his remark stuck in his throat, and his smile faded.

In the place of his followers, he saw proud Rathian Knights. They were in shimmering silver body armor, their faces concealed with armor veils. Their chest plates were engraved with their five tenets, written in the long dead Rathian language, but understandable to Shelon. *Live fidelity. Say the truth. Love your comrade. Fight with courage. Freely sacrifice yourself for the whole.*

"Rathians treat their prisoners with respect. It is immoral to do otherwise."

The one who'd spoken, the one that should have been Praj, unfastened the armor veil from his helmet, and dropped it away from his face. His features were identical to Shelon's. He stared at Shelon, amusement sparkling in his eyes.

His gold eyes.

Shelon dropped back a step, shook the vision out of his head, and rubbed it out his eyes with the knuckles of both hands.

He looked back, willing it be Praj standing there, rather than the Rathian that looked like him with Ver dala Ven eyes.

It was Praj. He had stepped forward, concerned.

"Shelon?"

"I'm tired," Shelon said, breathing a sigh of relief. Fatigue, that was it. He was hallucinating because of fatigue. He glanced at Edise, and terrible pity for the forgotten Janti overwhelmed him. His tone sober, his taunts dead in him, he said, "Feed them, water them, and refrain from kicking them for your pleasure. We must stop behaving like Janti. Treat them like you would treat a Shodite who had committed a terrible crime."

"Hide them from the Janti and pat them on the back?" Praj offered with a grin.

"Don't let them loose." he amended, "But do treat them humanely."

"As you wish."

Edise listened and watched the Shodites distrustfully, even as they brought food and water. The Janti and the Shodites will never trust each other, Shelon mused. Their hatred would live on, even after the Shodites were freed. And what kind of life would a Shodite have in Janti society were the social elite looked down upon the lower classes of their own kind? He'd wanted to work

326

Edise into an anger, to see the man realize how devalued he was in the eyes of the dakas, but instead, he had unwittingly pointed out to himself that even in a free society, men like Edise would be considered a better class of citizen than a Shodite.

Shelon was left wondering, again, if that was what he ultimately wanted for his people.

જ્જ-જ્જ-જ્જ-જ્જ-જ્જ-જ્જ-જ્જ

Gella considered rolling out a mat to sleep on the floor, but remembering Shelon's pleasure at sleeping in a Janti bed, she instead shook the dust out the bedding, and fluffed the mattress and pillows. She wandered through the common room, not certain what it was she was looking for until she found it, the small room Korba told her about that had a well pump. She pumped, and pumped, and pumped the handle until she was ready to give up on the prospect of having water to bathe in and drink, when it poured out into a wooden basin. She ran back to the bedroom, found a ceramic pitcher, and returned to the well room to fill it with water.

Washed and naked, she climbed into the bed. She planned on waiting up for Shelon, but she was too tired, and sleep was too inviting.

In her dreams she was again in Shodalum, following Cobo around as he did his chores on the farm. He spoke to her endlessly in that strange language. She tried to understand him, begging him to speak Shodite to her.

Crossing their paths in the middle of the yava field was a man she'd never seen before. A man with dark features, amused eyes, gold eyes like Cobo's, and an imposing stature. Him, she understood. He said to her, "Good day, warrior woman." and he chuckled and walked on.

જ્જ-જ્જ-જ્જ-જ્જ-જ્જ-જ્જ-જ્જ

Shelon woke her as he loudly let himself into their room, though he was trying to be quiet. She was fresh from her strange dream, and happy to see him bearing down on her, a grinning and disheveled drunken fool, smelling of wine and a fire pit. Amorous intentions twinkled in his eyes as he clumsily mounted her. She half-heartedly complained of his smell, and his appearance, while eagerly accepted him between her legs. Their attempt at lovemaking didn't last long before the wine and fatigue claimed Shelon. He fell asleep on her almost as soon as he lay down.

She didn't move him off her, rather held him greedily, all too aware their nights together were numbered.

The next morning, Shelon woke with a tremendous moan.

Gella had been awake for hours, standing at the crevice window looking down at the village. She looked fondly at the man in the bed.

"Too much reveling into the middle of the night."

He put both hands on the sides of his head, as if to keep it from cracking wide open, and squinted at her. "Did Praj bring me upstairs?"

"No," she smiled, "You brought yourself, and jumped me the minute you pulled your pants off."

He grunted. "Wish I remembered."

"You were incredible," she said, amusement twinkling in her eyes, "You did acrobatics. I'm sure my screams woke the whole castle."

He laughed in earnest. "You are a wicked liar."

She went to the bed, and took his head into her lap and smoothed his cheeks, compelling him to drop his hands away. His hand landed on her hip, and he caressed a hollow he found with his thumb.

"I didn't offend you last night, did I?" he asked, looking upwards at her.

"Your desire would never offend me."

He stared soulfully into her eyes. If she tried, she could have seen more for her than lust, more for her than the affection of a passing love affair. She wished for more, and savored the wish.

"Help me." he said abruptly. He rolled up and with her pushing at his back, he sat up. He stretched his back and moaned. "A hard climb that gets harder with each passing year." Glancing at Gella, he added, "I don't suppose you ache this morning?"

"Horribly." Her feet hurt, her back and legs were wobbly, and her head was made light by the thin air and cold. "But I will survive."

Amusement brightened his eyes. "I have a sight to show you."

They dressed, and he took her downstairs, through the war room (where several men were on the floor still sleeping off their drunk), and through the archway at the farthest end of the hall.

Beyond the archway was a circular antechamber, and from it branched seven corridors. Shelon said, "This one," meaning the one directly across from the archway, the only one lit by oil lamps, "leads to the kitchen. I'll show you later. Come."

He took her arm and walked her into a darkened corridor. "I repeat my warning, Gella, I want you to stay out of the unused corridors in the castle, like this one, unless I guide you. The castle is crumbling. In places, it is very dangerous." He paused, standing before a plain stone wall in the corridor. He found the place in the wall he was looking for, a loose stone, and he pressed on it. The wall opened, rock scraping against rock. A newer looking wooden staircase was revealed. They entered, and mounted the stairs. Looking down through the open rungs, she could see the original stairs, or what was left of them. Stone, and crumbling, as Shelon had warned.

They reached the top of the stairs, and emerged into clean, crisp, frigid air. It was the watchtower. The tower was a simple platform surrounded by a waist high railing and a cap to break the rain. A man leaned on the balcony, staring out at the sunrise, smoking leisurely.

"In a trance, Tobe?" Shelon said as he stepped onto the platform.

Gella followed behind, and it was the sight of her that caught Tobe's attention. He was young, very dark, slender, and looked very much like a Janti. Though his eyes were on her, to Shelon, he said, "I'm ready for sleep. Been a long night, and Praj is late for his shift."

"Take off. I'll wait for Praj."

Tobe nodded, and throwing one last, long glance at Gella, he left them in the watchtower.

He walked her to the railing, and holding her close, he showed her magnificence, and glory, as she had never seen. She could hardly breath, as she looked out on the world below, just waking. Below Moom, dwarfed by the castle, were sloping hills painted with too many variations of green to count. The sky was blue, with striations of red and gold along the horizon where the sun was struggling to make an appearance.

"I've never seen such splendor."

Shelon smiled, and pulled her away from the rail, turning her, and even before they reached the opposite rail, her breath caught in her throat for the sight that lay on the other side of the castle Moom. Beyond a hollow valley of green was a tranquil sea.

"I never minded watch duty." he admitted. "I could stay up here all day."

"Yes," she breathed.

"I've lived here often," Shelon said, "since escaping from prison. The first time I came up here, I'd only been out of prison a few days. I was still like an animal then, made insane by hunger, and fear, and bitter hatred. I somehow ended up with night watch, the first night I was here. That morning, I saw the sunrise......and my sanity returned. Raal, Monca, Solien, Grethian, they were distant, so distant. I felt happiness for the first time in my life, standing here and looking out at the greatest beauty I had ever seen."

She understood. She, too, felt happiness overwhelm her, and distant in her mind was the uncertainty of her future with Shelon, and her longing for her brother's voice.

"I wish this moment would never end." she said, molding herself snugly to Shelon's body.

He breathed his satisfaction, and stroked her hair. "Gella, my precious one. My precious one." he whispered.

Praj relieved them once the sun was higher, and the view was bright. Carrying with them the happiness, the love offered to them by nature, they went back to their bed, and they made love. There was no play, no raunchy words or pretty words; no talk at all. Only sighs, and long, tender gazes, and kisses with depth and meaning.

For the first time since leaving Cobo, she did not dream of him as she slept in Shelon's arms.

330

Chapter 16

The caravan journey through the Coulcubannha mountain range followed broken trails and dried riverbeds. The climate in the northern mountains was much colder than the Janti Center-plex, and far colder than the equatorial black desert in Shodalum. Cobo and Surna piled on their clothing, layer after layer. When it became clear they would not be able to shut out the cold, they asked a Huntress to rein the beast that pulled their cart, and climbed in to huddle together for warmth.

The Huntress, named Krep, sneered at them, snug in the cart, and slapped the beast on the flank, moving the oversized hairy beast forward.

Staring at the scanty outfit worn by Krep, Surna shivered involuntarily and cuddled deeper into the warmth of Cobo's arms. "Do you think they are acclimatized, or does it have something to do with their differences from us?"

"A little of both, I suspect, and throw in a healthy dose of their culture." he smiled at Surna, "Those women are respected for being tough. They'd suffer the cold until they froze to death in order to prove themselves worthy of respect."

"How dreadful." she murmured, and she chuckled, "I don't imagine I inspired much respect, the way I hopped in here with you."

"It wouldn't matter if you trudged through the cold naked all the way to Zadoq," he replied wryly, "You aren't a Huntress, therefore you aren't worthy of respect."

She frowned contemplatively, the creases of her face deepening.

"I don't actually want respect that badly." she said, and she laughed at herself.

The highway took them through the ruins of many old cities. Cobo learned their history and names from the Ryslac slaves, who seemed to be the only ones who endeavored to remember the history of Dilgopoche. In one such city, Rito-Sant ordered that they rest the slaves. The city was called Eudoxos and had been like Montrose, a resort community housing the Alliance elite on holiday. In the days before the Dome of Silence was put into place, Eudoxos was evacuated in secret. No one remained but the Dilgos, who, none the wiser, went on with their normal lives until the fateful day that the sky turned orange. In Eudoxos, and other cities in the higher elevations, being so close to the Dome wiped out the entire population in less time than it took its inhabitants to take one breath.

The city, itself, was untouched and well preserved under the cloak of the Dome, though the exterior had been blackened by lume. Cobo and Surna explored as much as they could of the sprawling city in the short amount of time they were there to rest. The lowliest of homes were like museums, filled with dusty antiques.

"Do the Dilgos know of the treasures they own?" Surna asked Cobo as she ran her hand over a footstool made by artisans of Redd's era. "So little wear in the fabric. How can it have remained in good shape for this long?"

"The lume killed everything, including pests that eat fabric. The rest is probably due to climate conditions. But really, I'm guessing. I don't know."

Surna straightened and hugged herself as she looked around. "It is eerie to wander inside their homes. I can almost imagine a family living here, living happily. It is so sad how they died."

Cobo glanced to the wisp of spirit essence hovering nearby. "Many never left Eudoxos after their death. I've never encountered a place so inhabited by restless spirits."

She shuddered.

Amused, he asked, "You aren't afraid of spirits, are you?"

"Of course not." She retorted lightly, but also made it clear was no longer interested in exploring the homes of ghosts.

Through his exposure to Dilgo minds, he learned their language quickly and passed on his knowledge to Surna. They made speaking in Dilgo a game to pass the time, though it served an important purpose. A few days into their journey, Surna was able to understand the Huntresses as they spoke to her without having to rely on Cobo's translation.

"You see that valley there," Cobo said in Dilgo.

Surna looked at the expanse below the narrow notch alongside the mountain they traveled, bit her lip, and did her best to respond. "See valley, yes?"

Cobo suppressed a smile at her broken Dilgo, and went on, speaking slowly for her. "That valley held the village, Maltana. It is the place where the abnormal births began. The Dilgos believe that the valley is cursed, and won't cross through. That is why we travel this dangerous route, instead of taking the valley. Though if we took the valley, our trip to Zadoq would be shorter."

They watched as Krep stopped to catch a snowflake in her mouth.

Surna said, with fondness, in her broken Dilgo, "Like child."

"She, all Dilgos, have never seen precipitation in any form."

Surna's mouth slipped open, and forgetting herself, in Janti she asked, "How is that possible?"

He gestured around them. "The Dome shut everything out, including the movement of storms. The heat of the lume evaporated rain clouds on contact."

"No, I mean, how is it possible that the Dilgos survived without water?"

Repeating the remarkable story Drell told of their survival, Cobo said, "It took time for their lakes and wells to dry up, and in that time the Dilgos devised an irrigation system, drawing water from a portion of the Tendalti Sea left exposed by the Dome. They built a series of self-driven pumps that are still in use today. The pumps draw in seawater, processes it, cleanses it, and pumps it to a reservoir near Zadoq. The Men and Women do their best to control water use." Grinning wryly, he continued in Janti so that the Huntress near them would not understand if she overheard. "The Men and Women didn't solve Dilgopoche's water problems. The Ryslacs engineered and built the pump and reservoir, as well as the canal system that moves the water from community to community."

She slid a glance to the Ryslac under a Huntress whip, being made to pull a cart. "And that is how they repay those who have accomplished so much for their kind? They did nothing less than save their people!"

"Yes, that is true. And it was easy for them. Genetically, the Ryslacs are born with superior minds, and they know it. They may act humble before the Men and Women, because they fear them, but they are not humble about what is obvious. And the Men, in their own way, fear the Ryslacs for their intelligence, because they are not intelligent. In fact, the giants are quite slow in some respects."

"How can the stupid rule the intelligent?" she asked incredulously.

"It is a matter of brute strength versus physical weakness." he said, "If you had a choice between crossing a Huntress to prove an intellectual point, or keeping to yourself and possibly avoiding retribution, what would you choose to do?"

"I understand."

"Good." he said in Dilgo.

As they traveled along the crest of a lengthy plateau, looking out at the valleys that were made in the elbows of the hills, they could finally see the canals Buhj and Drell spoke of, looking like slender veins of vital fluid reaching precious farmland.

"We must be close to Zadoq."

Surna resituated herself beside Cobo. "I hope so. That thing smells, and I can't sit in this cubby another day. Not that I mind the company." she said quickly, and ruefully.

Cobo chuckled. "Understood. And that thing is a honig." he said of the beast, "It was once a protected species kept in a Coulcubannha nature preserve. Another antique, my friend, priceless and yet treated by the Dilgos as mundane."

Surna nodded at the information. "I recognized it from pictures in a zoology program I had at the temple. I suppose even a protected species has its uses."

It took half the day for the caravan to negotiate the narrow path that twisted down the face of the mountain. As they reached the valley, they traveled alongside a canal, offering Cobo a closer look. It was wider than he'd imagined, controlled by a series of water locks. The depth in each lock varied to high, or very low, down to dry. The wider, deeper locks were connected to irrigation canals that ran across the farmland, the latter connecting to many more canals that were smaller still, and poured the water into field grids.

At the moment the fields were frozen. The unseasonable cold snap was due to the Dome's destruction. A few days before, they saw snowfall for the first time, an occasion for celebration if the crops hadn't been damaged.

The community of farmers tending the fields was drawn to the roadside by the sight of Rito-Sant's caravan. From the distance, the farmers looked smaller than average for a Janti, but this close it was obvious they weren't just small, they were miniature people. They were no larger than two or three year old Janti children, though they had the body symmetry and appearance of adults.

"Ryslac-Denmen." Cobo explained, and he paused, and listened to their minds. His eyes widened. His voice hushed, he said in Janti, "Some of them are over one thousand years old."

"They look like children!"

"Yes...eternal youth.....they don't suffer the ravages of old age......they don't suffer at all," he said with wonder, "They do not suffer from diseases, they are impervious to the aging process. They will stay young for as long as they are alive....and in their community, the only ones who have died are the ones who were murdered by the Huntresses for sport." A fleeting vision passed through him, of the little people being set loose out of cages and hunted like small animals for the pleasure of the Huntresses.

"They don't seem afraid of the Huntresses." Surna observed.

"It isn't the right season for hunting Ryslac-Denmen."

Surna watched the sober and wise faces of the Denmen as they passed, and decided, "The Huntresses have no consciences."

A strong mind among the Denmen caught Cobo's attention, nearly tapped him on the shoulder. He heard clearly a thin, child-like voice say to him, *"Welcome to Dilgopoche, Ver dala Ven Cobo."*

Cobo bolted upright to see over the crates that sheltered them, and searched the faces of the gathered Denmen.

"What is it, Cobo?" Surna asked.

Again, the thin, childlike voice only he could hear said, *"My name is Kiitur. I am the healer of the Denmen."*

A woman stepped forward from the rows of little people. Her features were as elegant as those of the satin and glass dolls Jishni used to keep in her room as a girl. Her skin was pale pink, her

337

cheeks rosy, her enormous eyes were thickly lashed, and her hair was blue-black and hung in plaits on either side of her face. She wore coveralls, in the style the laboring Shodites wore. Her tiny, bow shaped mouth was set in an amused smile.

Cobo held onto the sight of her gold eyes as the cart passed her. Her strength of mind, and fluid thought patterns reminded him of Taen, a Ver dala Ven untrained. He wondered if she was his kin, and in response to his fleeting thought she released to him a flood of personal information. She was two thousand and ninety years old, born one hundred years after the Dome of Silence was put into place.

"During the time my great-grandmother was a maiden," she said, projecting her thoughts to him as easily as he remembered communicating with his own father, *"Ver dala Ven Maxim visited Dilgopoche. He came here in search of the Masing Star. He never found the Star, but he did find abundant pleasure in the company of many young maidens."* The childlike crone let out a peal of laughter.

Impossible. Maxim had his one Ver dala Ven child, the child allotted to him by Betnoni's curse, Locat.

"More and more impossible, I was born an Ordinary One." She continued, her voice still greatly amused, *"My brown eyes turned gold when I was but six years old, after having heard the song of the Masing Star."*

She let him hear the peal of the song as she remembered it, sounding like a thousand gongs. The tiny Spirit of the Star passed along to him by Thib reacted to the song, and swelled inside his body in time with the music, and revealed to him the truth of Kiitur's claim.

Cobo sat back down with Surna, dumbfounded.

Surna was watching him quizzically. "What was that all about? You see someone familiar?"

"No....maybe....." and he fell into a broody silence.

She prompted him, asking, "And?"

He seemed to wake. With a crooked smile that he used to mock himself, he said, "Sorry. I was just considering the wayward lusts of my forefathers."

Chagrinned, Surna chuckled. "Please remind me not to probe your silences again."

ళు ళు ళు ళు ళు ళు ళు ళు ళు

"Zadoq is near," Baru announced loudly outside their semi-private room.

Taen dressed quickly and left his sleeping wife to join Lodan, Rito-Sant and Baru on the rooftop of the moving carriage, eager to get his first sight of his new homeland, the land he was to rule.

He first saw a community that was built into a cliff face, the homes looking like rustic caves, though by the square lines of each structure it was obvious they were made by the Dilgos. Ladders lead to the upper levels, and from those more ladders were used to reach higher levels. He saw men his size, climbing down, or up, moving from one level to another in their vertical city.

"Is that where I will live?" he asked in dismay.

Rito-Sant had chuckled at Baru's translation. Baru said to him, "The Inferes live like animals, not the Men and Women. Wait....you will see our palace. It is by the Lake of Tears."

The narrow canyon walls gradually fell away, and the last of the Coulcubannha mountains gave way to an endless valley. From the foothills of the mighty Coulcubannha, the Lake of Tears appeared as a deep blue stamp against a mainly tan background. Seven canals ran from the heart of the lake, feeding water to the entire country. A building, shaped like a crooked finger, rested alongside the lake, and a canal ran through its length. That canal emerged from the building, and disappeared again inside an enormous structure built in the shape of the Masing star.

The star was richly red, as dark as the streaks of red on the canyon walls. The center of the structure, or core, was rounded like half a moon set into the ground and easily as large. Running from the core was the sacred ten arms of the Masing Star. Each arm was attached low on the center, a quarter of its height. From the tip of each arm, Taen could see activity, tiny dots in motion that he realized were animals and people, entering and leaving the city.

"Zadoq." Rito-Sant said, gracing him with a proud smile.

Taen was thrilled. The shape of the city seemed to validate Riar Sed's claim. He would find the Masing Star. He would find it here, and he would possess it, and once in possession, he would be the most powerful man in the universe.

"The palace of Sant lies in the center." Baru said, though he was hardly listening, so rapt in his own fantasy. "The rest is left to the under classes. The Men and Women live under one roof, as a family. It is the only civilized way to live."

"It is the Masing." he whispered to Lodan.

Overheard by Baru, she vehemently corrected him. The shape, she told him, was that of their god, the sun.

Aside to Lodan, Taen whispered, "It's as plain as the sun in the sky....that is not meant to represent the sun."

"I agree."

Taen asked Baru who had built the palace.

"God, of course." she replied, as if he were obtuse.

He glanced wryly at Lodan. "Of course."

As Rito-Sant's coach approached the tip of one of the arms, Men and Women poured forth, cheering their return home. Rito-Sant stood with Baru at the bow of the ship, his arm draped around his sister's shoulders. He proudly displayed himself, and his renewed legs, to his people.

The noise of their reception woke Danati, and she emerged from their private quarters dressed in a robe Taen had brought from Janti for her, one of many gifts he'd given to his wife. (at his mother's suggestion) She climbed onto the deck, and as she appeared, Taen felt compelled to go take her arm. He treated her gently, as if she were a lady that might break, though she was taller and heavier than he, and perhaps stronger, judging from their rambunctious marital activities. She was, by far, the lustiest woman he'd ever been with, making him wonder if Dilgo women were, by nature, lustier than the shod.

Their reception followed them into the arm of the Masing. This close, Taen could see that the city was built with smooth, carefully formed clay, like a monument, or a sculpture. The artistic lines seemed incongruous with the hole hacked into the end of the arm, and the primitive windows roughly pecked out of the exterior walls.

Inside, the high dome of the arm's ceiling was braced by thick beams, set cross ways and buried into the clay foundation. They traveled beneath the first crossed supports, and the cool air from outside became a sultry tropical heat. The heat radiated from multitudes of lamps hanging from the braces. The city looked like a sky lit by a million suns.

The valley outside was barren, but the inside of the city was an explosion of plant growth, following streams and pools of water. Trees lined the wide cobblestone road, and they dripped with ripened fruits. Creeping vines covered the faces of homes, and stores. The living quarters, buildings, were built closely together, some stacked on top of each other for the sake of room, and built shabbily, without the elegance that was the star, itself. The dimensions of the buildings, doorways, windows fit the oversized Dilgo, yet among the Men and Women that were cheering their arrival, there were smaller Dilgos. Taen's eyes quickly passed over the deformed ones, those Men and Women used as pack animals and labor, but caught, and held onto the sight of a luscious raven-haired breeder. She wore a shapeless white robe, and her hair was left long, and loose.

The woman did not look away, but stared at him with big dark eyes that were filled with interest.

Danati noticed where his gaze had lingered. Her nostrils flared with indignation. Huffily, she said, "It is death for any man who defiles a breeder. Might you be ready for death?"

Her comment held the definite air of a threat. She, unlike the Huntresses who seemed to thrive on sharing their men with each other, was the jealous type. Reluctantly, Taen found her eyes, glancing up at her, and he smiled sheepishly. "I was surprised to see another woman like you....but so obviously inferior to your beauty."

Mollified by his trite compliment, she allowed him to hold her arm. As her eyes turned to the crowd, he stole a backward glance at the forbidden breeder.

Her speculative stare was fixed on him.

Taen's lips curled into a smile for her, and he glanced away in time to avoid being caught by Danati.

The caravan stopped as they neared the end of the arm. Dozens of musicians rushed out of the corridor leading into the palace, playing a light and happy song. Rito-Sant climbed down off the ship-carriage, and Baru-Oclassi instructed Taen to follow, without his wife. He did, and Baru descended after him, followed by Lodan, and then Danati, who hung back, her head down submissively.

Baru pushed Taen to Rito-Sant's side. Taen glanced over at the hairy leg of his father-in-law, then slowly upwards to the shaggy face that peered down upon him with a mix of grudging pride, and distrust. Taen would never grow accustomed to the giants, and wondered how he could rule men who towered above him. For the first time since his marriage to Danati, he considered the weighty implications of being a Dilgo sovereign.

His stomach trembling, he stepped through the thick entrance into the palace at Rito-Sant's side.

The palace common was a dozen times larger than the Congress plaza in the Center-plex, but with a lower ceiling than he expected. The common opened to the city's ten arms, with hacked out corridors like the one they just crossed through, and from them grew well worn foot paths crossing over each other in the rotunda. A jungle of plant life thrived, seeming to spring from the clay walls and floors. Sculpted trenches with running water linked ten expansive pools, each of which were in the shape of a bosnii flower, a flower that had hundreds of evenly jagged petals. The pools were set in a wide, irregular circle. Taen remembered the symbolism of a circle of ten bosnii flowers from his Suma lessons. They invited the return of the Masing Star.

In the pools, naked Men and Women waded waste deep in smoky red water, splashing, and copulating. Taen almost laughed out loud at the sight. If the Chancellor could see how the Dilgos defiled the sacred bosnii, Taen was certain he'd faint dead away.

At each opening into the city, the curtains were pulled aside, and Rito-Sant's people crowded in and cheered. The guests in the common cheered as they saw Rito-Sant, and the men stomped their feet in approbation.

Flower petals and aromatic leaves rained down on their heads as they crossed a bridge over a wide stream, and Taen looked up to

342

see an opening in the ceiling. Above them was a round gallery, and Taen could see many galleries above, many upper levels to the palace. At each gallery, crowding against a clay barricade, there were breeders, as lovely as his Danati, throwing fragrant plant parts down on his head and shoulders.

Rito-Sant guided Taen to a dais that overlooked a pool. A throne larger than Rito-Sant himself was on the dais, and several pillows littered the floor where his feet would rest. Two nubile, young Huntresses lay nude on the pillows, waiting to attend their ruler.

Directly behind Rito-Sant's throne was a narrow doorway, covered by a curtain of vines and heavily guarded by Huntresses. Taen touched the minds of the Huntresses in order to find out if he was correct, that this was the way to the upper levels of the palace, but he brought back images and gibberish that made no sense to him. He resorted to touching Baru's mind, but her mind was on a man in the pool who was beckoning obscenely for her to join him. Baru's mind, like most of the Men and Women, was a quagmire of base impulses, of violence and sex and need for control. Like an animal, she was instinctive, with little need to understand the world around her.

She fought the urge to leave Rito-Sant's side to satisfy her lusts, and threw her resentment and frustration at Taen. She was obligated to set aside her own needs to translate the conversation between Taen and Rito-Sant.

Danati, who could translate just as well, was taken away by the Huntress guard that accompanied them to Dilgopoche. Taen found her eyes, touched her mind, and learned that she was not permitted to stay among the Men and Women, even as the wife of her father's heir. From Danati, he found the information he'd been seeking from the Huntresses. The doorway was the opening to the upper levels. Just inside the walls was a purposeful space, unlike the hacked out openings, a gradual ascending ramp, a lengthy walk circling the palace many times to reach the upper levels.

Danati's memories were of living with the breeders in the upper levels, near their temple. She was excited, because her marriage had elevated her to living on the same level with her father and his brothers and sisters, and Danati's many sisters who were lucky enough to have grown into Huntresses.

Before Danati disappeared into the eleventh portal, she caught him looking at her, and she smiled, her thoughts running fluid with desire. She was content with Taen. She had thought she'd be revolted to bed a Janti male. Taen was proud of himself for having turned her thinking around on the matter.

Rito-Sant called out to a few good friends, and stomped a tribal dance to prove his legs. He spoke rapidly in Dilgo.

Taen understood one word. Ver dala Ven. A hush fell over the crowd, and eyes drifted toward the Janti Ver dala Ven. Cobo entered the palace, trailed by that hideous looking Suma Mistress. Though Cobo had maintained a deferential distance behind Taen in the caravan, he'd still managed to upstage Taen with his presence. Taen forced a smile that did not hide his resentment.

Rito-Sant addressed Cobo, his voice warm, friendly. Baru, started to translate, but Cobo said to her in Janti that it was not necessary, and went on to reply to Rito-Sant in Dilgo.

Flushed with shame and anger that Cobo had learned the language so quickly, while he was still dependant on a translator, Taen again felt upstaged.

Baru made it worse by coming up behind him and translating. "Rito-Sant has welcomed Ver dala Ven to stay at the celebration as an honored guest, and sit with us at the feast. Ver dala Ven accepted."

"Fabulous." Taen said dryly.

Rito-Sant spoke again to Ver dala Ven, and Cobo again replied in Dilgo.

Baru, fuming at the injustice of being saddled with an oaf that couldn't pick up her language as fast as Ver dala Ven, translated in a stilted tone. "Rito-Sant has informed Ver dala Ven that his breeder is not welcome at the feast, and must take her place in the fertility house. Ver dala Ven said that she is his attendant, and has asked that she be housed in his quarters, ...and Rito-Sant has complied." she added, as Rito-Sant nodded his agreement to Ver dala Ven's request.

Taen sighed his boredom for the inane conversation, and glanced at Lodan, who stood at the base of the dais among men who dwarfed him. He seemed completely at ease, as if he'd lived in Dilgopoche all his life. Taen felt a touch envious of the Kai'gam master. His calm was ever present, his mind sharp and focused and uncluttered.

As Surna was taken away, Rito-Sant finally got around to presenting Taen, and in doing so, he stripped Taen of whatever dignity he felt standing among the massive Dilgos. Rito-Sant took hold of Taen under the armpits and lifted him, like a small child, to the seat of the massive throne so that he nearly stood level with Rito-Sant's height.

He released Taen, and stepped back, grinning triumphantly. He then turned to his people and said clearly, "Taen-*Sant*," and with a gesture he encouraged the crowd to cheer for his heir.

The prompted stomping and cheering started half-heartedly, but by the end grew so loud it threatened to bring the roof down on their heads. Taen sensed among them a myriad of emotions thundering with their cheers. His entry into their society, and Janti patronage, would bring a new standard of living for the Men and Women. For that much, they were happy.

Hatred for Jantideva, and especially for him, was also present, but he couldn't find the roots of the emotion in the thousands of Dilgos.

The celebration went on with hardly a break. Rito-Sant, through Baru, offered his chair to Taen, and joined his people. Taen sat on the arm of the chair sullenly, and watched the Dilgos revel in their victory. Rito-Sant stripped himself of his loose groin wrap and danced in a huge, undulating line of men, while his organ hardened and thickened. Abruptly, he left the line dance and grabbed hold of a Huntress by the waist. He carried her to the pool and tossed her in, going after her with lust in his eyes. Taen turned away as Rito-Sant coupled with the Huntress among the swimmers.

He laughed at himself. He was far more prudish than he cared to admit. Watching Dilgos couple was not as enjoyable, or titillating, as Danati promised him it would be.

He glanced upwards at the breeders he could still see from the dais. They looked down at the carnal melee with longing. They could never join in, it was physically impossible for them to mate with the Men. Taen had felt in Danati's mind the frustration, and ache, and pain of being forbidden pleasure among the Dilgos. He touched the minds of the breeders above him, and felt the same frustration, ache, and pain, and longing....and lust, as their eyes greedily drank in the sight of three Men who were the right size, the right dimensions for them. Their eyes went from Taen, to Lodan, to Cobo, their minds rushing with the possibilities.

"Now.....this is titillating." Taen muttered to himself.

His raven-haired beauty appeared among the breeders. He wondered lightly how she'd gotten past him in the common. She, like the others, yearned for pleasure.

His eyes upturned, intensely connected to the hungry females above him, he was oblivious of Rito-Sant's two younger brothers stalking their way to the dais.

৵৵৵৵৵৵৵৵৵৵

Cobo saw through the thoughts of the brothers before they made their move. He tossed an urgent warning to the mind of Lodan, who reacted immediately. He took the scabbard off his back, sliding the blade out of it and tossing it aside with one motion. He put himself between Taen and the approaching Dilgos, brandishing his kai'gam before their eyes.

Taen seemed to break from a trance, and he shot to his feet, standing in the center of the throne and staring in horror at the scene unfolding before him.

The brothers were momentarily taken aback by Lodan's fierce show of courage, then broke into laughter at the little man with his little kai'gam.

The sight of Lodan holding the two brothers at bay caused a hush to riffle through the gathering. Shouts drew Rito-Sant's attention. Scowling, he left the group of Huntresses servicing him in the pool. Dripping wet, and disagreeable, Rito-Sant pushed through the crowd of Dilgos to the eye of the storm.

"What is this...traitors!" Rito-Sant shouted furiously at his brothers.

The younger, his name Seamus, flew into a rage. "You'd give your seat to a Janti, who cannot even climb into your seat without help....like a little boy!"

"You are the little boy, Seamus." Rito-Sant growled, "A selfish boy would deprive his people of salvation in order to call himself Sant."

"It was my right to take your throne!" the elder brother blustered.

"Blaec, you have no rights, but those that I give to you." Rito-Sant retorted.

Blaec removed his blade, a weapon as long as Lodan was tall. "B'lianza." he snorted, a word in Dilgo meaning he demanded a challenge to the death.

Rito-Sant threw his head back and he glared at his defiant sibling. "Are you challenging me, Blaec?"

Blaec glanced warily at his restored brother. Cobo sensed Blaec and Seamus feared their brother's strength.

Blaec turned his venomous glare on Taen. "No, I challenge him."

Baru, breathless with the anticipation of bloodshed, translated.

Taen laughed his disbelief. In Janti, he said, "They're insane!"

"Accepted!" Lodan said in a loud voice, his white blue eyes sharp and fixed on Blaec, "I will act as Taen-Sant's proxy."

Cobo felt a heartening flow of genuine concern from Taen for the welfare of his hero. "No, Lodan!"

But it was done. Baru translated. Lodan's acceptance of the challenge cleared the floor. The brothers backed from the dais, each of them wearing a knowing grin. They expected to kill the Janti easily.

Lodan stepped down from the dais. On the floor, he warmed up with a few lunges, and swung his kai'gam in circles to prepare his arms.

Blaec propped the tip of his blade on the stone floor and leaned on the handle casually, laughing at the little Janti. The Men around him laughed, too.

Lodan took a defensive posture, and shouted "Aiy ha!" at the men, indicating he was ready.

Blaec laughed louder.

347

He stepped toward the Janti, and he sneered a grin, saying in Dilgo, "Give it your best, little thing. Make your people proud before I kill you."

Though he did not understand the language fully, Lodan replied in Janti, his tone mocking, "You are free to step back before we begin, if you fear for your life. I will not hold you in low esteem."

Blaec took a few half-hearted swings at the Janti, toying with the man he saw as his inferior to amuse his cronies, and Seamus, who was holding his sides and roaring with laughter.

The laughter became shocked silence as Lodan swung his kai'gam upward, it screeching its song, and he disappeared from their sights.

Cobo could still see the master. He ducked under Blaec's blade, and through the giant's legs. Emerging behind him, Lodan swung his weapon upwards, swatting Blaec's hanging genitals soundly with the flat side of his blade.

The blade stopped singing with the contact, and Lodan seemed to appear out of thin air to the Dilgos, now standing behind their champion. Blaec dropped his blade, it clanging on the hard clay floor, and he crumpled to his knees, holding his smarting, and bleeding, privates.

Seamus's features twisted with dismay, and clouded with fury. He flew at Lodan, attacking in earnest. The force behind the blade Seamus swung was ten times that of an average Janti, but was met by Lodan's blade easily, as if his opponent was a Janti and not a Dilgo that towered above him. Lodan allowed Seamus to charge, pressing him into defensive retreat that formed a broad circle around the ailing Blaec. Out of habit, Lodan drew out the match for the entertainment of the crowd. He performed well, matching Seamus's blows gracefully, his acrobatic movements to avoid direct lines of attack were like a well-learned dance. Lighter, and poised, he seemed to dance on air around the larger, clumsier Dilgo.

Blaec recovered, faltering to his feet. He retrieved his blade, and joined his brother, attacking Lodan from the back as Seamus swung his blade in a frontal assault.

Lodan reacted to the two pronged assault by dropping easily to the floor, allowing the blades of the two brothers to crash together above him. He rolled away and popped himself onto his feet as if pulled up by a string, or a spring, for he then jumped high in the air, twisting his body around as his enemies swiped their blades through the air where he once stood, missing him by a breath. Descending, Lodan swung his legs down, and his feet struck the floor with perfect grace, placing him before both opponents, ready again to defend himself. His face was flushed with pleasure, bordering on glee, for the excitement of a less than mundane kai'gam match.

The brothers stalked him as one. Lodan held his ground, looking from one to the other as they raised their blades. Amusement sparkled in his eyes, and he rose his blade upward and made it sing.

For the Dilgos, he again seemed to disappear. The brothers took a faltering step forward, and shouted their dismay. Seamus lunged to the place Lodan was last seen, swiping through the air and taking the head off a shaped bush.

Casually, Lodan strolled around the brothers, holding his blade aloft and continuing to made it sing its mesmerizing song. He stood behind them as they ineffectually railed against the thin air in an attempt to kill their invisible opponent.

Once they'd spent themselves on fruitless combat, they stood back to back, in fear and frustration, waiting for their Janti opponent to appear.

Lodan retreated toward Taen, then ended the kai'gam's song and shouted, "Ha!" to wake them from the enchantment.

They blinked, and saw Lodan standing near the dais, grinning at them, and rotating his blade in a lazy manner.

Blaec, enraged by the game Lodan played, let out a wrenching battle cry and lunged at the Janti.

The sense of play left Lodan. Seriousness entered his face, his eyes. He held his ground, and swung the kai'gam around his head with the ease he'd used in his preparatory exercise. Two long steps and he leaped off the ground, performing a flip that propelled him to Blaec's height. In mid-air, he twisted and struck out with his blade. As before, he stuck his landing, and struck a pose, ready for a continued assault.

Blaec was a handful of steps away from Lodan as he jolted to a stop. He dropped his weapon, both hands grabbing for his own neck, and spun to face his opponent. Blood flowed freely through his fingertips from the opening Lodan had cleaved. A hissing sound escaped the wound, and Blaec fell to one knee. His expression reflected his shock at being bested by a little Janti. He fell forward, and was dead as his face hit the ground.

Lodan brazenly leaped onto the back of his victim, and fiercely shouted, "B'lianza!" at Seamus, gesturing at the giant with his bloody kai'gam.

Seamus was stunned by his brother's sudden death. Lodan's shout caused him to flinch, and he dropped his blade. The gesture meant the same in Dilgopoche as it did in the kai'gam arenas of Jantideva. He'd surrendered.

Rito-Sant stepped into the circle, his features sober. He proclaimed Lodan the superior, the winner, and offered Seamus's life as payment for the bad manners shown by his brothers.

In reply to Baru's translation, Lodan said, "I don't want his life. I want his service. He will vow his loyalty to Taen-Sant before all of Dilgopoche!"

Cobo suppressed his amusement. Lodan was shrewd. Seamus may choose death over such a vow, because in vowing himself to Taen, he completely abdicated his right to the throne.

Seamus wasn't happy with either prospect, death or becoming the underling to a Janti, but he chose the latter. Before the entire population of Zadoq, he knelt and vowed himself to the new monarch of Dilgopoche.

Without emotion, Lodan stepped off the back of his opponent, and went to Seamus. Using the loose wrap Seamus draped across his loins, Lodan reached up and wiped the blood from his kai'gam. In Janti, he said, "For desiring the death of Taen, you must bear the guilt of your brother's death."

Seamus clearly did not understand the Janti custom, but it upset him nonetheless to have his brother's blood on him. He shot to his feet and fled the palace.

Lodan again took his place before Taen as his protector. Cobo felt the awe, and the respect of those present, but not just for Lodan. Before Lodan's demonstration of his prowess, Taen was sparingly accepted into Rito-Sant's court, but Lodan, acting as Taen's proxy, had proven to them that Taen was worthy to stand among the Men and Women.

He was a part of them now, and he didn't even feel it. His awe for his hero, who had saved his life, blocked out all else.

Rito-Sant stood on the dais with Lodan, and for his bravery offered the Kai'gam master his choice of Breeders.

Lodan glanced at Cobo, and asked him to confirm Baru's translation. Amused, Cobo said, "Breeders....as in as many as you can handle, Lodan."

Lodan paled slightly. "Tell him I decline the offer."

"You cannot decline," Cobo said, "it is an offer that stands. Thank him and leave it be, if it is your choice."

Clearly discomfited by Rito-Sant's offer, Lodan took Cobo's advice and thanked the Dilgo leader.

In Dilgo, Rito-Sant officially announced Lodan's entry into the court. With that, the celebration resumed.

Taen climbed off the throne. He glanced at Blaec's body as four Dilgo Men carried him out of the common.

"I'm ready to retire." he said to Baru.

Irritably, she motioned for him to follow her to the portal behind the dais.

Cobo wished to retire, as well, but lingered a moment, his eyes scanning the crowd. He'd felt Riar Sed's presence, and in tandem, he felt the restraining influence of the Star's Spirit, which lay deep in his heart. He was too eager to encounter the dark sorcerer who had a hand in tainting his son, reacting like a common father who wanted to blacken the eye of the man who'd hurt his child. But it was not his decision when and where and under what circumstances he'd encounter Riar Sed. His life was in the hands of the Masing Star, and his purpose was no longer his own.

Laying his anger to an uneasy rest, Cobo trailed behind Baru to retire to the apartment he'd share with Surna.

જ્યજ્યજ્યગ્યગ્યગ્ય

The breeders had pressed themselves closer to the railing, their bosoms heaving as the sight of a Janti besting Blaec and Seamus in battle. Melish-Benu watched, too, with baited breath, but not for the same reason as the twittering dunder heads that crowded around her. She wasn't interested in the possibility of bedding the warrior. She loved the action.

She was a peculiar breeder. Her brother had even acknowledged her difference. In private, Rito-Sant called her by her Huntress name, Benu, and requested her company often to speak of matters that were usually reserved to the Huntresses. She maintained she was a Huntress, in her heart. The idea of giving birth never appealed to her, and war excited her mind. Rito-Sant did her the service of waving her commitment to breeding, dissolving the contracts she had with four Men. Among the breeders, she was the oldest to never have given birth. And, she was safely the oldest breeder to never have laid with a male for pleasure. Benu didn't yearn for the pleasure of Men. Hers was a higher calling. She was a warrior.

She watched the way the Janti moved, her liquid blue eyes sharpened by interest, her wide mouth partially opened in awe. He seemed to disappear, but he didn't, not really. The first time it happened, she heard the scream of the kai'gam and lost sight of him with everyone else. The second time, as she heard the scream, she quickly focused on the curly pale hair on his head and willed herself to see through the trick he performed. As the rest of the gathering lost sight of him, she alone watched him casually walk away from her brothers, those flailing fools. She laughed aloud, and her excitement grew. He was brilliant.

His brilliance made her want to fetch her kai'gam and challenge him.

Rito-Sant had a kai'gam forged for her, and allowed her the luxury of time in practice in the Gaarlot loft, above the fertility temple. While other breeders sat around their quarters, waiting for their turn to enter the temple and become impregnated, growing fat and soft and lazy, Benu shadow danced with her kai'gam, honing skills that seemed innate. Too bad they were destined to go to waste. Rito-Sant would never allow her to challenge the Men or

352

Women, nor would he now allow her to challenge the Janti warrior. He respected the warrior hidden beneath her softer flesh, but that didn't change the fact that she was still a breeder, and not permitted to practice the ways of the Men and Women.

Once the battle was complete, her eyes rested on the proud Janti warrior.

Next to her, Patra said, "I will bed him, I swear I will."

Patra's constant companion, Caltha, said, "No, I want Taen-Sant. He looked at me.....I felt he wanted me...."

Benu pursed her lips, and threw a disapproving glare at the young girls. "Patra, you are a hairy honig, the Janti warrior wouldn't want anything to do with you. And Caltha," she said, directing her sharp glare at the dark haired girl, "take another look at Taen-Sant! See how small he is? I doubt if what he has between his legs is enough to satisfy a Denmen."

Caltha seethed with the desire to make a retort, but knew she couldn't, not to Benu. As the sister of Rito-Sant, Benu held the highest rank among the breeders.

Throwing a last glance down at the Janti warrior, whom was now being addressed by Rito-Sant personally, Benu walked away from the breeders, assured that they would say nothing nasty about her until she was well out of their earshot.

With a rather imperious gait for a breeder, Benu went to her brother's quarters to wait for him. She knew he'd want to see her once he was done with the Huntresses at the celebration. He called Benu his confidant. He'd want to tell her about the Janti medicine that restored his legs, and his opinion about Taen-Sant, and, best of all, stories of the battles that lead to the reunification of Dilgopoche with the evil Janti honigs that had left them to die under the dome.

The Huntresses guarding his room readily let her inside, without question or comment.

Benu strolled casually to the water rest, where Rito-Sant used to lay his feet when they were in terrible pain, and she looked out the shaft portal overlooking the Lake of Tears. A cool evening breeze drifted into his room, along with smells she'd never encountered until part of the dome came down. They were the smells of Jantideva, of progress and richness, and they drifted into Dilgopoche, ready to bless the Dilgos.

Rito-Sant promised a new life for everyone. Everyone, except the breeders. Her eyes drifted to Rito-Sant's dold chambers. He entertained his Huntresses in this room, sometimes several a night. Each night, the Dold Huntress would arrive to collect his seed, and take it to the temple. Rito-Sant's twenty-two breeders had born him thirty-nine children in the past twenty solar years, thirty-eight of which were Women. Impressive for any Man, and Rito-Sant loved bragging on the fact. Sometimes he gave the credit for his success to his beautiful Huntresses, and their ability to inspire the clean seed out of him.

How Benu envied the Huntresses! Their lives were so free! They warred, and hunted, and copulated with the Men.....and as the latter thought crossed her stream of envy, she staunchly dismissed it. Better to be a focused warrior, than a rutting, open legged animal.

Sadness overwhelmed Benu, and she leaned on the portal to stare, unseeing, at the lake and the desert beyond.

A chill raced over her back.

"Good day to you, Melish."

A chill trickled into her stomach, and she flinched around to face Riar Sed. He was an old man, Janti sized, his body was bent and his face was ugly. He was Dilgopoche's first contact with a species they'd only heard of in myths. He claimed to be a Ver dala Ven. Rito-Sant christened him a God-sorcerer. Riar Sed had been with Rito-Sant for as long as Benu could remember. His ghostly presence in the palace never failed to frightened her.

"Why aren't you at the celebration?"

"I tire of frivolity." he said smoothly. His dark eyes seemed to shine malevolently. His lips were purple, thick and moist, his face puffy and deeply lined. A tendril of spittle tugged between his upper and lower lip as he said, "Why have you left the celebration?"

"Boredom."

"Lie." he accused lightly, "You come here with a Janti man on your mind. Craving the flesh, Melish?"

"If you know my mind so well," she retorted, "then you must know I only want to ask permission to challenge the Janti in kai'gam."

Riar Sed harumped, and shrugged, as if to say he knew all along, and turned away to sit on a floor pillow. He feigned disinterest in her presence.

"Are you staying?" she asked incredulously.

"I have business with Rito-Sant, far weightier business than your desire to play warrior with a Janti." he said pointedly.

She felt dismissed. She was tempted to stay, to prove to him that he had no right to order her about, but she didn't like the idea of being alone with him for however long she'd have to wait for her brother. She didn't like the way he looked at her, like a hungry Ryslac-Yesvectu visually judging her flesh for tenderness. Wordlessly, she stalked out of the room. As she passed him, he reached out and let her robe trail across his fingers. She halted, and yanked her robe away from him on principle.

He grunted a laugh, and again shrugged, turning his eyes to the portal.

Shakily, she fled Rito-Sant's quarters and dashed recklessly down the curved corridor. Like the levels below and above, the palace quarters were circular, and in the center of each level was an over grown common where the balcony looked down on the main common linking the city. Behind a screen of flowering xas bushes, she heard the cooing of the breeders. The object of their yearnings didn't interest her, she was too intent on getting away from Riar Sed, but as she went past the xas bushes, she glanced toward the breeders, to be sure they wouldn't see her disgraceful flight. She was unnerved to find they all were looking her way-

-and she slammed, full body, into an immovable object. She bounced back, and fell hard on her backside.

She looked up at the offending party, ready to shout anger at a breeder, because the size of the oaf she'd struck was the size of a breeder, but her words stuck in her throat as she saw the Janti warrior standing over her, concern in his features.

He said something to her in a language she didn't understand, and offered a hand to help her to her feet. She took his hand, and he lifted her easily. Standing before him, she saw he was the same height as she, a physical equal. She would have thought his diminutive stature, in comparison to the Men, would have revolted her. Quite to the contrary, all she could see was his attractive features. His blue eyes, a color she adored in all Men. His build, not too garish but firm and strong. His touch, electric. With a jolt, she realized she had fallen into noticing their compatibilities as male and female.

She yanked her hand away, and angrily snapped, "You aren't to touch a breeder!"

He replied in Janti. It was evident her anger confused him. Behind him, also speaking Janti, was Taen-Sant. He stared at Benu with unnatural gold eyes. Taken aback by his Denmen eyes, odd, so odd to see a man her size with Denmen eyes, she stepped away from him.

Baru came up behind them, and said, "What is it? What trouble have you caused, Melish?"

Benu tore her eyes from the odd new Sant. "This man touched me." She gestured to the Janti warrior.

Baru snapped at the Janti, berating him soundly in his own language.

His blue eyes flashed sardonically at Melish-Benu. He leaned toward her, and with an imperious air said something meaningful, something she did not understand, that made her tingle all over. It didn't matter that she didn't understand his language, it did not matter what he had said. His tone, his exotic tongue, the lift of his mouth and brow, the way his eyes twinkled with fury, it all served to excite her traitorous breeder body.

Baru's jaw tightened, and to Melish-Benu, she said, "Melish, you will stay away from these Janti men. They are disrespectful, and they too easily mock our laws."

"Yes, sister." she agreed readily.

Benu hugged herself, and watched her Huntress sister guide Taen-Sant and the warrior to their quarters. Taen-Sant had the apartment next to Rito-Sant, proof of his position in court.

The warrior didn't bother to look back at her. For some reason, his emotional distance tantalized her further, even hurt her pride a bit.

Throwing a cold glare at the breeders who stared at her, a few with knowing expressions on their faces, she turned and went up the ramp to her quarters.

In the privacy of her own room, she slid her kai'gam out from under her bed, and postured with it, mimicking movements she'd seen performed by the Janti warrior. She swung her kai'gam above her head as he had......and could not produce the same high pitched singing.

She tried again, and again, and again.......

<center>~~~~~~~~~</center>

"You certainly angered Baru-Oclassi." Taen said once they were alone.

Lodan pursed his lips. Baru had all but accused him of trying to seduce the breeder, pointedly informing him of a breeder's fertility, as if his fear of impregnating a breeder should supersede his fear of being killed for having relations with one. "Baru over reacted to an innocent gesture."

Taen laughed ruefully, "Still, asking a breeder if she is so fertile she could be impregnated with a touch," and he shook his head doubtfully, "It's offensive, don't you think?"

"No," Lodan stated flatly.

"Rito-Sant gave you permission to impregnate all the breeders you want, or so it sounded to me, can't imagine why Baru would threaten you with the law like that." Taen replied, and he threw a rueful grin at Lodan. "I wish he'd given me such freedom."

"I don't want to impregnate breeders." He replied contemptuously, and in a dismissive manner, he went about exploring the apartment. The space had the feeling of a cave, with clay walls and floors. Impossibly huge interconnected rooms opened to each other with primitive holes knocked into the thick, clay walls. The main receiving room was filled with sitting pillows, obviously made for the Men and Women, and a window was hacked through the outer wall, opening to a view of the Lake of Tears. A corridor led to four interconnected rooms, two that were furnished with huge pillows, and one filled with Taen's belongings. A Dilgo version of a bathhouse lay at the fore of the sleeping quarters.

In the main receiving room there was a square alcove, very narrow, with narrow walls and a low ceiling. It was the only room

357

with clean lines, and an opening that looked as if it was meant to be an opening, and not an assaulted hunk of clay. The dimensions, and bareness, made it look like a monk's quarters. Its location in Taen's apartment made it an ideal place for Lodan to sleep.

To Taen, he said, "This is will be my room. You and Danati will have some privacy, and I will always be on hand, in case you need me."

Taen glanced dubiously into the alcove. "There must be a better arrangement. You won't be comfortable."

"It is all I need," Lodan replied, "and now, I need to rest."

Danati softly called out Taen's name. Lodan looked toward the bedchambers. He saw the corner of a huge pillow, Taen's Dilgo bed. He smiled slightly, and nodded toward the sound, dismissing his young charge into the arms of his wife.

Taen slapped him on the back. "Have a good rest." and as an afterthought, he said, "Thank you for preventing Rito-Sant's brothers from slitting my throat."

"It is the reason I am here."

Moments after Taen retired to his marriage bed, Lodan heard Danati's sighs.

Lodan slowly removed the belt from over his shoulder. He held his kai'gam in his hand a long moment, looking at the blade. Though he'd wiped it on Seamus, blood remained in the fine etchings.

He went through the crude tunnel leading into the unused bedroom. He felt an abrupt drop in temperature. The walls, floor, they were cool to the touch and radiated their cold.

The warmer bathhouse was made for a Dilgo, and by Janti standards was primitive. The giant, oversized toilet basin was a pit that dropped waste into an unimaginable depth. Their version of running water was a constant stream erupting from a hole in the wall, rushing through a deep trench cut in the floor and drained out another hole on the opposite wall. The water was cold, clear and rushed quickly. Dilgos used their water extravagantly, as if their people had never suffered from scarcity.

Lodan dipped his sash in the running water and washed the blade clean. As he did, he looked at each symbol and meditated a moment on their respective meanings. Peace. Awareness. Control. Patience.

In the alcove, he lay his kai'gam on the floor next to the pillow. He sat down, and stared at the wall. He knew that he'd done the right thing in killing Blaec, but his conscience continued to torment him. He struggled to find a peaceful place within, away from the new scar he'd torn into his own heart. His mind insisted on dwelling on his decision, on the moment he knew he was going to kill.

The decision had come too easy.

His meditations complete, he lay down and sleep came quickly.

He vision-dreamed, a rare dream where he knew he was asleep, but conscious, too. He was in a kai'gam arena with Pletoro. The great master was an old man in Lodan's dream, slender with an upright body, and a shock of white hair on his head. Pletoro held Lodan's kai'gam, placed his finger on the blade, and ran it down the edge, cutting himself. Lodan watched the blood trickle along the etched side, pooling near the tip.

"What does this mean, master?" Lodan asked, staring at the blood as it sunk into the etchings.

Pletoro smiled kindly. "You missed a spot."

Lodan next found himself in Taen's apartment. The apartment was quiet and brightly lit with day. He sat up, and reached for his kai'gam. He looked at the length of his blade, to the point where Pletoro's blood had pooled. He saw he had, indeed, missed a spot. Dried blood was embedded in the crevices of the symbol meaning defense.

"I acted in defense of another." he said softly. Incredulously, he asked, "Acknowledging the circumstances of my act is supposed to ease my conscience?"

Pletoro stood at the alcove's opening. "No," he said, "Acknowledging life as precious will increase your peace."

"Master," he countered, "my guilt stems from my belief that life is precious."

"Wrong," Pletoro chided, "Your guilt stems from the knowledge that taking a life was easier than preserving life."

Shaken by the truth, Lodan threw his blade down on the stone floor. It shattered.

Lodan woke to the sound of clattering metal.

The apartment was dark, but not quiet. He heard whispering voices. He tensed, listened. Woman and man, whispers and sighs.

Taen and Danati, he thought. He relaxed.

Remembering his vision-dream, he reached down and touched his kai'gam. It was intact. It shattering was a symbol for his decision to never again take a life. He would defend Taen, employing any and all methods of defense at his disposal, but he would not take a life.

The whispering continued, moving from the main receiving room, to the secondary sitting room. Taen's voice was obvious, but Danati's voice sounded altered.

He realized she was speaking in Dilgo. He sat up, and listened. There was movement, sighing and soft, muffled moans coming from the secondary receiving room, the cold room. It took Lodan a moment to realize that the woman with Taen was not Danati. She called him Taen-Sant, and spoke no Janti whatsoever.

Lodan rested his back on the wall and languished in disappointment. Heeding Ver dala Ven's warning, he didn't allow himself to fully trust Taen, but a part of him enjoyed seeing Taen fall in love with his new bride. His Janti sensibilities were wounded by Taen's easy infidelity, though he imagined that infidelity was a concept the oversexed Dilgos would never understand.

Perhaps Taen didn't understand the concept of fidelity, either. He obviously didn't understand the severity of the Dilgo laws concerning the breeders.

Their dangerous tryst culminated with the mystery woman's guttural, muffled moaning. Their rustling moved, this time toward the door. In whispers, Taen made an effort to extract from the woman her name. She finally understood his laughably horrible Dilgo and responded, "Caltha."

They kissed for a long time at the door before Taen finally had the sense to send her away. He closed the door on her, and sighed.

"With Danati sleeping in the next room?" Lodan reproached. Though he pitched his voice low, it carried well enough to Taen.

Taen hushed him, and hurried to the opening of the alcove. He leaned in, and whispered, "You saw nothing."

"I saw nothing, but heard quite enough," Lodan said sardonically.

"Lodan...." he pleaded, "It was experimentation. How can I be blamed? She practically attacked me the moment I opened the door. They are all so.....hungry," he said, wont for another word.

"And you have taken it upon yourself to feed them all? Or just Caltha?" Lodan countered.

Taen hushed him again, feeling the bite of shame and the worry that Danati may actually wake.

Taen whispered, "The Dilgos have a different morality here. They don't have marriage....the ceremony Danati and I went through was a formality to make my mother happy. Danati says the Men and Women trade mates often."

"Is this what Danati expects? To be traded often?" Lodan asked pointedly, "And have you thought about the laws, Taen?"

"I am Taen-Sant."

"Meaning you are above the law?"

"Meaning I can get away with what I want." he said flatly, "Besides, if the law threatens me, I have you to protect me."

"I agreed to protect you from diabolic plots against your life," Lodan said stiffly, "not from the natural consequences of your own stupidity."

The boy seemed abashed. He shrank from the doorway.

He whispered, "I will be discreet. I want the same from you, Lodan. Be discreet with my secrets."

Lodan turned away from the sight of Taen's outline in the darkness. He said, "If it serves to protect you, Taen, I will guard your secrets."

Satisfied by Lodan's promise, Taen returned to his own bed, and his sleeping wife.

Lodan rose, and left the apartment. He felt the need to separate himself from Taen.

In the common, in a place where he could see Taen's door, he went through his morning exercises. Though dawn was imminent, the celebration below continued, unbridled. The common was full of drunken Men and Women coming and going, and breeders, who had been looking down at the party from the balcony. As Lodan stepped out, and began his routine, he immediately drew a crowd. The breeders called out to him in Dilgo, their tones suggestive, and a few Huntresses milled about, watching his movements with interest. A few tried mimicking him, but lacked the balance needed from some of the movements.

Lodan ignored them as he searched for a total peace within.

As he raised his kai'gam upward, he noticed the tip of the blade was still soiled, just as he'd been shown in his dream. Defense, but now he noticed that blood had also soiled the Suma glyph for justice. He stared at the blade.

Juxtaposed by the tip of his blade, standing alone in the balcony above, he saw the breeder he'd bumped into the night before. She was holding her arms upward, mimicking his movements, as the Huntresses had tried, though she did not hold a kai'gam. She watched him intently for his next move.

As their eyes met, she quickly receded from the opening, disappearing from his sight.

Dismissing the woman from his mind, he went on to complete the first cycle of his exercise. Starting his second, at the same place as the first, he again saw the breeder above him, mimicking his movements. He took care not to look her way, but watched her out of the corner of his eyes.

A student. The involuntary thought surprised him, and he faltered in the movement he was performing. He stopped and repeated the movement perfectly, and moved on, growing accustomed to the idea of taking students in Dilgopoche. They were certainly interested.....ah, but the Huntresses lost interest too quickly. They were easily discouraged and distracted. They were wandering away.

The attention of the breeders didn't falter, but their minds weren't on kai'gam.

On the third cycle of his exercises, he again saw the woman on the balcony above, mimicking his movements.

ৡৡৡৡৡৡৡৡৡ

Rito-Sant laughed thunderously as he entered his apartments. He had a beautiful Huntress on each arm. He hadn't enjoyed life like this since losing the use of his legs. The young Huntresses tended to ignore an old man who couldn't chase them in the pools, even an old man with Sant behind his name. Ver dala Ven had made him whole.

He was pushing the Huntresses into his dold chambers when he noticed Riar Sed sitting near the watering pool, glowering at him.

His high spirits plummeted.

"Welcome home." Riar Sed said lowly.

Sharp pain pierced his hips and legs, and his strength seemed to rush down, out of him, into the floor. He lost control of his legs, his bowels, his water. His waste ran freely down useless limbs. He cried out in horror as he fell forward.

The Huntresses stood over him, asking if he needed help. He couldn't see their true concern, he could only see the pity in their eyes for their poor, lame ruler.

"Out!" he screeched at them, furious at once for the return of his infirmity. "Go bed a Ryslac!"

His mighty Huntresses ran from him, cowed and hurt by his harsh words. As they flew out his apartment, Baru flew in. Seeing him on the floor, she rushed to his aid.

"No," he said, slapping away her hands. She'd cleaned and babied him for too many years. "leave me to wallow in my own filth, Baru!"

"Rito," she whispered, "it is undignified."

"Yes," he growled, "I am aware of my indignity. Get away!" he thundered.

Baru flinched, and stumbled backwards. She rushed out of the room, slamming the door hard behind her.

Rito-Sant slapped his aching legs. If he'd had a kai'gam, he would have chopped them off in his fury.

"Ver dala Ven's spell is easily reversed." Riar Sed remarked.

Rito-Sant rolled onto his back and threw a furious glare at Riar Sed. "He healed me!"

Riar Sed's brows shot up in amusement. "Oh, yes, you look well healed."

"I am no fool! It is you who inflict me! Mighty sorcerer," he spat, "you who cannot win a war, though you promised victory. Ver dala Ven is far more powerful than you, and is with us now, we have no need of you!"

Riar Sed clicked his tongue. "Be careful not to deify Ver dala Ven Cobo. He's nothing in comparison to his ancestors. Look at me! I am a nothing, indeed of the family line of Thranlam'Sum but an Ordinary One with only the powers my mother gifted me, and I reversed Ver dala Ven's artful work on your corrupted body."

Rito-Sant closed his eyes, his misery taking away his senses.

"I trust Ver dala Ven."

"And you prove it by keeping him very close to you, granting him your full favor, which is more than you ever gave me. I take hearty offense at being usurped by another sorcerer, especially Ver dala Ven. Where do your loyalties lie, Rito?"

With difficulty, Rito-Sant retorted, "You know!"

Riar Sed sighed, disappointed. "I understand Cobo has a certain mesmerizing charm. It is those gold eyes of his, reflecting the world he sees. Most people enjoy looking at themselves in his eyes, if they think well of themselves. With your legs restored, you saw yourself as a Man again, and the flattering reflection held you captive." Riar Sed rose and walked to Rito-Sant. Leaning over the giant, twisting slightly to look into his face, mocking concern, he asked, "How do you see yourself now, Rito?"

Rito-Sant recognized the cold glint in the sorcerer's eyes. He'd seen in hundreds of times, just before a kill. He managed a slight smile though he suffered. "He restored me," he said huskily, "I was a Man again. I can face death without bitterness. I am no longer afraid of you, or death."

Riar Sed snapped his fingers, and pain gripped Rito-Sant's chest.

"Then, by all means, do die." Riar Sed hissed.

Chapter 17

Trev kept watch on Ul Zub's boat. Agart was none to happy to have been assigned to his services. Her sharp professional veneer had dropped days ago, and she bluntly told him that she thought he was a drunkard and an idiot. True, he was a drunkard. Maybe an idiot, too. But he had a hunch, and Bail trusted his hunches more than he trusted his court's well thought and well researched advice.

Trev observed her walking along the docks in Bilk, early in the morning. He milled about with the Shod dockhands, lending a hand on occasion, wearing their uniform, unshaven and unclean, blending in well. She didn't give him a second glance, even as she passed right in front of him. He waited until she boarded Ul Zub's boat.

Trev casually strolled to the boat. His hands went into his pockets. "She's here." he said to the open com he'd had sewn into his work shirt.

Before he reached the boarding plank, Captain Agart's command dusted down on the dock in a narrow transport. Iada popped out of the cabin, and looked as though she were going to try to run. To her surprise, a common looking Shod drew a lume out of his pocket and brandished it at her.

⋘⋙⋘⋙⋘⋙⋘⋙

Bail received news that the medic, Iada of the house of Yuini Vol, had been found.

"She was in Bilk," Echo Agart reported. The woman was Bail's new Captain of the Security Force, taking over for Varian. She was thirty, sleek, with short dark hair and cruel eyes. She had distinguished herself with eight years of service in the Pliadors, all of those years working on patrol in Shod City.

Hope sprang painfully in Bail's chest. "Did she have a baby with her?"

"No, daka Bail, she did not. We did find Captain Edise's comm controller on her person, and his identification. Unfortunately, there is no sign of Edise."

Bail nodded curtly. "Take her to the Keep, under heavy guard. But do not harm her," he stressed, fearing they might again lose a lead to Archer. "Remember what I did to Varian after he killed that Shodite girl. I will send any officer who harms a hair on Iada's head to a Raal work camp to keep Varian company. Understood?"

Her features were stoic. "Yes daka Bail."

⚞⚞⚞⚞⚟⚟⚟⚟

Harsh questioning did not loosen Iada's tongue, not even after being confronted with her husband's confession to his part in aiding Shelon's escape. She claimed to know nothing of a baby.

Captain Agart questioned Iada forcefully, one session lasting nearly twenty hours. As her silence endured, and Bail's desperation mounted, he authorized Captain Agart to use whatever means at her disposal to make the woman talk. She was denied water and food, and tortured. Mistreatment seemed to strengthen Iada's resolve not to speak.

Trev urged Bail to use a less heavy-handed approach. He suggested they put a lume marker on her, and release her into Shod City. The lume marker was ultimately dangerous to her health, but was a perfect tool to keep tabs on her for up to three days. The marker acts on body heat, emitting a low level of the lume chemical, but enough that it was easily picked up on a detector in a windrider. Trev believed that Iada hadn't known the baby she was caring for was Archer, and now that she did know, she'd go straight to where ever she left him in order to use him as the ultimate hostage to her cause.

Bail conceded to Trev's approach, even though he had reservations about the effectiveness of releasing Iada into the Shod population. He was at a point where he would have tried anything to find his son, for himself, and for Jishni's sake. Jishni had ceased to go out into public, staying obsessively with Janus, night and day. She'd begun refusing to take the calming medications that Doctor Poulin prescribed, fearful she wouldn't be alert in case of an emergency. She wasn't eating, or sleeping. Missing Archer was driving her to the brink of sanity. Bail couldn't bear to watch her disintegrate.

The night before releasing her, they exposed Iada to the lume marker while she slept, introducing lume gas into the airshaft of her cell. Once she breathed in the chemical, she was marked. She woke feeling tired, but so far as Bail could see she seemed fine. She was told she was to be released for lack of evidence.

Iada was surprised, and suspicious. Too suspicious, Bail thought.

High above Shod city, Bail and Trev tracked her movements on a lume isolation monitor that was generally used to detect accidental exposures to the deadly chemical. She returned to her illegal flat in track four, and spent two days there.

Bail was ready to call an end to the experiment when, in the middle of the night, Iada finally left her flat, and Shod City. They tracked her into the Center-plex, to an affluent village named Nysus.

Trev put down on the private docking bay of a Nysus citizen, and there they tracked her on foot with a portable lume detector. The colors in the monitor changed from gray to bright red the closer they came to a lume presence.

As they passed the servant's quarters beside the home of a wealthy Janti socialite, the monitor turned red.

"She's here." Trev said.

Casually, Trev walked up to the building, and placed a disc on the wall. The listening device transmitted sounds to the earpieces they both wore plugged into their ears. Hearing nothing of consequence, Trev picked the disc off the wall and moved down ten feet, and tried again.

This time, they both heard Iada speaking excitedly. "How could you turn your back on an orphan who needed you? You, Marta, who cried day and night that you were too old to have more children! You heartless-"

"Iada," a man's gruff voice cut in apologetically, "Lady Edina refused to allow us to adopt. We couldn't defy her!"

"You could have petitioned the council of Shodite affairs!" she retorted.

"And be expelled from this household!" a woman countered hotly. "I was born to this household, my children work in this household."

"Where is the child?" Iada demanded.

"We had no choice, Iada."

Iada's tone turned dangerous. "Where is he?"

There was a pause. Euphoric anticipation tensed Bail's body, and he felt ready to knock through the wall and wring the truth out of Marta with his bare hands.

Marta said, "We left him at the Suma temple, in the Nysus spiritual common."

Trev removed the disc. Bail backed away from the wall, whooshing out a sigh.

"Next stop, the glorious Suma temple." Trev said wryly, removing the earpiece from his ear.

They rushed back to the windrider, and from there Bail contacted Captain Agart, who was hovering in a windrider above them with a force of nine men, waiting for instructions.

"Move in, and arrest Iada." Bail ordered.

As they lifted off, Bail watched Agart and her men descend on Lady Edina's property, the windrider's blowers destroying a portion of a fountain garden, the force of their exhalation blowing apart stone walls and taking down trees.

The commotion outside caused Shodites from all the households in the area to break away, scurrying off like panicked animals in fear for their lives.

ళళళళళఌఌఌఌఌ

Realization descended on Iada as the Pliadors descended upon the quiet Nysus neighborhood. The fevers, the rash under her arms and in her mouth, the breathlessness, they'd poisoned her in the keep! They'd placed a marker on her before releasing her, but she hadn't recognized the symptoms, though they were enough to make her too listless to travel for two days. She berated herself for her stupidity, leading them straight to Marta and Turq.

She made it outside, and ran, knowing too well that it didn't matter how far she ran as long as she carried the marker. She'd been sick two days, which meant the marker had another day's strength.

Her only hope for escape was to mask the marker. There was only one way possible. She needed to get to a lume manufacturing plant. There, if she found a hiding place, it'd be days before she could be detected, and by then she'd be clean again, unless she was re-contaminated at the plant. In that case, the Pliadors were the least of her worries.

A crackling noise brought her attention around, and she saw, under a patio dome, a portable warming table. A lume warming table. Before the tumult began, Shodites were preparing for a party. Now they were gone, hiding, and the warming table was left unattended.

Iada ran toward the table. She thought about hiding...under it? Behind it? Too open, they'd see her if they searched the patio.

Inside it? If she turned the table off, she'd be safe, and the Janti, when they picked up the lume marker, they may assume it was the table.

She turned off the heat, and waited for three agonizing seconds for the lume waves to die inside the large warming oven. All the while, she could hear Captain Agart shouting, "She went this way, the marker is getting stronger!"

She opened the metallic oven doors and pulled out the trays of bite sized meats left inside to keep warm, placing them carefully on the counter top above. She peeked over the counter in time to see Agart rounding a stone fence, her eyes on the lume monitor.

Iada climbed into the oven and hooked her fingernail into the crevice of the outer lip of the door, a place where the manufacturer had welded the inner and outer door together, and she quietly closed herself inside.

Immediately, the remaining heat inside the close space overwhelmed her. She pulled herself into a tight ball, breathed shallowly, and did her best not to faint.

She heard the sharp clacking of heels on the tile of the patio. Several pairs of clacking heels, as the Pliadors passed through. A person paused over the lume table. Iada's heart raced and she buried her face in her knees, waiting to be discovered.

"Renout!" Captain Agart shouted sharply.

Iada flinched.

"Get away from the food, you fool, and find that woman!"

The clacking of heels continued around the circle of the patio. They detected the lume marker, but the table was confusing their readings.

"Thoroughly search this household." the Captain shouted, frustration clearly in her tone.

The clacking heels grew distant, and the shouting muted as the Pliadors entered the house.

Iada couldn't take the heat inside the oven any longer. She knew it was just a matter of time before one of the officers happened to peek into the oven, if for nothing else than to snoop and steal another bit of food.

Risking capture, she pushed the door open with the weight of her body and tumbled out of the oven. She struggled to catch her breath, and scrambled to her feet. Her short sleeved tunic exposed her arms, and she noticed her skin was bright red, cooked raw. She was flaming hot, raw over every inch of her body, but her discomfort was a secondary problem. She looked around the patio. She was alone. She glanced to the house. She saw the back of one of the Pliadors, probably the one that was supposed to be watching the grounds.

Taking her chances with being caught, she trotted across the patio toward a wooded common that fringed this residence and the next.

In the woods, she splashed through a stream of cool water, and acting on instinct, she threw herself into the water and let it run over her to cool her burning skin. She was tempted never to leave the soothing stream, but shouts coming from the patio she just fled compelled her out of the water.

She ran, trying to stay in the cover of the trees where she could. She headed north, instinctively toward Shod City, as if she'd forgotten her original plan. In the back of her mind, a dismal voice uttered doubts that she'd ever make it to the lume chemical plants. They were far west of Shod City, on the other side of the Pril.

Even as she found herself on a public windrider, taken from the Nysus Public Square, she expected apprehension.

In Shod City, she allowed herself to feel a modicum of hope.

※※※※※※※※※

Chavva Tathal completed the preliminary reports on a group of babies brought in right after the second surge of reprisals in Shod City. The babies without parents were last. There were so many, she mused. More than normal. The riots, and the reprisals in Shod city had left many Shodite babies orphans.

Those without parents or family were kept in the center's nursery and cared for until they were placed in a household. Once they were placed, their benefactors would elect a Shodite nanny to raise them.

As was expected, twelve of the orphans were well suited for plant work, and the rest were suited for a variety of service positions.

For one, a scrawny boy she'd tagged with the name Birdy because he was so small, the tests produced a negative result. His profile indicated he was an undesirable, with no proficiencies to a needed service, and genetically inclined to succumb to the Shodite wasting disease.

Officially, it was the Center's policy concerning undesirable Shodite children to remand them to care facilities in the northeast, where they would serve as farmhands. In the wide area of farmland in the north, the air was cleaner, and there was less of an environmental impact on people prone to the wasting disease.

Unofficially, Chavva was instructed by her supervisors to discard the useless Shodites. There were already too many on the farms. To send more would be a waste of Janti time, and resources. She was to inject them with a fast acting toxin, and deliver their bodies to the crematorium.

She'd never been able to bring herself to euthanise a baby, not even a Shodite. She wasn't an activist, or a liberal, or a Shodite lover. She was the mother of seven. Birdy reminded her of her second son. He was premature, very tiny, and a quiet, sweet boy.

She was alone until the morning shift came on board. With utter impunity, she erased Birdy's record from the center's library. According to the center's records, he had never entered their facility.

371

She retrieved him from the nursery, informing the nurse that he was to go to the incinerator. She assured the woman she would take care of the record of his death. There was no reason for the nurse to distrust her. Chavva had been a senior staff member at the center for twelve years.

From the center, she contacted a Zarian national she'd met while still in school. Her friend, who was a liberal and an activist, talked her into accepting a position in the center to do exactly what she was doing for Birdy. To protect the lives of those who could not protect themselves.

She left a message, in code. It was a saying, in Zarian, that meant "A drop of rain in the sea." The saying was referring to the Zarian's belief that every person on the planet was like droplets of rain, and the Guardian was like the sea. In their philosophy, all people were equal, and the Shodites had as much a right to live as the Janti.

Chavva wasn't as sure about how she believed the Shodites should be treated. Some of them were vulgar, and ignorant, and they were all dirty. But she was sure about the babies. None of them had to die.

Her heart always beat hard and fast against her ribs when she delivered a baby into the arms of a Zarian. Chavva was committing a horrible crime in the eyes of Janti law, contributing to the escape of a Shodite. She'd heard of Janti being consigned to Raal work prisons for less. But she mustered her courage for the sake of Birdy, and behind the landing bay of the center she handed him into the arms of a tall Zarian man she'd never met.

As she walked away, she prayed for Birdy's life and his health. She prayed she'd done the right thing. And she prayed she wouldn't be caught.

৵৵৵৵৵৵৵৵৵

The Nysus Suma Temple was a replica of the Suma temple in Ona. It was decagonal building covered in carved glass that reflected sunlight and starlight. A crystal fountain shaped like the Masing Star was the centerpiece of the Suma plaza, which lead into the nave arena. Nysus was small for a temple, the arena built to

372

hold five or six hundred people at a time. At the moment there were about one hundred devotees sitting in the seats close to the alter, listening to a Suma priest teach the six precepts of Thranlam'Sum.

Bail strode urgently around the arena toward the corridor leading to the Suma's private quarters and prayer center. He'd already sent a message forward to the temple. The Chancellor, expecting his arrival and hearing the windrider dock in their bay, was waiting anxiously for Bail at the mouth of the corridor. He was Bail's age, a large man in black robes and a red sash, denoting his rank. His Suma name was Unesto. Seeing Bail, he hurried out to meet him.

"Daka, we are honored," he said, starting a bow.

"Take me to Mistress Ladina." Bail demanded, urging him to forget the formalities.

"As you wish." Chancellor Unesto replied uncertainly. He turned, his robes billowing out, and quickly led Bail and Trev down the corridor. Non-Suma was not permitted into the private sanctuary of the priests, but a Chancellor did not dare to refuse access to a daka.

Mistress Ladina was sitting in her dressing chamber, a chamber that led into the altar room of the Star. She stood as Bail entered her room, and bowed deeply. Because of the scarring on her face, her age was difficult to judge without the benefit of the yellow band she wore around her bald head. A headband was given to a mistress after fifty years of service. She held herself erect, and her features were stoic as Bail questioned her about a child she'd found abandoned in the nave.

"I've found many children left to the Guardian in the past weeks," she said, her voice wavering slightly with old age, "I don't remember a specific little boy. Many were small and undernourished. But I did take them all to the same testing center to be placed. I assumed they were all Shodites.....a Janti wouldn't leave their child in a Suma temple."

The thought of Archer going through a testing center with a drove of Shodite children cramped Bail's middle. "Which center, Ladina?"

"The Nysus center, of course."

∾∾∾∾∾∾∾∾∾

Jishni handed Janus to Nan and she carefully scrutinized each of the babies in the center's nursery. She found one that had Archer's features....but no, the fingers were too stubby. Archer had long fingers, and perfectly formed nails. Another had Archer's hands and fingers, but a complexion too pale. Archer had ruddier, darker features, much like Bail's.

"He's not here." Jishni said, her voice gruff from holding back her tears.

"He may have been sent back to a benefactor if a Shodite has claimed him as her own," Doctor Merl said compassionately. "Please, let us test Janus. If Archer came through our center, we can pinpoint the household he is now living in by comparing his genetic code to that of the babies we have processed."

Bail placed his hand on her shoulder. "Jishni, it is the only way."

She pulled out of his repellant touch, and moved toward Nan as if she'd meant to take Janus from her secretary all along. She blamed him, still, that Archer was missing this long. Illogical, irrational, she told herself, but she wasn't feeling terribly logical or rational lately. She needed to blame someone other than herself, and Bail was the easiest scapegoat. If only Jem Jin had lived.....

She took her son from Nan, and caressed his fuzzy head. "Janus, they need your blood. I'm sorry, my love, but it will hurt."

She handed Janus to the nurse, and the nurse placed him in a warming bed and held him still with gentle hands as Doctor Merl pricked Janus's toe. Janus started at the pain, and wailed, a sound that broke Jishni's heart. The doctor and took a smear of blood for the testing.

Merl was saying, "The tests will take up to ten days to be complete. The comparisons may take another ten to twenty days."

"A month," Jishni said miserably. "I have to live without my child for another month."

"A month is an unacceptable length of time," Bail snapped, "We want Archer back quickly."

374

"We will rush the results, daka," the doctor amended, eyeing Bail warily.

The nurse, a woman in her thirties, dark with curly black hair, picked up Janus, and as she turned to hand him back to Jishni, she stared at him as if she recognized him.

Hope sprang into Jishni's heart. "You've seen a baby that looks like my Janus?"

An absolutely horrified look came over the woman's face. "No, of course not." she breathed, and she handed Janus over to the daka. "Doctor, if you please, I will take the blood sample to Chavva. I have health records to leave off with her, I'm going there now, I can save you a trip."

"Very well, you are dismissed."

The nurse hurried off, carrying Janus' blood. Jishni watched her leave, and looked into Janus' face, wondering what it was she had seen that had disturbed her.

⚛⚛⚛⚛⚛⚛⚛⚛⚛

Swiana practically ran to the records center.

She found Chavva in the break room, drinking tea. As Chavva noticed Swiana approaching, she seemed to cringe with anxiety.

Swiana sat at Chavva's table, and glanced worriedly around the room to the rest of the resident technicians at other tables who were taking their breaks.

"The child you euthanised today...." and she had trouble going on. If Chavva was on break, she knew it was already too late.

Testily, Chavva said, "What of him?"

"You have already taken care of him?"

She squirmed in her seat. "Of course. You'd think I'd put off-"

"No, Please the Guardian, no." Swiana hissed, "He may have been the daka's missing son. They've traced him to our facility."

"We've had a multitude of children go through our facility in the last weeks," Chavva retorted defensively. "Why do you think Birdy was the daka's son?"

"I saw the daka's twin, Janus," she hissed, "just now. Chavva, he looks identical to the one you took for destruction."

Chavva bolted out of her seat. Glaring down at Swiana, she shouted hysterically, "Impossible!"

Her outburst silenced the break room. Swiana was uncomfortably aware than all eyes were on her.

Chavva continued, "All babies look alike. You are seeing things that are not there!"

Swiana stood, and handed Chavva a blood sample. Lowly, she said, "Compare the throw away infant with the daka's blood. It is the only way to be sure."

She left Chavva quickly. If there had been a horrible mistake like this made, she did not want to be associated too closely with Chavva. It wasn't her doing, or her decision.

જાજાજાજાજાજ

Chavva had no way of comparing the blood of the child with the daka's, unless she found him.

She called her Zarian contact, and left her message. Within an hour, she was meeting with a Zarian in the usual place. The man they'd sent this time was short, round, bald. He looked at her empty arms, and into her eyes suspiciously as she approached.

"I must speak to someone about the baby I saved this morning." she said shakily.

The Zarian backed away, looking as if he was ready to flee.

"No, no!" she exclaimed and she grabbed hold of his arm. "Listen, the child may have been daka Archer. I must see him, and take his blood again. I must know that he is not the daka's child!"

"I know nothing of a child given to the underground this morning," he told her, his tone pleading, "I know nothing except that I am to take into my charge a child. Where is the child you promised?"

"There is no child, fool!" Chavva shouted, "I needed to speak with you about the child I delivered this morning! Where is he? You must take me to him, I must see him!"

"I have no information." he countered, and his eyes were moving manically around them, as he waited for one of the docking crew to hear their argument. "If you gave the child to the underground this morning, by now it has a new identity. A family, who will cherish it."

Chavva grabbed his robes and shook him, though he was twice her weight. "I don't care to hear your political rubbish, all I want is the daka back, in my hands! If you do not take me to the child I gave you, I will inform the daka of your activities. I have names, I know faces-"

The Zarian pushed her off him, and dipped his hands beneath his robes. As she saw the lume in his hands, she regretted her threats.

She screamed for help.

Thunder erupted around them as he set off his weapon.

The sensation of being stabbed with a million needles erupted from her core and spread. She knew how the lume worked. Her internal organs were cooking, melting. Her legs turned to rubber, and she fell. She rolled down a slope and came to a rest on her back. Her limbs trembled as the lume's effects spread.

In seconds, the center's security force pounded down the ramp. Thundered floated above her, sounding far away.

One man knelt down by her side. She heard a disembodied voice say, "She is dying."

With effort, she hissed, ".....Birdy alive...."

The sensation of needles spread up her spine and in her skull, paralyzing her full body in a cocoon of agony. Tears slid down her temples and into her ears. Her sights dimmed. Her thoughts dwindled to one. Daka Archer is alive!

 જ્જ્જ્જ્જ્જ્જ્

The office was brightly lit and antiseptic white. A woman sat in a corner, weeping.

Bail hunched forward, his head in his hand, and he stared at the floor as she told them that Chavva, the lab technician, took a baby that resembled Janus for euthanasia that morning.

Trev was beside him, slouched in his seat, leaning the back of his head against the wall, his ankles crossed casually, and his features slack as if he were bored. Apart from them both were the

377

captain of the center's security force, a very nervous man at this point.

"I had just given her the daka's blood sample," she said gruffly, "no more than an hour before she was.....killed."

"Why didn't you tell Doctor Merl about your suspicions?" Trev asked, his voice slow, malevolent. "Instead of running to a tech?"

"I thought Chavva could quickly test the blood, matching it against the Shodite child, to prove me wrong.....without having to concern the daka...I didn't want to cause her unnecessary pain."

"Liar," Bail said lowly, and rising from his dejected position, he went on, his voice becoming progressively strident as his control slowly unraveled, "You were afraid of the law. Afraid you'd cause a scandal, because you knew it is forbidden to euthanise Shodite children. You feared you would be arrested and tried and convicted before the Alliance for the murder of innocents! You feared for your life, not daka Archer's!" He thundered, his whole body rigid with accusation.

"Yes....yes!" she cried out, sobbing, "I was afraid, but I never hurt those babies, I never did that terrible thing, I took care of them!"

"Did you know who the Zarian was who killed Chavva?" Trev interjected crossly.

"No....I didn't know she had Zarian friends...I didn't know her well at all." She was scrambling verbally, like a drowning woman. "I knew her in passing because we worked the same shift."

The security Captain asked, "Can you account for the missing records on the child in question?"

"The child in question," Bail fumed at the Captain, "has a name. Use it."

The Captain cringed a bit, and amended himself, reposing the question, calling the child by name, as ordered.

Bail frowned his deep anguish, and steadied his glare at the woman as she replied.

Her dark eyes flicked nervously from Bail, to the Captain. She was struggling to stop crying. "No......Chavva was in charge of the records."

378

"But you were in charge of the baby." Trev said, a trace of unkindness in his tone.

"I signed him over to Chavva.....personally...I gave him to Chavva.....I don't know what became of him...."

"You appear," Bail interjected, "very guilty Swiana."

She trembled at the accusation. "I'm not." she vowed, "I only took care of the babies." She closed her eyes, shunting huge tears from them. Miserably, she said, "You already think I am guilty."

"You turned a blind eye to the eradication of helpless infants," Bail said evenly. "You are guilty!"

She shuddered. She was afraid, of her situation, and of Bail, who appeared ready to leap out of his seat and throttle her with his bare hands.

"I was following orders...I didn't do anything to the baby...it was all Chavva's doing!"

"There are rumors," Trev said, and he shrugged in a friendly fashion, "but rumors, you know how they are, prone to exaggeration. I heard that there are a few subversives working in the testing centers around the Center-plex, funneling Shodite children out of the country through an underground. A Zarian underground."

She fiddled with a button on her smock, sucking in shallow breaths as she found control.

"I never suspected Chavva of anything subversive," she started, her voice less tremulous, "but I always thought it was unusual that she did all her own reports. The lazy techs usually put off the report writing onto us nurses, because they think we have nothing better to do with our time. She was never like that."

"Ample control over the record keeping." Trev said to Bail.

Bail nodded grimly.

"And...." the nurse offered, "there was something else about her I thought was strange. She got very attached to the babies in the nursery. She used to give them her own pet names. I used to think she was......obscenely corrupt......for the way she could dispose of the little ones she grew attached to. The one you are looking for.....she used to call him Birdy. She told me it was what she'd called her son when he was that small, and then she took him away to be....." she looked into Bail's eyes, and she swallowed

379

hard before saying, "I hope for the sake of Birdy that she was a subversive, daka."

It was Bail's turn to avert his eyes. He didn't like being put into the uncomfortable position of feeling gratitude for a political subversive's actions.

To the commander, he said, "Keep this woman in custody until further notice."

Swiana's tears refreshed themselves.

He continued, "What is the director's name?"

"Lora Uil'Paoratic."

"I want her placed under arrest, and delivered to the Captain of the Pliadors." Bail growled, "If she has the audacity to ask why she is being arrested, tell her that she is charged with sedition and murder under Alliance law."

"Yes daka."

Bail stood and stalked out of the office and down the corridor. Involuntarily, he came to a halt at the nursery. He stood, and stared at nothing, struggling with his despair and fury.

Feeling Trev's presence behind him, he said, "What if it wasn't him, the one Chavva Tathal gave to the Zarian? What if he has been placed in a Shodite home?"

"You'll know for certain once the records are completely checked. If there isn't a match, then there is a high degree of certainty that your son is in the hands of Zarians."

"Or dead."

"No. We won't let that be." Trev elbowed him, urging him to move forward. "Come on, then. I've got some strong brandy in the windrider that'll give you a bit of hope, or at least untrouble your mind for a time."

Bail let Trev pass him by, and he followed, placing heavy hand on friend's shoulder. He felt as if he was ready to collapse.

In the windrider, on the way home, he received the information that the Zarian killed on the center grounds was related by marriage to Plat L'Otu, the Zarian minister to the Alliance Council.

Plat of Zaria was brought to the palace under heavy guard. He was treated with respect, as per Bail's orders. It was Bail's original plan to meet with Plat alone, but Jishni insisted on being a part of the meeting, as well as including Avee and Dai. Bail's desire for a sedate initial meeting with the Zarian minister turned malevolent with the presence of the mindreaders.

They waited for him in the Orin reception hall. Jishni sat in an uncomfortable and garishly ornate chair that had a back that towered above her head. Bail sensed she wanted to silently remind Plat who he was dealing with by the chair she chose, a chair that had been her father's favorite. Avee stood to her right, and Dai to her left.

Bail stood apart from them, sensing he'd have no control of this interview, feeling very much like an interloper in the daka's affairs. Jishni had made it clear that she didn't want nor need his company. He was undecided if he'd even participate in Plat's questioning.

Plat was put off by the sight of the mindreaders, as Bail suspected he would be. His pace slowed as he crossed the distance from the entry to Jishni's chair. His eyes went from Jishni, to the mindreaders, to Bail.

He hesitated to an uncertain halt, about ten feet from Jishni. He smoothed the front of his clothing, a brightly striped costume of his native land, and tried to smile. "To what do I owe the honor of your summons?"

Jishni waited to the count of five to respond, an imperious tactic taught to her by her father and never employed until now.

"One of your family members was killed today in Nysus." she said smoothly. "Vrel L'Otu Cull."

He was genuinely distressed. "Have you informed his wife?"

"She has been informed." Jishni said. Her voice was low and smooth, and too controlled. Bail detected the undercurrent of her rage, and he saw that Plat had noticed it, too.

"What happened to Vrel?" he asked, staring warily at Jishni.

"We will get to that in a moment," Jishni promised, "first, I'd like to discuss your relationship with Vrel. Were you close?"

"We were family," Plat offered, "We weren't confidants, but we did see each other often. He lived in my home."

Jishni glanced to Avee. Avee nodded that Plat was being truthful.

"Daka Jishni," Plat said, his voice hushed with disbelief that she chose to consult the mindreader, "what did Vrel do?"

Bail chose this moment to join the interview. He stepped forward easily. "Plat," he said in a relaxed tone, "do you know anything about Vrel's affiliations? His friends, his political allies?"

"His friends.....yes, I know a few of his friends, but daka Bail, I don't understand--"

"We want their names." Jishni interjected sharply.

"Jishni," Bail warned in a soothing tone.

Dai leaned down to Jishni and said to her, "He is worried about turning over Vrel's associates."

Jishni's eyes narrowed. "Why, Plat?"

"Before I answer any more questions, I want to know what happened to Vrel!" Plat demanded.

"He was killed," Jishni replied evenly, "while in the commission of a crime. He murdered a woman."

"No, not Vrel." he whispered. "He venerated life."

"The woman he murdered was smuggling Shodite children to him from a testing center." she continued harshly.

Understanding flickered on his features a moment, and was gone. Bail did not need the confirmation of mindreaders to know that Plat knew something about the underground.

"My son Archer," Jishni said, her voice cracking with emotion, "through the caprice of fate, ended up in a testing center in Nysus. He was to be euthanised, but we believe that before that criminal act could be completed, a woman at the center saved him. The woman your cousin killed."

Plat spread his hands apart helplessly. "Daka Jishni, I know nothing of the underground."

"He has lied." Dai said calmly, his sharp eyes leveled on Plat's face.

"Nothing of consequence." he restated firmly, "I knew Vrel believed in the fair treatment of the Shodites, and I suspected he was taking affirmative action to uphold his beliefs, and of course I am aware of the underground, but I did not participate!"

"He is being truthful." Avee said. His eyes were equally sharp as Dai's, but perhaps less cruel, less anticipatory.

"Who else is in this underground, Plat?" Bail asked, "Give us a name of someone who can help us find our son."

Plat stepped back, placing his profile to Bail, as if he was getting ready to leave. His features miserable, he said, "You ask too much of me."

"No, I do not!" Bail bellowed. "One name is not too much to ask, considering you all but admitted that you knew about Vrel's illegal activities and did nothing to stop him!"

Plat shocked him by turning on him suddenly in anger. "At least I knew of my people's criminal acts! You are insensate to the stench of corruption that is beneath your noses! Do you know how long my people have been saving the Shodite innocents, while your people continue to murder them because their deaths are more convenient than their lives? Four hundred years!"

"There are channels you should have gone through before breaking Janti law and stealing Shodites!" Jishni retorted.

"We went through all the channels, all of them!" he shouted, "Just this year, we filed another criminal law suit against the Dorn testing center, offering a din of witnesses and proof of euthanised children and what do the Janti do? The Janti fired the director, restaffed the center, and the center went on doing its business, euthanising children under a new leadership!"

"I can't control all my people!" Jishni retorted, tears standing in her eyes, "I can only punish the ones that break the law."

"Ah, but you don't." he replied harshly, "Do you know where the former director of the Dorn Center is these days? He is running a smaller center in Thorley, no more than twenty spans from the testing center he'd been fired from!"

"That can't be!" she retorted.

"It is true," he threw a finger at Jishni, "by the grave of Thranlam'Sum, you authorized his transfer! He served three months in a detention center, and was reassigned and forgotten."

"I wouldn't have put him in charge of more children," Jishni rejected emotionally.

"You check the records, daka." Plat said, and he again, fearlessly, threw a rebuking finger at her, "Your people see you as

383

a barometer of their moral conduct. You say to them it is all right to kill Shodites, because you do not punish the men and women who do kill Shodites. You condone their base, evil behavior with a nod, and a bow, and a blind eye!"

Bail strode forward, putting himself between Plat and Jishni. "That will be enough."

Plat backed off, but his anger did not recede. "Zaria has always been outspoken against Shodite slavery in Jantideva. And we will stand firm on the rights of those who cannot protect themselves for as long as Jantideva's leadership forgets their hungriest, neediest citizens."

"Plat," Jishni pleaded, "I vow, I will take aggressive action against the directors of the testing centers that are misusing their power. Please, give us a name. We will not prosecute your confederates if we find Archer."

"No," Plat said lowly, stepping aside to see her beyond Bail, "I have no names to give you. I was not lying when I said I have no affiliations with the underground. And if I did, you could not buy a name with a promise like that, Jishni. Jantideva is notorious for breaking promises. Shall I cite the promise made to the Shodites by daka Redd? `Come into our arms' he told them, `we will care for you.' He cared for them by making them Jantideva's slaves!"

"Thousands of years before Archer's birth!" she retorted, "Must my child, an infant, pay for Redd's evils?"

"A time worn and trite excuse used by daka apologists for generations and generations. The Shodites have been paying for Redd's evils since they were first enslaved. Why shouldn't you pay for his crimes, too?"

Jishni stood and came up beside Bail. Angrily, she said, "If you want the Shodites, Plat, you take them! Take them all into your country! Let Zaria nurse them for awhile, then face me and tell me that Jantideva has done wrong."

Plat smiled unkindly at her. "Why, daka, I do believe that is what we are doing....one threatened Shodite baby at a time."

Without being properly dismissed, he turned on his heel and walked away from them.

"Plat!" Jishni called after them, "One name! One name or we will expel Zarians from Jantideva!"

Without slowing, Plat threw a reply over his shoulder. "Do what you must. I cannot help you."

Furiously, Jishni turned and asked Avee, "Did you hear anything in his mind at all helpful?"

Avee apologized, "I can't pull more than images from his mind, I'm not Ver dala Ven."

Jishni turned, and stared at Bail.

Bail knew what was going through her mind. She wanted to consult Cobo.

"I will go to Cobo." he relented.

"Yes." she said lowly, "And you will bring him home, to me. I must ask the questions, Bail." She gripped her stomach as if she were in pain. "I must hear the answers he gives with my own ears."

"Jishni," Bail said softly, "He may not be willing to leave his new home."

"Bail, I need him." she hesitated, and groaned, punching herself in the stomach, "He won't come to me! I know he won't and I know why he won't! My dirty, evil spirit drove him away eighteen years ago, and repels him still. I split this family, just as my forefather split the Alliance. I ruined Ver dala Ven, it was my doing! I robbed you of a brother, I robbed Taen of a father. I robbed myself of happiness."

"Jishni, my love," Bail intoned, trying desperately not to soak in her pain, "please, stop punishing yourself."

"I am the daka of Jantideva," she retorted, "I am the overseer of millions of slaves. I am the killer of children, evil incarnate, daughter of daka Redd and daka Corrinne. It is my curse to lose a child. I am so sorry Bail, I am so sorry I forced my curse upon you."

Bail was shaken by her outburst, and he tried to reach out to her. She bolted from his hands, and bolted from the room, running as if a demon were on her heels.

Bail glanced to Avee. Tonelessly, he said, "We're done for the day."

Neither men would meet his eyes as they left.

Chapter 18

The mood in Zadoq turned somber once the Men and Women heard of their leader's death. Rito-Sant's body was laid out on a carpet of greenery in the city's common. For days the mourners lined up continuously to see him, and weep, and throw flower petals on his rotting body. Baru informed Cobo and Surna that the mourning period would last one hundred days after Rito-Sant's body was immolated. During that time, there would be no public carousing, nor would the breeders be fertilized. The dold Huntress was expected to remain in seclusion. Baru explained their custom, saying the interim was to give Rito-Sant's soul release. If there was no happiness in Zadoq, there would be no reason for him to want to stay.

Cobo told Surna confidentially that he felt Rito-Sant's spirit lingering despite the sadness among his people. He was with many Dilgo spirits, walking the city as if they were still alive, confused and trapped within the stone walls.

Surna was made uncomfortable by Cobo's talk of the walking spirits of Zadoq. Now, in the darkness, if a chill overtook her, she was eerily reminded that she was never alone, even in the privacy of Cobo's apartment.

On the evening of a full moon, the Huntresses placed Rito-Sant's body on a funeral pyre near the Lake of Tears. They set him ablaze, and as he burned, the Dilgos prayed in song to their sun god to take his spirit up with the smoke. Baru, in a fit of ecstatic grief, threw herself onto her brother's burning body and let the fire consume her. She embraced death as she embraced Rito-Sant, suffering in silence as the flames devoured her living flesh.

Surna turned away as Baru sacrificed herself. Cobo put his hands on her shoulders to keep her from running out on the funeral. She knew the importance of maintaining good relations with the Dilgos, and running out on Rito-Sant's funeral would have been considered an insult to the leader.

Weeping was acceptable, and she did weep, but not for Rito-Sant. She wept for the woman who felt she could not live without him.

The mourning period did not postpone Taen's coronation. On the morning after Rito-Sant's immolation, leaders from each Alliance country began pouring into Dilgopoche to see the Janti daka take Rito-Sant's newly vacated throne. Notably absent was Taen's own family. Members of the court attended, provincial governors who'd arrived in the daka's stead to witness the coronation, explaining that the search for Archer consumed the dakas' time and energy.

Taen seemed unconcerned with either his family's absence, or the fruitless search for his brother. He was full of himself, strutting around, pleased with his quick ascension to leadership. His pomposity matched Durym's, who had arrived with the court. Durym was in attendance to bless the ceremony properly, according to Suma practice.

Surna had done her best to avoid Durym. She didn't attend the reception of guests, and had stayed in Cobo's quarters until the time of the coronation, specifically to avoid the sight of the ambitious young priest.

The ceremony took place in Zadoq's common. There was little ceremony to it, in comparison to Suma ceremonies. Seamus placed a black band, made from Rito-Sant's crown to fit Taen (it probably could have been a ring for Rito-Sant's finger, Surna mused) on Taen's head and declared him the ruler of Dilgopoche.

Surna had watched the coronation with the rest of the breeders from the balcony that was directly above the dais. Once the dold Huntress had completed presenting Taen to the Dilgo people as their new leader, it was Durym's turn. He stepped up onto the dais, stood behind Taen and started to say the blessings. He looked out at his audience as he spoke, as was his habit. His eyes traveled to around the common, then he glanced upwards. Seeing Surna, he stammered. For a few seconds he seemed out of touch with what he was doing, but as he averted his eyes from hers, he quickly recovered.

Surna frowned. Pious idiot. Standing around him were pungent smelling giants, yet it was her presence that disagreed with him, and why? Because she betrayed his calling.

Surna chose to retire to Cobo's apartment directly after the coronation. When she wasn't attending Cobo, she studied. Cobo had encouraged her to use an ariq stone he'd brought with him, to read all she could on Dilgopoche, or any subject she chose. She was most interested in great literature, but as a Suma Mistress never had time to read. In the ariq stone she found a library of classical novels, and mused that Cobo must have known of her thirst to read. Placing her hand on the stone, the script appeared in the air before her, inky black against the backdrop of the reddish wall. Currently she was reading a lengthy historical piece, a love story, set in a windswept coastal city in romantic Dacha, written by a Dachian who was notorious for bittersweet twists in his tales. She loved tales that made her cry.

She had just settled into her pillows and summoned the story when she heard a clapping outside Cobo's door. She knew it had to be a Janti. The Dilgos slam their fists on the door to gain the attention of the residents.

She quickly went to the door, to inform whomever it was that Cobo had planned to stay with Taen, to protect the new leader. Cobo worried that Seamus might forget his oath to do no harm to Taen, or that another Man might try to act in Seamus's stead.

She opened the door, and seeing Durym, her stomach immediately tightened.

"Cobo is not here." she said bluntly, and she moved to close the door.

Durym blocked the door with his foot. "I'm not here to see Ver dala Ven."

She grimaced. "I was afraid of that."

"Please, Surna, I must speak with you."

"We've nothing to talk about." Surna threw her back against the door and tried pushing it shut.

In a most disgraceful fashion for a priest in full ceremonial dress, Durym threw his entire body against the other side of the door to prevent her from shutting him out, "Surna, please, I am begging you, give me a minute."

"I do not wish to hear you spout Suma dogma at me, Priest!" she retorted, "I am happy! I am never returning to Jantideva, and I am certainly never returning to the altar!"

"That's not what I want to talk about!" he pleaded, "For the sake of all that is holy, Surna, let me in, and hear me out!"

It became a battle between their relative sizes and strengths, a battle that Durym was destined to win. In frustration, Surna shouted, "Priest, what would the Chancellor say if he knew you were behaving like a common thug!"

"Probably the same thing he said when I volunteered to live with Taen-Sant as his Suma spiritual advisor." he shouted back., "That I am crazed beyond belief!"

Shock threw her away from the door. Durym's force caused the door to fly open, and Durym stumbled into the apartment. He found his ground, and faced her, his chest heaving with the exertion of having physically fought for the right to see her.

Her disbelief worked its way into her expression. "You are here to stay?"

A hint of anger crossed his features. "I know how it must repulse you to live in the same city with me, but, yes. The Chancellor was concerned about Taen's spiritual needs, and asked the order for volunteers. I volunteered."

"Why did you throw your ambitions away?" she asked thoughtlessly. It was common knowledge that missionaries never went far in the Suma priesthood. It was those who stayed close to the court that became Chancellors.

She'd struck a nerve. His ambitions had meant much to him. With difficulty, he said, "I felt a higher calling."

She had to do a quick review her opinion of him, and decide whether or not her pride permitted her to feel a shred of respect for the status seeking little boy.

Mainly, she felt skeptical. "There must be some reward for you, Priest."

Apprehension drew his brows together. "None, but knowing that Taen is being guided properly by a Suma." and he grimaced at the opened door, and the sounds of a Dilgo couple indiscreetly engaging in sex in the corridor. "And now that I am here, I know I did the right thing. Dilgopoche is an unholy land."

She huffed a laugh and crossed her arms before her in a confrontational manner. "How typical of a Suma to look down upon the customs of a foreign land without trying to understand them."

"What should I try to understand?" he said hotly, his righteous indignation rising, "Dilgos disrobe, and engage in private commerce in public. What is to understand?"

Pique dropped her lids half closed. "At least they are open about their lusts. They possess an honesty that most Janti do not. One can never fail to know where one stands with a Dilgo. Janti, on the other hand, use subterfuge and out right lies in order to hide themselves from the world. They think they look pious, but in truth, their amorality is as obvious as a the amorality of the Huntresses and the Men."

Durym reddened. "I honestly didn't come to argue moral issues with you, Surna." he said tightly, "I came to ask you a favor. Ver dala Ven told me you are well versed in Dilgo, and you have befriended many in the city. I'm here to ask for you help. I need to learn the language, and the customs, and it would be helpful if I knew some of the people."

Cobo purposefully exaggerated. Surna knew a smattering of Dilgo, and encountered a few people willing to talk to her on her evening walks, mainly to ask her what horror befell her causing her scars. She had learned from those encounters that the Dilgos were far more accepting of her appearance, and her former calling, than any person in Jantideva had ever been. They didn't stare at her scars, or avert their eyes in disgust as they imagined her sexual purpose in the temple. In fact, as she described her service to the priests, a few of the Huntresses had looked at her with respect for her copious ability to service many men. Respect was something she'd never known as a Suma Mistress. She rather enjoyed being respected by the Huntresses.

Making silent note to speak with Cobo about her dislike of Durym in order to avoid having him put the priest off on her again, she refused Durym with a shake of the head.

"I'm far too busy with my duties as Cobo's attendant." she lied easily.

Durym's features softened. "I spoke with Ver dala Ven about your arrangement. Surna, he said if the idea pleases you.....I would like you to consider being my attendant."

The very thought of being the servant to a priest made her eyes grow hot. "It does not please me. I have no interest in being a Suma Mistress, especially not for you."

The insult made Durym look away. His face was vulnerable with hurt. "I don't want you to act as a Suma." he explained, "Your only duties will be in teaching me not to behave like idiot in front of the Dilgos."

"You should ask Ver dala Ven to help you personally," she told him dryly, "he is the one who performs miracles."

"I know you hate me, Surna." he said gruffly, "I accept your hatred....on behalf of...all you lost in your service to priests. Please, believe me, I am not asking more from you than courtesy, from one Janti who is far away from home to another. Help me learn my place here."

She felt a twinge of conscience for hurting his feelings. It wasn't his fault she'd grown to hate the priests for taking her life away from her. His only crimes were his insufferable youth and his blind ambitions. Both crimes were forgivable. While she was a Mistress, he did her the favor of regularly requesting her as an attendant for social gatherings. She appreciated that he at least afforded her the chance to get away from the temple, though she rarely enjoyed his company.

She felt herself giving in.

"You may accompany on my evening walks," she said flatly, "and I will teach you Dilgo. But we will not be constant companions, Durym. I have a full life already with Cobo."

He glanced at her, a hopeful gleam in his eyes. "Of course, I wouldn't infringe on your life."

"Nor will you infringe on my choices." she stated firmly, "You will not attempt to lure me back into the Suma. In fact, if you say one derogatory word about my new life, I will never speak to you again."

He nodded his understanding.

"Meet me here tonight after the evening bell has tolled."

"Thank you Surna." he said softly, and he left her.

She closed the door on his back and cursed herself for her sympathy. Now her pleasant evening walks would be spent with the last person on the planet she would have chosen for company.

There was a simple solution. She would have to take two walks a day. In the morning, and evening. Rohn was usually tending the children early in the day, in any case.

He was not a slave, but rather like a nanny. In Zhun, the fifth arm of the city, the children of the Men and Women were cared for, and raised. The Huntresses and the Men did their part, in a way, playing father and mother to their children, but it was the Inferes who really raised the children. They came from their cliff village and into the city each morning, and stayed until the evening, and taught the children songs, and games, and crafts, and play.

Rohn was Inferes, a genderless being. Not a man, not a woman. Surna had a crush on him, a giddy crush. He was smart, funny, handsome, and virile. But not a man, not a woman. She would see him in the mornings, now, instead of the evenings. She would be with him as he tended the children, rather than walking him out of the city as he went home.

She went back to her novel, and read the story of a bittersweet love, her thoughts gilded by Rohn's smile, and laugh, and masculine form.

∞∞∞∞∞∞∞∞∞

In the secret darkness of the room Danati had called the dold chamber, Taen felt his way into Caltha, and as the ruler of Dilgopoche he made love to his mistress.

And in darkness, she left him.

"I must speak to the dold Huntress about changing the laws concerning the breeders, don't you think, Lodan?" he whispered from the doorway, believing Lodan was awake and listening. "Sneaking around is unbecoming for a ruler."

If Lodan was awake, he wasn't replying.

Taen smirked. Lodan was a puritan, and probably didn't even condone temple priests making love to the Guardian surrogates, though there was no purer an act.

He looked in on Danati. She was laying buried in covers, and breathing heavily through her mouth. It had been a long and hard affair for her. She was exhausted, and emotionally overwrought after having lost her beloved father. Taen had been properly supportive of his wife during the day, and for the night....he had encouraged the Dold Huntress to prescribe sleep herbs to help Danati sleep.

Danati was perfect, but lacked something intangible that Taen couldn't put his finger on. That something intangible was in Caltha, who lacked nothing, except a decent grasp on the Janti language. They were getting better at communicating with each other, however.

Taen lit the lamps in the bathhouse, and slipped into the water. Sitting on the second stone step that led into the tub submerged him to the chest. He washed away the smell of the Dilgos with Janti soap, and after drying he scented himself with Janti cologne. He was a Dilgo now, but he was not accustomed to smelling like a Dilgo.

He dressed in a knee length bed shirt, plain white with the emblem of the Masing star on his left breast embroidered with gold thread, and climbed into bed next to Danati. In her drugged sleep, she reflexively reached for him. He avoided her touch, and her grasp coming up empty, she recoiled to her side of the bed.

He lay on his back and relaxed, willing himself to sleep.

From outside his window, far below, he heard a familiar voice.

He scrambled out of bed and hurried to the window. He crawled through the depth of the hole chiseled in the outer wall, and lay his full length on the cool clay. Hanging his head out the window, he saw Riar Sed standing far below.

"Where have you been?" he called out to his teacher, "I've been looking for you."

Riar Sed cracked a laugh. "I haven't been under Caltha's gown!"

Taen pursed his lips. "You spark my interest, then never come and see me! What am I to think?"

"Think anything you like, boy." Riar Sed snapped. He complained, "Craning my neck to speak to you is uncomfortable, and we are on the verge of waking your blasted protector. So shut up, and come down to me!"

"There's no way I can get past Lodan without waking him!" Taen retorted.

Riar Sed beckoned to him, and abruptly the clay became slippery, and he sailed out the window into open space. Taen cried out loudly in a panic.

"Shut up, stupid boy!" Riar Sed rebuked, "You may not be Ver dala Ven, but you do have some powers at your disposal. If only you'd learn to use them. Instead, you spend your days scheming ways to get inside a woman."

Taen did not fall. He lay suspended in midair, facing the ground. He caught his breath, and tried to control his panic in front of his teacher. He hated Riar Sed too much to show his fear. The sorcerer kept him aloft for too long, Taen thought, to test his courage. An evil smirk bent Riar Sed's lips as he finally beckoned to Taen, beginning his gentle descent. Taen landed on his feet in soft sand before Riar Sed.

Riar Sed sneered at him, "Pah!" he spat, "I wasted my time with you. You have the powers of Ver dala Ven streaming through your veins, but if I had not been here to save you, you would have plunged to your death. The Guardian would have had a time laughing at your stupidity."

Taen's eyes flashed with the rage he felt. "Perhaps my teacher was lacking."

"Enough of this," Riar Sed, waving off Taen's anger. "We have much to discuss, and little time to argue."

"Yes, we do." Taen said, reigning in his anger, "I am Dilgopoche. Now, I want the world. Show me the Masing Star."

Riar Sed laughed. "You act as if it is yours to possess."

"It's here, isn't it?" Taen asked excitedly. "That is why the city is in the shape of the Masing. The pools in the shape of the bosnii flowers.....that means it resides here!"

"No, wrong, incorrect!" Riar Sed bellowed. He pressed Taen to walk with him and they started toward the canal connecting the city with the Lake of Tears. The sand was easy on his bare feet, though occasionally he found a rough stone and flinched a step.

Riar Sed said, "This structure was built after the Dome of Silence was in place, by the poor souls contained within. They thought they could please the Guardian with their offering, but of course the Guardian wasn't listening. He let them suffer. And because he let them suffer, they spited him by breaking down the walls of their offering, and living inside. Years later, the Men and Woman began worshiping the sun. Their minds are too feeble to remember historical facts, stupid animals that they are, but the Ryslacs remember."

"Then.....where is the Masing Star?" Taen asked, completely uninterested with Riar Sed's impromptu history lesson.

Their course turned and they walked along the canal toward the building that contained the water pumps. Taen could hear the pumps whirring from where they were, a clever invention of the Ryslacs. A pumping system that was weighted, and once the water began flowing through the many cogs and wheels, the motion of the machine would not stop unless the water stopped flowing, and of course the water would not stop flowing unless the machine was stopped. It moved without fuel, electricity, heat; and generated the water flow through the canals and city, and generated electricity for the lights, and warmed the interior. The Men and Women believed the amazing invention of the Ryslacs was a gift, given to them by their god.

Riar Sed was right, they really were quite ignorant.

The water undulated as it moved, black and starless as the night skies above them.

"Not here." Riar Sed told him, "but it is in Dilgopoche. I believe that Betnoni left her son a clue how to find it in her secret prophecy, for Ver dala Ven Max came to Dilgopoche often, as did his son, Maxim. They were both searching for something, something they did not find."

"You don't know where it is?" Taen asked, irritated with the old man.

"I know it moves. It travels from place to place, on a path that seems set." he replied, "I don't know how, or why it moves. I know the ordinary man cannot see it. But Ver dala Ven can see it."

Taen stopped and threw his hands in the air. "What you are saying is you don't know where it is, nor can we see it?"

"Ver dala Ven can see it," he stressed.

"You think my father is going to share the Masing with us if he finds it?" Taen asked dubiously, and he shook his head, "My father is presently disenchanted with me, Riar Sed. He won't share the knowledge of the Masing with me."

Riar Sed's eyes narrowed shrewdly. "At first, I was upset with Rito-Sant for bringing Ver dala Ven to Zadoq, for that very reason. Then I heard a most amazing story from the mind of Baru. Ver dala Ven Cobo healed Rito with a gold light that came from his body."

The truth still stung Taen's pride. "Cobo told mother that it was the Spirit of the Masing Star, given to him by Betnoni to guide his destiny."

"The Spirit, yes." Riar Sed murmured, and grinning, he said, "Yet again inhabiting a Ver dala Ven. And where does it take him? To the resting grounds of its Body."

"Then it was meant for Cobo, and not us, is that what you are saying?"

"No, think of the prophecy, boy! Cobo is here to prepare the way, not to take possession of the Star. My boy, your father is here serve our needs."

Dryly, Taen said, "I'd bet he'd rather bed a Huntress than serve us."

Riar Sed chuckled despite himself. He glanced toward the city. "Is that so, Ver dala Ven? Would you prefer mating with a Huntress to helping us find the Masing Star?"

Taen glanced to where Riar Sed was looking, and saw the dark outline of Cobo watching them from the depth of his bedroom window.

He heard Cobo's voice around them. "I'd prefer to bed a hundred Huntresses than align myself with an amoral sorcerer."

Riar Sed's eyes narrowed. "Yes, yes, well, we shall see, won't we?"

"He heard us?" Taen asked incredulously.

"He is Ver dala Ven, stupid boy," Riar Sed growled, "If it were his will, he could have heard us if he were in Jantideva."

"But.....what does he know...?...."

"There are no secrets among Ver dala Ven." Riar Sed smirked. "And whether he likes it or not, my boy, he is a partner in our quest."

He glared at Riar Sed for his easy inclusion of Cobo in their plot. To hurt him, he said, "If that is the case, I have my father, and he has me. Why do we need you?"

Riar Sed's eyes narrowed. "I have spent my life searching out and compiling stories about peculiar occurrences in Dilgopoche-- mass healings, sudden blinding flashes of light, shifts in weather, and births of geniuses among the Ryslacs. The occurrences come in cycles, and near the same locations, year after year. I believe they are the result of the Masing Star coming into contact with our kind. I have mapped the locations of these occurrences, and I have committed them to memory." Nastily, he sneered, "I know you can't wrench the map from my thoughts. Ver dala Ven can, but he won't. I've written my map on my heart. If he tries to extract it, I will die." Riar Sed glanced back to Cobo. "And you won't kill me, will you, Ver dala Ven?"

"Not without just cause." was Ver dala Ven's reply.

To that, Riar Sed let out a throaty laugh.

Taen stared at Cobo's form, uncertainty and doubt working through the anger he felt toward his father. "How can we trust you?" he asked Cobo.

"How can I trust you?" Cobo countered.

"You can't." Taen replied sharply.

"I won't." Cobo said, and his dark outline sunk away from the window.

Riar Sed stared hard at Taen. "After the mourning period is done, you will begin preparations for a traveling tour of your country. Your people will expect it. The tour will take us to the four corners of Dilgopoche, and to each of the sights I have mapped. We will find the Masing, Taen, you and I...and Ver dala Ven, as well." he added grudgingly.

Soberly, Taen said, "If it were that easy, Ver dala Ven Max would have found it centuries ago."

Riar Sed scowled. "Stupid boy. Haven't you heard? Haven't you been listening to the world? The first signs of Betnoni's Prophecy have been fulfilled. We are going to find the Masing, you and I, and the Masing will be ours. Make your plans and try to keep an optimistic thought in that ignorant head of yours."

Feeling the need to prove himself to a man who never failed to make him feel lower than a bug, Taen calmed himself enough that he was able to levitate off the ground. He rose high above Riar Sed's head.

Riar Sed watched him, amusement curling his lips.

Imperiously, Taen said to him, "Don't you forget I am Taen-Sant."

An evil glint jumped into Riar Sed's eyes, and he whirled his fingers.

Taen felt his own control slip away, and he began to spin. He saw in succession the lake, then the palace, and the lake, then the palace, spinning progressively faster, until the faint image of where his feet once were left a streak of brown.

In his head, he heard, "Don't you forget who is stronger than you, boy."

He abruptly stopped spinning, and fell to the ground with a crash. He pulled himself out of the dirt, his knees and arms smarting from the fall, and he vomited his supper.

After he was finished vomiting, he began spouting curses at Riar Sed.

Looking up, he found he was alone. Riar Sed had vanished.

He rolled back on his heels, and glanced at the window where he'd last seen Cobo. A clear, pure yellow light came from his room, unlike the undulating pale orange glow of the artificial light that shown in the windows above and below. He suspected that the glow came from the Spirit of the Masing Star, conjured by Cobo. He'd not seen the Spirit yet, only heard descriptions of it from the peace envoy that had witnessed Cobo use it to heal Rito-Sant's infirmity. He'd asked Cobo to show him the Star, only to have his request denied with the lamest of excuses. Cobo had claimed that the Star's Spirit had its own objective and did not answer to his command. Taen flattered himself by suspecting that Cobo was trying to keep the Star to himself, for fear that he might lay claim to it.

The truth of the matter was harder for Taen's ego to accept. Between the dark sorcerer Riar Sed and Ver dala Ven Cobo, he was the weakest of the three.

He hated feeling weak.

Though he was trembling, he was able to make himself rise off the ground. He projected himself toward his window, his room, and reached out his hands as he glided gracefully toward the opening.

Landing safely inside, he glanced to Danati. She was still sleeping.

He returned to the bathhouse to clean the blood and dirt and vomit off him, and to try to find his river. Ever since Cobo broke through, he'd been left with a barren place in his soul. Until now, he hadn't missed the succor of his river. Danati had been his succor, and Caltha, and the promise of finding the Masing.

The prospect of having to share the Masing with Cobo enraged him. He thought might die if he actually had to endure losing power to his father.

Ver dala Ven Max knew of the Masing's presence in Dilgopoche. He had to have known from his mother's prophecy. Taen decided he would study her writings, but not with Lodan. Lodan was schooled in Suma, but not as fluent as a priest. And, among the priests, there was no one as fluent in Suma as Durym.

Taen had always despised Durym. Though they were close to being the same age, he'd always felt Durym looked down upon him as if he were ages older, and wiser. Taen had felt his mother's spite in sending Durym to be his spiritual advisor. She knew how much he hated the priest.

But, Durym was a brilliant Suma. The elder priests, even Aton, had consulted with Durym when there was a troublesome translation or interpretation of the old writings. Durym had given speeches on Ver dala Ven prophecy, and won acclaim for his thinking. He bragged about himself enough, but there had been some reason to brag.

Taen was not the strongest of the three, but he wasn't a stupid boy, either. He would use Durym, and his own wits, to discover the secrets of the Masing. Not even Riar Sed read or spoke Suma. Taen's priest leveled the playing field between he and Riar Sed.

Ultimately, the battle would be between he and his father, whose instincts and training made him stronger than any man or sorcerer. Taen intended to be victorious, and take back what was stolen from him by Cobo's thoughtless abandonment. After fighting his destiny for a year, he finally wanted to become Ver dala Ven. He deserved to be Ver dala Ven. It was his birthright.

జ్జ్జ్జ్జ్జ్

400

Cobo withdrew from the distressing conversation between Riar Sed and his son.

He sat on a pillow in the corner of his bedchamber and ruminated on Ver dala Ven Maxim's journey to Dilgopoche. It was a footnote in the history of a man who accomplished a great deal, though he'd been crippled by the loss of his grandmother and the stunted training given to him by his father. Maxim worked tirelessly for the humane treatment of expatriated Shodites, and he frequently traveled to other countries on missions of mercy. Historically speaking, his journeys to Dilgopoche weren't note worthy. His son, Locat, in old age would betray the secret prophecy to daka Corrinne, and Dilgopoche would become hidden from public historical record altogether.

"Show me," he asked the Star, and a vision quickly came upon him. In his vision he saw Ver dala Ven Max as a young man, traveling into Dilgopoche. He went from town to town, visiting burial grounds. He interviewed countless spirits of dead Dilgos. He seemed to be looking for those who might have met his mother, whether in life or after. None could help him. None had seen Betnoni.

Years later, Max's son, Ver dala Ven Maxim, also toured Dilgopoche, taking the same route as his father, seeing the same sights and making the same inquiries. He did not travel alone, however. He had an affair with a local woman in Zadoq and gave that woman a daughter. He never learned of the child. Maxim's daughter became a healer, and had many children, before and after the Dome of Silence was in place. One of her daughters had invited the blessings of the Masing Star.

"Kiitur," Cobo said aloud as he saw the tiny grandchild of Maxim.

His vision cleared, and before him a tiny star appeared. He hadn't summoned the Masing's Spirit, it acted independently of him, expanding and enveloping him into its glow.

Kiitur was within the star.

"Did you summon the Masing?" he asked, incredulous that an untrained Ver dala Ven could have this ability.

"I heard you call me." Kiitur said in her childlike voice. Her expression registered her awe, her shock, as she stared at the star around her. "And suddenly I am here."

The energy of the Masing vibrated through his mind, showed him that in Kiitur's case, she could not summon it for her use, but rather, it summoned her for its use.

Kiitur quickly accepted the strange journey she had just made, her attention turning to Cobo. "What troubles your mind, Ver dala Ven Cobo?"

He smiled at her use of his title, knowing he should address her in same, if for no better reason than to honor her as an ancient elder.

"Ver dala Ven Kiitur, very soon, I will embark on a journey to find the Masing Star."

She nodded thoughtfully. "Many have sought that prize. A few have had a taste of it, such as I, changed forever by its touch." She lifted her hands out to indicate the star that surrounded them, "Its spirit moves in us, Ver dala Ven Cobo. Why do you want to own its body? Do you crave its powers, like our kin?"

"I do not crave the Masing for power." he said earnestly, "I oftentimes crave to hear its song sung again in Ona. But I do not seek it for myself. I seek it because I feel it is my destiny to seek it. Yet, I do not know why. Why must I be the one to fulfill the prophecies, Kiitur? I am a dishonorable runaway."

Cobo released his past to her, hiding nothing, confiding all, and Kiitur breathed in his life, his story, his loves, his history, and nodded that she understood. "It is you because it is the Star's will."

"Too simple an answer, and too true."

"I have heard the Masing Star's song." Kiitur said, "It filled our lands with its magnificent song, a song so beautiful it struck me with gold eyes. Later, near the same place as I had been blessed, the Song struck a Ryslac-Vubushi blind. The Vubushi was pregnant at the time. The child she birthed spoke his first word only moments after being born. His name was Locuren, he too had gold eyes, and he became our savior. He conceived our pumps and irrigation systems, ending the deadly droughts caused by the heat of the Dome. He also encouraged us to segregate ourselves into

402

clans, according to our differences. He said that in doing so, we would strengthen as a people. He was right. There were less diseases and still births among our own kind. We all thrived."

"It is like the legend of Thranlam'Sum, touched by the Star and made Ver dala Ven."

"As Betnoni protected your adopted homeland, the Star protected us in our time of need. It made Ver dala Ven by necessity. There have been none made in this way since Locuren."

"None? You've not heard the Song since?"

"On the rare occasion I hear the Star, but not the Song." she replied, "I have heard it pass through our village. It thinks It is silent, but it hums softly, so softly that most people can't hear it. A pretty sound. Like the vibration of the tunca. Soft, yet enough to awaken me, and those like me."

"Ver dala Ven, you mean." Cobo questioned quickly.

"Of my children, twelve are like you and I, born with gold eyes. There are far fewer among the many generations of my descendants. Those that are of our kind number in the hundreds."

"So many," he breathed, pleased in a giddy way to know there were more his kind, "Now I understand why my appearance didn't spark Rito-Sant's interest. He behaved as though I were an Ordinary One, until I admitted to being Ver dala Ven. Do the kin of Locuren also show the sign and the gift?"

"Locuren was his mother's only child, and he was a vyesevk, a holy man who did not seek the pleasure or company of females. With his death died the Vubushi lineage."

"The Denmen lineage lives on."

"As does the lineage of Thranlam'Sum." She insisted.

Dejected by the thought that his son would sire the next Ver dala Ven, he replied, "That remains to be seen."

"The spirit of the Masing directed you to Dilgopoche for a reason. It brought you here, to Zadoq. Do you know what the name *Zadoq* means in the old language?"

"The last gate." Cobo replied. He knew, and understood the significance of the coincidence. "Ver dala Ven Itza made a number of outlandish prophecies concerning the last of Thranlam'Sum's line. Do you know of her?"

Indicating that she knew the history of the rejected lineage, she said, "Itza prophesied that the Star would die and be resurrected to silence, and that Ver dala Ven would nearly fade away, only to reemerged. She called the one to bring Ver dala Ven back to life the *last gate*."

"The last gate will be the last Ver dala Ven able to be possessed by the Star."

"Zadoq was so named because it was the last civilized city before entering the wild extreme north. The name had nothing to do with Ver dala Ven."

"And so the shape of the city is a coincidence?"

Kiitur gestured to the walls around them. "After my special children were born and our gifts alleviated much of my people's ills, we Denmen built this structure to honor the Star."

Dubious that so small a race could build a structure of such great size, Cobo placed his palm on the wall beside him, looking for confirmation in the stone. In it, he felt the invisible hands of a Denmen Ver dala Ven fitting it snugly into its place, and brushing a mixture of dung and seeds on the walls. The city took several hundred years to build and was to be a living tribute to the Masing. A living being. He saw the Star city in its original state before the Men and Women took up residence. Natural springs rushed beneath the city, soaking up through the walls, feeding the plants that grew in profusion under lights inspired to glow with the energy generated by Locuren's amazing water pumps. As Dilgopoche died in the drought, its unique plant life thrived within the walls of the Masing. The city was, in effect, a giant greenhouse.

The cubicles the Men and Women now used as living quarters were once closed off compartments, and each compartment was filled with its own magic, a vibrant force of life giving itself to the health of the plants it grew. As the walls were broken down, some of the magic retired into the stone.

"I had felt an enchantment in these walls." he said softly, "I didn't realize the source."

Kiitur screwed her pretty, doll like face into a sneer. "The Men and Women broke their way inside and live here like an infestation, breaking through walls as they saw fit, tearing down what we carefully built, clearing away growth as they chose."

"From the dimensions of the rooms, and the thinner walls leading into the cubicles, the thinner walls of the cubicles, themselves, you'd almost think the Masing wanted the Men and Women to reside here." Cobo commented.

Kiitur sighed, and glanced upward at the high ceiling. "There were moments of despair when I thought so, too. The Masing takes care of the feeble, and none were more feeble minded than the Men and Women. Before their god erected this city for them, they lived in the wilderness like animals. Now they are animals with a civilization."

Cobo detected scant evidence of higher reasoning abilities in the giant Dilgos, except in Rito-Sant, who, in life, had been the wisest of the Dilgo giants. Cobo had wondered who among them had conceived of the science of artificial insemination in order for the giant men to impregnate their fertile females, the small breeders. Now, in Kiitur's presence, he sensed the magic in the Star, and how it had moved through the Men and Women in the past. The knowledge of a few became mindless ritual to the generations to follow.

"The dold chambers and their temple," he said to Kiitur, "emit a vibration that enhances fertility."

"It does?" she asked incredulously.

"You don't feel the vibration?"

"Yes, but I had no knowledge of its purpose." she said, "Tell me more, Ver dala Ven."

He nodded, and allowed the magic of the city walls to speak to him.

"I am sorry, Kiitur," he said genuinely, "But it appears you did build this city for the Men and Women. The specially designed chambers were to enhance their chances for survival."

Clearly disillusioned, Kiitur averted her eyes.

"No...don't feel the Star has used and discarded you," Cobo entreated, "It hasn't. There was a purpose to it all. I feel it.....His purpose is present with us, right now. What you started two thousand years ago is being completed in our times. You've built a home for Taen." He said, feeling it with certainty. "Taen belongs here, Kiitur. If it weren't for the giants, how else would he have found his home, and fulfilled prophecy?"

Grudging, she said, "I can find solace in being a part of the plan."

"Kiitur, come with us on our search of the Masing Star. You are the only person alive to have heard it....you have made friends with it. Your knowledge would be useful."

Her features softened. "We will search for it together, Ver dala Ven, though the joke is it will not be found unless it wills itself found."

Cobo let himself laugh at the truth.

Kiitur began to fade. She looked down at her translucent arms, and smiled. "The Masing has decided we are done with our visit." and as she disappeared, she said, "I will meet with you again, Ver dala Ven."

Alone, Cobo returned to his pensive thoughts, but now they centered on Taen, Riar Sed, the future of Ver dala Ven. He felt his destiny trembling, ready for release but reigned by a force beyond his sight and control.

Searching for a sense of his future, a vision opened before him. He stood upon an impossibly high precipice. His future was one step away-

-into an abyss, black and deep, and lined with the skulls of those who had gone before him. Beside him, ready to take the leap with him, was his brother, aged many years, and with gold eyes, impassively staring into the depths of the abyss.

As his room resolved around him, he could only wonder what that might mean.

In the depth of his meditation, he missed the arrival of yet another transport to Zadoq. All through the day, windriders had come and gone and the unusual sound had become too usual for Cobo's ears in too short a time.

A pounding at his door interrupted his quiet mind, and the curt voice of Kreb, announced the arrival of Daka Bail.

As soon as he let his brother into his apartment, he knew Bail did not come to see Taen. The coronation, the death of Rito-Sant, the events that had rocked the Dilgo people had become a second thought for the dakas. Jishni could only think of Archer, and Bail could only think of Jishni. Swallowing his pride, a hard thing for a proud man to do, Bail had sought out Cobo for the sake of his wife.

406

Bail began telling Cobo of Jishni's infirmity. Surna chose that inopportune moment to return from her evening walk. She was ready to leave the moment she saw Bail, a sensed something amiss between them, but Cobo bid her to stay. She did so, retiring quickly to her small room, her head bowed in Bail's presence.

Once their privacy was restored, Cobo said, "I can't go back to Ona with you." And earnestly added, "As much as I might like to, Bail, Taen needs me here. My obligation is here."

Bail cast aside all measure of his pride in his entreaty. "She means more to you than this, Cobo. I know it. She needs you. I want you to go to her. I am begging you to go to her, and as much as that pains me, stabs me through the heart," he said, and he pound on his chest to emphasis his torment, "I want you to heal her in any way you can. Restore her hope, her spirit. Bring her back to life."

He once thought no one could love Jishni as he had throughout his life, but was proven wrong in Bail's gesture. It didn't matter to Bail how much pain he might feel at the prospect of Cobo and Jishni resuming their affair, only that it might benefit her, heal her.

Just as Bail had loved the son who wasn't his, he fell in love with the wife he never had wanted, a clean love that was not desperate or longing, but enduring. Abashed by his brother's selflessness, he once again decided that Bail was a better man than he could ever aspire to be.

"I wish I could help her." Cobo said truthfully, "But nothing can replace Archer, but to have Archer found and placed in her arms."

"Then find him for me." Bail begged.

Cobo sat with Bail, and he went spiritwalking, leaving his brother to watch his vacant form. He tried for hours to follow the thread left by Iada, something that might lead him back to the baby. The trail was cold.

"Betnoni's prophecy." Bail whispered low once Cobo had admitted defeat, "She spoke of Janus and Archer, didn't she? One to the Guardian, one to the Invisible. Archer is gone, thought to be a Shodite. Invisible. Janus…..Janus, my son, is the curse going to take him? Is he going to die?"

Cobo had no way of predicting death, for fate was sometimes capricious enough to bend or break the divination of Ver dala Ven.

He could only ease Bail's mind, keep him in the present moment. "Remember the fifth sign, Bail, and have hope. *He will see himself in the invisible, and what is lost is returned.* It is my belief that the fifth sign speaks of them, and of a future time when they will be reunited."

Bail rocked very slowly, like a little boy, his eyes closing with relief, hope, and utter fatigue. Cobo urged him to rest, and he did, lying on the pillows in the receiving room, falling fast to sleep as soon as he got comfortable. Cobo watched over him the way their mother once watched over them when they were ill. Protective, tireless, concerned. "Rest, my brother," because more trouble was to come.

Part Two

Chapter 19

He wore a work tunic that Ksathra's father loaned to him for his trips into Shod City, wearing the hood up to shroud his face. Ksathra always piloted him through the narrow streets, her bright and youthful face shining with beauty that stirred more than his manhood. She was the love of his life.

"Here is the building," she said, and she drew him into a tenement. A rodent crossed his foot as he stepped through the threshold. He jerked back, and stomped on the thing's head with the heel of his boot, cracking its skull.

"Damned capybas." he muttered. "When you said she moved into a better place, is this what you see as better?"

Ksathra grimaced at the carcass. "They are in a cleaner flat." she offered. She motioned him forward. She held his hand as they mounted the steps to the eighth floor.

From the open window, across from the stairwell, a woman was emptying a waste bucket into the alley below. He grimaced and chuckled, pitying in a wry way any poor soul that happened to be walking through that alley.

The flat they visited was filled with three children under the age of five, and one bone weary mother. Seeing them, her weary features brightened.

"Ksathra, daka Bailin!"

Ksathra hushed the woman with a finger over her mouth.

Bailin was less concerned with being found out. Grinning, he said, "Hail Gilmer." and embraced her. "How is your health?"

"Good!" she lied. He could feel her spine. She had lost more weight since the last time he'd had seen her.

"Are you eating?" he demanded.

"Of course! For an educated boy, you ask stupid questions." Gilmer glanced askance at Ksathra, "How does this obtuse dolt hold your attention, Ksathra?"

"He's good company on a cold night." Ksathra replied boldly, and she grinned playfully at him.

Gilmer laughed so hard that she began coughing. Bailin's light manner was gone instantly, and he held her sides as the coughing

411

fit faded. He helped her sit onto the mat in the middle of the floor, and instructed her to lie down and rest.

He sat next to her, at a loss for what to do for her. Ksathra's sister was only five years older than him, but she looked much older. The wasting disease had lined her face, whitened her brown hair, and stolen her youth. In the meantime, she continued to work daily as a seamstress, and was the sole caretaker of three children. Her husband had been killed in an iron works the year before. Bailin had tried to talk his mother into employing another seamstress at the palace, so that Gilmer could work with Ksathra and live in Dralon, but they didn't need another seamstress, and Gilmer's benefactor was loath to lose one of his best in his tailor shop. So Gilmer suffered in unclean conditions, dying all the faster.

Ksathra knelt on the mat and put Gilmer's head in her lap. She stroked her hair, and told her about the goings on at the palace, idle chitchat that calmed Gilmer and kept her company.

Bo, Gilmer's five-year-old son, sidled up to Bailin, and smiled shyly. "Bring me something?" he mouthed, knowing that if he openly asked for something from Bailin, his mother would rise and slap him for begging from a Janti.

Bailin suppressed a smile, and affected a serious demeanor. He glanced surreptitiously at Gilmer, and while her face was turned away, he produced a bag from beneath his tunic. He handed the bag over to Bo, as if he and Bo were exchanging government secrets, and not sweet cakes and fresh fruit. Bo took the bag and opened it and gasped his pleasure.

"Share with your sisters." Bailin ordered sharply.

Gilmer glanced at her children, all emptying a bag of goodies, and she clucked at Bailin. "You spoil them."

"It's nothing they don't deserve." he said, watching them eat their treat with relish. It was a mundane dish at the palace, one Bailin used to take for granted. But there was much that Bailin used to take for granted before he fell in love with Ksathra. He never gave much thought to the world she came from until she introduced him to its immortal heartaches. He was once as blind as his family, all far too preoccupied by their own petty intrigues to see the real troubles in Jantideva.

They weren't oblivious anymore, Bailin mused regretfully. Jantideva's troubles came right through the palace doors and stole his brother. Now, the Shodites had the daka's attention. Only now.

It was too late for Gilmer, and so many more that were already dead.

He held Gilmer's hand, and feigned gaiety as he described the snippet of the Dilgo wedding celebration his mother and father allowed him to view, of the giants and their open orgy, and the odd shaped human named Buhj, who was a Ryslac-Toscocti. His mother spoke of defining each Ryslac clan as a race unto itself, and offering them Janti representation on the Alliance council.

She embraced the warped humanoids easily enough. But the Shodites? They were not people, they were subordinates, animals to be used and stabled.

He kept the latter to himself, afraid of voicing his own caustic opinions too loudly. He held a hot anger in his heart for his family, his ascendants. To voice his anger would give rise to his rage, and he wasn't certain what he wanted to do yet with his rage. He wasn't like Taen, prone to sudden bursts of violence when crossed. He was smarter. He thought in terms of strategy. Someday he would rule Jantideva, and he'd see that the wrongs against the Shodites were corrected.

And Ksathra would be his bride. He held firm onto that dream. No one would take Ksathra away from him, and no one would take Jantideva away from him now that it was to be his.

Gilmer fell asleep on her sister's lap. They stayed while she napped, talking about nothing important, joking with each other half heartedly while a question hung between them. How long before Gilmer faded away?

It was twilight as they left her flat, and they held hands and walked silently from the tenement in Track five to the windrider station in Track four. Usually, Bailin kept his head down to avoid recognition. Shod City was a dangerous place for a Janti, especially for a daka. Though he supported Solien's Soldiers, he could easily fall prey to the rebels. He was the enemy.

Tonight, he happened to glance up in time to recognize a woman going into building forty-eight. She was covered with

413

blisters, but her features were unmistakable. She was Iada, the woman his father was searching for all over Jantideva.

His heart pounding, he gripped Ksathra's hand, and pulled her off course. He didn't know why he followed Iada. He wouldn't turn her over to the Pliadors. Besides, his father had admitted, lamented really, that she no longer knew where Archer was located. No one knew, except, perhaps, the Zarian that had rescued him from the clutches of death.

"Then why hunt her?" Bailin had asked his father the day before.

Bail answered with utter seriousness, "She is a criminal."

"But she didn't have anything to do with Archer's kidnapping, did she? She just happened to find herself with baby, a Shodite baby, she thought.....right?"

"Bailin, don't be impudent at a time like this!" Bail had shouted.

His parents had been shouting too much, of late. At each other, at Bailin and Voktu, at the servants. They were out of control.

He entered the building and caught sight of Iada as she disappeared into the stairwell leading into the basement.

"Rav'el," Ksathra said, calling him by his code name for their Shod City excursions, "Where in the name of your consha are you taking me?"

"I saw someone I know." he replied, and he hurriedly led the way down the narrow, and crowded, steps.

"Who?"

He didn't reply.

In the subbasement, he jostled through the crowded corridor to reach the flat he'd seen her enter.

The door was open, like all the doors on the floor. Without announcing himself, Bailin entered, towing Ksathra inside behind him.

Iada was sitting in a corner, resting. She glanced at the apparently Shodite couple, and frowned deeply. "Are you children to live here now?"

At a loss for words, Bailin faltered.

Ksathra jumped in and said, "Yes. Is the room clean?"

"As clean as any." she replied without moving to rise. She didn't look as if she had the strength to rise. The blisters on her arms and face were drying. They were obviously lume burns.

Bailin's eyes went from the burns on Iada's arms, to the scratchings on the wall. Words, in rough script. Recognition of the ideas conveyed caused his jaw to slacken. He released Ksathra's hand, and touched the score marks.

"Shelon," he whispered.

Iada nodded. "He lived in this flat for a time." she said casually, though there was a tinge of pride in her tone.

"See how his ideas have evolved." Bailin said to Ksathra, "He must be the foremost thinker of our time. Why won't my parents listen to him?"

"The older Shodites are set in their ways," Iada said, "but as long as the youth is attentive to Shelon's ideas, Shodites have a chance."

She struggled to rise. Bailin went to her and offered her an arm. She took his hand and once she got to her feet, she caressed the tell tale softness of his hand and looked warily into his face.

"A daka," she growled tiredly as she recognized Bail's features in Bailin's face. "So, the lume marker is still with me. Fine, kill me now, I don't care. I am not leaving my home."

She sneered at him and moved back into her corner. She leaned against the wall, and winced as she made contact. She was in obvious discomfort.

Bailin peered earnestly into her face. "I'm not one of my father's heartless lackeys, Iada," he said, "I won't turn you in. I didn't find you because of your lume exposure. I happened to see you in the street."

"You come to Shod City often, daka?" she interjected sarcastically, and she glanced at Ksathra. "Are you trading for quilts, or wraps for your lady?"

"We were visiting my sister." Ksathra replied.

Iada looked at her mournfully. "So you've sold yourself for his affections. Better you should prostitute yourself on the streets of Shod, earn your name as a craven whore among your own."

415

"Don't speak with disrespect to the woman I love," he chided calmly, though her insult against both Ksathra and himself rankled. "her name is Ksathra, if you wish to address her at all."

Iada's brows shot up, and she laughed ironically. "A Janti defending his Shodite whore. I am impressed, Ksathra. You hold his affections in a tight grip. Ah, but he is a young boy. He'll grow out of his liberalism in time to marry well. Won't you, daka?"

Bailin chose to ignore her insults. She had slurred her words. She was not a well woman. "You are suffering from lume sickness, Iada. If you come with us, we can take you to someone who will medicate you and look after your burns."

"A-ha....in the Keep, right?"

Ksathra stood at Bailin's side to look into her eyes. "My mother is a nurse, of sorts."

"A tremendous nurse." Bailin agreed. Felda had kept Gilmer feeling well far longer than the average victim of the wasting disease could expect to function. "Ksathra's family has a cottage in Dralon. It is safe there, now that my mother has forbidden the Pliadors from harassing the palace staff."

"It was enough they burned half the village, wasn't it?" Iada asked Ksathra pointedly.

Bailin gently took her by the arm. "You can lean on me."

"Wait, Bailin," Ksathra said, "If you recognized her so easily, won't it be dangerous to take her on a public transport?"

"Yes......what should we do?"

"My shawl"

"No." he said, and he removed the hooded Shodite tunic that hid an expensive silk shirt. "We are almost at the docking bay. If I am recognized by the Pliadors, we won't be stopped, or questioned."

"If you are recognized by my people, you could be assaulted!" Ksathra objected.

"Better listen to her, Janti," Iada slurred. "She's right, you know!"

Bailin shook his head soberly at both women, and offered his tunic to Iada. "It's a chance I'll take for you, Iada."

416

Iada's sarcastic demeanor slackened to disbelief. Her hand wavered as she reached for the tunic.

"This is a strange way to make an arrest, daka."

"Call me Bailin," he invited, "And you aren't under arrest."

Bailin adjusted the cowl hood so that her face was concealed, and he and Ksathra took her by the arms to lead her out of the building. He wasn't recognized as a daka as he emerged into the trading center, but a few eyes did travel from his expensive shirt to the baggy work pants he wore. Through the trading center they were given a wide berth. Bailin suspected that the traders believed he was a robber. They met with no harassment at the public docking bay, nor did the Shodites who were also on their way to Dralon, after having recognized the daka among them, make a move to greet him with anything more than a stare of disbelief. He worried only about the latter gossiping about his being out with Ksathra, rather than their recognizing Iada. He feared nothing but the threat of his mother trading his lover away to another house before he could reach a legal age, and he knew she would if she discovered that Bailin was sneaking out with Ksathra.

He got off in Dralon with Ksathra and Iada, and though he was late for supper he walked them the distance to Ksathra's home. Her cottage was one that wasn't damaged by the Pliadors. It was on the outskirts of the Shodite village, near the seaside and Master Lodan's premises. The latter probably saved their home. Lodan was so well respected that no one cared to disturb his home.

Ksathra's father had built their cottage sixteen years ago, when he and Felda, and their daughters were traded to palace service. It was a cozy cottage, several times larger than a flat in Shod City and with amenities that rivaled the lower class Janti homes in the Center-plex. The Ona Shodites lived well in Dralon, those who still had homes.

Ksathra let Bailin help Iada into the warmth of the cottage, and followed, closing the door behind them. Ksathra's parents were sitting by the fire, eating fresh bread. Seeing daka Bailin with Iada brought them to their feet.

"She is suffering from lume sickness. Can you help her, Felda?"

"I will try." Ksathra's stoic mother replied.

Felda drew Iada into the bathhouse, and sat her down on a bench to look at the burns. Iada told the story of how she'd received them without rancor, nor any emotion. "Unless you have a lume anti-toxin, there is nothing you can do for me," she slurred after finishing her harrowing story, "I'm not even certain I'll respond to the anti-toxin at this point. Better not to waste the medicine and let me die."

Felda pursed her lips. "You may feel like you are going to die, Iada, but you aren't going to die, not now or soon after." She got up and went through a cabinet, pulling out a box of medicines. She glanced soberly at Bailin, "You did the right thing, bringing her to me. I can help her. But you! You need to get home!"

"Yes ma'am." he said obediently.

Ksathra walked him out, and paused at the cottage door. They'd been lovers for a year, yet their goodnight kisses outside her parent's home were always hesitant, shy. He tasted her lips, and put his hands on her waist, then broke away as he heard her father's voice calling her inside.

Ksathra stared into his eyes, smiling wistfully. "The night after next, I will be in the palace late. I can stay over, and not be missed here."

His heart, and his groin, quickened at the prospect of being with her in two nights.

He kissed her again, despite her father, who was still calling for her to come in.

"Until then." he whispered.

She went inside, and closed the door on him.

He took the footpath that a few of their servants used, leading from Dralon to the palace. It was half a span, an hour walk, but enough time and enough of an exercise to work out his immediate need for Ksathra.

By the time he reached the palace his mind was on Iada, and Shelon. Cleses.....but only the Janti authority class saw him as a demon. Bailin saw him as a powerful figure, misguided in his earlier attempts to get the attention of the Janti. The murder of Pliadors sent a powerful message, but lacked refinement. Now, the sit-downs in Eller, there was an action that got attention. Ksathra had heard from a cousin that Shelon had organized the sit-downs.

A surprising change of pace for the man that wrote, "Kill the Janti who owns you, and you are a free man. War with the country that cages us, and we will be a free people. The Janti are not worth the air they breathe. Let them die, and make room for New Shodalum."

He was no less radical, but the sit-downs spoke of a genuine feeling for human life, regardless of their enemy's place in society.

Unlike the daka's methods, Bailin thought caustically. He couldn't exorcise Iada's accusation against his father from his mind. "I woke sick, in the Keep. I should have known that daka Bail wouldn't have released me without placing a marker in my lungs."

His father had practically killed her to find Archer. Bailin wanted his little brother back, too, but didn't understand why his father couldn't see how wrong it was to hurt people to that end. What made daka Archer's life more important than the life of Iada, or the hundreds in Shod City who were slaughtered during the search for Jem Jin? Because Archer was a daka? Or because Archer was a Janti? And why would either circumstance give daka Bail the right to choose who lives, and who dies?

Strolling through the palace, comparing his home with Gilmer's, he wondered what gave him the right to live as he did, while so many lived in abject poverty.

"You're late for supper." Haggins reproached as Bailin entered the dining hall. At the table were Voktu, their Uncle Kinn, aunt Sual, and their cousins. He was relieved to note that his father was not home yet, to question his whereabouts. Nothing was worse than submitting himself to his father's wrath.

"I know and I am sorry, Haggins. But, where's mother?"

"With Janus, in the nursery."

"Again tonight?"

"I'm afraid so."

He took his place next to his brother, and ate in silence, listening to Kinn and Sual discuss a play they'd recently seen, then the color they'd like to have in their apartment when they redecorate. Idle talk for idle people.

419

Before retiring to bed Bailin went to see his mother in the nursery. She was laying down, but not sleeping. She didn't look well. Janus slept in a warming bed nearby.

"How are you this evening, mother?" he asked, sitting her bed.

She let out a airy groan, and grabbed his arm tightly. "Bail....where is Cobo?"

Chilled by the glazed look in her eyes, he replied, "I'm Bailin, mother. Father hasn't returned yet from his mission to Dilgopoche."

She released his arm, and squinted at him. "Oh.....Yes, I see now. You look so very much like your father did when he was your age. Just as Taen took after....." and she faltered, laying back and placing a hand to her head. She mumbled, "I have Ver dala Ven on my mind. Your father should be coming home with him soon.....is it day or night?"

"Night." he replied.

"Night." she repeated numbly. "My dear one, you should retire. You have your studies to think about."

"Yes mother." he said, and he stood, and bent over her and kissed her on the forehead.

She patted his face, looking him in the eyes, and she smiled at him. "Did I ever tell you that I am very glad you are my son?"

Bailin paused, a frown crooking his mouth. No, she never had. Taen was always their favorite, the son they doted on, the heir apparent. Bailin was the second son, the runner up, and nothing he did merited much attention. Hearing her acknowledge him, even in a drugged state, filled him with emotion.

"Thank you for saying so," he replied thickly, doing his utmost to keep control of his emotions. "Sleep well."

"If I fall to sleep at all, it will be a better sleep than I've had in weeks."

"Archer will be found." It was the only comforting thing he could think of to say.

Dry eyed, sad, she shook her head. "They will not find him, Bailin. He is the sacrifice." she looked at him, her expression earnest and sane, though her remarks made her sound unbalanced. "All through the history of the Silence, the Guardian has required the daka to make a blood sacrifice to pay for our evils. It is the

420

curse of the dakas. My own parents lost a child. My sister was four, and killed in a windrider accident. My father's brother died young. My great grand parents lost a child.....you look through history, Bailin, and you will see. Each of us must make a sacrifice. Someday, you will make yours. I hope when that day comes, you are stronger than I am to face it."

"Mother," he said lowly, "wouldn't it be better to try and appease the Guardian, rather than wait for his wrath?"

She huffed a knowing laugh and closed her eyes. "You are young and naive, Bailin. Now go. Get a good night's sleep."

He went to his room, but instead of going to bed, he entered his study theater, a smaller version of the entertainment theaters in the High Room, and setting a light hand on the oval ariq stone by his desk, gained access to the Alliance library. He requested the historical records of the dakas. His genealogy went back nearly ten thousand years. He didn't bother to read that far back. He went back ten generations, and just as his mother warned, there seemed to be a "sacrifice" under every rule. Every daka lost a young child.

Bailin scanned the history of each daka. Written by Janti librarians, the history predictably lauded their actions, and played down their atrocities.

He was deep in his reading about his own Grandfather as his brother quietly entered his study theater. Seeing Voktu out of the corner of his eyes, he didn't bother looking up. With a sneer he often reserved for his pesky younger brother, he said, "I didn't hear you announce yourself, Vok."

Voktu sat on a chair near Bailin's desk. He was darker than Bailin or Taen, and many remarked that he was the image of their grandfather, Janus. "What were you doing that kept you so late tonight?"

"I went to hear Gilibea at the Edan theater." he lied easily.

"Oh...." he nodded as if he accepted the lie, but countered with, "Then why did you walk in from Dralon?"

Bailin flicked a wary and irritated glare at Voktu. "What were you doing, spying on me?"

"Haggins sent me looking for you. I saw you from the High Room garden."

"What business is it of yours what I do with my time?" Bailin snapped. "You aren't father, or mother. You are just a boy, hardly old enough to ride."

Voktu wasn't fazed by the taunt. He quipped in return, "Amazing that my eyes are open, I am so young."

"Get out of my room." Bailin ordered impatiently.

Voktu looked at the scrolling information that surrounded the image of their grandfather Janus, and winced. "You're studying the Declaration of Old Rathia? How boring. I hope I never reach your level in schooling."

"You'd rather remain an ignorant slank than study a few boring subjects?" Bailin countered hotly.

"I don't need to know much to be Kai'gam'Mod."

Bailin barked a loud laugh.

Voktu straightened, mocking indignity. "I have been practicing! You watch! I will someday be a master, rivaling Master Kru Dok."

"You'll never be anything more than my sniveling little brother." Bailin shot back, still laughing.

"So say you, daka Bailin!" he shouted heartily, and he leaped to his feet and performed a few smart kai'gam dances for Bailin's benefit. It was enough to make Bailin laugh all the more.

"Stop, stop it, you clown!" he begged, "I can't study with you prancing around like an Olla girl at the follies."

Voktu stopped, and genuine admiration for his older brother crossed his features. "So, you've been to the follies?"

Bailin brushed chagrin off his face with a quick swipe of his hand, and answered as if it were the most mundane show he'd ever seen. "Of course. I'm a man, all men go to the follies at least once."

"Hoo!" Voktu shouted, "Father wouldn't agree! He'd have your tail if he knew you were sneaking off to watch women disrobe at the follies! Was that where you were tonight?"

Bailin, suddenly presented with a perfectly appalling alibi, decided to let Voktu draw his own conclusions. "It's none of your business."

Voktu mocked an Olla girl dance, swinging his shoulders provocatively. "And to think Haggins was worried you'd been kidnapped, too."

Bailin's humor sunk. "He was worried about me?"

Voktu continued to dance like an idiot. "Dreadfully worried. But, everyone has been jumpy since Archer was snatched." Finally, he stopped dancing, and his own humor plummeted. "Me too. Next time you run off to ogle Olla girls, have the decency to come home before dinner."

"Yes, of course." Bailin replied, hushed by the seriousness in his brother's face. "I'm sorry I worried you."

Voktu shrugged as if it weren't a problem. "I forbid anything to happen to you. Without you, I'd be heir apparent, completely ruining my chances at a decent career in the kai'gam arena."

Bailin suppressed a laugh. "Don't forget your career as an Olla girl."

Voktu's wide mouth grew a wide, almost churlish, grin.

"You wait and see. I'll be a warrior."

The thought of his jokester baby brother as a warrior made Bailin laugh in earnest.

❧❧❧❧❧❧❧❧❧

She woke that morning with the need to pull herself together. She feared spending one more day wallowing in her horror of depression, fearing in the back of her mind that if she let one more day go by, she would spend the rest of her life huddled in the corner of some dark room, unable to function as a daka or a mother to her children. Despite her fatigue, she dressed grandly in a purple multi-layered gown, had her hair done, her face painted, and adorned her gown and hair with a glimmering array of gems. She was going to the Alliance Congress today, to confront the mounting problems she had been ignoring, and she intended to look the part of a daka.

Though she intended to act as a daka today, she had no intentions of leaving Janus at home, vulnerable. By her chair, a warming bed for Janus had been placed, and it was there that he slept as her first appointment of the day arrived.

Jishni was still groggy from the sedatives she'd taken the night before, but she felt capable to face Bery Erd'Als, Director of the office of Shodite Affairs. However, if she'd known that Grav Tulkue has also planned on attending this meeting, she would have canceled it, outright.

Bery was a diminutive man in stature and nature, and easily intimidated and cowed. As soon as he began speaking, informing her of the abundance of grievances from Shodites that his office had been receiving since the announcement concerning the testing centers, Grav began interrupting him and dominating the conversation. Bery seemed unable to take charge, and finish his presentation. It was as if Grav did not want the daka to hear about the numbers of Shodite parents complaining of missing children.

Jishni had read enough of Bery's initial report to know why he stood before her on this morning. The Shodite mothers and fathers were told a variety of lies about their missing babies, that they were traded to different benefactors, or that the babies took ill and died of natural causes. Never the truth, nor did the center directors and techs ever bother to prove themselves to the Shodites with documents or the corpse of a child. Parents were left to grieve, and wonder.

Her temper shortened by her own grieving, Jishni quickly had enough of Grav's stupidity, his defending the honor of the professionals at the testing centers. She sharply told him to shut up and sit down.

Grav paled, and obeyed her, but not without glaring at her as if she had no right to steer a meeting that was being held in her private chamber.

"Bery," she said, "I want you to continue recording the information on the missing children, and do your best to match them with the records at the testing centers. Those who do not have apparent records, we will assume they were rescued by the Zarian underground. The list of those children we suspect were rescued will be given to all the Alliance council members, so that whoever is aiding the underground can pass the list on. Perhaps we can reunite a few Shodite families."

"Ludicrous," Grav interjected, "As if the Shodites do not have enough children. You'd bring home the lame and useless? At whose cost? Will their benefactors take in the lost ones?"

"Grav," she said, her tone even and controlled, "I will have you ejected from this meeting if you do not keep your mouth shut."

"Do you think that in your delicate condition, you are strong enough to make the important decisions for Jantideva?"

She threw her head high. "Would you prefer it was Bail sitting here, Grav? For, if so, I would be happy to have him take my place as soon as he returns from Dilgopoche. But until then, you are stuck with me. And unless you would like to be physically ejected from this meeting, and barred from the Council until further notice, I suggest you not second-guess me again. I am the daka. You will do yourself a favor by remembering who it is you are speaking to in such an insufferably impertinent tone."

Reluctantly, he sunk back into his seat and remained silent.

She said to Bery, "Contact the Crier, as well. I want the Crier to publish the names and ages of the missing. I want Jantideva to see the appalling numbers of children that may have been eradicated. I want our people to open their eyes, their hearts." she added huskily.

Bery lowered his gaze, unable to look at the slivers of tears standing in her eyes.

Nan, who was waiting in the antechamber for Jishni to need her, entered the chamber. "Daka Bail is here." she said with an assistant's calm.

Hope flew through her that he'd returned with Cobo. "We will continue our meeting at another time." she told the two men abruptly, and she rose from her seat. "Bery, I have your reports, I will read them."

"I will make a rebuttal." Grav promised gravely.

"Looking forward to it," she lied, knowing she intended to erase whatever communication she received from him the second it was received.

The two men crossed paths with Bail. Grav muttered that he was happy to see the daka had come home.

In their privacy, Jishni allowed herself to rush to Bail. "Is he in Ona?" she wanted to know, "Or did he come with you?"

Bail's weary frown deepened. He looked tired. He hadn't shaven in several days. His rust flight suit smelled of the Dilgos....and his breath smelled of spice brandy. Heavily of spice brandy.

"What is it?" she demanded when he didn't answer her quickly enough, "Where is he? Take me to him."

"Jishni, sit down."

She placed her hands on his chest. "I don't need to sit."

Bail sighed, and took her hands into his. "He didn't return with me. He's not coming."

She pulled her hands away from Bail's, and touched her forehead. "Not coming?"

"He's been busy with Taen," Bail explained, "since the coronation. Our son is a monarch, and Cobo is his....Ver dala Ven. He doesn't have time for our problems."

"No time for Archer?" she asked dully.

"He tried to find Archer." Bail told her, "But without luck. There are numbers of babies in the world that are about Archer's age, size.....appearance...."

Incredulously, she demanded, "Surely he can tell my son apart from other children? He is a daka! He is kin! His mind should shine like a beacon for Cobo!"

"Jishni, you know the limits of Cobo's abilities. He can pull the truth out of an individual, but if the person he is probing doesn't know the truth," Bail looked away. Patiently, gently, he went on to say, "Archer didn't have enough time with us to make a lasting impression of us in his mind. His memories are now of strangers, not us."

"I cannot accept that Archer is lost to Ver dala Ven." she whispered, "And why wouldn't Cobo come to me? Why?"

Bail's lips trembled with anger, and sorrow. "For the same reason he left us eighteen years ago, Jishni. Because you love him too much."

Warily, she turned on Bail. "He said that to you?"

"You've said it to me."

Fuming, he abruptly turned on his heel and intended to stalk out of her chambers. He flung the door wide open.

Grav Tulkue, and a throng of his supporters impeded him. The gathering had obviously been planned in advance.

"What is this?" Bail questioned sharply of Grav.

Grav met Bail's eyes defiantly. "If the daka continues to take the grievances of the Shodites, I demand that she record the grievances of her citizens, as well."

Her frayed nerves could take no more. She pushed past Bail, and forced her way out of her office, driving Grav and his supporters back. "Have these people lost children in the testing centers?" Jishni demanded hotly.

"They have lost money on defective Shodites, and wish to lodge their complaints to the daka." he said with utter seriousness.

Jishni's ears became hot with a flash of anger. In as controlled a tone as she could muster, she said, "Very well then." and in a loud voice, she said to the gathering, "As it is Grav Tulkue's responsibility to look after the affairs of the Janti, you will make your complaints to him."

"Daka!" he reproached, "How could I possibly meet my duties to the council and take on such a horrendous task?"

She cocked a brow at him. "Indeed. I was wondering the same about my own duties, not to mention the infant still in my care." she gestured into her office, and to the sound of a newly wakened baby in a warming bed, "If you wish to have me hear out their grievances, you will do what Bery has done for me with the Shodites. You will screen their grievances, and make out a report summarizing their difficulties as well as graphing their losses. And, in the interest of fairness, their grievances will also be heard in the Crier." raising her voice again, she said, "We can have the Crier publish your sorrowful tales of lost profits right next to the names of missing babies. I am sure all Alliance subjects will sympathize with your horrible suffering, indeed, I am sure the Shodites will, too. Perhaps they will pass over your ancestral homes during their next riot."

Grav's allies flicked glances to each other. She could see a few shifting on their feet. None of them were willing to put themselves in a compromising position for their own cause. Too many people, Janti included, were sickened at the idea of babies being destroyed, even if the babies were Shodites.

Bail stood at her side, and firmly dismissed the gathering by saying, "Grav Tulkue's chambers is at the end of the corridor, on your left."

And in a low malevolent tone, he said to Grav, "I will summon the Watchers if you do not leave immediately."

Grav cheeks turned crimson, and his mouth set in a grim line. "You have not heard the last of this, daka."

He turned, and made his way through the crowd. His supporters lost heart, and filed out after him, throwing wary glances at Jishni and Bail. Jishni could read in their faces their concerns about their social standings, and their political standings, now that they'd angered the dakas. She expected that few of them would follow Grav to his office, and she was proven correct. Grav turned one way down the corridor, and his supports went in the opposite direction.

Bail's moment of anger with Jishni was spent on Grav. Now, as he looked at her, he just seemed weary.

"I'm leaving for Zaria tomorrow morning." he said abruptly, and in a way that made her feel like it was a spur of the moment decision. "I got a lead on Archer. It is probably nothing. It came from one of Trev's contacts. They usually aren't very reliable, but it's a lead."

"Is it something you should follow up on your own?"

He averted his eyes guiltily. "It's something I want to follow up on, Jishni."

"When are you returning?"

"I don't know." he replied. Wordlessly, he walked away from her, his gait relaxed.

Watching him leave, she was suddenly overwhelmed with the notion that he was walking out of her life. Though their marriage could never be dissolved, it would be easy enough for him to leave her. He had his life as a military commander. He could live as a soldier on any military installation and no one would question his duty, or dedication to Jantideva.

In the beginning, when they were first married and Jishni still had hopes of maintaining her love affair with Cobo, she used to wish he would leave. It would have been better to live without a husband than to live in a cold and loveless relationship under the same roof, as her parents had for twenty-nine years. Her mother's death seemed to be a relief to the seventy-two year old Janus. He took lovers, and learned to laugh again. Jishni hated that her sweet mother had made his life a misery. Better that she and Bail live their lives in utter separation, than to eventually wish each other dead.

The friendship they'd built between them in the place of marital love was far more than she had expected. Before Cobo had resurfaced, she would have fought hard to maintain his friendship and companionship.

She took a few hesitant steps toward his retreating back, and stopped. She didn't want him to leave, but didn't know how to ask him to stay. If she were to tell the absolute truth, she'd have to admit that she still loved Cobo. He would certainly leave her, then, and never return. The only lie that would make him stay with her was that she was in love with him, and no longer wanted Cobo. A lie like that would only hurt him, and her, once the truth was discovered.

And still yet, she almost shouted at his back the lie.

She wondered at the tangle of her own emotions as he disappeared around the bend of the corridor.

ৡৢৡৢৡৢৡৢঌৡঌঌ

Through a night of study, and a day of thinking, Bailin came up with an idea. It was legal, and it served the Alliance, though he knew it would be unpopular with Jantideva, and probably scorned by his own parents. Despite the latter, he decided he'd present his idea to them, nonetheless, just in case the Guardian had opened their ears to listen.

He'd planned to speak to them at supper that night, but was put off by their tense and uncommunicative mood. His father announced his trip to Zaria, but nothing was said of his trip to Dilgopoche and questions on the matter were fended off with uneasy haste.

Later in the evening, Bailin found his mother in the sitting room of their suite, looking out the windows at the Tronos sea. He

429

hesitantly intruded, clapping as he entered the room to announce himself.

She turned toward him, and he saw that his mother had tears in her eyes. She wiped them away quickly, and gestured that he join her.

"Are you done with your studies already?" she asked him, as if it were any night.

"Yes....where is father? I have something important to discuss with both of you."

"He is preparing for his trip." she demurred, and her eyes wandered to the sight of the sunset over the Tronos. "If you have something of import to share with us, let me be the first to hear it. I'm afraid your father won't be available to us.....for a long time to come."

Uncertainty caused him to hesitate. He realized by the crease in his mother's brow as she spoke of his father's leaving that she wasn't weeping for Archer tonight, as she had every night since his disappearance, but for his father. He felt a fresh surge of anger toward Bail, piling on top of the anger simmering in him for how Iada had been poisoned. His mother desperately needed him, and he was leaving with Trev for adventures in Zaria. "You don't need him, Mother," Bailin said firmly, and he reached out for his mother's hand. "I am here."

She was taken aback to be read so well by her son, and she smiled self-consciously. Squeezing his hand, she said, "I'm glad for your strength, my son."

She gestured for him to sit, and she sat in her favorite chair. Bailin's stomach trembled as he sat across from her.

"Mother, you suggested that I should research the deaths of daka children through the generations," he started, "I did and I found you were right. Every generation has had to endure their own sacrifice, and since Betnoni left us, it usually happened after a daka purposefully, and maliciously, harmed the Shodites in some way."

His mother watched his face knowingly, but said, "I was heavily medicated when I said those things, Bailin. It was the drugs talking."

430

"No, mother, listen. I've been studying the Declaration of Old Rathia," he cracked his knuckles nervously as he spoke. "I found an....error in the Declaration. It might have been overlooked by accident, but I tend to believe it was purposefully ignored because Old Rathia would have brought a high profit to Jantideva. In the Pact of Zren Rouge, in article forty two, subsection three, concerning the rights of Shodalum; Even if the rights to the land was granted to a country other than Shodalum or Jantideva, both Shodalum and Jantideva reserved the right to decide what was done with that land.....in a sense, we became partners with Shodalum concerning Old Rathia. Of course that was before Shodalum left the Alliance, but even in that case, the pact still stands. In short, when Grandpa Janus laid claim on the land in order to expand the industrial complex of the area, he ignored article forty two when he didn't inform the Shodalum Elders of his claim, and didn't gain their approval for its use."

"Yes. I seem to remember that the Alliance Council overturned Article forty two on the basis that under Old Rathian laws, the land would have been ours, anyway."

"But, according to Alliance law, we disposed of all laws that stood before, including the Rathian Laws of Conquest. The Pact of Zren Rouge was clear on this. In Article twelve, it specifically states that the laws of Conquest have no meaning to the peaceful World Alliance. If that is true, then the original claim Rathians had on Northern Shodalum is also nullified, therefore the land belongs to Shodalum."

"Shodalum is no longer subject to the laws of the Alliance, because they are not in the Alliance." Jishni replied.

"But they were when the Pact of Zren Rouge was put together. At that time, had the Alliance not been influenced, or maybe intimidated by daka Corinthian's Rathian slaying army, the Alliance may have ruled on behalf of Shodalum, and given back their land, instead of leaving the land in limbo for thousands of years."

"Yes, perhaps," she conceded, "It can be a compelling argument, if Shodalum ever insisted on being heard in the matter. But they have abdicated whatever rights they had to that land by turning their back on the rest of the world."

431

Bailin moved forward in his chair and looked significantly into his mother's eyes. "Days after Grandpa Janus overturned the Pact of Zren Rouge, Aunt Kama was killed."

Jishni recoiled from him, putting her back into the chair. "They were unrelated incidents." Jishni replied quickly, though she was clearly shaken by his remark.

"During the four year famine in the twenties," Bailin continued, "Great grandpa Herd strictly rationed the food given to Shodites in order to feed the Janti. Many Shodites starved....during the famine, his six year old son died after eating bad meat."

"I remember my father telling the story of his brother's terrible death." she conceded, adding, "It was an ironic coincidence."

"In the generation before, daka Talla died at the age of six after being hit mistakenly with a lume. A few days before his death, his mother, daka Cosima, had secretly employed the Pliadors to randomly eliminate six hundred thousand Shodites from Shod City, and they did so with a lume bomb, because they could think of no easier way to control their population. It was called an accident, but the truth came out years after Cosima's death. And then there was Cosima's father, Brig-"

"I see your point, Bailin," she interjected, "and I do know the history." She lowered her head into her hand. "What did I do, Bailin?" she asked softly. "Tell me my crime against the Shodites, and I will make recompense."

"Well...." he said, "I'm not sure, Mother. For a daka, you a very liberal, though your Pliadors still employ brutality in order to keep the peace in Shod City. Can't say that is anything new. You condone the unfair treatment of Shodites by your inaction, which, actually, isn't new either-"

"Stop," Jishni said, "I've heard these words, only they came from a Zarian's lips. I will not hear them from yours."

"Archer isn't dead." he continued with certainty, "Don't you see how significant that is, Mother? The Guardian has let you off with a warning. I bet if you were to heed the Guardian's will, Archer would be returned."

"What is the Guardian's will Bailin?" his father demanded sharply, "I suppose you've had His lips to your ear lately?"

432

They both started, and looked toward Bail. He was dressed casually, and carried his travel log.

"In a way," His confidence was decidedly shaken by his father's sudden arrival. He could tell that he had been reaching his mother. Reaching his father would be harder.

To his mother, he said, "Like Uncle Cobo said, it's your duty to free the Shodites. Until you do, Archer will not be returned."

Bail flung his travel log on the desk in the corner, the clatter of it made a contemptuous sound, and he stalked to the windows. Looking at Bailin, he vehemently said, "Uncle Cobo isn't here to guide us, yet he asked; No, he demanded us to destroy Jantideva, and to do so without his wisdom, his influence. Personally, I think Cobo has gone mad. And so have you if you believe that freeing the Shodites will bring Archer home!"

Bailin stood. He was the same height at his father, a slenderer version of the man he'd admired his whole life, and perhaps resented as well, for he was daka Bail's second favorite son. He was no longer nervous or tentative. He knew he was right, and his righteousness spoke for him.

"I can't count the times I have heard one of you openly disagree with the slavery of the Shodites!" he retorted.

"In private, we can say what we want!" Bail countered, "Before the Alliance, we must speak for Jantideva!"

"But you are right! Slavery is wrong! The Shodites must be freed, and I have come up with a way to do that, without it hurting Jantideva!"

His father's brows had shot up with amusement that was skirting irritation.

"By all means, enlighten us," he invited sardonically.

"The Janti-born Shodites want their freedom," Bailin said urgently, "but the Janti don't want to pay for their freedom, right? They are afraid that freed Shodites in our society will not flourish, but give rise to an impoverished criminalized underclass that our government will eventually have to support without the benefits of having services in trade. So what if we were to give them their freedom, and give them a chance to leave and live in their own country? If we were to give the Shodites Old Rathia, send them there, start them out, and let them fend for themselves as free men

433

and women, it would cost us no more than our initial investment, and the returns would be in knowing we did the right thing for the Shodites!"

Jishni, her eyes gentle, said, "Bailin, your heart is in the right place. But I am afraid that what you are suggesting is not as easy as you might imagine."

"Call it what it is, Jishni," Bail growled, "It's impossible. We cannot advocate giving a homeland to people who have a homeland. Like it or not, what Cleses said is true. They are our brothers, Janti-born, and do not wish to be ejected from Jantideva. Trying to eject them would only cause uprisings and insurmountable diplomatic problems. And what about the Jantidevans living in Old Rathia? Or the squatters that deem to call themselves Rathians? Are they to leave the homes they have known for hundreds of generations so we have a place to put millions of Shodites? Can you imagine the war that would cause? Compare it to the conflicts in Borysenka between rivaling factions, and I think you have a fair assessment of what relations would be like between Old Rathian residents and the Shodites if we were to throw them together."

"I'm not talking about pitting enemies against each other," he said, "I'm talking about adding to the existing settlements. Those Janti don't really live like Janti, and there are so few that live there, they might welcome more settlers, especially Shodites, who are adapted to hard work."

"And what about the Shodites who want to stay in Jantideva?" Jishni asked, "What will we do with them, Bailin? The Janti see them as chattel...that attitude will not change overnight."

"It can change with us." Bailin replied,

Bail huffed his disgust.

Jishni sighed. "Can't you see the broader implications, my son? If we were to abruptly terminate their services, and set them free, and they were to decide to stay in our country, who would feed them until they began to manage on their own? Wouldn't turning our backs on them be a worse crime? We've made them terribly dependent on us."

"As dependant on us as we are on them." Bailin agreed. "If we freed them, and was forced to pay for labor in our factories and

434

in our homes, half the Janti would have to live a less extravagant lifestyle. Some of them may even have to learn how to dress themselves, bath themselves, and feed themselves."

"Your insolence is unwarranted." Bailin countered evenly, "Your mother and I did not set our co-dependence with the Shodites in motion. It was here when we were born. It is not an easy problem to solve."

Bailin felt ashamed of his parents. They knew keeping the Shodites in slavery was wrong, but would do nothing to end the slavery, because it was too complex a problem for them.

Bailin glowered at his father. "I wish to be dismissed."

Jishni looked saddened. "Bailin, don't leave angry."

He may have been swayed to leave in a less abrupt fashion if his father, who was not in the mood to coddle him, hadn't snapped, "Dismissed!"

Without looking into either of their eyes, he stalked out of the sitting room.

ৡৡৡৡৡৡৡৡৡ

"He's headstrong." Bail said contemptuously.

"He thinks with his heart," Jishni said, staring after their son. She smiled. "He'll make a fine leader, someday."

"He'll have to." he replied coldly.

Jishni reluctantly looked to Bail. He was staring out the window, standing nearly in the same place she had been standing earlier. His back was to her. For Jishni, it was a replay of a moment between her parents. If they were forced to speak on some matter concerning the children, Janus's back was invariably put to Lana.

"So, it begins." she said softly.

Bail turned his head slightly without looking at her, his only acknowledgement that she had spoken.

"You wanted to speak to me?" she said flatly, squelching the hurt she felt. She could only feel hurt by his distance if they were in love. They weren't in love. They'd never been in love.

"I want you to keep my travel plans to yourself." he said, "Trev and I are going into Zaria unannounced and incognito. I

435

don't want Plat knowing we are snooping around for Archer. I'm worried they might move him around, and our trail will go cold again."

"You can count on my discretion."

He returned to the view, and a long silence passed between them.

He finally said, "Trev and I are leaving at dawn. If I don't see you before then, I'll say my goodbye now." He turned, and glanced her way as he walked by. "Be well." was all he said.

Jishni returned to the window after he left, and looked out at the sea, her vision distorted by a return of tears.

&&&&&&&&&

Early the next morning, Bailin met Ksathra on the path between the palace and Dralon. She was on her way to work. He was on his way to see Iada. Finding each other was an irresistible coincidence, and they decided, nearly involuntarily, to take advantage of the coincidence and run off into the woods for a stolen moment of intimacy. In soft grass, hastily unclothed, they urgently made love.

Near the end, he whispered to her, "I love you,"

and, "Be my wife, Ksathra, have my children."

And she breathed in reply, "I love you."

and, "It is a fine dream."

Her lack of hope for their future added to his overall blue funk. He felt her hopelessness. His parents would never free her to be his wife. Her freedom and position in the court would imply that Shodites are of equal value to the Janti, a message they'd never allow Bailin to send.

"I will abdicate my position as daka," he replied earnestly, "We can go to Zaria, and marry, and have ten children."

"Ten!" she laughed, "I will grow fat and frumpy if I give you ten children!"

"And I will go bald working all my jobs trying to feed ten children, and a fat, frumpy wife." he replied, smiling finally.

She giggled, and touched his face. "You say such beautiful things to me."

436

"Flowery words are my specialty." he replied wryly.

She peered directly into his eyes. "If you decide to run away to Zaria and take me with you, I will go and be your wife. And, if you decide you must stay here and rule Jantideva, I will stay, and be your concubine. You can come to me when you grow weary of the spoiled girl your parents pair you with."

Her lightly stated remark hurt him, and he rolled away from her. He grabbed his clothing and dressed irritably.

She sat up, looking beautiful in the soft morning light, like the first woman ever created. "Bailin, what is wrong?"

"I don't want you as a concubine, Ksathra."

"My dear, I am just being realistic." She huffed a cynic's laugh. "Besides, what do you think I am now if not your concubine? What do you think the household staff says about me when they notice me leave your room before the dawn? They don't see love. They see you as a lustful young man, and me as a whore."

"Who says those things about you?" he demanded, "I'll personally set them straight!"

Ksathra's cynical features softened. She moved to him, and put her arms around him, propping her chin on his shoulder. "If I am destined to be your concubine for the rest of my life, I will happily serve you."

As his chattel. As his slave.

"No, that can't happen." he said lowly. "If I cannot rule Jantideva with you as my wife, I don't want to be a part of this country."

She caressed his face, a worldly smile on her lips. "You are so easy to love."

She moved away from him and dressed. He watched her, how her hair hung down her back, and draped across her face as she buttoned her work smock. He tried to imagine her as an old and fat and frumpy woman. It was easier to imagine her like her mother, fit and active, and cheerful, with a face that aged gracefully. He wanted to see her age, but not as a slave. He wanted her to be free.

He let her walk out to the path alone, and he waited several minutes before returning to the path himself.

He avoided the busiest center of Dralon, where reconstruction was taking place, and stuck to a less often used path by the sea, through the woods.

He found Felda outside, weeding her garden. In the palace, she was a part of the kitchen staff, and not required to arrive for work until the early afternoon. In the spring and summer, her mornings were usually spent in her garden, producing vegetables for her own family, and many others in Dralon. The Shodites in Dralon had learned how to self govern, and share themselves with each other, like any community. Bailin imagined the Shodites living in their new land as they did in Dralon, but free. They could survive. He saw the Shodites' potential, growing in Felda's garden.

Felda straightened as she saw him, and slapped the dirt off her hands. She greeted him with a smile. "You've just missed Ksathra."

He averted his eyes to the sky, the pleasant tingling afterglow in his crotch causing chagrin that turned his features pink. "I suppose I'll have to see her at the palace later." he replied. "Actually, I came by to see Iada."

"Oh, well, she is doing much better." Felda said, and she gestured toward the house, offering him entry. "She's up and around."

Bailin went into the cottage, and found Iada sorting beans into a kettle. The blisters on her face were peeling, and her skin tone had normalized. She looked up as he entered, and didn't seem surprised to see him.

"Hail to you, daka." she said, and went back to her beans.

"Hail to you." He sat near her, and watched her deft hands pick through the tiny beans. "What are you making?"

"Soup." She said simply.

"Ah ha." He replied, trying to sound casual.

She threw a canny look at him. "What is on your mind, daka? Is it about time for me to go to the Keep, you think?"

"No, not at all." Bailin replied, and suddenly he felt uncertain and boyish with Iada. "Actually, I came to ask you to pass on a message from me, to Shelon."

438

Her fingers stopped working. "I will not lead you to Shelon, boy." She said bluntly, "Kill me now, because I will be no more service to you."

"I don't want you to lead me anywhere, Iada," he said quickly, "It's just….....I think I can help Shelon, and Solien's Soldiers. At least, I hope so."

Chapter 20

In the massive war room of the Rathian Castle, Shelon drank bitter wine and studied his own writings. His manifesto, which he'd committed to heart, read like a Pliadors handbook on how to deal with the shod.

The stories his friends had told him about the mayhem of the riots, and the Pliador reprisals, gave rise to his anger, and angry, he felt an attachment to his old ways, like an attachment he'd feel to a past lover he'd want to bed for old time's sake.

But.......

"If we burn Derick" he said softly, to himself, "in exchange for the lives lost in Shod City, the Janti will strike us again. And we will strike back....and they will strike us.....where does it end? All we are right now is a thorn in Jantideva's side. The day after burning their benefactor's houses down, the Shodites were at work rebuilding. The bloodshed was for nothing. Nothing, and it made more work for us."

He stood and walked around the empty war room. Here, in this place, he'd made many plans. He had long ago urged his men to, *"Show your anger! Bare your fangs! Show them your strength and cause them to fear us!"*

His whispered words reverberated off damp stone walls.

"They recognize themselves in our actions when we turn to killing, and their reflection frightens them." Shelon concluded, "But they are not really frightened of us. We are only Shod, after all."

"Speaking to your Rathian friend?"

He turned quickly at the sound of Gella's voice, and grinned at her. He'd told her about his experience in the torture chamber, of seeing a Rathian that looked like himself. He'd shrugged it off to fatigue, and it made an interesting story to tell, though he half hoped to run into his hallucination again. He could do with some advice on handling the Janti from a people he considered allies of a sort.

"Talking to the walls." he replied.

She approached and leaned her body against his, a welcome touch from a woman who'd taught him more about being a Shodite in three months than he'd learned on his own throughout his lifetime.

"I've been waiting for you." she complained lightly.

"I was just on my way up." he said, though in truth, he'd lost track of time.

She grunted knowingly. "You rarely sleep. What is troubling you? Iada's disappearance?"

His mouth crooked in a frown. A recent arrival to Moom was one of Praj's contacts. He had told Shelon what he'd heard about Iada's arrest, and her escape after being hunted through Nysus. There were no reports of her demise, no reports of seeing her at all in months. Shelon preferred to believe she was well, until he heard otherwise.

"She'll find her way here when she can." he said with assurance, "No, it's Praj. He wants to incite a riot in Derick during the Holy Festival. Derick attracts a million people during the festival. He'd kill them all if he could."

"And you're unsure that it is the right thing to do." she concluded on her own.

"I can't stop thinking about the Eller sit down, and that woman we briefly overhead on the public transport as we were leaving. Remember what she said to her companion? `Why should we be their benefactors if they won't work?' She sounded as if she were ready to trade all her Shodites away. If we can make one benefactor feel this way, why not several million benefactors? Why not all the benefactors? If we could organize a sit down, a permanent sit down, we could shut the country down. The factories wouldn't produce, the farms wouldn't be tilled, the cattle wouldn't be cared for, the shipping lines would be shut down. A non-violent revolution." Shelon said, "It worked for Shodalum."

"Where did you hear that?" Gella asked, smirking.

He smiled into her green eyes. "You have good ideas, my pretty precious one, but there is a cost. If the Janti suffer, so do we. If the Janti go hungry, so do we. How brave will the Shodites be if their bellies are rumbling, and they are being beaten or threatened."

"You are questioning how badly they want their freedom?"

"Yes. Yes I am." he said, "Vengeance is fun and easy, Gella. The desire for vengeance galvanizes the courage of the most faithless and cowardly. I know many who have little faith in change, only a great reserve of hatred for the Janti and a desire to wreak havoc. After all, what are they fighting for? To live like Janti? Even if that was possible, which I doubt very seriously, is it what Shodites should aspire to?"

She caressed his chest. "I hear you thinking about going to Shodalum again."

"A return to our homeland." he said, as a way to confirm her accurate guess. "If only they will take us back. But there are so many of us. Our numbers alone may be too daunting for the Elders. Shodalum is a small country, with few resources." He frowned deeply. "I feel trapped between an ideal and nothing."

"I can take you there. I just can't stay."

He kissed the top of her head. "According to their laws, neither can I."

"Shelon, let's go to bed." she urged.

"Are you tired?" he asked.

"Yes and I want you next to me."

He smoothed her face with his hand, unable to hide his concern. His Gella, who never seemed to want for energy, had been struck with lethargy during the past weeks. She suffered from the first stages of the wasting disease; inability to keep down her meals, fatigue, weight loss. Shelon had started counting the minutes until Iada's return, though he knew if it was the wasting disease, there was no cure.

"Alright." he replied, trying to sound light, "I've grown tired of talking to myself anyway."

He let her cling to him as they went up three flights of stairs. In the common sitting room of their quarters Korba was throwing wood into the fire pit and Praj was speaking in low tones to him.

Shelon hailed a good night to them and took Gella into their room.

He slept for a few hours, and woke as the sky was paling with the earliest warning of dawn. He huddled near Gella for warmth, and felt the urge to wake her and seduce her. He kissed her face, her lips, her hair. She woke, and moved toward him, kissing his neck and cheeks, and abruptly wrenched away from him, her eyes wide with shock. Before he had a chance to ask her what was wrong, she bolted from the bed and knelt by the bucket she kept near in a corner of their room. She wretched violently, though she had nothing in her stomach from the night before.

Shelon got up with her, and held her hair until the last spasm contorted her spine. He rubbed her back, and felt tears come to his eyes, though he refused to let her see them. For her, he smiled, and offered to get her fresh water from the well, and made her comfortable in bed.

He lay next to her, and held her, and worried in silence.

৵৵৵৵৵৸৸৸৸৸

Shodites came and left Moom with frequency. Moom was a resting station for the weary, the fugitive, and those seeking Shelon. The watchman in the tower high above the castle sounded the alarm nearly daily, warning of the coming of travelers on the path leading up the mountain. Praj, Shelon, Korba, and a host of intimidating looking men would disappear into the cavern and wait, as either the welcoming committee for Shodites or an ambush for unwary Janti travelers.

Jurge had watch today. Late in the afternoon, he sounded the warning.

Gella was outside as the bell rang three times. Three people were on the path leading to Moom. She, like the rest of the inhabitants, weren't especially alarmed. Children continued to play. A woman continued to feed a bonfire. Gella continued to damn the muggy cold. She was in awe of the brilliance of the greenery inside the castle walls, but she was tired of the cold, and of her infirmity, which she blamed on the cold.

As Jurge sounded the alarm a second time, alerting them to the nearness of their intruders, the men prepared to defend Moom. They tied sashes on their waists to hold lume weapons, taken from the armory near the cavern entrance. They didn't seem serious. They joked with each other, and laughed. Even as they disappeared down the stone steps, they seemed like a group of drinking companions on their way to a local tavern.

444

Having been met by that force, Gella knew first hand how formidable they were when it was time to defend the castle.

She wandered toward the opening of the cavern, which was near the base of the castle wall, and waited with a throng of women as the new arrivals were greeted below. The wait dragged on for much longer than she'd expected. She drew the blanket she used as a shawl tighter around her shoulders to block out the cold, and pensively wondered if this time the intruders were the enemy. It was twenty, against three. Dispatching three men should have taken no time at all.

She was ready to go down into the cavern and see for herself what was going on as Praj emerged. He had his massive arms crooked around the necks of two men she'd never seen before. He wore a jubilant grin beneath his shaggy blond moustache.

"Moom, meet my brothers!" he shouted, and he grinned at Gella, "They are alive!"

She saw now how they looked like Praj. Blond, lank faces, long bodies, wide shoulders, blue eyes, but they were clean-shaven. They looked young, Korba's age, but rough.

A crowd gathered around the three brothers, and Gella backed away, watching for Shelon among the men disgorging from the cavern.

She caught sight of him, and Korba, and between them, walking with their arms around her, was Iada. She looked thin, and her dark hair had been cut fanatically short.

Gella was taken aback by the sight of her, foolishly so because she had long expected this day to come. She was not prepared to see them together, however, holding each other. The way Shelon's eyes sparkled with happiness made her heart ache. The cold of the outdoors seeped into her bones as she envisioned sleeping without Shelon tonight.

Shelon looked her way, and sobered. He slowed Iada's pace, and dropped his head down and said something to her. Iada glanced at Gella, her expression serious, and nodded knowingly.

Gella pivoted and swiftly walked away from the lovers. She didn't need Shelon to break the news to her, or ask her to leave, and certainly did not want to be told to leave in front of his lover. She knew her place well enough. It was the place she'd occupied with Cobo, as his second choice. She would leave, and she would leave without being told to leave.

She fiercely held back her tears.

"Gella!" Shelon called out to get her attention.

She looked back, and hated herself for doing so. Shelon was trotting after her, and Iada and Korba were close behind. He was intent on verbally ending their arrangement. Did he think she was a tender hearted romantic with foolish ideas?

She broke out into a sprint.

"Gella!" he shouted, this time with a ring of aggravation in his voice.

She wanted only her desert wraps. She could leave when she'd gotten her desert wraps from their room. She'd be happy to leave Moom! Cold, dank, moldy, spooky, Rathian death trap!

She'd trade Moom for her arid desert in Calli in a heartbeat. Or Dilgopoche. Cobo might take her back, if she found him in Dilgopoche.

She slapped her hand on the indentation in the wall, and used all her weight to slide the stone door open. She heard Shelon enter the castle, the others hot on his heels. She slipped through the opening before she had it open all the way and ran up the stairs.

She burst into their room, and went to the wardrobe. She flung open the doors and ripped her desert wraps out, tossing them on the floor at her feet. She looked down at them, panting, trying to decide what to do next. Dress and leave immediately? Whatever she did, she could not stay in this room. She gathered her wraps and turned to put them on the bed.

Shelon filled the doorway. The sight of him caused her to gasp, and a sob escaped her lips. Unable to contain her emotions any longer, she turned away from him, dropped the wraps and covered her face with both hands and wept.

She felt his gentle hands on her shoulders. She wanted too much to feel his touch, that to feel it pained her. She stepped away from his hands, going to the slit window in order to lean against the wall. She felt weak all over, like she was ready to fall in a heap and die.

"Gella," he pleaded, his voice sounding miserable.

She wiped the tears off her face roughly with the palms of her hands. "I know, Shelon. Iada has returned." she said harshly at him. The truth twisted into a painful knot in her chest. She felt ready to succumb to hysterical tears. She glanced toward his form, unable to look into his face. "You don't have to ask me to go. I'll go. Please leave me, and I will gather my things."

"Where do you think you are going?" he demanded, at once irritated. "And what does Iada's return have to do with you wanting to leave?"

She was angered at once for his insensitivity. "Are you enjoying my torment? Does it please you to know I am not as hardened or unfeeling a whore as you thought I'd be? I understood the arrangement. Once Iada returned to you, I was to leave your bed. I accepted it, and now I am leaving."

"Your tears....they are for me?" he asked incredulously, and his voice softening, he said, "I've never seen a woman cry for me, except my mother."

"Pardon me for loving you," she said bitterly, "it seems to be a bad habit of mine, loving men I can't have."

He stepped closer to her, and she reacted by turning her face to the wall. "Please go. Iada is waiting."

In a light and mocking tone, he demanded, "Did I ever, once, mention such an arrangement to you?"

She moved enough to see his presence in her peripheral vision. She was made wary by his sudden change in mood. "It was unspoken." she admitted, "I knew you loved Iada. Korba told me about your relationship with her. I accepted it."

"Ah, yes, Korba." he said, and he chuckled ruefully.

He took her chin in his hand and turned her face, forcing her to look up at him. His eyes were intensely bright, gazing at her in a way that gave rise to just enough hope that her heart hurt all the more.

"I don't love Iada." he said bluntly, "She is my friend. We comforted each other occasionally, a long time ago, but not since she met Praj. She is Praj's lover. Did that little consha tell you that, Gella?"

"No," she whispered, suddenly hurting for a different reason. "Korba lied to me? Why?"

447

"Why do you think? To sway you into his bed! I'd be tempted to kill him for causing your sorrow, if it weren't for the fact that he was the one who brought you to me." He wiped a tear off her cheek with his thumb, then framed her face with both hands. His eyes devoured her face. "You are mine, Gella. And I am yours. You aren't leaving me. I won't let you."

His earnest claim on her was a comfort that bathed her in warmth, and happiness. Without warning, Gella burst uncontrollably into fresh tears. She hated her tremulous emotional instability of late, and quickly covered her hands to hide her face.

Shelon wrapped his arms around her, hushing her, and guided her to the bed. She let him lift her off her feet, and gently lay her down on her back. He stroked her hair, his hand moving on to her arm, her waist, her leg, in one light, continuous motion, sending a thrill throughout her body. She expected they'd make love, but after he kissed her lightly on her tear stained cheek, he pulled away and looked seriously into her face.

"I want you to let Iada to examine you. I briefly told her about your symptoms. I didn't have time to tell her much, because you ran away like you were being chased by a Janti."

Her lips curled tremulously. "It was a shock seeing you with her. I would have fainted if I hadn't run."

"She's waiting to see you now." he said, and amusement sparkled in his eyes, "Will you see her? Or are you still in shock?"

She her lips bent in a smile twisted by relief. "I will see her, but I know what is wrong with me. It is the awful, relentless chill that hangs over this castle. I swear, if I don't see the sun soon, I will wither and die."

His amusement faltered. He quickly averted his eyes, and seemed to force himself into light mood. He stood and went to the door and bade Iada to enter, saying to her, "Your patient promises not to run away from you this time."

Iada closed the door on Shelon, giving them privacy. She looked haggard, and there were scars on her face that weren't there the last time Gella saw her. The bag she carried wasn't her black bag, but a faded cloth satchel. She set it on the bed, and looked down at Gella.

"You've been sick." she said, her tone assuming.

"Shelon thinks I am sick," Gella replied gruffly.

"His judgement is generally sound." Iada said flatly. She sat next to Gella. "Tell me how you have been feeling."

Gella recited her every symptom, a bit uneasy about admitting how terrible she had been feeling. She was trembling, and again feeling emotional.

Iada listened, and seemed to make a decision. She went through the satchel and found a short black wand. She pressed one end to the tip of Gella's finger, and Gella felt a sharp prick. She flinched, and looked at her finger. It was bleeding.

Iada pressed more blood out, and then placed the other end of the wand to her finger, drawing out the droplets of blood.

"What does that do?"

Iada smirked. "You'll find out, soon enough."

꒦꒷꒦꒷꒦꒷꒦꒷

Shelon ignored Praj's brothers ramble on about some trouble they had caused in Padra, his eyes repeatedly finding the closed door. His impatience was manifest in the tapping of a toe, and shifting in his seat. Occasionally, to take a break from his tension, he slid a glare toward Korba. He intended to corner Korba and have a chat with the boy, very soon.

Korba had noticed his glares, and did his best not to look Shelon's way.

As Iada opened the bedroom door, Shelon was on his feet.

"What is afflicting her?" he asked Iada in a hushed tone.

Iada glanced into the bedroom, and then smiled into his eyes. "She'll tell you about her condition."

"Condition. Is it serious?"

Iada sobered dramatically. "It is."

Disbelief crossed his features. He felt she was mocking him.

"Iada, if it is serious, you tell me about it so I can comfort her." he demanded.

Iada refused with a shake of her head, and walked leisurely toward Praj.

"Iada!" he called out incredulously.

Praj grabbed her by the waist and pulled her into his lap. She lay her head on Praj's shoulder, and looked at Shelon expectantly. She pointed to the bedroom.

Furious, he said, "Fine. Splendid doctor you are!"

He stormed to the bedroom door, amending his manner as he crossed the threshold. He closed the door gently, shutting out the shocked laughter that had burst from Praj.

Gella was lying on her side, and watching him. She reached for him, prompting him to go to her, and sit by her. She was clear-eyed, and she wore an enigmatic half smile. He took her hand, and felt she was trembling.

Lowering his eyes, he said, "Tell me quickly, Gella. What is it that has made you sick?"

"First, I must assure you," she said softly, "that I didn't mean for this to happen."

"No one ever means to get sick." he consoled.

"In Strum, with all those men and then with Cobo....I never once had a reason to think this could happen to me."

He looked into her face, truly perplexed. "What kind of illness do you have?"

She propped herself on her elbow, took his hand and placed it over her lower abdomen. Looking into his eyes, she said, "I'm having your child."

It took a few moments for him to comprehend that beneath the warmth of her flesh lay the beginnings of a new life that he helped to create.

"You're unhappy." she assumed by his stunned silence.

"No, no, no," he denied dumbly, "no, no...."

She curled her hand around his neck and made him look at her. "If I'd had a choice, I would have chosen you to father my children, Shelon."

"Yes," he replied huskily, "You would have been my choice, too, Gella."

He bent down and put his forehead on hers and caressed her abdomen. He had arduously avoided siring children throughout his life, a silent refusal to give the Janti yet another Shodite to exploit. His deeply held inner convictions marred his happiness. "My son must be born a free man, or I will never forgive myself for my carelessness."

Gella seemed to understand his regrets. She moved into his arms and they held each other tightly. The strength of their bond was made manifest for Shelon. Gella was more to him than a special friend. He loved her, more than he'd loved any woman, and now she was having his child. His happiness should have been complete.

He squeezed shut his eyes to prevent tears from falling.

Shelon was drawn from his bed by music.

He unfurled himself from Gella's naked body and found his trousers in the darkness. He went to the door to investigate, thinking Praj and his brothers were still up, drinking, and Praj had taken to playing his mouth pipes.

The public sitting room was empty and the fire pit, cold.

A trilling reed instrument echoed from the stairwell, leaping above the chords of strings and horns. Somewhere in the lower floors, a full orchestra played.

He padded barefoot across the frigid stone floor, and stood at the top of the stairs, listening. The music had an ethnic flavor, nearly like the antiquated Shodite tunes his mother had taught him.

Despite the sudden chill shrouding his bare back, he started down the stairs.

The second level, and the first; both public sitting rooms were dark, empty, silent.

As he started down toward the war room, the cheerful music faded, and male voices took over, chanting in deep, resonating tones. He recognized that the language they were using wasn't Janti, Suma, or Shodite, just as he realized he did not understand what they were saying. The chants sounded liturgical, and were entrancing. Shelon hummed, following the cadence of their voices.

The stone covering to the staircase was left open. An orange, fixed glow came from the war room, casting finger of light across the bottom step. In the light, there was movement.

451

Trepidation slowed his pace. He was afraid of no man, but he sensed that he was not about to encounter mere men in the war room. At least not living men.

He eased around the stone aperture.

The chanting stopped and the bright glow dimmed to the undulating substandard flickering of a small fire in the pit.

Iada sat alone, before the fire, in one of the fourteen, stone seats situated around the fire pit. Her hands were linked in her lap, her head lowered and her eyes were closed. She looked like she was napping.

"Praj get tired of you already?" he joked from the stairwell. His voice echoed in the empty silence, mocking his ears.

Her head came up, and her eyes opened, alert, and she pulled a sportive grin for Shelon. "If it isn't the cur that impregnated young Gella. By my eyes, Shelon, you aren't the doddering old man I took you for."

Shelon grunted a laugh, and his eyes skittered around the war room. Hiding his chagrin, he asked, "Did you hear something unusual just now?"

"Like what?"

He hesitated describing the music and the chanting to Iada. He'd tell Gella later, but he didn't care to tell anyone else about his hallucinations. Iada, and the others, would think the pressure had finally broken him.

"Nothing," he shrugged it off. He joined her in the war room, his arms wrapped around his chest to fend off the cold. He sat in the stone seat next to her, immediately aware of the chill the stone radiated. "Why are you down here when you could be with Praj?"

"I have a lot on my mind." she said, "Much of which I needed to talk to you about. In private."

The seriousness in her face made him forget about the cold.

"I met a man who holds a high position in Janti society who wants to help the Shodites. He is a boy, really, but in his heart he has the potential to be a great man."

"Name." Shelon demanded skeptically.

She pursed her lips. "I trust him, Shelon."

"Name," he prodded flatly.

"In Shod City, I was recognized by this man, and instead of taking me to daka Bail, he took me to a family in Dralon who nursed me back to health. While I was there, he came to me with some information he wished me to pass on to you. At first, I thought he was using me to get to you, so after staying in Dralon a week, I slipped away, escaping him. I found Tam and Ule in Bilk, and we moved all over causing trouble. I was never followed or found by the Pliadors. I believe he really wishes to help us."

"Name." Shelon repeated, incredulous that she would go to such lengths to defend a Janti of any stripe.

She averted her eyes to the flame. "Daka Bailin."

"Daka Bailin." he sputtered, and he broke into laughter at what had to be a jest. He slapped his thighs, he was so amused.

"He has suggested," she said ignoring his doubt, "that you send an envoy of representatives to Shodalum, to petition the Elders to remove their ban on expatriated Shodites."

Shelon's laughter died as Iada verbalized one of the fancies he'd toyed with on dull days. He sobered. "Does he."

"With that done, we can then petition the dakas to release us into the hands of our ancestors."

Shelon suppressed a droll smile, and caustically said, "Is that how easy it will be? By the Guardian, why have we languished in slavery this long when the solution was so easy?"

Iada's brow twitched irritably. "The heir apparent of Jantideva is on our side, Shelon. Perhaps he is not in rulership, but he has the daka's ear. Closer and more beloved is his voice to the daka, than your voice!"

Shelon waved off her flash of indignation. "Even if we could convince the Elders to welcome us home, I doubt Jantideva will release us."

Iada lunged at him, slapping his leg playfully, her eyes filled with enthusiasm. "By law they must! Daka Bailin has told me that one of the reasons we are held to our benefactors is because Shodalum will not take us back. According to Alliance law, once Shodalum removes their ban, Jantideva is compelled to relinquish rights of benefactorship. They are to send us home."

His heart skipped a beat. "This is written in law?"

"And can anyone wonder," she said with significance, "why Shodites are not permitted to study the Alliance laws and history? It isn't that they believe we are too ignorant to learn. They are afraid we are too smart and will understand too much."

His mind was on fire. Solien never mentioned this law to him, she'd only encouraged him to fight. Perhaps she, like the Janti-born Shodites, had given up hope that Shodalum would ever want them back.

Trying to stay grounded in pessimism, he said, "The number of Janti-born Shodites is easily double the mean population of Shodalum. If you were a council Elder, how would you view the possible influx of double your population? Imagine what they might imagine. Modernization, crime, disease. If I were an Elder, I would send our envoy home packing."

"Ah, but daka Bailin has a solution for this problem." she said, a smile creasing the fading circles in her cheeks where blisters once were. "If we encounter opposition, we must convince the Shodite Elders to contest the Declaration of Old Rathia. He says the claim Jantideva, and the Alliance, has on Old Rathia is illegal. The land originally belonged to Shodalum and should be released to Shodalum. Our people can populate Old Rathia."

Shelon nodded calmly, as if he were giving the suggestion thought, though his heart raced. Moom had given rise to all his boyhood fantasies about the Rathians, and their quest for world peace, which turned into a quest for world domination under the rulership of an evil Rathian Lord. According to the bedtime stories his mother used to tell him, eight thousand years ago the Rathians landed on the shores of North Shodalum. The lands were wild, sparsely inhabited, and beautiful. A mirror of Rathia, which was a mythical country that no one seemed to be able to find on a map. His mother told him (her eyes alight with amusement) that Rathia was once a large island in the Gryvly, and had sunk into the ocean. The survivors of Rathia arrived in Shodalum, looking like silver bodied gods in their armor. They met no opposition from the awed Shodites, and claimed the land along the Peril River, where they made their first settlements. Unable to resist the lure of Jantideva, they explored the huge rural country, taking with them urban

454

ideals, and urban civilization. The Rathians were the foundation of Jantideva, and Shodalum. The founding fathers of their world.

He felt a chill race around him, and a faint echoing of the chanting he'd heard earlier passed through him, an audio memory that touched his nerves, and he drew in a sharp breath and shivered.

"It's as if they are calling me home." he said softly to himself.

Iada's stare was steady, disconcerting.

"I've been considering visiting Shodalum." he revealed to her, "Gella has told me so much and still it hardly whets my appetite."

"You will lead us?" Iada asked grinning, "I want to go, and I know Praj, Tam, and Ule will want to go."

He rubbed his chin thoughtfully. An image crossed briefly in his mind, of the oafish, vulgar, drunken brothers standing around him, a criminal fugitive, petitioning the Elders to be permitted into their country. He smiled wryly. "As long as Praj, Tam, Ule and I hide behind you and Gella."

"What better way to let them know what they are getting themselves into?" she countered with a grin, "Too bad Yegi isn't still alive. Let them see the warriors our rejected ancestors spawned."

"We want to convince them to trust us." he replied flatly. "Not frighten them." He glanced upwards, and a quote of his own making caught his eyes. `Shun their beds, shun their children, shun their ways.' "There really is only one person who can help us. Our Native Daughter. Gella knows her people. She knows what they might accept, and what they'd reject out of hand. She must lead us, not I. It will be her discretion who goes, and who stays."

Iada nodded her agreement, but there was disappointment in her face too. Shelon smiled at her, and touched the side of her head with the palm of his hand. "I understand your desire to see our own country, if only for a day."

"I've decided I want the privilege for more than a day." Iada replied, and she amended, "I admit, I didn't take daka Bailin seriously, not at first. But as I thought about his plan, as I thought about living among my own kind, speaking the language my mother taught me, I'd give anything to be a Shodite who lives in Shodalum. I'd give anything for my family to have that privilege."

Shelon thought of his child, at the moment residing safely in Gella's womb, and he said, "I would, too."

The cold finally too much for him to endure, he stood. "I'm going back to my woman. You should get some rest, too, Iada. Come upstairs with me."

"I can hardly rest with Shodalum on my mind."

"Praj has been whining for you for months!" he exclaimed, "I cannot endure another day of his complaints! Take yourself up to him, this minute!"

Amused, she obeyed, and led the way.

As he started up the stairs, he glanced back, half expecting to see the otherworldly glow he'd seen earlier. There was nothing but the undulating glow of the firelight licking the walls, partially illuminating his written word.

࿐࿐࿐࿐࿐࿐࿐࿐

She'd been having nightmares about Shodalum. They were located variously; in Nari, Calli, her home of Nmar, and in them were a variety of family members she hadn't seen since she was a girl. Though each respective nightmare seemed different, there were two common threads weaving them together. In them, she was always with Cobo, and always she was searching for Shelon. She'd wake from her dreams weeping, consoled only by the presence of Shelon beside her.

Shelon presented her with the prospect of returning to Shodalum as she was picking through Moom's well tended garden for ripe vegetables. Because of her nightmares, her superstitions took over her reasoning, and before she had a chance to think his request through, she turned him down.

"Why?" he demanded, dismayed by her flat refusal. He was sitting on a rock, his elbows on his knees and his eyes on her. "It is an opportunity to help the Shodites win their freedom. For the sake of our son why won't you lead our delegation?"

"How you decided this child is a boy, I'll never know." she replied caustically.

"We need you to help us form our delegation, and to stand with us, Gella, or we don't have a chance."

"I am dead to Shodalum. Dead women cannot speak before the Elders." she said bluntly.

"You are the Chosen Sister of Ver dala Ven. They will honor you."

She paused above a plant filled with greens and grimaced at the truth. Thib did not like her, but would stand with her before the Elders to give her a voice, simply because of her family relationship with Cobo.

"You want our son to be free, don't you?" he prodded, thoroughly irritated. He'd expected her to agree to his plans simply because it was him asking.

She picked the greens off the plant, throwing them into the basket between her feet, and straightened, her arms akimbo. "I'm afraid." she admitted lowly, "The journey to Shodalum will be a long one, and dangerous. You thought I was not listening this morning as Iada described the mood of the Janti? They are forming militias to hunt down runaway Shodites. You, and I, and each person we travel with, are hunted. If we reach the border of Shodalum, it would be a miracle. And our journey doesn't end at the border, Shelon. There is the trek across Shodalum to Sidera. We cannot use Janti windriders to reach Sidera."

He stood and went to her. He looked deeply into her eyes. "I understand that the journey will be dangerous and hard. Don't worry, Gella. I will protect you and the baby." he pushed a strand of her hair behind her ear and caressed her jawline. "I will protect you with my life if I have to."

She touched his craggy face with her dirty hands, her finger finding a scar left over from his beating at the Keep. "But who will protect you?"

"The Guardian." he said with all seriousness.

She couldn't bring herself to voice her distrust in the nebulous being the Janti called the Guardian. Of all the gods worshipped, he seemed less likely to be of any aid to a single mortal. His mind was forever distracted with matters of more import, such as the timely spinning of the planets around the sun.

She'd ached for Shodalum, and the sands of Calli under her feet. Perhaps her dreams were telling her what she already knew, that she was homesick, but that to go home she had to make a choice; Calli, or Shelon.

It was no choice. She'd wanted Shelon.

Just as she was ready to refuse him again, nausea struck her like lightening. She ran out of the garden, and dropped on her knees near a vine growing out of the fortress wall, where she vomited the cooked grains Iada had made her eat that morning.

She felt Shelon's hand on her back. Once she was done, she wiped her mouth and glanced apologetically over her shoulder.

"Iada promised the sickness wouldn't last long. She gave me some herbs to soothe my stomach, and I had thought they were working."

"She needs to eat more." One of the women from the garden offered. Her name was Treasure. She was a dark skinned Shodite, dark as many of the Janti Gella had met, but had the most astonishing blue eyes. She was Gella's age, and already a mother seven times over, giving birth to five of her children while living in Moom. She carried her youngest, a toddler, on her hip as she tended the garden. She stared at Gella, and nodded knowledgeably. "You don't eat enough. If you eat more, you will vomit less."

"Insanely illogical." Gella retorted, and she winced and gripped her stomach. It ached.

Treasure wagged a finger at Shelon. "Feed her, now."

Shelon obediently nodded. He made Gella stand, and started her walking toward the castle.

"No more grains," she begged, "No more green things, no more wild bore meat." The very thought made her gag, and she clamped her hand over her mouth and gulped away the urge to vomit.

"What else is there?" he asked testily, "My son isn't going to grow strong on bread and water!"

"Yava," she said gruffly, "I crave it......dream about harvesting it."

"We have no yava on hand." and he grimaced, "I'd rather eat Ul Zub's fish than yava."

She could almost taste the fish, and the salt, and smell the boat, and she stopped behind a thatched roof hut and heaved again.

458

Done, she wept a little, saying, "I can't go on like this. I can't go on."

He hushed her tears, and embraced her and reminded her that her sickness would be temporary. Reluctantly, he also said, "Perhaps taking you with us was a bad idea, in your condition."

She gripped him. "You don't have to go, either, Shelon. It's madness. The Elders will never allow us to return to Shodalum. The law is strictly enforced."

She felt his shoulders slacken in despair, and thought she'd managed to talk him out of the insanity.

Wordlessly, he started her back toward the castle. A grim frown was on his face, speaking of his perseverance. Though he believed her, she sensed he would still go to Shodalum, and try to speak to the Elders. At once she felt ashamed for trying to take away his hopes, though she had spoken the truth. Her reasons were selfish. She didn't want him to leave her, utterly fearful of losing him.

The women of the castle were congregated in the kitchen, pounding out bread dough and talking, their manner relaxed until Shelon entered. They immediately abandoned their task to wait on their beloved leader, all except for Iada who watched the other women with an amused smile. Among the Shodites, even in the castle where he worked and lived as an equal among his people, Shelon was treated like a daka, and Gella was treated as a part of him. Once he told the women that Gella was hungry, they fussed over her like she was the most important person they'd ever met. The treatment never failed to make her feel very uncomfortable. She was seated at a table near the hearth, and served a bowl of vegetable broth taken from a simmering pot above the cooking fire, with a thick slice of freshly baked bread.

Shelon sat across from her and watched her eat. Though he was looking at her with his eyes, his gaze was far away. Without having to ask him where he was, she knew he was planning his route Shodalum. She remembered the route, in the reverse. She and Cobo rode on one of those blasted windriders for what seemed like years, but was no longer than the trip she, Shelon and Korba had made from Padra to Horp Row. The cities they passed through seemed monstrously large to Gella, though Cobo assured her they

459

were small in size compared to the sprawling Center-plex, which he described to her as twenty or so cities in one. She didn't believe there could be a city of that size, and was astonished to find he hadn't exaggerated.

She and Cobo had an escort to Ona, and had been shown every courtesy afforded Ver dala Ven. Shelon and his delegation wouldn't be given the same courtesies as they crossed Jantideva to Shodalum.

As if he was reading her thoughts, Shelon said lowly, "A pack of fugitives is an easy target. We should avoid busy centers of commerce on our way to Shodalum. But how? We certainly can't hike two thousand spans of wilderness."

Her heart leaped painfully in her chest. He really was her other half, their minds and souls one.

From the counter where Iada pounded out flat bread, she offered, "What about daka Bailin?"

Hearing Bailin's name, Shelon scowled and his eyes shot over Gella's shoulder to Iada. "I don't trust anyone who carries that appellation to his name."

"I trust him." Iada offered.

Shelon barked a cynical laugh.

Iada went on to say, "If anyone could provide us with safe passage to Shodalum, he could. The dakas travel without molestation. No one would check the passengers of his windrider, or our destination."

"If he is trustworthy."

"You know me well enough," Iada replied sharply, "to know that I don't trust easily."

Shelon stared at Iada for a long time, then let his eyes drift to the fire. Gella toyed with her soup, fearing Iada had convinced Shelon to take on the dakas, as well as the Elders. The last time he took on the dakas, he was nearly killed.

Iada passed the dough she'd been working to another woman and cleaned her hands on a rag, staring at Shelon, waiting for his verdict.

Finally, making up his mind, he stood, and crooked his finger to Iada.

"And where are we going?" Iada wanted to know.

Ambiguously, Shelon said, "Have some arrangements to make." His gaze dropped to Gella. Affectionately, he said, "You're not to leave here until you finish feeding my son."

His command, as well as his insistence that their child was a son, rankled her, and she scowled. "I will feed our daughter until she is no longer hungry." she retorted.

He smirked as he turned away. He grasped Iada lightly by the elbow and led her briskly from the kitchen. Gella quickly averted her eyes from the intimacy, jealousy adding weight to her already sour mood. She tried to dismiss her jealousy, over and over, reminding herself of Shelon's claim on her, and her claim on him. Unable to finish eating, she cleared her place at the table and went after them.

෪෪෪෪෪෨෨෨෨

The unused corridors of the castle were often dark, and they all looked alike, blank gray stone walls, with arched ceilings. Those that were well used, such as the corridors leading from the war room to the kitchen, or the well room, or the stairs to the upper levels, were lit continuously by battery lamps, or oil lamps that were hung from the ceilings. Without thinking, Gella followed the path of light from the kitchen, expecting to soon enter the war room.

The corridor was longer than she remembered, and twisted more, and did not break off into other corridors, instead becoming more like a gradually descending tunnel. Her mind mired in jealousy, she obliviously followed the lit lamps, never noticing that they were not the lamps installed by the Shodites, but the defunct electrical glass contraptions the Rathians left behind. Shelon bemoaned the fact that the wiring in the castle had been eaten away by rodents and time. He disliked the smell of oil lamps, because the smell reminded him that this was as much as the Janti would ever give Shodites to light their homes.

She hated the smell of the lamps, too, because lately the smell turned her stomach.

It was missing that smell that caused her to finally notice the lamps. She stopped and looked up at the gently glowing ball of light, and the moss clinging to the fixture mounted in the wall. Shelon had insisted the electricity no longer ran through the castle.

The four lights in the corridor ahead flickered, as if to beckon her onward. Beyond the four lights, there was a bend, and darkness.

Shelon had warned her not to get lost in the castle. There were dangers, especially in the lower levels where the supports beneath the stone floors were crumbling. The castle was built above a series of natural caves, much like the cave they entered when they first arrived at Moom. She imagined falling through the floor, and falling endlessly.

Unsettled, she backed away, ready to flee and find her way back to the kitchen.

The lights behind her extinguished, leaving the labyrinthine corridor pitch black. Panic caught her around the throat. Instinctively, she shouted Shelon's name. Her voice echoed down both ends of the corridor.

Shelon's reply traveled from the depth of the unused corridor. "Come to me, Gella," he said.

She gazed down the tunnel. He sounded close, though he was not in sight. "Shelon? Is that really you?" she asked, her voice tremulous.

"Come to me....." he beckoned.

She took a wavering step toward the sound of his voice. As she did, the lamp above her head went out. She paused, and looked again into the blackness behind her.

"Shelon?" she called out.

"Come to me." he beckoned again, but this time his voice sounded different. He almost sounded like....Cobo.

She started toward the next light, her pace quickening. Her mind raced with the possibilities. Cobo was Ver dala Ven, and Ver dala Ven was capable of miraculous acts, according to what she'd been taught by her parents and the Elders, although Cobo hadn't shown her this side of him. She imagined he could very well be in the tunnel, waiting for her.

Still, even with the promise of Cobo in the tunnel, having each light she passed extinguish as she reached it was unsettling. The darkness lay on her back, pushing her forward.

She paused at the last light, and glanced around the corner into the darkness. She stepped forward, and as if she'd crossed some magical threshold, the lights in the tunnel came on, and the one over her head flickered, and went off.

She stared down the lit corridor. She could see from where she stood that it ended ahead. Two more lights, and then a dead end.

"Cobo?" she called out, expecting him to appear.

The light at the end of the tunnel flickered, beckoning to her to continue coming.

Her pace slower, she walked cautiously to the next light. An acrid musty smell thickened the air, and the stone floor gradually turned from gray to black, stained by mold. The dampness made the floor slick. Gella guarded against losing her footing by placing her hand on the wall and clinging to the cracks and crevices opened by decay. The silence of the tunnel was accented by the soft padding of her feet, her quickened breath, and the melodic sounds of trickling water behind the walls. Her hand found damp openings in the wall where water seeped through, and saturated the stone.

A pit came before the dead end. Two stone steps were visible, the rest of the pit was under black water. She stood at the top of the steps, glancing from the water, to the tunnel behind her.

"Cobo?"

The lights in the tunnel extinguished.

She froze. The darkness made her blind. Her heart pounded against her chest. Nearly afraid to make a sound in the reverberating silence, she whispered, "Cobo, please don't tease me."

A scintillating light appeared next to her, taking on the shape of a man. Her trepidation was tempered by relief that she was no longer blind. "Cobo?" she said hopefully.

His image sharpened. His face narrowed and eyes appeared, golden like Cobo's, but he was not Cobo. He was taller than any man she'd ever met, his back proudly erect, and he wore a costume of metal. She cranked her head back to meet his eyes, and involuntarily took a step backwards. She felt the damp wall with her hands, and was suddenly aware that she was trapped.

"Lereh Kratlaftos, bseglin greifen malor." he said in a strange language, and he smiled at her, a smile that was not malicious, but seemed malicious simply because of the surroundings and circumstances.

Without becoming aware that she had understood him, she knew he'd addressed her as Warrior Mother and had said, "Welcome to my tomb."

Breathlessly, she said, "Who are you?"

He spoke to her in Shodite, now, saying, "I am Mo'ghan, the First." he said, introducing himself, "I was born of the Masing, made a Rathian, I died a Knight, and I was laid to rest here," he gestured to the water, then placed his fist over his heart, "I've been waiting a long time for your arrival, Lereh Kratlaftos."

She pressed her back into the wall, trying to put more distance between her and the wraith, imbued with the fear that Mo'ghan intended to take her life.

A sneer twisted his mouth into a contemptuous smile. "You are of far greater value to me alive."

Her throat was too dry to make noise, leaving her unable to voice her questions and fears. She stared, frozen in place, as he gestured again to the water. Before her eyes the water disappeared. A set of stone steps lead downward to an opening of the subterranean chamber.

Mo'ghan descended the steps and entered the chamber, taking his light with him, leaving her in darkness. Though his presence was terrifying, the darkness was equally terrifying.

Finding her voice, she said, "Mo'ghan?"

A sunny glow crept out of the chamber, up the steps, and reached out for her. The glow, once it enveloped her body, calmed her and entranced her senses. She started down the steps, drawn into the chamber by the glow of Mo'ghan's essence.

The chamber was smoothly round, the walls and ceiling adorned with colorful mosaic tiles, set in busy geometric designs. The ceiling's design bore the unmistakable depiction of the Masing Star, set in behind a black Rathian cross.

A stone sarcophagus was in the center of the chamber. A symbol was etched on the top of the sarcophagus, and she recognized it as the same symbol etched on the door of the room she shared with Shelon. One long vertical line, crossed by three shorter horizontal lines. She knew as she looked at the symbol that it was Mo'ghan's mark, his name in a language that was no longer spoken.

Mo'ghan appeared next to the sarcophagus. He placed his hand on the stone, on the symbol atop the stone, and said, "My home."

"You lay in that tomb?" she breathed.

"My bones lie here, as well as my spirit," he said solemnly.

Her eyes traveled along a band of black and orange mosaic in the center of the visually beautiful wall. "You must have been great to have such a tomb made for you."

"As I said, I was the First." he replied stoically. "I was not placed here as a tribute to my life, but to imprison my spirit. They were afraid of me." A touch of sadness entered his eyes. "Though I did them no harm."

"Who?"

"Those....I served."

He looked away, to the tomb. He again caressed the symbol. "Here, see this. They called me a warrior. Yet I killed no one. I warred....with no man."

"Who are you really?" she asked softly.

Mo'ghan's sad eyes turned up with his smile. "A spirit very close to you. I am the spirit you will usher into a new world, and a new life. For me, a fearful beginning, being not as I was, but as I will be......like you."

He raised his hand off the stone, and toward the ceiling mosaic of the Masing. "Thank you, Guardian, for Gella al Perraz and Shelon al Entlay. They please me. They please me very much."

A bright light assaulted her eyes, and she closed them, covering them with her hands. She felt warmth envelope her, burning in her lower abdomen, as if burning her womb. She cried out for her child, fearful he was being harmed.

In answer to her cry, the tomb melted from around her. The warmth was on her back, now. Cautiously, she took her hands away from her eyes. She saw she was no longer in Moom, but in Shodalum, in Calli. The black sand warmed her feet, and the heat rising off the sand baked into her body. In supreme ecstasy, she raised her face to the sun.

"Gella al Perraz," The female voice, so like her own, brought her attention to a woman standing near her. The woman was the likeness of herself, except she was easily twenty years older than Gella's present age, and she did not have green eyes. They were gold, as gold as Cobo's, and Mo'ghan's. Her likeness said, "I am Betnoni."

Her mouth dropped open in shock.

Betnoni smiled wistfully. "Ah, I know my dear Gella. You are agnostic. I don't mind your doubt, nor does the Guardian. In fact, the Guardian finds your doubting mind endearing."

"You are me," she whispered.

Betnoni held out her arms to present herself to Gella. "I came in your living form to honor you, my child."

"But...older...."

"Yes, older. As a promise, my dear, a promise you must not forget. I have chosen you, Gella al Perraz, to be my agent. One day you will sit on the council of Elders, and you will be a wise leader of your people. You will unite Shodalum, the Old and the New. But in order to reach your destiny, my daughter, you must now heed the will of the one you love more than your own life. You will hear Shelon, and obey him."

The final command curled Gella's lips. "Obey him? Am I his chattel?"

"No, my child," Betnoni admonished, "You are his other half. The completion of him, and he is the completion of you."

Betnoni dissolved, and a gust of wind carried her dust off to the sea. The same wind twisted and turned around Gella's legs, pressing her to follow. In the wind, she heard laughter. Many voices, as if many people surrounded her.

Afraid, she ran after Betnoni. She went through the fields of yava, over the cement foundation of a chemical plant that lay in ruin, and up the rocky crest overlooking the Gryvly. There, she stopped. Below, on the beach, a young couple played in the surf. Gella grew incensed that squatters had claimed their home, and was ready to storm the beach and set them straight about the ownership of Calli, until an old man passed her and trotted down to the beach. He was Cobo, and his face was alive with happiness.

"Cobo," she whispered, and her ever present yearning for him felt satiated.

And, just then, another person brushed by her, a woman, herself, twenty years older as Betnoni had shown her, with wrinkles and gray streaks in her long hair, and a body not so hard as it is now. Her older self went down to the beach, following Cobo, and the young man that had been playing turned to her and embraced her. He looked familiar to Gella.

"Shelon's son." she said softly, and she understood at once that she was experiencing a vision of the future. A vivid, glorious vision. "But where is Shelon?" she asked, her smile fading, and she looked for him all around.

As her eyes scanned the desert, she saw now that Calli was not so barren, but a thriving village, with many interconnected fields, growing many things. There were trees growing in the black sand, an orchard where there was once only dunes. All around Cobo's original home, more and more homes had come into being.

And near the sea, there was Moom. Not a structure as huge as a castle, but the largest home Shodalum had ever seen, with three stories and slender windows. On the massive double doors, a symbol was carved. The symbol of Mo'ghan's name.

That is my home, Gella thought in shock.

"Shelon!" Gella cried out, "Shelon!"

No one heard her, or responded. She looked back at the grown boy who was to be her son of the future, and asked Betnoni, "Where is Shelon?"

The surf replied in hisses and whispers, "In your heart."

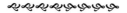

Chapter 21

Shelon pointed the camera tube at Iada. She stood with her back to a wall in the bedroom she shared with Praj. Shelon nodded at her to speak.

"Daka Bailin." she started, "can you hear me?"

Shelon had his eyes on the screen. Bailin shifted forward in his seat, and said, "Yes, I can." His voice was tinny and distorted over the antiquated comm link, as expected for the distance they were transmitting, but at least they were reading him clearly enough.

Bailin said, "I was quite surprised to hear from you, Iada, especially after so long. I had feared the worse had happened to you. Are you well?"

"As well as I have ever been." She replied, and getting on with it, she said, "I've been in contact with Shelon. He has formed a delegation to go to Shodalum, as you suggested, but Daka, we cannot get there without private transportation."

"What is it you need?" he said, "A standard windrider, or a double class?"

Shelon nodded to her, and she said, "Wait a moment, daka."

Shelon handed the camera to Iada, and traded places with her, putting his back against the wall. As he came into view on daka Bailin's screen, the daka's eyes widened with astonishment.

"Shelon of Solien's Soldiers." he whispered, in the same worshipful tone the Shodites used.

Coming from a daka, it thoroughly unsettled Shelon.

"Daka Bailin, are you aware of the political prisoners we have in our possession?"

Bailin seemed to waken from a trance. "Oh--yes....yes, I heard something about it. You captured ten men...three were found dead in the Pril, seven are still missing. Are they still alive?"

Reminded of Vold and Vere's inhumanity, Shelon grimaced. "Yes, seven of your men, including the Captain of your father's personal guard, Edise, are alive and well. I suppose your father has already replaced Edise?"

"Twice, so far." Bailin admitted.

Shelon shook his head at the idea of Edise being irreplaceable. "You realize then how important these men are to your father?"

"Yes." Bailin replied, and seemed ready to ask him what Edise and his men had to do with transportation to Shodalum.

"Then we will come to an understanding, right now, before we make further arrangements." Shelon said evenly, "If you turn on us and have us arrested or killed, those seven men will be executed and your name will be carved in their chests."

Bailin's mouth slid open. His voice hushed, he said, "I mean you no harm!"

"Are you certain?" Shelon prodded, affecting a casual tone, "You aren't luring us into a trap to impress your father, are you? Although, I imagine the capture of Cleses would be quite impressive, don't you think?"

Defensive anger crossed Bailin's brow. "I don't care for my father's approval. All I care about is freedom for the Shodites."

Shelon stared at the young man's resolute features, and felt a stirring of hope. The hope set him ill at ease. "That better be true, daka, because I am putting many lives into your hands."

"You can trust me." he assured Shelon earnestly. "Tell me what you need, and I will make sure you get it."

"An unmarked double class windrider,"

"Give me a time, and your coordinates," Bailin said, "and I will send someone."

"Have your pilot leave it in the public transport station in Horp Row," he said, "Understood?"

"Yes." Bailin said earnestly.

Shelon cut off contact, and glanced to Iada. She was pursing her lips at him.

"You still do not trust him."

He was ready to admit it was true, but was cut short by Korba's frantic shouting.

"Shelon! Iada! Someone, help me!"

Shelon darted out of Iada's room in time to see Korba carrying Gella into the common sitting room. She was limp, unconscious, and very pale.

470

Behind Korba were Praj and Tam, Treasure and several children. His shouts had drawn attention, and more were coming upstairs.

Shelon ran to him, and took Gella out of his arms. Her clothing was damp, and her whole body felt cold to the touch. "What happened to her?" he demanded.

"The children heard noises from the one of the forbidden corridors-" with a catch in his voice, Korba said, "We found her like this. Iada, I couldn't hear her heart."

Iada drew them into her room, and Shelon lay Gella on the bed. As Iada felt for a pulse in her right arm, Shelon held onto her left hand, rubbing it, trying to bring life into her. Her skin was too pale, and her lips were blue.

"Iada," Shelon demanded huskily, "tell me she is alive."

Gella's blue lips parted, and she whispered, "Shelon,"

He gripped her hand tightly, and held on as if he were holding her to life. He caressed her face. "Gella, precious one, open your eyes."

She opened her eyes, and seeing his face, she smiled. "I thought you were dead."

Shelon laughed unsteadily. "My dear, I was just wondering the same about you."

Iada threw a blanket over Gella. "She needs warmth. Put her by the fire."

Shelon tucked the blanket around her, and lifted her. She buried her face into his neck.

"Never leave me." she demanded softly.

"Never." he replied gruffly. He walked her quickly to the fire pit, and sat her in a Janti sling back chair that one slave or another had stolen from their benefactor and carried up the mountain. Praj threw wood onto the fire, and sparks flew, the smoke trailing into the flue.

Shelon knelt at her side, and gazed at her face. "What happened to you?"

Tears came to her eyes. "I was lost."

"I told you to stay away from the unlit corridors." he admonished gently.

471

"I think....Mo'ghan must have saved me," she said softly, her eyes closing slightly. She seemed senseless.

"Mo'ghan?" Shelon questioned, "What did you say about Mo'ghan?"

"He is here.....he wants.....he wants me to go to Shodalum with you, Shelon. I must go or they will not listen to you. They will listen to a Chosen Sister."

Her voice was so weak, and he worried she would slip away from him. "Iada, are you sure she will be alright?"

Gella opened her eyes and looked at him. "Shelon, promise me. Promise you will never leave me."

He framed her face with his hands, and oblivious of all those who listened, he said earnestly, "Gella, I will not leave you, never leave you, not until I die."

Her tears spilled over. "Do not die." she ordered.

Wryly, he said, "If I made that promise, it would be a lie."

"Lie to me." she insisted.

She was trembling with fear. Iada warned him that Gella would experience strong emotional reactions now that she was pregnant. He squelched his sudden irritation with her in order to comfort her irrational insecurity.

"I promise, I will not die."

Her relief was shallow. Though she physically relaxed, apprehension remained in the depth of her green eyes.

৵৵৵৵৵৵৵৵৵

They couldn't have picked a finer day for their journey. The weather was balmy, and Horp Row was burgeoning with summer visitors. The public landing stations were active. Special notice of the double class windrider that landed in bay sixteen caused a slight stir. The windrider bore the daka's insignia on the side.

No one noticed, however, that daka Bailin was the pilot. Not yet, at least. He had disembarked from the windrider, and looked about.

Iada's heart quickened. This was nothing of the plan Shelon so carefully devised. As calmly as she could, she walked toward

472

Bailin, hoping he would not see her in the teeming crowd of travelers.

He did notice her and his mouth grew a big grin. He waved, calling attention to himself and her. Iada dropped her eyes to the ground and kept walking toward him. A pair of station security officers strolled past her, their stink causing her to break out in a cold sweat. She forced herself to remain casual, relaxed. She was dressed in a Janti gown, and though it didn't fit her as well as it had fit Gella, it did enough to camouflage her in the throng of lower middle class Janti.

Holding her skirts, she mounted the metal steps to bay sixteen.

She was met at the top landing by Bailin.

"Good to see you, Iada!" he said enthusiastically.

Lowly, she hissed, "Shut up, boy, or are you trying to get me killed?"

Bailin seemed genuinely abashed. "I...I am just happy to see you."

"Usher me on board like a pilot would for a Janti woman." she instructed stiffly.

"Oh...yes." and he bowed, and flourished toward the ramp. She entered the windrider. Seeing Ksathra sitting in the passenger cabin, she grimaced. "What did you do, run away together?"

Bailin came up behind her. "It had crossed our minds." he said, throwing a secret grin at Ksathra.

Angrily, Iada said, "Shelon told you to leave the craft. What are you doing here?"

"I figured you'd need a pilot," he said as if it were obvious.

"Wonderful!" she snapped, "You assumed we did not have that part of our plan arranged? And just how long do you think it will take before the daka sends out the Pliadors to look for you?"

Bailin's humor faded, "She won't miss me. She thinks I've gone to the Suma Temple for lessons. I canceled my lessons with my tutor, and here I am. I have enough time to get you to Shodalum, and home before the dinner hour."

Iada stared at him in disbelief. "And if she misses you? What then? If we are in the presence of a daka when we are caught, we will be put to death. The Pliadors will automatically think we kidnapped you! They may even think Ksathra is in on the plot!"

473

"We won't be caught," he retorted, and he planted his hands defiantly on his hips, "Besides, just how many discreet pilots do you think I know? All of them are loyal to my parents, and they are members of the Pliadors. Not a one of them would leave a double class windrider here without asking a few questions, or at least reporting it to my mother. Face it, Iada, it's me or no one."

Reluctantly, she bent to his reasoning.

"Very well. Lift off." and to Ksathra, she said, "Help me off with this damnable costume."

The ramp closed, and the windrider made a wobbly lift off. Iada had to hold onto a handrail as she slipped out of the dress.

Iada shouted toward the cockpit, "If you please, a steadier hand! I am starting to feel like I am on a seafaring vessel!"

"I'm sorry!" Bailin shouted back, "I've only had my license a month."

"A month?" she countered incredulously.

"He is a very good pilot, for a beginner." Ksathra assured her.

"You are a blind and dumb fool in love." Iada admonished.

She kicked off the last of the underskirts. Underneath, she wore a coverall, and her satchel was tied to her waist. She joined Bailin in the cockpit, sitting in the copilot's seat.

She took over the controls. "Release them, daka," she ordered, "I will take us to the meeting sight, and from there you may fly at my discretion. If you frighten me with hapless recklessness, I will take over again."

He stared at her incredulously, "You can fly?"

"Indeed," she replied, "I learned about twenty years ago. I took a fancy to my benefactor's pilot. I made him happy, he taught me to fly. I believe he might be the father of my second son, but," she shrugged, "I could be wrong, too."

"A Shodite that can fly a windrider." he said, his eyes bright, staring at her able hands, "You are amazing, Iada. You prove them all wrong."

"Who needs to prove anything?" she snapped, "Shodites are not animals. Are we Ksathra?" she asked the young woman standing behind them.

"Bailin understands us."

Iada pursed her lips at the defensive words. In the week she was with Ksathra's family, she'd seen how the two young people loved each other. An impossible love, with a predictable outcome. She wondered what Ksathra expected from Bailin, or in the reverse, what Bailin expected of Ksathra. A couple of romantic, idealistic children.

Holding reign on her opinion of the young lovers, she took the windrider higher than a normal flight path. She took a west course, then turned east. She turned again, northeast. After a while, and watching her viewing screen closely for windriders that might have followed her, she turned due south.

"Strange course." Bailin commented, his arms crossed. His eyes held a canny glint in them.

Abashed, Iada said, "I had to be sure we weren't followed, daka."

"You still don't trust me." he said flatly.

"I trust you," she admitted, "but I do not trust your mother. Would she have let you leave the palace without a guard?"

"I didn't," he said, and he grinned slyly, "I signed up six men for the guard. As far as mother knows, I am covered."

Iada threw him a questioning look.

"Shelon's political prisoners." he edified, "The names didn't cause alarm. No one ever looks at those manifests, anyway."

Iada had a bad feeling in the pit of her stomach.

Abruptly, she changed course, heading northeast.

"Where are we going, now?" he demanded.

"I'm taking you and Ksathra to Dralon." She said, "I want you to go home, and change that manifest. Then make an appearance before your mother. Tell her your plans were canceled. I can only hope the windrider isn't missed right away."

Bailin wore a petulant frown. "You don't want me to fly you to Shodalum?"

"You made a mistake," Iada explained evenly, "putting the names of political prisoners on your flight manifest."

"I told you, no one ever checks the manifests."

"Before your brother's kidnapping, or after?" she demanded sharply.

He stared at her, uncertainty working in the tick of his cheek.

"Ah, you don't know!" she accused angrily, "If someone were to double check your manifest, and recognize one name on that list, they would automatically believe you had been kidnapped by Solien's Soldiers. The Pliadors will not only hunt us down, but enter Shod City and kill hundreds of innocent people to make their point!"

Bailin winced and turned his stare to the oncoming sky.

Finally, he said, "Ksathra wanted to see her homeland."

"She can come with us." Iada offered.

"She only has today. My mother's seamstress expects her to be in the palace tomorrow morning."

Iada threw a harsh glare at Bailin. "Can you let her go to experience freedom, or are you too selfish?"

"What kind of freedom is living as a fugitive?" Bailin retorted.

"From my experience, it is better than living as a slave."

"Do I have a say?" Ksathra interjected. She stood between them, looking from one to the other. "You argue about me like I am not here."

Bailin became repentant. "What is it you want, Ksathra? Do you want to run away from the palace? From me?"

"To freedom, Ksathra." Iada added firmly, angry at the daka for putting a selfish spin on what her leaving might mean. For all his liberal views, he was still a self-indulgent daka. "There are places in Jantideva that the Shodites live in relative freedom. After we leave Shodalum, we can take you to one of those places. You needn't sew your fingers raw to please a Janti designer, Ksathra."

She dropped her eyes to consider her options. Bailin stared at her, his hope fervent on his features.

Ksathra reached for him, and said, "My place is with Bailin."

His relief was visible. He took her hand and kissed it, and held it to his face.

Iada again pursed her lips. "Very well. I will drop you both in Dralon. You remember what you must do, daka."

"I will change the manifest."

"I can only hope it isn't too late by the time you get home." Iada said, and she gestured to him to take the controls. "Hold us at this altitude."

"I've never flown this high." he admitted.

"It's the same as skimming rooftops, daka," she said, getting up from her seat, "Only safer. We're not likely to crash into another foolish young man who only earned his license last month."

He frowned like a boy, like one of her sons might have under the same harsh adult criticism, and took over the controls.

She brushed past Ksathra, and went through the passenger section to the communications cab. She disabled the beacon attached to the on board data base, just as Shelon had shown her, then sent a brief message to Shelon, informing him that she would be ten hours late for their rendezvous. "I will explain upon arrival."

༄ ༄ ༄ ༄ ༄ ༄ ༄ ༄ ༄

Bailin returned home early in the afternoon.

He went, first, to the docking bay to change the manifest. As he brought the manifest up on the data screen, he found that his manifest had been referenced three times since he left early this morning, twice by Captain Agart, and once by his own mother. He punched in his mother's private voice line. Her tremulous reply told him she'd been under stress.

"Mother? It's Bailin." he said nervously, "I'm calling to inform you that my classes were canceled, and I am home for the day."

"Bailin!" she exclaimed, "Where are you?"

"In...at....I'm...." he glanced over his back to the day shift docking crew, and knew at once that he could not lie. "I'm at the docking bay."

"Agart will meet you there." she said flatly, and she cut him off.

He was greeted by a ten man squad, led by the grim Captain Agart, and escorted to the day room under the Spire of Ver dala Ven Siddhar. There, his mother waited for him, looking regal in a red gown, her hair upswept and garnished with hanging baubles of gold.

With her was the Pliadors investigative team that had been working on Archer's disappearance.

477

Jishni was angry. She strode toward him, her full skirts billowing at her sides, and before he fully entered the day room, she demanded, "Where have you been since this morning?"

"I went to the temple, but my classes were canceled."

"No you did not!" she thundered vehemently, "Captain Agart and her men have been to the temple. Chancellor Yana said you contacted him yesterday to cancel today's lessons!"

"I didn't see the Chancellor, because I didn't actually go to the temple. I went to the library, directly and spoke to Aton."

"Aton did not see you, either." she interjected, incredulous that he could lie to her, and in front of the Captain's guard. Her ears and cheeks were furiously red, growing as bright as her gown. "You left here with a guard of men who haven't been seen in months. Just how did this come about, Bailin?"

His mind went blank. No suitable lies came to mind, at least not until he glanced at his brother, who was hovering in a doorway, unnoticed. Steeling himself, Bailin said, "I didn't go into the Center-plex, mother. I went to Plaetesus, to the follies, to watch Olla girls."

"What?" she breathed, absolutely appalled.

The truth came tumbling out around the core lie. "I didn't want you to find out where I was going, so I took a windrider on my own. I used the names of those men because I didn't think anyone would double check my manifest. I honestly didn't think I'd be missed for a few hours."

His mother did something to him that she'd never done in his entire life. She raised her hand, and slapped him soundly across the face. Bailin was so taken aback that tears came to his eyes, and not for the pain. The humiliation reverberated long after the sting faded.

"How dare you make me worry about you." she fumed, "When Captain Agart reviewed your manifest, we were certain you'd been abducted. Our forces went on high alert! I called your father, and he is coming home from Zaria!"

Bailin knew he was in deep trouble. "Can't you call him back, tell him I'm alright?"

Jishni's mouth set in a frown. "Absolutely not. I will let your father deal with you, Bailin. Until he returns home, you are to stay in your room. You will have no visitors, nor will you have communications with your friends." She narrowed her eyes shrewdly, "And, perhaps our sewing staff will have some time off. They've deserved a long vacation, don't you think?"

At once, he understood that his mother suspected he was having a relationship with a seamstress, and she intended to make his life a misery by cutting him off from Ksathra, too.

He reflected on how he and Ksathra had joked about running away together while on their way to Horp Row. He wished heartily he'd followed his impulses, and whisked her away.

Captain Agart chose this moment to interject an inquiry about the missing windrider.

Bailin had planned to report it as being stolen, but not for another day, in order to give Iada time enough to get to Shodalum.

Though his back was erect, and his heart strong, his voice wobbled like a little boy's as he responded. "I left it on the docking bay. Right where it belongs."

The woman's mouth pursed in a grim line that seemed natural for her face. "I looked myself, daka Bailin, when we fetched you. I didn't see it."

"The crew must have moved it for repairs." he said with a shrug, "I ran into a transformer outside the club and creased the body." A half-truth. He ran into a transformer in Horp Row, and creased the body. The docking crew looked the damage over, and declared that more was damage done to the transport than the immovable transformer. It helped that Ona's insignia was on the transport, the docking crew was willing to overlook almost anything for the daka's pilot.

"Have you been drinking, too?" his mother demanded.

"No!" he defended, "I just wasn't looking where I was going! It was a slight crease!"

"Captain Agart," Jishni said abruptly, "Escort this young man to his room. I want sentries posted outside his bedroom door. He is not to leave, and no one is to see him without my authorization."

"Yes daka."

Bailin's jaw dropped. "Mother! Is an armed escort really necessary?"

479

Her lips trembled. As she looked at him, he could see her disappointment in him. "You've already proven to me you are not trustworthy."

The outrage of youth fed by the unfairness he felt was inherent in this situation made him cocky. "Why don't you lock me up in the Keep? And while you're at it," he gestured at Captain Agart, "have your thugs beat me, as well."

"I've had enough of your insolence, Bailin," she said, her tone dangerously low. "If you ever want to see the light of day again, you will shut your mouth this instant, and leave me."

His anger was tempered by a fear that his mother could do far worse to him than embarrass him in front of the security staff. She had the power to separate him from Ksathra, for good if she chose.

Reluctantly, he obeyed her and followed Captain Agart to his private quarters. He sulked the entire way, hoping that Iada appreciated the sacrifices he'd made for the cause.

෴෴෴෴෴

Gella had instructed Iada to stay clear of landing anywhere inside Shodalum, though it was permissible for windriders to cross the airspace above the country. Perhaps not as low as Iada flew, but she, Shelon, all of them, were eager to catch a glimpse of their homeland.

As dawn lightened the sky, Gella brought points of interest to their attention. The wild high lands of Shodalum. The central flood plains, where their country's grains were grown. The black desert, where nothing lived but slanks and bugs, and nothing grew except yava; Calli was in the most forbidding section of the black desert, on the coast. "It is my home," she told them proudly as they crossed over the abandoned desert, "with Cobo."

Shelon's heart was immediately eaten by envy. He envied the life Gella had led with Ver dala Ven, and the years his beloved spent with that man, and he also envied their freedom. He envied all Shodites living in Shodalum. He longed to know himself as a free Shodite.

Iada put down in a flatland, on the border between Shodalum and Old Rathia. It was an uninhabited grassy plain, with no trees in sight, and skies that went on forever. From their landing sight, they could see Peril Bay.

Shelon tied his pack of supplies to his back, and stepped off the windrider. He halted at the bottom of the ramp, and stared at lands he'd never seen.

Gella came up beside him and took his hand. Her features were bright with anticipation. "Let me be the first to introduce you to Shodalum."

She guided him to the broken down fence that marked the border. Together they climbed over the wooden planks, and set their feet down on Shodalum soil.

For Shelon, it was an indescribable moment. The grasses didn't look different, or smell different, nor did the soil seem improved, but the air did seem clearer to his nostrils. He broke from Gella and reached out his arms, as if to embrace the land, and went forward, breathing in Shodalum's air.

With a grin, he shouted, "I know this land. It lives in my blood. I am home!"

Gella had started down the gradual slope to the beach. She beckoned him to follow. She was on her way to get into the water, to ritually wash Jantideva off her skin and out of her clothing. Shelon followed, eager to experience the ancient custom of his homeland.

Behind him, Praj and Tam crossed the fence and broke into a run toward the beach. She'd told them all of the washing custom, and its meaning, the reaffirmation of being a Shodite.

As they sprinted past Shelon, laughing gleefully, Shelon was inspired to run after them. Passing Gella, he turned and trotted backwards a few steps to blow her a kiss. She laughed, and waved him on.

He dropped his pack on the beach and ran into the surf. The waters of the Gryvly were brutally cold. Shelon's breath was taken away as a wave washed over his thighs, but he refused to be pushed back because of his own discomfort. He threw himself over the wave, and let himself be drawn under the water.

In the cool, rushing quietness of the Gryvly, his thoughts focused involuntarily on Betnoni and how she'd given her life to protect native Shodalum. He'd always rejected her as a patron saint, because she was no patron to the Shodites of Jantideva. But in the water, as if he were in the frothy movement of Betnoni's mind, he felt he understood her patronage. She loved all Shodites. She welcomed them into her protection.

The water around him warmed, and he imagined that it was Her arms welcoming him into her protection. He opened his eyes, expecting to see Her spirit. In Her place was the blue sky. He'd risen to the surface.

He kicked himself upright to tread water, and watched Gella on the shore. She undid her pack, the one she insisted on carrying despite the objections of every man on the delegation, and set it beside Shelon's. Walking toward the water, she held her hands toward the sky in supplication, and recited a Shodite prayer for forgiveness, one Shelon had learned as a boy and had forgotten as a man. Her body defined by her Shodite wraps, and the sun shining through her red hair, she looked as striking as a goddess. Shelon's heart raced at the sight of her.

She entered the water, doing as he had, throwing herself into a rolling wave to experience the shock of cold all at once. She let the water wash over her without fighting the waves.

Shelon swam to her, and as she bobbed to the surface, he twined an arm around her waist and pulled her to him. She wrapped her arms around his neck, and her legs around his waist, and let him keep them afloat. He stared into her face, into her brilliant green eyes, at once feeling happier than he'd ever felt in his life.

After a brief swim, the chill of the waters chased them back onto the beach. The four of them staggered onto dry land as Iada and Korba walked Forsythio to the water's edge. Forsythio was an Elder, of sorts, among the Shodites in Shod City. He was a judge for those who needed counseling on moral matters, and he was a teacher and scholar. The Shodites considered him to be one of the wisest men alive. The Janti, however, didn't have much use for him after he turned eighty-seven. He was released from his benefactor, his home taken away from him, and since forced to live on the kindness of his fellow Shodites. In the following years he lost his sight, but never his acuity of mind. Among his own, he continued to act as a judge, and had made many sound rulings from

482

the alley where he lived. Shelon found him in Shod City, begging on a corner in Track three twelve for food, and presented him with the opportunity to travel with them to Shodalum. He eagerly jumped at the chance, without question.

And now, as he felt the sand beneath his feet, he was as eager to have Iada walk him into the water.

"The water is cold," Praj informed him, his teeth chattering loudly, "It'll make your bones ache."

"I don't care." Forsythia said hoarsely. He shook Korba off his right arm, and his milky white eyes seemed to scan his surroundings. "Native daughter," he said to Gella, reaching out in her general direction. "you take me to the water."

Gella obeyed him, and let him wrap his arm into hers. He was smaller than Gella, stooped and frail. Shelon had no doubt that Gella could carry him to the water if she took a notion to try.

They followed Gella and Forsythio. As they went, Gella described the scene to Forsythio, and he asked questions.

"The water is gray-blue, and calm today." she said.

"Is at always gray-blue?"

"No. In Calli, it is as green as a fine gemstone. Imagine a green sea against black sand. It is beautiful."

"Is the sand here black?"

"No, it is white."

"White sand and gray-blue water. Yes, I can see the Gryvly," he said and he smiled a toothless grin.

"The water is coming up to us now. It will be cold." she warned.

With Gella's gentle direction, she steered the elderly man into the water and had him kneel and let a wave wash over him. It knocked him about, but he laughed with the same glee they all felt for being free. Korba leapt into the water to help Gella keep Forsythio from being washed away like a twig, shouting a curse at the freezing water, which in turn made Praj laugh out loud and taunt the younger man's lack of fortitude.

Iada came up beside Shelon. "I don't like the idea of leaving the windrider unprotected. We should take it with us."

"And earn the wrath of the Elders before we manage to get an audience with them? I think not." Shelon replied flatly.

483

"There are spans and spans of empty space in Shodalum. We could put down in a discreet area, where no one would find it."

"Janti technology is strictly forbidden in this land. We may as well get used to doing without it now. It's a small price to pay, don't you think, Iada?"

"Perhaps," she said, "I would hope that in the future, we could persuade the Elders to loosen their laws against certain technologies."

Shelon looked askance at Iada.

She shrugged, "What harm would it bring to have some helpful technology. Imagine, if you will, Shelon, the trek we must take to reach Nari. Gella said it is a full day and one half of walking. Then to Sidera, which could take us months! None of us will make it."

Shelon sniffed the air, and wrinkled his nose as if he caught a bad scent. "I think," he said ruefully, "that you stink of Jantideva, Iada."

Without warning, he scooped her off her feet to throw her over his shoulder. She protested loudly and beat on his back as he walked into the surf. As a large wave swelled and rushed toward them, he tossed her off his back and into the water. She rolled behind the wave, still screaming obscenities at him.

Shelon found his footing in the wave, and watched Iada as she rose from the shallow water, soak and wet and chilled. His laughter was involuntary.

"You'll pay," Iada promised as she trudged to shore, her teeth chattering. "I'll get you back."

Shelon sniffed deeply, and smiled his satisfaction. "You're smell has improved."

She snorted contemptuously, and trudged toward Forsythio and Gella. Shelon's gaze shifted from Iada's wet black hair, to Gella's face.

She held an arm out to steady Forsythio, though her attention was on Shelon and Iada. Amusement sparkled in her eyes, and as she found Shelon's gaze, she smiled. She was as genuinely happy to be in Shodalum as he, so happy she'd forgotten to be jealous of his playful moment with Iada.

How happy would she be if the Elders turned away their request for citizenship, and ejected her from the only country she has ever known?

The thought sobered his mood.

They hiked a far enough distance from the border so that they wouldn't be seen if the stolen windrider was found. On the grass above the beach, they made camp for the day. Lying spooned with Gella and facing the sea, he broached the unpleasant subject of eventually leaving Shodalum. "If the Elders turn us away, we will live in Moom."

"They won't." she said with assurance.

"But if they do, we have a home. I know you hate Moom, but we will be free there."

"They won't turn us away," she insisted irritably.

He was silenced by her obvious rejection of the very thought that they might not be successful in their mission. He toyed with the ringlets of her hair and brooded about their future beyond Shodalum. If Shodalum did not want them, their next recourse was to continue with their struggle with the Janti, one battle at a time.

One Shodite life at a time.

Sleep did not come easy for Shelon.

Chapter 22

Bail arrived to the palace early the next morning. He came through the servant's entrance. Unshaven and dressed as a Zarian peasant, in britches that were full in the legs and tapering to the ankles, sandals exposing dirty feet, and a layered cloak over top a gray smock, he wasn't recognized by the few kitchen maids that were up, preparing bread for the next day. A cry of alarm did not impede his progress to the service lift.

He took the service lift to his family's private wing.

As he suspected would be the case, Jishni was not asleep, but waiting up to see him. Sometime during the weeks he'd been gone, Janus had been moved from the medical wing and into their private nursery. He was in her arms as she paced.

She stopped as she saw him. A mingling of relief and uneasiness came over her features. No welcoming smile, he noted bitterly. Brushing aside his hurt that she didn't rush into his arms like a lover, he gruffly asked her where he could find Bailin.

"Perhaps we should talk first."

He was in no mood to spend time with Jishni. His life was torment enough. Wordlessly, and assuming that Bailin was in his room, he left her, and took the steps up to the private rooms of their apartment.

"Step aside," he ordered the two sentries on duty outside Bailin's door. It took a second glance for them to recognize this rough looking Zarian to be their daka. They obeyed him, while trying not to stare at his low class dress.

He clapped and announced himself.

Bailin opened the door, and peered fearfully at his father. "You came home." His reply was cheerless.

"Step aside and let me in." Bail ordered lowly.

Reluctantly, Bailin did as he was told.

Bail entered the room, and slammed the door hard behind him. Without so much as a hello, he attacked. "I left you in charge, Bailin. I expected you to watch after your mother, to at least cause her no grief while I was away. Apparently, that was too much to expect of you."

"Father," he objected angrily, "You don't understand!"

"Do not tell me I don't understand!" he countered, "Your interest in Olla girls, I understand! Your desire for unrestrained freedom, I understand! You think I don't remember what it was like to be seventeen? Damn you!" he thundered, his anger exploding inside, not just at Bailin, but for their restrictive place in Janti society. After experiencing unrestrained freedom in Zaria, to return to the palace pained him, as if he were brought back in chains. "You had a duty to protect yourself, and this family! You let me down, Bailin. You let Jantideva down!"

Bailin trembled with unexpressed fury, but held it in check. His arms were crossed over his chest, and his eyes were on the floor at Bail's feet.

"I spoke to Agart," Bail continued, a tick working in his jaw. "She informs me that you took out a double class windrider, and returned with nothing. You recorded in the manifest that you brought the windrider back, but every crewman she interviewed swears that the windrider didn't return. Where is it, Bailin?"

"It was stolen." he said sullenly.

"Stolen?"

"In Plaetesus."

"Stolen?" he repeated incredulously.

"I was stranded. Rather than call Mother, I took a public transport to Dralon, and walked home from there. I knew she'd be angry about my canceling classes to go to Plaetesus, so I tried to alter the manifest. I didn't think you'd miss one windrider."

The confession had the ring of a memorized alibi.

"A double class windrider isn't like a handful of coins, Bailin," he said, carefully modulating his tone, "it can't very well be misplaced. Especially one that has our family's insignia boldly printed on the side. I'd think a thief would want something smaller, and less conspicuous."

Bailin shrugged, his eyes still focused on the floor at Bail's feet. "How should I know what that thief wanted?"

"Look at me, Bailin." he ordered.

Bailin hesitated, his mouth crooking into a frown.

"Look at me." Bail ordered evenly.

Bailin met his eyes. Defiance burned brightly within their depths.

He took a step toward Bailin, holding his son's defiant glare. "I will send Agart to Plaetesus to ask questions. Which Olla cabaret were you patronizing?"

Bailin broke their eye contact for a second, pausing as if coming up with a name. Finding Bail's eyes again, he said, "The Zunnzer Club."

Sardonically, Bail said, "The Zunnzer? Pretty rough club for a young man. I've heard the women there perform live sex acts with each other on command."

Bailin's defiance broke long enough to express his shock.

Bail laughed loosely at his son's innocence. The anger in his face made it look like he was baring his fangs at Bailin. "You've never been to the Zunnzer. You weren't there yesterday morning. Where were you?"

Warily, Bailin said, "I was with a woman."

"Who?" Bail prodded doubtfully.

"An Olla girl. You wouldn't know her."

Bail planted his hands on his hips. "Try me."

Bailin's defiance fled, and apprehension creased his face. "It's private! What difference does it make, she had nothing to do with the windrider being stolen!"

"What is her name?" Bail insisted.

He faltered lightly, "Ciana. I don't know her full name. She is from Garma."

"A Garmanite, named Ciana?"

"It may be a falsified name." he offered. "She is pretty, uh, black hair, black eyes, dark skin, like a Garman. I met her through Hyan. I meet her outside the Zunnzer a few times a week. The windrider was there when it was stolen."

More, and more lies.

"If a daka's windrider was parked outside the Zunnzer a few times a week, the journalists from the Crier would make certain all of Jantideva knew about it." Bail snapped irritably.

"The Crier turns a blind eye when your men kill Shodites by the hundreds." Bailin retorted defensively, "Why would they care if I have sex with an Olla girl?"

Bail's frustration was peaking. "You answer me this," he asked through gritted teeth, "Why take a double class windrider to meet your mistress, instead of a standard? Eh?"

"I.....I.....it was the only one available!" he declared.

Bail smiled mirthlessly. "I can easily find out if that is true, Bailin."

"You don't believe a word I say!" Bailin accused.

"I'll believe the truth when I hear it!" he shouted.

"Fine! I gave the windrider to Cleses and Solien's soldiers!" Bailin retorted hotly, "The Shodite fugitive named Iada is a pilot, and she flew it out of Dralon yesterday afternoon!"

Feeling outrageously mocked, Bail growled, "We aren't finished with this." and he stalked out of Bailin's room.

Jishni waited for him expectantly in the hall. "What happened between you?" she asked, "I heard shouting,"

Unable to abide her presence, he stalked away, saying over his shoulder, "I will contact you as soon as I know more. In the meantime, Bailin is forbidden to leave his room!"

Jishni insisted on following him out. "Bail, please, we need to talk."

"Our son is defiant." he snapped, "What is there to talk about?"

"Dilgopoche." she said, "I want to travel there."

His step quickened. "Go and see him, I don't care." He reached the stairs, and plunged down them, desperate to escape her eager plans to spend time with her lover.

"Bail!" she demanded of his back, "I need you to come home!"

He paused, a glimmer of hope pulling him back, but before he could turn fully to face her, she added:

"I need you to stay with the children to free me to go to Dilgopoche. Trev could take me, I'd be perfectly safe. Having you here is the only way I'd feel secure being parted from Janus a few days."

"You want me to watch our children so you can run off and meet your lover. No wonder our son is laying with Olla girls."

"Ridiculous, I am merely going to...." and as she processed the fullness of what Bail had said, she demanded, "Is that what he told you? He is seeing an Olla girl?"

He shook his head. How he resented her today! He continued on, unwilling to listen to more of her demands, her needs.

"Bail!" she shouted after him, "Is that what he told you?"

"An Olla girl is a perfect mistress for a young man," he replied flatly, "a trite mistress, an obvious mistress, a terrific alibi!"

"What are you talking about?" she demanded, "Bail! Please, wait, can't you at least give me a minute of your time?"

He entered the lift, and pulled the lever to close the door. Looking into Jishni's face, gruffly, he said, "No."

The door closed, and he was immediately relieved to be out of her presence.

Trev waited for him in the dark blue windrider they'd bought in Zaria. Blue, in Zaria, is said to invite the protection of the Guardian. Zarian houses are blue, and they fly blue windriders, all for the sake of a centuries old superstition. Bail had wanted to blend in, and he could not have done so flying his silver and white windrider, replete with the Masing Star on the side.

Landing in the docking bay near Zunnzer, among hundreds of small, unmarked, darkly colored windriders, he noted again that there was no possible way his son could have landed one of Ona's double class windriders here, or anywhere in Plaetesus, and not be noticed.

In Zunnzer, he and Trev mingled with the girls, drank, watched the shows; establishing themselves as patrons while casually inquiring about the famous people that came through. Councilmen? Leaders? The Olla girls were as eager to talk about their experiences as they were to dance. None of them ever remembered seeing a palace windrider in the docking bay, or meeting an actual daka, except-

"Daka Kinn," a tiny Olla girl told Bail. She looked fourteen, or fifteen, and was pale, like a Rysenk, with dark eyes. "He come incognito, but I recognized him from a picture of the dakas my boss has in his recreation room. He paid me off with a few drinks, and I promised to keep quiet about him being here."

"Obviously he didn't pay you enough."

She smiled slyly and leaned her full body against his. "I don't tell all my clients about him, just the few I find extremely attractive."

Bail fended her off with a gentle hand on her arm. "I'm just here to drink and pass the time."

"Oh," she pouted, but amusement lay behind the pout, "too bad. If you change your mind, I'll be around."

Hours later, Trev joined him at a table. "If Bailin was here, he wasn't here this morning. And no one knows a Garmanite named Ciana." Trev laughed loosely. He was drunk, and his clothing was loosened. He'd been enjoying the delights of the Zunnzer Club. "Have you ever heard of a Garmanite named Ciana? What kind of a lie was that? If he is going to persist lying to you, he needs to improve his lies."

Bail grunted his agreement. His eyes were pensive and on his drink, only his second of the night.

Trev frowned, and slapped Bail on the shoulder. "As long as our work here is done, you should go have fun. I haven't spoiled all the Olla girls for you," he grinned roguishly.

"I'm not in the mood for fun." he replied, "What could Bailin have possibly done with a windrider that he felt compelled to lie about it?"

"Ditch it in the Tronos?"

Bail hadn't allowed himself to consider a scenario where Bailin had avoided near death. The whole idea made him too nervous.

Like a demon voicing Bail's fears, Trev went on, "And what if he wasn't alone? Maybe he ditched the thing, and was the only one to survive. That, in itself, is enough to fear disclosure."

"He lied on the manifest," Bail replied, "about his security team. He left the palace alone. Why?"

"You check and make sure all your young Shodite women are accounted for, and intact?"

"Are you saying he was taking a Shodite woman off somewhere to be alone?" and then it struck him, "No, Bailin wouldn't do that, he's too idealistic about the Shodites. He wouldn't use one, not like that."

Trev shrugged. "Fiery idealism can be doused by a healthy dose of lust. Especially if it is wet enough."

"Jishni isn't keeping an eye on him," Bail said vehemently, "Her mind is on Janus, and Cobo, and not with her older sons, who need her. And they need me, too, and where am I?"

"Acting like a dead man in Zaria." Trev offered.

"Jishni wants me to watch the children so she can run to Cobo." he said wrathfully, "Well, I think I will. But not here. In Zaria."

Trev's brows tweaked upward. "And what of your search for Archer."

Bail looked at his drink, his eyes unfocused. "I will never stop searching for Archer. But my life must go on, too. I have a home in Zaria."

"A rented bungalow." Trev corrected, "That is hardly large enough for you and that black cloud that follows you around."

"We will find a larger home." Bail insisted, "On the Sochen sea."

"Jishni won't allow it." Trev said flatly.

Bail's mouth curved with distaste for his wife as he ruminated on the correctness of Trev's assessment. Jishni would never let him take their children away from her, even for only a few weeks. It wouldn't matter to her that Bail missed them. She'd tell Bail to come home, which, under the circumstances was inconceivable.

Bail finished his drink, and considered how he might be able to get around Jishni.

જ⊷જ⊷જ⊷જ⊷જ⊷જ⊷જ⊷જ⊷જ⊷

Bailin's decision to run away was made in haste, and in anger. His parents didn't understand him, nor did they respect him enough to allow him a modicum of freedom. He was as much a prisoner of their will, as Ksathra was to the will of Jantideva. He waited until the whole house was sleeping, including the kitchen staff, to avoid being seen. He packed lightly. He didn't care for his possessions as much as he cared for his freedom. He took a few items of clothing, those made by Ksathra's hand and a handful of tokens for public transport, enough to get them to Old Rathia. From there, they could either go into Shodalum, or lose themselves in the wilderness along the Peril. They will settle, build a home, have children, and live as commoners.

He pulled down the sashes from the drapes on the windows and tied them together. Measuring them with his arms, he found they would bring him short of the ground by sixty-five feet.

Thinking rashly, he decided his only recourse was to climb to the roof, and let himself back into the palace. No problem, he thought. The outer walls of the palace were amply decorated with statuary, providing safe foot holds and hand holds. Once he reached the roof, he could let himself back into the palace through an attic window, and from there, slip out of the palace and to Dralon.

He tied the end of his makeshift rope to his bedpost. He flung open his windows. As he looked down at the sheer drop to the fountain, the pads of his feet and his consha tingled with apprehension.

He rechecked the knots in his rope, and tied it to his waist.

He tossed his bundle of clothing out the window. He watched it as it sailed to the ground, landing on a patio beside a fountain with a nearly inaudible thud. The bundle broke open and a tunic popped out, its arms and torso laying flat on the ground. From his room, it looked too much like a headless body lying broken on the patio.

"Not an omen." he asserted to himself, shaking off his fear.

Breathing shallowly, he sat on the window ledge, and flung a leg over the side. He let his leg dangle there a moment, languishing in indecision. If he left now, he mused, who would be here to speak on the behalf of the Shodites? Daka Jishni, who is nothing more than a socialite with a title attached to her name? Daka Bail, who is a blood hungry war general? Daka Voktu, who (by his own admission) would not make a proper daka?

"It's not my problem." he said aloud. "I was never meant to be daka. That was Taen's place."

Reaching forward, he took hold of carving in the stone and climbed the rest of the way onto the window ledge.

He squatted there a moment, and made the mistake of looking down. He grunted a moan, and clung to the design on the palace walls with a vice like grip. His breaths came in short, intermittent bursts. He fought for calm, and looked for his next handhold. Above him was the head of a long forgotten saint. Large enough to provide a decent hand hold, but.....his eyes fixed on a crack in the stone. A small, thin crack.

He looked for another handhold. The next statue over, the head of yet another saint, was similarly cracked. The damage of time, damage that no one fixed, because who in their right mind would take a stroll on the ledge and notice?

"Can't go up." he hissed to himself.

He looked down again. Below his room was his mother's study, and below his mother's study, on the next floor down, was a guestroom. An empty guestroom.

If he could not go up, he would go down.

He grabbed hold of the makeshift rope, and let his legs dangle off the ledge. Fighting paralyzing fear, he willed his hands to move on the knotted sash, one hand after the other. He descended slowly.

By the time he reached his mother's study, he was properly terrified. A breeze had picked up, and curled around him, causing him to rock and sway madly. He pulled himself onto the ledge, and leaned heavily on the wall to rest and catch his breath.

He was faced, now, with a choice. He could either continue down another floor, dangling by a sash that was not made to hold his weight, or re-enter the palace through the study, taking the chance of being caught by his mother. Neither appealed to him greatly.

The drapes in the study were parted, revealing muted darkness. His mother had gone to bed hours ago. No one would be in the study. She sometimes left a light on in her study, forgetting to turn it off as she left the room.

He crept to the window and ran his fingers down the seam where the two hinged windows met. It was unlocked, and parted to his touch. He opened the window wide, cringing as its hinges protested. The sound seemed to rip the quiet of the night.

He paused a moment, listening for movement in the study. Positive the study was empty, he stepped inside through the part in the curtains.

And came face to face with his father.

Bail's expression was stormy. He grabbed Bailin by the seat of his pants and yanked him into the room forcefully.

"What exactly do you think you are doing?" he thundered, "Trying to get yourself killed?"

Bailin noticed many things at once. The muted light he'd seen was the glow of his mother's private communications theater, and beyond the glow, in the darkness, another figure stood in the room with them. He'd thought a moment it was his mother, until he heard Trev's sardonic voice.

"Going out to hook up with his Olla girl, more like."

"Disobedient child!" Bail shouted. "You were told to stay in your room!"

Bailin was already in enormous trouble. He didn't feel like he had much to lose, so he let himself be led by his anger. "I am not a child!" he shouted in return, "I am a man, and I deserve more respect than you give me!"

Trev burst into mocking laughter.

Unfortunately, his father wasn't as amused by his bid for independence. His features were malevolent with fury. "A man are you? You are not enough of a man to take your punishment when given, or to tell the truth! You are no more than a boy in a man's body. I've spoiled you too long. As of tonight, you will go into the service."

"No!" Bailin retorted, "I do not want the service!"

"I don't care what you want!" Bail fumed.

Jishni's theater chimed, breaking through the tense moment. His father twitched, and glanced over his shoulder.

"I got it." Trev said, and he moved to the ariq stone and took a copy of the message.

"What are you doing?" Bailin demanded.

"I am taking care of my family." Bail replied evenly.

Trev shut down the theater. "Done."

His father grabbed him by the arm to escort him out of the study. The sash he had tied to his waist hampered them for as long as it took Bailin to untie his own knot.

Jishni met them in the corridor. She wore a dressing robe, and her hair was down, spilling in silky curls over her shoulders. Bail's eyes reflected involuntary appreciation for her appearance, then hardened angrily again.

"What is this?" she demanded.

"Bailin tried to escape us by climbing out of his window and into your study."

"Bailin!" she exclaimed, her face paling slightly.

Bail nodded at Trev. "Take Bailin to his room, and stand over him until I get there. I need a word with Jishni."

Trev took Bailin by the arm to escort him away. Bailin shrugged off the insistent hand, and threw an angry glare at his father. "You can't make me go into the service."

"The service?" Jishni questioned.

"You go to your room," Bail ordered, "or I will find a more repugnant punishment for you, Bailin."

"Anything is better than living in this house!" he declared, and he tried to stalk off.

"Trev, make sure he goes to his room." Bail ordered sharply, "Use force if necessary."

As Trev came up beside him, Bailin threw him a warning glare. "Don't touch me."

Trev held out his hands in surrender, an amused grin on his face.

Bailin thoroughly hated Trev for the grin he wore.

His sentries were surprised to see him walk down the hall, and fell all over themselves to discover how he'd escaped, to somehow deflect blame from themselves for letting him slip away while under their care.

Trev stayed in his room, and ignoring Bail's glare, he casually pulled the tied sashes inside and followed them to the bedpost they'd been tied to. The bedpost was split. It looked ready to give way under Bailin's weight.

Bailin was caressing the split the wood, feeling a bit sick to his stomach, when his parents entered his room. His father was no less furious with him, but the force of his fury had drained away. His mother was stoic, though her eyes were red rimmed from crying.

Her voice was subdued as she gave their collective verdict. "Your father and I have decided you will go to Odhran to train for the military."

His heart sunk. Odhran was the military outpost closest to Rysenk, in the middle of nowhere, and thousands of spans from Ksathra. "But mother....I have a life here I don't want to leave!"

"A woman, you mean?" she asked sharply. "You are too young to be so enamored. A few years in the military will remind you that your first responsibility is to Jantideva."

"You will not be alone in Odhran." Bail said, "I will be there to personally oversee your progress, and Voktu will come, too."

Bailin looked at his mother quizzically. "What about our family here?"

Jishni dropped her eyes and abruptly left the room.

Bail said, "We have a home in Odhran. The three of us will live there for now, while you go through your training, and Janus will visit often."

"And mother?"

The hardness in his father's eyes faltered, and he looked away. "She has responsibilities which tether her to the Center-plex."

In other words, she isn't coming. Bailin felt sicker by the minute. In one twenty four hour period, he'd managed to tear his family apart.

"Father," he said earnestly, "I will train here if you like. I will do so voluntarily."

"It is done, Bailin. Once our home in Odhran is ready, we will leave." The hardness in his eyes returned, "Until then, you are not permitted privacy. The sentries will be posted inside your room. Understood?"

"Yes," he replied softly.

After his father and Trev left him in the company of armed guards, he sat on his bed and stared off into the disaster he'd created all around him.

ৼৼৼৼৼৼৼৼৼ

Gella took her place in front of their group, setting their pace. They followed the beach, walking through the early morning hours, and rested through the heat of the afternoon.

For much of their journey, the men took turns carrying Forsythio. Two men would make a seat for him by clasping their hands together. Praj and Korba carried him longest that morning, assuring Forsythio often that he was so slight they hardly noticed his weight.

Gella saw the strain in their faces after a few hours of carrying the slight man. Korba especially, though he was kindest to the older man. He treated Forsythio as a sacred being, as her own countrymen treated an Elder. Finally, she saw the Shodite in the handsome young Janti-born man.

After their rest, and as evening approached, they were on their way again. Shelon and Tam took Forsythio. Korba objected, insisting he could continue to carry their Elder.

Gella took Korba by the arm. "Let them." and before he could object further, she said, "Walk with me."

He seemed taken aback that she wanted to walk with him, much less speak to him. She hadn't shown an interest in his company in weeks.

He fell into step beside her, seeming unsettled.

Once they were far enough ahead, and out of Forsythio's ear shot, she said, "I respect how well you treat Forsythio."

"He is our Elder," he explained, as if his treatment of Forsythio needed no explanation.

"Not many Shodites of Janti-birth seem to understand the sacredness of the Elders. Wouldn't you agree?"

"No, not at all," he asserted, "I know few Shodites who disregard our Elders."

"But, when you took me to Shod City, I saw many old people on the streets, begging. Is that what you consider well cared for?"

"They weren't Elders."

"Of course they were." Gella replied, "Perhaps they weren't wise enough to sit on a council, or hand down judgements in disputes, like Forsythio, but they were the Elders of their clans. Of their families. Here, in Shodalum, we take care of the very old and sick. They serve a purpose in our society."

"Yes, here you only throw away your youths." Korba replied pointedly, "Like you, Gella. Did you deserve to be abandoned?"

She prickled at his reminder of her family's callousness. "I suppose I would have been better off with a benefactor, that way I wasn't thrown away until I was old....and too frail to earn a living doing more than begging for food."

Korba suppressed a smile at her sarcasm. "I see Shelon hasn't dulled your talons."

"No man could." she retorted lightly.

They were silent. Korba looked back at Shelon and Tam, the two of them acting as one to carry Forsythio. Praj and Iada was arm in arm, and Ule trailed behind them, occasionally stopping to throw a stone into the water.

"I still love you." Korba admitted as he turned forward. "Call me a fool-"

"You are a fool," Gella replied irritably. "Korba, it is insanity to pursue me now. I am Shelon's."

"I hurt you by pursuing you." he said, "I won't make that mistake twice. How was I to know that Shelon would-" he faltered, and sheepishly, he went on, "I honestly thought I was doing you a service, warning you off Shelon. He was never one to form lasting attachments with women, and that opinion comes from Iada, not me. But that has changed with you, and there is also the child to think of. You child needs you to be happy in order to grow strong. Shelon makes you happy. I can only hope you do not hate me for what I did."

She sighed, submission to the uncomfortable topic of conversation. Matter-factly, she admitted, "A week ago, I would have loved to throttle you with my bare hands. But love is a strange beast, Korba. I can sympathize with your motives. Of course I do not hate you."

"I am relieved to hear you say that," He threw a quick glance over his shoulder at the sound of Shelon's full voice as he spoke to Forsythio. Regretfully, he said, "I only wish Shelon felt the same. He made it perfectly clear how he felt about me. And, of all people, he is the last I would have wished to displease."

"He will forgive you in time." Gella said with certainty.

As if to mock her assurance, Shelon barked Korba's name. "You are taking Gella too far ahead!" he reprimanded.

Korba obediently stopped, and waited for the group to reach them. Gella went ahead a few more steps feeling the need to be defiant, then stopped, and impatiently waited, too.

She fell in step beside Shelon, and Korba walked with Iada and Praj. Gella noticed Korba was careful to avoid looking her way once with the others. Shelon did not tell her what he had said to Korba, but she could guess readily enough, judging from how Korba had avoided even looking her way. She made a mental note to try to soften Shelon's heart toward him.

When the sun went down, Ule lit the oil lamp Gella had allowed them to bring, and they followed the dancing circle of light it created.

They continued on well into the night, until Forsythio lay on Tam's shoulder and began snoring loudly. Tam commented that he was ready to begin snoring, himself.

Shelon suggested they rest. They made camp on a sandy outcropping in the elbow of gentle hills.

After they'd eaten, Gella took a leisurely stroll up a gentle slope above the camp. The grassy plain was giving way to a desert. The light sand sparkled in the night.

She saw Shelon ascending to her out of the corner of her eyes. As he stood at her side, his head tilted to the sky, he said, "I've never seen stars like this, Gella. I am in awe."

She looked up at the sky she had been missing, and smiled. "It is the world as the creator meant it to be."

She looked down and pointed to the horizon. "There, do you see the lights in the distance?"

"Nari?" he said hopefully.

"With a quick pace, we'll be there by morning." Her eyes traveled the length of his Janti clothed body. "We will begin seeing my people. You, and the others, will have to wear your wraps."

"We would gladly do handstands for you if it meant an end to our trek." he said. He put his hand on the back of her neck and rubbed away the tightness there. "You seem to be holding up well. Are you?"

"I'm tired," she said, and she tossed a brilliant grin over her shoulder at him, "but I am better off than you, with your wobbly Janti legs."

He chuckled. "Yes, indeed, I will have to toughen if I am to live in Shodalum."

She leaned into his body and let herself relax. "Our walking is not done once we reach Nari. If Thib agrees to be our voice before the Elders, we have to go to Sidera. It is a very long trek."

"I would walk one hundred days, if it meant a chance for freedom." he said firmly.

"I believe you would."

They stared at the desert for a long while, resting in each other's silence. Her thoughts were on Nari, seeing Thib, and begging for a mouthful of pickled yava, for which she had a mighty craving.

Shelon's thoughts were pensively caught in their future. Quite suddenly, he said, "If Thib cannot convince the Elders to act on my people's behalf, is there a chance she can at least convince the council to allow you to stay here, and resume your life as a citizen?"

Despite the warmth of the night, she went cold. Her vision of future in Shodalum without Shelon flooded her mind, and an emotion akin to panic flooded her senses. "You promised you wouldn't leave me." she said abruptly.

"Gella," he said rationally, "it may be the only way my son will be born free."

She pushed off his chest and glared up into his eyes. "You promised."

His eyes flickered away. Repentant, he said, "I know. I will keep my promise. But I couldn't help the thought. Call it a.....weak moment."

She gripped his tunic with both hands, and fought her tears. After the shock of encountering Mo'ghan had worn off, she had told herself that none of her vision had been true. That it had been a delirious nightmare brought on by guilt for refusing to support Shelon's plan to address the Elders. But, faced with Shelon's weakness, she feared he might succumb, and leave her for the good of his son.

Though she was exhausted, she slept poorly. Every time she closed her eyes, she saw herself living alone in her cottage in Calli.

After resting, they prepared for the final leg of their journey. The Janti-born wrapped themselves in the strips of cloth Gella had made for them in Moom. Gella had demonstrated how to use the wraps while they were still in Moom, but faced with actually putting them on, she was forced to verbally talk them through the process. Wrapping one leg tightly, then tying off that piece at the waist. Wrapping the other leg with a strip long enough to continue covering the torso to the middle chest. Wrapping one arm with a short piece that wrapped around the neck. Wrapping the other with a long piece that finished covering the upper torso. The loin wrap was a wider piece, which went around the waist and hips, forming a sort of skirt. Last were the wraps for the feet and hands, which were long enough to go half way up the calves, and forearms, respectively.

Apart from the others, Gella helped Shelon tied off his hand wraps. Once he was dressed, she stood back to look at him, a smile on her face. "You are handsome."

He grinned ruefully. "I feel like an Iladdatha monk being prepared for my final rest."

"You'll get used to it," she told him, "the wraps are more comfortable than Janti clothing, and by far more useful."

Ambivalently, he fondled the edge of his loin wrap. "I feel a bit exposed."

Gella frowned at him. "Not a bit of your skin shows, except your face, and those ears." she pointed out with a smile.

He grinned, and sardonically he replied, "The absence of underclothes, and being able to feel the breeze on my consha is enough to make me feel exposed."

She shook her head in dismay. "After a day in the desert, you won't feel so modest. You'll be happy for that breeze on your consha. You may even desire to behave as a real Shodite, and go natural."

"I doubt that very much."

He did like the others, and wore his Janti pants over top the wraps. His modesty baffled her. He, like all the Janti she'd met, were oddly proper. They did not like exposing their bodies to the sun and the air, but they conducted their private lives like the street whores in Strum. If a man can lay with numerous women, why does exposing his consha to warm air bother him so?

She decided she would never understand that side of Shclon, nor would she try. It really was too confusing.

They walked deep into the night, Forsythio snoring all the way. As the sun rose, Gella pointed out the distant sight of Thib's home.

Forsythio, awake and intent on Gella's description of Nari, straightened in the arms of his helpers. "Quiet," he said, cocking his head as if he were listening to something. "I hear singing."

They stopped, and listened, wary of the bandits Gella had warned them they might encounter on their trek to Nari. Soon, they all heard what Forsythio heard first. A single voice, singing at the top of his lungs.

"There, over there." Praj said, pointing down the beach.

In the distance there was a lone traveler. He wore wraps, and carried a small satchel.

"He's harmless." Gella decided.

They walked on, and as they got close enough to see him, Gella recognized him as the man she and Cobo first encountered in Strum.

"Hail, Radi il Ubay!" she called out to him.

Praj's jaw slackened. "....il Ubay?"

Gella threw a curious glance his way.

"Hail fellows!" Radi called out, with a wave. As he came closer, he grinned broadly at Gella. "Oh yes, I recognize you! Gella al Perraz, of Calli!"

Gella felt curiously carefree and happy for meeting a countryman on the road, though she barely knew this man. She grabbed his arms, and grinned. "I hardly recognize you! Last time I saw you, you were a wasted man. Look at you! You've fattened!"

He smiled knowingly. "I was healed by Betnoni."

She took his hands, so strong now, and looked into his face. He was not an old man, after all. The wasting disease had made him look ancient, but now he looked young. Perhaps thirty.

His eyes went around the group that had assembled behind Gella. His eyes rested on Forsythio, and his gaiety faded. Looking soberly into Gella's eyes, he said, "I hope you are not returning to the blessed sands for healing?"

"No, we are going to see Thib. Why?"

"So many have congregated on the blessed place that Betnoni could not accommodate them all. She healed as many as she could, and left the sands. I was one of the lucky ones."

Gella wouldn't have believed that Betnoni would heal one person, much less many, but here was proof, in Radi's sparkling blue eyes. "I'm very glad for you, Radi."

"You are il Ubay?" Iada asked, her voice tremulous.

Radi glanced at her, and smiled. "Yes, of Lot." and he looked into Gella's eyes, "I am not surprised to have encountered a friend this morning, Gella. Last night, Betnoni came to me in a dream. She told me to rise and walk and she showed me the way. She told me I was to be a guide for her again, this time to my kinsmen. Do you think she meant that you and I are now kinsmen because I guided you and your brother to her once, before?"

"I, and my brothers, are il Ubay." Praj said softly. "We are your kinsmen."

Gella's threw a quick glance at the brothers, then to Shelon for confirmation. She hastily remembered Cobo telling her, a long time ago, that nothing in life happened by chance. She thought he had spun the philosophy in jest, because he had been chewing yava all day and was laughing drunkenly as he said it, and crying too, as he usually did when he had too much yava. Laugh and cry at the absurdities of their existence.

Radi looked curiously at Praj. "You do seem familiar, but I don't know you from Lot. Are you kin from the Rwezd tribe of il Ubay?"

Praj's voice choked as he said, "I am Praj of the house of Xxirius Xsang, your kin from Jantideva returned to see my homeland."

Radi's mouth formed a shocked oh, and he went to Praj. He took Praj's arms, and looked into eyes that had a similar shape and shade. Gella was struck by the resemblance she saw in the two men, though over two millennia separated Praj's branch of the il Ubay tribe from Radi's.

Radi smiled. "Then, welcome home, my brother!"

He embraced Praj, and the large, burly, dangerous man Gella had grown to know as a droll cutthroat began to weep. In turn, Radi welcomed each of the brother's into Shodalum with an emotional embrace, Tam next, then, once he'd set down Forsythio, Ule.

Shelon watched the reunion, longing in his eyes.

Gella took his hand. "You will meet your kin, too." she said lowly, "I will take you to your home, myself."

Shelon's eyes were trained on Radi and Ule. Radi touched Ule's graying blond hair, then his own, remarking on how similar they looked. "My only home is with you." Shelon said. His stoic demeanor could not hide his underlying sadness from her, and she sensed his mind was on Tuv Grethian, the Janti who'd sired him, and whom he most resembled.

She reached up and caressed his cheek, and he turned into her hand to look into her face. "You are my home, too, Shelon."

He attempted a smile, and kissed her hand, but his eyes returned to the il Ubay kinsmen, and the sadness returned.

Enthusiastically, Radi took charge of their trek and had them follow him to Thib's house by the sea.

The throng of Betnoni worshippers had built a massive shrine in Her honor on the beach where she had appeared to Thib. A large, natural rock face had been carved meticulously into Betnoni's likeness, and offerings of food, flowers, clothing, and water were left at her feet. There were six devotees at the shrine, laying prostrate in the sand, praying to their goddess. One had hold of Betnoni's feet, and was begging for her son to be healed of an illness.

Radi guided them beyond the shrine, and into the field. On Thib's land, the temporary tent city had turned into a community, and permanent homes were being built.

"The ones who are staying intend to devote their lives to Betnoni," Radi explained.

Her eyes on a mud hut in progress, Gella asked, "What does Thib think about all this?"

"It was she who invited us to stay and build!"

Thib's home came into view, a simple hut set apart from the village growing nearby. Thib was outside, seeming to watch the progress of the village. Gella realized as they approached, that Thib waited for them.

Her eyes were sharply on Gella. "Sister of Ver dala Ven, you have returned."

Gella had to fight off her temperament. She hadn't liked the way Thib had treated her the last time she encountered the old woman, and she didn't like the way Thib looked at her now.

"We've come with an Elder of the Janti-born Shodites, seeking your wisdom." Gella said, carefully modulating her tone.

She flicked a glare at Shelon, who stood at Gella's back expectantly. She behaved as if she knew this was the man Gella had chosen as a mate. "And where is your brother?"

"He is attending to his family." Gella replied.

"Hmm." she replied noncommittally, and her shrewd, black eyes found Forsythio's face. Ule and Korba had put him down at his direction, and he now stood by Shelon, clinging lightly to Shelon's arm. "Bring your Elder into my home. I will communicate with him in private."

Shelon objected, saying, "We are a delegation, and all wish to be heard."

Thib's glare returned to Shelon, her eyes flicking over his Janti trousers, clearly displeased, then reaching his face. "And who are you?"

"Shelon....al Entlay." he said, saying his whole name with reluctance.

Her brows shot up. "Shelon? Fighting Devil, are you? Are you a fighting man, Shelon?"

"I am."

"I will not hear a fighting man," and her eyes traveled around the delegation, "or his disciples. There is no war in Shodalum. I will hear the Elder, only."

Shelon pressed his lips together, suppressing a retort, fighting to remain diplomatic. Gella had warned him not to anger Thib. She was their only chance of reaching the Elders.

Ule put Forsythio's hand on his arm and led him to Thib's door, allowing Thib to take over from there. Shelon followed, and hovered at the threshold until Thib told him to leave.

Walking away, he grumbled, "I wished to be a part of the negotiations."

"This is why we brought Forsythio." Gella reminded. "Thib will respect the words of an Elder before she respects ours."

He nodded curtly his understanding, yet tension remained bunched in his shoulders.

Hours passed. In the interim, Gella and Shelon went to the beach, and Gella made an offering of the last handful of yava flowers she'd carried with her to the shrine of Betnoni. In prayer, she humbly asked that her child be born healthy.

As if answering her prayer, a devotee offered Gella a bowl of pickled yava root. Gella took it gratefully, and ate it with relish. It was sour, and salty, and the best tasting yava she'd ever had in her life.

Shelon stood over her as she ate, pensively looking into the face of Betnoni's likeness.

A shout from Iada compelled them to leave the shrine, and return to Thib's home.

Forsythio and Thib stood outside, and were surrounded by Shelon's small delegation.

Iada greeted them as they approached. "Thib has agreed to speak for us to the Elders."

Shelon grunted his satisfaction.

Thib found his eyes. "We will leave in two days. Time enough to gather your strength, and to prepare. It will be a long and treacherous journey. Be warned. You may make this journey for nothing. I doubt the Elders who are presently sitting in judgment of our land have the courage to lift the banishment from your head. Are you prepared for that end, Shelon al Entlay?"

Shelon stared down at her. Firmly, he said, "No."

Her thin lips crooked in a knowing smile. Gella could only wonder what Forsythio told Thib about him.

Thib instructed Radi to find their group accommodations in their village, then she waved them away with both hands. As Gella followed Radi, she glanced back at Thib. Her shoulders were stooped, her body, frail, yet she was surrounded by an indomitable strength. Despite Gella's earlier resentment, she found she respected Thib.

They celebrated, all but Shelon and Gella. He lay outside by a fire, silent, melancholy, staring at the stars. Gella lay her head on his legs, and let his silence be, feeling with him a nag of anxiety for being so close to their objective, yet as far away as ever.

ৰ৴ৰ৴ৰ৴ৰ৴৹৹৹৹৹

The report wasn't false. The daka's windrider was in a field near Peril Bay, next to the Shodite border.

Echo instructed her squadron to systematically circle the craft while scanning for signs of life. Her brown eyes searched the land around the craft, her logic working quickly. Because the craft was so near the Shodalum border, she now suspected that subversives, perhaps Zarians trying to make a point, had stolen it.

"No signs of life." Her tech leader reported flatly.

Her thin mouth pressed in a hard line. "Have you scanned the region?"

"No sir."

"Then do so." she ordered flatly.

"Yes sir."

The handsome tech looked away from her and went about his duty. They were the same age, and went to school together. In those days, Echo was a young society woman and wore the gowns, the accoutrements of a young society woman. He, Lomen is his name, was her lover until they graduated from the academy. In school, she had bested him in grades, physical challenges, and weaponry. She graduated with a rank, he graduated as a tech. At that point, it didn't matter how broad his shoulders were, or how pretty his eyes were, or how good he was in bed, he was a subordinate. A person in her past.

Besides, Echo's career left her no leisure to be a constant lover or a wife. Her black uniform was her life, and she wore it with pride. More pride than she would have felt as the wife of a handsome security tech.

"The region is clear for two spans in all directions." Lomen said.

"Expand your region scan," she ordered, and to the pilot, she said, "Land, but be sure to stay clear of the scene."

509

"Yes, Commander Agart."

They went down slowly into the field.

Inside the daka's windrider, her investigative team went to work. A search team went through the entire craft, in search of the thieves, or evidence to their identities or whereabouts. Nothing was found, and nothing was missing, except the medical supply box. Its contents had been emptied on the floor of the cockpit.

A tech team extracted the flight data from the on board computer. She expected it to tell her what she already knew. Once she had reported the craft missing, possibly stolen, her office had been flooded with communications from Security offices as far south as Horp Row, and as far north as Old Rathia. She connected the times and places of the multitudes of sightings, and concluded that the craft left from the palace, landed in Horp Row, next in Dralon, then was flown to a Pril garbage incinerator near track four hundred in Shod City. From there was flown to the Shodalum border.

Instead, she found that the person who took the windrider had disabled the recording systems. "Whoever did this knew what he was doing." Lomen said, "It might have been an insider. Maybe someone on the daka's repair crew." he offered.

"If it was an insider, the bi-lo detectors will be off line, too. Check them." she ordered curtly.

The bi-lo detectors were a fairly recent addition to the security devices installed in the daka's windriders. They scanned the full body systems of whoever sat in the pilot and co-pilot seats, and snapped a picture of them for record.

"Bi-lo is online." Lomen said with a grin. "Processing now."

Echo stood over Lomen's shoulder, tapping her finger impatiently on the back of his chair, her eyes eagerly on the data screen.

Five faces appeared in five boxes on the screen. Daka Bailin's face was expected, but the following four took Echo fully aback. She recognized three. Ksathra, of the house of Jantideva. Iada of the house of Yuini Vol. Cleses of Solien's Soldiers.

Her voice carefully modulated, she said, "Have the bi-lo place them in order."

510

The screen changed. Daka Bailin was the first pilot, and sitting with him was Ksathra of the house of Jantideva. Next, Daka Bailin was sitting next to Iada of the house of Yuini Vol. The next sequence, Iada was in the pilot's seat, alone in the cockpit. On the next, the co-pilot's seat was taken by the fifth, unidentified male. The last set of pictures to come up was of Cleses and Iada.

"Daka Bailin is a subversive." Echo whispered.

Lomen glanced at her, a horrified expression on his face. "He can't be....he is the heir apparent. Guardian help us."

She gritted her teeth. Making a decision she knew she had to make, she said, "Give me the bi-lo chip."

Lomen removed the unit for her, his hands shaking slightly.

She took the chip, and glanced over her shoulder. They were alone. She removed her lume from her sash and shot Lomen in the neck. He died instantly, though the effects of the lume continued to cook him, causing his body to convulse. He fell out of the chair and onto the floor at her feet.

Having heard the lume detonation, her men came running. She quickly hid the chip in her sash, and kicked Lomen's lume off his body. Her men arrived, ready for the heat of battle. Their eyes fell on Lomen, and confusion caused them to stop short.

"I caught him destroying the bi-lo. He threatened me with his lume." she declared, "He must have been in league with the subversives who stole the windrider. Now, we may never know who took the ship from daka Bailin."

"Lomen?" one of her men questioned.

Another said, "He recently took a vacation to Zaria."

Taking advantage of that convenient information, Echo shouted, "He was a subversive! A traitor! A Shodite lover!"

For his crimes, Lomen was treated with the disrespect a subversive deserved. He was stored in the waste receptacle, and kicked a few times for good measure.

Echo left a team on the scene to search for the subversives, reminding them in a pointed way not to encroach on the border of Shodalum. She'd given her order with a smile, and they smiled back at her, understanding her perfectly.

Her report to daka Bail was the same written report she made to her Major General, the report that became public record. Lomen was a traitor, aiding forces unknown and unseen, to escape Jantideva for an unknown purpose. In her report, she suggested it might have had something to do with the recent troubles with Zaria, but her conjecture did not interest the daka. In fact, the daka didn't seem the least bit interested in her investigation and its conclusions. As soon as the windrider was returned, he had Trev Morley and a special crew of techs take the craft apart.

As always, she had to fight for the attention and respect she deserved. Being a woman in the Pliadors was a chore at times.

Placing a protective hand over the chip that was tucked in her sash, she left Ona's landing bay, a grim frown on her features. Her instincts were on target. Had she turned over the bi-lo chip to Bail, daka Bailin's subversive ties to Cleses would have no doubt been buried. No one in Jantideva would have guessed their future daka to be so evil.

Echo knew. And with the knowledge in her hands, Jantideva did not have to worry about daka Bailin ruling their land.

✤✤✤✤✤✤✤✤✤

Max stepped over the border fence, following his superior officer and flanking his best friend, Wenda. Agart had left them six strong, well armed, and empowered to act independently of her will. Their superior, Yed, had them follow the footprints found in the sand at the sight of the stolen windrider, and the footprints lead them to the Shodite border. Alliance law forbade them to cross into Shodalum, but Yed conveniently forgot the law and they crossed. Those that crossed with him, went with an air of impunity.

Max felt guilt the moment his foot touched Shodite soil. He took the Alliance laws seriously. His father was an Alliance judge. He was raised to respect the Alliance above, and before Jantideva. His father would be disappointed in him for breaking the law, especially now that he was an upholder of the law. But he was a first year officer, and had no say. If he disobeyed orders, he may as well quit the Pliadors today.

512

Wenda smiled at him, her eyes crinkling pleasantly at the corners. "We're in Shodalum, and haven't been struck by lightning."

Yed heard her comment, and called out over his shoulder, "Less chat. Pay attention."

Wenda pressed her lips together, masking a smile and suppressing yet another smart remark. Wenda enjoyed inviting and inciting trouble. Max decided long ago that her rebellious nature was the reason he liked her. He was a mild person, with aspirations to be a rebel. Out right rebels appealed to him.

The footprints took them to the beach, and disappeared from there. Yed pointed out that the surf might have obliterated them.

They followed him to the water, all but Max, who had to stop and urinate. Wenda offered to lag behind if he needed help. She loved embarrassing him, and she had succeeded, once again. Max told her to get lost, and finished his business.

As he turned to head down to the beach, he noticed a giant wave rising from the bay and surging toward the team. No one on the team seemed to notice the danger. They loitered on the beach, as if to take a break. Max called out to them, but his voice was drowned in the thunder of waves.

The massive wall of water reached out and grabbed the five of them as one, and wrenched them into the Gryvly.

Max ran down to the water's edge, screaming Wenda's name. He shucked off his battle gear, his weapon, his sash, his boots; again screaming Wenda's name. His only thought was to save her. Forget Yed and the others; they were men he hardly respected. But Wenda, he had to save her.

The wave came again as he prepared to leap into the water. He paused, and watched it, awed and terrified at once, expecting, as it crashed down on him, to find Wenda faster than if he'd simply dove into the Gryvly.

The wave reached upward into the sky, and against all laws of nature, it came to a standstill, a pillar towering above Max. The spray of the mist surrounded him, and he felt he might drown from the density of the air. He took two quick steps back. The mist tightened on him in a vice like grip and prevented his escape.

Just then, he noticed a dark thing floating in the pillar of water. The thing floated to the surface, and Wenda's face popped out for a moment, level with his face. Her expression was serene, eyes partially open, mouth pouting. She was dead, claimed by the Gryvly.

She floated back into the massive body of water, disappearing.

Max screamed, and trembled, and waited to become a part of the sea.

The wave receded abruptly, washing away the dead. Left behind was the mist holding him in place. The mist took on a form. It was a woman of incredible beauty, wearing Suma robes. In his panic, he was still able to notice her big ears, peeking from under long, straight, black hair.

"Your name is Max." she said.

Max was numb, and unable to reply. He stared.

"For whom are you named?"

His mouth moved, but he made no sound. He was thinking about his great-grandfather, who was named Max, and who'd been named for his grandfather Max, and so on.

The woman nodded that she understood. "I was hoping you were named for Ver dala Ven Max."

He remembered the story, remembered her name and her Max.

"Betnoni." he whispered.

"I have spared you, Max," she replied, "so that you may return to Jantideva and remind your people that the Janti are not welcome in Shodalum."

The woman turned to mist, and the mist released him and returned to the sea.

Gasping for air, he backed warily away from the water. His thoughts of rescuing Wenda were cold. She was dead, he was certain of it. Carried to the bottom of the sea by Betnoni.

Finally gathering the courage, he turned and ran up the beach and to the border, and leaped over the fence. He didn't stop running until he reached their transport.

Bail tried a civil approach to questioning Bailin. He took him to a comfortable recreation room, served him ale, (which his mother had strictly forbidden him to drink) and did his best to ingratiate himself to his own son.

"I have many unanswered questions about the windrider." he said easily at one point, "I'm not looking to punish you, Bailin. I just want answers."

After a few drinks, Bailin seemed less cautious, less suspicious. "Okay. The whole story. I'll tell you everything." Bailin proceeded to tell him that he was taking food supplies to Shod City. "I couldn't very well take a guard with me. They would have reported back to you, and I would have been in trouble for interfering with the affairs of other benefactors. I left the windrider in the private bay of Sturgei Textiles, and when I returned it was gone."

Bail suppressed a smile. Finally, the ring of truth. "Are we so terrible that you'd rather have us thinking you are seeing Olla girls than caring for hungry Shodites?"

Bailin's brow darkened, though his tone was moderate. "I've seen how your men treat the Shodites."

His son had managed to make him feel ashamed.

Wiping his shame off his face with a swipe of his hand, Bail went on, "I have one more question, a minor detail. Why did you remove the bi-lo chip?"

Bailin's ignorance was not fake. "What is a bi-lo chip?"

"You really don't know." Bail said, more to himself than to Bailin, though Bailin replied that he did not.

The missing bi-lo chip was a mystery in and of itself. Agart reported that Lomen had sabotaged the bi-lo. Trev could find no damage to the unit, other than the missing chip. And if the chip was damaged, where was it? Trev had questioned Agart on the matter, and Agart continued to maintain that there was no chip to be found on the windrider.

Bail was forced to assume that whoever took the windrider knew about the bi-lo, and it was that person who'd taken the windrider to Old Rathia. The thief could have wanted the craft for any number of reasons. Considering it was found on the Shodalum border, it may have been a trafficker in Shodites. Benefactors had been known to pay mercenaries to wait for Shodites to cross the border.

Whoever it was, they didn't get far. Not according to a Pliador named Max.

Agart scoffed at his story of Betnoni's wrath, and jailed him for leaving his post and for suspicion of murder. She sent another team out to search for the first, and they, too, disappeared. Bail stopped her from sending a third. "Surely you don't believe in that old tale about Betnoni protecting Shodalum?" Agart demanded.

Bail believed. He had to believe. His own father was Ver dala Ven. He'd witnessed first hand his father's amazing control over the elements. He was twelve when the summer rains came with such frequency that the Pril threatened to flood, and destroy Shod City, as well as the multitudes of factories in the industrial quarter. Each day, as the storm clouds gathered, his father would stand on the seventh spire and produce a wind strong enough to turn the clouds in another direction. In the reverse, he'd seen his father produce rainstorms during droughts. He'd seen him clear the Pril of toxins with a hand gesture. He'd seen him heal sick people with a touch. Bail took the reports of Betnoni's emergence from the Gryvly very seriously. Ver dala Ven was a force he could not fight, nor would he try. At this point, he didn't care if he ever discovered who stole the windrider. All that mattered was his son's honesty.

He could now concentrate on his move to Odhran.

He had expected Jishni to fight him harder on his move. She was distressingly pliant on the matter, until they discussed his taking his sons with him. Bailin was easiest for her to release. He was nearly grown, and she knew Bail was right. Bailin needed his father to guide him through his passage to manhood. Voktu was another matter, though he too was reaching maturity quickly. They'd argued heatedly before coming to an uneasy agreement on Voktu. He'd spend time equally in Odhran and Ona until he was of an age to choose where he wanted to make his permanent home.

They were still negotiating on custody of Janus. So far, she'd only agreed to leaving Janus with Bail if she took trips out of the country. In other words, to Dilgopoche.

516

At least she wasn't presently communicating with Cobo. Bail went through her personal messages thoroughly, expecting to find proof that they'd continued their love affair where they'd left off. Instead, he hadn't found one note, one message received from Cobo, or sent to him, since he left for Dilgopoche. It was a small conciliation to know she hadn't thrown him over for the promise of being with Cobo. He was left to know she had thrown him over......period.

Bail decided he should be content that he got what he wanted out of Jishni with relative ease.

"She is eager for her freedom,"

Trev blurted the remark thoughtlessly once Bail told him about their new living arrangements.

More so than I, Bail mused.

Chapter 23

Cobo sensed Jishni's intention to travel to Dilgopoche long before she actually arrived. Her official motive for the visit was to see her son, and to press Ver dala Ven for further information concerning Archer.

She had another, underlying motive, one touching Cobo from her heart. She was on her way to Dilgopoche in order to rekindle their love affair. An aura of freedom surrounded her, unfettered by Bail or the court or the ghost of her father. Cobo's moral determination to honor his brother's claim on her was weakened by the stink of hope, and the silence of the Star's spirit. He wondered if the time for their love had come, finally.

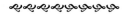

Taen's schedule was hectic. The Men and Women looked to him for guidance on every mundane matter pertaining to their city, from waste removal to the distribution of breeders. They seemed unable to make a clear decision on their own, except when it came to the water. On that issue, they were possessive in the extreme. A new season had begun, and the time had come to set the trade price for goods brought in by the Ryslacs. The trade was made in water, nothing Taen understood with great clarity. One, two, three locks a day? Four, five, six?

Lodan suggested to Taen to allow the Ryslacs to set their own prices. They were the farmers who'd best know how much water they'd need in the coming year. His suggestion was greeted harshly by the Men in charge of the water distribution. Taen was told that distribution was figured on the quality of the goods brought in by each Ryslac farmer. Taen was forced to hold an audience with each individual farmer, and negotiate each case. Invariably, each case became a battle between the Men who'd controlled the water, and wasted most of what they controlled, and the needs of the farmland.

Lodan expected that Taen would be too harassed and tired to entertain Caltha in the evenings. He was wrong. Each night, a few hours after Taen fed his wife her sleeping medication, there would be a pound on the door announcing Caltha's arrival. Taen carried on the dangerous affair with the relish of a thief that stole for the pure enjoyment of committing the crime.

Lodan generally planned evening exercise around the time of Taen's date with infidelity.

Tonight Caltha did not come, and Taen paced. Lodan did not ask why Taen did without her company. He stepped outside the apartment as usual, to perform his exercise. He glanced from right to left at the Huntresses guarding Taen's apartment, and wondered briefly what they thought Caltha was doing in Taen's apartment every night. Attending to Danati? That was probably what Taen told his sentries, and they were obtuse enough to believe just about anything.

In the relative quiet of the common, Lodan moved slowly through his meditation exercises. As he did, he surreptitiously watched for his student to appear on the upper level. She had not missed a morning or evening exercise since he'd first spied her practicing with him.

Tonight she did not immediately appear.

As he started his second cycle, he noticed his student at the portal to the corridor. She waved to get his attention. He paused in the movement he was performing, and looked her way. She threw a worried glance at the sentries at Taen's doorway. Noting they were not looking her way, she showed Lodan that she carried a crudely forged Kai'gam.

She beckoned to him to follow her, and ducked back, disappearing into the corridor.

His heart lightened the moment he saw the kai'gam she held. She was ready for an earnest lesson. But not here. The breeders were severely limited to their freedoms. Wielding a kai'gam was probably forbidden to the smaller Dilgo women.

He hesitated. Glancing at the sentries, he wondered if he could trust them with Taen's safety in his absence. Making a decision, he went to Ver dala Ven's apartment, the next apartment over from Taen's, and clapped.

Surna quizzed warily, "Who is it?"

"Lodan."

The door opened immediately. Lodan looked past Surna to Cobo. Cobo wore a knowing smile. "I'll watch over him." he said without Lodan having to express his desire to teach his student personally, versus his fear for Taen's safety.

Lodan bowed appreciatively at Cobo. "Thank you, Ver dala Ven."

"Good night to you, Lodan."

Eagerly, Lodan entered into the corridor. His student waited half way to the next portal opening. Seeing him, she turned and quickly walked away. He followed.

She led him to the top most level of the palace. This level was as large and open as the city common, but was empty. There were no plants, waterfalls, pools. No resting Dilgos on pillows. Four pillars supported the dome roof, and crude torches attached to each pillar lit the area.

His student walked to the center of the room, turned and faced him as he approached. Her mouth held firm to a wry smile, and her eyes sparkled. She held her kai'gam before her, ready to begin.

"Do you speak any Janti?"

She said something to him in Dilgo that sounded derogatory, and she'd said it with a gleeful smile.

"I wonder if that was a yes, or a no." he replied dryly to himself.

She tapped the end of her kai'gam on the ground and grinned wider at him. "B'lianza."

That word he understood. "Challenge to the death? You want to challenge me? B'lianza?" he asked incredulously, and he couldn't help himself. He laughed.

His student took offense. Her eyes darkened with fury. Belting out a war cry, she lunged toward him. He easily deflected her attack, and their blades clashed. The challenge had begun.

Her form was excellent, better than some of the challengers he'd played in matches during his career as Kai'gam'Mod. She held her kai'gam with a firm grip, her arm flexible, and her movements were controlled as well as graceful. But in her form, he found two faults. The first was in the ferocity of her attack. She threw her blade across his with all her strength in a relentless attack, without leaving herself a reserve of energy in case the challenge lasted longer than a few minutes. The second fault was the placement of her eyes. She diligently watched his kai'gam to anticipate his next move. A common mistake.

He bounded backward two long steps, breaking the rhythm of her attack and giving himself the space he needed to swing his blade above his head. The light play off the etchings in the blade, as well as the subtle vibration it made as he swung it, instantly mesmerized her. Her eyes unfocused, and she froze.

He took eight quick steps forward, and held the blade above her collarbone, mocking the deathblow as he would in the arena. He shouted, "Ha!" to wake her.

Becoming alert, she faltered backwards a step as she saw his blade so close to her neck.

He lowered the blade and chuckled scornfully.

Her fury re-ignited, and she lunged for him, renewing her attack.

"If you want to learn," he shouted at her in Dilgo above the ringing, clanging cacophony of their crossing blades, "I will teach you! End the challenge!"

Fiercely, she snorted, "B'Lianza!"

And as he defended himself, he harnessed a stream of her thoughts. She was determined to prove herself worthy of the Huntress name....Benu.

"Alright, Benu," he retorted, gritting his teeth, "B'lianza!"

He reversed their joust, going on the attack, crossing her blade with as much ferocity as she'd used to attack him. She was not cowed, but excited by the play. She defended herself nicely, and broke from their volley to find refuge by placing a pillar between them. They stalked each other slowly around the pillar, their chests heaving as they each caught their breath. She wore an exhilarated grin, and spouted things in Dilgo at him, challenging words, he thought.

He too, was exhilarated by the exercise. He mocked her in the same tone of voice she used with him. "Are you tired? Are you ready to quit? You will not win, Benu. You will not best me. I am Kai'gam'Mod! I am Lodan!"

She faked a step to the right. Seeing her plan, he moved with her, and let her sprint away in the opposite direction. She laughed as she escaped him, as if she'd ended their contest with a victory.

Casually, he went around the pillar and followed her, swinging his kai'gam in jaunty circles, passing it from hand to hand, and wearing a grin specially made to gall the proud Dilgo woman.

She said something contemptuous at him that he didn't understand.

"B'lianza," he replied, mocking her.

Reddening with fury, she rose her kai'gam over her head and struck a pose. She moved the kai'gam in her hand, a subtle movement. Nothing happened, which frustrated her. She swung the kai'gam in a large circle, ending in the pose, and she attempted the move again.

She was trying to make her kai'gam sing.

"Your form is good," he said in Janti, watching her twist her wrist, "If you had a decent kai'gam, you might be able to make that work for you."

Thinking he'd insulted her, she gave up on the magical move of the kai'gam artist, and threw herself into another full frontal assault. She swung her kai'gam at him, level to slice his body in half. He sprang back, and met her next swing with his blade. As their blades made solid contact, he shoved forward, preventing her from pulling back to swing again. He slid his blade down hers, circled her kai'gam with his and hit the underside of her hands with his hilt. The movement lifted her kai'gam from her hands, and tossed it over his shoulder. It flew and hit the floor behind him with a clatter.

She grabbed her smarting hands and gasped her shock. Apprehensive, she backed away from him. He sensed her expectations. She expected he'd finish the challenge with her death, as he had with Blaec.

He backed away from her, stepping carefully over her kai'gam. Without taking his eyes off her, he picked up her kai'gam and showed her both blades. Wordlessly, he gestured to her plain, flat blade with the tip of his, then reversed the gesture, showing her the curve of his kai'gam, as well as the etchings along the smooth sides.

He then tossed her his blade. It sailed through the air, turning end over end. She reached up and effortlessly caught it by the grip.

He posed for her, as she had for him, encouraging her to try to make his blade sing.

She did as he instructed, swinging the blade overhead, and the blade let out a high pealing whine. Her image faded from his sight.

He suppressed his excitement and concentrated on his opponent, ready to test skills he'd been honing his whole life, but never had the chance to test until today. He felt, rather than heard, the sound of her rapid heartbeat.

As she realized her success, her heart began to beat faster with her own excitement, and she moved, stepping cautiously toward him. He maintained his position, listening to her as she moved around him. The song of the kai'gam flew into an aria, and he instinctively knew the blade was in motion. He brought the Dilgo kai'gam up and perfectly blocked the downward slice of the blade.

As the blades clashed, she appeared to his sights. Her expression turned from triumphant to incredulous disappointment. She hoped to kill him and prove herself, and she could have, if she were a bit more practiced in the art.

A thrill raced through him, and beamed from his expression. He'd waited his entire life for a worthy opponent. The danger she posed to him meant nothing. He wanted more. He pushed her off, and backed away, and with a grin and a beckoning hand, he invited her to try again. She lifted the blade, and again disappeared from his physical sight. He opened his senses to hear her heart beat, but this time he could also feel her breath, her body temperature, her aura. He closed his eyes, and visualized her movements as if he was seeing her with his eyes. She stalked around him, with the intention of attacking him from the back.

From somewhere below, a bell tolled.

She halted. Listened. He felt her intention falter.

She moved toward him, and gently lay the blade of his kai'gam over hers, ending its song and allowing him to see her. He opened his eyes to find her bright blue eyes were steadied on his. They were full of the intelligence and the intensity of a true warrior. The rest of her didn't look the part of the warrior. In the billowing robe worn by the breeders, she looked deceptively soft, and womanly. But he knew better, now. She was a warrior. She had earned her Huntress name, if not before the fullness of the community of Men and Women at least in her own mind.

She said a Dilgo word he understood. "Concede."

From below, the bell tolled again. The breeders were being called to the temple. Their hundred-day period of mourning was over. Only yesterday Taen was complaining of being forced to decide how many breeders were to be impregnated on this auspicious day.

She flinched toward the sound, bared her teeth and uttered a grotesque sounding curse. She walked toward the sound, gesturing to it angrily with her fist.

"Benu," he said to her, calling her by her Huntress name, and in the best Dilgo he could muster, he said, "Don't leave. I will teach you all I know."

A sober expression pulled her mouth into a frown. She said something in Dilgo he struggled to understand. He made her repeat it, and still didn't understand.

Frustration entered her expression, and she patted her stomach, and pulled out her gown, making it grow.

"They are fertilizing you....tonight?" and he repeated the latter in Dilgo.

He understood her reply. "Morning."

She handed him his kai'gam and walked away, leaving him holding both blades, a gesture he took to mean that she was walking away from the discipline.

"Benu," he called after her. She turned, and stoically met his eyes.

He searched for the right words in Dilgo. Finally, he said, "What do you want?"

She pointed at the kai'gam, and said, "To learn."

He went to her, and pressed the grip of his kai'gam into her hand. "I will teach you."

She patted her stomach and threw her hand to the side, denoting with a sneer that she thought it was an unreasonable idea. He tried to imagine what she might say, in her own words, and wished he had tried harder to learn Dilgo.

"I will teach you, even if you are with child." He said, and he held the grip of his blade in her hand, "As a gift, this will be your kai'gam. Understand?" He gently moved it toward her, trying to make her understand.

Her fierce, warrior's eyes became wet, and she shook herself from his grip. She forcefully dropped the kai'gam on the floor, and fled.

He gave chase, losing her immediately as she entered the level where the breeders lived. Two stalwart Huntresses blocked the entrance. He could go no further, and his shouts for her attention drew malignant glares from the Huntresses.

He couldn't give up on her so easily. Pregnant or no, he'd teach her. In Jantideva pregnant women were often very active. Especially the Shodites. He only needed permission, and that was easily obtained, through Taen.

ৡৡৡৡৡৡৡৡৡ

Lodan strolled through the apartment, frowning slightly at the ever-deepening hole in the thick wall between Taen's secondary sitting room and Rito-Sant's old apartments. It was Taen's intention to have more space. He complained often of not having enough privacy in his apartments of gigantic rooms. Lodan suspected Taen's bid for a larger apartment had something to do with Caltha.

Lodan found Taen soaking in the bathhouse. His mind was focused only on Benu, not on Taen's state of undress. Being in Zadoq had a numbing effect on Janti modesty. Taen didn't seem to mind that his privacy was broken, nor did he seem surprised by Lodan's sudden intrusion. He treaded water in the center of his tub, and turned to look up at Lodan.

"Daka Taen, I need a favor from you," Lodan said urgently, "I've met a woman who shows tremendous potential as a kai'gam, but I am afraid she is in the unfortunate position of being a breeder. I need permission to take her as a student."

Taen swam to the side of the pool. "I was actually thinking of you, Lodan, just before you came in to see me. I believe I can help you, if you help me."

"How?"

"Tonight, the dold Huntress, Mira, is conducting a fertility ceremony, and the breeders will dance the Joy of Seduction before the Men. Even Danati is expected to attend and dance, though she will not be receiving seed." Taen explained, dismally adding, "The dold Huntress is seeding a slew of breeders in the morning. Caltha is among them."

The mention of Caltha made Lodan uncomfortable. "What has this to do with me?"

Taen's shrewd eyes glanced upwards at him. "I can get your breeder for you. You will have to take her as a mate, however, in order to break her contract with whatever Man seeds her."

He hesitated. He badly wanted to teach Benu the art, but to take her as a wife struck him as wrong.

"Very well," Taen shrugged, "Perhaps you should look to the Men and Women for students, Lodan."

"I'll do it." He replied, making his decision too hastily for comfort.

Taen grinned knowingly. "Wonderful. Then I will do this for you, but only if you agree to also take Caltha as your wife."

Lodan nearly choked on his own shock.

"It's perfect," Taen was saying, trying to sound convincing, "she can always be near me, and we can carry on our affair without fear of reprisals. There are no laws against adultery in Zadoq. Of course, we will be discreet, nonetheless. I fear Danati would kill Caltha if she learned of our affair. Apparently, she is the only Dilgo in Zadoq that has embraced the idea of fidelity."

Recovering, Lodan said, "I can't do that!"

"Of course you can." Taen said, "According to Rito-Sant's own declaration on the day he died, you are free to take many wives." Taen pursed his lips. "I have given this much thought, Lodan. It really is the only way to protect Caltha, and my child."

"A child," Lodan replied, hushed by the news.

"Caltha is pregnant." Taen confirmed, "And, if the dold Huntress suspects she was impregnated before her ceremony there is a possibility she could be beheaded. I don't want that to happen to her, but I can't protect her either."

"Unless you want to be beheaded with her," Lodan said stiffly.

"Exactly. But if you marry her, she is protected, and so is my child."

Lodan turned away from Taen, and his intrigues.

"Lodan, the child Caltha carries could be Ver dala Ven."

"How could you?" Lodan asked harshly, "If only you'd let yourself be happy with Danati."

"I don't love Danati, I love Caltha, and besides, Danati must be barren. She is still not pregnant, for all the work I've done on her. The dold Mistress is unhappy with her state, I can tell you." Taen chuckled, and continued, "I want Caltha. I'm proud it is she who is carrying my child. If you aren't willing to help me protect her, and the future Ver dala Ven, then may her death be on your head."

Lodan's anger rose quickly. He spun around and said, "No, her death would be on your head, adulterer."

"Will you do it, Lodan?" Taen asked, as if no oath had been hurled at him, "In exchange for the breeder with potential, will you protect the future of Ver dala Ven?"

He stared down at Taen for a long time. He had no loyalties to the daka, but he did have loyalty to the line of Ver dala Ven. An instinct within him urged him to protect Ver dala Ven at all costs, even at the cost of his own comfort.

Finally, he said, "I will protect Caltha. But I will have Benu, too, if it is her choice to live a lie."

Taen smiled, and he pulled himself out of the water. As he dried, he said, "We'll go now and tell Mira, before she has impregnated your new wives."

Lodan left the bathhouse and waited in his alcove as Taen dressed. Helping Taen in his deception with Caltha troubled him deeply.

The only bright horizon was the possibility that Benu would agree to become his wife, in order to become his student. He hoped that training her was worth the uneasy feeling left in him for the lies he'd have to tell.

৵৵৵৵৵৵৵৵৵

The fertility temple was cold and bare, save for the rows of resting beds near the tranquility pool. The breeders scheduled to be blessed in the temple each chose a resting bed, and waited for the dold Huntress to attend to them.

Mira went to Benu first, giving her a tea made with the ancient herbs that was thought to encourage new life to grow.

"Mira," Benu whispered huskily, trying to avoid being overheard by rows of women sitting in the breeding chambers with her. "Can't we wait until next cycle?"

Mira looked down on her sister with distaste. "Rito-Sant treated you like a Huntress, but you are not one, Melish," she said evenly, "It was his instruction that you be bred after he died. It is your time. Accept it. And drink your fooghum."

Benu looked into the white cup, and the dark fluid inside. She threw a quick glance at Mira, who was attending the breeder in the next resting bed, a dark skinned girl who was at least half Benu's age. The girl drank her foogham, and grimaced.

Benu glanced at the moving water beside her. The stream sprang from the overflow from the tranquility pool, and ran into a drain in the floor.

She glanced again at Mira, who still had her back to her. Quickly, she poured the tea into the running water. The tea diluted, and turned the water dark green.

And it ran down the drain.

When Mira returned, and she found Benu's cup empty, she smiled at her younger sister. "Very good, Melish. It is an honor to serve your purpose."

Benu thought not.

After they'd all had their tea, Mira instructed the breeders to bathe in the tranquility pool. The water was warm, and scented. As Benu moved through the shallow pool, she heard snippets of conversations carried on by the breeders around her. Many of the women here today expected to be impregnated with Rito-Sant's seed, after hearing one of the Huntresses comment that they still had some of his from the last cycle. Some expected Taen-Sant's seed. One, the cheekiest girl Benu even met, Caltha, claimed she was certain she would give birth to Taen-Sant's child. Insolent thing.

Benu didn't want to know who Mira planned on using to impregnate her, but if she were to guess, she would assume she was receiving the seed of Arcos, the Man she belonged to in contract before her brother ascended to the throne and removed her from the breeding schedule. The breeders of Arcos usually gave birth to Men and Women, and of the latter, mainly Huntresses. She supposed she should be grateful to be receiving strong seed.

Benu found an isolated corner of the pool and studied the undulating water. Once, when she was a girl, before it was known that she would grow to be a breeder rather than a Huntress, she witnessed a Huntress take her own life in a tranquility pool. The Huntress was distraught over the death of her favorite lover. She threw herself into the pool, and breathed the water until she lost consciousness, and slipped away into death.

Benu reasoned that she'd lived a good life. And, tonight, she'd learned she was a fair Huntress, even pitted against a man like the Janti, Lodan.

Her eyes grew hot. He'd offered to make her a better than fair Huntress. He'd offered to teach her, even though she was a breeder, and worthless. He'd offered her the world, and as he did so, he looked on her with open admiration.

She stared at the water and considered what it might feel like to breathe it into her lungs. Would it hurt any more than having all she wanted within reach, yet never being able to take it into her hands?

She held her breath and submerged into the water. It took the courage of a Huntress to take her own life. She thought of Baru, the greatest Huntress Zadoq had ever seen, and how she'd chosen death with their brother. She'd be lauded for generations to come as a hero.

Benu opened her eyes, to look death in the face.

Through the wavering water, she thought she saw the Janti warrior standing at the edge of the pool. A trick played upon her by her hopes, but her hope forced her to the surface to investigate. It was no trick. Lodan stood at the edge of the pool, and Taen-Sant

530

stood beside him. Mira knelt and sat on her feet to bring her height level to Taen-Sant. She spoke to him in labored Janti.

Lodan found her in the water, and their eyes locked. He said something in Janti to Mira, and pointed at Benu.

Mira said to her, "Benu, get out of the water." The breeders around her stared enviously.

"What does the warrior want, Mira?" she asked.

"He wants an old useless breeder to be his lover." Mira said, "I told him to pick another young, fertile girl, like Caltha, his first choice. But he insisted on you."

Benu looked at Caltha, who was being dressed by Danati and two other attendant breeders, then at Lodan. She was his first choice? That impudent little girl? Benu couldn't decide if she wanted to feel insulted, or elated, because either way she was escaping the duties of being a breeder.

She rose out of the water and let herself be dried. As she stole a glance over her shoulder at the warrior, she found his eyes were steadied on her, and not Caltha.

She suppressed a pleased smile. Second choice, indeed!

෴෴෴෴෴෴෴෴෴

During their walks in the city, Surna taught Durym the Dilgo language much the way Cobo had taught it to her, by initially teaching him words for things and incorporating the words into Janti conversation. However, unlike her spirited and interesting conversations with Cobo, her conversations with Durym were stilted and aloof. Her interest was not raised unless they crossed the path of one of her acquaintances, at which time she was compelled to introduce her companion. Her Huntress friends, once discovering he was a Suma, asked her the anticipated question....was he one of the many she serviced? She answered honestly, and without translating either question or answer for Durym's sake of modesty. The truth was that she wasn't certain. Durym's age would have made him too young in the eyes of the priesthood to make daily devotions on the Star altar, but his eminence among his priests may have waved the required years of celibacy. She preferred to think of him as too young. The very idea of Durym on the Star made her skin crawl.

Tonight, walking through the seventh arm of the Star, their conversation was interrupted by the birthing bell. Surna's heart quickened, and she automatically took him in the direction of the birthing center.

"What is happening?"

"There was a birth." she replied, "The children born to the breeders that are Ryslac or Inferes are discarded. The Ryslac-Vubushi are kind enough to take in all Ryslac breeds until they can be adopted by their own kind. The Inferes take their own, too, and raise them."

"Inferes?"

"The genderless Ryslacs, though they aren't considered a breed of human, but a mistake of the Guardian, which is nonsense. They are more human than most Janti I've known."

"Genderless....how is that possible?"

She ignored his silly question and looked among the Ryslac-Vubushi for her friend, Rohn.

He stood at the front of the gathering, holding a basket. Rohn was a statuesque person that had the appearance of a healthy Janti male, his shoulders broad and his arms rippling muscle. His complexion and curly hair were dark, his eyes pale gray, and his skin was deeply lined, a common trait of his kind. The skin around his eyes creased pleasingly when he smiled.

He happened to look her way, and he smiled broadly.

She couldn't help herself, she felt giddy all at once. She waved.

"Who is he?" Durym demanded.

His tone irked her, and she crossly replied, "A friend."

The dold Huntress appeared in the doorway. In one massive hand, she held three writhing, screaming newborns by the legs. The Huntress carelessly tossed the newborns into the air above the crowd of Ryslacs.

The Ryslacs, and Rohn, scrambled to catch them before they hit the ground.

One child was not lucky to find the saving grace of a pair of adult hands. It was flung long and hard, and hit stone floor headfirst. It quieted, and lay still as a doll.

Durym shouted his horror, and he rushed to the child with more urgency than the Ryslac-Vubushi that had missed catching the child.

Surna rushed behind him, feeling as sickened as she had the first time she saw the treatment of the Ryslac babies born to breeders.

Durym gently picked the child up and cradled him. He touched the child's slack face, and each of his four loosely hanging arms.

"He is dead." Durym choked.

Tears stung Surna's eyes. "The Huntresses do not value life, unless it looks and acts like them."

"Horrifying." Durym said, and he bent his head close to the child. His grief was real, and all encompassing, and wholly unexpected. Surna had grown to know Durym as a self-involved boy who was like the Huntresses, lacking humane compassion for anything that did not serve him.

Feeling contrition for having judged him so harshly, she bent down and put her arm around his shoulders to comfort him.

"Ai, Surna," the Ryslac-Vubushi who'd missed his catch said, "I will care for the broken one."

"Yes, of course, Renstali," She touched Durym's dark hair to bring his head off the child. "Let the boy's people care for his body."

Durym seemed reluctant to release it to Renstali's arms.

"His mother won't even mourn him, will she?"

"It is the way they are." Surna offered, at a loss for a better explanation for their careless and heartless behavior. "The strong live, and weak die."

"We all die, Surna." he retorted, "The strong should protect the weak."

Rohn had drifted toward them, and had heard Durym's heartfelt remark.

"But often physical strength has nothing to do with real strength." Rohn said easily, "We should pity the Men and Women for their weaknesses, and forgive them their ignorance."

Durym threw a hot glare at Rohn, and seemed to size him up.

Rohn's attention turned to Surna, his eyes twinkling. "I am pleased to see you. I missed you this morning in Zhun. The children also missed you. They played 'catch the Inferes,'" he laughed himself, "I am exhausted!"

"You look wonderful to me." she replied, smiling shyly. She felt like an idiot around Rohn, but the feeling was delicious.

He seemed to share her uncertain shyness, and to cover he showed her the child he'd caught. He lifted back a blanket from the basket he carried, to show her a tiny pink baby, eyes wide and alert. "Not a scratch, not a bruise, but probably hungry."

Surna was immediately lost to everything around her but the sight of Rohn's prize. She squatted down to the basket and cooed at the little one.

Rohn smiled at her fondly. "Will you be escorting me to the end of the city, Surna?"

"Oh yes." she breathed. Without question, she gently took Rohn's child from the basket and cradled it in her arms. The anatomy of the Inferes child appeared male, except they lacked testicles and nipples. Their chests were bare and unmarked, and their penis no more than a device for urination, lacking the muscles for erection and the highly sensitive nerves that made it an organ of pleasure. Most adult Inferes had the appearance of a man, though, as Rohn explained to Surna on their first meeting, they lacked all glandular specifications that made them either female or male. They were born sterile, impotent, and without a desire or drive to mate. Still yet, she couldn't help but see Rohn as a man, not a sexless person. A sexless person wouldn't have the ability to turn her knees weak with a smile.

"He is beautiful." she said of the baby in her arms.

Durym, a presence she'd momentarily forgotten, stood over her shoulder to gaze at the child. "Will you raise him as your son?" he asked of Rohn.

"I have room for this one, though I am not the only caretaker among my kind." he said, and he smiled self depreciatingly, "We Inferes are mothers to all, fathers to none."

Surna laughed at the lighthearted joke.

Durym introduced himself, saying afterwards, "It is good to meet someone in Zadoq that speaks Janti."

"Yes? I thought I was speaking Inferes." and Rohn winked playfully at Surna, for the same remarks had passed between them a few months ago, during their first meeting.

"Oh." Durym replied, and he glanced at Surna, "Like the Ryslacs, he speaks a language that is similar to ours?"

"Ah, but I am not a he," he said, directing the comment to Durym, "I am Inferes. If you must attach a gender on me, keep in mind that in my society, I hold an office that is generally held by females of your kind. So, you could as easily call me she."

Durym stammered his response. "I--well...of course, which ever makes you most.....comfortable."

Surna saw the bright playfulness in Rohn's eyes, and realized he was having a great deal of fun with Durym's sudden discomfort.

"Don't let Rohn tease you, Durym," she said, without looking away from Rohn's twinkling eyes, "Rohn can be a wicked tease."

A Huntress hulked over them, and spewed Dilgo at Rohn. She urged him to leave the city, spitting a variety of curses that Surna recognized but still did not fully understand.

"Time to go home." Rohn said ruefully.

Surna fell into step beside her friend as they started down the path leading through the seventh arm, and to the opening of the city.

"Where do you live?" Durym asked, scrambling to keep up with them.

"My village is in the cliffs." he replied easily.

Surna turned to him, "You remember, the cliff dwellings in the hills above."

"I remember seeing them, yes." Durym replied. "Mos'm Drindle has his pilot circle the cliffs twice in order to get a good look at them. They are magnificent. I'd never seen anything quite like it in my life."

"Thank you for your kind words."

535

Durym did his best to move in between Rohn and Surna. "So, how did you meet Surna?"

"I care for the children of the Men and Women. We met by chance." he looked affectionately at Surna, chuckling. "She was basically assaulted by the children, and pulled into a game of repta."

She felt the need to explain repta to Durym. "In repta, the objective is to stack blocks with a team as fast as you can. Who ever finishes first, without knocking their tower down, wins."

Rohn said significantly, "She is quite a good player, and not with just repta."

"I sometimes go Zhun, it is in the fifth arm of the city," she explained, "and Rohn allows me to play with the children."

"Oh no. Play?" Rohn shouted a laugh. "She slaves for those children. They have convinced her they are the neediest things on the planet!"

She suppressed a smile. "Rohn is always accusing me of spoiling them." She held the precious bundle protectively. "How can a child be spoiled when they are born perfect?"

Rohn looked at her appreciatively. "Perfection is as inconceivable a concept for an Inferes as lust."

She had a hard time believing he couldn't conceive of lust. Not with the way he looked into her eyes.

Durym seemed to notice the sparks crackling between them, as well. "If an Inferes knows no lust," he said testily, "then why do I get the distinct feeling that something is going on between you two?"

The petulant question shocked Surna. He nearly sounded jealous, though she attributed his jealousy to his faith, and his belief that once she took the vow of a Suma she was forever obligated to live as a Suma.

"I believe your question is inappropriate, Durym." she chastised lowly.

Rohn frowned, and glanced at Durym, measuring him anew. "Is he your Janti lover, Surna?"

The innocent question had a startling effect on Durym. He lunged forward between them and defensively retorted, "I am a Suma priest! We are a celibate order!"

Rohn's brows flew up, and he slid a quizzical eye at Surna. "Was that not the order you served as a love goddess?"

Surna laughed at the way Rohn saw her vocation. "Yes, it was, and Durym was a part of the temple."

"Must we speak so freely about temple practices?" Durym asked severely.

"But I was hardly a love goddess." she said wryly, disregarding Durym's discomfort. "I was more like a relief station for sexually frustrated priests."

"Surna," Durym chastened in a hushed tone.

Sternly, she said, "Durym do not start trying to convict me of your faith."

Durym's lips pressed together with his disapproval, but he threw up his hands in surrender.

Rohn glanced back and forth between them, and sensing their tension, he steered the subject away from Surna's former vocation. "And what might you name this one, Surna?"

She gazed down at the child's face. He'd quieted, but his mouth still pouted. "This one I think I will name Dex. He looks like a Dex, doesn't he, Rohn?"

Rohn suppressed a smile. "I do hope the other children won't make fun of Dex for having such an odd name."

"You think they will make fun of him?" she asked, concerned for the young Inferes future happiness.

Rohn laughed throatily, "The children may not, but I might. Dex in the language of the Men means pointy."

Surna grimaced. "Pointy what?"

"And therein lies the crux of the joke, doesn't it?" he asked her, amused.

She looked fondly at the child, and shook her head. "We cannot name you pointy, can we?"

Behind her, Durym offered, "Ruela. It is my sister's name."

"Ruela," and Surna glanced to Rohn for approval.

"Ruela," Rohn said slowly, and he shrugged, "No taunt comes to mind. Ruela it is."

She glanced at the baby and whispered its name. "Thank your uncle Durym for a beautiful name, Ruela." She glanced back at Durym and said, "You are considered the baby's relative now,

Durym, for naming her. If she ever needs you, be prepared to be there for her."

Durym seemed instantly charmed by the prospect.

At the city gate Rohn hesitated long enough to allow Surna the time to say goodbye to the baby. She gently replaced the child into Rohn's basket.

He stepped closer to her, ignoring Durym's sudden tension, and looked tenderly into her eyes. "I'd be happy for your company in the village, Surna. I have no duties with the Men tomorrow. Will you come see me?"

Her heart thrilled, but she was careful not to seem too eager, heeding what she remembered about her mother's advisement on how to handle a man. "If I can make time."

He caressed her face with his open hand, a touch that caused her to vibrate from head to toe. "I hope to see you. Please make time."

"I will." She promised.

He smiled winningly at her, waved to them both, and trudged into the darkness of night with his newest charge.

Durym followed him out a few steps, staring at Rohn's retreating back. "He doesn't look at you like a genderless being." and he threw a hard look at her. "And you don't look at him like he is a genderless being."

Irritated by what she perceived as his pious Suma judgement, she angrily stalked away from him. How dare he judge her for forming a perfectly innocent friendship! But how innocent was it if she harbored secret longings? Her pace slowed as she realized she wasn't angry with Durym, but herself. She'd developed a crush on a person who wasn't a man or a woman, and would never look on her in the same way. A nice, uncomplicated crush that was never destined to move forward, never destined to hurt her emotionally, because how could she expect more from Rohn than friendship?

She wasn't ready for more, she decided. Her heart was virginal. First she'd fallen in love with a faceless man, a priest, now she found herself wanting to fall in love with a man who was not a man at all. She spent too many years in the star, she decided. Her exile from affection had muddled her senses.

Reaching the palace, she hazarded a backward glance at Durym. His eyes were trained on her, and she saw the hurt in his face that was becoming familiar to her.

"Ah Durym," she sighed to his spirit, "You are too Suma for your own good." and she entered the corridor leading to the upper palace.

She passed through a throng of breeders, who silenced as she went by. In Janti, women were silenced by the ugliness of her appearance. In Zadoq, breeders were silenced by their envy. They believed she was the mate of Ver dala Ven. Surna and Cobo allowed them to think what they wanted. Cobo had endured a number of awkward moments with breeders hoping for his favors. He was well disposed to avoiding more awkward moments.

Well away from them, she heard their coos and ahhs over Durym, who fended them off indignantly, but in Janti. Finally, he called out to Surna. He sounded panicked.

She paused before the portal leading into the first level, and turned to see that the breeders had Durym pinned against the wall. They picked at his clothing, and smiled wantonly at him as they pulled aside their gowns to expose themselves. He pushed their hands away, treating them with care he'd show a lady in the Janti court, though he probably needed to shove them firmly away in order to escape their clutches.

She crossed her arms and smirked at Durym. "They find you attractive."

He grimaced at her. "They'd find Tidio attractive!"

She couldn't help but laugh at his remark.

"Surna, please!" he pleaded, "Help me!"

She addressed the breeders in Dilgo, and with as sharp an edge to her voice as she could effect. "Release him, or I will find Mira!" she threatened. The invocation of the dold Huntress' name was enough to ease them away from Durym.

He quickly trotted toward her, and stood behind her as if a beast threatened him.

"They are frightening." he commented breathlessly. "I know now why Lodan accompanies Taen where ever he goes."

"Come along, young man," she said in a motherly fashion, "I'll escort you to the safety of your chamber."

Durym cocked a brow at her. "You must know how it effects my male ego to need the escort of a woman to feel safe? I am devastated....not that I'd turn down an escort."

Despite her earlier irritation, she managed to laugh at his joke.

She walked him to his apartment, then to her own. Cobo was inside, standing at the window in his bedchamber.

"You are up late."

He turned, a grim expression set in his features. "Go get Taen. Tell him his mother will be arriving in less than hour."

Surna's mouth fell open, and she turned and ran out of the apartment to find Taen-Sant.

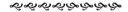

Chapter 24

The Huntress guard lined the gate at the second arm of the city, closest to the Lake of Tears, waiting for the arrival of the Janti daka. Taen and Cobo stood side by side, watching the skies. The silence of the land around Zadoq announced the blowers in the windriders long before their running lights were sighted in the starry sky.

Taen fidgeted nervously. "What does she want?"

Cobo would not reply.

Jishni's luxury Starling landed in the same clearing used by previous Alliance visitors, followed by two compliments of Watchers in four transports. The armed Watchers disembarked first and formed lines on either side of the Starling's boarding ramp. Jishni emerged from the Starling alone, without her court or the usual entourage of aids and keepers. She stepped down the ramp in regal style for the benefit of no one. The barbaric Dilgos didn't appreciate her layered gown of silky blue, or her ostentatious jewels. The Dilgos held her in low esteem despite her manner and appearance, for she was a Breeder. They were curious about her Watchers, their useless weapons, their soft appearance and garish purple uniforms, unbecoming of warriors. Their curiosity held them at the city gate, but not her importance.

She'd come without her children, and without Bail. Cobo easily drew in her thoughts and feelings, as easily as breathing the air. Fear of her son staggered through the constant worries for Archer and newer frets over Bail. Until she caught sight of Cobo, and then her thoughts shifted to the moment they could be alone.

Cobo tried to remain neutral, to keep his desires in check, but weakened as she started toward him, her eyes never wavering from his. His eternal longing to caress her skin, breathe her sweet scent, be one with her again came alive.

"Welcome to Zadoq, Mother." Taen said stiffly, his eyes darting between them. Their dynamic eye contact was not lost on their son.

She tore her eyes away from Cobo, and bowed slightly to her son. "I am pleased to be in your presence." By her formal manner, and the flat dislike in her eyes, Cobo knew she did not mean the sentiment. She still harbored ill feelings toward Taen for his part in Archer's disappearance.

"What brings you to my home?" Taen wanted to know, and he cocked a brow toward Cobo, as if to imply that he already knew.

"I've come to see you in your rightful place as ruler of Dilgopoche." she said, and she timidly glanced at Cobo, "I have also come seeking the talents of Ver dala Ven."

To that, Taen stifled a knowing laugh.

Cobo shot a glare at Taen.

He ignored Cobo, and to his mother said, "Would you like a tour of Zadoq, Mother?"

"It is a bit late and I am tired," she replied, her eyes still on Cobo's face, "perhaps tomorrow."

"Very well." Taen snapped his fingers to his Huntress guard, an angry gesture. "Straight to the guest apartments."

Cobo fell into step beside Jishni, and Taen took her other side as they followed the Huntresses through the city. Behind them were her Watchers, marching in two single file lines. Jishni took in her surroundings as all outsiders had, with no small measure of dismay, while at the same time asking her son stilted questions about his rule, and his needs.

"I haven't given much thought to what I'd like Dilgopoche to have, besides an updated military." Taen replied blithely.

"It is written into treaty," Jishni replied tersely, "that Dilgopoche is to become a part of Jantideva, and therefore would not need an independent military."

"I don't see how that is possible." Taen said flatly, "The Dilgos are as set in their ways as the Janti. The two societies will never mix."

"We will not war, either." she stated resolutely.

"And what about defense?" Taen questioned curtly, "Will Jantideva protect us from outside invaders?"

"Who in the Alliance would invade your little country, son?" she replied with a laugh, "We are a peaceful society, but even if we were not, no one in the world wants anything to do with Dilgopoche."

Taen reddened with impotent fury. "Are you saying you have given me a useless country to rule, mother?

"My son, I said no such thing," she replied easily, "In fact, I have been approached by a wealthy man who would like to utilize Dilgopoche's natural resources."

"Who?" Taen asked, his interest piqued.

"Shea Roseno."

Taen's mouth slid open.

She nodded. "Now that the Dome of Silence is down, he wants to extend his mining operation from the lower Coulcubannha Mountains, into the interior of Dilgopoche."

"And what do we receive in return?" Taen asked quickly.

"In trade, you can have whatever you want." she said flatly. "Goods, services, free trade."

"I am tired of living like an animal." he said harshly, throwing his arms at the city. "I want a proper palace."

"Is that all?" she replied expectantly, "Surely Dilgopoche has needs beyond your desire for a palace."

"I also want windriders." he added, "Rito-Sant hated Janti technology, but I do not."

"The Coulcubannha is populated, Jishni." Cobo interjected, glancing at his son pointedly, "Perhaps the population should be consulted before Shea Roseno destroys their land."

"Fine, consult any one of them that has a Sant after their name." Taen replied harshly.

Jishni frowned. "If there is a conflict, it must be resolved before I can give Shea permission to expand. Shea doesn't want trouble from the Ryslacs, and neither do I."

Taen fumed like a boy who did not get his way. "Of course mother. Perhaps I should let you take care of the negotiations for me."

"Cobo might be a better choice." she replied smoothly, "It sounds as if he at least cares for the needs of the Dilgo people."

Taen shot Cobo with a glare. Sardonically, he said, "Perhaps I should make Cobo my minister of the Interior."

Perfectly serious, Jishni replied, "Perhaps so."

They entered the public common of the palace. The area was being readied for Lodan's wedding celebration. Cobo casually informed Jishni of the upcoming affair.

"Two wives?" she asked incredulously. "What is it about the Dilgo women that suits him so well?"

"They are a finer breed than Janti women." Taen retorted evenly.

Jishni took the insult at face value. She halted and swirled her skirts angrily as she confronted Taen. "I already regret saying hello to you, Taen. Don't bother seeing me on to my apartments. Cobo will suffice as a guide."

His eyes narrowed. "In case you forget, mother, this is my home, my palace. I will do as I please, and it pleases me to see you to your apartments."

He snapped his fingers imperiously, and the Huntresses started the procession forward.

In defiance to her son's will, she held back, keeping Cobo's pace and not Taen's.

Her apartments were next to Cobo's. Standing outside the door in a line were Durym, Surna, and Lodan, each performing a bow to honor their daka's arrival. She greeted each warmly, especially Lodan, congratulating him on his upcoming event. "I wish you every happiness, for both you and your," and her pretty brows crinkled, the only sign that she disapproved, "wives."

Lodan accepted her best wishes imperturbable expression on his face, hiding his very real discomfort at becoming a polygamist.

Before entering her room, the Watchers stormed in and searched it thoroughly. Taen glared at her for her lack of trust. "If I was going to plot against you, mother, those Watchers of yours couldn't prevent your demise."

"I know that far too well." She slipped her hand into Cobo's, lending her complete trust in him to protect her from Taen's sickness.

Taen grinned sardonically. To them both, he said, "Enjoy your evening," and with a perfunctory bow, he left them without asking leave to do so.

Once the Watchers were satisfied that the rooms were secured, she was allowed to enter. She invited Cobo inside with a glance.

She closed the ill-fitting door, and leaned on it, drained by her confrontation with Taen, and waiting for her strength to return.

"He is nothing like the son I knew and loved." She said low of Taen, "How can I feel such hatred for a child I brought into this world? Something is wrong with me, Cobo. I can feel it, deep inside. Something of me has died."

"Grief feels like death." He assured, "In time, your load will feel lighter."

"No, never. Never again will I feel carefree, or light."

"I hope that isn't true."

"Bail told me that Archer is lost to us."

"No, not lost to you. Not forever."

"The prophecy. Yes. I wish I could trust your interpretation of the fifth sign. I am sorry, Cobo, but I cannot."

"I understand."

She closed her eyes, shunting tears down her cheeks. "I wish there was real hope, but I have come to accept that I will never see him again. Just as I have come to accept that his disappearance is a punishment."

"Jishni, please don't think that way." he admonished gently, "Not every tragedy that befalls us is punishment. Most of the time it is unfortunate circumstances beyond our control, only that, unfortunate circumstances."

"No." she said softly, and she smiled, a sad smile that aged her before his eyes. "We both know better the events leading to Archer's disappearance. It was my love for you that lead to Taen's evil. And even knowing this is so, I can't help myself but to continue loving you, and wanting you. As I said," and she laughed harshly at herself, "there is something deeply, disturbingly wrong with me."

She opened her eyes and finally looked into his face. Making a decision, borne from desperation and need, she pushed off the door and strolled toward him, casually unleashing her hair. Dark tendrils of auburn dropped to her hips and fanned over her shoulders. Cobo couldn't help himself. He took a lock of her silken hair and ran the length of the lock between his fingers. The scent of her was exquisite, and he let it draw him closer. Her purpose was clear as she began to unsnap the bodice of her gown.

Cobo fell into a trance as he watched her disrobe. With instinctive movements, he touched the skin of her collarbone as it was exposed, and sliding his hand under her loosened bodice, he felt the heat of her breast. Her head dropped back, relishing his caress, and her sad smile widened. "Cobo." She whispered, "Heal me as only you can."

He kissed her lips without staying her hands, once and then twice, and on the third time he sensed the fullness of her pain and longing, longing that was not exclusively for him. She had imagined him, for a brief moment, as another man.

He drew away, understanding how to heal her. Regretfully, it was not through the resuming of their love affair, as Jishni thought. He took hold of her hands and prevented her from dropping her gown off her bare shoulders.

"Tell me what has changed, Jishni."

"I am free." She told him, and her eyes averted to the floor, "Bail has left me. He lives in Odhran now. We will never live as man and wife again."

The tight emotion coiled in her voice alerted him to her true feelings. "You are not separated by your choice, but by his." Cobo realized. The soft words made her cringe. "Please, look at me, Jishni, as you did only moments ago, and tell me I am wrong."

"What difference does it make?" she questioned, and a smile faltered over her lips. "I've dreamt of being with you forever. My attraction to you is complete. I love you, with all my heart. Please, Cobo, let's continue."

She pushed her fingers through his hair and rose on her tiptoes to kiss him, and for a moment he let himself forget Bail, the world, their past, and held her as she wished to be held, and melted into her body as she wished, and liberated his ancient desire in a fervent kiss. He wanted her so that he ached, an ache that dulled his senses, his reasoning. He ignored how wrong it felt to be in her arms, and how her thoughts edged away from him when she closed her eyes, finding someone dearer to imagine. Cobo ignored a promise he made to his brother, and he urged her toward the large pillows furnishing the room, with an intention to lay her down and soothe his ache with pleasure.

Reading his intentions, she broke from his arms and pulled away, put her back to him and covered her face with both hands. She shook, her back trembled, her hands trembled. The sudden separation from her brought his senses back, and he saw through her, as he always could, to understand her sudden reluctance to reconfirm their love.

"We are still one, Jishni," he acknowledged, and trying very hard to keep a harsh tone from ruining his gentle words, he added, "I feel your heart being torn in two, and it is not over the love we once shared. Bail hurt you by leaving."

"He took our sons. That hurt." she replied caustically, "But he? Hurt me? How could he, I don't love him."

Her denial vibrated painfully through his spirit. It was plain enough to see without his gifts of insight that she'd fallen deeply in love with his brother and it hurt her to lose him. She would never admit it was so, not even to herself. Desperation brought her to Cobo, and not the desperation to find Archer or to be with him. She was desperate to prove that her feelings of love for Bail were false.

He drew close to her back, and though she stiffened she did not pull away as he placed his hands on her shoulders. Gradually, he drew her into a gentle embrace, buried his face into her hair and with his gift sought the wound that needed healing. Her love for him had become an obsession that blocked her ability to live naturally. He began to sense the depth of the wound he'd left on her heart when he'd abandoned her and Taen. She suffered in silence, allowing pride and a pining love to become her shield, and though her heart tricked her into falling in love again with Bail, her pride refused to let that love express itself. She wished for Bail to love her in return, but would never take the chance to tell him of her feelings. To protect her pride, her entire body of emotions, she'd made the bitter resolution to steel herself against love for the rest of her life.

It took all of Cobo's strength to refrain from weeping for her.

"I've taken so much from you," he murmured, "how can you still want me, even now?"

"Who else do I have to turn to?"

"Bail."

She turned in his arms, and there were tears on her face. "He never loved me."

A sad smile crossed Cobo's features as he realized what he must do to heal her heart. "Bail loves you. I sensed it clearly when he came to see me about Archer. If only you'd let him in, Jishni, not be so afraid of him, he can make you happy."

She shrugged off his hands. "I did love him, and he left me. The way you left me."

He eased away to put distance between them, troubled by the bitter stain in her spirit. "Tell him but once of your true feelings, and he will never again leave your side for as long as you live. I promise."

She looked at him over a bare shoulder, her vulnerable heart exposed. "Once?"

"One time, and he is yours."

Her brow crinkled as she considered Cobo's advice. Her distrust of love, and fear of being further wounded was a fortress surrounding her, and for her to heal, the fortress had to come down. Cobo could not pull down the walls for her, it would have to be her own doing. He'd given her the key. It was all he could do for her.

He left her apartment, leaving her this time for good. He couldn't help wonder what miracle might heal his aching heart. Nothing, and no one, he suspected. He'd grown too accustomed to being alone.

In his own room, the Spirit of the Masing Star finally made an appearance, moving within him, a gentle sway that eased his broken heart, embraced and rocked him into a peaceful slumber, and offered him contented dreams of Shodalum, Gella, and a tribe of thousands living in Calli.

కళకళకళకళకళ

Durym wiped his brow with a cloth. "The heat is oppressive."

Taen stopped his pacing and glanced askance at his priest. Durym's apartment was compact, windowless, and once used by a Huntress. Her smell was still in the walls, in the pillows. Though Taen would not have personally tolerated the uncomfortable accommodations, he tired of listening to Durym's ceaseless complaints. In three days he left on his traveling tour of Dilgopoche. He had to gain an understanding of the prophecy concerning the return of the Masing Star before the tour began, or remain the weaker of both Riar Sed and Cobo.

"The sixth sign. I want to hear it again." he urged Durym.

Durym threw a contemptuous glare at Taen, but he obeyed. He placed his hand on the compact ariq stone, and Betnoni's smooth, calm voice intoned, "The sixth sign of the Rebirth is fear. Mo'ghan Awakens! The Rathians Rise with him, and revitalize their mission in secret and dark places."

"She has to be speaking of the Men and Women." he muttered to himself, chewing his thumbnail mindlessly. "It is obvious, don't you think? The Rathian influence is all around us here, and it was here that Lord Crag completed his career as a warmonger."

Durym displayed a moment of impatience that was quickly covered by his smooth, priestlike demeanor. "It could be taken in that way, yes."

"But you don't think so?"

"As I have said before, Betnoni's primary interest was Shodalum. In all her writings, she speaks of them with respect and much regard. Never once does she allude to Dilgopoche. I would think her reference to Rathians had more to do with Old Rathia, myself."

"Do you think the Masing Star could possibly reside there instead of here?"

"Wouldn't it make more sense? Old Rathia is a part of Shodalum, and in lore she protects Shodalum's borders. She calls out for the dakas to free the Shodite people. Her focus is on Shodalum, not Dilgopoche."

Taen's back stiffened a bit as he reminded himself that his country did not even have an empty seat on the Alliance Council, whereas Shodalum's seat remained at the Congress for thousands of years, unmolested and empty. Dilgopoche had become Jantideva's newest slave. Jantideva was the benefactor, or so his mother seemed to believe, breezing into his palace, issuing her orders.

"Somewhere in Betnoni's prophecy," Taen said with angry malice, "she hid clues to finding and possessing the Masing Star. I am certain of it. Why else would her son and grandson spend so much time here before the Dome was put into place?"

A bit self righteously, Durym pointed out to Taen that if the Guardian wished the Masing to be found, it would have been found long ago.

"According to Ver dala Ven Cobo, now is the time." Taen replied evenly, his hatred for the priest glittering in his eyes. If he hadn't needed Durym, he would have had him beheaded on the spot.

"Where are we in the prophecies? What sign?"

Durym shrugged slightly, and offered, "Yana believed the third sign came and went when your brother, Archer, was kidnapped. 'One to the Guardian, One to the invisible' the latter could be a reference to the Shodite nanny who kidnapped him, at least one could construe it in such a way."

"'The fourth sign of the Rebirth is death.'" Taen quoted, "Rito-Sant's death, obviously-"

"Far from it, Taen-Sant." Durym countered, "Rito-Sant was not placed in a tomb, he was burnt, his ashes scattered to the four winds. The Masing Star did not appear on the day he was immolated, did it?"

Taen burned. Durym could be so insufferable!

Durym continued without noticing that Taen was furious for his highhanded interruption.

"I believe she used tomb as a metaphor, pointing out that with the disappearance of the Star, Ver dala Ven was placed in a sleeping death. As for the mention of death, it could mean almost anyone, or anything. The death of a belief, the death of silence, the death of our separation with the Guardian Spirit of Creation."

"Perhaps it means that the Masing is dead." Taen retorted.

Durym looked at Taen as if he were obtuse. "I cannot see how you can read such blasphemy into Betnoni's Prophecy. Never did she intimate that the Masing was not living and breathing."

"Blasphemy?" Taen laughed out loud. "You do not know the meaning of the word! The Suma have taken the prophet's writings and twisted them for far too many eons to endure!"

"Taen-Sant!"

A dangerous glint shone in his eyes as he glared at the priest. "I know the Masing Star lives, buffoon! I wish to possess it, don't I? Now, open your mind and be a service to your master."

Durym glared his disbelief at Taen. He disliked Taen with as much fervor as Taen disliked him. They were equals in that respect. It was the only common ground they shared.

Durym said, "Wouldn't it be helpful to have Ver dala Ven offer his wisdom on Betnoni's prophecy? At least you'd have a more insightful view."

"Perhaps later." Taen replied, conceding that he may need Cobo, after all.

Tori, the commander of his Huntress guard, pounded on the door. "Taen-Sant, your mother has arisen and wishes an audience with you."

Taen went rigid.

"Very well, tell her I will be with her shortly!" To Durym, he said, "I will return as soon as I am done with that crone."

Durym gasped at the term he used for Jishni.

Taen rolled his eyes at Durym's loyalty to his mother, as if to question his very naiveté.

"Do some research," Taen ordered, "find references to Dilgopoche made by any and all Ver dala Ven prophets. Especially those referencing a tomb. Itza's prophecy, and all the prophets of her lineage, for instance. Understand?"

As much as Durym disliked taking orders from Taen, he held his tongue and nodded his obedience.

Despite spending days looking deeply into Betnoni's prophecy, he felt less in control of the situation than ever. He'd felt cocksure that he'd crack the prophetic riddle on his own, after all he was the Chosen. Betnoni's riddles confused him, breaking his confidence. Once his tour began, he would not have time for study. They would ride in Rito-Sant's huge carriage, pulled by a hearty herd of smelly honigs, and tour the country, and if he understood Riar Sed's intentions they would search every inch for an intangible force that Durym could not even define. On the positive side, he'd be away from Zadoq for half a season, which became a drawback, too. He was forced to take Danati on their tour.

His only comfort would be Caltha's presence, but even so, his time with Caltha would be severely limited. There were no hiding places in a few carriages, and Danati would have seeing eyes. She stopped taking her sleep herb.

It would be no end of frustration during the trip, if the trip lasted too long.

He wanted it all. He'd dreamed of having a home for himself, Caltha, Danati, and a harem, the full body of breeders, if possible. Eventually, he would have his way. Danati would accept Caltha into their family, and more, if he chose. There were quite a few breeders that had caught his eye lately.

And he wanted his own Shodites. He was tired of looking at the Ryslac slaves. They were simply too peculiar. Hideous might be a better descriptive. The Ryslac-Yesvectu female who cleaned his toilet facilities had an absolutely evil appearance. Reptilian Yesvectu's slitted irises and skulking manner were threatening. Tori, in her broken Janti, had told him that the Yesvectu were a delight to hunt because of their speed and agility, and the Yesvectu male's willingness to attack predators added an extra thrill to the game.

Tori assured him that the female Yesvectu were less aggressive, hardly enough of an assurance to placate Taen. He wanted out of Zadoq, and into his own palace, surrounded by his own people.

He returned to his apartment to prepare for his meeting with his mother. He expected to find Danati up, and dressed. Instead, she was still asleep. Lying next to her on their bed was Caltha. She was nude, and waiting for him.

She smiled as he entered the room, and caressed herself.

Shocked, worried that Danati might wake, he hissed, "Get out of here!"

Caltha reached over to Danati and poked her hard in the side. Danati groaned in her sleep, but did not move.

"She was fed sleeping elixir, a bit more than normal." Caltha said in Janti. She'd put him to shame by learning his language faster than he'd learned hers. "She won't wake."

"You drugged her?"

552

Caltha shrugged one shoulder, not a denial and not an admission of guilt, and she smiled again, rolled up and patted the sheets between her legs. Their child had already started showing in the low of her belly, adding a delicious curve to her body that he simply could not deny touching.

"Come," he beckoned, and he moved to pick her up off the giant pillows.

"No, here." She insisted.

"With her next to us?" he asked incredulously. Through his shock, he was abruptly titillated by the prospect. The Men and Women routinely enjoyed each other in public. It was custom. But to Taen it seemed so.......bad. So deliciously bad.

Caltha crooked her finger at him and lay back down.

Carefully, he climbed onto his mistress, his eyes on his wife. He found refuge in the heat of his lover, and at that moment Danati moaned his name as if he had entered her, exciting him tremendously. The pillow rocked Danati as they pleasured each other, and Danati responded in her sleep by again moaning, as if she were somehow involved. Lust overwhelmed him, and he reached for Danati, and fondled her breast. Soon, faster than ever before, he was done with Caltha. But he was not done.

It was an instinct, a Dilgo instinct, that caused him to leave Caltha, and enter his wife as she slept. As he rocked between Danati's lax legs, Caltha lay on his back, moving with him. It was sublime.

Yes, this is what he wanted. He wanted a harem of willing Calthas to lay with, when he chose, as he chose. He wanted to live a Dilgo life of accepted debauchery, while living in a Janti palace, with Janti servants to wait upon him. He wanted to have his Dilgo life, in Ona.

If he possessed the Masing, he would have all he desired. And the crone would lose her precious country.

On that thought, he exploded inside Danati, his climax lending him the false sense of utter omnipotence.

Afterwards, spent and laying between two women, his feelings of weakness, and insecurity, returned.

ॐॐॐॐॐॐॐॐॐॐ

"The Vubushi is a large community." she commented as the windrider circled the mountainous Ryslac city. "Has there ever been a census?"

"None that I know of." Taen replied. They stood side by side on the enclosed observation deck, observing the sights of Dilgopoche from the air. Despite his contrary attitude the night before, Taen behaved himself during their morning meeting, acting as host and dutiful son. Her suggestion to see the country from the air was eagerly accepted, and he even seemed to enjoy the impromptu tour. "The Men and Women don't think very highly of the Ryslacs."

"Have you been contacted by the Ryslac leaders?"

"I am their leader." Taen replied guilelessly.

"They must have leaders within their community." She replied easily, "Buhj spoke of having elected leaders among the Toscocti."

"I've spoken to every Vubushi farmer, in turn," he said wearily, "negotiating water usage. None ever mentioned having a leader. I wish they had, it would have saved weeks of having to listen to every single farmer whine about their certainty that a the coming heat will kill their crops this year."

"The heat?" She crooked a smile. "It's mild....well, rather cold, I'd say. The weather is wonderful, compared to the Center-plex."

"The Vubushi are alarmists." he dismissed, "Since the Dome came down, the weather has been a bit different. The temperature has been erratic. But, like I told them, the weather is normalizing."

She let her eyes follow the hills and valleys below. "The land is barren. A result of the dome?"

"As far as I am told, yes."

"We've already destroyed their land. I can only wonder if the Vubushi would be agreeable to a foreigner strip mining their hills." she said aloud, thinking of the diplomacy involved.

"I've already said yes, mother." Taen said flatly, "We don't need to consult with the Vubushi."

"Of course you do!" she said sharply, "They are your people. You must at least give them consideration before making such a decision."

554

"They are like the Shodites. They are our slaves."

"The Shodites are not at issue here!" she retorted defensively at a subject that was a fresh irritant under her skin,

Laughter bolted from Taen. "How many considerations do you give the Shodites? If a factory is to be built, does it matter that a Shodite lives on the land?"

"I cannot control how the Benefactors treat the Shodites under their care." She replied, still feeling too defensive for comfort.

He shrugged, "Then call me the Vubushi's benefactor. I welcome Shea Roseno. They will welcome him too, in fact, they can work in Shea's mines. With four hands per man, Shea never had a better work force."

"Four hands per man can also hold weapons in a revolt."

He glanced quickly at her, seemingly ready to retort, but the retort dying on his lips. A worried look crinkled his brow as he looked again to the sizable Vubushi city.

"Take my advise, Taen," she urged, "present Shea's offer to the Vubushi, don't force it upon them. There are many benefits to having a mine here, and you can list them all to make your case. The Vubushi may well surprise you and accept your proposal."

"I can't." he shook his head, "I dislike their kind. I'd rather not spend time with them, or look at them , or even listen to them. They are hideous, unnatural creatures."

A bolt of anger struck through her, but she suppressed the urge to berate him for his bigotry. In a calm tone, she said, "Then it might be advisable to have an intermediary, someone who can speak to the Ryslac-Vubushi in your stead. Someone they will trust."

"Another Ryslac?"

"Actually, I was thinking about Buhj." she said, "He is a talented communicator. He certainly did prove himself during the redistribution of the Ryslacs after the Montrose War. He might prove useful to you."

"Yes, he might." he conceded.

"I'd like to see him," she said casually, "Do you know where the Toscocti are in the plains?"

"We can visit him now if you like."

"Will you ask him to be your intermediary?"

Taen didn't seem at all threatened by her suggestion. He considered his options. Finally, he said, "If I agree to have Buhj as my intermediary, will you meet my present personal needs?"

He was as grasping as ever. Disappointed in her son, she said, "The arrangements will be made as soon as I return to Ona."

෴෴෴෴෴෴

Buhj avoided his grandfather by going into the grain fields and participating in the harvest. Not one to labor hard, the fields would be the last place in Dilgopoche his grandfather looked for him.

Of course, the fields were Drell's idea. He didn't mind physical labor, mainly because it wasn't him doing the laboring. Buhj hated working the fields. The plants were spiny and lashed at his faces, and the farm hands treated him poorly because he'd courted many of their daughters, leaving a string of broken hearts in his village. Love was a game for Buhj.

His grandfather's Other believed it was time for Buhj to marry and settle into a vocation. He encouraged Drell to take up teaching, through Buhj. The village children needed more teachers. Not only had his Grandfather's Other chosen his vocation for him, but he'd chosen a woman for him, as well. Her name was Trina, and she'd just come of age this season. True, she was a comely young woman with an interesting mind, but marriage?

Imagine your torment, being wed to a comely woman with an interesting mind, Drell thought at him scornfully.

"I'm not ready for marriage, even to a pretty girl."

She likes us.

Buhj chuckled lowly. "I've heard she likes many."

She is experienced. She won't bore us.

Irritated, Buhj demanded, "Just whose side are you on? Grandfather's or mine?"

I like Trina, and I like her Other.

"If I didn't know better, I'd think you were conspiring with Grandfather." Buhj grumbled.

If I were the pilot of the body, Trina and I would have been married by now.

"Well, you're not! I am! And since I am in charge, I will decide when we marry!"

His raised voice brought the attention of the farm hands around him, and they looked askance at him. It was very impolite for a Toscocti to speak aloud to his Other, especially in the presence of his own kind. Chagrinned, he lowered his head and continued to cut down the grain.

Yes, you are in charge of the body, Drell fumed, *but you forget that I can make your life very unpleasant.*

Drell began to recite Dilgo war poems, boring, long winded poems that usually put Buhj to sleep. He did his best to ignore his brother's intrusive thoughts, humming a song to himself, concentrating on slapping down the grain, but Drell's ceaseless droning sent irritation shivers up his spine, driving him to distraction.

"Stop it, will you!" he shouted, not able to take it any longer, "Stop it, stop it now!"

The farmer in whose field he was hiding stalked toward him, holding a scythe in his hand like a weapon. His operative face scowled angrily. "Get off my land!"

Horrified, Buhj sputtered, "I apologize for my outburst, it won't happen again."

"The youth of today!" he shouted angrily, "You have no manners! In my day, I would have been beaten for speaking to my Other in public! Now go! None of us want to listen to you argue!"

In the row Werned fled, the sight of the trail in his hand, following the fingers to another land, conquest beating a path to him, battles roaring side and stim-

Buhj grimaced, threw down the scythe and he started out of the field. Low, under his breath, he snarled, "Now see what you've done?"

Over the Coulcubannha he rode, charging through the cloud of death, immortal and invisible in his stealth, a victory at his side, a dark knight in the fore-

Buhj rolled his eyes and sighed. Drell was relentless.

An odd sound rumbled in the air above him, silencing Drell and causing the other farm hands to stop their work, and look at the sky. Buhj recognized the sound.

557

Jishni!

Buhj smiled at the prospect. As he caught sight of the white and silver windrider and noticed its general direction, he started running to meet it.

It landed in a clearing outside his village. The Toscocti poured out of their homes, and abruptly Buhj was surrounded. He followed the crowd to the landing sight, and was in time to see Taen-Sant disembark with Jishni.

"Jishni!" he shouted happily.

She grinned wide as she saw him. Her Watchers preceded her as she disembarked and cut a path for her through the crowd. Reaching him, she took his much wider hands into hers and gushed, "I am so happy to see you again."

"As I am to see you." he replied, and he felt his cheeks turn red. "I have missed your company."

"And I, yours. And Drell's, too. How are you both?"

Drell prodded him to ask about her twin son. "Us?" Buhj said incredulously, "How are you? Did you find Archer?"

The sadness that swept her features told him all he needed to know. "You will." he said with assurance. "I feel it in my bones."

Her smile returned, but with less sparkling enthusiasm in her eyes. She reached up to take him by the face, and kissed his left cheek, then Drell's right. "Thank you for your timely encouragement."

Touching his tingling cheek, he said, "You should know that I'd say anything for a kiss."

Cannily, she replied, "You are a good boy, Buhj."

Feeling properly let down, he said, "Perhaps this would be a good time to introduce you to our village senate?"

"I've come to speak to you." she replied, "But, it might be a good idea to meet with your village leaders." She turned a cocked brow to her son, "What do you think, Taen-Sant? As long as we are here, would you like to see the machinations of local government with your own eyes?"

Taen-Sant seemed a bit uncomfortable, and reluctant to step off the ramp of the windrider. His eyes followed the semi-circle of Toscocti that surrounded them, distaste clearly in his face. "If I must."

Jishni took Buhj's arm, and let him guide her through the throng of onlookers, while Taen-Sant followed. Jishni behaved regally, greeting each Toscocti who made eye contact with a smile and a decorous nod of her head. Buhj at once felt proud to have the Janti daka on his arm.

He noted that Trina had come out with her mother to watch. She was dark and sultry, with black eyes and curly black hair, and an operative face on her right side. She was a stunning beauty that Buhj might have chased if it weren't for her expectation they'd marry at the end of the chase. Damn his grandfather's meddling.

Look at her, she's jealous!

Buhj glanced away from her, and smirked.

She cares about us.

Casually, and for Drell's benefit, Buhj asked, "Have you come to take me back to Jantideva?"

you wouldn't dare

"As you recall," he continued, "Drell was very interested in working with your people."

before we met Trina!

"Absolutely, the offer still stands," she said readily, "if that is what you'd like."

"But that is not why you came to see me." he assumed, ignoring Drell's angry voice.

"I had something more local in mind." she confirmed.

"Ah, there is the town hall." he said, and he pointed at their magnificent new building in the center of the village. It was meant to be a replica of Zadoq, a building with a round center and beams of light, but their architects could not replicate the city's beams of light. Instead, they built patios made with cut stone, fashioning them like beams of light. From the rooftop of the building, one could see the design clearly enough.

Three elderly Toscocti males and two females waited for them outside the hall. Buhj introduced them each in turn to Taen-Sant and Jishni, and each welcomed the visitors to their village.

Bril, the chief senator of the Toscocti, seemed rather nervous. He tweaked the ear of his Other's face. "We have not had a visitation from Zadoq since before the border war. What brings you to our humble village, Taen-Sant?"

559

"My mother." Taen replied with a churlish smile.

"If I may." Jishni interjected, "We've come to speak to Buhj about a position in Taen-Sant's government."

An excited murmuring flew through the crowd, and all eyes were on Buhj.

Taen-Sant wants us?

As bewildered as Drell, Buhj mindlessly followed along as Bril escorted Taen-Sant and Jishni into the town hall. Behind them, the throng entered the hall and filled the upper spectator galleries.

The five senators took their seats. It was custom that those addressing the senate would stand, but in this case seats were hastily brought for their guests, and they were placed before the senate.

Buhj stood off to the side, waiting to hear more about Taen-Sant's request.

Jishni did most of the talking. "The Janti wish to begin industrializing Dilgopoche, but to do so, we need Ryslac cooperation. Taen-Sant and I are seeking an intermediary, someone who can communicate with both the Ryslacs and the Janti investors, insuring that all sides will be content with their respective arrangements."

Bril viewed her speculatively. "It sounds like a solemn responsibility. Are you certain you want Buhj for the post?"

"Buhj proved himself worthy of the post during the disbursement of Ryslac prisoners of war." Jishni asserted, "He has a talent for diplomacy. I, for one, trust him implicitly."

Jishni looked to Taen, prompting him to speak.

He cleared his throat, and stated, "I, too, trust him."

did he seem to hesitate?

Buhj stifled an urge to tell Drell to shut up out loud. What did it matter that he was hesitant? He was Jishni's son, therefore trustworthy.

"Question!"

Buhj's eyes darted to his grandfather, who was in the gallery above. Buhj inherited his good looks from his mother's side. The family resemblance between he and his maternal grandfather was evident, for Guillin looked like an older version of Buhj.

"Yes, Guillin, what is your question?"

"Will my grandson be forced to live among the Men and Women to perform his solemn duty?"

Bril looked to Taen-Sant for an answer to the question.

"He may live where he likes," Taen-Sant offered. "As long as he performs when he is needed by the court. Presently, he is needed among the Vubushi. Until matters are settled there, he will reside among them. I will want him to report to me often, and to do so he must come to Zadoq."

"You will ensure his safety among the Men and Women?"

"I will."

Bril looked at Buhj. "And what have you to say, Buhj?"

Diplomacy appeals to us, but do we want to leave our village?

Buhj replied inwardly to his brother, *It's not as if we are leaving Dilgopoche.*

"I want to serve my people, and my clan." he said aloud.

have you lost your-

Thoughts of Trina filled Drell's mind. Buhj looked upward and found Trina's faces. Tears streamed from all her eyes. *Brother, if she wants us*, he told Drell, *she will still be here when we return.*

Buhj had a good feeling about the appointment, as though he'd been waiting all along for Jishni to come and give his life a purpose. .

A destiny, for the likes of you and I? Drell questioned, and he mused on the possibility that his brother was right, that they had a destiny beyond what was offered them in their village. *It would be quite an adventure, and we'd see Jishni more often, I'd bet.*

Buhj was happy that his brother finally came around to his way of thinking.

Chapter 25

Surna climbed the last ladder and from there she scaled a rock face to reach the peak of the butte. From above, Rohn offered his hand to bring her the rest of the way. As she stood next to him, he gestured to the land around them. The view of the canyon, and in the distance, Zadoq, was magnificent.

"Beautiful."

"Wait until the sun sets." he promised, "You'll see more stars than you've ever seen."

He rolled out a mat in soft sand, and sat down, patting the place beside him. She sat with him, facing the lowering sun. The muscles in her legs rippled and twitched from her exertion. She breathed in the fresh air and grinned.

"I feel wonderful."

Rohn looked at her appreciatively. "You are radiant. Climbing agrees with you."

She took the compliment as she would have taken a compliment from any man she liked very much, smiling shyly and turning away.

"Do you spend a lot of time up here?" she asked, diverting the compliment so she could again look into his face.

"Don't tell my family." he said with a smile, referring to the village of Inferes he lived with in the cliff dwellings below. "I need time away from the children on occasion. The peace I find here fills me and energizes me so I can be a better parent."

"I wondered where your patience came from." she commented lightly, "I'd thought a few times today that you were actually a god of some sort, sent to Dilgopoche to lovingly discipline Inferes children."

He smiled apologetically. "Oh, yes, they were terrors today, weren't they? I am sorry you had to come on a day when nothing seemed to go right."

"No, don't be sorry," she replied quickly, "if they were always perfect, I'd be worried, and mainly about my own kind, because children of my own kind are definitely not perfect."

"What are children of your own kind like?"

"I have no personal experience with children of my own, but I have been around other people's children....and they are very much like your children, Rohn. They play, and dance, and sing, and occasionally misbehave."

"Then we're not so different, are we Surna?"

"No, we aren't."

They watched the sun go down, and the sky turn to fire. Rohn told her that before the Dome was deactivated, the sky glittered gold during a sunset. By his wistful tone, she could see he missed the spectacular sight.

The stars lit the sky before darkness was completely upon them. Rohn lay back with his hands behind his head, and invited her with a smile to do the same. He seemed utterly relaxed.

Lying next to him, she was less relaxed. She crossed her hands over her stomach protectively and stared at the sky, all the while she was tormented with the awareness that her arm lightly touched his side.

"Do you miss Jantideva?" he asked her suddenly. His eyes were steadied on the sky, and his manner was casual.

"I think of my family, occasionally," she replied, "but I don't miss Jantideva."

"I can't conceive of leaving my home and not missing it terribly."

"I was very unhappy in Jantideva." Amending her statement, she added, "More like I was dead there. I came to life here. I've never been happier than I am right now."

He was silent for a few long moments.

"I am happy with you." he finally said.

The significance in his tone turned her head and she looked over at him, finding him looking at her.

"In my culture," he said, "Inferes live in pairs."

"Like mates," she acknowledged breathlessly, "I noticed."

His face crinkled with a smile and he rolled onto his side, propping his head in his hand to look down into her face. His face was half lit by the stars, and shown pale blue. He was closer to her now, and her heart beat faster. "Not like mates. We do not mate, as you already know. We prefer to live with a partner than alone. Someone we can confide in, and talk to, and share our life with."

"I'd think you could confide in your friends." she offered, "Your community is so closely tied, and you have so many friends."

His brows hooked together. "Are your kind more like the Men and Women? Are you able to live without a constant partner? I thought...marriage, is it called? I thought marriage was a partnership between two of your kind."

"Yes, but it is also linked to mating. Two people fall in love, and want to spend their lives together, and start a family."

"Then our partnerships are similar to marriage."

"No.....how can it be similar? In many ways, the instinct to mate brings males and females together. They are attracted to each other, and fall in love."

"Is that what love is to the Janti?" he said, disappointment in his features, "The instinct to mate?"

"For many of us." she conceded.

"For you?"

As her eyes roamed his masculine face, the grip of sexual desire tormenting her, she had to question her own definition of love. She'd always believed that sexual attraction was nothing more than carnal instinct. But now she wondered. She was attracted to Rohn, physically and emotionally, and the two elements interlinked to become love.

"Mating, for my kind, is not a purely sensual act guided by instinct in order to reproduce." she said finally, "For many, it is a way to become one with another person. It is a sacred act, to be guarded and cherished."

He seemed to consider her explanation.

"We have a ritual," he said, "we perform with our partners that we hold sacred. May I show you?"

Abruptly, she was alive with anticipation. "A mating ritual?" she asked hopefully.

He smiled at her knowingly, detecting the hope in her eyes and tone. "Not as you might expect. But a ritual that is our way of becoming one with our partner. May I?"

"Yes," she allowed, unable to take her eyes off Rohn's face.

His expression became tender. He reached for her face. Lightly and slowly, he caressed her cheeks with his fingertips. The

565

nerves still alive in her face quickened. His caress moved to her neck, and he explored the hollows of her collarbone.

As his fingertips traveled down her arm, he leaned forward and placed his cheek next to hers. His skin was smoother than it looked, soft. He rubbed his cheek against her rougher, scarred cheek, and moved on to her neck. Finding a place that had made her shiver when he'd touched her with his fingertips, he again found it with his lips and gently licked her skin.

She drew in a jagged breath, prompting him to pull away.

"Do you find this unpleasant?"

Trembling with the pleasure of his touch, she laughed unsteadily at his question. "On the contrary, I find this very pleasant. But I have to wonder, where is this leading?"

His face was close, and his scent exotic and alluring. "Inferes are not sexual beings."

"I know," she interjected quickly, "I don't expect that from you. Actually, I didn't expect touching, either. Not like this-"

He went on as if she hadn't interrupted, "But our skin is very sensitive to touch. If you stimulate my skin," he ran his hand up her arm again and it came alive with mad tingling, "I will feel pleasure. In our ritual, partners stimulate each other until the pleasure consumes them both."

She glanced at his hand, then back at his face, her confusion on her features. "Inferes *make love?*"

"Make love," he said, allowing the words to roll of his tongue slowly. He smiled at the term. "Yes, that is what we do. We make love."

"But Rohn," she said uneasily, "you are a genderless being. I thought sexual pleasure was out of the question."

Interest sprang in his eyes. "Am I causing you to feel sexual pleasure?"

She faltered, suddenly shy.

"You must know," she said awkwardly, "that I....I find you attractive. I know you don't think the way we do, or view your own kind in that way. Still, it's hard for me to recognize that you are sexless, because I....I can't stop thinking of you as a man."

His hand was on her chest, caressing through her tunic the concavity made there by the Suma initiation that had removed her breasts. Her disfigurement did not seem to have an affect on how he looked into her eyes.

"I am drawn to you, Surna. I think of you often and yearn for your company always."

His hand moved to her belly, and a cascade of fresh desire thrilled her heart and trickled into the heat between her legs.

She closed her eyes at the sheer pleasure of his touch. "I feel the same for you,"

His hand went under her tunic, and he rubbed her belly, making her squirm.

"What does sexual desire feel like, Surna?"

Her eyes flew open as she realized she'd been obvious. With another man, she may have felt too mortified to speak, but with Rohn, the truth became easy. "Like.....my insides are being torn apart, down inside, and right where you are touching."

"It sounds painful."

"Not in the way you might think," she replied haltingly, "it is....a delightful ache. I don't mind it, not at all."

"Sexual feelings are an aching, but this is good?" he asked dubiously.

"Very good." she replied, and using both hands, she touched his face as he had touched hers, lightly with her fingertips. His eyelids drooped as he felt pleasure.

"What do you feel?" she asked him.

"A warming vibration beneath my skin," he breathed, "which spreads. Grows. It feels like.....a red sun shining from my heart."

She lifted her face and rubbed her cheek against his. He answered her movement. She felt his breath quickening in her ear. Feeling his excitement pulsate between them aroused her further. She moved to his neck, licking him as he had licked her neck, eliciting a soft noise from Rohn.

Eager to pleasure him, she lifted herself up and urged him to lie on his back. She rubbed her cheeks against his as she untied the thin sash at his waist and freed him from his thick woven mantle. Beneath the mantle, he wore a cloth the Inferes called a geckle. It tied loosely at his waist, and draped to his knees like a skirt. Feeling bold, she released him from the geckle, as well. Rohn did not object, not even as she paused to look at his body. The skin of his body was like his face, wrinkled in folds and soft. Like the babies she'd seen, he did not have hair, nor did he have nipples, and his navel was close to his pelvis. He had one attribute of the male of her kind, the stubby penis that was nothing more than a passage for urine. It lay, unmoving, against his hip.

Pulling her eyes away from his groin, she trailed her fingertips over his midriff. She followed the valleys between the folds to his chest. As she reached the area over his heart, he sighed content. She rubbed his chest the way he'd done hers, and he moaned and closed his eyes. She repeated the motion and watched his face. He seemed to experience some type of cathartic pleasure. He arched his back, bringing himself up to meet her fingertips. She repeated the same motion, and he grunted his pleasure and trembled, and he touched her, reaching for her to share his pleasure. She couldn't help but to smile with delight. Giving pleasure was fabulous!

"What does that feel like to you?" she whispered.

Huskily, he said, "Pulsating warmth, where you touch."

"Where else can I touch you that will make you feel this way?"

"My shanks." he said opening his eyes to her. He looked at her in the way she imagined her whole life a lover might look at her while making love. Eyes filled with the agony of rapture. "Less intensely, my arms and neck."

She moved to kneel over his legs, and trailed her fingertips down his shanks. He moaned, and she noticed the skin beneath her fingertips warmed. She caressed his legs with her full hand, and Rohn's skin became feverishly hot.

She moved to his arms, and caressed their length to his hands. His skin cooled slightly as she paid attention to his arms, but was still very hot to the touch. She met his eyes, and moved her hands to his chest and caressed him between the folds of his skin. His eyes darkened, his breath quickened and his skin blazed with fever once again. She continued rubbing his chest, and before long, his chest muscles began to twitch and vibrate in climax, and as quickly subside, his entire body relaxing in sweet afterglow. He smiled tiredly at her.

"You are not asexual, at all." she accused softly, and she smiled, "You can't procreate, but you do feel pleasure."

"All beings feel pleasure." he replied breathlessly, and in a graceful movement, he sat up and brought their faces close. He rubbed her cheeks in what she was beginning to define as an Inferes kiss.

She placed her hands on his face, and held her lips on his, and he let her, and she experienced her first kiss with a lover.

Releasing her, he lay her on her back and loomed above her. In a voice softened by desire, he said, "I can bring you pleasure, Surna. My partner was once a member of the court, a consort to the breeders. Eegan taught me how-"

The mention of a partner caused her to pull away. She looked into his face. "You have a partner? Which one is your partner? Have I met her?"

His passion faltered a moment as he realized she was upset. "Long ago." he admitted quickly, "My partner is dead."

"You are a widower." she said, feeling relief, as well as compassion, flood her at once.

He smiled uncertainly. "I don't know what that means."

"It doesn't matter." she replied, and she touched his face. With her touch, she immediately mended the moment, and Rohn's earlier passion returned. He rubbed his cheek against hers.

"After Eegan died, I thought I would never want another partner." he whispered. He sat back to look into her face. Emotionally, he said, "I love you."

She trembled, and whispered, "I love you, Rohn."

With both hands, he touched her face, her neck. She reached for him, their arms crossing, and touched his face, his neck.

"Surna, may I ask you to leave your people, to live with me and my children, to be my partner?"

The night, the setting, and her feelings for him, lent magic to the moment. She was positive that every event in her life, including her pain, had been preparation for this moment. If she'd been another person, lived another life, she may not have been able to look past their differences and recognize the beauty in Rohn. Indeed, if she'd married as she'd wanted in her youth, she would never have come to Dilgopoche. Imagining living her life without ever meeting Rohn brought tears to her eyes.

Overwhelmed by happiness, she replied, "I will be your partner."

He laughed his relief, and embraced her jubilantly. She realized he'd been nervous, fearful she'd reject him. She held him tightly, trying to assure him in her embrace that he never needed to worry about her rejection.

He released her and caressed her arms. Wearing a grin, he tugged at the sleeves of her tunic. "Take this off. I want to see your skin."

Struck by shyness, she warned, "I am different than you."

Amusement danced in his eyes. "Is that so? You are not Inferes under this frock?"

"Don't tease me," she chided, smiling, and she stood. Holding his eyes, she undid the sash at the waist of the work trousers she wore and dropped them off. She was more reluctant to remove the tunic top, but did so at Rohn's insistence.

For was seemed like an eternity, he looked at her. He touched her legs with his fingertips, tracing over the rumpled scars, seeming to find each pockmark left from her graining. He touched the mound of her groin, her hips, her waist, and lifted himself up to trace the half moon scars on her chest where her breasts once were. She watched his face as he looked at her, waiting for his disgust, or pity, but never seeing either reflected in his eyes. In his face was interest, and curiosity.

He urged her with his hands to kneel on the mat with him, and he embraced her nudity. The contact of his skin against hers was a sweet sensation, and she savored him.

He lay her on her back and looked deeply into her eyes. "I've never pleasured a being other than Eegan. My only reference to your kind is what Eegan told me about the breeders, and you are a bit different than the breeders he described. If I am clumsy, will you forgive me?"

"What are we going to do?" she asked, smiling gamely.

Rohn answered by parting her legs, and performing as her lover priest had performed. She felt an instant of shock that he would know such a technique, one that had been unknown to her until her lover priest came along, but her shock was soon swept aside as bliss took over.

Jishni chose to leave Zadoq early the next morning. She felt she accomplished a great deal for Taen in placing Buhj in contact with both the Vubushi, and with Shea Roseno. She'd now feel comfortable monitoring the negotiations from afar, knowing the Ryslacs had some form of representation.

Cobo felt her sense of peace as he bid her goodbye and watched her board her windrider with her escort. She was at peace with the promise of a relationship between the Vubushi and Roseno, and she was at peace saying goodbye to Cobo.

Cobo stood in the sunshine outside the city's gate long after he the roar of the windrider's blowers faded in the distance. He had not yet come to terms with letting her go. He had to abide with the possibility that he may never come to terms with losing her.

Gella had been companion enough to ease him through a lifetime of missing her. Gella was gone. This time, he would have a grandchild to keep him occupied.

As the child in Caltha grew, he strongly sensed the spirit of it. Touching it with his mind, he came back with visions of a little girl with a lopsided grin, and pale gold eyes. Caltha carried the hope for Ver dala Ven's future. A living gate, and a difficult situation. Because she was to marry Lodan, Ver dala Ven did not have the right to take the child and train her. The right extended only to Taen's children. Cobo was certain Taen had no intention of claiming this child as his own. To do so would put Caltha's life, and that of the child, at risk, for Danati would murder them both.

Ruminating on Jishni, Caltha and the child, and the future of Ver dala Ven, Cobo did not hear, or sense, Surna walking toward him. As she hailed him a good morning, he started, and spun around.

His reaction made her laugh. "You are jumpy!"

Cobo noticed at once a change in Surna. She glowed with happiness.

"Are you just getting home?" he questioned with the mock severity of a father.

571

"As a matter of fact, yes." she said without contrition, and she smiled widely. "Did daka Jishni leave already?"

"Her mission here was done." he confirmed. He tried, but he was unable to fully mask his overall despondency concerning Jishni.

Surna noticed, but did not comment on his mood. Instead, she deftly changed the subject. "I am glad to have found you first thing, Cobo. I need to know if I am permitted to leave your service."

His mouth crooked in a smile. He'd been expecting this day since the first time she mentioned Rohn's name to him in passing conversation. The two were a gift to the other. "Have you found a better post with the Inferes?"

Her smile turned brilliant. "I am Rohn's wife."

"You bring me wonderful news." he said, and he embraced her. "I hope you will be very happy."

She returned the embrace heartily. "I know I will be."

They turned and entered the city together.

Cobo asked, "When can I expect you to leave?"

"I assumed you might need me to help you prepare for your trip with Taen-Sant," she said, "I am willing to stay as long as you need me."

He sensed her urgency to return to her beloved. Understanding her perfectly, he told her, "I have few needs. So few, I hardly need assistance. You may leave today, if you wish."

She turned giddy and took hold of his arm. "Rohn will be so pleased!"

He smirked. "As pleased as you?"

She laughed gaily, and he was reminded of the girl he once knew who had brown hair and gleaming eyes and broad hopes. He'd thought the Suma had smothered that girl, but he saw her now, resurrected.

He mocked a stern brow. "I expect to meet Rohn before you leave my service. You are my responsibility. I can't leave you to a man I have never met."

She giggled. "I'd love for you to meet Rohn."

He patted her hand. "Tonight, then. I will escort you to his village, and give you away, in the name of your father."

Her grin faltered somewhat. "My father already gave me away once." she replied, "I'd prefer that you give me away in your name, Cobo."

He felt the resentment in her bubble up for the way her father had given her to her brother, then allowed her brother to give her to the Suma. It was a scar that in Rohn's hands would heal in time.

Cobo consented soberly to give her to Rohn.

ও্ও্ও্ও্ও্ও৯৯৯৯

Surna's mood was bright as she packed her things into her trunk. Her features grew animated as she spoke about the children in Rohn's care. Cobo listened with interest, laughing occasionally at stories about the children's antics.

Clapping at the door drew him away from Surna. "It is Durym," he announced before opening the door.

She let out a resigned sigh as he allowed Durym to enter the apartment.

"Good day Ver dala Ven." he said, though his eyes were riveted on Surna. As always, his stare made her exceedingly uncomfortable.

"Surna," he greeted with a nod, "I missed our walk last evening."

Surna gently closed her trunk. Durym's eyes fell on her personal belongings, packed and set in the receiving room, and confusion marked his brow. "Are you moving to separate quarters?"

"Surna is leaving Zadoq today." Cobo said easily.

Durym's shock was real, and it was tinged with hope. "Are you going home?"

Surna threw Cobo a wry frown for revealing her plans to Durym. Telling Durym a piece of gossip was like telling a reporter for the Alliance Crier. By nightfall all of Zadoq would know of her move to live with the Inferes.

Sardonically amused by the thought that he would ultimately save her a great deal of explanation in the long run, she replied, "No, I'm not going back to Jantideva."

"Then, where?"

573

Cobo chose this inopportune time to remember that he had something to do. "And while I am out, I will arrange for a cart and a honig for your journey." He threw an apologetic look toward her before heading for the door. He knew she did not like being alone with Durym, but that did not prevent him from *leaving her alone with Durym*.

Ruefully, she stared at the door as it closed.

Softly, Durym asked her, "Where are you going, Surna?"

She looked into his face, and she felt herself assume a defensive posture. She expected his Suma disapproval. "Rohn has asked me to live with him as his wife. I have agreed."

Struck dumb by her announcement, Durym did nothing more than stare at her.

She shifted uncomfortably. "Cobo has given me his blessing." she said firmly, "I would hope you wouldn't make a misguided attempt to sway my decision, Durym. I'm in love with Rohn, and I am happy."

He turned away, as if to leave the apartment. He hesitated by the door, his arms akimbo.

Lowly, over his shoulder, he said, "What can he offer you? He isn't a man."

Her memories of the passionate night she spent with Rohn washed through her, and she couldn't help but smile. "He is all I need, and all I want."

Durym turned slightly. She could see in his face his deep conflict over her decision to live with Rohn as his wife. A part of her felt exasperation with the strict Suma priest, but she also felt compassion for him, for his devotion to his vocation.

"Durym, I know you find my actions unholy. I imagine I must be the first Suma Mistress to leave the temple, and marry." she said gently, "If it will make you feel better, you may bless our union in the name of the Guardian. I'm sure Rohn won't mind."

His eyes flashed indignation, and he shot her with a glare. "I will not bless your union." he retorted, "You told me he was a genderless being. How can a genderless being engage in a marital union?"

Defensively, she replied, "We are not actually entering a marital union, we are becoming life partners. He may not have a gender, but he is a vital person with whom I share a deep love and respect."

"You do not love him!" Durym sputtered. His angry facade shattered, exposing a hurt and vulnerable man. Fervently, he accused, "You love another."

His intensity pushed her back a step. Incredulously, she demanded, "Are you accusing me of romantic duplicity?"

"No, not duplicity," he replied quickly, taking a step toward her, "It is a mistake. Only a mistake, and it can be rectified. You do not love Rohn. You love *me*."

She took another step back, certain he'd lost his mind.

"I want you to leave me, Durym." she said tremulously.

"You love *me* Surna," he insisted.

"I do not!" she retorted hotly, "All I ever did for you was teach you Dilgo. I never led you on, Durym, I never did or said anything that would bring you to your erroneous presumption."

His intense gaze refused to let her go. "You told me you loved me, Surna. On the day you left the star, you revealed to me your feelings."

She gasped, realizing that he'd confessed to being her priest lover. Revulsion shot through her stomach, and she grabbed her midriff and turned away.

He came up behind her, and lightly touched her arms. She bolted away from him as if he'd threatened her with bodily harm, and slapped at the air to keep his hands away. "Don't touch me!" she cried.

"Surna, I love you, too." he said ardently.

She warily faced him, but she couldn't meet his eyes. She felt embroiled in her worst nightmare.

"I have loved you since I was first paired with you for a state dinner at the Dacha embassy." he continued, "I remember that night well. You were surrounded by aristocrats who refused to look upon your face, but you held your head high and stared at them in turn, as if daring them to reject you. I saw your strength, and instantly fell in love with you."

"No." she whispered miserably, "You can't be him."

His voice broke. "I shouldn't have allowed the Chancellor to assign me to your altar, Surna, but I couldn't help myself. My weakness caused me to violate the trust of the star."

"You violated me, Durym." she said shakily, "The star did not bare itself to you, I did! You violated my trust!"

"You wanted me!" he retorted, "I waited for you to expose me. I even wanted you to expose me, but you never did! For a year, you let me do what I did, and in the end you admitted to loving me, Surna. You love me! Not that Inferes!"

"I loved an ideal, not you." she replied, and she swept a tear off her cheek. "How could I love you? You never once spoke my name. Even as we traveled together, attended functions together, I was nothing more than a mute doll on your arm. Much as I was in the star, a mute doll to be used."

"I didn't know what to say to you," he said weakly, "and I was afraid of your rejection. I knew you didn't like me. You behaved distant to me, always. But after you left, I wished I had told you. I thought.....You might learn to like me if you knew it was I who you really loved. My life is empty without you, Surna." He pressed his fists against his forehead and grimaced. "You hated my ambition, so I threw it away and came here, seeking a second chance. But still, you hate me. What can I do to make you stop hating me?"

"I don't hate you," she offered half-heartedly. "Durym, look at us. You are a priest, and I am a Suma Mistress. What you are suggesting is morally reprehensible."

Tears fell from his eyes. With jerky movements, he undid the snaps of his priest's cape. He ripped the cape off his shoulders and threw it at her feet. Beneath, he was clothed in a fashionable pale green, floor length tunic.

"I will resign from the priesthood!" he declared. "I will become a scholar. I will not be able to offer you a lavish life, but I offer you myself. It's all I have to give."

Her revulsion for him tempered as she was struck with a burst of insight, caused by his removal of his priest's cape. "Durym, leave the priesthood and marry if that is really what you want to do with your life. But do not make me the excuse you use to leave the priesthood. And do not use me to ease your conscious."

"Excuse?" he countered unsteadily.

She peered deeply into his eyes, seeing him fully for the first time. Bemused, she said, "You violated the star hoping I would go to the Chancellor. You said those very words. But if I had, what would it have accomplished for you and I, Durym? You would have been ejected from the priesthood, and I? I would have gone on as a Suma Mistress."

"You hated being a Suma Mistress," he replied evasively.

"I was respected," she said, "by all the priests for my constancy. I was the only Mistress in your order that had gone to the Chancellor in the past to report violations to the star. You took a terrible chance coming to me, and doing what you did. Do not tell me you did not want to be ejected from the priesthood, Durym."

He stared at her warily.

"You hate being a priest, nearly as much as I hated being a Mistress." she said softly, compassionately, "My dear, we are the same."

The hurt in his face would not leave so easily. He dropped his eyes to his cape.

"My father often bemoans my inability to tap minds." He admitted, "Reading minds was an ability that ran in my family, but did not come to me. Instead, I was intelligent. My father decided I could best serve the daka as a Suma. And because the highest position I could ever hope to hold was Chancellor in the Janti Temple of Ona, that is what he expected me to aspire to. I wanted to please my father, but I dreamed of being an Alliance scholar. A simple researcher of details." He met her gaze. Earnestly, he said, "It was never my intention to use you to be ejected from the priesthood. I did fall in love with you. I am in love with you, Surna."

"I don't doubt you." and in a conceding tone, she said, "I loved the person who brought a bit of mystery into my dull life, and by far the most pleasure I'd ever felt. But, a love like ours is not enough to carry us through a lifetime, Durym. We're not compatible. What you need is a woman your own age, who can bear your children, and who will adore you for who you are." Her voice softened, "And I need Rohn."

His eyes glittered with unshed tears. "It's impossible to conceive that I might find happiness without you."

"You will." she assured him.

An uncomfortable silence passed between them. Surna shifted feet, trying desperately to think of a graceful and humane way to dismiss him from her presence.

She finally broke the silence by saying, "Durym, I have so much to do-"

"I will leave," he said softly, "if you close your eyes, Surna."

She shot him with a curious look. Thinking he wanted to somehow preserve his dignity by not having her watch him leave, she complied. She closed her eyes.

She heard him pick up his cape, and heard it rustle as he placed it over his shoulders. She heard each snap close. She heard him step closer to her, and felt his presence standing over her. She fought the urge to back away.

His voice low, and close to her ear, he said, "Thank you Surna, for changing my life."

Durym left her. She opened her eyes after the door softly shut behind him.

Cobo returned later. Seeing her sitting on her trunk with her head in her hands, he said, "How are you?"

"You knew about Durym and I, didn't you?"

"I knew." he conceded.

"Why didn't you warn me?" she demanded, "I wouldn't have spent so much time with him if I had known how he felt about me."

"It wasn't my place to interfere in your private affairs." he said guilelessly.

Piqued, she said, "What is the use of being in the employ of Ver dala Ven if I cannot count on your guidance occasionally?"

He smiled slightly. "You've made your peace with Durym. Now you are properly prepared to move on. What guidance could I have given? The Guardian had the matter well in hand."

Her anger fizzled, and she couldn't help but smile at Cobo. "How can I argue with you?"

Cobo cocked an amused brow. "You can't." He gestured that he wanted her off the trunk. "Tori found a cart you can use. And I

578

happened to run into an Inferes at the city gate. He said he was waiting to see you."

"Rohn is here?"

Cobo looked affectionately into her eyes. "He is eager to have his wife home."

Jittery with happiness, she finished gathering her belongings, and Cobo helped her set them outside the door. He added his library stone to the pile. "I have no use for it." he explained with a shrug. It, or rather the masses of reading material it held, was the one thing she knew she'd miss while living among the Inferes. She placed it in her trunk, and embraced him for the thoughtful gift.

Cobo lead the honig pulling her cart, and walked her to the city gate. Rohn stood in the sunshine, waiting, just at Cobo had told her. Once they crossed the threshold out of the city, Cobo took Surna by the hands and offered her to Rohn, saying, "In my name, Ver dala Ven Cobo, I give this woman to you, to cherish for all your natural life."

Rohn took her hands, and smiled into her eyes, and promised Cobo he would cherish her. It was not a traditional wedding, nothing like she used to daydream about as a girl, with a gown and a party, a golden rope around her neck and a Suma blessing, but she didn't need all those things as long as she had Rohn.

Before departing with her Inferes husband, she caught a glimpse of Durym. He stood deep in a gathering crowd of curious onlookers, some of whom were Huntresses she had befriended over time. Seeing she'd seen him, he waved his goodbye. She waved back, then turned away, ready to go home.

࿐࿐࿐࿐࿐࿐࿐࿐

Taen burst into Durym's apartment unannounced. He felt it was well within his rights, the palace was his domain. Durym sat at his desk, slouching actually, and stared vacantly at the wall. He wore casual clothing, and looked rumpled.

"Have you found anything of worth to me in the old prophecies?" Taen asked curtly.

Durym hardly lifted his head to acknowledge Taen's presence. "I've searched all writings of the Ver dala Ven in Itza's lineage, tirelessly I might add. I found nothing worth reporting. Her lineage was not notable for accurate prophets. It was a fruitless search that gave me a headache."

"No, there must be something." Taen rebutted, irritated at once with Durym. "Didn't Itza utter something about a tomb as she was consumed and transfigured by the Star?"

"As I recall, she beckoned death, for she thought she was about to die. After the transfiguration, she went quite mad. The Suma have never trusted her ravings, nor the writings of her lineage." Durym replied lethargically, "If you'd done your studies in Ona, you'd know this already."

Taen felt sorely ridiculed. "My studies are of no consequence. You are my Suma, it is your duty to translate what I wish translated, and render no opinions unless they are requested."

Durym slid a weary glare at Taen. "I am no longer your Suma. I am leaving Zadoq tomorrow, after I have performed Lodan's wedding. I will tell the Chancellor you need another priest, and a scholar, if you like. I am sure he will send someone qualified."

Taen's hands went to his hips. He couldn't say he was disappointed. Durym was not being as much a help as he had first anticipated. Besides, a few more days with the Suma, and he would have put him to death, simply for the sheer pleasure of the act. "What brought about this sudden change?"

Durym stared at him, and he chuckled mirthlessly. "A personal revelation. That's all I'll say on the matter."

Taen didn't appreciate his high handed dismissal, nor could he deny his own curiosity. He concentrated on focusing his thoughts, and touched Durym's mind. His focus did not last long, but it did last long enough to bring back Durym's dark mood, and erotic memories about......Taen shuddered. The Suma mistress's face flashed before his inner sight.

"Durym, not only are you boring and tedious, you are sick, too."

Durym's brows hitched together in a confused scowl. "What?"

Taen took his leave as abruptly as he arrived, in part because there was nothing else to say to Durym, and also to relieve himself of the images of Durym's twisted, warped lusts.

He returned to his own apartment. His apartment was empty. Danati was with the breeders, preparing them for their wedding. Lodan had been at the blacksmith's for the past two days, preparing a gift for his bride of choice, his student, Melish. Since reaching Zadoq, Taen was so seldom alone that to find his apartment empty was disconcerting.

Riar Sed had admonished him often to meditate, to practice his focus, and prepare for the day they would encounter the Masing Star. His teacher had warned him that as he got older, his focus would be harder to control. Touching minds and manipulating the elements would become laborious, and someday he may lose his gift altogether. Taen promised Riar Sed that he would practice his focus, then made excuses for never having the time. He had a country to run, and then there was Danati and Caltha, two women with hungry sexual appetites. He'd noticed that his focus had thinned. Touching Durym's mind had left him tired, mentally scattered.

He paced through the apartment, looking for an excuse to ignore his inner urging to meditate. Nothing came to mind.

Resigned, he sat down in the bathhouse to be near the water, and studied the stream that ran from the overflowing pool into the drain. The water was clear and pure, thanks to the pump and water purification system built by the Vubushi. The thought of the Vubushi took his mind to thoughts of Shea Roseno, and the mines, and Buhj, and his anticipation of all the benefits Shea's wealth would bring him. A palace, finery, windriders, Shodites, and perhaps, eventually, an influx of Janti.

Many minutes passed as his fantasies carried him away, until he finally realized he was no longer focusing on the water. He ruefully dismissed all his pleasant thoughts to again seek the purity of the water flowing from the pool into the drain.

And again he was pulled away by random fantasies, this time about a breeder who'd brushed against him this morning as he left his apartment to join the wedding celebration in the common below. Her skin was pearl, luminous, and her eyes green. Her hair was as black as Caltha's, but longer, straighter. She was smaller than Caltha, and younger, fresher.

Arousal woke Taen to his mindless diversion, and he shook his head roughly to break himself from the fantasy.

Again, the water. He focused on the purity of the water.

Flitting, frustrating thoughts continued to cloud his mind, but he refused to allow them to consume him. He discarded them as they appeared.

Eventually, the distractions ceased, and he became one with the flowing water.

The vision of his river enveloped him. He stood and walked into the water. It was only ankle deep, and flowing weakly. In the center of the river, there was a place where the water no longer flowed at all. It was the place Ver dala Ven had dug into Taen for the truth about Jem Jin. The water avoided this place, and the sand there was dry.

Though his river had weakened over time, Taen's concentration immediately brought him a clear vision. He felt it had to be the future. He saw Thranlam'Sum standing on a cliff, chanting in singsong words he did not understand.

Uuina'merloa'treloara'zalewra'alo

He listened carefully, doing his utmost to commit the words to memory. He turned his eyes down to the waters, chanting. His focus grew intense, and he missed the subtle changes in Thranlam'Sum's features. The face narrowed, the body grew taller, the gold eyes changed size and shape. Cobo turned his head slightly to watch his son attempt to put the chant to memory, and sadness overwhelmed his expression. He lifted his hands in supplication, and the breath of a great spirit reached down from the sky, encircled him, and bore him away from Taen's river of consciousness.

Taen involuntarily emerged from the vision without realizing that the vision had not been brought on by his own focus, but by the will of another. Thrills raced through him for his masterful ability to calm and focus his mind, and his newfound ability to summon forth a great teacher from the past. Sitting on the cool bathhouse floor, he repeated the words he'd heard chanted. He stood and paced around his apartment, saying the words over and over, moving his lips dramatically, enunciating the words carefully.

He still did not understand the words, but felt they were consequential. He became intent on putting the chant to memory.

⚚⚚⚚⚚⚚⚚⚚⚚⚚

On the third day of the wedding celebrations, Lodan was permitted to see Benu, accompanied by Ver dala Ven Cobo. He had Cobo translate his words clearly for her, so that she understood the purpose of their wedding. As he spoke to her, he made certain to guard Taen's secret, and made no mention of his agreement with Taen concerning Caltha. He told Benu, through Cobo, that in their marriage she could expect no more from him than for him to be her teacher. If that arrangement didn't please her, she could refuse him.

"But tell her," Lodan said, "that with our partnership she would have other freedoms that she might prefer over being a breeder."

Cobo translated. Lodan thought, at first, that she seemed a bit disappointed about the boundaries he laid down for their marriage, but she accepted the arrangement, in exchange for the freedom he promised.

He took Caltha as his first wife, a union that was sanctioned by Durym. The ceremony was much like Taen's and Danati's in Montrose. Caltha danced for him, and lay on the floor before him, writhing in fake ecstasy. Lodan focused his eyes on his co-conspirator, Taen, who watched her antics from the dais, jealousy shading his features.

Durym refused to reside over the ceremony between Lodan and Benu, as the Suma did not condone polygamy.

Their Dilgo wedding was different, too, from the ceremony he'd been through with Caltha. Benu did not dance, but instead she shocked the Men and Women by arriving onto the common floor with her kai'gam. She went through a cycle of the exercises she'd learned by watching Lodan, while a boy played a tunca in the background. Lodan found her dance beautiful, and far more enjoyable than Caltha's sexually explicit display.

Once Benu was done with her dance, and had knelt before Lodan on the marriage pillows, Lodan presented his gift to her.

583

He'd spent the days before the wedding forging and carving a kai'gam for her, a perfect replica of his own, a perfect counterpart for their sparring matches.

"May the spirit of Pletoro guide you as he has guided me." he said in carefully rehearsed Dilgo as he placed it into her hands.

She fondled the kai'gam, her eyes glittering with exhilaration.

In Janti that was thick with a Dilgo accent, she said to him, "I will learn, and make my teacher proud."

The final portion of the ceremony was the public consummation, which, like Taen's wedding, was modified for the Janti. Lodan and his wives were expected to retire to their apartment directly after the ceremony to finish the nuptials in private.

The hole in the wall that separated Taen's apartment with Rito-Sant's was complete. He gave his old apartment to Lodan and his wives, while taking Rito-Sant's larger quarters. He'd told Danati that he broke through the wall in order to keep his protector within shouting distance. As they entered the apartment, the three separated almost immediately. Caltha took the bedroom Taen had once shared with Danati, and Benu claimed the dold chamber, which was now open to Rito-Sant's main receiving room through a large, crude hole in the wall.

Lodan retired to his alcove.

In the middle of the night, Lodan woke to the sound of Taen and Caltha making love.

A shadow moving outside the opening of the alcove brought his head up. The shape was a woman, and he knew without seeing her face that it was Benu. She had just been at the doorway of the bedroom, and was now entering the alcove.

She knelt down and felt the pillow where she'd last seen Lodan, and grabbed hold of one of his ankles. Releasing him, she said lowly in Dilgo, "Caltha was not your first choice."

So now she knew Taen's secret. Lodan didn't know how Taen had expected to keep his relationship with Caltha a secret from Benu, not with him skulking in and out of their apartment.

"No," he whispered in Dilgo, "She was not."

Benu grunted contemplatively, stood and left him.

584

He lay down, and tried to get back to sleep. They all needed their rest. Tomorrow, they'd leave on their journey, and begin their search for an ancient treasure.

Lodan stared into the darkness, an uneasy feeling settling over him.

∾∾∾∾∾∾∾∾∾

Taen-Sant's caravan assembled outside the city. His carriage took the lead, pulled by a hundred honigs, instead of the hundreds of Ryslac slaves Rito-Sant had used in the past. Lucky for the Ryslacs, Taen-Sant was made squeamish by their aberrant appearance. He also left behind his Huntress guard. He told Tori that he needed her Huntresses to stay in Zadoq and protect the city, but admitted to his traveling companions that he was tired of the Huntresses gamy smell.

They left Zadoq in the evening hours, striking out into the desert, a desert that had been transforming into a grassy plain since the rains had begun to come inland. Cobo stayed on the top deck of the carriage to watch Zadoq grow smaller in the distance. The Spirit of the Masing Star had been restless the last few days, making him restless. It took him on impromptu trips into the dreams of the Dilgos, to future and past events, in Dilgopoche and beyond. The Star also had him exploring the depths of the city, and the underground palace deep below Zadoq that had been built by the Rathian, Lord Crag. The palace was deserted long ago, left to erosion and forgotten by the Dilgos. The caves it made hummed, as though they were alive.

The restless spirit of the Masing Star abandoned him entirely as soon as their journey began, returning to Zadoq, and as he watched it expanded and took the entire city into its embrace.

"Ver dala Ven," Kiitur said low to him, deep in the night, "We are gathering the dead."

Kiitur stood by his side, looking out toward the horizon where Zadoq was last seen. She gestured in a wide circle, to the numbers of discarnate spirits that followed their progress. They were pale outlines of shadow on an otherwise darkened plain.

585

"They are the spirits who have been trapped in Zadoq since the city was built by your kind." Cobo explained, "The Spirit of the Masing Star ejected them from their home, and they cannot return. I suppose they follow us because they do not know where to go."

"They are liberated, they should pass on into the next world."

"It's not so easy for them. They've been hostage in the city for a long time, living on as if they'd never met death." Cobo knelt down to Kiitur's level, and confided, "I am unsettled. What if the Masing Star is really dead, Kiitur? What if its Spirit lives, like those, only thinking it is alive?"

"Then we journey for nothing," she replied soberly, "and we have nothing to await." She placed a reassuring hand on his forearm. "We've survived without the Song for this long. We should not fear a continuation of the silence."

He accepted her wisdom with a nod, but was not consoled.

Chapter 26

The Elders held their congress in a natural clearing in the Sidera forest. During the Reformation, the Elders chose Sidera to be their seat of government because it was untouched by Janti progress, the last untouched place in Shodalum. The forest was said to be the oldest in existence. The vrenmaa trees were gargantuan in circumference, and they grew through slate rocks in the highlands. Their broad, stiff, spiny leaves formed a canopy high over head, allowing in no more than dappled sunlight to the forest floor. The village of Sidera was built in the hollows of the tangled vrenmaa root systems. Central to the village, around a broad, naturally carved stone that the Elders called the Rotoriam, they held their government.

"I am Shelon. My Shodite name is al Entlay."

Shodalum's twelve Elders took a vote on whether or not they'd hear this speaker. One by one, their voices reached up in affirmation. Shelon was given permission to mount the Rotoriam. His demeanor was calm as stepped up onto the stone. The Elders were seated below, on hand carved stone stools around the Rotoriam. They turned their eyes upward and gave Shelon their full attention.

Shelon pivoted, acknowledging each of them in turn with a slight bow. He had waited for months for this moment, his opportunity to address the Elders of Shodalum. He was well prepared.

Gella sat on the ground next to Iada, and surrounded by many others. She was nervous for Shelon, and as a response to her jittery nerves her stomach growled. She grimaced and rubbed the growing lump in her middle. She'd been feeding her hunger so often that her weight had increased rapidly, still hunger would not leave her alone. She felt like a bloated jug of yava jelly. An emotionally unstable bloated jug of yava jelly. Shelon had, one time and never again, good naturedly teased her about her rounder form. She'd humiliated herself by bursting into tears. From that point on, Shelon took great care with the words he used in her presence, especially if it had to do with her appearance.

"In Jantideva, I was born into the House of Tuv Grethian," Shelon began, "where I was trained to serve as a houseman to the Grethian family."

Gella knew the speech as well as he. He'd recited it to her often enough, practicing for this day. Occasionally, as he recited his speech, he would succumb to his own brand of unstable emotional outburst, simmering fury, goaded by frustration and impatience with the Shodite system of government. Thib had spoken on their behalf long ago. The Elders agreed to hear the testimony of the Janti-born Shodites, then set a date far flung in the future, explaining that the business of Shodalum took precedence over the business of outsiders. While they waited for their day to be heard, their delegation had separated. Praj and his brothers, with Iada and Korba, went with Radi to Lot to meet more of the il Ubay clan. Forsythio was placed in an Elder's home in Sidea for the interim.

Shelon and Gella returned to Nari with Thib, and put in her crops in exchange for room and board. Shelon worked harder than he had ever worked in his life, and Gella ate more yava than she ever remembered eating.

Shelon was content with their life, until he began reciting his speech to Gella, at which time he was harshly reminded that his happiness, and his freedom, may not last.

"My mother served the Grethians, as did her mother, and hers before her," he went on. "We are a Shodite family born into slavery. Those who called themselves our benefactors used us as they would use animals, and housed us as they would house animals. The Janti genetically test us at birth, as they do their cattle, to place us into the positions we'd serve them best. Recently, in the Alliance Crier, the daka confessed to atrocities committed against the smallest, and weakest of our kind, the children, while in the care of such testing centers. The Janti routinely disposed of those children who were not suited to the tasks they were born to perform, as well as those who were predisposed to incurable diseases, treating them like garbage, murdering them and incinerating their bodies. One can only wonder if this scandalous evil committed against the Shodites would have ever come to light if the daka had not inadvertently lost her own son to the system."

Shelon's words had the impact he'd hoped. The panel of twelve Elders threw wary glances at each other.

He held out his hands in supplication, and slowly turned to address all the Elders. "My own child is to be born soon. If we are sent back to Jantideva, my child is destined to have the same system imposed upon him. Against my will, and his, he will become the slave of a Janti. He will not be permitted to have dreams, or to forge his own destiny. Whatever good he is destined to contribute to his kind will be smothered."

He paused for a moment, and looked into the eyes of Feld, the one elder who had originally objected to Thib's introduction to the Janti-born to the Rotoriam. Feld's round and wrinkled visage held on it reluctant sympathy.

"My son is a Shodite." Shelon gestured to the audience, where the rest of his delegation sat among the Sidera residents. "We are the sons and daughters of this land, your cousins, your kin. On behalf of our ancestors, we are asking for your forgiveness, and asking for you to welcome us home."

He'd finished just as his allotted time ran out. Gella knew Shelon had so much more to say, another frustration of this meeting among the Elders. They gave each in the delegation a short time to speak, and no more. Forsythio was first to speak, and Shelon last.

Shelon bowed to each of the Elders and stepped down. A frown creased his face. He returned to Gella's side and placed an arm protectively around her shoulders, and, as had become his habit since he'd first been able to feel the child moving, a hand on her belly. Gella patted the hand over her belly, and met his eyes, and gave him a supportive smile.

Shelon shook his head pessimistically.

Thib climbed the steps to the Rotoriam without waiting for permission to speak. Her voice pitched high and fierce, and her mouth crooked in a challenging scowl, she said, "Before you begin your deliberations, I will remind you of Betnoni's solemn undertaking to protect us, and her desire that we extend ourselves to protect our kin. Whatever fears you have concerning the great changes their coming will afflict on our society, you must weigh them carefully against your devotion to Betnoni. She is watching us, brethren. She is watching us."

She nodded, and stepped carefully down from the Rotoriam. Arms were offered to her, for guidance and balance. She refused them with a wave of her hands.

Feld stood. "The Elders have heard your supplications. It is time for us to depart and think about what we have heard. We will congregate in the house of Umo at dawn."

Umo, a spindly old man in his nineties, bowed his acceptance. He, and his eleven counterparts, separated, leaving for their own homes.

Shelon sighed. "It is done."

Thib patted Shelon's arm reassuringly. Her affection for him had grown tremendously during the months he and Gella had lived in her home, even to the point that her affection spilled over and touched Gella, as well. "You've done well. You had their attention. Usually, if they are not interested in a speaker, they pick at their toenails, or daydream."

Shelon managed a smile.

Thib patted his arm again, "Come along, children. My friend Umo has invited us into his home. We will rest easy tonight."

Shelon helped Gella stand, and held her arm as they descended the rocky forest floor to Umo's home beneath a particularly large vrenmaa root.

The interior was carved out by hand, and smelled rich of the living tree. Umo, as other residents of the Sidera forest, had to often trim down new growth from the interior of his walls. This day he needed to repair the hearth's flue. Sucker roots had closed off the hole he'd carved into the roof and lined with stones. He drafted his male guests for the job, and together they pulled out all the stones, trimmed and re-bored the vent hole, and replaced the stones.

As they worked, Gella went out with Umo's wife, Lona, and Thib and Iada, to gather food for their supper. The Sidera village shared a common crop on a lower lying plateau, where the massive root systems of the trees converged as one. The bark of the roots were spongy, and welcomed seeds sown in its body. The crops flourished on the roots, as extensions of the trees themselves. The Siderans grew yava; as well as tunguli, a fern like yellow vegetable, yellow grains, and various berry bushes that were indigenous to the forest.

Gella was drawn to the yava. Umo instructed her to pick only the leaves of the plant for their meal, but she couldn't help herself, she pulled up a whole plant for the root. The root was large, and juicy in appearance. She brushed it clean, and smiled. "This will be my supper." she told the other woman, smacking her lips at the prospect.

Thib cackled. "I think that baby she carries must be a Shodite, eh, Lona?"

"Or a black sand worm. That is the only thing in Shodalum that loves yava as much as your young Gella."

The two elderly women laughed at the comment.

Having her child compared to a black sandworm was enough to bring tears to her eyes. She turned away quickly, as if to resume picking the yava leaves. She was unwilling to make a fool of herself over an innocent comment, but could not stop the tide of tears that ran down her face.

Lona went on as though she did not notice that Gella was moved to tears, though all the women noticed and watched her with a knowing eye. "With each of my children, I craved different foods. It is said that we can tell our children's future dispositions by the food we crave during pregnancy."

Thib snarled her skepticism.

"It is true!" Lona asserted, "With Waes, I craved chino seeds, a mild flavor that settled well on my stomach, and see? He turned into a mellow man who arbitrates troubles for others. And with Mounon, I craved sweet things, and she turned out sweet, and with Qait, I craved breads, and he turned out to be a stable, organized man."

"Pah," Thib laughed, "What silly nonsense."

Her curiosity piqued, Gella wiped her face of tears and turned slightly to Lona. "What could craving Yava roots mean?"

Lona cocked her head to one side as she considered the possibilities. "The root of the Yava is least bitter, yet the toughest portion of the plant. One needs to chew and chew to get it down."

Iada laughed. "You will have a child like Shelon, Gella. A tough, hard headed child who doesn't know when to quit or say no."

The prospect of having a son like Shelon appealed to Gella.

Lona agreed. "Yava roots are also the strongest portion of the plant. You can replant a yava root, year after year, and it thrives, no matter the climate. Yes," she smiled, "you have a strong child, I think."

Gella touched her stomach, and smiled.

By the time they returned to Umo's home, the men were done with their chores, and sitting around outside, telling tales. Shelon sat cross legged on the ground next to Umo, listening raptly as the old man recounted an old Shodite tale that Gella had heard a hundred times. Shelon seemed so young that Gella had to stop and stare. It wasn't that the men around him were far older, though they were, but his devotion to Umo made him seem young. Like a son, perhaps. So young, so bright, were his eyes, and so quick, his smile. For a moment, she thought back on the vision in Moom, of the young man who called her mother. That young man was Shelon, a Shelon of the future.

He caught her staring at him, and she smiled for him, feeling mysterious for her thoughts about their son, and she turned away to follow the women in. She was starving for her yava root.

ഷെഷെഷെഷെഷെഷെ

They were given a tiny, private room in the loft. A thin mat on the spongy floor was their bed. Shelon spooned into her back, his arm around her. As she was ready to drift off to sleep, he began caressing her bosom. Gella turned her head, finding his chin with her forehead, and she sighed her content.

"If I weren't so tired, I'd make love to you." Shelon whispered, and he laughed at himself. "As a slave, I never worked as hard as I have worked here. But, for all the hard work, I've been happy. I love this land. I want to stay."

She wrapped her arm over his. "Please, don't worry about their decision, Shelon."

"It's hard not to. We have so much to lose."

"Umo is on our side."

"He is one of twelve. The decision must be unanimous."

"Thib seems confident. Shouldn't that waylay your worries?"

"It should." he replied, implying that it would not.

She turned part way in his arms. Touching his face, she said, "If they turn us away, we will return to Moom, and next season, we will come back to Sidera and petition them again. We can petition them until the day we die, Shelon. They will let us in, eventually, simply to avoid hearing our testimony repeated."

His eyes were dark liquid in the dim light of their room. He stared into her face, his love for her plainly revealed. He kissed her, a long and lingering kiss, and his hand caressed her breast.

"I thought you were too tired." she whispered.

"I was wrong." he replied wryly, and he kissed her lips again.

He drew her back to his chest and tenderly made love to her. Their passion had changed during the course of her pregnancy, due to the unwieldiness of her body and Shelon's fear of harming her, but their passion had not cooled. Gella responded to the motion of his body, reaching for him, stifling the cries she knew would raise brows if she'd let them be heard.

In the aftermath, as she was still shuddering in his arms, he whispered, "My woman, my life," into her ear.

Gella hugged the arm he had around her chest, and fell asleep happy.

Shelon lay his hand on her belly to feel the movements of his son. Together, they stay awake and worried about the coming day.

అఅఅఅఅ౯౯౯౯

The delegation of Janti-born Shodites milled about outside Umo's home as the Elders held their meeting inside. The morning became the afternoon. The delegates first paced, then rested, then paced again as night grew near.

Finally, Thib emerged, followed by the twelve Elders. The Elders quickly walked off toward the Rotoriam, while Thib approached the delegates.

"They have come to a decision. You must stand before them on the Rotoriam to receive it." she said. Her expression was inscrutable.

Shelon glanced at Gella, and shook his head, rendering his own verdict.

As they reached the Rotoriam, young men were lighting lanterns and hanging them from the low laying branches of nearby trees. The entire village was arriving, drawn by the light of the lamps.

Once the Elders were seated around the Rotoriam, Feld stood and said, "Will our Janti-born cousins step forward."

Thib urged them up onto the Rotoriam. Her face was still expressionless, but now Gella sensed buoyancy in the old woman's manner. Her stomach fluttered as she watched Shelon step up on the Rotoriam with the rest of his delegates.

Feld did the speaking. His sallow face was as severe as his tone. "Praj il Ubay," he said formally, "step forward."

Praj did as he was told.

Feld said, "Will you respect Shodalum as if it were your mother, and the laws of Shodalum as if they were your father, all through to the end of your life?"

Praj hesitated, and glanced backwards to Thib.

"Speak, boy!" Thib shouted at him, "Say yes!"

Her outburst caused a rustle of laughter among the Sidera residents, standing about.

Praj grinned uncertainly, and looked back to Feld. "Yes, I will."

Feld nodded. "The Elders of Shodalum recognize this man as Praj il Ubay of Lot."

As one the Elders raised their voices in affirmation.

Gella's mouth slid open. Praj had just been made a citizen of Shodalum.

Shelon found her eyes. His shock prevented a grin from forming completely on his mouth.

Feld repeated the ceremony on Ule, then Tam, il Ubay by birth. Iada and Korba were accepted into Shodalum under their name, ud Hiil. Forsythio was accepted in his Shodite name, od Morne.

594

As Feld came to Shelon, he paused, and glanced toward Gella. Thib put a hand at her back. "It is time for you to join Shelon."

Gella mounted the Rotoriam, barely able to breathe. Shelon reached for her hand, and smiled. She could see now the tears of joy standing in his eyes.

"Shelon al Entlay" Feld said staidly, "Will you respect Shodalum as if it were your mother, and the laws of Shodalum as if it were your father, all through to the end of your life?"

"I will." he said, his voice clear and proud.

"Thib has informed me that you do not wish to be consecrated to the soil of your tribe, but to Calli. Is this correct?"

Shelon threw a wry glance at Thib. "Yes. I remember saying something to that affect over supper once, long ago."

Thib nodded her head graciously.

"Are you aware that Calli is owned by this woman, Gella al Perraz?"

"I am aware."

Gella blinked. Feld had spoken of her as if she were still a citizen.

"In order to be consecrated to Calli, you must join this woman's tribe."

Shelon looked into her eyes. Happiness glowed from his face as he asked, "May I join your tribe?"

"You don't have to ask for something you already have, Shelon."

To Feld, Gella said, "I take this man into my tribe, and into my home."

"No time like the present." Feld said, ruefully glancing at her round belly. "The Elders of Shodalum recognize Shelon al Perraz of Calli."

"Wait!" Gella said loudly, "No, that is not right. I wish to have my name changed to al Entlay."

Shelon's hand tightened around hers to gain her attention. She refused to look away from the Elder. "Shelon has waited a lifetime to be known by his Shodite name, and frankly, I have no affinity to mine. I want Shelon to have his name."

Feld's brow furrowed. "It can be done.....but you do realize that you will have to have your child, and all subsequent children, consecrated to Calli, or they will be at risk of not holding legal citizenship?"

"Gella," Shelon whispered, "my name doesn't matter to me as much as my freedom."

She looked into his eyes. "Having our children consecrated to Calli is a simple matter, Shelon." she took both his hands in hers. "I want our son to be al Entlay. Like his father."

He lowered his head, his eyes still steadied in hers. She thought he might refuse her, but he did not. He said, "I love you, Gella."

A slight smile curled her lips, and to Feld she said, "I will take al Entlay."

"Very well." To Shelon, he said, "The Elders of Shodalum recognize Shelon al Entlay of Calli, taken by Gella al Entlay of Calli."

Twelve voices shouted yay, and Shelon was made a citizen.

Shelon burst into laughter, and grabbed Gella into an embrace. Reaching over her shoulder, he pulled Iada into their embrace, and she pulled in Praj and Korba, and Korba pulled in Forsythio, and Praj, his brothers, until they all clung to each other, celebrating their happiness.

Feld cut through their celebration by tapping a stone on the Rotoriam to gain their attention.

Still clinging to each other, they looked down upon the Elder respectfully.

"Tomorrow morning, we will meet with you to discuss the feasibility of accepting other Janti-born Shodites into Shodalum. For now, we rest."

The Elders abruptly left.

As the others resumed their celebration, Shelon stilled, his expression turning pensive. Pulling Gella along, he descended the Rotoriam. To Thib, he asked, "They haven't decided whether or not to accept more Shodites into Shodalum?"

"They have many concerns they must first address." she confirmed.

"Then, we aren't free yet." he said, his tone hushed with disbelief.

596

Thib took hold of his arm and peered upwards into his eyes. "They have taken an important step, Shelon al Entlay of Calli. Rest easy tonight, brother. Rest well."

She nodded toward him, and beckoned to Gella and Shelon to follow her and her friends, Umo and Lona, back to their home.

"Rest easy tonight," Gella implored, holding his hand tight.

Shelon nodded mutely, but concern furrowed his brow.

৵৵৵৵৻৵৻৵৻৵৻

The Elders met in Feld's expansive home the next morning. Their newest immigrants were invited to attend, and instructed to sit aside and listen, not to interrupt unless addressed. The Elders, including Thib, sat in a casual circle on the floor, and drank tea and ate meat cakes. For the longest time they talked about personal matters, of the crops and their grandchildren, and the squabble over land rights between the ol Ralds and the yu Yiggi in Nari.

Shelon sat perfectly still during their idle chat, though Gella could see by the tick in his cheek and the increasingly grim frown that he was growing wearily impatient.

Thib was the one that finally broached the subject of the Janti born, sparking a round table discussion. Gella suspected that the Elders were waiting for Thib to begin all along.

The Elders listened without interruption to Thib's recounting of Betnoni's appearance on the beach of Nari. "She gave me a spark of her life to hold until Ver dala Ven claimed it, and while it was in my possession, I saw the horrors the Janti had put our people through in Jantideva. She instructed me to soften your hearts to the Janti-born, so that all our tribes will open their arms to their brothers held in slavery."

She finally indicated she was done speaking by knocking her knuckles on the wooden floor.

"What of the Janti mind set they bring with them?" Feld asked, his tone subdued out of respect for Thib. "Will they be able to adhere to our laws, or will they desire to change our laws, our ways?"

Thib replied, "Hasn't each generation made changes that the last did not approve?"

Olva, a relatively young Elder at sixty nine, said, "Ah, yes, but they weren't changes that disrupted Shodalum's basic structure of simplicity."

"Very true," Feld remarked quickly.

"What if they miss their technology?" Relez questioned, and she knocked her knuckles on the floor.

"Then they can return to Jantideva, or go on to another country of their choice." Thib replied, "It is my understanding that Zaria is willing to take immigrant Shodites, and treat them as citizens, rather than chattel. By accepting the Janti born into our country, we are freeing our kin from slavery. It is the right thing to do."

Acoba said, "Betnoni would wish us to accept our brethren. She will no doubt ensure that we will be able to accommodate them."

"Or it is as Forsythio suggested," Doro interjected, "that we must work in cooperation with daka Bailin to secure Old Rathia."

"And what of the Janti living in Old Rathia?" Umo asked, "Shall we eject them from their homes? It would cause a range war! Is that what we want?"

Zodia frowned. "With the Janti born on our side, we could handily eject the Janti, and Shodalum would be whole again."

"Why did the daka believe we wanted Old Rathia?" Doro asked.

"He says it was stolen from us." and Thib shrugged and laughed, "What's new? The Rathians long ago stole North Shodalum from us....and now the Janti has laid their claim. Who here believes the land was ever ours?"

Amused approbation rose around the circle.

Ualtar spoke up. "How would we go about accepting into our country so many Janti born? Brother Shelon estimated over twenty million to welcome and indoctrinate to our ways; it's a daunting prospect."

"Oh yes, indeed, but I believe if we take them by tribe, that would be best. And each tribe can sort out their own hierarchy accordingly." Umo offered, "Of course, a census would have to be taken of the Janti born who wish to come home, and their names divided among their tribes."

"There will be tribes who will not accept new blood." Sena warned, "They will not want to divide their properties among themselves, much less newcomers."

"The il Ubay did not mind." Thib reminded.

"The il Ubay accepted three sturdy men into their tribe." Lantro said, amusement twinkling in his gray eyes. "I believe they needed a few sturdy young men."

Laughter traveled around the circle at the expense of the il Ubay.

Feld said, "Ah, yes, but imagine the shock of a tribe being forced to accept one hundred, or many hundreds, or many thousands of men, women and children. There are only a few tribes."

Umo, piped in, "Of the Line of Twelve, there are one hundred sub-groups, with several thousand more branches in each family line. If each are taken as independent tribes, there are over seven thousand to consider."

"Divide them," Feld went on pointedly, "by the millions of Janti born, and imagine, if you will, being forced to divide property, and food, accordingly. We will undoubtedly face famine."

"The first seasons may be hard." Thib agreed, "But we were born for struggle. We will adapt. I, myself, look forward to having my tribe grow."

"You have Nari, Thib." Feld replied reproachfully. "What of the tribes that do not have your wealth of land?"

Bane said, "There are the lands in the Black desert available. In fact, land as vast as to hold millions. The last measurements made," he glanced at Gella, and smiled slightly, "were made about eighteen years ago. There are approximately two million parcels in the Black Desert. If the Gella's tribe took in that many families, she could ease the burden of our tribes, considerably."

"Who in their right mind would want land in the Black desert?" Feld retorted.

"Perhaps you should ask Gella al Entlay of Calli?" Thib said coldly.

Feld faltered, and threw an apologetic look toward Gella.

"I'm told," Thib said, "that most Janti born would much prefer the Black desert to slavery. If that is true, they will forge a life here. If it is not, they can leave."

Relez leaned forward, and addressed Gella. "Will you accept newcomers to your tribal land, Gella al Entlay?"

They all turned toward Gella. She was at once uncharacteristically shy. In Strum, she'd grown hard, defensive, wearing the armor of a blustering maverick, an unrepentant whore, a woman without the acceptance of her tribe. She would never have expected acceptance from any of those sitting in Feld's home. It struck her suddenly that she was among the Elders, and they wished her to speak among them. Awe and respect dried her throat.

"I will accept as many into my tribe who will come."

Feld hummed a response.

Olva said, "If it is our fate to accept the Janti born, then how can we disobey Betnoni? She has protected us for all these centuries."

Agreement traveled around the circle, and this time, even Feld nodded.

Shelon's grip tightened on Gella's hand.

Ovu said, "Then are we all agree to accept the Janti born into our country?"

A great yay filled the room, and a smile curled Shelon's lips.

"First order of business," Feld interjected, "we must organize a census to evaluate tribal land holdings, and to inform our people of our decision."

"We will also need to collect the twelve tribal crests, as the law requires, to be presented to the Alliance." Doro interjected.

"Would you?" Feld asked.

Doro rapped his knuckles on the floor in acceptance of the task.

"All there is left to do is to elect a representative to speak for us before the Alliance Council." Feld said, "But who?"

Thib said, "I suggest Chosen Sister Gella al Entlay. She has already had prior contact with the dakas, and by the nature of her family ties she has leave to speak before the council."

"No." Shelon said sharply. "It is too dangerous."

All eyes switched to him, and the Elders stared at him as if they could not believe he'd have the audacity to meddle in their affairs.

Thib rose, and in a condemning tone, she asked Shelon to step outside.

He seemed cowed by Thib. In a cajoling tone, he said, "Thib, I cannot condone delivering my beloved into the hands of the enemy."

Gella rose, glancing apprehensively at the Elders. "Shelon, we will speak outside."

He let both women usher him out. Thib emerged wagging her finger at him. "I warned you not to interrupt! Have respect for the process, fighting man!"

"I don't want my wife in Jantideva ever again!" he thundered suddenly, silencing them both. Arms akimbo, he paced away from them.

"It isn't your choice." Thib retorted coldly, "It is Gella's. She is the matriarch of your tribe. You bend to her will. It is the Shodite way, and you may as well get used to it."

Shelon looked back at Gella longingly. She understood his fears. Entering Jantideva would be dangerous for any Shodite, but especially so for her since becoming a recognizable fugitive. She no more wanted to return, than he wanted her to go.

The baby kicked her as she made her decision, and she mindlessly caressed her assaulted belly. "I choose to obey Shelon's will."

He sighed relief and turned away.

Thib nodded, plainly disappointed in them both. "I will tell the Elders."

Thib returned inside the house, leaving Shelon and Gella outside, their invitation to sit with the Elders silently revoked.

Gella went to Shelon, and touched his back with both hands. "Will we return to Calli, and leave the politics to someone else?"

"Why not?" he asked, "What more can I do for the Janti born than I have already done? Once the daka learns that Shodalum has lifted the banishment, they are compelled to release the Shodites."

"And if the daka doesn't listen to the representative?" Gella asked pointedly. "Perhaps Doro is right. Perhaps I am the only one the daka will listen to, Shelon, because of my connection to Cobo. Shouldn't I be willing to do my part in freeing the Janti born?"

Shelon tipped his head to look at the green canopy swaying above their heads. She couldn't see his expression, but she felt she knew him well enough to know that he was pensive.

Finally, he turned and looked intensely into her eyes. "Your only concern should be growing a hearty son to help us with our farm. And learn to grow him well, because I am planting another one in you as soon as he is born."

Amusement cocked her brow. "Don't I have a say?"

He abruptly embraced her, burying his face into her neck. "Yes, you do, Gella. You do." he said, his voice husky with fear.

She had a feeling he wasn't talking about the conception of their second child.

৵৵৵৵৵৾৽৽৽৽

The Elders assembled the tribal crests needed as proof of Shodalum's intent. Though they needed only the crests that belonged to the tribes in power during daka Redd's tyranny, many more tribes sent their mark, wishing to be counted among those accepting their kin. The tribal marks were burned into small squares of animal hide and carefully rolled and tied. Gella added her crest to the collection after having redesigned it with the help of Shelon. Her crest once held her mark, a circle within a circle, and Cobo's, a curling Janti glyph expressing his name. To it, they added Shelon's chosen mark, a cross with three intersecting lines. It was the Rathian name for Mo'ghan the First, and it meant Peaceful Warrior. Gella tried to talk Shelon into using a form of the al Entlay crest, instead, but he would not hear of it. The ancient Ver dala Ven represented to Shelon the embodiment of the Rathian Creed of Honor, a creed he respected and likened to Shodalum's gentler ways. She bent to his will, though having the same mark on her crest as she'd seen in Moom, and in her frightening hallucination about the long dead Ver dala Ven, disquieted Gella.

The Elders appointed Thib to be their Alliance representative. Praj, his brothers, Iada and Korba volunteered to accompany her to

Jantideva, to protect her and to carry the proof of Shodalum's intent, a simple bag filled with rolled parchments.

Shelon and Gella left for Calli shortly after Thib was named, accompanied by their friends and a legion of census takers. Reaching the Sidera lowlands, the latter broke from them, dividing into many small groups and heading to the settlements on the east and west shores to begin the census of the mid-lowland tribes.

Their friends were staying behind, in Sidera, until Thib was ready to leave for the border. Shelon embraced each of his friends, and bid them good luck. To Iada, he added sardonically, "And after you deliver Thib to the Alliance Council, do release Edise and his men from Moom. Although I wouldn't mind the thought of Edise rotting in Moom for his part in the death of Solien di Haveran, it doesn't seem like the Shodite thing to do."

"It won't be my first order of business, but I will get to it." She said with a grin.

"I wish I could see the daka's face when Thib takes her seat on the Alliance council." Shelon lamented, still grinning, "I've no doubt that it will be a priceless sight."

"You could come." Iada reminded.

Shelon glanced at Gella, and more specifically, Gella's belly, and shook his head. "I've a family to think of, Iada. And a promise to keep." With that, he found Gella's eyes.

"I'll be sure to visit you in Calli very soon," she promised, "to give you the details."

For a long time after leaving their friends, Shelon did not speak or smile.

"You want to go, don't you?" she asked finally.

"I'm not going." He replied evasively.

That which he had left unsaid spoke louder to her than his curt words. He dearly wanted to go to Jantideva and see the fruits of his labor. All he needed from her was a release from the promise he'd made, a bit of encouragement to go. A shock of guilt coursed the inside of her arms and into her stomach as she realized how her fear of losing him had robbed him of a gift, one he'd earned. But no matter how acutely guilt bit her, she could not bring herself to let him go.

603

"Are you sure this is the landing site?"

Iada shot Praj with an irritated look. He threw his hands in the air in surrender.

"Someone found the windrider and took it." Korba said blandly.

"Obviously."

"You don't think daka Bailin came back for it, do you?"

"How would he know where to find it, Korba?" she asked pointedly.

"No matter." Thib replied. She leaned on a walking stick that was taller than her. Her face and wraps were dusty black from their trek through the black desert, yet she had a smile on her face. "Betnoni's blessing is with us, children. Let us keep moving."

She took off toward the Janti side of Peril bay. She moved fast, and with a definite spring in her step.

"I don't believe she is one hundred years older than I." Korba complained. "I am exhausted. How does she keep going?"

"Determination." Praj commented wryly.

"Catch her, tell her to hold back." Iada told Praj, "We still have an option to walking to the Janti Center-plex."

Praj started after her, trotting to catch up.

Iada searched the ground. She'd left a marker. Not an obvious marker. A rock, and she remembered on one side there were pale gray striations running through the center. A luck rock.

"There it is." she muttered to herself, and she went to the rock, and kicked it over. She got on her knees and began to dig.

"What do you have there, Iada?" Ule asked, standing over her shoulder.

"Korba and I buried a relay that I'd found on the windrider. Just in case we were tracked. I suppose I didn't have as much faith in daka Bail's stupidity as his son did."

Korba dropped down on his knees at her side and helped her dig. At an arm's depth in the soft soil they came upon a metal box.

"The medical kit?" Ule questioned.

She brushed off the sand, and opened the box. It was empty, except for a palm-sized relay, a tranny, a voice only communicator. Praj and Thib were making their way back as Iada switched it on.

"It still works." she said, relieved. Relays were tricky, and easily ruined by dampness. "Betnoni must be protecting us, Korba. I didn't expect it to survive."

"What have you got there?" Thib asked, and she looked at the item over Iada's shoulder. "Hmmm, it's a doowiddle."

Iada glanced at the old woman's face. "A *doowiddle*?"

"It is a Shodite term," she said in utter seriousness, "for a gadget we don't understand."

"Ah--well, with this *doowiddle*," Iada told her, "we can contact daka Bailin, and perhaps he can help us get safely to the Center-plex."

Thib knelt down, and watched Iada with interest as she operated the doowiddle.

Chapter 27

Bailin wished Ksathra could see him in his dress uniform. He looked fine in black. He'd completed his cadet training, with honors. They had been the longest months of his life, but he'd worked hard and did well. He did not want to repeat his training. Being parted from Ksathra was agony.

"Come Bailin. Your mother and Janus should be arriving soon." his father called from the hall. Their home in Odhran was less ostentatious than Ona. Bailin could have heard his father's voice from any part of the mansion, had he pitched it loud enough.

"Yes, father." he said formally. If he'd learned anything in the past months, it was to at least show respect for his father, though he may not feel respect. Showing respect kept him out of trouble.

He smoothed down his jacket for the last time. It would be different from his classmates. Black, with gold piping. Fit for a daka.

"Bailin!" his father shouted from the stairs.

"On my way!" he shouted back.

His relay chimed. Greedily, his eyes shot to the screen in the facing wall, blinking blue and white to denote and incoming message. He and Ksathra had been communicating daily since he'd been taken away from Ona. He'd expected her to contact him today, or, rather, hoped she would contact him.

"Bailin! We will be late for your mother's landing!"

He flinched. His father's voice came from the hall. By the gods, why was father so intent on meeting mother today? His parents had hardly spoken to each other since Bail had moved to Odhran. Mother came to visit once a month, for a few days at a time so that father could spend time with Janus, and she could spend time with Bailin and Voktu. Notably, the two of them neglected to spend time with each other. In the beginning, Bailin thought that their separation was his fault, but over time he discerned that there were troubles between them that went beyond his mistakes and entrance into military training.

607

He backed away from the insistent chime. The caller would have to leave a message. "Ksathra, I love you." he whispered, hoping his sentiment somehow reached her heart.

He trotted from his room, down the wide hall, and plunged down the steps. His father and Voktu were both waiting for him in the entry hall. Bail wore his dress uniform, also piped in gold, with a gold sash, but encumbered with a number of medals and patches, denoting his years of service, rank, and successful campaigns. Voktu looked presentable in a new full-length dark blue tunic.

Bail seemed impatient.

"Well, what took you so long?"

"I apologize for keeping you waiting." he said quickly.

Bail nodded his acceptance of the apology, and led them out of the hall, his pace quick. Two Watchers opened the double doors leading to the west patio. Walking through the patio, they picked up the honor guard of cadets, who also hurried to keep up with daka Bail's frantic pace.

A team of Pliadors was stationed at the landing bay, Trev among them. As they reached their positions, just below the landing bay, his mother's windrider came into sight. The young cadets stood at attention. His father fairly crackled with nervous tension, and ordered that Bailin and Voktu stand up straight, as well. Trev sidled up to Bail, said something lowly to him that Bailin could not hear, and then chuckled as the elder daka threw an indignant glare over his shoulder at his friend.

"What did he say?" Bailin whispered sideways to his brother, who was closer to Bail and Trev.

"What did who say?" Voktu replied, oblivious of everything except the near perfect landing of their mother's Starling.

"Silence!" Bail insisted, which earned Bailin a glare from Voktu for getting him in trouble.

Jishni looked striking. Her curly hair was free around her shoulders and face, and she was adorned with sparkling jewels and flowing silk the colors of spring, pale blue and yellow. Her eyes swept the young men, and finding Bailin's eyes, she smiled proudly. She started down the steps.

Behind her, Nan carried Janus. He was getting big. Nan carried him on her hip, with Janus facing the world. He kicked his legs madly and smiled at each face he saw.   He looked funny, dressed in a baby sized tunic that matched Voktu's.

Jishni kissed Bailin on the cheek then stood back to look at him fully. "You are handsome." she said, and she grinned happily at him.

"Thank you mother."

She moved on to kiss Voktu on the cheek. Bailin turned his head slightly to spy his parents as she moved on to greet their father. He saw their eyes lock, and for a moment they said nothing, but it seemed they'd spoken volumes.

"You look well."   Jishni said to Bail.   Was her voice constricted? She certainly did seem nervous.

"You look beautiful, as usual." Bail replied. His tone was more formal. Controlled and casual. There was nothing anxious about him now. He acted as if her arrival meant nothing to him.

Bailin turned his eyes away, discouraged. They were being civil for his benefit, and for the benefit of her court and his honor guard.   Nothing had changed between them.   His father's impatience must have been for the formality of greeting daka Jishni on this special day. After all, what would their subjects say if they attended Bailin's graduation separately?

At Bail's directive, the honor guard moved out, and guided them to the assembly hall of the training center. The hall was already filled with parents waiting to see their sons and daughters graduate from the military consortium. They stood as the dakas entered their private gallery above the main hall, and bowed as the dakas took their seats.

Bailin followed the honor guard to the front of the hall, and sat with his classmates. Before he sat down, he stole a glance at his parents. They weren't sitting beside each other. Voktu and Nan sat between them. His father held Janus, bouncing him lightly on his knee. His mother watched his father. Bailin thought he saw yearning in her expression. For Janus? Archer? Or father? He wondered.

The ceremony began with a Suma blessing, given by an elderly priest named Eres.

Bailin fidgeted, his thoughts so entrenched on his missed call that he didn't hear his name announced. His neighbor, a pretty and curt girl he didn't know well, elbowed him. "Your turn."

He stood and rapidly made his way to the stage. His commanding officer held out a sash for him to accept, white like his classmates except for the red fringe on the ends, denoting that he graduated with top honors.

He put it around his waist, and tied it, and glanced at his family's gallery. He couldn't see their faces for the lights in his eyes, but he could see that his parents' hands were in the air and they were snapping their fingers in approbation. Soon, the entire audience was snapping in time with the dakas.

Bailin lowered his head and smiled his appreciation and left the stage so that the next graduate could be called.

❦❦❦❦❦❦❦❦❦

The post graduation celebration was held in the Odhran ballroom. The cadets and their families were invited into the daka's home to eat, dance, sing, and drink their fill. The special entertainment was a surprise performance by Bailin's favorite singer, Gilibea.

As Gilibea began to sing, entrancing his audience, Bailin took the opportunity to slip out of the party. He assumed that he wouldn't be missed. He'd lost sight of his parents, and his friends were hypnotized by the voice of the superstar. No one seemed to note his casual exit, and he kept his pace casual until he reached the first landing of the stairs leading to their private rooms. From there he took the steps two at a time.

Locked away in his room, he found not one, but ten messages. As he prepared to view them, eager to see Ksathra's face, yet another message caused his relay to chime.

Quickly, he answered.

The screen was black, and the voice connection choppy. Still, he recognized the woman's voice.

"Iada! You are alive!"

"I just spent twenty seven days walking across Shodalum." She replied wryly, "If I am alive, it is just a reflex."

"Where are you? And how did you find me?"

"A better question would be what happened to the windrider you gave us?"

"My father's people found it the day after you left Dralon." he informed her, "I was forced to report it stolen, Iada."

She countered in a business-like tone. "Daka Bailin, we have just returned from seeing the Elders. They have agreed to lift the banishment on the Janti born."

"Iada!" he shouted, "Excellent news! Ksathra will be so happy."

"We've brought with us a Shodite Elder as a representative of Shodalum. We need to transport her to the Center-Plex so she can address the council."

Bailin shrunk in his seat. "Transport? I don't know if I can, Iada......You can't imagine how much trouble I got into last time....I mean, I just graduated from the Military Consortium, if that gives you any idea how much trouble I got into!"

"Daka Bailin, you have no choice," she countered, "You set us on this course. You are partly to thank for our being in the company of a Shodite Elder, and you are very much responsible for her welfare in your country. You know the dangers, and you certainly know all that is at stake."

He squirmed, at once feeling like a childish boy for having put his own comfort ahead of the future of Ksathra's people.

"I can't get away right now. Can you stay where you are for another day?"

"We are safe for now." Iada confirmed.

"Contact me this time tomorrow." he said, "I will try to think of something."

"Very well. Out." she said simply, and cut their connection.

Bailin noted that his hands were shaking. He'd stopped castigating himself for helping Iada and the others long ago. He'd learned a valuable lesson, he thought. Leave the heroics to the heroes.

But he could not turn his back on Iada now, no matter what the price. Any price was worth Ksathra's freedom. Including losing the fleeting respect of his parents.

He stood, and smoothed the front of his well-earned uniform. It was time to inform them of the truth about his political actions, and of the special visitor waiting to be seen by the Alliance Council.

ৡ৵ৡ৵ৡ৵ৡ৵ঌ৵ঌ৵ঌ৵ঌ৵

Gilibea's song was about lost love.

It struck Jishni in the heart, and her eyes grew hot with tears. She felt compelled to leave the celebration and find a private place where she could think, and pull herself together.

She went outside, onto the balcony above the east gardens, and found support on the curved railing. Wiping her tears away she chided herself for being overemotional. She felt as if she couldn't help herself. Not when she was this near Bail, yet unable to approach him. There were moments when she thought she saw in Bail's eyes the love Cobo spoke of, but then he'd return to the aloof and distant man she'd always known, chilling her heart and soul. She'd come to the conclusion that Cobo was mistaken about Bail's love.

Her love for Bail, however, was true enough. She'd finally recognized its age and durability, though it seemed too new and fragile to risk divulging to an indifferent man. She remembered too well her youth and the ease in which she shared herself with Cobo, and the outcome. She hadn't feared the risk then, but then she'd been young. Loss hadn't yet tormented her until she was numb with insecurity.

She followed the railing along the meandering ramp leading down to the fountains. There was a chill to the night air, but it was not enough to send her inside. She was tired of keeping up appearances before the strangers in her own home. Smiling and making small talk had become an oppressive duty. She reached the path in the garden, and stepped off into the grass, to edge closer to the large pool fountain.

"Bored with the party?"

His voice startled her. Standing in the darkness, smoking a manua leaf like a common Shodite, was Bail. The ember of his

612

manua was close to his face, lighting his eyes. He stared intently at her.

The sight of him caused her heart to jump into her throat. Breathlessly, she said, "I was weary of Gilibea."

A knowing laugh preceded him as he stepped into the muted light falling from the windows above. "I listen to it night and day now that Voktu is also a fan. It is monotonous noise. The man sings like a woman."

His approach sent pain coursing through her arms, her gut, for the rejection she felt from him, for his coldness through out the evening. "Voktu....is a fan?" she said, struggling to sound as casual as Bail sounded, though her heart raced and her throat tightened.

"There isn't a young person between the ages of twelve and twenty that isn't." Bail replied dryly. "Gilibea is something of a phenomenon, I am told."

She fell into making small talk, repeating the same inane conversation she'd been having with a pompous aristocrat, a mother of one of the cadets, a conversation she'd only just escaped, unable to think of anything else to say to Bail as though they were strangers. "Chancellor Debbin believes he is a danger to our children."

Bail sputtered a sardonic laugh. "Chancellor Debbin thinks everything is a danger to our children, unless it involves the Suma temple. Gilibea is just a poet. I find nothing about him disturbing, except the way he sings."

She drew a shaky breath and smiled. "I agree with you."

He grunted a laugh, and replied, "Fancy that. We agree on something."

Bail held her eyes for a long moment. The moment filled with intimacy. She felt an urgency to say something, anything to him, knowing intuitively that this was her chance to somehow bridge the gap between them. Her hands and legs trembled, and she wished with all her heart that she didn't fear being vulnerable.

She glanced away, the words dying on her tongue, and the moment died, too.

Abruptly Bail's mood changed from amiable to brusque. "I should return to our guests, and play host." He tossed the manau on the ground and walked away, his shoulders bunched near his ears. She recognized the posture. He was angry, too angry to stay in her presence, because he was angry with her. Nothing had transpired to incite his anger, except her withdrawal. As if opening her eyes for the first time, she confronted their similarities. She and Bail had similar dispositions, they agreed on most all matters, and protected themselves in the chill chambers of their own emotional fortresses.

Perhaps......perhaps he is as vulnerable, awaiting her to make the first move and hoping she loves him, too....Perhaps......and she let her musings guide her into following him with the intent of catching him before he got too far away from her. She wasn't certain what she might do if she caught him, only that she had to try. Excusing herself as she worked through a throng of gossiping teens, she scanned the crowd for him, and seeing his back still retreating from her, her thoughts grew calm, focused. *Trust me.* She closed her eyes, and heard Cobo's voice as if he were with her, standing next to her. It was a memory, she told herself, of his entreaty right before she'd presented him before the Alliance. *Trust me.* And yet it felt closer than a memory.

As she opened her eyes, she acted without thought. She called Bail's name. He didn't hear her at first above the music and chatter, not until she shouted his name loud enough to make her voice ring in the open dome of the ballroom.

Bail pivoted on his heel to face her, disbelief open in his expression. The crowd parted around them, most bowed as though that was what Jishni had demanded, and yet their heads tilted up so they could stare at their dakas. The quiet that broke out around them became oppressive, and caused Bail to cast his eyes about, before turning his curious gaze on her. "Yes dear?" he replied, a stilted and softly stated reply that carried well in the silence of the ballroom.

She tried not to see the people about them, only him, and tried not to listen to her own nasty, evil inner voices, and focused on trusting Cobo. He was with her, she was certain of it now, for she felt him embrace her spirit and urge her forward. She started toward Bail, loving the sarcasm in his reply, for it made her want to laugh. She tried finding the right thing to say, and as she grew closer to him, she opened and closed her mouth as she started and faltered over many words.

"Are you alright?" he quizzed. True concern smoothed the sarcasm from his voice.

"No." she replied, easy enough to say. She neared him, and suddenly was made aware of the people standing about him, watching, listening. A chill enveloped her. "Can we go somewhere private?"

"Certainly."

And she became aware of how exposed and vulnerable she felt in his presence, and how her hope ached throughout her body, in the depths of her mind and heart. The old fear crept around her, and this time she did not feel Cobo's strengthening presence or influence to assuage her fear. It was as if he'd touched her to encourage her forward, then left her to stand on her own.

"No," she said very softly to Cobo, wherever he was, "I can't do this. I can't. Not alone. I am too much of a coward."

Bail prevented her from leaving, fleeing, by taking gentle hold of her arms. Still confused, though his confusion tempered by slow understanding, he gazed into her eyes and asserted, "You aren't alone."

It could well have been sarcasm, for she was not alone at all, but surrounded by her court, friends and family. But it was not stated with sarcasm, rather it was simply stated, a reminder that he had stood with her in the worst of times, the best of times, and right now, he was with her. She looked upward into the earnestness in his eyes. Her history lived in his depths, but what of her future?

"I need you." She replied involuntarily, this time loud enough to be heard by him, indeed, everyone around them heard and had the audacity to pass it back to those who weren't in the center of the drama. The whispers around them unnerved Jishni. Placing her hand on her head, she said, "I am feeling a bit tired."

Bail's interest was piqued by her first reply. "What do you need me to do for you?"

Trembling, skirting the edge of emotional control, she moved closer to him. "Are you happy in our new arrangement?"

The strangest look went through Bail's face, calculation, something more, something she'd never seen in him before.

615

"No." he said finally, and he waited.

"Neither am I."

"Why?"

He'd cornered her, and she realized he'd done it on purpose. He wanted at her motives, for they were important to him.

She faltered, trying to form lies to cover her true feelings, that it would be better for Jantideva, for their sons, for the Alliance that they reunited. She feared being crushed, and in front of their court it would be a mortal wound. She feared his rejection, especially a dispassionate rejection.

As if he knew her thoughts, her misgivings, he urged her on. "You've nothing to lose in telling me, Jishni. Tell me."

"I miss you." She whispered, and she waited for him to crush her spirit, to rebuff her feelings, to remind her that she was as much an unwelcome entity in his life as he seemed to her during their first years of marriage.

"Yes," he agreed, his voice hushed, his eyes bright and intense, " I miss you, too."

His earlier aloof demeanor had lifted, and beneath was warmth, and expectancy, sparkling eyes and a looming presence that had the power to awaken her mind and body. He had swayed forward, waiting intently for her to admit the truth, a truth he wished to hear.

The armor of bitterness she'd used to fend off the very leanings of her heart melted under his steady eye. She admitted the truth quickly, got it over quickly.

"I am in love with you."

Bail drew in a sharp breath. The pleasure that warmed his expression undid her fears. "Cobo?" he countered in a low whisper, wanting to know where he stood, for Cobo was the only entity that stood between them, in the past and in the present. But never again in the future.

"We are done. We've been done since the day he left Ona, all those years ago." she said, and it didn't hurt as much as she thought it might to admit that it was true. "You are the one I chose. You are the one I have shared half my life with, without regret. You are the one I want."

Bail enveloped her tenderly into his arms. In her ear, he whispered, "I love you, Jishni, I always have loved you, from the moment I first met you." and she heard his voice tighten, as if he were ready to weep. She never knew that he shared her heartache, secret and alone, pining for the one he loved as she wasted much of her life pining for Cobo. Building his fortress to hide and protect himself, as she built hers.

"We are one." She said to Bail, a sentiment she couldn't have conceived of sharing with another man but Cobo, though it was entirely true. She'd become one with Bail's heart, and it felt wonderful to acknowledge that he was a part of her.

A burden was relieved, loosened from her chest, and happiness filled her, washing away entrenched bitterness. She held Bail's neck tight, vowing to never release him for as long as she lived.

The moment they held each other, the onlookers broke their dazed silence, and erupted in applause.

Bail's head came up, and he laughed unsteadily.

She smiled crookedly at him, and invited him to kiss her with an upturned face, and as he did, the applause heightened. They both laughed, but it would not end their embrace. Bail deepened the kiss, and she melted in his arms. While in his arms, the crowd around them disappeared, the applause faded, until it was only she and Bail.

ఆఆఆఆ

Bailin was as stunned, and elated, as the guests in the ballroom at the sight of his parents locked in a passionate embrace. Seeing them broke his purposeful stride, and he stood, frozen in place, yet another voyeur to his parent's reunion.

Bail released Jishni, and swept her off her feet to carry her out of the ballroom. The cheers where deafening. Gilibea burst into a love song, obviously dedicated to the lovers running off to be together.

Bailin's cheeks tinged scarlet as he realized what they were probably running off to do. Nothing he hadn't done with Ksathra, but they were his parents, for the sake of the Holy Guardian, what did they think they were doing?

"I don't think mother and father are angry at each other anymore." Voktu quipped.

"Terrific timing." Bailin muttered.

He couldn't interrupt them with his news now. He resigned himself to living with his stomach nerves through the night, and making his confession in the morning.

And from there? His parents would hear the Shodite Elder, and release the Shodites from bondage. Ksathra would be free, and as soon as she was free, they'd be wed. Bailin tried to feel pleased, but a dark omen of doom hovered over him.

He grabbed a glass of ale, and left the party to return to his room, where he planned to ruminate alone on his uncertain future.

"Good evening, daka Bailin," a low female voice purred as he rounded the ballroom entrance. He paused, and turned to see Captain Agart. She was sleek and beautiful in her black uniform. He bent his head toward her courteously.

"Congratulations on graduating with top honors."

"Thank you." He glanced ruefully toward the hall leading into their private home.

"I am certain you will be an asset to the Pliadors."

Bailin smirked. The last thing he wanted was to be an asset to the Pliadors.

"I imagine Cleses and his like might think so, too," she said smoothly, "don't you think?" She smiled cryptically, and sauntered away.

His brows hooked together, and he stared after Captain Agart, baffled, and unsettled, by her remark.

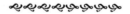

Chapter 28

Bailin's mother and father stared at him, stunned. He stood before them in their private sitting room, his hands secured behind his back, his back erect, his expression grim, waiting for their reaction.

"Is Cleses with them?" his father finally asked, as if it had any importance to his profound news that Shodalum had finally opened Her borders to Her banished people.

"I don't know. Iada didn't say."

"You helped her escape us," Bail said numbly, as if finally putting it all together, "when you knew we needed her to find Archer."

"She doesn't know where Archer is," Bailin retorted, "and you know as much."

Bail's features darkened with fury. "What I know is my son betrayed me."

His father hadn't shouted, hadn't moved toward him, but Bailin felt compelled to take a step back. "Not purposefully, father," he replied quickly, angered that he felt cowed by daka Bail, "she was suffering, due to the lume marker you infected her with. I wanted to help her."

"You helped a terrorist." he growled.

Mustering his courage, he replied, "I helped a Shodite! By our own law, as soon as the Shodite Elder stands before the Alliance and proclaims Shodalum's forgiveness, you must set the Shodites free. Including the terrorists who have fought for their freedom at a great price!"

Jishni, her mouth agape, reached for Bail's hand. His father's demeanor changed immediately, growing tender for his wife's touch.

"Bail, he has done what no daka dared to do," she said softly, "he has freed our slaves."

Bail looked askance at her, for her observation, and for the language she used to describe the Shodites.

Bailin looked eagerly to his mother, finally feeling he had an ally.

619

She said, "Who are we to fight our own laws, Bail?"

"What are you saying?"

She smiled large at him. "We have a Ambassador from Shodalum to welcome into our country. Shouldn't we welcome her personally?"

Bailin's heart pounded hard and fast in his chest as he waited for his father to agree, and when Bail did agree, he couldn't help himself, he jumped and whooped for joy.

꽁꽁꽁꽁꽁꽁꽁꽁

Trev circled above the sight twice. "Looks like a camp. They had a fire, and I see bedding, but no people....no, wait, here we go....look down there."

Bail looked out at the border, where a broken fence lay on the ground. A man lay over the fence, face down. The soil around him was black.

"Lume," he said thoughtfully. To Trev, he said, "Take us down."

Bail instructed Bailin and Jishni to stay inside the windrider, just in case there were bandits in the area. Old Rathia was replete with rugged types who didn't recognize law, nor did they recognize they were under the rulership of dakas. Trev, Bail, and the Watchers disembarked. Bail told the Watchers to spread out and search the area.

Bail and Trev headed for the man lying on the fence.

Trev kicked him over with the toe of his boot. He was a young man with blond hair, and white blue eyes that were opened and staring in death. Trev whistled, and shouted To the Watchers, "Need an identification data base!"

To Bail, he said, "He's not a Shodalum Shodite. He's wearing blues."

Bail nodded. Factory workers wore blues.

The team leader scanned the corpse's face with the camera, and they waited for identification.

Bail wandered around the sight, not certain what he was looking for, until he spotted an unusual object on the ground, nestled in a thatch of tall grass.

620

As he picked it up, he knew from his childhood history lessons it was parchment, though he'd had never seen parchment in his life. The smell of leather wafted from it as he opened the tightly rolled square. An emblem was burnt into the animal hide. Two circles, a Rathian like cross, and a Janti emblem he knew all too well.

"Oh, this cannot be." He whispered low.

"Ule of the House of Xxirius Xsang." the team leader reported as the identification popped onto the screen of his database. "He is wanted in five Janti provinces for crimes against the Alliance. He is suspected of being linked to the bombing of Judge Iusco's windrider."

"A friend of Iada's, no doubt." Bail muttered. He held out the parchment for Trev to see.

"Shodite crest."

"With Cobo's name on it."

"Gella was with them?"

"For Cobo's sake, I hope nothing happened to her."

He looked up and saw his son outside of the windrider, wandering around the campsite, looking at the items the Shodites had left behind. "That boy is a trial." he muttered angrily.

Trev glanced at Bailin. "Not so much a boy, as an irresponsible young man. But he has fortitude enough to defy his father for what he believes in. For that, you should be proud."

"Oh yes, I am proud of my defiant and stubborn son." Bail grumbled, for it was true. He was proud, and furious with his son. He stalked off toward Bailin, and in the same instant, Bailin started toward Bail, his eyes on the corpse.

Bail blocked his way. "Just where do you think you are going?"

"Is he one of Iada's confederates?"

"Unfortunately, yes."

"Damn." and he looked across the border. "Maybe the others went back to seek refuge."

Bail grabbed Bailin's shoulders in time to prevent him from crossing the border.

"We have to look for them!" Bailin insisted.

"We can't." Bail replied. "It isn't permitted."

Bailin looked at him as if he were mad. "Father, I believe the Elders will understand our breaking their law forbidding us from entering into their country. We have to make sure their Elder hasn't been hurt by the bandits!"

Bail glanced over the border, haunted by the story Max Nuninhar had told his commanding officer as he resigned his commission to the Pliadors, of Betnoni rising from the sea and destroying Janti invaders.

"We will search by air." he said to mollify his son, "We can cover more ground in less time."

Bailin nodded and hurried back into the windrider. Bail called his men in with a whistle, and with one last look at the body, he followed Trev into the windrider.

&ى&ى&ى&ى&ى&ى&ى&ى&ى

"We can't leave without contacting the Elders!" Bailin retorted. "At least allow them to send another representative!"

Jishni sighed. They'd searched for hours, flying in a tight, systematic search pattern, and found nothing, and no one. "Bailin, we understand your frustration. Trust me, we are mortified that this has occurred. But it is strictly against Shodite law for a Janti to enter into their country."

"Then I will stand before the council, and I will relay Shodalum's wishes."

"You cannot." Jishni replied tersely, "You know the law better than I, Bailin. Tell me, what is the protocol to be used to free the Shodites?"

Bailin turned scarlet. He knew that the Alliance would not free the Shodites unless an Elder stood before the council to personally relay Shodalum's wishes. And then there was proof needed, proof that the Shodite people approved of their Elder's actions.

"You don't want to free the Shodites, mother!" he shouted, "You are just another slaver, holding the Shodites under the weight of your law."

Bail shot out of his seat. "Enough! You will not speak to your mother in such a disrespectful tone!"

622

Bailin didn't flinch, or cower. He stood his ground. "I will not rest on this issue. As your heir, I have a voice. I will not remain silent. I will speak my mind before the council, and before the Janti people."

"Speak your opinion!" Bail replied contemptuously, "But don't count on the support of the Janti."

"I don't need it. I have the law." His face, so serious, his demeanor, so dignified, he looked years older than his approaching eighteen years. Jishni couldn't help but feel pride for his strength, and convictions.

Bail was clearly annoyed with Bailin's strength and convictions. "If you speak before the council without a Shodite representative at your side, you will shame yourself."

"I am already shamed, by how we treat our Shodite citizens!"

"I have heard enough." Bail said, his tone dangerous. "You will leave us. Go, and sit in your cabin. Now!" he thundered.

Bailin hesitated, glaring at his father. He flicked a look at Jishni, as if to seek her support. She remained silent, unwilling to let him turn her against Bail. Never again would she turn against her husband for anyone.

Simmering, he skulked out of the forward deck.

Bail paced, agitated.

"My love," Jishni said gently, "he is willful, yes, but he is also idealistic and young. I see in him the potential for greatness."

Bail stopped and looked at her quizzically. Then scowling, he said, "Oh. Yes, Bailin, he is insufferable to me now, but at least he is a man, and not a boot licking cur like Kinn." He paced to a window, and looked out at the sky. "What could have happened to them?"

Jishni rose. "The Shodites?"

Bail nodded and glanced at her, worry creasing his brow. "Something must be done, but I am at a loss. Bailin is right, the Elders need to be notified. But how? Betnoni was my ancestor, too. Would she block me if I were to enter her land on a mission of peace?"

"Betnoni?" she asked incredulously.

Bail turned away, grimacing. "If the old legends are even true. Who believes them anymore? Do you?"

She went to him and put her hand on his arm. "What is on your mind, Bail?"

"Nothing." he said, shaking his head. "The sooner we get home, the better." He looked over his shoulder and a smile broke through the worry in his features as he realized that home meant Ona, with Jishni. He enveloped her into his arms and they looked out at the passing clouds, the pleasant thought of home soon replaced by pensive reverie.

ঌঌঌঌঌঌঌঌ

Despite a slank's unwelcome tenancy, nothing was disturbed in their home. Gella brought out the left over casks of pickled yava leaves and roots she had tucked away in the cellar after their last harvest. There was enough to feed the two of them, sparingly, into the next harvest. Providing they could revive their crop.

They spent their days digging up yava roots and placing them in a soaking tub with water. The live roots would sprout in a few days, the dead roots would stay hard as rocks. Gella didn't expect many to sprout, but to her happy surprise, most of the roots had survived the full season they'd spent untended in the sand. They stored the live roots in casks of damp sand, to await planting. The season to plant was coming soon, and Gella was determined to be ready.

Weeks after their arrival home, the male slank that had been using their home as a refuge during their absence returned to re-stake its claim to its easy haven. She and Shelon had been fishing, and left the door wide open to air out the small hut. It was late in the afternoon when they went back to the house for an afternoon nap, and found the territorial slank in their doorway hissing at them. The squat reptile was smaller than a female of the same species, with long toe claws for digging, and a long jaw filled with sharp teeth to pull apart its prey. The males were scavengers, eating the leftovers of a female's kill. A female slank was dangerous, she would attack unprovoked.

Gella wasn't afraid of the male slank. They were slow and lazy. Instead, she felt like a female slank herself, her brood, her home, threatened and defiled by the male. She threw rocks and

624

screamed at the beast. Shelon faltered, for only a heartbeat, then shook off his dismay and did as she did. They chased it out of their home, but it wasn't content to retreat, and turned on them as if to defend its squatter's rights, swinging its whip tail, hissing at them, cranking its jaws wide to display his rows of teeth. It was easily as long as Shelon was tall, but no match for Gella. Once she had it out of the house, she snatched up the sharp ended sand hoe that she'd left by the door, and plunged the metal tip into its mouth, deep into its throat. Blood erupted from the soft tissues, and the slank convulsed violently. Gella pulled the hoe out and began thumping the beast on the head, following its movements as it tried to avoid her assault. She managed to knock the sense out of it, and it stopped convulsing, and moving. It lay on the ground, groaning.

Using the gutting blade that Cobo had made for her years before, she stepped over the slank, grabbed it by the snout and lifted its head, and slit its throat. Pale red blood gushed, and saturated the sand by her feet. The blood had a rancid stench, as if the slank was a rotting carcass.

To Shelon, who stared at her agape, she said, "Help me turn him over."

"And was that a lesson on how to kill a slank?" Shelon said, and he grunted a laugh at her as he grabbed the slank by the snout and flipped it onto his back.

"A male slank." she informed him with a pleased smile. "Steer clear of the females. They'll eat you alive."

He glanced up and winked at her. "True for all types of females."

She smiled wryly, and handed him the gutting tool. "I kill them, you clean them."

He chuckled, and bent down to slit the animal's underbelly.

A shout brought both their heads up. They looked at each other, and Shelon straightened.

"Shelon! Gella!" the shout came again, from far off. It seemed to come from the direction of the beach.

"Korba." Shelon said, and he dropped the gutting tool and ran toward the sound of the shout.

Gella went after him, holding her belly and trotting at a much slower pace. Shelon was far ahead of her, already crossing the

625

foundation of the Calli ruins, a chemical plant that was weathered and falling down into the sea. As she reached the foundation, he'd reached the rise above the beach, where he paused and looked for Korba. He glanced back at Gella, and motioned for her to come, and disappeared down the rise.

She reached the rise in time to see Shelon meet Korba far down the beach. Korba was bent over, holding his knees, seeming to gasp for air, but she could see he was also speaking to Shelon. At his feet was the tied sack in which Feld had placed the precious rolled crests.

Shelon shouted, something she could not hear but she knew his shout, knew it was a curse. Something terrible had happened.

ৡৡৡৡৡৡৡৡৡ

"I went swimming." Korba wept, "I didn't hear them come. I heard a lume when I got out of the water. I ran up in time to see them arresting Thib. They bound her as if she were a dangerous fugitive."

"Daka Bailin turned on us." Shelon assumed.

"They killed Ule." Korba sobbed, "I did nothing. I grabbed the proof, and lay in the grass and hid like a coward."

Shelon grimaced. "What good could you have done arrested, or killed, Korba? You did the right thing."

Korba straightened, and scowled. "The dakas will pay for this outrage!"

As furious as he was at the dakas, Shelon stilled as he considered retaliation. It would be easy to return to Jantideva, and strike out at the dakas. A well placed lume bomb, and their point would be well made.

He looked at Gella, standing on the ridge, pensively watching them. Her hands rubbing her belly, soothing their child.

"No violence." he said lowly, "The Janti may be corrupt, but they are our brothers."

"What?" Korba demanded incredulously, "Are you in your right mind, Shelon? Didn't you hear me? They arrested Thib!"

626

Shelon turned a sharp eye on the younger man. "We are no longer Janti-born. We are Shodites. Would a Shodite advocate murder to make a point?"

Korba's eyes narrowed. "They took Thib. Perhaps the Shodites would advocate murder if they knew that their most revered Elder had been kidnapped."

"No, they wouldn't. They would assume it was the will of Betnoni, and wait for a sign. I am sure Thib accepted her fate without a fight."

"You can't tell me you believe in a master plan." Korba retorted contemptuously. "Nothing comes to a Shodite without struggle. Why did we think it would be easy to win the freedom of our people?"

Shelon leaned close to Korba. Lowly, he said, "I feel your frustration. I know it well. But it isn't hopeless. Nothing is ever hopeless."

Even as he said the words, he felt the patient Shodite sensibilities take over, leaving him peaceful, and contemplative. There was a solution to this new problem. Eventually, it would make itself clear.

Korba seemed to want to retort, but instead swooned. His knees weakened and he fell against Shelon. Shelon caught him in his arms, and he held the younger man up. Korba was soaked with sweat, cold as ice, his face pale. He'd been in the heat too long without water to drink, leaving him dehydrated and exhausted.

"Come to our home, Korba." he said gently. "You must rest."

Gella met them on the beach. At Shelon's directive, she fetched the bag, and followed as Shelon carried Korba to the house.

এওওওওওওওও

Korba was unconscious by the time they lay him on their mat.

Gella placed rags soaked with water from the well on his forehead and trickled water into his mouth, which she made him swallow by gently petting his throat.

"What are we going to do?" Gella asked softly.

Shelon gazed down at Korba's slack face. "For now, we nurse Korba back to health. I am going to finish gutting that slank."

627

"I meant about Thib and the others." she countered crossly.

"I know." he replied obliquely. He threw a sideways glance at the census, sitting in the corner, as he left her to return to the task at hand.

He quartered the slank's carcass, then thinly sliced the meat off the bone. He lay the slices over racks in the sweltering heat of the drying shed. Gella assured him that in a few days the meat would be ready to store, or eat. Shelon was a bit squeamish about the prospect of eating slank, especially uncooked. He sneered at the smell of the meat as he treated it with the herbs Gella prescribed. Throwing his head back to escape the smell, he noticed cracks in the roof of the drying shed.

He climbed up onto the roof and surveyed the damage. Cobo had used thinly cut slate to make the roof. Corners of the squared off tiles were crumbling, and needed to be replaced.

He found the slate Cobo had used in the ruins of the Calli factory. He'd mined it from a thick wall that had once been the core of a lume reactor. Shelon hesitated and inspected the wall before breaking off slices of the slate with the hoe. It was obvious the lume chemicals were inert. Cobo and Gella was a healthy pair, and lume did not take years to kill a victim. Minutes, days, months if it was the wasting disease, but not years.

He made the number of slate tiles he needed, taking pains in perfectly forming them, and took them back to the drying shed.

He straddled the roof and repaired the holes. Afterward, he sat on the roof and stared off at the ocean's horizon. Though he was still worried about Thib, and Iada, and Praj, and his people, he retained the peace he'd felt earlier. It was almost eerie. For months, he'd listened and watched the Shodites. With the exception of the swiftness in which they acted to free their Janti-born kin, their lives were generally lived at a slow, plodding pace. There was wisdom in taking things slowly.

And as he stared at the ocean, he was reminded of Thib's teachings on Betnoni. She'd tried to indoctrinate him in the Shodite religious practice of worshiping Betnoni, and he'd listened, quietly amused, because he was a sophisticated city person who once believed that worship was an act of the superstitious. But here, worshipping Betnoni was nothing like the gilded Suma

628

worship of the Guardian. To the Shodites, Betnoni was the sea, and the air, and the land of Shodalum. Betnoni's spirit surrounded all things. To love his home was to worship Betnoni. To love Shodalum was to worship Betnoni.

His peace was grounded in his love for Shodalum.

He considered their options. Of course, the Elders would have to be notified. More important, they'd need to deliver Shodalum's message to the Alliance.

He felt a nag of anxiety as a random thought crossed his mind. With Thib no longer able to stand before the Alliance Council, the duty fell to Gella. And as Chosen Sister to Ver dala Ven, she had rights that superseded law. Getting her to the Center-plex would be easier, and she would have access to the dakas.

"I have to let her go to Jantideva." He said aloud, "Don't I, Betnoni?"

A breeze whipped around him, singing an affirmation.

৵৵৵৵৵৵৵৵৵৵

Her sleep was restless. The baby's movement, her back aches, her burning stomach, her aching legs. She was miserable, yet happy to be miserable. Strange. She thought the only pleasure her body could give her was through the act that had given her a child. She never suspected a higher, purer pleasure could be had through pregnancy. She'd usually viewed pregnant women, with all their myriad of aches and complaints, with pity.

They lay on their mat, Shelon at her back and rhythmically rubbing her belly, pausing as he felt the child squirm and kick, chuckling lowly in her hair and kissing the top of her head as if it were she that inspired the child to move. His dotage was the sweetest pleasure of all. She imagined he'd be a wonderful father, and tonight let her mind wander into a future where they had many children, and grand-children.

An image of Shelon aging, his sterling hair turning white, his craggy face growing deeper lines, his body stooping, narrowing, gave her comfort as she drifted off to sleep.

"Gella," a soft voice beckoned to her.

She opened her eyes. She was on her back, alone in her bed. "Shelon?" She sat up with ease, and noticed her belly was flat. She smoothed her stomach with the palm of her hand. "Shelon?" she called out, her alarm raising her voice an octave.

"Gella." a woman whispered.

She stood and glanced upward at the loft, where Korba was sleeping. "Korba, are you up there?"

"Gella." the woman whispered.

Hesitantly, she moved to the door. She crossed the threshold, stepping into sunlit washed day.

"Shelon!" she shouted, pitching her voice so that he could hear her if he was in the fields, or the drying shed.

"Gella."

She recognized the voice, and turned, as it had seemed to come from behind her, and as she turned, her surroundings changed from the Black Desert, to the interior of a building.

As she recognized the cell quarters of the Keep, Thib's voice called to her again. "Gella."

She started down the corridor, glancing from side to side into each cell, her heart pounding furiously. The sight, the smell of the place, brought back the intensely painful memory of being violated right before Shelon's eyes.

"That perverted molester is not here Gella." Thib said, "Do not be afraid. It is only me."

Gella slowed as she came to the cell that had been Shelon's. The cell came into view gradually, and as gradually, she saw that Thib was being held in Rathian chains, just as Shelon had been held.

Thib smiled at her sardonically.

"Too bad you are just an apparition," Thib said with a throaty cackle, "I have an itch on my face that is driving me mad. Beg as I may, Betnoni won't scratch if for me!"

Gella entered the cell. She glanced to the ground where the prison guard had died. The body was gone. On the wall behind her, there was a blackened lume outline. She glanced at the outline, sensing there was someone behind her, yet no one was there.

"Well, come on, come on," Thib encouraged, "No need to be bashful."

"Why am I here?"

"My dear, can't you guess?"

Gella stepped closer to Thib, staring into the old woman's intense eyes.

"To free you?"

Thib's features crinkled with amusement. "They cannot chain my spirit or my will, or my mind, only my body. They've got my body in a goodly knot, that much is certain. I cannot fulfill my duties to the Elders. Someone must take my place." Her eyes were bright, and fixed on Gella. "The Proof has fallen into your hands for a reason. You and Shelon must take my place, and stand before the Alliance to free our Shodite brothers from bondage."

Gella touched her flat stomach. Before her eyes, it grew in vast measure until she was as round as she remembered. "I can't, Thib. My son will be born soon. He must be born in Shodalum, and consecrated to Calli. He cannot be born a Janti."

"Trust Betnoni, my child." Thib offered, "She has your welfare, and your son's welfare, well in hand."

Thib, and the cell, and the Keep, dissolved around her. She was again in the Black Desert. Standing outside her home. In the distance, she saw Cobo walking up from the beach. He waved at her.

And she woke.

She reached for Shelon. He was out of their bed, and building a fire in the hearth. She struggled to sit up. Unlike her dream, there was nothing easy about changing positions.

Shelon noticed she was awake, and hurried to her side to give her an arm. "You sleep well?"

She crooked her mouth in a smile. "I dreamt of Thib, that she was in the Keep, in the same cell as you were held. She was talking nonsense, about our needing to take the census to Jantideva."

Shelon stared warily at her, and knelt down to look up into her face. Holding her hands, he said, "Perhaps your dreams are talking to your conscience. I know my dreams have been talking to my conscience. I had a similar dream."

Just then, Korba came in from outside. He was stripped to the waist and wet, his ringlets of dark hair dripping water on his face. He shuddered, and reached for his shirt, which was hung on a wooden peg beside the door.

Gella couldn't take her eyes off Shelon's earnest stare.

"What shall we do?"

"Return, and stand before the Alliance."

Korba paused by the fire, and listened.

"But, Shelon, it may take more time than I have. What about our child?" she objected, "If he is born in Jantideva, he will be landless. We cannot pass Calli to him, and if anything happens to us, he will be left to fate." She squeezed her eyes shut on her own horror of her child being left to fate, as she had been at a tender age.

"All that is required of you," he said, "is to present the council with the Proof, and to make Shodalum's welcome clear. Afterwards, you will come home and I can stay in Jantideva to see to whatever needs to be done."

Her eyes flew open and narrowed. "No. I cannot return home without you."

Cajoling, he said, "My pretty precious one, haven't I proven my steadfastness to you yet? I will return."

Her vision of a future living without him tormented her mind. "Your steadfastness is not in question." she replied softly. "If anything were to happen to you,"

"Nothing will happen." he assured her, and earnestly, he said, "The Janti-born need me. I am their leader. Should I abandon them, Gella? I feel that, no, I shouldn't. I feel it too strongly to deny, I must be part of my people's liberation."

"Shelon," she moaned, unable to argue with him. He was right. Fate had them in its grasp.

"You must promise me, Gella," he said intensely, "once the Shodites are free, you will return to Shodalum so that our child will be born in his homeland, and consecrated to Calli."

With difficulty, she agreed. "I promise to come home in time to have our child....with or without you, Shelon. Though I pray you come home with me."

632

He smiled his relief. "Of course I will. Of course I will." He rubbed his full hand on her belly, rousing the child.

"Do you feel ready for a hard walk across the desert?" he asked her softly.

She smirked. "I dare to say that you will have difficulty keeping up with me."

Shelon laughed easily.

She smiled, though she did not feel the smile. She was shrouded by a dark future, a future she feared.

❧❧❧❧❧❧❧❧❧

Shodalum's seat on the Alliance council remained empty for twenty four hundred years. The council had voted, numerously through the years, on a proposal to remove the seat, and remove Shodalum from the rolls entirely. The proposal was always voted down, due to Zaria's sponsorship. Their legal analysts continued to remind each generation of council members of the laws that prohibited Shodalum's permanent expulsion from the Alliance, namely the laws concerning the Janti-born Shodites.

Bailin made history by standing before the council and announcing that Shodalum had decided to lift its banishment of its lost citizens. On display before him, in a tight fitting glass case, was the Shodite family crest found on the border. In a passionate speech, Bailin asked that a search be made for the missing Shodite representative, while also vowing his support to the freedom of Shodites.

His most vocal opponent was Jantideva's council representative. Grav Tulkue lodged a dozen objections during Bailin's brief announcement, much to Bailin's chagrin. As a daka, he was accustomed to being shown reverential courtesy. In the council chambers, all men were equal, wealth or social standing was set aside and courtesy checked at the door.

Once he stepped down, a boisterous argument broke out between Tulkue and Plat. The remaining council members took sides, and joined the argument.

Bailin was gratified that the majority was with him, and wanted to see the Shodites freed.

His father leaned close to his ear and said, "I've never seen Grav turn that shade of purple."

The comment, which was made in jest, was the first words his father had spoken to him in days. It was nonsense, but for Bailin, it was so much more. It was his father reaching out to him, in acceptance. Some of the tension he'd been feeling since leaving the Shodite border was alleviated, and he felt like he was a part of his family once again.

His mother sat on his other side. Her hand rested lightly on his arm. It was her brand of support. With his parents at his side, Bailin felt strong.

"If you will just consider the consequences! What are these people going to do in Shodalum? Farm?"

"They will survive, Grav." Plat snorted derisively, "Despite what you think, you are not their keeper! The Guardian is their keeper, and He says it is time to release them!"

Grav shouted angry laughter. "What do you know of the Guardian's desires? And I don't see a Shodite in that seat!" he said, pointing at the empty seat between Della Ston and the Iladdatha representative. It was new, replaced each year as the other council seats are replaced. "By law, a representative from Shodalum must sit in that seat, and show us proof that they welcome their kin home."

"She was to be here," Bailin interjected, "but as I have said, she and her party ran into trouble at the border. And see here, this is the proof that the census was taken."

"A single crest is hardly a full census." Grav replied dryly. To the Council, he said, "All we have here is one Shodite crest of dubious origins and the word of a young pup fresh out of the Military Consortium!"

"A daka," Bail reminded him tersely, "lest you forget of whom you are speaking."

Grav looked askance at Bail. "That crest has Ver dala Ven Cobo's mark on it, and is obviously not from one of the Twelve Tribes. It doesn't count as proof that Shodalum wishes to welcome their kin home, indeed Ver dala Ven could have left that parchment to you before leaving Dilgopoche! How am I to know that this isn't a conspiracy to trick the Janti into releasing the Shodites?"

"To what end?" Bail retorted, his control taut.

"You tell us, daka Bail." He invited, brows cocked.

Jishni stood, demanding attention by her actions alone, and she opened her arms to include all of the council members, "Don't you understand what has happened? Shodalum has indeed reached out to us. We should be celebrating, not bickering."

"I disagree." Grav said gruffly, "I am afraid that it is a conspiracy. A conspiracy concocted by Cleses to free his people, and carried out by daka Bailin."

"How dare you accuse our son of treason!" Bail retorted hotly.

Della Ston looked on Grav with dislike. "You had better have proof of your accusations, or weigh your words with more care."

Grav opened his purse, reached in. A bi-lo chip was between thumb and forefinger as his hand emerged from his purse.

"May I offer this as proof?"

Bail threw a quick look at Bailin, his mouth tense.

Bailin's eyes never left the chip as Grav handed it off to an underling, who delivered it to Aton at the other end of the council chamber. Aton, after seeking permission in a glance from the daka, which was given as a terse nod, dropped it into the image projector. A disc rose in the center of the circle of seats, and above it the information on Grav's stone was projected. There was a hushed murmur of shock.

"Several months ago," Grav said smugly, "a windrider was supposedly stolen from daka Bailin. Here, you see proof that it was not stolen, but given to Shodite terrorists by daka Bailin. The woman sitting next to daka Bailin is Iada of the house of Yuini Vol, a known co-conspirator of Cleses and linked with the disappearance of daka Archer. Now, I know you all recognize the likeness of Cleses. Once daka Bailin gave his windrider to Iada, she and Cleses took the windrider to the Shodite border."

Grav threw a dubious glare at Bailin. "I ask you, daka, was your trustworthy source Iada, or Cleses, himself?"

Bailin's mouth slipped open. Mentally, he madly scrambled for a reply that would not sound damning, and was not a lie.

"She is trustworthy." he said softly, involuntarily, then winced as Grav Tulkue chuckled harshly.

"Iada, is it?" To the rest of the council, he said, "Daka Bailin is young, so we must forgive him his idealism. But we cannot trust him, much less the source he deems reliable. There is no representative from Shodalum present here today, because there is no representative from Shodalum!"

જ⁓જ⁓જ⁓જ⁓જ⁓

As soon as Bail saw the bi-lo chip, he knew that someone close to Ona had betrayed his family. Someone who was technically adept, who knew of the secret security device placed in palace's fleet of windriders. And someone who was privy to the content of Bailin's announcement to the council.

The missing bi-lo chip had always bothered Bail. Indeed, several odd coincidences surrounding the entire incident set the hairs on the nape of his neck on end.

He had thoroughly investigated the man accused of sabotaging the bi-lo on the stolen windrider. Lomen was his name. He came from a lower class family. His father was a foreman of Shodites in a textile mill in Starna, a small town across Lake Pril. His family was not wealthy. It was his school grades that landed him a place in the Military Consortium after he enlisted. He showed an aptitude for tech work. All through school, his only interests were in bi-lo functions, and related devices. He had few political affiliations, few friends, and one girlfriend. Echo Agart.

During her initial debriefing, Agart behaved as if she didn't know Lomen well enough to know why he might have sabotaged the bi-lo. The discovery that they were once lovers and that she had lied by omission stuck with Bail, even though under subsequent questioning Agart admitted to her relationship with Lomen. She said that she was afraid to admit to the affair, especially under the circumstances, where she may be considered his accomplice. "It was a long time ago," she said with a shrug, "after school we both went our own ways. Essentially, I know very little about Lomen."

A perfectly reasonable explanation.

But, then there was the problem of the missing chip.

After the council meeting was adjourned, Bail called Tulkue into Jishni's office for questioning. Tulkue strolled in, head held defiantly high, until he noted the Pliadors standing just inside the door.

Bail gestured for him to sit

"Am I being interrogated?" he asked as he took his seat.

Bail got right to the point. "Where did you get the chip?"

Grav evaded the question by saying, "What difference does it make? A person who is a true patriot has delivered Jantideva from a plot to free the Shodites. Whoever gave this chip to me should be deemed a hero."

"You and your accomplice betrayed the House of Jantideva before the council." Bail retorted, his voice overly controlled, "You should have brought the chip directly to me, instead of humiliating my son before the world. You have made an enemy of the dakas, today."

Grav's face twitched, breaking his smug demeanor.

"Janus appointed you," Bail went on evenly, "and I kept you on because I once trusted your judgement and your loyalty. But I no longer trust you. You are dismissed from your seat on the council."

Grav squirmed. "But, daka, surely you can see that I had the welfare of Jantideva at heart."

"If you truly believe your source is a hero, name her, and I will rethink my decision."

"I keep my confidences to the grave."

Bail snapped his fingers, and the unit of the Pliadors stepped forward, a quick, smart, march to Grav's side.

To Grav, he said, "You will be escorted to your chambers, where you will gather your personal items. From there, you will be escorted to the landing bay. By the time you lift off, your name will be stricken from the Congress library. From this moment forward, you no longer have clearance to enter this, or any, government facility."

Grav paled. "But, I have a right to be heard before the Alliance before I am dismissed."

"At my discretion. You've been comfortable," Bail said, baring his teeth, "under Jishni's easy rule. Her father was harsh, but not she, she allowed you far more freedom than any minister to ever sit in your seat before you. But no more, Grav. You are out! And if you choose to cross me again, I will exercise my sweeping legal right under Alliance law to have you executed for treason."

Aghast, Grav remained silent.

"You will be escorted home," Bail continued, "and be under confinement until I decide what punishment befits your crime."

"And what of daka Bailin's crimes?"

Bail smiled unkindly. "As you so aptly pointed out to the council, he is a boy to be forgiven for idealistic foolishness."

He snapped his fingers again, and the two men flanking Tulkue compelled him to turn around, and, each grabbing an arm, marched him out of the office. Tulkue went without argument, his face ashen.

Bail contacted Trev. As Trev's face appeared on the screen, he said, "I need two things." His tone was terse, angry. "I need to know if there has been a tag placed on Bailin's relay in Ohdran, and I need to know where Agart has been since Bailin's graduation."

"Done." Trev said, and switched off.

৵৵৵৵৵৵৵৵৵

According to Agart's flight manifest, on the night Iada contacted Bailin, she had taken sixteen enlisted men from Odhran, and returned to their home base in the Center-plex. The bi-lo and the directional recorder in the windrider she used had mysteriously fell off line on that day. Trev had a tech measure the fuel core, and he found that the solid fuel burned that day corresponded with the distance spanning from Odhran to the Shodite border, then on to the Center-plex.

Under strenuous questioning, her personal pilot cracked, and gave them the details of their ambush on the Shodite border, and the location of their prisoners. Agart had hidden the Shodite representative in the most conspicuous place possible, in the Keep.

Trev raided the Keep with a small compliment of men. Bail's instructions were to arrest all Pliador officers on the premises, and charge them with treason. The innocent would be weeded from the

638

guilty later. For now, their objective was to round up Agart and her people, and hopefully find the Shodites they abducted, alive and well.

Trev stalked through the hold, glancing into each cell. He slid to stop once he saw Iada, sitting in a corner of a cell, and gestured to his men to release her and take her into custody. She stood, with difficulty, as the lume cell trap was unlocked.

Praj of the House of Yuini Vol was found next.

Last, Trev found the Shodite representative. She was a tiny elderly woman with a shock of silken white hair lying against sun blackened skin and a calm smile pressed into her thin lips. Trev was disgusted to find her frail arms and legs locked in heavy irons, naked, and lying in her own excrement.

"Madam, are you the Shodite I seek?"

"I am Thib," she replied, her voice stronger than he thought it might be for having been neglected and abused, "I have come from Shodalum to sit on the Alliance Council."

He immediately went about releasing her from the irons. Her arms were covered with bruises, and sores. He was not one to feel compassion for any person, Janti or Shodite, his heart was closed. But the sight of Thib's mistreated body infuriated him beyond his own comprehension. He called for the medics. To Thib, he said, "Lay still. We will carry you out, and care for your wounds. And rest assured," he added, "we will punish the persons who did this to you."

Her arms released, she reached up and touched Trev's bristled face. Her fingers were long, and bony, and being touched by her was like being touched by a skeleton. "My son," she said, "you are the image of my husband at your age. So many years ago, but I remember like it was yesterday." She tugged at his face, turning him as if she were looking for something, tugged at his ear, and then sighed, seeing his blood red birthmark.

"So, Yesho," she said, "You returned as a Janti. Not that I mind, I really don't. And I don't mind that you didn't wait for me, either. I am starting to think I'm doomed never to die," she said caustically. "It's really rather irritating at times but, it is Betnoni's will."

Trev frowned, and worried about her. She was raving. Delusional. He gently smoothed matted hair from her forehead, and looked into the depth of her dark eyes. She smiled at him, and for a moment, he had the strangest feeling that he'd known her from somewhere, met her in his past.

The feeling fled him as the medics arrived and took over. He returned to his duty, and left Thib to their care, refusing himself a second thought about the old woman.

∾∾∾∾∾∾∾∾∾∾

Grav Tulkue's home was one of the first places Trev Morley and his troop of snarling vigilantes searched. Grav endured the search, expressing righteous indignation, but not objections. If he was nervous, he hid it well.

Echo had watched the search from a vent hole in the floor. She was narrow enough to fit in the old, unused heating ducts of Grav's home. She knew no one would think of looking for her there. No one in the military had her imagination. Consider the ease in which she'd slipped past the four Pliadors guarding Grav's estate. If they were her men, she would have had their sashes.

After the search was over, and Trev and his men were gone, she crawled out and spent the rest of the day lounging in Grav's sitting room. She listened to the news, and watched military communications. She learned of the results of the raid on the Keep. It was announced on the Crier that an Anti-Shodite faction of the Pliadors conspired to keep a Shodite representative from taking Shodalum's seat on the council.

"That's it, then." Grav said, downfallen. "The dakas have betrayed us completely. The Shodites will go free."

Stunned, Echo folded her hands in her lap and stared at the screen as Trev Morley reported to daka Bail that Thib was on her way to a medical care facility.

After taking the Shodite representative into custody and listening to her rail on about the Janti-born being released, Echo couldn't help but think about her father and his lume refinery, and what would happen to him if his workers were suddenly stolen from him. Her father treated his Shodites well, but reminded Echo

640

always, they were not really people. If they were, the Guardian would have released them long ago. They were just drones, in place to serve the Janti. Nothing, no spirits, no real intelligence.

And what would they do if they were released? Knock about in Shodalum? Starve, suffer, die. A waste of good labor.

She was scared for her father, who'd be ruined if he didn't have his shod to run his factories, and for herself, she couldn't fathom the changes that would come to Jantideva. She didn't want the changes.

"We can still stop this." she said, her tone measured. She turned a malevolent glare upwards. "May the guardian supply us with opportunity, and strength."

"What will you do?" Grav asked softly, sitting carefully in a seat near her.

A cruel smile upturned her mouth. "I will do what I must to preserve Jantideva."

ৰ৶ৰ৶ৰ৶৽৽৽৽৽

They went, as Thib suggested, to the original landing sight, and waited. Mid-morning, the day after they arrived, Chosen Sister Gella al Perraz appeared in the distance, followed by Cleses. The latter carried a long, full bag slung over his shoulder.

Seeing the windrider, and the Janti milling about around the windrider, the travelers stopped, and watched, wary.

Thib instructed Bail to trust Betnoni, his ancestor, and to cross forth into Shodalum and greet the delegation. Stifling a moment of fear, he untied his sash and left it, along with his weapon, with Trev, and stepped over the fence with his hands held high. He took to the beach, his manner one of surrender, approaching them alone, and vulnerable. Occasionally, as a particularly large wave would crash to shore, he'd skittishly jump away from the reach of the water, his heart pounding in anticipation of Betnoni's wrath.

He reached them, unscathed. Once he was close enough to see their distrusting expressions, he stopped, and lowered his arms. "Gella," he said, glancing surreptitiously to the hugeness of her pregnant belly, "Thib sent me for you."

"Thib spoke to you of my coming?" Gella replied dubiously.

641

"Yes."

"Is she well?" Shelon asked.

Bail threw a chagrinned glance his way. He was not used to the idea that Cleses was to be the true Shodite representative. Thib had named him, personally, before the council. Bail did his best to behave toward Shelon as he would any dignitary, a dignitary with all the rights and respect due to him, though it was hard to not think of Shelon as a murderer, a traitor, a terrorist.

"She is. She has already addressed the Alliance Council. They await you, and the census."

"And you came for us, personally?" Shelon asked sardonically. "Is this a trick?"

"No trick," Bail assured him, "I am here to assure that nothing happens to you and your party."

"Iada and Praj?"

"They are alive and well, guests of the Zarians."

Shelon stepped forward, glaring at Bail directly in his eyes. "We come to you with the will of Shodalum." he said, "Will you heed your own laws, daka?"

"We have no choice," Bail said tiredly. Since his son's initial announcement, legal analysts had been working night and day to find a loophole that they could jump through and escape this end, but there was nothing. They were bound, by law and by the majority feeling of the Alliance Council to release the Shodites and deport them to Shodalum, despite the will of the majority of Janti.

Shelon nodded, understanding that Bail was being forced into action, that he did not wish to release the Shodites. In spite of the distrust in his eyes, Shelon said, "We will go with you."

Bail sensed heaviness in the air, and interpreted it as his own sense of the history being made. He walked beside the Shodite representative destined to change Jantideva forever.

As they stood before the council, where Thib introduced the Shodite representative (much to Shelon's surprise), Bail again felt the air grow heavy. Jantideva braced Herself for catastrophic change.

With aplomb that belied his initial surprise, Shelon took his place at the council table, and spilled the contents of the bag he carried.

In a bold voice, though less harsh than the tone he used in the Vass chamber, he announced, "I present Shodalum's census. The banishment leveled on the heads of the Janti-born Shodites has been lifted. We demand that you free our people, and send them home."

Distant thunder made Alliance Congress tremble at that moment. The sound was dismissed as the thunder of a monsoon storm looming above the Tronos. No one noticed the difference in the pitch and rumble, except Bail and Shelon. Their eyes locked, concern ripping through both their faces. They, as one, recognized the aftershocks of a lume bomb.

જાજાજાજાજાજાજાજાજા

Bail's lume weapons specialist, Captain Grey, reported that a lume bomb had erupted in Shod City at the moment Shelon's announcement, killing all the residents of Track four, an estimated eighty thousand Shodites.

The terrorists responsible did not come forward to take credit for the mass murder. Instead, they lurked in the shadows, threatening the shod with their silent presence.

Bail's loyalty to his people tugged at his sense of duty toward the innocents killed. He feared discovering what he already suspected. Like the perpetrators of the abduction of Thib, he suspected that the terrorists were his own men and women, Pliadors, people he respected, trusted, cared for, desired to protect.

Bail rationalized that he vigorously protected the Shodites by assigning his best investigators to ferret out the Janti terrorists, while ignoring his lurking suspicions about each and every one of his personnel. Their fury with Shelon and their apathy for the fate of the Shodites was all too clear, and yet he left the investigative team intact, and unsupervised.

જાજાજાજાજાજાજાજાજા

Shelon had kissed her goodbye, a lingering and sensual kiss that left her longing for him. Releasing her, he promised to be

643

home to see their son born, while in the same breath repeating to her that it was too dangerous for her to stay.

She didn't speak during their trip. Iada and Praj kept to themselves, content to be in each other's company. Thib rode by the pilot, thoroughly enjoying the ride, and his company. The old woman flirted with him, and the man, who was easily eighty years her junior, flirted back. All in fun, Thib had said as Praj mocked her for having a crush on a younger man. All in fun.

Their mood was ambiguously hearty. They felt triumph for having had a part in freeing the Janti-born, and deep sadness for the many deaths their own. They had discovered, rather harshly, that freedom would still come at a price.

Trev landed the windrider near the border. Thib was audacious, and gave the pilot a kiss on the lips. Rather than pull away, he returned the affection, and embraced her. It was odd to see the two behaving as if they had known each other forever.

Gella hung back as the others went down the ramp. Superstitious fear gripped her. She knew she couldn't cross the border without Shelon, that if she did, she'd lose him forever.

"I'm not going." she told Thib, and she felt a tug of regret and guilt. "I am returning to Shelon."

Thib shook her head. "I'm not surprised. Stubborn girl! Shelon has his hands full with you!" She turned and started toward the border.

Praj and Iada hesitated.

Iada said, "Gella, are you sure you want to do this? You can't have too much longer-"

"You and Praj go on." Gella urged, "You can reach the Elders in half the time that Thib can travel, to assure them of our success. If you walk hard, you may even be able to catch up with Korba before he reaches Sidera. He was ailing, I doubt he has kept a hard pace since we parted."

"I doubt I can keep a hard pace required to catch him." Iada quipped, and she smiled uncertainly. "Are you sure you want to go back? Home, and freedom, is close, Gella."

"My place is with Shelon." She replied, "I will return when it is my time. And I will bring Shelon home with me."

Iada and Praj accepted her decision, and crossed the border, following Thib, who was already over the border and walking down to the beach.

"Will you take me to the Zarian embassy?" she asked Trev.

Trev simply shrugged his indifference to her presence, and ordered her to prepare for lift off.

During their trip back to the Center-plex, Gella napped. In her dreams, she saw Cobo. He was standing on a cliffside, in a snowstorm, shouting at an icy sea.

The fourth sign of the Rebirth is Sacrifice. The Masing Star emerges from its isolated tomb, and the last gate is opened. To take the hard path, the daka must have faith in Ver dala Ven.

Chapter 29

Cobo abruptly ended his meditations by standing on the edge of the snow capped rise over looking the ice caves below and shouting for the spirits that surrounded him to, "Be quiet, all of you, be quiet!" in a voice that was hoarse and ragged from the cold.

The spirits were entirely inconsiderate. Brooding around him night and day, murmuring in his ears their hushed complaints about their lives, the ones who weren't fully oblivious of their state pestering him for answers. *"Tell us the meaning of our existence, Ver dala Ven. Tell us the meaning of our deaths. Tell us, if we are truly dead, why hasn't the Guardian called us to His arms?"*

Cobo did his best to accommodate the spirits, especially those who'd been spirits in the times of Ver dala Ven Maxim and had spoken with him during his journeys. But there came a point when their constant badgering had a draining affect.

"Begone, spirits!" he ordered often, making the sign his father used to make to ward off the dead. They'd disappear for a time, and splendid silence would descend upon him, and he would sigh, and smile, and relax.

But they always returned, and usually in greater numbers. During their lengthy and aimless travel through the hills and valleys of Dilgopoche, they'd gathered too many spirits to be counted. Cobo detested passing burial grounds, knowing that the spirits of the dead who rested there would leap out of their graves and surround him, prattling questions in both his ears. It was enough to drive him insane!

The spirits were thicker, and more intrusive, around the ice caves on the northern shoreline of the arctic Tandalti Sea.

They reached the ice caves in time for a brutal storm, and made a camp in the cave they'd come to explore, to escape the bitter cold. The antechamber at the entrance of the cave itself was warmer than being in the icy wind, but still very cold. The stone and slate were covered in a fine film of reflective ice, which like warped mirrors distorted their features, elongated their bodies, reflecting them all around.

Like fingers of a hand, the antechamber of the cave broke off into many directions.

Following Riar Sed's lead, the travelers went through a narrow passage, where the floor was an icy bed of course sand. The air warmed as they progressed, quieting the complaints of Danati and Caltha and Taen, the latter who'd scornfully pointed out that the carriage outside was warmer than the ice mirrored antechamber of the cave. The passage narrowed before it opened into a huge gallery, with slick walls and hovering clouds of steam. A faint blue glow touched the rocky walls, and pillars, the fringed ceiling, a glow that emanated from a steaming hot spring of milky water bubbling in a giant bowl made from the cave's concave floor. The heavy, humid, cloying heat warmed their frozen skin, and they at once removed the wraps and capes they'd used to protect themselves from the cold. The rest of the troop waited in the warm chamber as Taen-Sant and Riar Sed explored the cave. Cobo listened to their progress with his inner ear, listened to their joy as they found another mark of Ver dala Ven Maxim, sure of their success. He listened, and at the same time, he tuned his senses outward, to the storm. It settled into the palm of the mountains, and dumped snow and ice until their route was completely blocked. It was an apt end to an endless, tedious journey.

Riar Sed had originally set their course according to old legends and recent claims of sightings of the Masing Star. He had them traveling in circles that sometimes overlapped, linking one circle to another. They often stopped at points of interest for days, or weeks, where the Masing Star was said to have appeared. It was in these places that Cobo could not hear the Masing's song at all.

Before reaching the Tandalti Sea, they had crossed through the territory of Middrilrich. The Ryslac-Middrilrich were diminutive beings, but unlike the Denmen, who had well proportioned bodies and pretty doll-like faces, the Middrilrich had squat legs and arms and torsos, and their heads and hands and feet (and, some lasciviously implied, their genitals) were oversized, larger than the average dimensions of a non-Dilgo. They looked like a Janti that had been made compact. They were farmers, and as prolific as the Vubushi. They were also the keepers of the pumps by the sea.

They maintained the works and the locks leading to the Lake of Tears.

Stories among the Middrilrich of the Masing Star were as prolific as the people themselves. In their largest village, Cobo, Kiitur and Bulbode sat with the Elders to hear the stories, while Riar Sed insisted that the rest of their party remain on the outskirts of Middrilrich territory. (Apparently Riar Sed had a nasty reputation among the Middrilrich as a thief. He made idle promises to heal their ill in exchange for supplies, then never kept his promises.) The Middrilrich told many stories of the Masing, including stories about Ver dala Ven Maxim, and his interest in the ice caves.

Son, the village storyteller, a man with a long face and long ear lobes and a hang dog expression, told Cobo that Maxim had lived in the ice caves for a while, taking a Middrilrich named Po with him as an attendant.

"Ver dala Ven Maxim searched the caves day and night, mumbling that he could feel the vibration of the Masing beneath his feet, and in the air that he breathed. After many weeks, Po woke one morning to his master's shout. He was deep in the caves. Po chased after the sound of his voice. Before he reached Maxim, he heard a great rumbling, and a high pitched whine, unlike anything he'd ever heard before, and saw a light, brighter than the sun, but it was shining from deep in the cave. In fear, he ran away, leaving his master."

Son concluded, saying, "It is written that for his crime of leaving Ver dala Ven, the Guardian shrank our people to the size of Po's courage."

The intriguing tale sent them north to explore the caves.

Each day, Riar Sed and Taen-Sant searched the caves for the elusive Entity, the Masing Star, and as they did, Cobo went out to his ledge to find peace enough in order to command the elements. He wished to end the storm, to clear their path so they could escape the frozen hills on the Tandalti Sea. He sensed danger and death lurked in the caves, though try as he might to aid their escape, the chattering spirits overwhelmed him, and each day he retreated from his mission, having failed.

649

ஜ ஜ ஜ ஜ ஜ ஜ ஜ ஜ ஜ

Cobo, wrapped in the temporary silence he'd won by chasing off the chattering spirits, could not return to his meditation. The lull in the storm was done, and the wind whipped him in the face with sleet. He gave up on solitude, and made his way down the ridge to the cave entrance.

Lodan and Benu were just inside, and engaged in their evening exercises to the light of a torch. The air was still and frigid at the cave opening, and their breaths streamed from their noses and mouths rhythmically, yet they were unaffected by the cold. The two practiced kai'gam constantly, until their movements, thoughts, their energy seemed melded to one. Away from the practice, they moved as one. Eating, sleeping, speaking, dreaming, they had become one. The line between teacher and student had blurred, as they learned from each other, taught each other. They had achieved a peace in their practice that raised them above the petty conflicts that actively took hold of their troop from the moment they left Zadoq. They scarcely seemed aware that they were trapped in a cave by the weather with disagreeable people.

Cobo passed them without interrupting their flow, and passed by the antechamber holding the herd of smelly, and restless, honigs.

Halfway down the passage leading into the warmest chamber, he heard the sound of Caltha's petulant voice. Caltha was again jockeying for Taen's attention. The fatter she grew with child, the less Taen paid attention to her, and the more outrageous she behaved. Danati was not as blind as Taen had hoped. She knew the child in Caltha was not Lodan's. Lodan hardly gave Caltha a second look, hardly made time for her at all. Yet, there she was, fat and pregnant, and insisting on Taen's attention.

Did you have luck, Ver dala Ven?

Cobo glanced upwards to Kiitur. Along the edge of the chamber wall, there were several gradations of ledges, where they had made their camp. Taen and Danati took the lowest ledge, closest to the warmth, Lodan and Benu took the next level, with Caltha sleeping at their feet. Cobo, Kiitur and Bulbode took the upper level, though it was slanted at what appeared to be a

650

dangerous angle. They risked the danger of the slope to escape the nonsense of the trio, Taen and his women. Kiitur looked down from their ledge, her divine face expressing curiosity.

He shook his head, and glanced toward Caltha and Danati. The two women were fighting over a blanket, each of them gripping opposite sides in a nasty tug of war. Taen's blanket from Taen's bed. Caltha needed more comfort for her bed, and had claimed the blanket as if she were Taen's woman.

Taen ignored the two, sitting naked as a Man by the spring, making an attempt to focus and calm his mind. Anger rose off him in waves. He was weary of both his women, and ready to return to Zadoq, to another woman he'd taken as a lover before they'd left, one he felt he loved more than Caltha. Of course, he loved the woman in Zadoq because she was an agreeable concubine, and not a jealous and screeching wife, which is what both Danati and Caltha had become to him.

Cobo might have laughed at Taen, and his immature indiscretions, if he didn't have to worry about the future of Ver dala Ven. More and more, he sensed an active source of power emanating from Caltha's child. He did not doubt that the child was Ver dala Ven. He only hoped that Danati didn't kill Caltha before it was her time to give birth. He sensed Danati's murderous impulses, and he had warned Lodan. He would protect Caltha, if he could, but Caltha seemed determined to provoke Danati to the limits.

Such as with the blanket issue.

Cobo went by the two women, and discreetly touched Danati's mind, doing what his father taught him was wrong, manipulating her will. She abruptly calmed, and graciously allowed Caltha to have the blanket.

Caltha, stunned by her rival's sudden change of heart, reeled back, clutching the blanket. "And another pillow, too!" she cried, not yet willing to win this argument.

Before Danati's fury rose, Cobo again touched her mind with no more a gesture than a glance, manipulating her into an agreeable state. She gave Caltha a pillow from her own bed.

Holding her prize, Caltha threw a venomous glare at Taen, who was still ignoring them, and stalked to her private, and lonely, nook.

Cobo climbed up beside Kiitur and Bulbode. Kiitur, standing, was still much shorter than Cobo sitting. She crossed her arms and eyed him with disapproval.

He grinned sheepishly at Kiitur. "At least we'll have silence."

She suppressed humor. In a chiding tone, she said, "A sorry trade for abandoning one's ethics."

"Well, I don't care if what you did was ethically wrong," Bulbode said, leaning conspiratorially close to Cobo's ear, "the peace is a joy beyond measure."

Bulbode was seated on a rocky outcropping around the ledge, a perfect seat for a Denmen but merely an elbow prop for a Janti. Cobo leaned back, propping his elbow on the outcropping, glancing to Bulbode in silent, and appreciative, accord.

Bulbode was as beautiful in face as his mother, bright and pink as a porcelain doll, with golden eyes and a thatch of curly dark hair on his head. He had a paunch in his middle, and often rested his tiny, dainty hands there. Presently, he placed his hands on his middle, and asked, "How is it you are able to change a person's mind, Ver dala Ven?"

Much like Riar Sed, Bulbode could read minds, speak to spirits, and heal. But unlike Riar Sed, his interest in knowing what his kin could do was strictly academic.

Cobo said, "I diverted her jealousy to a quiet corner in her mind, with memories she doesn't visit often, where it will take time for her to sort it out and grab hold of it. I didn't end their conflict. I could have, perhaps under better circumstances. It is very difficult to spirit away a negative band of emotions, and there is always the danger it will root itself in the soft soil of another receptive mind, and I fear there is much loose and soft soil present among those four." he nodded toward Danati and Caltha, Taen and Riar Sed.

"Indeed," Bulbode replied, "The dynamic between the women and Taen is most disturbing."

"We should leave here." Kiitur concurred with a shake of her head. "Caltha is too close to the end of term to be sleeping in a cave."

Cobo agreed silently. "Have you heard the song yet?"

Kiitur frowned. "Not even in my dreams."

It sings to me each night. I think it is trying to tell me where to find it.....and if I find it, what then? Taen and Riar Sed have conspired to possess the Masing, together and apart from each other as rivals. I must not let that happen. I must resist....but, it is hard. Sometimes, I feel very weak.

"I trust your strength, and your judgment." Kiitur replied, patting the stubble on his face with the palm of her tiny hand.

Cobo had more trust that Danati would eventually kill Caltha.

❧❧❧❧❧❧❧❧❧

After their evening exercises, they chose to spar in an unused chamber near the entrance where the honigs were hitched. The chamber was not warm, and rather narrow, but enough room to spar, and work up a sweat. Lodan removed his shirt for the exercise. Benu stripped down to a flimsy undergarment that covered her from her breasts to the tops of her legs.

Their sparring began as practice, and soon hastened to passion. Movements that were violent, were also tender. The clashing blades became a substitute for clashing bodies, their breath heaving, their sweat pouring, and their faces resplendent in ecstasy. Lodan slid his blade the length of hers, a caress. Benu lunged for him and locked her blade with his, an embrace. Their minds fluid in exchanged thoughts of devotion to the art, and each other, the highest love and respect possible to pass between two people. They were equals, and combatants, and lovers, but not of the flesh. Of the mind and soul, but the flesh remained waiting, wanting.

As she moved, the sinews of her muscles worked in concert, a symphony of perfection, which Lodan watched from behind half closed eyes. He drank in the sight of her legs, her arms flexing and extending, the taper of her waist most evident as she raised the kai'gam over her head, the flow of her flaxen hair, the sharp flash of her eyes, the grimace of concentration etched into a pretty mouth.

Lodan smiled at her as she bested him in a movement he felt he had perfected in his youth, and he tarried too long savoring her brilliance. She slashed at him, too close, close to his ear, close enough to cause a breeze, to stimulate his senses, to bite at him, and he bit back, swaying to the side and bringing his blade up, slashing aside her face, purposefully missing, but making his blade sing in her ear, a song of love.

Her heart raced. His followed. They were one, combatants and lovers, crossing their blades in the rhythm of carnal love, thrusting, thrusting, faster and faster, harder, harder. Lodan felt himself become aroused for her, though it was his blade that touched her, becoming an extension of his body. He felt each contact with her blade in his physical body, the electricity of the contact biting his flesh, and his nerves, and his senses. Arousal, he once thought it was folly and a waste of his strength. With Benu, it sharpened his senses, his abilities and strengthened his body, making him man before her, not just a teacher or a sparring partner. A man.

Hours, their practice lasted hours, neither wanting it to end, but it did end. As always at the end of their matches, they stood apart from each other, at a good distance, their kai'gams lowered, their breath heaving, their eyes locked, each waiting for the other to succumb to the lure of passion, waiting for the other to make the decision to end their celibate ways. Each waiting for the other to turn away first.

Benu was usually the stronger. She was bred for celibacy, Lodan told himself. It was easy for her to turn away, turn her back to him, to dress as if they'd copulated as strangers, and to return to meditations, lofty thoughts on Pletoro and Kai'mai, lofty and above the baseness of the physical.

Lodan had known women, but not one as alluring as this woman. Benu was his equal, and his partner, and his nemesis, all in one. Turning away from her was madness, he'd tell himself, but he'd done so, even though he found that in his desire for her, he did not break the peace of Kai'mai thought. His desire seemed as intertwined in the peace of Kai'mai as the practice of kai'gam. He never thought it was possible.

He was learning, still, learning from the masters of the past, and of the present, and from the master that stood before him, a goddess slick with sweat, her transparent undergarment clinging to her damp skin, revealing to him every line and curve of her, revealing all but that which he coveted most.

Yearning was in her eyes, in the parting of her soft lips, in the high blush of her cheeks. He felt it in her aura, in her thoughts, a fleeting brush with her appetite for flesh. But, no. Again, she turned away. Slowly, resigned, she turned away from him, and dressed, and left him in the gallery alone.

He closed his eyes, and tilted his head back, still trying to catch his breath, and now trying to recover from her rebuff. His manhood did not as quickly relax, not as he thought of sleeping at her side, and waking with her in the morning, and sparring with her tomorrow, and the day after.

Sweet, precious torment, it was his, and he wanted to suffer, if only to suffer in her presence.

He went outside the cave, stripped and bathed his heated body in snow, the freezing shock enough to cool his passions.

She was sleeping as he lay beside her in the sweltering humidity of the cave. She was nude, her head on his pillow, like an invitation. He lay next to her, fully clothed though the heat of the cave was uncomfortable, for he did not trust his own nudity against hers.

In sleep, his hand drifted to the curve of her waist.

ॐॐॐॐॐॐॐॐॐ

She awoke at his touch, and sleepily curved her back into his chest, glad he'd finally decided to seduce her.

Feeling the material of his shirt against her bare skin, hearing the steady lowing of his breathing, she twisted her head to see he was fast asleep. She turned under his arm, and watched his face as he slept, gazing at the long yellow lashes that fringed his cheekbones, and the perfect shape of his mouth. She was ready to give in to her ache for him, to be the first, to beg for him, if only he

655

would wake and see she was willing, and ready. She lightly touched his face, bearded now for weeks, but no, he would not rouse. He slept hard, unless he sensed danger. He was in no danger in her arms, except, perhaps, the danger her wanton virginity presented, the danger of thrilling abandon, of her weakness for his flesh.

She slipped closer to him, and lightly tasted his lips, and waited for him to stir. His brows moved up, and for a moment he looked like a little boy, a cherub, reacting to his mother's goodnight kiss. Charming, but far less aroused than she wished him to be. Making herself comfortable in his chest, she fell quickly into a dreamless sleep.

જ્જ્જ્જ્જ્જ્જ્જ્જ્જ

Sleep settled the cave. The honigs quieted. Sound was limited to the swaying rumble deep in the earth, and the hissing whispers of Riar Sed deep in the chamber.

Cobo lay near Kiitur and Bulbode. Mother and son slept. Cobo stared restlessly at the crusty slope of the cave wall, listening to Riar Sed talk to his spirit slaves. The sorcerer spoke in conspiratorial low tones, whispers that wouldn't be heard by Taen, or Caltha, or even Lodan, who had trained his ears to hear the slightest sound. Cobo, however, heard every word as if he were sitting with Riar Sed.

He heard the song of the Masing, as well, its exquisitely sweet voice filling the stone, and ice, and water, and his mind.

And before his eyes, a tiny point of light appeared.

Cobo sat up, and the light moved with him. The Masing's Spirit had returned to him, unbeckoned.

spirit walk with me

He heard his father's voice as clear as if he were sitting with him on the ledge.

Without question, Cobo left his body, and as he did, the star expanded and enveloped his physical form to protect him from evil.

And he was face to face with his father.

"Am I sleeping?" Cobo said, his tone hushed with shock.

"No, my son."

Ver dala Ven Voktu drifted away from Cobo, indicating with a nod of his head that Cobo should follow. Together they drifted down, passing Caltha's sleeping form, Lodan and Benu in close embrace, to hover over Taen and Danati. Danati had her back to Taen, and Taen was on his back, his sleep resolute.

Ver dala Ven Voktu gazed downward at Taen. "Taen's soul can be cleansed of evil," he said, "but, in order to do so, you must do as I instruct. You must not weaken."

"Of course father." Cobo agreed readily, hurt that his father could think him so weak he could not do what was necessary to save Taen.

"You have been touched by the Masing, guided to the heat and the light?"

"Yes. It beckons to me."

"And yet you do not respond. Why?"

Cobo was loath to describe to his father his weaknesses, his fear that he was not strong enough to keep the Masing from Taen and Riar Sed.

"Help us to escape the caves, Father." He asked, evading his father's line of questioning, "If we stay too long, Taen's child may suffer grave consequences."

Ver dala Ven Voktu explained, "The defenders of the Masing have held you captive in these caves, waiting for you to act on the lure of the Star. Once you act, you will be free to leave this desolate place."

The multitudes of spirits that had badgered him during their journey surrounded his father. Cobo looked upon them now, their visages serene, their mouths shut and silent. He understood at once their purpose. They gave their eternal lives in order to protect the Masing from unclean spirits, and men like Riar Sed.

"The Star isn't for me." He argued, and he glanced at Caltha's belly, at the child within who was still, and listening to their ethereal conversation.

"Nor is it for this child. This child is not the Gate. But she is equally important, my son, for she is to be the *mother* of hope."

Cobo understood, and was downfallen. The Star would not sing upon the birth of this one, nor at her elevation, not as he

657

hoped. There was yet another generation to wait, for as short a time that had passed between the first sign of Betnoni's prophecy and the fourth, the wait for the fifth sign to appear would take twenty times longer.

"The fifth sign will appear, only if we keep her alive." Cobo retorted, feeling danger shadow him from all sides.

"Not to worry." His father assured, "She has many protectors. Today, we worry only about Taen." Ver dala Ven Voktu drew them toward Taen. "This day is the day you will touch the Masing Star, Cobo. Remember, no matter what happens, do not interfere with the Masing Star, for it is guided by the Guardian's heart, and will."

"I will remember." Cobo said solemnly.

His father nodded, equally as solemn. "Follow the heat, follow the song. It will lead you to Holy Ground. Once you are there, Cobo, you will know what to do."

Cobo let the song fill his heart, and mind, and immediately, he was drawn into the glowing pool of milky blue water.

❧❧❧❧❧❧❧❧❧

Yu and Ret were once Ryslac-Toscocti, a two faced monster with two souls. Even in death, they insisted on acting as one, living in one form. Except, in death the immobile face of Ret, the silent twin, was alive and active. Two sets of eyes, affixed in a split face, stared at Riar Sed.

"We've searched all the caverns." Ret reported, "We find no star, only empty spaces, water flows and molten rock shifting in rivers beneath the caves."

Ret was the learned one, the intelligent one, and the one Riar Sed least liked. Ret had no voice in the bargain struck between Yu and Riar Sed. In life, Yu had sought out Riar Sed to heal his wife. Riar Sed saw the opportunity to add to his growing number of servants. Yu bargained away his soul, or souls as it were, and Ret got stuck in servitude to a sorcerer.

"We hear the song," Yu added, an ingenuous expression on his face. "at least, I can."

658

"I cannot." Ret snapped. "All I hear is the little demons chattering at Ver dala Ven night and day. How does he stay sane?"

"Who says he is?" Riar Sed muttered.

"He spirit walks each night, just as you suspected, master." Yu said.

"I knew it." he fumed.

"We've never actually seen him," Ret countered, "but we hear the legions of ignorant souls who follow him. They actually hope he will give them relief, life.....*freedom*."

Riar Sed threw a canny look at Ret. "A wish you share with the ignorant, I am sure."

"You promised us freedom if we protected daka Bail from acting on his son's spells. We did as you asked, and you have not kept your promise!"

"Ver dala Ven ultimately saved daka Bail's life from Taen's misguided spells." Riar Sed countered maliciously. He had never intended to release the Ryslac-Toscocti, but promises of freedom generally made one or the other work harder for him. "If you do not fail me this time, I will honor my promise."

Ret sneered dubiously, and glanced at the mean little demons on his right. Riar Sed's multitude of servants enslaved long ago. They'd become weak, and oblivious of their own beginnings, their own egos, wills. Over time, Ret and Yu would be like them. Ret was aware of his fate.

Yu's eyes blinked, and widened, and he cocked his head as if to listen with physical ears. "The legion is on the move, master."

"Ver dala Ven must be spirit walking." Riar Sed replied impatiently, "Follow him." The Ryslac-Toscocti vanished.

Riar Sed glanced around at the vague outline of his slaves. "Come, my children. We will rest while they labor."

Riar-Sed drifted silently from behind the natural colonnade in the cavern, and his private space for meditation. His eyes fell to Taen. The useless boy. He was as blind and deaf as the others. Nothing of Ver dala Ven existed in him, except the lust for forbidden fruit. That flaw, father and son shared.

Above, Ver dala Ven sat on the edge of the ledge, his legs crossed, his eyes opened and fixed, his body waiting patiently for his spirit to return. Around Cobo's body was a bubble, shimmering gold. It was protecting Ver dala Ven from attack, physical or spiritual.

"That insufferable man, he again possesses the Spirit of the Star!" he hissed angrily.

And as his anger and envy rose, a bright light hit his eyes painfully, causing him to throw his arms over his face and turn away. He growled. It protected Cobo from even the taint of his hatred.

Angrily, he tossed his arm toward the figure and growled a Kanaki curse, "Bluleslamali!" A black, hot burst of energy flew off his hand. It hit the bubble around Ver dala Ven, ricocheted, and struck the opposite wall. The impact was thunderous, shaking the entire cavern. The sleeping ones woke as one, bolting off their beds, Danati crying out in horror.

"What happened?" Lodan demanded, rolling easily to his feet. His wife/protege was up with him, naked and proud, grabbing hold of her kai'gam and holding it aloft, prepared to do battle.

Riar Sed's eyes were on Ver dala Ven Cobo, resting in repose, unharmed, undisturbed. He sneered. "It is nothing. The earth shifted, that's all. Happens."

Kiitur stared down at him with her golden eyes. She knew he'd lied.

"Turn your eyes away from me, freakish thing!" He shouted at her.

"Master Lodan," Kiitur called out. "It was not the earth shifting that woke us. Riar Sed tried to do harm to Ver dala Ven. But his magic was not strong enough to pierce Cobo's protection."

Lodan and Benu both turned a distrustful glare on Riar Sed. "Is that so?"

"The Ryslac speaks nonsense." Riar Sed said, feeling abruptly uneasy for the way the two warriors glared at him. "It is a curse of their kind. They have tiny brains, you know. They are the least intelligent of all the Ryslacs put together."

"Ver dala Ven Cobo prefers their company to yours." Benu retorted contemptuously, "Exactly what does that say about your brain, sorcerer?"

"Speak not to me, Breeder!" Riar Sed countered.

Benu took a menacing step toward him, murder in her eyes.

660

Lodan blocked her path. "No violence, unless we are in physical danger."

"Pletoro was never a breeder, how could he understand the insult?"

"You are not a breeder, you are Benu." Lodan replied easily.

That reminder was enough to mollify her rage. She eased back. Her glare did not lose its fire, however.

Lodan's face was stone as he turned on Riar Sed. His tone bland, he said, "If you again attempt to do harm to Ver dala Ven, or any person in this cave, and I will defend them, even if it means ending your life."

He'd made enemies. Nothing new. He had enemies at all corners of the globe. His own kin were his enemies. His brothers, sisters, children, grandchildren, they were all his enemies, but he didn't care. He would possess the Masing, and he would become all powerful, and they would know his wrath.

Indeed, this golden haired god and his glaring consort would know his wrath immediately.

Taen, hearing his intentions, shouted, "No, Riar Sed!"

"Bluleslamali!" Riar Sed fumed, and another black, hot burst of energy flew out from him, this time from the hatred in his eyes, and it flowed toward the kai'gam master and his woman.

Lodan swept aside, and hooking Benu by the waist with his arm, he dropped to the floor. Benu landed on top of him, and rolled away as a burst of energy streaked above them. Riar Sed's missiles pounded the wall near where they stood with two thunderous booms.

Taen rushed to Riar Sed, disbelief and fury twisting his features.

"Do not harm Lodan!"

Riar Sed sneered. "Ah, what harm did I do? Your hero looks alive and well."

"No thanks to you." Lodan retorted, and he helped Benu to her feet.

A heady sigh from Caltha drew their attention. She knelt in her pillows, staring wide-eyed at the golden light descending from Cobo above her, encasing her in his protective shell. Her hands were out and she smiled, as though the sun cast its rays on her face.

661

Danati stared hatefully at Caltha, fuming. "Why does Ver dala Ven embrace her?" She turned on Taen, "Why does he embrace her with his protection, and not me?"

"Shhh, do you hear that?" Riar Sed muttered, and he strained to hear a distant humming as the bickering of the others continued.

"She is Lodan's wife," Taen retorted hotly, "and Lodan is his ally."

"She is like Melish, nothing but a breeder." Danati replied contemptuously, fixing Caltha with a spiteful glare, "Nothing and no one lusts after her. She is nothing, nothing at all!"

"I am enough to carry Taen-Sant's child." Caltha retorted cattily, "What are you but a barren Inferes?"

Danati gasped at the truth, though she knew the truth in her heart. She grabbed a stone from the floor and hurled it at Caltha. Caltha covered her head and ducked, but the stone would not pierce the protective bubble. It bounced, and flew back at Danati, striking her on the head. She fell to her knees, wailing, and holding her bleeding forehead with both hands.

"Taen, Taen, I am hurt!"

"I'm sorry you're not dead." Taen replied angrily, and to Caltha, he shouted, "You dreadful wench, how dare you betray me?"

The ground shuddered. Taen threw his arms out to his sides to keep his balance. He glanced backward at Riar Sed.

"Tremors?"

Riar Sed laughed aloud, staring past Taen at nothing. Soft as a whisper, a song surrounded him. Finally! He could hear the song of the Masing Star!

❧❧❧❧❧❧❧❧❧

Cobo's sight fluctuated between blindness and clarity. Through the milky waters of the wandering, bottomless hot spring he could see, intermittently, human skulls embedded in clay and stacked ritually, each painted with the Rathian emblem of peace, a cross in a circle. A burial ground! Taen's intuition was correct. The Masing had retreated in exile to a tomb of fallen Rathian soldiers.

Cobo felt heat surround his spirit. In the heat was the song, the light, and a heart beat, slow and steady. He was carried downward by the will of another, greater force. A hand, enveloping his spirit, pulled him into the core of white fire.

A healing fire.

He was not blinded. In the fire he saw the host of past Ver dala Ven, each of them with their hands outstretched to touch his spirit, welcoming him into the fold. *i am to die among them* he thought happily, and he surrendered to the sensual joy of being one with his own kind, and with the heart of the Guardian.

But no, the tether that connected him to his physical body was strong, and secure, and kept him apprised of the goings on in the cavern he'd left behind. He felt the blows against the protective force set around him by his father.

He sensed danger.

He sensed....a birth to occur...

...far too early...

"Say the words!" The Ver dala Ven shouted at him, their faces animated with approbation. "Say the words! Say the words!'

He was close. The center of the world, the center of the universe, the center of creation lay before his eyes.

The words were involuntary. The language was nothing of this world, but of the Guardian. The spell had been born into him, rather than taught, a birthright.

"Uuina'merloa'treloara'zalewra'alo"

Yes....he understood them....*hear me, come to me, swallow me, create me, alive.*

The core of Masing formed around him. Had he been in the flesh, he would have been burned away in an instant, the heat was so intense. A beautiful aria filled the Star, and he felt peace surround him, and he felt his true purpose. His purpose had been born with the birth of the Masing Star.

Born with the birth of the universe.

He reached out with his hands, and touched the inside of the Star. It had been empty of Ver dala Ven too long. It embraced Cobo with hungry love, ready to move with his will.

He understood. It was a craft, able to transport Ver dala Ven's soul beyond the confines this world, this time, this reality, to the places of gods, or of legends. The stars, to the future, to the past, to alternate realities he scarcely comprehended.

"I can change it all," Cobo thought, drunk with the power of the Star, "I can return to my beginnings, I can avoid my mistakes, I can take a good wife and I can train my son."

In the Star, visions came with ease. A picture of the world he conceived emerged around him in brilliant color and detail, and he lived a new life in a flash. As a young man, he resisted his love for Jishni. He married Surna, and she gave him many children. Taen was born their eldest. He is born an innocent, but wickedness soon collects around the weak places in his spirit. Cobo trained him. Though Taen has the love of both father and mother, and absent the lure of being a powerful daka, he still takes longer to train than any before him. Cobo tried to impress upon Taen the ethics of Ver dala Ven. His success is marginal, and Taen grows dangerously powerful, empty of morality.

Shock electrified Cobo as he witnessed, as if in a dream, Taen conspiring with daka Janus to murder him, in order to gain his place in court as Ver dala Ven.

He saw next, as a restless spirit, Taen presiding over the court for Janus, as well as Jishni. In this timeline, Shelon would not live long enough to make a difference among his people. Taen has no mercy for the Shodites. Taen has no mercy.

The image shifted to a Strum street. Gella, after living a short life as a prostitute in Strum, dies of a filthy disease in the streets. No one mourns her death.

"Gella," he whispered, "I cannot let you die for a lost cause." The truth hurt him. Taen was born a lost cause, lost to Cobo.

He understood his mission, and no longer resisted.

The Masing moved. He felt it take direction from his mind as fast as he made decisions, that he was its pilot and it was his guide. The Masing became his body, and he became the Masing's soul.

He ascended through the watery grave of Rathians, reaching out for Taen.

∽∾∽∾∽∾∽∾∽

A piercing, unearthly scream filled the chamber.

The form of a man rose from the depth of the hot spring, and hovered over the water. His image was brighter than the sun, and blinded their eyes; they turned away as one, throwing their arms before their faces.

Riar Sed struggled to see through the opening between his frail arms. His eyes ached, but he would not look away. The brilliantly illuminated man that had appeared had six arms, and four legs, and three faces; one youthful, one middle aged, one old. Ver dala Ven transfigured in the Star, and the faces were of Ver dala Ven Cobo.

"No!" he mewled.

He rushed to Taen. Over the piercing note being sung by the Masing, he shouted, "Your father has found it and entered it! We must do something!"

Taen stared at the monstrosity Cobo had become. The light burned through his eyes, but in his hatred, he felt no pain.

"As one!" Riar Sed ordered, "As I taught!"

Riar Sed threw a curse at the Masing. A burst of energy flew from his hand, and struck Cobo, and was absorbed into the Star. The Star grew brighter.

"I said, as one!" Riar Sed berated Taen contemptuously.

"I don't need you," Taen replied, his eyes fluttering dreamily. He stepped forward, toward the heat of the Star.

Riar Sed grabbed him by the arm. "You do need me, you stupid boy."

Taen shook off his insistent hand, and in a loud voice, he chanted. Riar Sed had never heard these words, did not know the language, and was surprised Taen knew the language, ignoramus, rutting lout that he was.

"*Uuina'merloa'treloara'zalewra'alo*"

The song of the Masing brightened, hurting their ears.

Cobo's voice boomed through the cavern. He sounded saddened, regretful. "My son accepts the embrace."

The glow of the Masing became intense. Try as he might, Riar Sed could not keep his eyes open.

665

For a moment, he shared the space with his father. He felt his father's thoughts, and fears, fears for his son, and another, not himself.

"You are about to die." Taen assured him, hoping to inspire Cobo to fear for himself. Fear, to taste it was delicious. Hate, to feed it was easy.

"I've already tasted death, my son," Cobo said, "I died the day you were born."

With that, Cobo voluntarily left the Star and returned to his physical body.

The Masing formed a body around Taen. Through the eyes of three faces, he watched his father re-enter his own body, and stand on the ledge above him, and wait, stone faced, for his fate.

Taen laughed, his laugh rumbling through the cavern, shaking the earth. Ver dala Ven Cobo has surrendered! I am all powerful!

He felt the heat rise around him, so hot he stopped laughing, choking instead. He receded, became blind to his surroundings, curled into the core of the Masing, and demanded to know what was happening to him.

discarding the useless, came the sung reply.

Taen realized too late that his body would not survive being one with the Star.

৵৵৵৵৵৵৵৵৵৵

The Masing lost the shape of a man, and became a Star again with thousands of undulating arms. They swelled, and recoiled, feeling with Taen his pain, because Taen was the Masing, and the Masing was Taen.

Fine ashes and bits of bone and teeth were dumped from the underside of the Star, forming a pile on the cave's stone floor.

"For the good of his soul," Cobo reminded himself, "to cleanse him, and our lineage, of evil." But it did not assuage his sorrow, or end the steady stream of tears wetting his cheeks. He'd helped make Taen only to suffer this fate. Ver dala Ven had diminished, in gradations, through time, each more self serving than the last. They were destined to reach a point when Ver dala Ven could no

666

longer resist the lure of evil. Taen would be the last Ver dala Ven to know such weakness.

He found his cape at his feet, and climbed down from the ledge with it in his hand. He was the only one among them that could look upon the Star without pain, approach without feeling the intense heat. The Star had changed him, he felt it deep inside his soul. He was the beginning, a teacher, a spirit brother with the Star. For the rest of his life, he would be connected to the Star, and he would spend his life preparing the coming generations for its return. The joy he should have felt was marred by grief. He ducked to get underneath the Star and lay his cape on the ground next to Taen's ashes. Lovingly he scooped the ashes and placed them in the center of the cape. He then folded the material over, and over, until the ashes of his son were safely secured and would not leak out. He embraced the bundle, and mourned for his son.

In the star, he sensed that Taen was beginning to wake from his suffering. Taen was strong, indeed, with hatred and fury.

"Kiitur, Bulbode, climb down, get out of the cave, Lodan, Benu, protect Caltha, get her out!"

The Masing again formed a body for its pilot. Taen emerged, still in mortal pain, but taking control. His fury and pain dampened the Star's tremendous light, relieving the others of the torment afflicted on their eyes. His strength rose, and ebbed, but not fast enough. In this state, he was beyond superhuman, and they were in incredible danger.

Cobo glanced ruefully their escape route, which was now blocked by Taen.

"If only you hadn't been swayed by sentiment," Taen replied to his thoughts, his three faces grinning. "You might have lived to see another day. Now you will all die."

"Yes, yes, kill them all Taen." Riar Sed hissed, avarice glittering in his eyes, "All of them, do it now!"

Taen's anger turned on Riar Sed. "You do not tell me what to do, old man! Stupid- old-man!"

Riar Sed looked gracelessly astonished. "You will turn on me? After all I have done for you? I made you!"

Taen's six arms came together, hands together as if holding a lume, the way he used to play as a child with his brothers. He was

667

always the criminal, the runaway Shodite, and they were Pliadors, or his victims. Again, he was the criminal, but his pretend lume was deadly. A flash of lume like energy, created by Taen's imagination, snapped from the star, striking Riar Sed in the chest as thunder rocked the air. Riar Sed was thrown backwards, slammed against a stone column, his broken body an empty sack once it hit the ground. His chest smoldered where he'd been struck, and his spirit hovered, senseless, nearby.

Filled with the satiation of the kill, Taen turned on his father, and shot his pretend lume again. The burst of energy struck Cobo in the chest, knocked him on his back, but did not have the power to kill Ver dala Ven. He was not immune to pain, however. Cobo felt like a Huntress had punched him in the chest. He struggled to get catch his breath, and get back on his feet.

Taen's strength waned. Quickly, acting out his vengeance, Taen turned on Caltha, and the bastard child she carried. The next of the line, who would one day give life to the Gate. He knew now that his place was not to own the Star, but cleanse the line for the future. His covetousness of the baby's destiny was murderous. He aimed for the womb.

Lodan reacted instinctually. He grabbed Caltha, and they dodged the strike of the energy pulse. He made his kai'gam sing, and they both became invisible to Taen's eyes. The effect was enough to confuse Taen, though he knew that they were near. He'd been trained well enough to know to listen for the song. He shot off his pretend lume randomly, aiming for the song of Lodan's kai'gam.

Lodan helped Caltha dodge the bursts of energy as he tried to get her to the cavern's entrance.

Benu, to confuse Taen further, raised her kai'gam and made it sing. She rushed past Lodan and Caltha, and faced her enemy as a Huntress. She dodged the energy bursts Taen lobbed at her, boldly making her kai'gam howl to get his attention. Now Taen had two singing sources to shoot at with his pretend lume. Her diversion worked to draw fire.

Momentarily.

A burst of energy blew up between Lodan and Benu, causing Caltha to scream. The attention of Taen's three faces twisted quickly toward the sound.

Lodan roughly shoved Caltha off him, and toward Benu, making himself visible.

Taen lashed out at Lodan, striking him in the face and causing him to fly far and high, backwards into the darkness of the passage leading out of the cave.

Benu cried out his name, dropping her defensive cloak. She grabbed Caltha by the hair and rushed her toward the passage, toward Lodan, her back to Taen.

Taen prepared to take another shot.

Cobo was wobbly, but he was on his feet and nearly able to breath once again. He pointed at Taen, and a stream of lightning flew from his arm, the force of it wrenching him forward several steps. It was a trick of defense his father taught to him but one he'd never tried. The sensation was something akin to having his skin ripped off his body. He cried out his pain.

The bolt of lightning hit Taen's three faced head, snapping it aside and causing him to lose strength and fade into the star, but not before he shot off a burst of energy at Caltha, striking her in the head. She fell just inside the mouth of the cave. Benu stumbled with her, righting herself quickly to drag Caltha the rest of the way, into the waiting darkness.

Taen reformed quickly, and as he saw Cobo still alive, he screeched his outrage. He shot six bursts of energy in succession, one from each arm, striking Cobo's chest with fists of flame, throwing him back, but not off his feet.

"I will not die, Taen!" he gasped as he fought crushing pain.

"I do wish you would try, father!" Taen retorted angrily, and prepared to hit Cobo with another salvo.

Two streams of light flew at Taen from the ledge above Cobo's head. Kiitur and Bulbode directing their energy, like an electrical currant, at Taen. The currant webbed over his body, burning him. He drew back, and roared as he sunk into the star to escape the sensation.

"Kill him!" Danati screamed hysterically, "Kill him!" She was on her knees, cowering, covering her bloodied head with bloodied hands. "Kill him! Kill him!"

Cobo felt Taen's desire for vengeance turn on his wife. "Run Danati!" Cobo ordered, and he threw another lightning bolt at Taen, the force of which pulled him forward and threw him onto his face.

The outer shell of the Masing Star absorbed the lightning, making Taen too weak to throw bursts of energy at them, but not too weak to do harm Danati. Taen moved the star toward Danati, and reached out for his wife with the Star's many arms as she ran past him. Caught by the demon, Danati screamed with her whole heart.

Taen embraced her, enveloping her into the vicious heat of the Star.

Cobo reached up from the ground, and the lightening he hurled at the Star traveled through his full body, pulling him across the slate until he was at the edge of the hot pool.

This time, he'd released enough force to knock the woman from Taen's grip.

Too late. Danati-Zuna fell, a clump of burnt flesh, on the stone floor. Danati's spirit fled, still screaming.

Taen lost form, and growled his frustration. He pressed on the inside of the Masing, trying to push his arms through. His hands were outlined here and there, his feet, here and there, but nothing happened.

He no longer had enough strength to act as the Masing's pilot. "You killed me!" Taen accused, as the truth flooded him, the truth of his father's deed, and of his own destiny. "You killed me!"

Finally, it was over. Taen's true torment had begun, his power gone. "Yes, I did. I killed you, my son." Cobo admitted huskily.

"Ver dala Ven!" Benu shouted. Her voice was miserable, and held a note of panic.

Cobo forced himself to his feet, and ignoring the tormented wails of his son, he dashed toward the sound of Benu's voice.

In the antechamber, by the muted light of a torch nearly ready to die, Benu held Lodan's head in her lap.

Near Lodan, Danati lay still and quiet, her eyes partially open, unseeing.

Lodan was alive, but his face was badly burned. In the place of his sky blue eyes were empty black sockets. His eyes were burned away.

"Help him," Benu cried, and her tears fell on Lodan's face.

"No, save the child!" Lodan ordered, moving his burnt lips with care. Indeed, he was alive. Blind, but alive.

"No, you cannot live like this, master." she wept.

"I can, and will," he reached up for Benu's face, finding it easily as if he was looking at her with seeing eyes, "My warrior wife, I can still see. I see with my heart. Hold me now, and let Ver dala Ven save Taen's child."

Benu pressed her face to his, her lips to his, and wept for him, unconsoled by his reassurance.

Cobo went to Caltha. She was dead, and her spirit gone, never to return. But the child in her womb lived. He ripped away Caltha's garments and lay them aside, ready to swaddle a child. He took up Lodan's kai'gam, and held the blade over her belly. An anxious sweat beaded his brow, and he moved to press the blade into her skin, only to pull back, a shaking mess of indecision.

"You must take the child out." Kiitur said as she approached.

"I've never done anything like this before."

"Here," Kiitur told him, making a mark with her fingernail across the lower half of Caltha's belly, and she took the tip of the kai'gam, "I will guide you."

He again raised the blade, with Kiitur as his guide, and pressed it into Caltha's flesh. "Continue, the womb is tough." Kiitur advised, and he pressed through several layers of flesh, to the tough shell of the womb. Sliding the blade forward with enough force to open the womb, the waters spilled forth and a foot, the length no more than Cobo's thumb from knuckle to tip, flopped out.

"Reach in and take it out." Kiitur instructed gently.

She grabbed hold of the skin flap and pulled it up as Cobo reached with both arms into Caltha's womb. He swam his fingers through thick wetness, and gently cradled the child between his arms.

671

"It is tiny." he said, his voice hushed with the awe of new life. He carefully extracted the baby. The feet, the legs, the hips, the abdomen and umbilical cord, the head, and arms. She was covered with blood, and mucous, and her eyes were matted shut.

Her mouth opened, and she let out a thin, high pitched wail that filled the cavern.

They laughed their relief as one. Cobo gingerly set the girl child on her mother's garments. Kiitur took over, wiping the mess off the baby, out of the eyes, and nose, and from around her mouth, off her legs and arms.

Bulbode pinched off the umbilical. "Cut it here," he instructed, and Cobo used the tip of the blade to cut the baby free from her dead mother. Bulbode, who obviously had some experience with caring for a newborn, bent over the end of the umbilical cord, and held it, waiting for the cord to fuse shut.

Under their care, the baby calmed, and whimpered quietly, nearly cooing a newfound content.

"It is a girl." Benu whispered to Lodan. "She is alive, but small. Too small. I've never seen a small one like this live long. And here, with no milk, no warmth," She wept, her heart breaking now for the baby.

Cobo wiped his hands and arms on his clothing, and moved to Lodan's side. He placed his hands over Lodan's face, and healed the burns, but could not restore his eyes. Eyelids turned from charred black to pink, fusing over empty sockets.

Regretfully, he said, "I'm sorry, Lodan, I can do no more."

Benu again began to cry.

"You must have restored my eyes," Lodan countered, "I can see."

Bemused, Cobo held his hand before Lodan, and shook it in front of the fused lids.

Lodan smiled, and seeming to look around, said, "I see your hand, Ver dala Ven. And I see the baby, and Kiitur, and Bulbode," and he reached for Benu, "I can see my Huntresses wife weeping for me."

"But your beautiful eyes," she sobbed, "they are gone."

"It is true, Lodan." Cobo replied.

He smiled, "Pletoro once said that only a blind man can understand the unseen, because a sighted man only believes what he sees. I am grateful that I have learned that lesson well. Benu," he said to his wife, "Will you stay with a blind Kai'mai?"

"Forever." she whispered.

"Then I am content to be blind."

He caressed her face, she caressed his, their love passing between them, an entity that lived in and around them, binding them, one to another.

Cobo was reluctant to intrude, but he had an important favor to ask. "Benu, I can cause you to give milk. Will you allow me to do this, so that you can feed Kaitlin?"

The name of the child came involuntarily, as if she had chosen her own name. The name belonged to Cobo's mother. Kaitlin. A beautiful name for a beautiful girl.

The baby chortled, as if to approve of the name given to her.

Benu was startled by his request, and glanced at the tiny baby. "I have no affinity for children, and no experience."

"Benu," Lodan whispered lovingly, "you hurt for Kaitlin. I feel you, you want this child to your breast."

She blushed. "How can you know me like this?" she asked, smiling her incredulity.

He laughed, a hearty laugh of a man who was genuinely happy. Blindness had given him a greater gift than sight, the gift of soul reading, the gift of seeing truth.

Benu glanced again to the baby, whose eyes were open, and as gold as Cobo's, and seemed now to be watching her.

"I will give the child succor." she agreed.

Eerily, the newborn smiled at her.

Benu shivered.

"Don't be afraid of her," Cobo said, "Kaitlin is a strong spirit, but pure, and good. She needs you."

"I'm not afraid." she lied. The warrior, afraid of no man, could not admit fear of a baby.

Cobo reached out, and touched her cheek. Benu's eyes widened as she felt her breasts grow large with milk.

Kiitur guided her in the gentle art of feeding a baby, and the baby suckled greedily at the breast of her surrogate mother. Once

673

Benu got over her fear of the baby, she grew tender toward Kaitlin, touching the soft fuzz on her head, and toying with her tiny feet and hands.

"Hold her to you, Benu," Kiitur told her, "Even when she is not feeding. Your warmth will keep her alive."

"Your warmth," Cobo said, standing and looking down at his grandchild, "and her own vitality, of which she has plenty."

"Will she live?" Benu asked hopefully.

"Oh, yes, she will live."

Pensively, he returned to the mouth of the passage. The Star was gone, having taken Taen and returned to its place of rest. The cavern was dark, except for the bluish light of the spring, and seemed colder. He found his son's remains, wrapped in his cape. He picked it up, held it to his chest, and wandered into the gallery. He could still hear the Masing's song, and Taen's cries of torment. A tormented soul. Another he had been responsible for, one he'd failed horribly.

"Father," Cobo whispered, "Guide me as I train Kaitlin. Be sure I miss nothing in her education."

He felt the whispering voices of the defenders of the Masing push past him like a breeze. With them was his father, and as his father passed through him, he gave his blessing, and his forgiveness.

Cobo buried his face into the folded cape, and he wept for the loss of his son.

◈◈◈◈◈◈◈◈◈

The snowstorm lifted, leaving the skies blue and clear, and the air cold. Cobo climbed to the peak where he retreated to meditate.

Lodan followed, slowly and without needing help. His eyes were gone, but he could still see where to put his feet and hands. It had been one day since he was blinded, and already he was alive with the confidence of a man with sharp eyes. This morning, he had picked up his kai'gam to do his exercises and afterwards Benu goaded him into a sparring match. He could never resist her, especially when she snorted, "B'Lianza," as she had, that fateful day they shared their first match. He sensed she was testing him,

674

for she did not attack as she normally would with the passion he so loved. He put her concerns to rest by sparring with more skill than he'd ever displayed. He learned that his ability to see wasn't like the physical sight he'd taken for granted. It went far beyond seeing form and color and movement. He could "see" her heartbeat, her scent, and her aura close to him. He could "see" her thoughts, her emotions, and even their united future. He moved with her as though their movements were made by the same mind, and in the same body, with the same intentions. It was the most exhilarating match of his life.

The baby's cry abruptly ended their match.

He expected Benu to step back, and pause, to uphold their uneasy custom of measuring each other, resisting each other. He could see her, in his way, watching him, noticing his visible state of arousal beneath his exercise togs, and making a decision. She came closer to him, and in her movement, he sensed she had chosen to relent, to be the first. She tossed aside her weapon, allowing it to clatter on the stone, and embraced him, kissing him, a kiss filled with promise. Her luscious mouth, the feel of her warmth, the sexy smell of an exercised body, and the stream of her erotic thoughts combined to strip him of his control.

The cries of the baby caused her to reluctantly break from his lips.

"Kaitlin is hungry."

He held her fast and pressed his lips to her ear. "I am also hungry for you, but I can wait."

He felt the way she trembled, how her heart jumped, and savored the delicious feel of her in his arms for as long as they were permitted.

"Benu!" Kiitur called for from the outer chamber.

Benu groaned. "Maybe you can wait, but I am mad for you, I can't,"

He loosened his arms, and chuckled as he pushed her away.

"Feed the child," he said, "and return to me."

Benu hurried out of the gallery, breathless with anticipation. Lodan waited, passing the time testing his senses, his instinctual depth perception. In his mind, he had a perfect image of the cave walls, of each sharp rock, of the distance from one protrusion to another.   He tested his accuracy, measuring with his inner site from one place to another, then measuring with paces or lengths of his arms. It was all clear, so clear.

Benu returned to him, carrying rolls of blankets, and he helped her lay them down, and they stripped, and they lay down together, and they cast off celibacy together. Their lovemaking was like their kai'gam matches; smooth, passionate, at times combative, and wholly exciting.

The sleep that came with the aftermath of their passion was interrupted again by the cries of Kaitlin. Benu woke with a groan, and rose to feed the child.

Lodan layered himself with clothing and blankets, protection from the cold, and stepped outside of the cave for fresh air.

That was when Ver dala Ven asked him to climb with him to the peak above the cave entrance.

"The skies are clear, I can feel the sun on my skin." Lodan commented as he stood by Cobo. "And the sea is gray, I hear it striking the shore roughly. There must be a storm on the horizon. Is that a ship in the distance?"

"Yes," Cobo said appreciatively, "In the far distance. Farther than the eye can see."

Lodan smiled at himself. "I can smell it. A Rysenk freighter, they still use fuel oil to power their engines. We are returning to Zadoq, aren't we?" Lodan asked abruptly, sensing the subject that Cobo had needed to broach with him.

"Actually, I was hoping you and your wife would want to return to Jantideva with me, and Kaitlin." Cobo replied, "I believe that none of us will be safe in Zadoq, now that Taen is dead. And I have to return, to take my....Taen, to take Taen's remains to his mother, and to introduce her to her granddaughter."

He felt Cobo's sorrow, and the secret he carried with him. The secret of Taen's paternity, a secret he hadn't dared to guess about but that had been a rumor for years. Wordlessly, he vowed to keep Ver dala Ven's secret.

"I trust your instincts about Zadoq. But I will have to ask Benu before I can give you my decision about returning to Jantideva."

"Of course." Cobo replied, "She may not want to leave Dilgopoche, and that I understand. Kiitur and Bulbode will not leave Dilgopoche....no matter how hard I tried to convince them to come with me. They are leaving for their village in the morning. If you decide to return to Jantideva with me, we will leave in a week, or two, depending on how hardy Kaitlin becomes. If you decide to stay, I will stay with you until Kaitlin is older."

"And Benu is forever attached to her?" Lodan questioned, concerned for her emotional well being once separated from Kaitlin. Already, she had formed a strong bond to the baby, and it had only been a day.

"Benu's heart will not be irreparably harmed," Cobo replied, "and it won't be long before she has her own child to suckle."

Lodan grinned at the prospect of being a father.

In the weighty silence that followed, Lodan sensed in Cobo pangs of loneliness, and of his desire for a place that was dry, and hot, and for a woman with sparkling green eyes and a mean wit.

Chapter 30

Gella did her best, but could not get comfortable.

She blamed the bed. It was too soft, the bedding too silky, the pillows too fluffy, the scent too floral, the bed too high from the ground.

She blamed the surroundings. The guest quarters in the Zarian embassy were overdone, too lush, much like Ona, and as closed up as a Shod city tenement. Traditionally Rathian in design, the grand mansion had few windows, and the few that were built into the embassy were tall, thin slits enclosed in glass that could not be opened to allow in air.

She often felt like she was suffocating. In order to get air, she had to dress as a Janti and sit in the patio garden, surrounded by well meaning, and curious, strangers who insisted on making conversation with her, and touching her belly. In Shodalum, no one would be so presumptuous to touch a pregnant woman's belly. Here, especially among the Zarians, it seemed a common, and accepted practice.

Shelon told her she should feel grateful for the Zarian's hospitality. They were more than glad to take in the newly appointed Shodalum representative, and wife. Even in the face of threats, and the very real danger posed to the Zarians.

The danger. Yes, that was the real reason she could not get comfortable. Each day Shelon left the Zarian embassy, he was taking his own life into his hands. Before the last tragic terrorist attack, the Crier was kept informed of where and when Shelon and daka Bailin would be speaking. They were traveling around the country together, in a show of unity, overseeing the census process and speaking to the Janti who would listen about the change that was in the air. They were to speak in Blaxen, in the south, almost as far south as Horp Row. At the last minute, their speech was canceled. It was a fluke. The weather was foul, and their pilot didn't want to take the chance flying through high winds. Someone didn't know the speech was canceled. At the time Shelon would have been introduced, a lume bomb went off. Several thousand Blaxens were killed.

679

It was the third lume bomb detonated since Shelon took his seat on the council. The second, like the first, had been set off in Shod City, killing tens of thousands who were, at that time, participating in the census.

Today, Shelon was speaking in Loxyn. The speech was impromptu, and the Crier was not informed. Shelon refused protection from the daka. He suspected the Pliadors were behind the terrorist attacks. He'd say so to Gella, then laugh as if it were a joke, though she saw the fury and frustration in his face. "Not so long ago, I was the terrorist. Now I am the victim. It's rich!"

Shelon's opposition was unquestionably brutal, though not all who opposed him were Janti terrorists with bombs. Each day, a band of Janti-born calling themselves Nationalists flooded Shod City to preach to the masses. They urged the Shodites to stay in the slums, to insist on their rights as Janti citizens. They preached on the difficulties that living in Shodalum offered, and of the hardships they faced if they were to transfer to Zaria. "What of our rights as brothers and sisters to the Janti?" One especially vehement leader shouted to a throng of eager followers. Draco Ullioc quoted from Shelon's day of fury, and convicted his followers of his beliefs that they should force their way into the good graces of the Janti. The young revolutionary had started his share of riots in Shod city, as well as in front of the Alliance Congress, and attracted a good deal of hatred from all sides.

Shelon usually arrived home at this hour. Each day, Gella listened for the return of his windrider, trying not to worry if he was a little late.

He was on time today. She struggled out the bed.

Damn...squishy.....bed....knees   sink...belly   impossible   to maneuver....feet struck the floor...nude...she was sick of clothing.....

Her gait was comical. Her back was slung in an arch, her child hung low, and her legs bowed with each step. She sensed that her day was coming, soon.

Gella had tried to convince Shelon to go home with her, now, leave for Shodalum, never return. But he would not hear of it. She knew that he would not go back to Shodalum without his people.

Another week. Maybe two. His assurances didn't cut through her apprehension that she'd return to Shodalum without him, bear his child without him.

She walked to the window, and looked out to the landing bay beyond the woods that surrounded the embassy. The sight of him disembarking from a Zarian windrider brought tears of relief to her eyes.

He looked up at her, and as if he could see her in the narrow window, despite the reflection of the afternoon sun off the glass, he waved. He knew she'd be waiting for him to return.

જ્જ્જ્જ્જ્જ્જ્જ્જ

Laughter went around a table on the other side of the dining hall. Gella looked away from the food she was picking apart, to the Zarian girls at the other table. Their heads were close, their faces bright with smiles. They were sisters, and they looked much alike. Brown hair, brown eyes, brown skin, the same nose, the same eyes, in six different variations. Plat's daughters.

His many sons were at another table with their grandparents.

"We now have four million Shodites who have registered their family names with the census, ready to return to Shodalum." Plat said proudly.

"And another five million who have added their names to the Zarian registry. Many of them intend to stay in Jantideva, as Zarian citizens." Shelon added, discontented. "I'm disappointed in my own people, Plat. They don't want Shodalum. Not even after the way they've been treated in Jantideva, and by the Alliance."

Plat nodded thoughtfully. "We expected a much higher number to request Zarian citizenship, to be honest."

"They haven't all been counted, yet." Shelon replied grimly.

Plat smiled, and patted Shelon's arm, "Don't be disappointed in your people, Shelon. They know nothing of Shodalum, except that they've heard the life is hard. And they've heard that bit of good news from your own lips!" He said with a laugh. "They are tired, my friend. They want a life not too unlike the one they have, but with choices and self- determination. Isn't that so?"

681

Shelon grunted, and nodded that Plat was correct. He turned to Gella, and touched her hair, bringing her attention back to them.

"Should I have lied to them about Shodalum?" he asked, a half joke.

She smirked, "You saved the lazy ones the shame of fleeing the country before the first harvest."

Shelon smiled at her comment. "None are as stalwart as my Gella."

"Really? I'm not feeling very stalwart at the moment."

Concern creased his features. "Is it time for us to retire?"

"You stay," she said, "I'll go up, if Plat will give me leave to go."

Plat cocked brow at his own wife. "I think...two more days?"

Standish, Plat's wife, giggled. She was like her daughters, brown hair and eyes, pretty, somewhat round. She slapped Plat on the arm. "You think you are such an expert."

"I believe I am quite the expert." he bragged. "After seeing you give birth thirteen times, I'd say, yes, I am."

"Thirteen." Gella groaned, glancing at Standish, who was not much older than her. "How horrible for you."

Standish giggled again. "Oh yes, you say so now. But you will want more. All women do."

"Go on with your wife," Plat urged, "we have no business at the moment that is more important than her comfort."

Shelon needed no encouragement. He stood and helped Gella out of her seat.

In the lift, he chided her for not eating.

"I don't feel like eating." she defended.

"You must eat." Shelon replied tenderly.

"Shelon, what if I only have a few days?"

"When we go home for the birth of our son, he will be born right on the shore where I had my first taste of Shodalum. Appropriate, don't you think?"

"And? What then? I make the trek to Calli with the baby, alone, and you rush back to your duties as savior of the Janti-born?"

Shelon pressed his lips together, reluctant to reply to her sarcasm.

"You will return here, won't you?" she demanded.

Shelon looked at her directly. "Blame Thib. She made me Shodalum's representative."

"I do." she said vehemently, "And I blame you for accepting."

"Gella, my pretty precious one-"

"Oh, please, Shelon, do not pamper my ears!" she retorted hotly.

The lift stopped and the doors opened, and Gella stalked out, as best as she could under the circumstances, leaving Shelon to trail in her fury.

Shelon sauntering into the room, watching her as she irritably tugged off her clothing. He had the audacity to watch her with a veiled expression of interest.

"You are staring." she said flatly.

"I have a right to stare." he replied blandly, though amusement sparkled in his eyes. "You are my wife. In some countries, you'd be considered my possession."

He'd said it with a straight face.

She viewed him narrowly. "Are you purposely inviting my wrath?"

"And what exactly could you do to me in your condition?" he replied, cocking his head to the side, his eyes trailing down her backside, "I may be an old man, but you are burdened."

"I can still kick your scrawny behind out of my bed." she replied angrily, and she removed the last of her underclothing. Nude, finally free and comfortable, she sat on the bed and covered her face. She started to cry.

He grimaced. "Oh, Gella, I hate tears." He knelt on the floor in front of her, placing her feet between his knees. He touched her arms, and noticing the child inside her moving around, he placed both hands on her belly.

She sniffled, and threw her arms down to her sides to look at him. "I fear for you." she told him, "I fear living without you."

He lightly caressed the valley between her breasts with the backs of his fingers, as he ran his hands upward to place them on both sides of her face. He looked soulfully into her eyes. "Once the census it done, I will return to Shodalum, and I will raise my

683

son, make him more like me than you can stand. I vow to you, Gella, I will not allow my life to end here, in Jantideva."

"But my dreams...in them, I am in Shodalum, searching for you, always searching for you...."

"Nonsense," Shelon retorted snappishly, and he stood, and paced to the end of the bed. The subject vexed him now, as it did on the day she finally told him about her the frightening nightmares she had while in Moom, about losing him and grieving for him. It was as if he shared her fear that he'd be taken from her too soon, so much so that he needed to vehemently reject her fears, in order to reject his own.

"I can't be swayed by your nightmares, Gella. There is a higher calling, here. The Shodites need a leader to take them home."

"But you said it yourself, more than half of them don't want Shodalum." she countered tearfully. "They want Zaria, or Jantideva, or nothing at all. They are cowards, and sheep, and I can't lose you to their idiocy!"

Reproachfully, he said, "I am here for the ones who do want Shodalum."

She had to look away from him.

"Gella, try and understand." he pleaded. "Before I met you, I made a vow to myself and my people that I would see them be free. I must keep my vow. And the day is here! I can't leave now. My people would lose heart to hear that I had run home because of the danger we all now face."

"I do understand." she said softly, "But I am still afraid for you."

He went to her, and took her chin in his hand. Staring into her eyes, he said, "One more day, and we will go home. And I will accompany you to Nari, where you will stay with Thib until I return for you. And, before you miss me, I'll be home for good. Trust in fate Gella. Trust in me."

"How can I trust fate?" she asked, and her eyes grew hot, "I am happy. Fate has always hated it when I was happy."

He released her chin, and crooked an uneasy smile. "Me too. I've learned to live in the moment, because my happiness is always fleeting. I've often behaved selfishly, taking happiness when I could, because I was sure fate would send me plunging, any minute, into the depths of misery. I never looked into the future, because I didn't know I had a future." He returned to her, kneeling before her, looking earnestly into her eyes. "In Shodalum, I felt my future grow, Gella. I will live there, in the future, with you. I feel it, I feel it so strongly, I feel I can impose myself on the future, simply to be with you. Don't you see? Your nightmares have no meaning, because my will is stronger than your fears."

She embraced his neck, setting her head on his shoulder. She felt his strength.

The chime of the relay in their room broke them apart. Gella sighed. "Can't they let us alone?"

He caressed her face, as if to apologize for the interruption, and stood, went through the opening in the screen around the bed.

The chiming stopped, and Bailin's voice reached her ears.

"I need you and Gella to meet me at the temple in Ona at dusk. It is gravely important."

"Gravely?" Shelon asked sardonically.

Bailin chuckled. "For me, personally, it is gravely important. I'd appreciate your presence in the temple."

"Very well. We will be there."

Gella glanced at her discarded clothing and sighed.

Shelon stepped through the screen.

"I suppose the time is now."

"We did make a promise to him, didn't we?" Shelon smiled at her. "And it is important to keep our promises."

"May I go like this?" she asked, with an upraised brow.

"I wouldn't mind, but you may scandalize Jantideva."

ৰঞ্ঞৰঞ্জৡৡৡৡ

Bailin hadn't spent his day in Loxyn with Shelon, as was planned. He had his own impetuous agenda.

That morning, Bailin met Ksathra in the woods where they'd once made love. It was there he gave her a gold bracelet, and asked her to marry him, immediately, that day. She happily agreed to become his bride.

685

Bailin left Ksathra in Dralon to prepare for their wedding, as he went to find a Suma that he was sure would perform the ceremony for them. This priest had become a nihilist. After having spent several months in Dilgopoche, Durym, son of Avee, returned a changed man. He reviled the priesthood, and spoke out against the use of Mistresses in the temple. He described the pain and loneliness the women endured in shocking detail, causing uproar in the temple community. He demanded to be released from his vows, but was compelled to live as a priest until Chancellor Yana was certain Durym couldn't be turned. To that end, the Chancellor gave him the lowliest position in the temple, that of a prayer monk, and spirited him off to a temple in Raal Two, a free city surrounded by work camps.

Bailin didn't dare land in the city, itself. Even the free inhabitants of the city, the guards, and their families, were usually men and women who were as dangerous and desperate as the prisoners they guarded. Raal Two was a city of shadows, dirty, rampant with crime.

Bailin landed in the temple, which was a fortress in the eye of the city. Before he'd lowered the ramp to disembark, a number of Suma had lined up to greet him. They were clearly delighted by a daka's unexpected, and rare, visit.

The Chancellor offered a meal of tea and cakes, and expected the daka would attend a hastily planned prayer vigil.

Bailin asked that he be taken to Durym, immediately. The Chancellor of the temple was taken aback, and insulted, that Bailin chose to speak to a fallen prayer monk before sitting with the important priests, and praying, but he held his tongue and obeyed his daka.

The prayer boxes were no bigger than a kneeling man, with air holes in the sides. A circle of ten inhabited a cramped room, and playing soft from each corner was a recording of Suma monks chanting the Twelve Holy Precepts. From some of the boxes, tired voices chanted along.

The Chancellor unlocked Durym's prayer box.

Durym crawled out. He wore a beggars wrap around his waist, and no more. The light was too much for his eyes. He covered them with a hand and he struggled to get to his feet. Bailin

686

wondered how long Durym had been in the box, and stopped wondering as Durym's pungent odor reached his nostrils. Bailin knew about the boxes, that the prayer monks prayed in them as a way to show their total devotion to the Guardian, recreating the legendary conditions inside the star. A beautiful concept, but with a grittier reality. The prayer monks rarely left the boxes to eat, to sleep, to relieve themselves, to bathe.

The knowledge of their suffering was nothing to Bailin until now, as he smelled Durym, and saw his weakness.

"Can you stand on your own?"

Squinting at the voice, still unable to see, Durym countered with, "Who is asking?"

"It is I, Bailin."

He stiffened. "Daka Bailin! What are you doing in Raal Two?"

"I'm here for a favor, but before we can speak, you must bathe." he said ruefully.

౸౸౸౸౸ఞఞఞఞ

As Durym met Ksathra, his eyes lit with appreciation.

"She is a vision of loveliness." he complimented, making Ksathra giggle. She crossed her arms before her chest, covering the immaculate beadwork of the brilliant yellow gown she'd hand made, hiding shyly.

Bailin put his arm around her, and smiled proudly. "She is a goddess."

Durym gazed at them as they held each other, and he nodded contemplatively. "I see you were meant for each other. And you are brave to want to love each other in the open. I admire you, and I envy you." And he said, "Bailin, if you are ready, the cowl."

Bailin flashed one last grin at Ksathra, and covered his face with the cowl, attached to the hood of the black robe he wore. The wedding robe was the same Taen had used, and his own father had also used it to marry his mother. Bailin had stolen it--*borrowed* it-- from his father's things.

Ksathra covered her head, and part of her face with her veil, not so much for tradition or style, but for secrecy. They left the

687

wedding rope behind, because it seemed akin to a symbol of slavery, and Bailin would not allow Ksathra to wear a symbol of slavery.

Durym escorted them into the temple proper. Through the sheer black material over his face, Bailin saw the guests he'd invited. Plat, with his wife and children, were in the front row. Shelon and Gella stood at the altar, waiting for their part in the secret wedding to be done. The adults smiled as he and Ksathra emerged with the priest. The rest of his guests were mainly journalists. None of the latter knew the identity of the mystery couple to be wed. He'd made sure they knew only the time and place. He knew that none would refuse an invitation to the temple in Ona, especially a mysterious wedding invitation.

Far in the back, hidden in the shadows, were Ksathra's parents. He couldn't have had them in the front row when so much depended on secrecy. His mother surely would have asked questions.

His brother sat in the daka's balcony, and beside him were his parents. They were no doubt wondering who on their staff chose this day for an impromptu wedding. He imagined they recognized the guests in the front row, and hoped the presence of Gella and Shelon didn't give them away.

Due to Durym's new attitude toward the use of Suma Mistresses, he performed a duty that normally was left to a Mistress. He took Ksathra by the arm, and walked her to the altar. Bailin focused on her as Durym instructed her to kneel before the altar, and placed the black wedding cloak over her back.

Shelon and Gella, together acting as his mother, they guided Bailin to his place before Ksathra. Bailin knelt, and bent forward, placing his forehead on the floor, paying homage to the Guardian.

Durym blessed them, and began the ceremony. He was concise, kept the ceremony short and was careful not to use their given names, though his words about love and devotion were poignant. There was a point that tears came to Bailin's eyes for Durym's heartfelt enthusiasm about their union.

"Enjoy your life together!" Durym said as he closed the ceremony, "From this day, forward, you cannot be broken apart, ever."

Durym removed Bailin's cowl and Ksathra's veil, to allow them to look upon each other's faces. As their eyes met, they were official, legally married in the eyes of Janti law.

Their wedding had been perfect, until his father recognized him.

"Bailin!" he shouted from their family's balcony. The journalists in the main audience shot to their feet, and trained their ready cameras at the couple. The wedding was about to be recorded for posterity, and surely it would become best known for the initial confrontation between he and his parents at the altar.

Bailin prepared for a confrontation. He planted a firm arm around Ksathra's waist and held his head high, his eyes trained on his mother and father as they flew down the aisle at them. His father spoke first, and to Durym, who stood behind the newly wedded couple.

"Tell me that this is a charade! A joke!"

"It is a legal, and blessed union," Durym replied.

"Ksathra and I are married," Bailin said, and he raised his voice to be heard by the journalists, "Ksathra, who was once a Shodite slave of the House of Jantideva and is now a Zarian national, is my wife. Daka Ksathra of Jantideva."

Utter silence filled the temple, save the croaking of Shelon's suppressed chuckle.

Bail sneered at the journalists, then turned the sneer on his son. "You will not make this a public spectacle." To his sentries, he ordered sharply, "Clear the temple!" He glared dangerously at Bailin, and pointed to the priest's antechamber, off to the side of the altar.

"March."

Bailin obliged him. He took Ksathra by the arm and they strode to the antechamber, Durym and his parents trailing behind. Once behind closed doors, his mother was the first to start. She uttered a frustrated sigh. "Bailin, do you know what you have done? You have bound yourself to this woman until your death! How dare you enter into marriage without counseling with us! Without our blessing!"

"You wouldn't have given your blessing." Bailin accused, "I heard you, just yesterday, discussing my fate with Nan! You

689

intended to pair me with an important Tredallis heiress, a woman I have never met!"

"It was idle talk between friends!" she retorted.

"Just as it was idle talk when you gave Taen away against his will." Bailin replied hotly.

Bail interjected, "You cannot compare yourself to Taen, you are the heir apparent! And you have married a Shodite!" He swung around and pointed a lethal finger at Durym, "You should have stopped them!"

Durym pursed his lips. "Love should never be denied."

Jishni pressed her palm to her forehead, as if to quell a headache. "Durym! You served us! How could you betray our trust?"

"I did not betray anyone. I did what was right."

"That is it!" Bail shouted, "I am placing you under arrest!"

Bailin's jaw dropped. "You cannot arrest Durym! He was acting on my command!"

"You are not standing over my grave, yet, boy," Bail fumed, "You are not in a position to command the Suma to do your will, and Durym knows as much!"

Durym wore a smile as Bailin's father railed against him, a strange smile, as if he'd fulfilled some life goal that he'd not shared with another soul

"Ksathra is my wife." Bailin interjected lowly, "And there is nothing you can do about it. You must accept my choice."

Bail and Jishni found each other's eyes, incredulous.

His father suddenly looked at him, triumph taking the tension out of his brow. "She is Shodite. She cannot marry unless it is the will of the benefactor, and I am Ksathra's benefactor. As such, I say this marriage is nullified."

"You are no longer Ksathra's slaver." Bailin replied easily, though his father's claim of ownership over Ksathra infuriated him. "Ksathra is currently registered for Zarian citizenship. She is free, and I am free to take her as my wife."

Bail uttered a growled obscenity, in a language that sounded like Rysenk, but Bailin wasn't sure.

"You are too young." Jishni rejoined evenly, attacking with logic, cajoling logic.

"Perhaps, ideally, I am a bit young for marriage. But, legally," Bailin shrugged his triumph away. Marriage was legal the moment a Janti entered the teen years. It was poor form to marry young, only the lower classes married very young, but it was not illegal.

He'd thought of every angle possible. He'd studied the law carefully, and found many precedents where a daka had married young, or married a commoner, even a commoner from another land. What he'd done was binding, and legal, and permanent.

"You've put yourself in danger." Bail said, his voice hushed by his own concern. "Already, there are those who'd like to see you dead for your part in the Shodite exodus. But now that you've taken a Shodite wife-"

"Zarian, father." Bailin corrected, "She is a Zarian, now."

"Are you so naive to think that the terrorists that are against setting the Shodites free will recognize her new nationality? They don't recognize Alliance law on the matter!"

"Father, it is done." Bailin said stiffly.

"I can see that!" Bail shouted angrily.

Bailin glanced to Ksathra, whose head was lowered, her features sober. His heart quickened for her. "Ksathra," he said, and she turned her head sideways to look at him. "and I are in love. I would rather die than live without her."

Tears glittered in her eyes.

His father moaned his distaste, his despair.

Bailin frowned a bit, but could not tear his eyes away from Ksathra's gaze. "We have made arrangements to stay at the Zarian embassy until we have a home to call our own. We won't embarrass you, father, if that is what you are worried about. And, if you wish, I can abdicate. Voktu can take your place."

"Absolutely out of the question." Bail breathed furiously, "You have taken away our right to participate in the choice of your wife, you will not take away my right to put my eldest son in my seat!"

Jishni uttered a little gasp, but Bailin didn't hear it, or see his parents exchange a mortified gaze at the slip. Ksathra's moist eyes enchanted Bailin. He felt drunk on the elixir of having made his fondest wish come true.

"You will stay in the palace." Jishni ordered, having regained her composure. "I will not have you moving away!"

"No, mother," Bailin said, blinking, finally tearing his eyes away to look at his mother. "perhaps, if it is what you want, we can return to the palace later. But not now. Not until the Shodites are freed. Ksathra cannot live among her own as a daka. It wouldn't be right."

"Daka," Jishni whispered. His mother was stricken, ashen.

He smiled at her. "Mother, Ksathra may not be a Tredallis socialite, but she is more than worthy to be called daka. Please! Please welcome my wife into the family."

She shook her head. "Ksathra, I've always liked you, but," Unable to finished the sentiment, she said to Bailin, "I am your mother. You should have come to me. I could have at least offered council. I could have at least given you to her, instead you gave that honor to Shelon and Gella. Can you imagine how this hurts me?"

Overcome with grief, his mother swung her skirts around and rushed out.

Bail's mouth was tense, his tone hard. "I'll leave you to the Zarians, if that is what you want." He slid a furious glare at the priest. "You will come with me. I wish to sit with you and Yana on this matter."

The priest nodded his assent, and let Bail take him by the arm and drag him out of the antechamber. The sentries, left without orders, followed their daka, unquestioning.

"Oh, Bailin, that went horribly," Ksathra breathed ruefully.

He nuzzled her cheek. "I'm sorry, Ksathra. But they'll come around."

"And, if they don't?"

"We will live in Zaria." He grinned. "Wife."

"We did it." She murmured, sounding a bit shocked, "We really did."

The Crier announced the news all through the night. *Daka Bailin Wed a Shodite Seamstress!* Their wedding pictures ran in every article, pictures depicting a happy couple.

Echo stirred the spice brandy by rolling it between her hands. She'd heard all the articles. She knew all the details of daka Bailin's happy little affair. She understood, too, the significance of a Shodite being made a daka. The shod were being elevated from the lowliest of creatures, to the highest.

Her eyes trained on Bailin's picture, and she drank the brandy. The liqueur warmed her throat, her chest, cleared her mind. Dropping the bottle away, she returned to rolling it between her hands, and she considered her next act of defiance.

Striking out at the shod apparently had no affect on the status of their deportation. Millions of Shodites were already being deported to Zaria. The rest would be sent to Shodalum, and soon. A month, maybe less. Her father had lamented that his factories were empty, and his home, dirty. His shod were no longer working for him, not now that the Zarians were feeding them.

Meddling Zarians. Daily, they shipped in supplies to the millions of shod that were not working for their food and board. Grav commented that the Zarians were too well organized for this to be an impromptu effort. As if they'd been planning this for years.

She'd been concentrating her efforts on striking fear into the shod.

"Perhaps I have been impressing myself on the wrong people." she said aloud.

She set the bottle down, and brought up a picture of the Zarian embassy, from a camera she'd lodged in a tree in a park nearby. For weeks, she watched Shelon's comings and goings, plotting to kidnap him, to imprison him the way he had imprisoned Edise. Perhaps catch that woman of his, and cut his child out of her as he watched. Kill it before his eyes.

But kidnapping was an ugly affair. She had no time to dally with the shod, or the Zarians.

The Zarian guard was light on the embassy. No Alliance security, no Janti patrols.

She chuckled wickedly at the prospect.

そう

‱‱‱‱‱

For a change, it was Shelon who had trouble sleeping. His mind was too busy with his plans for the next day to rest. He intended to spend his day in Shod City, in the Tracks that had not yet submitted a completed census, to encourage those who had not registered to do so. He desperately wanted to be finished with the census. By all measure, it was not half done. At this rate, he'd be here forever. In Shodalum, it had been so much easier. For all their slow, plodding, backward ways, they knew how to rally their people.

The Janti born, however, were diverse in their ways and beliefs and desires, and far more fragmented as far as their family tribes. Rallying them was next to impossible.

They were Janti, all right. Without a sense of their past, their culture, too intimidated by the Suma, too set in their ways to get up and take action!

It was the middle of the night. He was dressed, and sitting in a chair, watching Gella sleep. The muted glow of the night lamps in the floors outlined her. She was nude, atop the covers, on her side. That boy in her belly squirmed around, doing his level best to wake her. Shelon watched her stomach awhile, fascinated. He swore he could see the outline of an arm and elbow, or was it a knee and leg? The child was held tight under her skin, and seemed impatient to escape.

Hushed, under his breath, he said, "I will be seeing you soon, young man."

He sighed, and let Gella's fatalistic omens nettle at him. How often had he found happiness, only to have it stolen from him? Too often for comfort. As little as one year ago, he'd wanted to die. Gella rescued him, and now all he wanted was life. Sweet, precious life.

He felt that by wanting, he was tempting fate.

His worries made him restless. He stood, and looked at Gella's serene face for a long time, then left to take a walk in the night air.

He strolled through the gardens, staring up at the stars. He was shrouded by darkness, wearing dark blue. No one could have seen him in the shadows.

No one did. Walking through a row of evenly placed trees, he happened on a man and woman, dressed in black and lurking near the building. They carried something Shelon recognized. He descended into the darkness, no more than fifteen, twenty paces away. They went on with their business, unaware they were being observed.

They placed the item, glittering silver in the moonlight, under the balcony of the ballroom. The placement really didn't matter. Once it went off, it would kill everyone in the village that surrounded the embassy, including those in the embassy. The placement was perhaps symbolic. They wanted the Zarian's to know, unequivocally, that there were those who were displeased with their stand on the Shodite issue.

He picked up two rocks. Weighed them in his hands. He'd grown adept at using a lume, but rocks were his first weapons. In Raal they were handy, and free, and he was an excellent marksman. As the two terrorists stood and stepped away from the lume bomb, Shelon stepped out of his cover and pitched one of his rocks with all his might. It struck its target, the head of the man. He uttered an *oofp* and fell flat on his back.

The woman reacted, simultaneously twisting to look at the man and ducking down and grabbing for the lume on her hip. Shelon tossed his second rock into his right hand and pitched it with as much force as the first. This one caught the woman on the side of her head. Her arms flew out, and she crumpled and fell to the ground.

Shelon ran to them. The man was dead, his forehead bloodied.

The woman drifted in a semi-conscious state, moaning, blood trickling from her ear and nose.

He took their lume hand weapons away, and shouted at the top of his voice for the guards. No one came. Cursing himself for refusing Alliance protection, he found the bloody rock he'd used on the man, took aim at one of the windows above, and threw the rock. It broke the window. He heard a startled shriek.

A second later, Bailin's face pressed through the narrow gap.

"Evacuate the embassy!" Shelon shouted upward at him, "A lume bomb has been planted here!"

"What--bomb?" Bailin said, stupid from sleep and bliss.

"Evacuate the embassy, now!" he repeated vehemently, "Wake everyone, Gella, Plat, the servants! Bailin, now!"

Bailin fell back

Shelon walked quickly, and lightly, to the bomb. He kneeled before it, and scanned the outside of the cylinder. He took a deep breath, and lifted the cover plate. The bomb was simple, less crude than the one he'd built in Eller, but similar in design. Five silver plates were set in a star pattern, and on them were glass domes. The glass domes were filled with wires. Standing erect on the top of each glass dome was a solid, thick coil of lume wire.

He saw that the remote triggering device that was normally built into the military's lume bombs had been replaced with a timer, and the timer had been activated.

৵৵৵৵৵৵৵৵৵

She was bent over, the sun at her bare back, her hands on the leaves of a yava plant. She stroked the spiny leaves lustfully. She hungered for yava.

She plunged her hands into the black sand, and dug for the root. She could feel it was the largest, juiciest root she'd ever grown.

Hands lay over hers, and help her dig, a man's hands that were long, and familiar, and she didn't pull away, or feel it was unusual, or that her space had been encroached upon. She expected him.

She uncovered the root, and lifted it out of the ground with his help. It was huge, heavy, and continued to grow under their hands. She looked up, laughing into his eyes. His gold eyes.

Cobo spoke to her, his lips moving slowly, his voice low and muffled by static. "Are you ready to share your home with me again?"

Gella woke with a start.

She heard shouting. She sat up in bed. "Shelon?"

696

The door to her room slammed open. "Gella!" Bailin called for her, and without invitation he rushed through the gap in the privacy screen.

His urgent manner shook her. "What is it?"

He threw her robe at her. "Hurry, Gella, we don't have time."

He whisked her out of her room, and into a rushing, half dressed throng of groggy and panicked Zarians asking questions that went unanswered.

Outside, they were hustled to the landing bays to a waiting windrider. Crossing the mosaic tiled plaza, Gella happened to glance toward the gardens. She halted.

"Shelon?"

He stood by a strange object, looking down, looking abject. Behind him stood a man she recognized. A tall Rathian with gold eyes, and an almost malevolent smile.

"Mo'ghan."

The sight of the spirit caused her to quake with fear for Shelon, and for herself.

"Shelon!" she screamed, and she started toward her husband.

Bailin grabbed her by the shoulders, and urged her along with the rest. "He found a bomb, we must evacuate now."

"We must not leave him, Shelon!" she shouted for him hysterically.

Bailin's grip tightened on her waist now, biting into her skin. "No, Gella."

"Shelon!" she shouted as she was forcefully moved forward. "Shelon!"

He glanced over to her. He urged her to go, waving her forward.

She fought Bailin's hands, but his grip was cloying, and suddenly his was not the only grip hastening her forward. There was Plat, and Plat's eldest son. They would not release her to follow her impulses.

She twisted her head so that she did not lose sight of him as she was taken up the ramp of the windrider. "Shelon!" she screamed, wishing he would abandon the object, and save himself.

෴෴෴෴෴

697

Gella's scream caused him to look away. His heart raced.

He looked again to the interior of the bomb. His eyes went from one wire, to another. It was like a combination lock. Pull the wires in the proper order, and the bomb is deactivated. Pull them in the wrong order.....Shelon had as much chance of de-activating the bomb as he did surviving its blast, were it to go off with him right next to it.

The timer continued to count down.

The woman's moaning had stopped. She was resolutely unconscious, unable to tell him what he needed to know, the order of the wires. Shelon's only consolation was that when the bomb went off, she'd die with the rest of them.

Running away didn't even occur to him. He knew he wouldn't be able to escape. He doubted the windriders that were taking off at this moment would escape the sweep of this bomb. He doubted that Gella.....

"Gella," he whispered, "I made a promise to you. I am not allowed to die. And neither are you."

Caprice in moments of crisis was his greatest personal flaw, or so he thought. He waited until a count of ten remained, in order to give Gella and the others the maximum amount of time to escape. Without contemplation, as soon as the timer began ticking down from ten, he started pulling wires. This one,(ten, nine) and that one,(eight, seven) and the one at the top,(six, five) yes, and this at the right,(four, three) and this at the left(two, one)--it was as if he could hear a voice in his ear telling him the order, as if the information came from another source.

(Zero)

The trigger snapped. Sparked impotently.

He rolled back on his heels and stared, dumbfounded, at the bomb.

He stood, still staring into the interior of the bomb. Shelon's lips turned up in a relieved smile.

Feeling a presence at his back, he glanced over his shoulder. He was startled to see the fierce eyes of a man he recognized, a man dressed as a Rathian Knight, and bearing his own features with gold eyes.

The Rathian crooked a smile at him. "It is honorable to keep your promises."

He disappeared.

Shelon gasped, and bolted backwards from where he'd seen the knight last.

෯෯෯෯෯෯෯෯

Bailin recognized Captain Echo Agart, though her face had been maimed by Shelon's well placed rock. The doctors told him that she'd survive.

Her dead partner was lume weapons specialist, Captain Ig Grey, one of his father's elite officers. Bailin had the presence of mind to know that the greatest scandal in Jantideva's history was unfolding at his feet. In his anger, and feelings of betrayal, he chose to use the scandal to his advantage.

He summoned his father to the embassy, telling him there had been an incident that needed his immediate attention.

Daka Bailin arrived with Trev in the middle of the night, tense, ready for anything, even the news that one of his most trusted specialists was a traitor.

"You suspected him all along!" Bailin accused as he read the guilt on his father's features.

They were alone in the sub-level of the embassy, facing each other over Ig Grey's body, which was laid out on the floor.

"Not openly." Bail replied, "But I knew his politics."

Bailin wanted to believe his father. Bail had been a hero, a man of honor, and as a boy, Bailin had looked up to him, and loved him ardently. He was left wondering if his judgement had been impaired. Had he seen a hero, instead of a fiend, because daka Bail was his father?

The conflict between his love for his father, and the bad taste of distrust for the daka that stood before him, caused his eyes to grow hot. "Regardless of your assertions, if this gets out, the scandal will rock the Alliance. The Alliance will take one look at the circumstantial evidence linking you to the terror against the Shodites, and assume you were involved."

Bail threw a worried glare at his son. "Is that what you really think of me, Bailin? That I am a terrorist?"

Bailin had to look away. "I don't know what to think, father." he said honestly, "I know only what I see. And I see a man laying here that took orders directly from you. He conspired with Agart to kill us all."

"If you think I sanctioned Ig Grey's illicit actions, you are wrong." Bail replied, impassioned, "I would never risk your life over a political cause, no matter how weighty the cause. Bailin, you are my son. You are more important to me than the Shodites, or the Janti Benefactors, or my own life. On my life, Bailin, I had nothing to do with their plotting."

Bailin sunk into the darkness of a corner, and looked at his father. Bail had been badly shaken by the breath of tragedy that had grazed them, discovering that another of his children had nearly been taken from him. Bailin could see the lines of pain in his father's face, left by missing Archer. Bail had grown old in a short time because of loss.

In the few minutes they'd spoken, he grew older still.

"I believe you." Bailin relented, his voice thick with emotion. "But I do not trust those that you trust. I do not trust any Janti, not with my life, or my wife's life."

Bail remained silent, understanding.

"Less than half of the Shodite population has been counted." he went on, "But it is becoming clear we cannot finish the census here, sitting as we are, in the jaws of the beast. Shelon needs a safe place to finish the census. A place where the population is sparse, and it is protected by.....forces we do not understand."

"What do you want, Bailin?" Bail asked quietly.

"Old Rathia." Bailin stated firmly. "By law, it belongs to the Shodites. Give them that land, and give them a new option. That way, those who do not wish to live in Shodalum, or Zaria, or to stay in Jantideva with their slavers, can make a new life there."

Bail thought about it for a moment.

"Are you blackmailing me, son? Old Rathia in exchange for your silence on the matter of Ig Grey?"

Bailin suppressed a tremor of nerves, and forced a mean smile. "Yes, I am."

His father cracked an ironic laugh. Some of the tension in his body loosened, but none of the stress in his face fled.

"Then what choice do I have," he replied lightly, "but to honor your request?"

"Then you will release Old Rathia to the Shodites?"

"Not all of it." he amended easily, "There are Janti settlements north of the Peril river. To the south, the land is wild, and relatively free of settlements."

"You're giving half?" Bailin asked incredulously. "You expect me to accept half?"

Bail shrugged, "Fine, take it all. And I will place you in charge of the conflicts between the Shodites and settlers out there that still call themselves Rathians. I hear the settlers north of the Peril are not the types to sit with a mediator. More the type to kill whoever happens to cross them."

Bailin paused long, thinking about the deal offered him. Again, playing hero to the Shodites might cost him a thousand sleepless nights. But he felt his duty to them far more acutely now that Ksathra was his wife, and his children would be part Shodite. If he became the champion of the Shodites, and mediator to a thousand conflicts, he would do so for love.

"You have a deal."

৵৽৵৽৵৽৵৽৽৽

Early the next morning, Shelon made his claim on Old Rathia on behalf of Shodalum. The Alliance had no choice but to relinquish their claim on the land, and did so in a brief vote. Daka Bailin was placed in charge of Janti-Shodite-Rathian relations, a charge he took proudly. Publicly, for the Crier, the release of Old Rathia was touted as the last philanthropic act done for the Shodites by the Janti, and recorded thusly for posterity.

The reality was far less benevolent. For two days, the Janti gathered before the Congress and threw taunts, and often stones, at whoever entered or left the building. The Alliance Congress was shut down for days. Hatred ran in rivers, cutting a deep path in Jantideva, pitting Shodites against Janti, and Janti against Janti.

Bailin watched the sight dismally, knowing the rift deepening in Jantideva may take forever to heal.

Shelon left with Gella the day after Old Rathia was made Shodalum's, with the first of many thousands bound for the New World. Gella was in the earliest stages of labor. Shelon was more nervous at the prospect of being a father than Bailin had ever seen him, even in the face of dismantling a lume bomb. Bailin saw them off, promising to visit soon to see the new baby. Shelon nodded, his eyes riveted on Gella's anguished face. Bailin doubted that Shelon heard a word that was said to him.

Less than a week after the New World was open to them, the Shodites left Jantideva in a massive exodus. Few went on to Zaria, to make a new life there. Still more stayed in Jantideva to assert their Zarian citizenship, and face a hard life as the lowest underclass their society had ever seen. There were leaders among them promising that one day they would be accepted as Janti brothers. Bailin hoped their predictions came true.

Ver dala Ven Cobo returned from Dilgopoche, long after the initial Shodite exodus, with news of Taen's death. He told a story that stunned them, of the Masing returning and taking Taen, leaving only his physical remains. He informed them that Taen's death was yet another part of Betnoni's Prophecy, fulfilled.

Bailin hadn't seen his brother since he left for Dilgopoche, and perhaps wouldn't have seen Taen for years had he lived. They were not close, nor did they get along, but they were brothers, and he grieved.

His parents were shattered, but they had a lifeline. Kaitlin. The baby was tiny, like the way Archer and Janus were at birth, premature, but strong. She let out a hearty bellow the first time Lodan's dilgo wife handed her over to Jishni. His mother cooed, and wept, and turned to Cobo for comfort while his father watched on, approving, and hurting. Bailin would never understand the special bond between his mother and Cobo. He knew only that it existed, and was sanctioned by his father.

They laid Taen to rest on a Holy day, the Day of Masing, placing him in the family crypt, near daka Janus. Cobo stayed with Taen's remains until the day he was interred, the way Bailin would have expected his own father to watch over Taen's rest. Again, it

702

was a dynamic bond, this time between Cobo and Taen that he recognized, but escaped his understanding.

Cobo, Kaitlin, Lodan and Benu stayed with them in the palace for several months, during the Reformation. Jantideva did not recover from the loss of their work force as easily as Bailin would have predicted, and relied heavily now on their new born Zarians to do the jobs the Shodites once held. With one change, the Zarians demanded wages and better living conditions than they ever received as Shodites. And because they were so desperately needed, their demands were met.

It was the first time in twenty four hundred years that the palace was completely staffed by paid help. And it was the first time in history that a Shodite lived in the palace as a daka. Ksathra made a beautiful, and benevolent, daka, and despite the numerous death threats made against her, or perhaps because of the numerous death threats, his parents made a special effort to treat her as a most welcome member of the family. His mother once told Ksathra she liked her, and by the way she treated her, Bailin believed she really did.

Bailin and Ksathra, and her parents, returned to Shod City on the day before destruction was to begin. They walked the empty streets in silence, each remembering individually the overcrowding, the rodents, the ugliness of crime, the raw sewage that ran through the streets, the hunger of the old. But mainly, they remembered Gilmer, Ksathra's sister, and her children. Gilmer had died in this city, of the wasting disease that afflicted numbers of Shodites. Her benefactor wasted no time trading her children away, and steadfastly refused to reveal their location to their Shodite relations, even after being petitioned by the dakas to do so. Ksathra's parents were heartbroken. A part of them knew they'd never see Gilmer's children again, though they refused to lose their hope.

Once the few Janti-born who chose to be Shodite citizens were absorbed into the tribes, Shodalum, again, retreated from the Alliance. Indeed, they retreated as well from the Janti-born that had formed their sister nation, which they now called New North Shodalum. Bailin begged Shelon to keep his Alliance seat, to do his utmost to change the Elder's minds. Shelon was tired of

Alliance politics. He wanted a simple life, and so he retreated, too, into the bosom of Calli, where he and Gella, and their son went on to live, as always, a simple life.

Bailin chose his mission in life, to be the daka who brought Shodalum back into the world. His cause stretched before him, a challenge of many twists and turns and knots to untie, and though he was already busy arbitrating the problems of the New North and the Janti and Rathians of the same region, his goal for Shodalum kept a fire burning in his heart for the Shodites.

ๆ๛ๆ๛ๆ๛๛๛๛๛

"Gella!"

She straightened, and shaded her eyes to see Shelon. He was across the field, near the foundation of the chemical plant, cutting sucker branches off the yava plants. At first she thought that Mo'ghan was hungry again. The child ate so often, it was easier for her to wrap him directly to his breast. But, no, Mo'ghan was still sleeping, laying cozily on Shelon's back, held in place by a pouch of Shelon's design.

Shelon was pointing.

Gella was near their home, and the ruins obstructed her view. She walked toward Shelon, still looking in the distance. She expected to see travelers. In the months they'd been home, they'd had many visitors to Calli, some who'd asked to stay. Small homes now dotted the Calli bay. Where they were once utterly alone in the desert, there was now a community coming to life.

Indeed, as she walked past the obstruction of the smokestacks, she saw three figures approaching. Two men and a woman. The woman held a bundle to her breast. A baby. Even from this distance, she could see that one of the men was as blond as Praj, but it wasn't Praj. His gait was graceful, very much unlike Praj, who lumbered. The second man...there was something familiar about him.

Her breath caught in her throat as she recognized him.

"Cobo," she breathed, and she broke into a sprint. "Cobo!" she shouted, laughing and crying at once. She'd been dreaming about him for months, and here he was. "Cobo!"

704

He laughed his happiness, opened his arms and also broke into a sprint. He was obviously tired from their journey, but he didn't falter. He ran to her, as she ran to him, until the met, and threw their arms around each other. Cobo lifted her off her feet and swung her around, and laughed, and laughed.

The adventures of Cobo and Kaitlin continues in **"Silent Star."**

About The Author

I was born in Arizona, lived in Tucson for most my life, and now reside in Michigan. I've always been an avid reader of all types of books, and I am of the opinion that in most cases, the book is better than the movie. I've been a serious writer since my early twenties, and have completed five stories. *The Last Gate* is the first of a three-part story involving some of my favorite characters.

I'd like to thank my husband and daughter for their infinite patience with my hobby, and especially my husband for his unending emotional and financial support, without which I would just be an average space cadet, and not the author of a finished work. I dedicate *The Last Gate* to Brian and Samantha, and to my dear friend Michele King, the first person to ever read my work, and who encouraged me so well I kept right on writing.